GRIM BIRTHRIGHT
THE JONAH BLACKSTONE SAGA

A Jonah Blackstone Collection by
JOHN DARR

The Jonah Blackstone novels are works of fiction. Names, places, and incidents either are products of the author's imagination or are used fictitiously.

Any resemblance to actual events, locales, or persons, living or dead, is entirely coincidental.

The Protector's Ring © 2014 by John Darr Books,
The Seeker's Compass © 2016 by John Darr Books,
The Amulet of the Goddess © 2017 by John Darr Books

All rights reserved.
ISBN-13: 978-0-9909740-7-9

CONTENTS

THE PROTECTOR'S RING   1

THE SEEKER'S COMPASS   336

THE AMULET OF THE GODDESS   640

ABOUT THE AUTHOR   1039
OTHER BOOKS BY JOHN DARR   1041

BOOK ONE

THE PROTECTOR'S RINGS

CHAPTER ONE
THE FALLEN

How long have we been enemies, Isaiah?

Isaiah Blackstone didn't bother to answer the question that had been projected into his mind. He brandished his gleaming Reaper blades—fifteen-inch, doubled-edged weapons made of single pieces of unearthly silver metal. His wife, Janice, stood beside him, her own blades held ready.

They stood in a wide, underground tunnel. The walls, floor, and ceiling were covered in onyx slabs, long since sullied by two millennia of dust and dirt. The normally close air and dank smell was exacerbated by the number of extra bodies currently occupying the space.

At least ten attackers blocked their way. All were dressed in grey pants and matching tunics with bone-white skull symbols on the left side of their chests. Each carried a curved, jet-black scythe with a handgrip. Their eyes were a solid, milky white that was the sign they were possessed by Wraiths.

Isaiah shouted and waded into their midst, blocking the swipes of their scythes with his blades. He ducked low and brought one of his blades into the underside of an attacker's chin. His long leather Reaper coat whipped around, taking hits on the enchanted fabric as he sliced. The eyes flared as the Wraith and its mortal host died. He stabbed another in the heart, used his augmented strength to kick a third guy into his fellow henchmen while cutting a fourth man across the chest.

Janice fought at his side like a beautiful Nubian princess. Always an agile woman, she'd incorporated acrobatic techniques into her fighting forms. She somersaulted, wrapping her legs around the neck of one attacker while skewering another with a blade. She twisted her body, whirling the trapped attacker into two more.

The Protector's Ring

Isaiah charged straight ahead, cutting down the last two men before reaching an ancient wooden door. The writing etched into the surface was in the Kikongo tongue, one of the languages of the surrounding countryside of central Congo. The inscription translated into *conversations with the gods.*

On the other side was a hidden underground amphitheater, used by the ancestors to receive enlightenment from the Afterworld. Isaiah and his allies had thought the location a fitting safe haven to train the first Protector in over two thousand years. But it had been compromised.

"You can't save him. Give up." Deyanira's voice penetrated his concentration again.

Isaiah shook his head, trying to ignore her. She was using an arcane enchantment to communicate directly into his mind. It was a holdover from their time together as part of the Kin: the Grim Reaper's personal guard. They had been friends, of a sort, reaping souls from worthless mortal bodies. But Isaiah didn't see mortals that way anymore. After all, he had fallen, giving up his station as a Reaper and marrying a mortal.

Reaching deep inside his soul, Isaiah shouted, "Sakoto!" The Yoruba wind evocation stirred the air around him. Within seconds, a torrent of air raced through the outer doors and into the antechamber. The wind slammed into the wooden door, flung it open, and banged it against the inside wall. The sound rolled across the amphitheater.

Isaiah's breath caught. A large magical shield surrounded the entire stage area. Inside, the current Protector huddled inside his own protective bubble while no less than twenty of the grey-robed attackers surrounded him.

They slashed and sliced with their jet-black scythes but so far, they couldn't touch him. When the boy turned in Isaiah's direction, his eyes wide with terror, Isaiah silently urged him to remember the training and listen to the ring. It could do so much more, if the legends were true.

Deyanira stood to the side in her flowing red Reaper's robes. She conjured a hex and sent it at Isaiah before ducking inside the protection of her barrier.

Kulinda, he thought, evoking the blocking spell with the Swahili word. His Reaper blades glowed brighter in the darkened space. The Angel script covering every square inch of the weapons flared as he brought them down in a crossing pattern to block Deyanira's attack.

Unlike most Reapers, members of the KIN despised their former lives. As such, they hated frail mortals and even reveled in the more hideous ways humans found to kill each other. Isaiah experienced a bit of shame from his time in the Kin. He'd been full of pain and sadness over his own first Death. Taking advantage of his pain, the Grim Reaper had twisted his mind and recruited him.

But I finally saw the truth to the Grim Reaper's plan. I rebelled. "Maybe you should fall, like I did, Deyanira. Become a Fallen Reaper. Step into the light."

Isaiah expected her to laugh, but her tone was sad when she spoke directly to him. "You forget. I was a powerful sorceress in my first life. I have no light to embrace."

"Then start a new course."

"You've grown so sentimental since you've left the Kin. I would never become a mortal again."

The restorative effects of crossing through a portal had reduced Deyanira's ritualistic scars to faint lines on her pale face. A full head of red hair that spilled down to her shoulders helped her look mortal despite her claims, and that hypocrisy galled Isaiah.

"You cross over into the mortal world more than any other Reaper. I wonder what that says about you?"

He wanted to goad her, but again, she came across as sad. "I miss our arguments, Isaiah."

"I don't."

Deyanira broke the mutual gaze to focus on the struggle inside the shield. "We all have our parts to play."

Isaiah mounted the stage, keeping his blades ready in case Deyanira attacked again. He moved back and forth along the outside of the barrier, unable to help.

The young man had lost his own protective bubble and had started to phase around, moving from one location to another in a blink of an eye. It was unfortunate, Isaiah mused. The boy had never known about the supernatural world or the After Life and didn't fully understand how to listen to the ring. Isaiah groaned, wondering how much could have changed if someone with training had activated the ring.

That was the catch: only certain mortals could access the power of a Protector's Ring. This young man had been one of them, maybe the last. Now it was all lost because of a traitor in their midst.

The would-be protector continued to phase around, but he couldn't avoid the attackers. There were too many, swarming around him like killer bees. Each time he appeared, he received a cut. Blood sprayed across the floor creating a macabre design.

Finally he dropped to his knees, unable to phase anymore. The attackers charged in cutting and opening new wounds. One held a scythe aloft and brought it down, intending to slice him open from left shoulder to right hip.

The boy's bloodied hand trembled as he held the ring close to his mouth and spoke to it. As the scythe bit into his body, he screamed out in agony. At the same time, the ring flared, engulfing him and the closest executioners in a brilliant light.

Isaiah blinked in horrid surprise. He snapped into motion and rolled off the lip of the stage. He pulled Janice with him against the stage's side. They huddled there, Janice curling herself into a ball so his larger body could cover her. Isaiah made sure to pull his long coat over them both.

The storm of power erupted overhead. The sound of stone hitting stone, and occasionally his back, was deafening. When the roaring decreased and the pressure relented, Isaiah peeked from under his coat. Half the amphitheater seats had been blasted to ruins by the release of power.

He lifted his coat away, gaping at the smoking spots where the blood had been baked on it. Except for a few rips, it was whole. He stood, slipped on the coat, and offered his wife a supporting hand. "You alright?"

"Yes." Janice stood.

He leapt up to the stage.

When Janice followed, her jaw dropped. "Oh my God."

It was like a bomb had gone off, Isaiah thought.

As the dust settled, a green bubble became visible on the far side of the ruined stage. Deyanira crouched there, the release of power having stripped away her human guise. Her face was more skeletal, her head bald except for a single red ponytail in the back. Most striking was the fully visible scars on her face.

Isaiah strode to the center of the stage and found the ring, gleaming and undamaged on the scorched floor. He crouched and scooped up the source of devastation.

"Give that to me, Isaiah." Deyanira had lowered her shield and stood facing him. Her frayed and smudged red robe swished as she gestured to the ring.

Isaiah rose to his feet. "I don't think so."

Deyanira's brilliant green eyes bore into his as she raised her right hand. Instead of casting a spell, she opened a vortex.

Isaiah didn't wait to see if more of her henchmen would swarm through. He reached back, and Janice clamped her hand in his. He nudged himself and phased from the amphitheater. He used his power to enter the aether, the stuff of the supernatural realm. It allowed him to bridge the gap between his starting point and destination in seconds.

The mortal world snapped into existence around them as they reappeared seven thousand miles away in a secluded courtyard. The closely packed brick surface, surrounding shrubbery, and the Lacebark pine at the center of the space reassured Isaiah. This was the sanctuary of Isaiah and Janice Blackstone.

He paused to take a deep breath of Georgia air. The sound of chirping birds and gently rustling branches was at odds with the death they'd just witnessed. But Isaiah had another reason for taking his time. He needed to let the dizziness pass. As a Fallen Reaper, phasing was second nature to him. But the distance, after expending energy fighting and carrying someone with him, took its toll.

Janice pressed a piece of hard candy into his mouth. The sweetness gave him an instant surge of energy. "Thanks."

A tall young man had been sitting on a nearby bench. He shot to his feet and hurried over, his own undamaged long coat swaying.

Isaiah nodded to him. "We're fine, Marcus."

Marcus halted, searching their bruises and raising an eyebrow at the sight of Isaiah's smoking long coat. "What about the Protector and the ring?"

"He's dead and I have the ring." Isaiah released his wife's hand and strode a few feet away, holding the ring in his right palm.

The Protector's Ring

Marcus stirred behind him. "We have to let the Alliance Council know."

"There're traitors in the Alliance. That's how they found the boy."

"But--"

Janice placed a hand on Marcus's shoulder. "He's right."

"Then what are you two planning?"

Isaiah turned. "I'm resigning from the Council."

"You can't..." Marcus sputtered.

"Yes, I can, and I want you to take my place." Isaiah held up a hand to stop Marcus from arguing. "A Council member can step down and name his replacement." Isaiah removed a golden shield from an inside pocket of his coat and held it out to Marcus. The shield's face featured three interlocking circles with outstretched wings above the center one. It was the same symbol branded into the left breast of both of their long coats. When Marcus hesitated, Isaiah skewered his fellow Fallen Reaper with his most severe glare.

Marcus's shoulders slumped a bit and he placed his slender hand on top of the shield.

Isaiah nodded. "Do you pledge to honor the Alliance and what it stands for, abiding by its edicts and rules?"

Marcus gulped. "I so pledge." Curving lines appeared on their forearms, hands, and the shield. The lines flared for a second before fading away. Marcus sucked in a deep breath, took the shield from Isaiah, and turned it over in his trembling hands. "What are you going to do?"

"The Grim Reaper wants the ring, and Deyanira will tell him I have it. So we're going to lead them on a goose chase."

Marcus slipped the shield in an inner pocket while giving Isaiah a hard look. "For how long?"

"Long enough."

Marcus furrowed his brow, making his lean brown face more hawkish in appearance. He pointed at the ring. "What about that?"

Janice slipped the ring out of her husband's hand and held it up. "We'll hide it."

Marcus shook his head. "I need to come with you--"

"You have a new job," Isaiah cut him off. "There has to be three Fallen Reapers on the Council to balance out the Mages and Mortals. You know that." He waited for Marcus to nod. Isaiah softened his tone. "And you're Jonah's godfather. You'll have to step into that role soon."

"What does that mean?"

"I'm sorry." Isaiah patted Marcus on the shoulders. "It's better if you don't know where we hide the ring." He looked away. "I have enough blood on my hands."

"None of this was your fault," Marcus said.

Isaiah didn't respond. Instead, he watched his troubled protégé come to terms with the situation. As a lawyer, Marcus had always been cool and calculating. It's why Isaiah wanted the young man to take his place on the Council. *And our son's godfather.*

When Marcus met his gaze, Isaiah sensed the final acceptance and understanding radiating from him. All Fallen Reapers could sense the emotions from others, except those trained to shield their feelings. Marcus didn't use one of those techniques, Isaiah noted, a clear sign of how close they'd grown.

Heaviness weighed on Isaiah as he stood beside Janice, and he used her nearness to draw strength. A chasm yawned before them, but they couldn't falter. He clenched his jaw, biting back the frustration. His voice grew tight as he said, "Tell the Alliance Council the ring was lost." He met Marcus's intense gaze. "Go."

A brief flash of uncertainty crossed Marcus's face. He swallowed and finally shut down his raging emotions. Squaring his shoulders, he gave Isaiah a respectful nod and phased away.

As soon as he was gone, Janice wrapped her arms around Isaiah's waist, resting her head against his chest. "We won't have a lot of time."

"I know." Isaiah wrapped his arms around her. "Maybe six months."

Janice sucked in a breath and frowned. "What about Jonah? Shouldn't we explain everything now?"

"If we do that, the others will focus on our son before he's ready." Isaiah tightened his embrace. "We can't do that." Janice nodded, rubbing her cheek against his chest. Isaiah shook her. "Are you sure about this plan to hide the ring?"

She tilted her head up to look into his deep brown eyes. He always loved the way her lighter brown eyes sparkled. He saw the certainty in them and knew it was a result of her gift to intuit things.

"Yes, it'll work," she said. "It's the last place anyone from our world would look for the ring."

CHAPTER TWO
A BOY NAMED JONAH

Jonah Blackstone stood at a shuttle stop, gazing intently through the glass cover of a Washington Post newspaper stand. He resembled any other twelve-year-old kid with his sagging blue jeans, loose t-shirt, colored sneakers and a ball cap on his short Afro. But unlike the other kids, off enjoying the start of summer vacation, Jonah carried his book bag with him.

He had paused in front of the newspaper stand, not knowing why the headline grabbed his attention. *Death Takes a Holiday?* Maybe it was the word *death* itself. Or maybe the cartoonish drawing of the Grim Reaper, complete with skull face and scythe, drew his attention. Perhaps it was the simple fact that he had an intense interest in the subject, ever since his best friend Oliver had died the year before.

Jonah had been able to sense something awful would happen, and he had seen a strange person wearing all black and hovering around his friend. When Jonah had tried to warn Oliver about the stranger, he discovered that no one else could see the man.

He leaned closer to read as he swallowed past the lump in his throat. That's why the article drew his attention. It represented a chance of finding an answer to why he could sense Death. According to the article, no person within a two-hundred-mile radius of Washington DC had died over the past two weeks. Victims of serious accidents, the kind that normally caused instant death, were hanging on. Terminally ill patients fought back from the brink of death. The phenomenon had everyone puzzled and a little scared.

Jonah's reaction had been his normal reaction to anything that puzzled him: he headed to a library. Even though he lived in Fairfax County, Virginia, he often came to the Arlington Central library because the manager knew his mom and treated him like a guest. He figured an Internet search would be enough to look up any previous occurrences of Death Holidays.

The research had provided immediate results. Jonah's excitement grew as he found articles about another such event. Tomorrow would mark thirteen years, to the day. Goosebumps rose along Jonah's arms: tomorrow was his thirteenth birthday. That meant the last time this happened was the day he was born. It had to be a coincidence, Jonah thought.

The wind gusted around the shuttle stop, snapping Jonah out of the troubling thought. He hitched the book bag on his shoulder as he waited. Another streak of silent lightning flashed overhead, and passing adults muttered to themselves.

A cold front appeared out of nowhere, taking a few hours to make the late June temperatures plummet twenty to thirty degrees. Bulging gray clouds blotted out the sun and the strange lightning flashed all day long, but no rain fell. The overall effect was oppressive, Jonah thought. Something strange was happening, and he could sense the crackle of tension in the air.

As Jonah gazed at the overcast sky, he hoped the strange weather wouldn't prevent his mom and dad from flying home. He missed his parents and hadn't seen them in over two weeks. They had promised to be home in time for his birthday, and he wanted to spend it with them.

He reached inside his jeans pocket, wrapping his fingers around his cell phone. Should he play his mom's message again? It felt like he'd done it a thousand times already, all the while wishing his dad had spoken in the message. Jonah longed to hear his dad's deep voice telling him that everything would be fine. The phone was out and in his hand when he experienced an annoying hitch in his stomach.

The sensation was not unfamiliar. It had been happening all this week, and each time his stomach hitched, he saw a person in black. They came in all races and nationalities. And the one thing they had in common, besides an intense fascination with him, was their unnatural stillness.

Jonah searched the people walking around him and saw a thin white man who stood on the other side of the busy Arlington Boulevard. Like the others Jonah had seen, he wore a black long coat, black pants, and black boots. Why did these people watch him? The wind kicked up a notch again and neither the man's long brown hair nor his coat stirred.

A group of office workers approached and walked right through the man as if he wasn't really there. Jonah blinked in surprise. That couldn't be right, he told himself, suddenly filled with the urge to talk with the man. He stepped off the sidewalk without thinking and a horn blared and brakes squealed.

The shuttle bus screeched to a stop just short of Jonah, and the driver started making angry gestures. Looking across the street, Jonah ignored the shuttle driver. However, the stranger was gone. That was the other thing about these people. They seemed to vanish in the blink of an eye.

The shuttle driver resorted to honking his horn as he motioned Jonah to get on or move out of the way. Jonah sighed, hitched up his book bag, and hurried around to mount the steps.

He worked his way to the very back of the shuttle to hide. His face warmed as every pair of eyes seemed to watch him. Jonah hated being the center of attention, and this was his worst nightmare. *Why do these things always happen to me?*

Even though it was rush hour and the shuttle was packed, he found an empty seat next to an elderly black woman. Being extra careful not to bump her, Jonah dropped into the seat and slipped the book bag on the floor between his feet. As he did so, the strange guy outside popped into his mind and he gazed past the woman and out the window.

His eyes hadn't played tricks on him. Those people walked through that man like he wasn't really there. Maybe there was something in the articles about strange people appearing around town. Jonah unzipped his book bag, intending to pull out the articles, but his new video game console tumbled out. He managed to catch it before it hit the ground and he placed the device on his lap. When he reached inside the book bag again, the elderly woman stirred and pointed a boney brown finger.

"That looks like an expensive little gizmo." She spoke with a squeaky little voice that fit her tiny body.

Jonah turned the small game console over in his hands. "It's a birthday gift from my aunt and uncle."

"Oh. Happy Birthday."

She offered to shake his hand. As soon as Jonah touched her, the woman's little body tensed and her free hand clutched the tiny ankh necklace she wore.

The Protector's Ring   11

"Are you okay?"

"Yes." She took a deep breath, and offered him a weak smile. "How old are you, young man?"

"I'll be thirteen tomorrow."

"I bet you have a big party planned."

"No, not really. It'll just be my mom and dad."

"What about your relatives?"

"They live in Georgia."

"No friends?"

Jonah shook his head no. The woman studied him for a moment, then glanced down at the book bag. "Summer school?"

"I'm doing research at the library."

"Bookworm, eh?" She laughed. "My second husband was a bookworm. He kept books everywhere. It drove me absolutely crazy."

Jonah wondered what she would say about his parents' study. Bookshelves covered an entire wall, stuffed with volumes from all around the world. His parents were archeologists, and the room was a bookworm's heaven.

The woman leaned closer, and the scent of some flowery perfume tickled Jonah's nose. "I never went in for big parties, myself. Better to keep it small, I say. More cake for you."

She gave Jonah a wink and went back to staring out the window while fingering her necklace.

Jonah thought about her comments as he slid the video game console inside the book bag. He hesitated before taking out the articles; the conversation also reminded him of the day he had discovered the name of his ability. That had also been the day his best friend Oliver had died.

Jonah was understandably upset with Oliver's death, so his parents had sent him to bed early that evening. Unable to rest, he had snuck out of his bedroom and crouched at the top of the stairs. His parents were in their study with the doors closed. Jonah's heart pounded in his chest as he descended the stairs, tiptoed to the closed study doors, and peeked through the crack.

He couldn't see his dad, but he heard the desk chair creak as his dad spoke. "I talked with Marcus and the others. They agreed with me. Jonah has Death Sense."

"Are they sure?" His mom moved into view. "He hasn't shown any other signs."

"You heard Jonah. He accurately sensed the danger around Oliver. I just wonder if our son is telling us everything."

"I'd be shocked if he wasn't. He is more your son in that respect."

There was a slight amusement above the clear worry in his mom's voice. His father let out a low grunt. Both his parents remained silent for a moment. Jonah had started to move when his mom spoke again.

"Maybe we should tell Jonah everything now." His mom twisted her hands together. His dad stepped into view and took her hands in his.

"No, Janice. He'll be thirteen in a year. We follow the plan."

Jonah's mom began to cry, and his dad hugged her. Sensing they would remain that way for some time, Jonah stepped back from the door and crept upstairs to bed.

His parents' conversation filled him with fear. *Death Sense?* He had never heard of the term. However, he already had experienced it twice in his life. The first time had happened when his second-grade teacher died. The second time occurred earlier that day, when Oliver died.

The sensation started with a buzzing in his head and a slight headache. This was followed by a whisper of a person's name and, when Jonah thought about the person in danger, his headache would spike.

Cold chills and vomiting followed as the headache built into a severe migraine at the moment the person died. It was the only time Jonah would ever get sick, which made it all the more unusual.

From that night on, his parents never mentioned Death Sense, and Jonah was afraid to let them know he had listened to their conversation. So he turned to the books in the library, trying to find anything he could about his ability. Jonah decided that it only happened when someone close to him, or who he liked, was in danger. It was the reason he decided not to make any new friends.

The Protector's Ring

Jonah glanced out the shuttle window again as he rubbed his forehead. He'd been trying to deny that his head buzzed today. That frightened him because the only people close to him were his neighbors the Garretts and, of course, his parents.

CHAPTER THREE
THE SEER

The evening commuters jostled each other as they rushed to catch metro trains. Jonah bumped along in the midst of the crowd until he heard someone call out his name.

"Jonah."

He stopped and spun around, causing several people to give him irritated looks as they hurried by. The voice sounded so near that Jonah wondered if someone had actually whispered in his ear. The initial rush of people thinned out, and he saw her. The little woman from the shuttle waited on the sidewalk, halfway between the shuttle stop and the gate. She beckoned to him.

As Jonah approached, he wondered if he had left something on the shuttle.

"Excuse me," he said when he reached her. "Did you call my name?"

She nodded. "I didn't want to say anything on that crowded shuttle."

"Okay..."

"When I touched your hand, I understood about you. It must be hard to be different."

"I don't know what you're talking about. I have to get home."

Jonah backed toward the gate, but the woman grabbed his forearm. "I know you can sense Death."

Jonah pulled his arm out of her grip. "You're crazy."

The Protector's Ring 15

"Crazy? Hah! I know about the other thing you can do. You are special."

"I'm not special. I'm just a kid."

"You want to believe that, but you were never just a kid. Deep down, you understand, yet you try to hide from it."

Jonah couldn't deny her words. In fact, he had thought the same thing about himself earlier.

"Who are you?"

"I'm a Seer. You were meant to take that seat next to me today."

"That just happened."

"Child, nothing happens by accident." The Seer motioned toward the sky with a gnarled hand. "Look about you, young man. It is no coincidence that Death is behaving strangely and you turn thirteen tomorrow." She pointed at Jonah's eyes. "You see them, don't you?"

"What do you know about those people?" Jonah sucked in a breath, catching the woman's larger meaning. "What does the weather have to do with me?"

The Seer didn't answer. Instead, she held out a knobby hand. Jonah shrank away from it.

"Take my hand, Jonah Blackstone."

"How do you know my name?"

The woman shook her boney hand. "Take it."

"Why?"

"I can only see by touching."

Jonah hesitated as two competing desires warred inside him. He desperately wanted to know about the people in black and the strange weather. However, this Seer could sense all those things about him just by shaking his hand. For the first time in Jonah's life, he was afraid of receiving information. This woman could destroy his hope of being a normal kid. No, Jonah decided. He didn't want to touch her again.

Perhaps the Seer read the decision on his face because she grabbed his hand with a surprisingly strong grip. Then she added her other hand to keep him from pulling free. Jonah's Death Sense began to buzz in his head as the woman closed her eyes. Her body jerked and stiffened. The ankh necklace begin to glow. When she opened her eyes, they were milky white.

Jonah struggled in the woman's firm grip. She opened her mouth and spoke in a deeper voice.

"Yes. You are different."

Her voice seemed to wrap itself around him, chilling him to the bone and freezing him in place. Jonah was frightened, yet there was something compelling about her, something that drew on his very soul.

"Yessss," she hissed. "You will become more powerful than anyone ever imagined. You are going to change things."

The woman let out a strangled moan as Jonah's Death Sense flared, causing him to wince. A shudder went through the Seer's little body and her head flopped forward. Jonah staggered as she sagged into his arms.

"Whoa!" He gently shook her.

"Hey!" The station manager called out, stepping from his kiosk. "Is she alright?"

Before Jonah could answer, the Seer stirred and lifted her head.

Her eyes were their normal deep brown color again. And she blinked several times as if trying to focus on him.

"I'm just a little tired."

"I have some water inside." The station manager paused by the gate, watching the woman with a skeptical look.

"I'm fine." She patted Jonah on the arm. "My grandson here is helping me."

"Let me know." The manager went back to his kiosk.

The Seer turned on Jonah with an awed expression. "Don't you realize how important you are?"

"You said I will change things." The Seer nodded. "Tell me. What will I change?"

"You'll change everything, young man." Her expression shifted into a deep frown. "Trust your feelings about your parents."

The Protector's Ring   17

"What about my parents?" Jonah asked, struggling to keep up with all the cryptic comments.

"I saw you in pain and great loss."

"No."

"Your pain will end, and things will get better. You will be happy again and among family." She patted his hand. "I'm sorry."

Jonah pulled his hand free and backed away from the Seer. When she reached out, he turned and ran through the gate to the station, trying to escape the finality in the woman's voice.

"Remember, it will get better!" she called out.

Jonah tried to block out her voice as he boarded an orange-line train. He found an empty seat and collapsed into it as fear rippled through his body. Curling up against the side of the car, Jonah pressed his head to the cool window. It took him several minutes to calm his heart and for the fear to recede.

When he reached his stop, Jonah exited the station and unlocked his bike in a sort of daze. The lightning flashed continually overhead as he rode down the sidewalk along Saintsbury drive. He didn't notice it. Instead, he filled his mind with comforting thoughts of his parents being home and waiting for him. Maybe they wanted to surprise him?

Despite grasping at happy thoughts, Jonah had to battle his own growing fear, and the frequent gusts of strong wind, as he turned onto his street. When his house came into view, Jonah's spirits drooped. The house was dark and his parents' car wasn't in the driveway.

The old woman's voice came back to him, mixing with the irritating buzzing in his head. He wouldn't accept it. She had to be wrong. His feelings were wrong. Jonah tried to push the troubling thoughts out of his head as he rode to the Garretts' house.

A bright yellow balloon narrowly missed Jonah's head as he entered the Garretts' kitchen. Little Tim, the Garretts' youngest son, let out an unrestrained laugh. A *Happy Birthday* banner hung above the entrance into the dining room and a large birthday cake was on the kitchen table.

"Ah," Mr. Garrett said. "There's the birthday boy."

Little Tim stifled his laugh, walked over to Jonah, and shook his hand. "Happy Birthday, Jonah."

"Thanks, Tim."

Mr. Garrett laughed at his son as he pulled the loosened tie from around his beefy neck. He hadn't changed out of his work clothes: a dress shirt, tie, and slacks.

"We know your birthday's tomorrow, but since you'll celebrate with your parents…"

"We decided to have a birthday dinner for you tonight," Mrs. Garrett finished, coming in from the dining room. Kim, the second youngest, followed her mom. Mrs. Garrett crossed over to Jonah and picked a stray leaf off his shirt.

"I hope you're in the mood for pizza."

"That sounds cool." Jonah slipped off his book bag and Little Tim grabbed it.

"I can take that to your room."

"You don't have to do that."

Little Tim ignored Jonah's protest, hefted the book bag, and staggered out of the kitchen. Jonah wouldn't be surprised if the curious little kid riffled through the bag. Little Tim found everything about Jonah interesting.

He stuffed his hands in his pockets, unsure of what to do with himself. He was grateful to the Garretts for letting him stay over, but he wanted to sleep in his own bed tonight instead of a daybed in the guest room again.

He knew his mom would disapprove of his negative attitude. He was about to offer to help with the balloons when Kim pointed a little finger at him.

"Mom, he's gonna see it before we're ready."

"No, he won't, Kim." Mrs. Garrett took plates from the cabinet and handed them to her daughter.

Kim balanced the plates and paused long enough to warn Jonah, "No peeking."

Mrs. Garrett nudged her daughter toward the dining room before saying to him, "Why don't you go watch the game with Tyrone?"

The Protector's Ring

Jonah's shoulders slumped. He considered going to the guest room and hiding out until dinner, but Little Tim came back to help his father with the balloons. Jonah knew he'd look stupid going back there after having the boy carry his book bag. So he nodded to Mrs. Garrett and shuffled off to the den.

Tyrone Garrett lounged on the couch with the TV remote in his hands. He was a thick boy, beefy like his dad. When Jonah entered the room, Tyrone gave him a slight nod with his rounded chin before focusing on the game again. Jonah crossed to one of the armchairs and sat down.

Stocky Mr. Garrett had played college football for Howard University. Tyrone played football in Middle School. Both were avid sports fans, but Jonah just wasn't into sports like that. Neither were his parents. He'd take a good adventure book over a game any day. He suspected that was one reason Tyrone didn't want to hang out with him.

Kim let out a squeal of laughter from the dining room. Little Tim answered with a shout, and both their parents told them to calm down. Jonah slumped in the chair, rubbing his forehead. He could never get used to all the activity of the Garretts' house. Even when younger, he had been a quiet kid. And being the only child of researchers made for a quiet house. His Death Sense throbbed painfully at the thought of his parents, and Jonah tried to ignore it.

The doorbell rang several minutes later, and Mr. Garrett's heavy footfalls vibrated up into Jonah's chair as the man hurried down the hallway to the front door. The noise of wind and rattling branches rolled into the house when he answered. The delivery boy looked put out and grumbled as he handed over two large pizzas.

Mr. Garrett paid the boy, then had to use his shoulder to close the door against the howling wind.

Mrs. Garrett took the pizzas from him. "I hope you gave him an extra tip."

"I did. It's getting worse out there."

Jonah didn't say anything as he followed Tyrone and his parents into the dining room. As everyone gathered around the table, Jonah had his first opportunity to witness the birthday decorations. He was stunned. In addition to the *Happy Birthday* banner over the entrance to the dining room, balloons were tied to the backs of the chairs. Multicolored napkins were placed next to each plate. The birthday cake took up the middle of the table.

Jonah thought the decorations a little young for him, but he kept that to himself.

Mrs. Garrett sat a pizza box on either side of the cake and opened them. The aroma of pepperoni and grilled chicken wafted over the table. Any other day, Jonah would have been the first to dive in. Tonight, he didn't think he'd make it through one piece.

"The birthday boy has the honor of taking the first slice."

Jonah smiled, trying to hide the grimace on his face. He chose a piece of chicken pizza, sat down, and watched the Garretts as he took his first, small bite. Thinking about the Garretts, picturing them individually in his mind, didn't affect the buzzing in his head. They weren't in danger.

A knot formed in his stomach as dread and sadness welled up inside him. He glanced out the dining room's bay window, watching the trees whip back and forth and hoping the feeling would pass. When he turned back to the half-eaten pizza on his plate, he saw Mrs. Garrett watching him. She gave him a thin smile before hurrying out of the room and returning a moment later with the birthday presents.

Kim and Little Tim were particularly excited. "Open ours first! Open ours first!" Kim bounced up and down in her chair while Little Tim tried to keep calm.

Jonah started to open the wrapping paper when Kim reached over and ripped it. "You're supposed to do it like that, silly."

Jonah smiled and pulled off the last of the paper. Inside, he found a set of bookmarks with images of famous African-Americans and with colorful tassels. Jonah suspected the gift was Little Tim's idea.

"We thought you could use these, at the library," Tim explained.

"Thanks." Jonah put the bookmarks aside and looked up to see Tyrone holding a thin, square present.

"Happy Birthday."

Jonah took the present and opened it. Inside was a music CD.

"You don't have that one, do you?"

The Protector's Ring

Jonah turned the CD over in his hands. It was the soundtrack of the latest action movie. "No, I don't." He would never have expected Tyrone to do something like this. "Thanks a lot."

The last gift was from Mr. and Mrs. Garrett. Their package was larger than the rest, and it was heavy. Jonah started to open the paper, paused, and held the package out to Timothy and Kim. "You want to open it?"

The siblings launched themselves on the wrapping and tore it off in seconds. The Garretts had bought Jonah a dark brown attaché case with gold fasteners.

"Wow. Thanks."

Opening the gifts took Jonah's mind off the dread for a time, but the cold sweats started, and he worried the Garretts would notice. When his stomach grew queasy, he put on a brave face. However, the sight of pizza threatened to make him heave.

"Can I be excused?"

Mr. and Mrs. Garrett traded glances and Jonah thought they would say no.

"It's my stomach," Jonah added.

"I can get you something." Mrs. Garrett began to raise from her chair. "Maybe some mint tea?"

Jonah stood. "I just want to go to my room." He saw the mixture of looks on everyone's faces, but he had to get away.

When the Garretts gave him silent nods, Jonah gathered up the smaller gifts and slipped them in the attaché case.

"Thanks for the presents," he said and ran off to the guest room.

Jonah didn't bother to turn on the lights. He dropped the case by the closet and lay on the daybed, watching the continual lightning flashes outside the window. He couldn't hold off any longer and allowed himself to think about his mom and dad. The pain hit him so hard that he cried out before he could stop himself. His body began to twitch and spasm at odd intervals.

Not my mom and dad. Not them! In desperation, Jonah grabbed his iPod. Maybe the music would help to drown out thoughts of his parents so he could rest.

It almost worked. Several times, he started to drowse, but an unguarded thought about his parents would enter his mind and the pain from the Death Sense would jolt him awake. Finally, fatigue won out and he descended into a troubled sleep.

CHAPTER FOUR
HIDDEN CHAMBER

Jonah dreamt that he stood outside on a round brick-and-concrete platform. Crickets chirped loudly, somewhere in the middle of the night. The tree branches rustled from an errant, hot summer breeze. The only illumination came from a full moon, which gave everything a haunted look.

About a hundred feet away, stood an old, abandoned brick building. Jonah thought the building was familiar, but he couldn't remember from where. As he puzzled over that, he sensed a change in the air pressure a second before his mom and dad appeared between him and the building.

Even in a dream, Jonah imagined that any other kid would have been surprised to see people appearing, but he wasn't. He'd seen his father do the *special thing* before.

He'd seen his father do it one night when someone threw a brick in the dining room window. His mom had grabbed him and dove to the floor. Jonah looked up in time to see his dad's body ripple, disappear, and then reappear right next to them.

Jonah could never forget because he'd done the *special thing* himself. It happened at the end of the school year, when bullies chased him into the boy's bathroom. When the bullies burst through the door, they knocked Jonah backward. Instead of hitting the cold bathroom floor, Jonah felt a rippling along his body and a second later, he found himself lying in the dirt on the elementary school's ball field.

He kept that and other experiences to himself over the last six months, feeling his parents were too busy with the move to their current house, as well as constantly coming and going on secret trips. Because of the constant travel, Jonah had spent more time as a guest at the Garretts' over the last month than he had at home. He was overwhelmed with the realization that maybe he should have at least told his parents about the people in black clothes. Shame and a little anger hit him.

Jonah called to his parents. "Mom. Dad."

His parents continued to look around without giving any indication that they heard him. Why couldn't his parents hear him? This was his dream. As he wondered about that, he began to notice other things.

His mom and dad, who normally dressed alike in jeans, hiking boots, and plain brown shirts when working, had on different clothes tonight. His dad wore a long black leather coat with a high collar that didn't hide his broad, muscular shoulders. Jonah had never seen the coat before nor the black military-styled boots, black jeans, and shirt his mother wore.

As he stepped off the platform and moved closer, Jonah became aware that his parents were also dirty and sweaty as if they'd been running. Maybe they'd been fighting, he thought. There was a patch of dirt in his dad's hair and smudges on his black coat. And his mom's naturally frizzy curls stuck out at odd angles and she had a rip on her right pant leg.

They finished searching the area and turned to face the building. Jonah followed their gaze. Now that he was closer, he could read the words carved into the crumbling stone facade: Free Public Library.

"Are you ready, Janice?" Jonah's dad took out a cylinder. With a flick of his hand, the cylinder gave off a metallic swishing sound and transformed into a bright silver blade. His dad muttered and the blade shone with a pale yellow light.

His mom nodded and made a quick movement with her right hand. Jonah heard the same metallic swishing sound and a second later, she held a long silver blade. Hers shone with a pale white light. Jonah stared at the weapons in amazement.

The blades were doubled-edged and made of single pieces of metal with strange symbols covering every surface. His mom twirled her blade once, bringing it to rest in a reverse grip. She looked like a true fighter, Jonah thought, as she mounted the front steps with his dad.

They reached the entrance, pushed open the old library doors, and disappeared into the darkness. Jonah rushed up the chipped and broken

The Protector's Ring

stone steps. When he reached the door, he skidded to a halt because his parents stood just inside.

"Mom? Dad? Can't you hear me?" Jonah raised his hands and waved to them, but his parents didn't notice. They moved off into the darkened space.

Jonah didn't like this dream. When he swatted at the doorframe in frustration, his hand went straight through. He reached out for the doorframe again, taking his time. Jonah thought he could feel something as the hand went through the wood. He was like a ghost. Is that why his parents couldn't see or hear him?

Jonah's heart began to race, and it was all he could do to keep from screaming until he reminded himself it was just a dream. He wasn't dead. He wasn't a ghost. While he was distracted with the doorframe, his parents had crossed the library lobby.

The old counters and railings were still in place, but the rest of the floor was empty. Jonah hurried around—and even through—one of the railings, to catch up to his parents. His dad stopped in a side hallway to jiggle a doorknob. When it didn't open, he stepped back and, raising a large boot, slammed it into the wood beneath the handle. The wood cracked and splintered as the door banged open.

Jonah couldn't understand this dream. It was like being inside a 3D environment instead of a real dream. All he could do was watch and follow as his parents entered the stairwell. They descended two flights of stairs and came out in a pitch black hallway.

His dad waved his bright blade around in graceful movements, sending rats scurrying in all directions. A blank section of mildewed wall stood before Jonah's parents. His dad moved the blade back and forth, mere inches above the surface, then ran his large hand over a particular spot.

Jonah's dad pulled a round object—a compass, Jonah noted—out of his shirt and, holding it against the wall, waited. Nothing happened for several minutes until a low rumble filled the hallway. The vibration rippled up through the floor and shook his parents, but Jonah didn't feel anything. The wall rippled like water and an opening appeared. Jonah's jaw dropped as the darkened hole expanded, sounding like brick sliding across brick. The opening stabilized into a perfect circle. His dad calmly held the blade inside the hole.

"You first?" His mom nodded toward the opening.

"Of course." His dad stepped through and paused just inside to reach back and grip his mom's hand. The dim light from the blades dropped below floor level as they descended out of view.

Jonah crossed to the opening, took a deep breath, and descended the long staircase behind his parents. He had gone down about half a dozen steps when he heard the sound of sliding bricks behind him. His parents continued on while Jonah froze, listening. The opening in the wall had closed.

He paused, wondering how they would get out. Maybe his dad could use the compass again, from this side. Yeah, Jonah thought as his nervousness eased. His dad would be able to get out. That made sense. Buoyed with that conclusion, he continued down the extremely narrow passage. It was longer than he expected, and a dim glow grew brighter until he reached the bottom.

His parents stood before two high metal doors. There was a gold symbol spanning both, three inter-locking circles with a pair of wings spread out above. At the heart of the center circle was a round hole. His dad placed his compass in the depression. It rotated ninety degrees, followed by a loud click, like a bolt being released. When his dad removed the compass, the massive doors opened on their own with a heavy, creaking sound. Lights flared on inside the room.

Jonah hurried forward to follow his parents, and his jaw dropped. The chamber was huge, with a surprisingly high ceiling. Bookshelves lined three entire walls and extended up, at least two floors. Every shelf and cubbyhole was packed solid with ancient-looking volumes. Most were vertical on the shelves, but here and there, some were laid sideways. Even the spaces between the tops of the books and shelf above were crammed with more books and rolled parchments. It was a hidden library below the old library.

"Whoa!" Jonah let out an amazed breath as he stumbled further into the chamber.

Even though everything looked ancient, modern electric lights were mounted along the entire lip that separated the walls from the domed ceiling. The illumination reflected off the smooth stone, creating a subdued yet even lighting throughout the space. Jonah thought it was like many of the libraries he had visited.

While he stared at the treasure trove of books, his parents' attention was on a large, circular ring that was positioned against the fourth wall. Jonah moved closer to give himself a better view. It was made of stone with symbols, like the ones on his parents' blades, carved into the surface.

"Why is a portal in this chamber?" His mom brushed her fingers along the ring.

"They used it to cross over." His dad pressed a large hand against the surface. "I can sense it."

"You mean her?"

Jonah's dad nodded as he rotated on the spot, scanning every inch of the chamber.

"We should leave here now," his mom insisted.

"In a minute." His dad raised his rich, baritone voice so that it echoed through the space. "Elder, show yourself. We need your help!" He waited a moment, then called out again, "Elder. We need you."

"I don't think he's coming, Isaiah."

"You're right. I had to try." He took her hand. "Let's go."

They had turned for the opening to the stairway when the sound of running footsteps grew louder ahead of two men, who came into the chamber. They were dressed in grey tunics and pants with bone-white skulls on the left side of their chests. Each carried a curved, jet black scythe with a hand grip. Their eyes were solid, milky white. As soon as Jonah saw that, his Death Sense spiked. What was it about these white-eyed people that bothered him? Were they Seers, like the old woman from the bus?

A taller, third person in a billowing red robe stepped through the opening behind them. The robe had smudges on it, and the hood was drawn forward. The three newcomers quickly fanned out, blocking the exit.

Jonah's mom made a quick motion with her left hand, causing the cylinder in that hand to transform into a second gleaming blade.

His dad pointed to the bandit in the smudged red robes. "What's the matter, Deyanira? You're looking a bit ragged. I suspect you'll have to cross back very soon."

"Give me the Protector's Ring, Isaiah, and I'll let you live." Deyanira's cold voice cut the air like a knife. Jonah marveled that his dad didn't flinch.

"Your master wants me dead."

"Perhaps. Give it to me and I can let you go." His dad began to shake his head and Deyanira snapped, "Think of your family."

"I am." Jonah's parents gave each other's hand a quick squeeze. His dad stood tall, puffing out his chest and brandishing his own blades. "You can't have the ring."

Deyanira threw back the hood and Jonah sucked in a startled breath. Scars covered her face and a single red ponytail hung off the back of her otherwise bald head. She glared at his dad.

"So be it."

The woman waved her arms in a smooth motion and conjured a greenish ball of flame. It floated in midair until Deyanira brought her hands together and shouted, "*Washa!*" The fireball shot forward.

Jonah's dad waved his blades and shouted, "*Sakoto!*" A sudden gust of wind rushed forward, snuffing out the ball of fire. His dad dropped into a fighting stance.

"Shall we finish what we started?"

Jonah heard the distinctive metallic sound as Deyanira drew out her own blades. The smooth motion made it appear as if the blades were already activated beneath her robes.

Deyanira pointed a blade at Jonah's mom. "You two take care of the woman. Leave him to me."

Panic gripped Jonah as Deyanira's henchmen closed the distance between themselves and his mom. Both men sliced the air with the scythes in practiced movements. The sound of the weapons, like an eerie whine, set Jonah's nerves on end.

However, his mom wasn't bothered by the sound, and she didn't wait for them to strike. She moved like a ninja with her blades as she rushed the nearest fighter. He swung his scythe, and she easily blocked the move. Sparks flew when the weapons connected. The fighter whirled and sliced at his mom again, but she ducked under his arm, cutting him across the leg. He leapt backward, favoring the injury.

She sprang forward, swinging at him with her right blade. He blocked that with his scythe, then was forced to use his hand to knock Janice's left

The Protector's Ring

blade aside. He succeeded in doing that twice more before grabbing her left wrist and using his body to push her away. Jonah's mom spun with the motion, came under the scythe, and scored a deep cut across his chest. The bandit spasmed, dropping his scythe to the ground. His milky-white eyes turned normal as he fell to the floor beside his discarded weapon.

A flash of light caught Jonah's attention. His dad and Deyanira whirled, slashed, and countered each other's blows. Their movements were interspersed with blurred attacks and strange pauses. Deyanira lunged, and Jonah's dad knocked her blades aside to land a kick to her midsection. She stumbled back, then turned the fall into a backward flip and came down on her feet.

Meanwhile, the remaining fighter rushed Jonah's mom, swinging his scythe. She managed to leap back as the weapon caught her shirt and sliced it open. The fighter brought the scythe up and down in an overhead swipe.

"Mom!" Jonah shouted.

His mom crossed her blades and caught the scythe, but the force of the blow drove her to her knees. When the attacker shoved her backward, his mom rolled with the motion, pulling the guy forward. Planting a foot on his gut, she heaved, flipping him over her head. The man landed on his back and tried to roll to his feet. Jonah's mom got to her feet first and kicked him between the shoulder blades. She followed that with a swipe across his back, and he slumped to the floor.

Green light flared as Deyanira weaved her arms, conjuring another fireball. "*Washa!*"

"*Sakoto!*" Jonah's dad shouted in response.

This time, the gust of wind stopped the fireball in midair. As his dad continued to mutter and weave his blades, the fireball turned back. It struck Deyanira, whose robe burst into green flames that she snuffed out a moment later. She spun on the spot to face the portal, a sneer twisting her face.

Five widely spaced symbols on the portal already glowed a rich yellow color. When the sixth symbol lit up, a rip formed in the portal's center. It expanded into a circular opening that grew until it reached the inner edges. Jonah shivered as a wave of cold air rolled over him. Several red-robed people stood on the other side. The portal was a doorway.

A cold, inhuman laugh filled the chamber. Jonah's dad raised his blades, staring through the opening. Deyanira flinched and dropped into a crouch.

Light flared on the other side of the device from a source Jonah couldn't see and then, a huge, brilliant, red fireball roared through and into the chamber.

His dad shouted, "Get down!"

The fireball sailed over his parents' heads and hit the far wall. Books, wood, and stone exploded in all directions. The ground shook as a wave of heat and dust rolled over Jonah. He feared the entire chamber might collapse. Nightmarish red flames began to burn the precious books and the old wooden shelves. Black smoke coiled along the high ceiling like an angry living creature, causing the chamber to fill with choking fumes and intense heat. In the middle of it all, Jonah's parents huddled together.

"Dad!"

His dad turned, peering through the smoke. His eyes widened in shock. "Jonah?" His mom looked around, apparently unable to see him, but Jonah's dad looked directly at him. He took a step forward. "Jonah! How?" His dad paused, lifted his mom to her feet, and pointed through the smoke.

Her blades slipped free of her grasp and clattered on the ground as she raised both hands to her mouth. "Jonah!" She darted forward, but his dad was faster, slipping an arm around her waist and pulling her back. She struggled in his grip, slapping at his arms and glaring up at him, but he held firm. After struggling for a moment more, she finally relaxed and leaned her head against his chest.

"Mom? Dad?"

His parents faced him, both oddly composed despite the nightmarish heat and destruction around them.

"We're sorry, Jonah," his mom said.

"Just remember," his dad added. "We did everything to protect you."

"We love you, sweetheart," his mom shouted.

Alarm rolled through Jonah and he started for them, but at that moment, another huge fireball roared through the opened portal, adding to the hellish red glare from the roaring flames.

Jonah's Death Sense hurt more than ever, forcing him to his hands and knees, and he threw up. His dad faced the oncoming fireball, weaving his hands in a complex motion and shouting, "*Sakoto!*"

Jonah reached out for his parents, but everything began to waver. The sounds warped as he felt himself being pulled away. The scene grew smaller as if he were sucked through a dark, scary tunnel until nothing but darkness remained.

CHAPTER FIVE
BEARER OF BAD NEWS

"No!" Jonah shouted, in his own bed again. He squeezed his eyes shut and tried to return to the dream.

"Jonah, wake up!" He opened his eyes to find Mrs. Garrett leaning over him in her nightgown. "You were shouting in your sleep."

"I have to go back!"

"Honey, you're in the bed. You haven't been anywhere."

"You don't understand." He struggled to sit up and realized his bedsheets were twisted around his body. He'd also thrown up on himself, and the soiled pajama top clung to his sweaty skin. Jonah trembled all over; the lingering smell of burning books irritated his nose.

"Jonah, what's wrong?"

"It's my parents."

Mrs. Garrett couldn't hide the look of fear that crossed her face. "I'm sure they're all right. They'll be here tomorrow." She helped Jonah untangle himself from the messy sheets and pointed to the pajama top. "Take that off."

"But something happened to them!" His words were muffled as he pulled the offending garment top over his head.

Mrs. Garrett frowned as she gathered up the bed sheet with his smelly pajama top and hurried from the room with the balled-up mess.

Jonah slumped back on his damp pillow and glanced around the darkened room. Despite what she said, he could tell Mrs. Garrett believed him. That meant she knew something about his Death Sense. He wondered why his parents would tell her before they'd even talk to him about it. He started to tremble all over again.

Not my parents, please!

The certainty about his parents threatened to overwhelm Jonah as he lay there. Mrs. Garrett returned several minutes later with a cup of warm mint tea and a clean set of sheets and pillow case. Jonah hastily wiped the tears from his eyes as she gave him the cup.

"This should help you sleep." She motioned him to stand, unfolded the sheets, and quickly remade the bed.

Jonah lifted the cup with a shaking hand, drank some tea, and frowned. His mom had fixed mint tea for him whenever he had a bad dream. Mrs. Garrett's had a strange aftertaste. Jonah tried to concentrate on that as he got back in bed, but his mind refused to work and his eyes closed. Immediately, flashes of images from the dream sprang into his head. He forced his eyes open and was surprised to see Mrs. Garrett standing in the doorway. Wasn't she just beside the bed?

"Try to get some sleep, Jonah." She closed the door.

Alone again, he rolled over and glanced at the clock on the bedside table. It read two in the morning. He had officially turned thirteen years old. Jonah curled up under the covers and tried to keep his eyes open. He didn't want to go to sleep.

He struggled to focus on the strange dream. He'd had them before, but never anything this detailed. That chamber, the sounds and smells, were so real. And his father truly looked shocked that he was there. How could that happen in a dream? And why couldn't he control anything?

With a start, Jonah realized that thinking of his parents didn't cause pain. The buzz and headache were gone. He wanted to believe that his parents weren't in danger anymore and they would be all right. As he tried to hold on to that comforting thought, his eyes overcame his resistance to keep them open, and sleep overwhelmed him.

A cry rang out, startling Jonah out of his sleep. He sat up in bed and blinked at the muted sunlight coming through the window. He listened as someone, probably Mr. Garrett, raised his voice for a second. Then the cry subsided into the low tones of a conversation.

Jonah peeked at his clock, groaned, and rolled over when he heard another muffled voice—a male voice. He sat up in bed again. That second voice sounded familiar. *Dad?* He hopped out of bed and pulled on a shirt as he left the guest room.

The hushed conversation increased in volume as Jonah neared the Garretts' den. When he reached the doorway, all conversation halted. His spirits fell because he didn't see his father. Instead, a tall black man dressed in a long, dark leather coat stood next to Mr. Garrett. The coat was just like the one his dad wore in the dream, Jonah thought. And he recognized the man, especially the large brown eyes that never seemed to blink as they watched him.

He offered Jonah a slender right hand with a bright silver ring on it.

"Good morning, Jonah. My name is Marcus."

"I know you." Jonah shook his hand. "You work with my dad. Have you seen him?"

Marcus's eyes widened and he shook his head no.

"Jonah." Mr. Garrett gripped Jonah by the shoulders. "We need to talk to you." He ushered Jonah into the den and sat him in a chair. Then he began to pace back and forth, looking solemn.

The man's sad face frightened Jonah. "What's wrong? Is it my parents?"

The question forced Mr. Garrett to stop. "Jonah this is difficult--"

"They're dead, aren't they?" Every detail of the dream came flooding back into Jonah's mind. His breath caught as the pain hit him.

"We're sorry." Mr. Garrett knelt in front of him. "There's been a terrible accident and your parents—well, your parents were killed."

Hearing the actual words stunned Jonah even though his mind already knew the truth. His body began to tremble, and he hugged himself. Mr. Garrett patted his shoulder. That didn't help. Images from the dream flashed through his mind, and he closed his eyes, trying to block them out.

The Protector's Ring

His mind wouldn't cooperate as it replayed the entire fight. *Fight!* He didn't see an accident in the dream. He opened his eyes, staring up into Marcus's face and ignoring Mr. Garrett.

"My parents weren't attacked?"

"Can I talk to Jonah alone?" Marcus also ignored Mr. Garrett as he focused intently on the boy.

Mr. Garrett hesitated, not leaving Jonah's side as he faced Marcus. Jonah could sense the tension between the two men. Perhaps Marcus felt it, too, because he finally shifted his large eyes to Mr. Garrett.

"I'm responsible for Jonah."

"That's funny," Mr. Garrett snorted. "I never saw you around when Jonah had to stay with my family."

Marcus squared his shoulders, and his eyes seemed to bore into Mr. Garrett. Although Marcus wasn't much taller than Mr. Garrett, something about the stare clearly intimidated Jonah's neighbor.

Mr. Garrett broke eye contact first and glanced toward the kitchen. Jonah heard a sniffle and realized that Mrs. Garrett must have been crying in the other room all this time.

"I'll be in the kitchen if you need me." He gave Jonah's shoulder a reassuring squeeze before leaving the den. Marcus moved a chair to face Jonah and sat down.

"Why do you ask if your parents were attacked?" Marcus stared at Jonah in his unblinking way. When Jonah didn't answer, he continued, "I worked with your father. And I don't know if your parents ever told you, but I'm your godfather. You can trust me."

Could he trust Marcus? His parents had talked with the man about his Death Sense, but the dreams were different, and he had never mentioned them to his mom and dad. He had to say something because Marcus watched him, waiting for an answer. "My parents worked in dangerous places sometimes."

Marcus scrutinized him for a several moments, and Jonah wondered if the man could sense his thoughts.

I don't care, he thought. *I don't care if you believe me. I don't care if you believe me!*

Marcus frowned and broke eye contact. After several quiet moments in which Jonah heard the Garretts' low tones from the kitchen, Marcus finally spoke. "Jonah I know you have a lot--"

"Can I be excused?"

Marcus narrowed his eyes. Jonah wondered if he'd gone too far, but again, he didn't care. He just wanted to be alone. Marcus closed his mouth and nodded.

Jonah ran out of the den and came face to face with Tyrone, Kim, and Little Tim sitting on the stairs. Everyone froze, looking at each other. Little Tim started to say something when his big brother clamped a hand over his mouth.

The movement shook Jonah out of his paralysis. He bolted past them and down the hallway to the guest room. One thought pushed all others out of his mind as he closed the door on the world outside. *My parents are dead!*

By mid-morning, Jonah had fled to his parents' home and the solitude of his own bedroom. He lay on his high, full-sized bed and stared up at his jet fighter mobile revolving lazily overhead. He tried to remember putting it together, but images of the terrible dream kept intruding, forcing all other thoughts away.

He sat up and looked around his room. Maybe a book would help. He jumped off the bed and scanned the books on his bookshelf, but nothing interested him. He crossed to the old wooden desk that had once belonged to his dad. A thick piece of glass covered the top. Postcards, tickets, and other collectibles from all around the world were arrayed underneath: every place his parents had ever traveled.

His eyes widened when he saw the postcard with the vintage image of a library on it, the same library from his dream. He lifted the glass, dumping his pencils and notebooks on the floor, and pulled the card out. How could he forget? Not all the postcards were from overseas. Some were from places in the US.

Jonah sat down in his reading chair and stared at the card. It was small, only three and a half by five inches. His mom had told him that the library was the first one built for blacks in that South Carolina county. As soon as

The Protector's Ring

he thought about the chamber, the entire dream returned. Jonah allowed it to play out in his head, remembering as many details as possible. He would never forget the milky-white eyes of the attackers. The old woman's eyes had become colorless. Were they connected, he wondered. And what about the woman called Deyanira, the portal, and the strange green and red fire? And who had laughed in such an evil way from inside the portal?

Jonah held the postcard limply in his hand. Why did his parents give him the library postcard, yet never tell him about the strange chamber beneath it? What did their last words mean? How did they protect him by dying? He sucked in a breath and held back the tears. He considered tearing up the card, but quickly rejected that idea. This is where they died, and they had given the card to him for a reason.

It was something from them, a part of them. And, Jonah realized, sitting forward in the chair, he had a whole house of things that belonged to his parents, including a library. He leapt to his feet and stuffed the postcard in a back pocket as he left his bedroom.

Jonah bounded down the stairs and stopped at the threshold to his parents' study. When he took a single step into the room, he paused again as a strange, sad sensation overcame him. A slight pressure touched Jonah's ears, like going up in a plane. Marcus spoke from behind him.

"Jonah?"

He whirled around. Marcus stood beneath the archway between the kitchen and den, watching him. Jonah's eyebrows drew together in confusion.

"Where did you come from?"

"I came in through the back door."

Jonah sensed that wasn't true. He couldn't explain how; he just knew it. Besides, he hadn't heard the back door open or close. Marcus, as tall as anyone Jonah had ever met, looked over Jonah's head and into the study.

"Why were you standing in the doorway?"

Jonah stuffed his hands in his pockets and wouldn't meet Marcus's stare. "My parents never let me in there while they were away."

"You think of going into the study as being disobedient." Marcus gestured around him. "All of this is yours now. Your parents left it all to you."

Jonah bit down on his lip and turned to gaze into the study.

"I'll leave you alone." Marcus nodded and walked to the front door.

Jonah thought his godfather made a show of opening the door and leaving. He hurried over and peeked through the door's little glass window. He didn't see Marcus outside, nor a car. It was as if the man had vanished. The idea didn't bother Jonah. His dad could do it, and Marcus worked with his dad. So why couldn't he do it too, Jonah decided as he backed away from the front door.

He didn't hesitate this time as he entered the study. His eyes were drawn to the large bay window on the right. It faced out on the front yard, and today, bright sunlight streamed through the patterned sheers. The little shapes cast weak shadows across his mom's desk and the front of the glass display case behind it. Both were opposite the door and closer to the window. To the left of the doorway, bookshelves covered the entire wall and were stuffed with books and journals from all over the world. His dad's desk was right in front of the huge bookcase.

Jonah crossed to the desk and pulled out the old leather desk chair. It creaked as he sat down, placing his hands flat on the desktop. After a moment, he reached over and picked up his dad's favorite paperweight, turning it over in his hands. It was heavy, even though it was a copy of an actual medallion. Every detail was faithfully reproduced, including a large crack on the side.

Next to it was his dad's gold magnifier, or eye loupe—the same kind jewelers used. As Jonah lifted it to his eye, he heard someone enter the house and move around in the kitchen. At first, he thought Marcus had returned, but when the back door closed a few minutes later, he set the magnifier down and went out to investigate.

Two thick turkey sandwiches, an apple, and a bottle of juice were on the kitchen counter. Mrs. Garrett had come over, and he'd been wrong to avoid her. She had been his mom's best friend. He promised himself to thank her and apologize when he went back to their house.

The sunlight outside had dimmed to a pale golden hue by the time Jonah left his house. Hoping to sneak into the guest room without being seen, Jonah decided to use the Garretts' front door. That plan backfired

The Protector's Ring   39

because Tyrone, Kim, and Little Tim sat at the bottom of the staircase. Tyrone quickly motioned for Jonah to be silent. An unusually quiet Little Tim and Kim sat on the stairs behind their big brother. For a second, Jonah imagined that they had sat in the same spot all day. Then he realized how dumb that sounded. Still, Tyrone's actions confused him until he heard Mr. Garrett's voice carrying from the kitchen.

"I don't think it's healthy for Jonah to be by himself."

"He's always been a quiet boy." Mrs. Garrett sniffled.

"That's my point. I don't want to speak ill of the dead, and I know Janice was your friend, but his parents should have done better. "

Jonah bristled when he heard that, but Tyrone held a finger up as Mrs. Garrett responded.

"They did fine, and Marcus is responsible for Jonah now."

"Well, I'm not too sure about Marcus, either. You've seen the way he looks at us. There's something off about that man. I can't put my finger on it."

"Jonah will be okay. He has relatives, you know."

"Thank God for that. I just hope they're good, down-to-earth people."

Mrs. Garret sniffled again before saying, "Despite what you think, those were Jonah's parents, and he loved them. So you be careful what you say around him."

"Alright. I will."

CHAPTER SIX
THE PLAN

Jonah hid in the guest room, ignoring the Garretts' attempts to get him to come out and eat dinner. When the third knock came, Jonah considered running back to parents' house until he heard a different voice.

"Jonah?" Marcus called out.

Jonah hopped off the daybed and threw the door open. "Why are you here?"

"I came for dinner. Everyone's waiting for you." Marcus held out a hand. "Let's go."

Jonah didn't think he had a choice, so he shuffled down the hall to the dining room. Marcus wasn't kidding. The Garretts waited, watching as he came in. Shame warmed Jonah's face when Mrs. Garrett gave him a sad smile.

"Thanks for the sandwiches, Mrs. Garrett," Jonah said, "and for letting me stay here."

"You're welcome." Her smile grew warmer, Jonah thought, and that made him feel worse.

He lowered his gaze. "I'm sorry I didn't come out."

"That's okay. We know you wanted some time to yourself." Mrs. Garrett glanced at her husband.

Mr. Garrett clapped his beefy hands together. "Well, let's eat." He gestured at the two empty chairs on Jonah's side of the table. Kim, Tim, and Tyrone were bunched up on the other side.

Jonah relaxed as dinner started and the adults talked among themselves. He was shocked to discover that Marcus wasn't just his godfather; the man would also function as the executor of his parents' estate.

He caught Jonah's stare. "I went by your home today to assess everything and make arrangements."

Once again, Jonah could sense that Marcus didn't tell the whole truth. He wondered if the man had gone through his parents' study after he had left. *It's mine now*, Jonah reminded himself again. He'd have to get used to that. Even so, he realized that, in his mind, all those things would always belong to his mom and dad.

After dessert, Tyrone took his brother and sister into the den to play video games. Mrs. Garrett, who had gone off to the kitchen, returned with coffee and motioned to Jonah.

"Why don't you go and join the others?"

Marcus gave him a slight nod, so Jonah rose and followed the others into the den. He didn't join in playing the videos, but sat to the side and watched. Soon he grew bored with that and decided to head back to his room. That's when he caught a part of the conversation the adults were having in the dining room.

"I think Jonah should see a grief therapist or counselor," Mr. Garrett commented. "I have a friend who specializes in that."

"I don't disagree with providing Jonah help," Marcus responded. "I only ask that you let me find a professional from our company. We have counselors on staff."

"What difference does it make?"

"Dear," Mrs. Garrett chimed in. "Let Marcus handle it."

Jonah's anger got the better of him and he whirled around—and bumped into Tyrone.

The larger boy stepped back. "You want to play me in a video game?"

"No."

Tyrone glanced at the dining room doorway. "Don't pay them no mind."

Jonah pushed past the boy, hurried to the front door, and stepped out into the hot evening. He had no clue where he was going until he stood at the bottom of the porch steps. Should he walk off around the neighborhood? Maybe he should go to the park and sit on the swings to think. Why bother? Whatever the adults decided, he knew his opinion wouldn't matter.

He walked to the driveway and leaned against the back of Mr. Garrett's sedan. Jonah stuffed his hands in his pockets and shuddered with pure frustration and loss. He wanted his parents back. He wanted life back to how it used to be. He wanted to be home, with his mom and dad talking in the next room, their voices reassuring and safe. A tear rolled down his cheek. He reached up to wipe it away just as the front door opened.

Jonah expected Mrs. Garrett to come out, but instead, Marcus walked to the driveway and stopped facing out toward the neighborhood. Jonah wondered if the man even noticed him. The sun had already set and he leaned in the shadows. As Marcus lingered, Jonah's frustration returned.

"I'm a freak," he said softly.

When Marcus slowly turned, Jonah knew the man had sensed him all along.

"You're not a freak, Jonah." Marcus stepped closer. "You a teen boy, like any other in the neighborhood."

Half-lie, Jonah told himself. "Then why are you afraid?" Marcus raised an eyebrow. "I know you're afraid of what I could tell a doctor."

"And what exactly could you say to a therapist?"

"You know. I'm different. My dad was different. I have Death Sense. I heard my mom and dad talking about it. He told you."

Marcus subjected Jonah to one of his unblinking stares for a full minute before he spoke. "What do you think a therapist would say about that?"

Jonah looked away. "They would think I'm crazy." As Jonah said it, he knew that he could never tell a therapist any of those things. That made him feel even more alone. "I can't say anything, so send me to a doctor." More tears ran down his cheeks.

"Jonah, you've suffered through a horrible loss." Jonah shook his head, but Marcus went on, "I would never send you to a regular therapist because you would need the freedom to talk about everything that's happened. And you'd need someone who would understand. I wasn't lying to Mr. Garrett. Our company has professionals. You could be totally honest with them."

The Protector's Ring

"So, are you gonna do it?"

"Do you want to talk to someone?"

"I don't know." Jonah swiped at his face, smearing the wetness across it. He was glad it was dark so Marcus couldn't really see that he'd been crying.

"We'll wait to see how you do, okay?"

Jonah nodded, even though he still had the sense that Marcus didn't want him to talk to anyone, not even someone from his company. It was all too much for him to figure out, so he kept quiet as Marcus checked his watch.

"I have to go. There's a million things to arrange."

When Marcus gestured to the house, Jonah's anger flared again.

"I don't want to play video games."

Marcus raised an eyebrow. "I wasn't going to suggest that you do that."

"Oh. Sorry."

"I was going to suggest that you go inside and get some rest."

Jonah pushed off from the car and started for the porch. Marcus subjected him to one of his stares before he turned and strode down the driveway. As soon as the man had turned away, Jonah paused to glance at his godfather. That's when he noticed the black sedan parked along the street.

"You have a car?" Jonah called out.

Marcus stopped at the end of the driveway. Even in the dimness, Jonah could see the smile on the man's face. "I assure you, Jonah, I travel like everyone else." Marcus lingered for a moment, then said, "Most of the time."

When Jonah awoke the next morning, the conversation with Marcus was still on his mind. He didn't want to think about wills, estates, or any of those things, so he avoided Marcus for as long as possible.

To occupy his time during the day, Jonah began to methodically go through his parents' books. *They're my books now,* Jonah had to remind himself. He stayed there all day long, only pausing when Mrs. Garrett brought him lunch. He ate dinner with the Garretts that evening and even played video games this time. Marcus never showed up, although Jonah couldn't be sure if his godfather waited until evening to go through his house again. Jonah was sure that Marcus was searching for something.

Despite his misgivings, he continued his self-imposed exile for a third day, searching through his parents' library. He had pulled books, gone through them, and even taken notes for almost two hours when came upon an old grey hardcover book.

The faded gold letters on the side read *A Manual of History*. Jonah pulled it off the shelf and carefully removed a brittle rubber band that had been wrapped around it. The inside front cover contained an imprint of the seal from the Public Library of the District of Columbia.

Jonah's finger brushed a piece of folded notebook paper stuck inside. He turned to the marked page and his eyes were drawn to an underlined sentence halfway down the page:

The Protectors possessed powerful rings which enabled them to carry out their duties.

Jonah unfolded the piece of paper. Two words were jotted down in his dad's slanted handwriting: *Protector's Ring*. Below that was the letter *H* with a question mark. Jonah wracked his brain trying to think of anyone his parents knew with a name starting with the letter *H*.

A light knock came from the study door, and Little Tim peeked into the room.

"Wow, nice library." Little Tim saw the books on the desk in front of Jonah. "Were you studying?"

"I'm researching." Jonah closed the history book and laid it on the desk, watching the younger boy enter the room.

"What are you researching?"

"I'm looking for stories about people with strange powers."

"Can I help?"

"Maybe later."

The Protector's Ring

"Oh, okay." Little Tim's eyes widened and he scooped up the magnifier, lifting it to an eye to look through. "Wow, this is cool."

Jonah quickly took the magnifier from the boy and sat it back on the desk. He considered taking it, the medallion paperweight, and a couple of other things and packing them now. He paused because he still thought of them his dad's things. They belonged here, on his desk.

Little Tim crossed to the glass display case behind the other desk and pressed his hands and nose against it, gazing at all the objects inside. The boy's breath quickly fogged the glass, causing Jonah to stir.

"Tim, does your mom know you're here?"

Little Tim turned around with a guilty look on his face. "Yes."

"She does?"

"My mom told me to come over."

"Why?"

"That tall guy wants to talk to you."

"Why didn't you tell me that?"

Little Tim shrugged. Jonah was sure the boy had begged his mom to come over so he could look around the house. He knew Jonah's parents were archeologists and thought that was really cool.

When Jonah considered it, he guessed his parents did have cool jobs. He ached with the pain of the loss, and his eyes teared up. Jonah leaned down, pretending to look in his book bag so he could wipe his eyes.

"Jonah?"

Little Tim stood beside the desk, staring at him.

"What?"

"Can I come back and see the library again?"

Jonah blinked and glanced around. "I guess so." He carefully placed the old rubber band around the grey book, slipped it in his book bag, and leaned the bag against his father's desk. A bit of fear gnawed at him, and he wondered why Marcus wanted to see him.

Jonah paused in the entrance to the den with his hands stuffed in his pockets. Mr. and Mrs. Garrett sat on the small couch while Marcus sat across from them in one of two armchairs. Mr. Garrett waved Jonah inside.

"Come on in and have a seat."

Jonah watched Marcus as he crossed to the remaining armchair. The lawyer gazed at the Garrett family photos on the fireplace mantel. As Jonah sat down, the man's large, unblinking eyes focused on him. After a moment, Marcus shifted his attention to a briefcase sitting on the coffee table and lifted a single page. Jonah noticed that he didn't disturb the other pages arrayed on the briefcase.

"Jonah." Marcus paused until Jonah focused on him. "You remember your aunt and uncle in Georgia?"

"Yeah, but I haven't seen them in a long time." Jonah glanced at the Garretts, both of whom looked a bit worried. "Why?"

"Your parents made arrangements. In the event of their deaths, and if you were still a minor, your aunt and uncle would become your legal guardians." Marcus paused. "You understand?"

"I have to go and live with my aunt and uncle in Georgia?"

Marcus nodded, watching him. What did Marcus expect him to say or do? He didn't have a choice. Then a thought occurred to him.

"What about our house? What about all my stuff and my parents' stuff?"

"Don't worry about those things. You won't move to Georgia until late July, giving you plenty of time to pack. By the way, school starts up the second week of August, so that should give you time to settle in."

"August? I'll lose a whole month from summer vacation."

Jonah was struck by Marcus's smile in response. It seemed genuine.

"I'm sorry about that. You should start thinking about everything you want to take. The company will ship and store the rest of your parents' things in Georgia so you and your relatives can go through them at your leisure."

"Does that include the library?"

"Yes. We will pack and ship your parents' entire library."

The Protector's Ring

"And," Mrs. Garrett spoke up. "You should try packing a little at a time. That way, you won't let the move date sneak up on you."

Marcus nodded in agreement as he leaned forward to read the next page sitting on his briefcase.

Jonah focused on the coming move and his relatives. He didn't hate them. In fact, he barely knew his aunt and uncle or heard from them except when they sent a gift. He remembered twin cousins, a boy and girl about two years older.

What bothered Jonah was a vague feeling that something strange had happened the last time he visited, seven years ago. Even though he couldn't remember the details, the thought of going back made him nervous.

"Now," Marcus paused and exchanged a quick glance with the Garretts before he continued, "your parents' memorial service is scheduled for tomorrow."

"What memorial service?"

"We would have told you sooner, but we didn't want to interrupt your solitude."

Mrs. Garrett reached over to touch Jonah's arm. "Are you okay with that, dear?"

"No." Jonah said it before he could stop himself. A memorial service would force him to think about his parents and the fact that they were gone.

"It was wrong of us not to tell you sooner." Mrs. Garrett shot an angry glance at Marcus and her husband. "We know this can be a little overwhelming--"

Jonah pulled his arm away from Mrs. Garrett's hand and stood up. Marcus watched him for a moment and then set his papers on the briefcase. "We can talk about the rest later."

Jonah nodded, but his heart raced and his hands were balled into fists. The Garretts looked miserable and avoided his direct gaze. Marcus remained calm and stroked his clean-shaven chin while subjecting Jonah to his strange stare.

After a few more awkward moments of silence, Jonah stalked out of the den and down the hall to the guest room. The conversation in the den flared up as soon as Jonah closed the door, so he blocked it out.

CHAPTER SEVEN
MEMORIAL SERVICE

Jonah's eyes snapped open. Something had awakened him: a loud bird call just outside his window. Jonah pulled back his curtain to find a large crow sitting in the rhododendron bush outside. The bird caught the movement of the curtain and tilted its head to watch Jonah. It let out another caw and took flight. Jonah closed the curtain and sat back in bed, rubbing the drowsiness out of his eyes. That's when he noticed the black suit hanging on the door handle.

Did I put that there? No, I didn't. Mrs. Garrett must have done that last night, after I went to bed.

Jonah slumped as the suit reminded him that today was the memorial service. He still believed that a service would make everything so final, but he also wanted to honor his parents. His mom had bought the suit for him at the start of the summer even though Jonah never wore it.

Now he would wear it for his parents' own funeral, Jonah thought as he dragged himself out of bed. He showered and dressed on autopilot before going downstairs.

As he expected, everyone wore solemn expressions when he entered the kitchen. Mrs. Garrett offered to make breakfast, but Jonah shook his head. He wasn't hungry. At ten-thirty, Mr. Garrett took Kim and Timothy to a friend's house. When he returned, Mrs. Garrett, Tyrone, and Jonah were ready to climb into the family car and head to the cemetery.

Jonah wondered if the memorial service would take place inside a chapel or at the graveside. He knew from Mrs. Garrett's conversation that his parents had chosen a historic black cemetery in Washington, DC. As

The Protector's Ring 49

Mr. Garrett steered between the large wrought-iron gates, Jonah gazed out at the headstones. Some were small and normal. Others were large and elaborate. He saw several with headstones capped with obelisks several feet high.

Jonah's Death Sense gave an unexpected twinge, and he scanned the few people scattered among the headstone. *There!* A woman in black stood absolutely still, looking down at a granite headstone that was smaller than all the rest. If not for her presence, he would never have seen the grave. A light breeze blew through the graveyard, and as he expected, the woman's black dress didn't move an inch. As Jonah concentrated on that, the woman raised her head to look directly into his eyes. In the space of an eye blink, she vanished.

Jonah sat back in the seat, thinking. His Sense wasn't as severe and intense when he saw these strange people. It was more like a warning or an alert. He nursed that thought until Mr. Garrett pulled the car to a stop.

His guess about a chapel or graveside service proved wrong. They had parked in front of a mausoleum. Rows of exterior burial crypts lined the visible side of the building.

He followed the Garretts to the front doors, where an elderly black man in a dark suit and white gloves waited. He nodded to everyone without speaking, then turned and led them through the dim interior to a bare, metal elevator. It creaked loudly as everyone stepped inside. This surprised Jonah, who had expected something fancier.

The elevator descended three floors, banged to a stop, and opened. The subdued lighting heightened the eerie feel of the place. Several people stood near an exposed niche about halfway down the wide central corridor. Four rows of folding chairs faced a simple podium and a cloth-covered table.

Mr. Garrett paused to look around. "The cemetery didn't provide enough chairs."

"Marcus told me that we'd be able to sit up front with Jonah." Mrs. Garrett started for the front row.

As they moved closer, Jonah's attention was drawn to a couple of ornate urns resting on a temporary shelf below an opened niche. They were shaped like books with widened bottoms. The urns would be placed side by side in the Blackstone niche, like books on a shelf. Tears stung Jonah's eyes and he fought to keep the pain of his loss under control. He wouldn't cry in front of everyone.

Marcus stood among a group of people Jonah didn't recognize. They were all dressed more or less alike, with the same button on their dark suit coats, so Jonah suspected that they all worked for the company. Although he was curious about the buttons, he was too far away to see their details. It took him a moment to notice a boy wearing shades standing among the group. Jonah thought he must be at least eighteen. After all, he also wore the same button.

Beside himself and Tyrone, the boy was the only other young person here. He glanced in Jonah's direction, then quickly looked away. That's when Jonah noticed the bald man with deep, dark skin.

Omar?

Jonah had met Omar three years earlier, on the same day he'd met Marcus. Omar placed a hand on Marcus's shoulder, whispering in his ear while nodding toward Jonah. Everyone in the group turned to watch as Marcus excused himself and strode over to Jonah and the Garretts.

"Thank you for coming and bringing Jonah." Marcus gestured toward the reserved seats in the front row.

Before Jonah could sit down, Marcus placed a hand on his shoulder.

"I need a word with you." Jonah thought Marcus would take him to meet his group. Instead, he walked along the front row of seats and down the main corridor. He turned to watch the small crowd as he waited for Jonah. "How are you doing this morning?"

Jonah shrugged. Mr. Garrett watched them with a curious glance, and Jonah recalled the man's comments about his godfather. He glanced up and caught Marcus giving him that unblinking stare.

"Is that all you wanted to ask me?"

Marcus finally blinked and shook his head. "I wanted to let you know this memorial will be a little different."

"What do you mean *different*?"

"Everyone will be invited to say a word or two about your parents. You'll be the last one to go."

The Protector's Ring   51

"I don't want to say anything!" Jonah's voice carried, and people turned in his direction. He lowered his voice. "Can't you do all the talking?"

"Jonah, you're expected to say something about your parents."

"But--"

"You'll know what to say when the time comes." Marcus guided him back to his seat, gave Jonah a final nod, and walked off to greet other people.

"Are you all right, Jonah?" Mrs. Garret patted his forearm.

"Yes, ma'am," Jonah lied.

The panic rose up inside him. This—being the center of attention—is what he hated. He began to shake, and he turned in his seat to hide the reaction. As he looked around the crowd, he fought to hold back the nervousness.

The central library manager, a Jamaican man with long salt-and-pepper dreads, stood in the back with two other people from the library. The man gave Jonah a friendly nod. Jonah considered waving back, then thought better of it because his hands shook.

As he battled with the nervousness, he sensed the change in the crowd before he heard Marcus clear his throat. He faced forward. Marcus stood behind the podium, waiting. Once silence settled over the gathering, he folded his hands together on top of the podium.

"We came here today to honor the lives and memories of two dear colleagues and friends: Isaiah and Janice Blackstone. They were brave, fearless, and tirelessly worked for the benefit of all human beings." Marcus paused, reached over to the table, and pulled off the covering cloth. Jonah stared wide-eyed at the table.

A collection of buttons, pins, framed pictures, ribbons, a couple of statuettes, books, and papers covered the table. Jonah suspected that all these things belonged to his parents. Marcus selected a small medal and held it up for all to see.

"Isaiah Blackstone taught me that true compassion transcends all boundaries, circumstances, and expectations. It's a lesson that I'm still learning. I will always remember Isaiah." Marcus lowered the medal and clutched it in his hand as he stepped to the side.

For several tense moments, no one moved until the library manager walked to the front and took a small manual from the table. He turned to the crowd and held the manual high.

"Janice Blackstone taught me that real knowledge begins with knowing yourself. Only then can you truly understand others." He looked briefly at Jonah. "I'll always remember your mother." He walked back to his seat holding the manual tightly against his chest.

And so it went. One person after another gave their remembrance until finally Mr. and Mrs. Garrett went up together. Once they finished, Marcus turned to Jonah and nodded.

Jonah rose shakily to his feet and went to the table. At first, he didn't know which item to take. Then he saw his dad's golden magnifier and he picked it up without thinking. Suddenly, an idea came to him. Everyone had chosen to honor either his mom or dad. Shouldn't he honor both of them?

Jonah glimpsed something feathery. He moved aside a postcard to reveal a large feather from an actual black eagle. It belonged to his mom, and he gently lifted it in his hand. And last, he selected a framed photo of his mom and dad taken while they were on one of their archeological trips.

Jonah stepped away from the table and turned to face the crowd. His mind went blank.

What could he say about his parents that others hadn't said?

He glanced down at the feather, aware of the quiet expectation of the crowd. As the silence stretched, he heard his mom's favorite saying float through his mind, and he knew what to do.

He held up the eagle feather in his trembling hand.

"My mom--" His voice cracked with nervousness.

He heard Mrs. Garrett say, "Give him strength," in a low voice.

Jonah began again. "My mom. She tried to teach me that being alone isn't living. She showed this by the way she lived her life and by the different people she knew." He found the library manager in the crowd and nodded to him. "I'll always remember my mom."

Jonah held up the magnifier. "My dad told me to never be afraid of the new and unknown. He said that if I learned new things, I would grow into

The Protector's Ring **53**

what I should become." Jonah's voice grew stronger. "I'll always remember my dad."

Next, he held up the framed photo. "What happened to my parents taught me that no one knows what will happen tomorrow. I think that we should appreciate what we have today. I will always remember my parents."

When Marcus stepped toward the podium, Jonah held up all three items. The movement surprised Marcus, who stopped.

"I remember my mom," Jonah intoned.

A couple of people from the company said loudly, "We remember your mother."

"I remember my dad," he continued.

"We remember your father." More people joined that time.

"I remember my parents."

The entire crowd responded with, "We remember your parents."

Jonah paused as the last words echoed down the corridor. Then he lowered his arms and bowed his head. Marcus stepped behind him, placing a hand on each of his shoulders.

"Well done, Jonah." Marcus gently guided him toward his seat. Jonah started to sit down, but he stopped because at that exact moment, his stomach fluttered and his Death Sense buzzed.

He quickly scanned the crowd and sucked in a quiet breath. A mysterious short man, dressed in dark clothes that made his pale skin stick out, stood back from the gathering. The man also scanned the crowd, and when his gaze came to Jonah, he blinked in surprise.

Marcus finished his closing comments and the memorial guests rose to their feet, blocking Jonah's view of the man. He dodged to the side to see around the clump of people, but the mysterious man had disappeared.

Wait, Jonah wanted to shout to the man, but his Death Sense still buzzed. The man was nearby. Jonah's excitement grew. Maybe this time, he could talk to one of these strange people.

Luckily, the Garretts engaged Marcus in conversation. Omar and the older boy stood nearby. No one paid any attention to Jonah. He made his decision and slipped away into the bowels of the crypt.

CHAPTER EIGHT
STRANGE VISITOR

The dimly lit crypt proved far larger than Jonah had anticipated. From what he could see, the crypt contained a main corridor with an arched ceiling. Then there were the four parallel side corridors and oddly spaced connecting side passages, creating a huge, underground grid.

Just when Jonah feared he would never find the mysterious man, his Death Sense gave him a jolt. He stopped and peered down one of the larger side corridors. The lights began to flicker and two bulbs went out, leaving half the hallway in shadows. *This blows*, Jonah thought as he took a step toward the darkness.

"What are you?" The voice came from the end of the hallway.

Jonah's knees shook with fear, yet something about the man drew him. He squinted into the shadows and could just make out the man's outline.

"I'm a boy."

"I can see that. The question is: how can you see us?"

"Why wouldn't I be able to see you?"

"Mortals can't see us."

Jonah shuddered, his quaking voice betraying his growing nervousness. "Why can't mortals see you?"

The man didn't respond, and Jonah began to think that maybe following him had been a bad idea.

"Who are you?" The man's voice wasn't menacing. He sounded curious.

"I'm Jonah. Jonah Blackstone."

He heard the rustle of cloth, and the mysterious man stepped under a flickering light. He had a short scar along his pale right cheek, and his stark white hair stood out in the light. The man didn't come any closer. He simply narrowed his hazel eyes.

"You're Isaiah Blackstone's natural son?"

"Y-yes."

"But that's impossible. Your father…" The man stopped, cocking his head to the side as if listening to something.

"What about my father?" Jonah moved closer, then sucked in a breath because he also heard something. It sounded like a distant call, a siren. As he tried to get a better fix on it, an image exploded in his head, causing him to grunt in pain.

He saw a young guy squirming on the ground, clutching his midsection and moaning in pain. He lay in the middle of a side street in some city, Jonah didn't know where. Another young guy knelt over him, trying, without success, to get his friend to stand. He would die soon. Jonah knew that. Despite the blood covering his shirt and ground and the ragged breaths, Jonah sensed it. Death.

Just as suddenly as the vision came, it vanished. Jonah groaned again and stumbled backward. The mysterious man darted forward, grabbing Jonah's arm and keeping him standing.

"How could you see that?"

Jonah twisted out of the man's grip. "What about my father?"

The man stared at him for another moment, then stepped back into the shadows and vanished.

"Jonah!" Marcus strode around the corner a second later, Omar and the strange boy trailing behind. "What are you doing here?"

"A man stood right over there." Jonah pointed at the patch of shadows. "He just disappeared."

Marcus turned quickly to Omar and gestured toward the spot.

Omar closed his eyes and raised a hand, palm up and fingers spread as if pushing against something. A moment later, he opened his eyes and looked at Marcus.

Realization washed over Jonah. "You can sense him."

Omar offered Jonah a little smile.

Jonah turned to Marcus. "Who are these people I keep seeing?"

"You've seen others?" Marcus traded a startled glance with Omar.

Jonah nodded, hoping that Marcus would finally tell him something. However, his godfather shook his head. "We need to get you back. The Garretts are worried about you."

"No. Tell me what's going on."

"Jonah…" Marcus reached for his arm. Jonah stumbled back and would have fallen if the boy hadn't grabbed him with a surprisingly strong grip.

Jonah glanced up into the boy's shaded eyes.

"Jonah, this is Kevin," Omar said, inclining his bald head toward the silent boy. "Kevin, this is Jonah."

Kevin raised his chin but didn't speak. Jonah wondered if the boy was angry because he had stepped on his feet.

"Jonah," Marcus began, running his large hand over his face and down to the back of his neck. "This is not how your parents would want you to act."

"You talk about honoring my parents. They never treated me like a kid!"

"Your parents didn't tell you everything."

"So there is something going on."

Kevin snorted.

Omar chuckled and said in his deep, African-accented voice, "He's definitely his father's son, Marcus."

Marcus glared at Omar, who simply crossed his muscular arms and returned the glare. Marcus let out an exasperated breath, turned, and strode off. As he reached the corner, he shouted over his shoulder, "Bring him along!"

Omar shook his bald head as he patted Jonah on the shoulder. "It's good to see you again. You've grown over the last three years." Omar held out an arm. "After you, Mr. Blackstone."

The Protector's Ring

"Can't you tell me anything?"

Omar paused, as if he might reveal something. Even Kevin turned his head to watch. Finally, Omar sighed. "I'm sorry. That's up to Marcus."

"Oh." Jonah hung his head and started back. At least Omar answered him, unlike Marcus. He didn't know if he angered his godfather and frankly didn't care. Whenever an adult treated him like a kid, his attitude jumped over rational and landed squarely on defiant and rebellious. That's how his dad described it whenever they butted heads. Depending on the degree of Jonah's stubbornness, Jonah's dad would get just as irritated as Marcus appeared to be. However, his parents took care to treat him like he had a brain.

Jonah's irritation with Marcus rose again. He saw the look Marcus and Omar had traded when he mentioned the others. Why did they try to hide it?

I'm glad I talked to one of these people.

That thought also produced more questions for Jonah. Why did the visitor say that mortals couldn't see him? He sounded as if he wasn't mortal. If he wasn't a mortal, did that mean he was immortal?

Jonah wondered how he could see immortals. He held up his hands, stared at them, and thought to himself, *I'm a person. I'm mortal. And I can see them.* As Jonah lowered his hands, the reality sunk in. He had just pissed off the one person who could possibly answer those questions.

Way to go, Jonah.

His parents' memorial service had been enough of an event. Jonah wasn't ready for the gathering at the Garretts' house. After more than one person told him how brave he had sounded, Jonah had to get away. This time, he decided to be a bit more clever because Mrs. Garrett and Marcus were keeping an eye on him.

He excused himself to use the hallway bathroom. When he came out, he paused to pretend to check his tie. Mrs. Garrett was in the kitchen unwrapping another gift of food. That left Marcus as the one to avoid.

Waiting for the right moment, Jonah was rewarded when a husband and wife came through the front door. He made a show of shaking their hands. As soon as the new arrivals moved off, he took a deep breath and slipped outside.

He set off down the street at a brisk walk, expecting someone to shout for him. He didn't breathe easier until he turned the corner and walked out of sight of the Garretts' home. Feeling safer, he slowed his pace and loosened his tie. Although he feared Marcus or Mrs. Garrett would come after him sooner or later, he didn't care as long as he had some time alone.

When Jonah reached the little neighborhood park, he crossed over to a wooden bench and sat down. Slipping in his iPod's ear buds, he lay back on the bench, and listened to the entire soundtrack Tyrone had given him for his birthday. He wanted the music to take him away, since he literally couldn't get away like he wished he could. That didn't mean he wanted to go to Georgia. He wanted another life of adventures like the ones he imagined his parents must have experienced.

The cold reality settled in and Jonah squeezed his eyes tight in an effort to prevent tears from rolling down his cheek. His parents' lives were far more dangerous than they had ever let on. And now they were gone. Could that be the reason Marcus wanted to keep him in the dark? Jonah shook his head, not wanting to let go of his anger toward his godfather. He didn't want to understand the man's point of view. He grunted in frustration as he stood.

Listening to music wasn't working, but he wavered, trying to decide where to go next. He didn't want to return to the reception, yet he didn't have a choice. However, going back didn't mean he couldn't take his time. He exited the park on the opposite side and proceeded to make a big loop through the neighborhood before reaching Sayre Road.

He'd make another right at the end of the street onto Saintsbury and head back to the Garretts'. Jonah managed to add at least ten more minutes of welcomed solitude to his walk. When he finally started up Saintsbury and his own house came into view, he slowed his pace. The urge to run inside and hide out in his room rolled over him. No, he had to tell himself. *That's the first place they'd look for me.*

He continued on, each step increasing the dread at being the center of attention. As he reached the Garretts', he didn't expect to find Tyrone standing alone at the top of their driveway, shooting baskets. The boy's tie had been loosened and his shirtsleeves rolled up to the elbow. Tyrone paused, waiting for Jonah to reach the top of the driveway before tossing him the basketball.

The Protector's Ring

"Mom told me to go find you, but I figured you wanted to be alone."

"Thanks," Jonah said, feeling a brief flash of gratitude toward the otherwise standoffish boy. He took a shot at the hoop mounted to the side of the house.

Tyrone grabbed the ball. "So, you leave for Georgia?"

"Yeah."

"That bites! I hear they still fly the rebel flag down there." Tyrone did a layup, then tossed the ball to Jonah. "Why can't you stay with us? My parents can adopt you."

Jonah shook his head and did a layup. "I have to live with my aunt and uncle."

"Sorry, man."

"Yeah. Hey, maybe you could come down and visit someday?"

"By then you'll have a Southern accent and all!" Tyrone's laughter was brief. "Oh boy." He motioned to the kitchen window where Mrs. Garrett looked out. "I guess we should get back inside before my mom freaks out."

Jonah glanced at the street and debated disappearing into the safety of the neighborhood again. Making his choice, he nodded and followed Tyrone around to the front porch. As they reached the top step, the porch light began to flicker. At the same time, Jonah's stomach gave a twinge and his Death Sense buzzed.

"What's wrong with this light?" Tyrone, at least three inches taller than Jonah, easily reached up and tapped it with a finger.

Jonah turned toward the yard and almost yelled. Three people stood in the middle of the Garretts' manicured lawn, watching him. He tapped Tyrone on the arm. "Do you see those people?"

"See who?" Tyrone looked over Jonah's shoulder and shrugged.

The front door banged open and Marcus stepped onto the porch, his eyes fixed on the three strangers.

"Jonah. I think you and Tyrone should get inside."

Marcus gently nudged Tyrone and Jonah toward the front door as he stepped past them to face the strangers. Jonah reversed course and positioned himself behind Marcus, peeking around the tall man's arm. Two of the strangers, a man and a woman, stood together while the third, a tall man in a grey robe, stood off on his own.

The man and woman bowed to Marcus, then the man spoke in a somber tone. "Please give our condolences to the boy."

They waited for Marcus to return the bow. Once the ritual was complete, the pair pivoted on the spot and vanished.

Marcus turned to the grey-robed stranger. "Your job is finished. File the information in your archives and tell your master it is over."

The man continued to stare at Jonah, which drew Marcus's attention. "I told you to go inside."

Jonah wanted to tell Marcus he wasn't his dad, but at that moment, Kevin came outside. The boy reached inside his suit jacket as he descended the steps. The stranger's eyes widened and a second later, he vanished. Kevin stood on the very spot the man had occupied, scanning the area as if he expected someone else to appear.

"Who were they?" Jonah tugged on Marcus's sleeve when the man didn't immediately answer.

"Not now, Jonah."

"But I could feel them, just like all the others. And you and Kevin can see them."

"Keep it down." Marcus glanced inside the house. "We'll talk later."

Jonah told himself that he'd get answers when most of the people had cleared out. He watched Marcus talk in urgent tones to the other people from the company; the strangers seemed to have lit a fuse under them all. Jonah tried to stay close to Marcus, just in case the man let a clue slip. Mrs. Garrett intervened, though, and pulled him in to the kitchen to thank the library people. By the time Jonah got away and came back into the den, Marcus and everyone from the company were gone.

The Protector's Ring

CHAPTER NINE
BLACK DOGS

Jonah wondered what would happen if he refused to pack or get ready for the move to Georgia? He had a right to be mad. Those strange people who showed up in the Garretts' yard wanted to see him. He deserved to know what was going on.

Jonah grabbed his pillow and hurled it across the guest room. He thought of all kinds of choice words to call Marcus in his mind but soon grew bored with that, so he got up, showered, and grabbed his book bag.

As soon as he stepped outside the Garretts' house and felt the sun on his face, Jonah's irritation got the better of him. He circled around the house to the backyard and got on his bike instead. Packing could wait until later, he thought, and he rode off. He didn't know where he'd go, so he cruised through the neighborhood. The park was full of kids today, but he didn't feel like being around a lot of people.

He continued to ride around his quiet neighborhood, not really thinking about anything. Eventually, he caught the metro into Arlington and the mall where he played videos games until he made his way to the Central library. After accepting condolences from a worker who knew him, Jonah sat down in his favorite study room. But he couldn't bring himself to study anything. His mind wouldn't focus, so he sat there, letting thoughts and memories slip in and out of his head. Nearly two hours later, Jonah's resolve to oppose the adults in his life gave out, and he headed back home.

When he entered his own bedroom, he stopped. Refusing to pack would not have worked because two bulging suitcases lay on his bed. He opened them up and stared in amazement. Mrs. Garrett had neatly stuffed them with all of his school and winter clothes. He imagined she did it while he was hiding out, and that meant she had stayed home from work. Guilt nibbled at his insides as he zipped the cases closed and slumped down into his reading chair.

What would my parents tell me to do?

His father would gently squeeze his shoulder and tell him to keep going. That was his dad. Never give up. His mom would point out the positive. *At least you don't have to pack your winter clothes. And remember to thank Mrs. Garrett.*

He looked around his room. Maybe Mrs. Garrett was right and he could do a little now to avoid the rush when the time came to leave. Deciding to start with the desk, he propped up the piece of glass and scooped all the postcards and tickets into a side pocket of his book bag. His father's magnifier, the black eagle feather, and photo of his parents were already inside, remnants of the memorial service. Jonah left the two suitcases on the bed and slipped the book bag's strap over a shoulder.

Downstairs, he paused in the archway to the kitchen, staring at a legal box on the counter. A large yellow sticky was affixed to the lid with a message on it.

Jonah, I thought you would like to go through these things and decide which ones you wanted to keep. Take your time. - Marcus

He slipped off his book bag, placed it against the archway wall, and peeked in the box. It was full of his parents' things that had been at the memorial service, things no one had chosen to use in their memorials. Jonah didn't need to go through the box; he planned to keep everything. He replaced the lid and rested his hands on it as he looked around the house.

They had moved here over a year ago, just after his best friend had died. The past year had been quiet for Jonah. His parents even seemed happier. Then the full implications of the move to Georgia hit him. This place was home. And just like his mom and dad, he would never see it again.

The Protector's Ring   63

Jonah's contemplative mood persisted for the remainder of the day and into that evening as he sat down to dinner with the Garretts. Everyone seemed in good spirits, and Jonah admitted he began to enjoy himself. His bouts of sadness about the coming move lifted. Everything went well until Mr. Garrett wrinkled up his nose during dessert.

"Do you smell that?"

"Must be a neighbor burning leaves." Mrs. Garrett sniffed the air and nodded. Now that the conversation around the table had stopped, Jonah heard faint shouts coming from outside.

"What is going on?" Mr. Garrett rose from his chair and thundered down the hallway to the front door. When he opened it, a wall of sound rolled into the house. "Oh my God!" He rushed outside, and everyone else followed.

Many of the neighbors ran or pointed down the street. Jonah looked in the same direction and froze. His house was engulfed in flames.

"No!" Jonah started toward the house, but Mr. Garrett grabbed him.

"Stay here, Jonah. It's too dangerous for you to go near it."

"I'll call the fire department," Mrs. Garrett shouted. She led Timothy and Kim back inside the house.

"Let me go." Jonah continued to struggle in Mr. Garrett's grip. "All my things are in there!"

I have to get there! The thought rolled over and over in his mind like a drumbeat. Mr. Garrett released him and spread his arms out, clearly prepared to grab Jonah if he tried to run for the burning house. Tyrone came up behind his father and also readied himself.

"My things are in there," Jonah shouted, the anger and determination surging through him. "I have to get inside!"

Mr. Garrett shook his head. "I can't let you do that."

Jonah let out a frustrated yell and darted for his house. As Mr. Garrett and Tyrone moved to tackle him, something strange happened. A rippling sensation raced over Jonah's entire body. Jonah braced himself for an impact that didn't come. He stumbled, lost his balance, and pitched forward onto the soft ground. The smell of freshly mown grass assaulted his nose.

When he rolled over and looked back, he saw Mr. Garrett and Tyrone several yards away on their own front lawn while he sprawled in the neighbor's yard. It had happened again: he'd managed to move in a blink of an eye, yet he didn't waste time pondering it and scrambled to his feet. A wave of dizziness hit, and he leaned against a lamppost in the yard to steady himself. It took Mr. Garrett and Tyrone calling out his name to clear his mind. Feeling stronger and more determined to save what he could, Jonah raced off toward his house.

Too many spectators had assembled to watch the blaze, and Jonah feared one of them would try to stop him. In fact, a few people had already noticed him running down the sidewalk. He ducked through the gate into his backyard and up to the kitchen door. He burst into the house and immediately began to gag on the smoke. Taking a moment to gather a breath, Jonah ducked low and moved through the kitchen. When he reached the entrance into the den and found his book bag, he gasped.

The fire engulfed that entire side of the house and the whole study. There was no way he could get through to save anything. When he grabbed his book bag, his stomach seized up and his Death Sense spiked.

A fierce growl came from inside the burning study. Jonah moved through the den, peered into the flames, and his heart froze. A huge, dog-like creature moved into view. It tore through the room, ignoring the smoke and flames, which reflected off its jet-black skin.

The creature paused to sniff the air, then twisted its head around to look straight at Jonah with a pair of glowing red eyes. It let out a howl, exposing double rows of sharp teeth as it moved into the study's doorway.

Jonah stumbled back, tripped, and fell on the floor near the entrance to the kitchen. The sight of the creature drained Jonah's will to move any further. Nevertheless, he tried to yell, but instead, he sucked in smoke and started coughing. His vision blurred, and it became harder to breathe. As he sank to his knees, Jonah saw the creature tense and prepare to attack.

Suddenly, the air in front of him rippled and a tall person in a long, black coat appeared, holding two silver blades. He whirled on the spot like a dark, avenging angel, slashing at the creature, which howled and rolled back into the study. The person turned around. It was Marcus! He shouted to someone behind Jonah, "Kevin, get him out of here."

Kevin stepped into view with a pair of silver blades in his own hands. He crouched beside Jonah and paused. "Maybe I should stay…"

The Protector's Ring

"Get him out of here now!"

Marcus whirled around just as another dog-like creature stepped into view.

The heat overwhelmed Jonah, and he resisted blacking out. He tightened his grip on the book bag. Marcus shouted again above the roar of the flames. Kevin snapped into motion, deactivating a blade and using that hand to grab a fistful of Jonah's shirt. A rippling sensation played along his entire body, and a moment later, he and Jonah were in the backyard.

Jonah succumbed to heavy coughs for several moments, his abdomen seizing up and cramping with the violent movement. Finally, he let out a last hoarse cough and caught his breath. From inside the house came loud crashes, howls, and the sound of scraping metal. Kevin cursed under his breath and whirled on him.

"Why did you go into the house, Jonah?"

"I needed to get my book bag. It's all I have left." His vision had cleared enough for him to glare at the boy. Jonah was about to say something when a pair of strong hands lifted him to his feet and he yelled, instead.

"Are you okay?" Omar turned Jonah around, giving him the once over.

"I'm alright."

Omar turned a worried glance on the burning house. Before Jonah could say anything, a shout came from the backyard gate.

"Jonah!" Mr. Garrett and the rest of the family rushed over. "One minute I'm about to tackle you and the next, you're in the neighbor's yard."

"It's just the excitement, honey," Mrs. Garret said. "I'm sure you're wrong."

She moved her husband aside and started brushing dirt off Jonah's clothes. However, Tyrone sputtered and pointed a shaking finger at him.

"I saw him ripple and--"

"We're just glad Jonah wasn't hurt." Mrs. Garrett gave her husband and son a worried look. Her attempts to explain things away were rudely interrupted when Marcus rippled into sight less than a foot from Tyrone. The Garretts' son yelled and tumbled back onto the ground.

Omar hurried to brush dirt and soot off Marcus's long coat. Marcus actually looked a little embarrassed at the attention as he scanned the waiting people. Even though wisps of smoke rose off his coat, he seemed unhurt. Jonah's eyes fastened on a burned spot on the coat's left breast. He corrected himself because the coat wasn't damaged from the fire. There was a symbol branded into the leather: three interlocking circles and a pair of wings spread over them. It was the same symbol on the buttons all the company people had worn at the memorial service.

He wanted to ask Marcus about it, the black dogs, and so much more, but at that moment, the loud cracking of wood drew everyone's attention. They watched as the Blackstone house crumbled in on itself. Jonah slipped around the others, lost for words as everything he and parents owned burned. All that was left was the book bag at his feet. Jonah barely noticed the hand that touched his shoulder.

"I'm sorry, Jonah." Marcus's words were soft.

Mr. Garrett was anything but soft-spoken when he bellowed, "What's going on?"

Marcus spared the man a glance before turning and speaking directly to Mrs. Garrett. "We need to move Jonah tonight."

"Okay," she answered. "I'll put some clothes together."

"Wait a minute." Mr. Garrett held up his beefy hands. "No one is going anywhere until I find out what's going on. Who are you people?"

"It's not safe for Jonah here."

That comment stirred Jonah out of his shocked contemplation of his ruined house. "Why isn't it safe for me?"

Marcus raised his own voice. "Kevin, take Jonah back to the Garretts'."

Mr. Garrett moved to block Kevin, but Omar stepped right in front of the man and crossed his muscular arms.

"Honey?" Mr. Garret gulped, glancing at his wife.

She gave her husband a worried look before turning to Marcus.

"He'll be fine," Marcus answered the unvoiced question. When Mrs. Garrett started to speak, he added, "Janice told you about us?"

She nodded. "Janice told me that you might have to…" She paused, glancing into Jonah's wide eyes. Then she squared her shoulders. "She told me you might have to take Jonah away at a moment's notice."

The Protector's Ring

"Then trust her decision, as she trusted you to watch over her son."

Mr. Garrett stared between Marcus and his wife. "What's this? What do you know about these people?"

Mrs. Garrett wrung her hands as she faced Mr. Garrett. "Marcus wants to talk to you, that's all." She avoided her husband's betrayed expression as she reached for her son's arm. "Come on, Tyrone."

"But Mom!"

When he pulled away, she grabbed his ear and twisted. "Now!"

Jonah was shocked by the tactic. He'd never seen Mrs. Garrett so much as raise her voice to her kids. His own mom had never done anything like that to him, either. Tyrone cupped his injured ear as he shuffled toward home, muttering to himself. He didn't dare say anything else to his mom, who marched right behind him. Jonah, following with Kevin attached to his arm, didn't blame him. Mr. Garrett remained in the yard, watching helplessly.

Jonah wondered what Marcus and Omar would do to the man, but his real interest was in Mrs. Garrett. Did she work with Marcus? Jonah knew his mom had told her a lot, more than she told him. That raised even more questions for Jonah as he walked down the sidewalk to the Garretts' house.

CHAPTER TEN
PARTING WAYS

Questions continued to overload Jonah's mind as he waited in the Garretts' kitchen. What were those two black dogs he had seen in the house? What were they doing, tearing through the library? And Marcus and Kevin carried silver blades like his parents'. They could appear and disappear. What did that mean?

All of these questions bounced around inside Jonah's head. Every time he tried to concentrate on one question, another swirled to the surface and took its place. He tried sorting it all out until Mr. Garrett, Omar, and Marcus returned.

Mr. Garrett sounded excited as he stepped into the kitchen behind Marcus. "That's going to be a real mess in the morning." He caught sight of Jonah and gave him a strange look, as if trying to remember something.

Mrs. Garrett returned to the kitchen with Kim and Little Tim trailing behind her. She had a bulging duffel bag in her hands.

"Here you go, Jonah. I packed a few of Tyrone's old things."

Tyrone, who had a dazed look on his face and never took his eyes off Kevin's deactivated blade, sat up in his chair. When he opened his mouth, Mrs. Garrett gave him a severe frown and said, "I took the clothes you outgrew and I had already planned to give away."

Tyrone settled back in his chair and kept quiet as his mom turned to Jonah. "These should hold you over until…" Mrs. Garrett glanced at Marcus, and he nodded. "Until you get to Georgia."

"Georgia?" Jonah's mind finally clicked into motion. "I thought I didn't have to go there until next month?"

The Protector's Ring

"You'll have to leave sooner than we planned." Marcus shook his head. "I wish it could be tonight, but tomorrow will have to do."

"Why? Is it because of those--"

"Jonah!" Marcus gave him a warning look.

Mr. Garrett stared between Marcus and Jonah. "Because of what?"

"Because of the fire," Marcus answered, never taking his eyes off Jonah.

"Well," Mrs. Garrett interrupted, setting the large duffel bag on the floor. "I'm sure your aunt can take care of getting you some new clothes."

She spoke as if his world hadn't been turned upside down again, Jonah thought. Everything was gone: his school clothes, coats, sneakers, even the ugly tie he and his mom bought for his dad for Father's Day.

Little Tim stepped around his mother. "You're going away?"

"Yeah."

"But what about all your stuff?"

"Tim," his mother cautioned. Jonah handled the stab of pain, even though tears threatened to follow at any moment. His sides were starting to ache with the effort to hold it in, and that made his back hurt.

Little Tim's worried expression reminded Jonah of what he had left. He unzipped his book bag and wrinkled his nose at the smell of smoke. He pushed that out of his mind and found the bookmarks Tim and Kim had given him as a birthday present.

"Don't worry, Tim. I still have these." Jonah knew his voice sounded weak. Little Tim didn't mind; he held out a hand for a shake. Kim surprised Jonah when she also insisted on a handshake.

"Jonah needs to rest," Marcus announced. His voice broke the silence that settled in the kitchen and people snapped into motion.

Mrs. Garrett nodded and motioned Jonah out of the chair. Tyrone stood but hung back as his parents said their goodbyes.

"Take care." Mr. Garrett shook Jonah's hand.

"I wish you could stay here," Mrs. Garrett whispered as she gave him a hug. "But your parents made other arrangements." Marcus cleared his throat and Mrs. Garrett hurried on. "Make sure you write and let us know how things are going."

"I will. Thanks." A tear ran down Jonah's cheek despite his attempts to hold it back. He turned and let Kevin escort him down the hallway and out of the house.

A tall woman with extremely short blonde hair stood next to a large black car parked in the driveway. She was dressed in the same clothes as the others: all black. And she wore the long coat complete with the symbol burned into the left chest. When she nodded to Jonah, several earrings in her left ear tinkled.

Jonah stopped suddenly, causing Kevin to bump into him. His curiosity with the symbol overrode his other feelings. He pointed. "What does that mean?"

The woman gave him a tolerant smile but refused to answer. Kevin reached around Jonah, opened the back door, and tossed the duffel bag on the backseat. Then he waited for Jonah to climb in before he followed.

The sudden silence of the car, once Kevin closed the door, shocked Jonah. Raised voices, and blaring emergency radios from the fire trucks felt distant and unreal to him. He watched the flashing lights through the shaded window until a dark shadow blocked the view and a tap came on the glass. Kevin rolled it down and Marcus leaned in.

"I know you have a lot of questions, Jonah. We'll talk tomorrow. Right now, I need to stay here and sort out things." Marcus shifted his gaze to Kevin. "Take care of him."

Kevin nodded.

Jonah didn't dare say anything because he knew he couldn't hold out much longer. For some reason, he didn't want to cry in front of Marcus. Fortunately, Kevin rolled up the window. A moment later, the car backed out of the driveway and pulled away. Jonah turned in his seat, watching the smoldering ruins of his house out the rear window.

His home was gone. His things were gone. His parents were gone. The enormity of the loss finally hit him. Jonah sank back into his seat, buried his head in his hands, and cried. He took great, heavy sobs and barely noticed Kevin patting him lightly on the back. When his body began to shake, Kevin pulled him close and wrapped a protective arm around his

The Protector's Ring

shoulders. The boy didn't say anything nor seemed to mind that the tears were wetting his black t-shirt.

Jonah lost track of time. Except for the quiet hum of the car's engine, his sniffles were the only other sound. When he grew quiet, the blonde woman spoke.

"You ready?"

Jonah thought the woman spoke to him until Kevin stirred and answered.

"Why do I have to babysit, Emily?"

"Because Marcus told you to take care of him." Emily had a no-nonsense voice. Yet when she spoke again, her tone had softened. "You're doing okay with him."

"He reminds me of my little brother." Kevin shook Jonah's shoulder. "Hold on to your book bag."

Jonah suspected what would happen next when Kevin reached over and grabbed the duffel bag with his free hand.

"We're ready."

Emily swerved the car off the highway and onto the shoulder of the road. As soon as it stopped, the strange ripple sensation spread across Jonah's body. Kevin shifted beside him and a moment later, the scene around them changed.

A thickly wooded area appeared around Jonah and Kevin a split second later. With the car, and Emily, gone, Jonah realized he sat in midair, and he yelled out.

He didn't fall on the ground because Kevin held him up. The older boy hissed in Jonah's ear, "Put your feet on the ground." Kevin waited until Jonah followed his order, then shook his head. "You don't know how to change your body position when you phase?"

"No."

Kevin stared at him like he had just said he couldn't tie his shoes. Jonah's face grew hot with embarrassment.

"I didn't even know it was called phasing."

"Well, changing your body position is hard to learn."

"You mean--"

"Quiet." Kevin held up a hand.

Jonah bristled. He closed his eyes and let it pass as he thought about learning to shift as he moved. His dad must have been able to do it, and Marcus as well as Omar. Then he realized he never actually saw Omar phase. He was already in the backyard when Kevin phased them outside his burning house.

"Omar can't do it, can he?"

"No, he can't. Marcus has to give him a ride, like I did for you."

"I can do it myself."

"You didn't know where to go. Now, shut up."

"Don't tell me to shut up."

Kevin turned his back on Jonah as he scanned the surrounding woods. Jonah didn't like how the boy bossed him around, like he was a kid. He wondered if Kevin could see anything with those stupid shades on.

Kevin stirred and pointed at the book bag, which Jonah had dropped when they first appeared in the woods.

"Pick up your bag."

"No."

"Stop acting like a kid, Jonah."

When Jonah crossed his arms in defiance, Kevin's body blurred into motion, snatched up the book bag, and shoved it into Jonah's chest. The impact knocked him back. In a flash, Kevin stood over him.

"Sorry. I didn't mean to do that." He reached down and offered a hand. Jonah wanted to tell him to get lost, but he accepted Kevin's help. The older boy pulled him to his feet like he weighed nothing.

Jonah backed away from him. Kevin might look like any other urban kid, wearing a printed black t-shirt and colored sneakers. And the jeans hung just right, exposing the required amount of underwear. However, Kevin was more than he appeared to be. He was clearly strong and super

The Protector's Ring

fast, Jonah thought. When he picked up the book bag in his free hand, Jonah noticed the muscles in Kevin's arms, like he worked out.

Kevin turned his side to Jonah and said, "Grab one of my belt loops."

Jonah didn't know why his heart skipped a beat when Kevin said that. He moved closer, hooked his middle finger through one of the loops, and was surprised by the heat coming off the boy's body.

"You're hot." He said it without thinking. Kevin searched Jonah's face for a moment. When he grinned, Jonah's own face grew hot with embarrassment for a second time.

"I didn't mean it like that."

Kevin didn't respond. He twisted his body and phased them out of the clearing.

Once they reappeared in a new location, Jonah squinted through the dimness. He could just make out lights from a building through the thick trees. But Kevin didn't move; he just scanned the surrounding forest.

Jonah grew impatient. "Why are we waiting here?"

Kevin made a dismissive sound before answering, "I needed to make sure the way is safe and we weren't followed. It's a good thing it is. Otherwise, someone may have heard you talking."

"I didn't know."

Kevin placed a hand over Jonah's mouth. When he knocked the hand away, Kevin laughed. "Let's go, little man."

Jonah glared at the older boy and waited. He expected Kevin to grab hold of him and use his ability again. Instead, Kevin set off on foot through the sparse trees, forcing Jonah to run and catch up.

CHAPTER ELEVEN
SAFE HOUSE

The lights that Jonah had focused on turned out to be a fifteen-story apartment complex. All the units facing them across the busy street sported gently curving balconies and windows. Judging by the cars going in and out of the parking garage, this was an upscale place.

Kevin paused, waiting for a break in the traffic, then led the way across the road. Jonah began to have misgivings about going inside such a nice place as they approached the double glass doors. He was a mess, and he noticed that Kevin had smudges on his shirt and a little dirt in his hair. The older boy didn't hesitate to enter the lobby of polished marble, smooth granite, and shiny metal surfaces. The concierge at the front desk dropped his evening newspaper and stood, giving the boys a suspicious look.

Kevin waved almost lazily at the man, saying, "Hey, Thaddeus." He continued across the lobby like he belonged in the place.

Jonah wasn't as brave and cast several nervous glances at the concierge until they reached the elevator lobby. Only when they stepped into a plush elevator and the doors closed did he relax. The elevator was done in gold and silver metal and the back wall was one large mirror. Jonah caught a glimpse of himself and averted his eyes. He looked worse than he thought.

He focused on the floor indicator and was shocked. The elevator had already shot up several floors without so much as a vibration or sound. It reached the thirteenth floor and whispered to a stop. Kevin exited onto a quiet and well-lit hallway. It took Jonah a moment to realize the door numbers had the numbers thirteen in them. He'd never seen that before.

The Protector's Ring 75

Jonah began to wonder if anyone lived on this level, it was so quiet. Halfway down the carpeted corridor, Kevin pulled out a real key and, unlocking a door, he waved Jonah inside.

The foyer was tiled in a light-brown slate. An entry table stood to the right with a mirror situated above it. A small closet was on the left. Jonah followed Kevin as the older boy moved into the unit. To the right, off the foyer, was an open kitchen done in stainless steel, dark cabinets, and granite countertops. Next to that was a large dining area, complete with a formal table made of dark wood that could seat eight people.

The living room had a white sofa and sitting chairs arranged around a large glass coffee table. Kevin maneuvered around these to a very modern dark green and black stone fireplace situated in the middle of a wall of floor-to-ceiling blinds. When he opened the stark white blinds, the illuminated Washington Monument shone in the blackness above darkened trees.

"Wow," Jonah said, wanting to reach out and touch the view. "Is this apartment yours?"

"It's a condo." Kevin paused, and Jonah wondered if he was going to make fun of his mistake, but the other boy simply shrugged and picked up the duffel bag. "This is Marcus's place."

He carried the duffel bag to a narrow bedroom just off the living room and dropped it on a full-sized bed covered in a red-orange spread and matching pillows. A floor lamp and table were positioned beside the bed. Jonah paused in the doorway, next to a small desk and chair. His eyes were drawn to the wardrobe beyond the bed. Beautiful color nature photos adorned the front of its doors.

"This is the guest room," Kevin explained. "The bed is all right." When Jonah frowned, Kevin smirked. "I've crashed on it a few times." He held out a hand for the Jonah's book bag. "You can leave that in here."

Jonah shook his head and wrapped his arms around it. "I'll keep it with me."

"Whatever."

Kevin slipped past him and back into the living room. Jonah followed and sat his book bag on the floor next to the white sofa. Afraid to sit down because the night's events had left him filthy, he settled on stuffing his hands in his pockets and watching Kevin. He wanted to ask questions, but Kevin turned to the window, staring into the darkness outside. Jonah glanced around, struck by how neat the condo looked, almost like a picture in a magazine.

His gaze came to a small bookshelf against the wall between the kitchen and a short hallway, just past the dining area. The bookshelf was one of those modern kinds that slanted against the wall. Instead of just books, small statuettes and pictures also occupied the shelves, including a three-sided picture holder. Jonah moved around the table to get a closer look at the pictures. Omar and Marcus stood arm-in-arm on a beautiful white beach. Marcus actually smiled.

Jonah lifted the frame, turning it over. Omar and Marcus wore cold weather gear and stood in front of a snow-covered peak with skis slung over their shoulders. In the last picture, Omar stood with a group of teenagers around him. All wore the same powder blue school uniform with *Alliance Academy* on the front. The kid's dark skin shone brightly in the sunlight and their high cheekbones and deep-set eyes resembled Omar's own features. Could this be his native country, Jonah wondered. He saw lush, green trees beyond the school that sat in the background.

The stand-alone framed photo surprised Jonah the most because it wasn't a picture at all. It was a reduced Beauty Essence magazine cover featuring Omar. He wore dark jeans and a printed shirt that opened down to his navel, exposing a well-defined chest and abs.

"Whoa."

Kevin glanced over his shoulder, his eyes narrowing when he saw the holder in Jonah's hands. "Omar's a model."

Jonah rotated the holder back to the first picture of Marcus and Omar on the beach, recalling the way Omar had fussed over Marcus. "Are they dating?"

He caught Kevin giving him that unblinking look, the kind Marcus did at times. After several quiet moments, a smile tweaked the corners of Kevin's mouth. "Something like that."

Jonah opened his mouth to ask more questions, but Kevin turned back to the window. Frustration flared inside Jonah, and like a bursting dam, the events of the night flooded into his mind. He forgot about being dirty and curled up on the uncomfortable sofa, hugging himself as he tried to hold off crying.

The Protector's Ring 77

Kevin heard him sniffle and finally turned around. "I can't tell you what's going on."

"Why not?"

"I'm Marcus's apprentice."

"So?"

"You really don't know a lot about our world, do you? An apprentice can't share anything his mentor forbids him to tell."

"Marcus told you not to say anything?"

Kevin nodded. "I'm sorry, Jonah. I think you should know."

The front door closed and Emily strode into the living room. "I left the car about thirty miles from here."

Jonah didn't understand and hopped to his feet. "Why couldn't you just phase here?" He turned to Kevin. "Why did we have to walk through the woods and across the street?"

"This condo is protected from that sort of thing."

Emily gave Kevin a sharp look, and he shrugged in response.

Realizing Kevin and Emily had let something slip, his determination to get more out of them peaked. "You mean it's protected from those black dogs? What about the Garretts? Aren't they in danger?"

Emily took off her long coat and folded it over the back of a kitchen stool. "The Garretts' house is protected. That being said, having you stay with your neighbors tonight may have created too tempting a target."

Jonah's eyes widened when he heard that. "Who's after me?"

Pressing her lips together, Emily moved into the kitchen without answering.

Jonah leaned against the breakfast counter, watching as she prepared coffee. "Are you Marcus's apprentice?"

Kevin laughed in the background and Emily stopped in mid-motion. "God, no."

"Then why can't you tell me anything?"

Emily placed the coffee pot on the machine and pressed the ON button. "It's Marcus's responsibility, Jonah. Not mine."

She refused to meet his glare. Jonah shifted and his hand brushed against her long coat, reminding him about the symbol.

"Can you tell me about that?"

Emily finally met his gaze before looking down at her coat and shaking her head. Her refusal made Jonah want to scream and he plopped down on the sofa again, knotting his hands into fists. He couldn't remember being so frustrated in his life. He wanted information; he needed it. That's how he was. His parents had always encouraged him to seek out the facts. Now they were gone and Marcus and the others didn't want to tell him anything.

The front door opened again as Marcus and Omar entered. Marcus stopped just inside the living room and scanned the glum faces in front of him.

Even though the man towered at least two feet over Jonah, he took a step back as Jonah ran up to him.

"What happened to the Garretts? Emily says I'm a target," Jonah shouted, not caring that his voice rang through the condo. "Tell me what's going on."

Marcus glared at Emily and Kevin as he spoke. "Jonah…"

"Tell me!"

Omar dropped their coats over the back of an armchair and placed his hand on Jonah's shoulders. Jonah struggled, but he couldn't shake Omar's strong grip.

"Jonah, calm down. I know you're angry. You have a right to be angry and afraid."

"I'm not afraid!" That was true. Anger burned inside him. He was angry with Kevin, the Garretts, and with Marcus for keeping information from him. And he realized he was angry with his parents for dying and leaving him alone.

Omar gently squeezed Jonah's arms. "You wanted to know about the Garretts?"

"Omar…" Marcus spoke up.

"Your way isn't working." Omar turned back to Jonah. "Well?"

The Protector's Ring

In truth, Jonah wanted to get away from all of them. But his desire to understand everything happening around him won out over the impulse to run. He wiped his eyes with the back of his hand.

Omar waited until Jonah nodded, then he said in softer voice, "I'm a Memory Charmer."

Jonah blinked. "A what?"

"A Memory Charmer. I can modify a person's memory."

Marcus let out a breath and leaned against the kitchen counter.

Jonah repeated the term silently to himself as he digested Omar's revelation. He thought he understood and asked, "You can erase memories?"

"No, I can't erase memories. I can suppress them or make them less prominent, and I can only affect very recent memories. Older ones are impossible to touch without serious damage to the person."

"You blocked Mr. Garrett's memories of what happened tonight."

When Omar glanced over his shoulder at Marcus, Jonah wondered if he regretted mentioning the ability.

"Yes, I blocked his and Tyrone's memories, but I like to say I charmed the memory."

Jonah's mind kicked into gear as something else occurred to him. "What about Timothy and Kim?"

"They never saw anything."

Emily spoke softly to Marcus as she handed him a cup of coffee. "Are we considering formally recruiting the mother?"

"She's more valuable as she is, I think."

Omar gave them an impatient look, and Jonah knew Omar wanted to keep him calm. That embarrassed him.

"I'm sorry."

"Jonah, you don't owe any of us an apology."

Marcus leaned over Omar's shoulder. "I think he should get some rest."

"No," Jonah objected. "I want to know what's going on."

"I'll talk to you in the morning." Marcus motioned to Kevin. "We have important business to complete tonight."

Kevin stalked over from the window and leaned over the sofa. "Come on, Jonah." He held out a hand. "It'll be all right."

Jonah reached for his book bag when Omar gripped his shoulder, stopping him.

"Marcus, you should tell him."

"Omar…"

"He has a right to know. He's going to Georgia tomorrow. Now's the best time."

Omar and Marcus locked gazes for several moments, during which Jonah noticed that Omar wasn't bothered at all by Marcus's strange stare. After several more moments, Marcus waved his hands in surrender.

"Fine. I'll tell him, but maybe I should talk to him alone."

"I think," Omar said, "he'll feel better with another teenager present."

Until that moment, Jonah hadn't realized that he'd moved closer to Kevin. He did feel better not being the only kid in this group.

Emily clapped her hands together. "I'll make more coffee."

Marcus nodded. "Maybe you should sit down, Jonah."

Jonah did and was relieved when Kevin perched on the arm of the sofa, hovering close by. Marcus took his time setting his coffee down on the breakfast bar. Jonah suspected his godfather was trying to find the right place to start. Finally, Marcus met his gaze.

"Jonah," Marcus began, "what do you know about Reapers?"

CHAPTER TWELVE
THE HALF-REAPER

"What do I know about Reapers?" Jonah repeated to himself, rather than to the group standing around him. "I know what they do. They take people's souls in the movies and TV shows."

"That's correct as far as it goes. What else do you know?" Marcus replied. When Jonah shrugged, he continued, "There are two additional things I want you to understand about Reapers before we go any further. When certain humans die, instead of their souls going on to their final destination, they are chosen to be Reapers. No one knows how or why those humans are chosen." Marcus paused again, and this time, Jonah realized he waited for a question.

"So all Reapers were human?"

"Yes."

Again, Marcus waited, prompting Jonah to ask, "So what's the other thing I need to know about Reapers?"

"Human souls normally move on to a final destination. Reapers help them along. And even Reapers move on, eventually." Marcus took a deep breath. "But some Reapers choose to go in the opposite direction."

"You mean Hell?"

Marcus laughed. "No, I don't mean Hell. I mean they give up their station as Reapers and become human again. It's called falling and Reapers who undergo the process are called Fallen Reapers. You need to understand both of these things to appreciate what's happening to yourself."

Jonah's mind raced with the possibilities. Why did Marcus focus on Fallen Reapers? "What does that have to do with me?" Marcus held up a hand as Jonah shot to his feet. The gesture stopped Jonah, reminding him to focus on what was happening: Marcus was finally giving the information he'd been so desperate to hear. He took a deep breath and let it out as he sat down.

Marcus nodded and continued, "You can do the things you do because you are half-Reaper and half-human."

Jonah required a full minute to process Marcus's actual words. He leapt to his feet and backed away before Marcus could stop him.

How could he be a half-Reaper? That meant that his mom or dad must have been a Fallen Reaper. All the things his father had done in the dream flashed into his mind and his eyes widened as he stared at Marcus. "My my dad was…"

"A Fallen Reaper."

"But that's… that's…"

"Impossible?" Marcus gestured to the sofa. "Jonah, please sit down."

Jonah obeyed, drawing up his knees and wrapping his arms around them. Something icy cold gripped his heart, and his stomach burned. *I'm a Reaper, a creature surrounded by Death. Is that why my best friend died? Is this why my parents died?* Jonah's breaths came faster and faster as it grew harder to breathe.

"I'm a Reaper," he said.

"Half-Reaper," Marcus corrected.

Deep down, Jonah thought that was just as bad. He squeezed his arms tightly around his legs. Slowly, the shock began to subside and he could focus on Marcus's explanation. His mind offered up a question.

"You said that when Reapers fall, they become human. Then how did my dad have powers?"

Marcus smiled at him. "You're very perceptive. Let us say that generally speaking, Reapers do become human when they fall. However, there are ways to retain or reclaim some of their former power."

"Wow." All thoughts and fears about being a half-Reaper were forgotten for the moment as the conversation switched to his parents. "Did my mom know about my dad before they met?"

The Protector's Ring

"Yes. That's why your father loved your mother so much. He found someone who accepted him. They eventually got married, and they decided to have you. That caused a lot of trouble. No Fallen Reaper ever produced a child. Many thought it impossible."

Marcus started to go on, but he stopped himself. He traded a glance with Omar, who returned an encouraging nod. Marcus focused on Jonah again.

"Your father and mother hoped that you would be normal and have a normal life. When you developed the Death Sense, they were frightened. Not everyone thought you should be kept in the dark at that point, but everyone respected your parents' wishes. They wanted to protect you from your supernatural half for as long as possible. They did it out of love, Jonah, not shame. And they sacrificed themselves to protect you."

Jonah sucked in a breath. That was exactly what his parents said to him before… Jonah shut his eyes, willing that memory away. He searched for something else to focus on as he thought about everything Marcus had revealed so far.

He glanced around at the others, none of whom watched him directly. A question came to mind, something that he'd mentioned to Kevin earlier. "Fallen Reapers like my dad can phase. And half-Reapers like me can do it."

Instead of responding, Marcus strode to the window to gaze out on the darkened view. He kneaded the back of his neck. Jonah felt a pang; his father had done the same thing whenever he thought about something important.

"You and Kevin phased tonight," Jonah continued, his mind putting more pieces together. "So, are you a Fallen Reaper or half-Reaper like me?"

Marcus shook his head. "You're the only known half-Reaper."

"Then you're like my dad."

Jonah watched Marcus as he lowered his hand, squared his shoulders, and turned to face him.

"Yes, Jonah, we are like your dad. We are Fallen Reapers."

Jonah gaped at Emily, Omar, and Kevin. It was like finding out something he knew all along but didn't recall until this minute. As usual, his mind kicked into gear as more questions occurred to him. "I can't sense you like I sensed the man at the memorial service. And I never sensed my dad or Kevin."

Marcus spread his arms to include everyone in the room. "We are essentially human now."

"But you said there are ways to keep some of the power? How, if you're human?"

"Even though we fall, we're always sensitive to the power as humans." Marcus paused and took a deep breath. Omar went over and touched his shoulder.

"Maybe you should show him, Marcus." Omar's deep voice was quiet.

Kevin stirred. "I'll do it." He stood, pulling his shirt over his head in one fluid motion. Jonah gawked at the boy, caught first by the fact that Kevin was muscular. Then Jonah's eyes were drawn to the intricate design on Kevin's neck, shoulders, forearms, and chest.

Jonah stood to get a closer look. "Are those tattoos?"

"Nah. They're patterns."

"They were etched into Kevin's skin at the time he fell," Marcus added from the window.

Jonah didn't like the sound of that and looked into Kevin's face. "Didn't that hurt?"

"Heck nah." Although Kevin tried to play it off, Jonah could sense that falling must have been very painful. Kevin slowly rotated his body so that Jonah could see that the patterns continued across his upper back.

"Why do it?" Jonah couldn't imagine anyone willingly going through extreme pain.

"The patterns are part of a binding spell and allow us to draw in power," Marcus explained. "When we're fully charged, they are black. When we use power, they turn brown." Marcus indicated Kevin's patterns; they were a deep brown. "After that, they turn deep red and finally, a light red. If one of us ever totally depleted our power, the patterns would disappear, leaving faint scars on our skin."

Jonah pointed at the intricate design. "You have patterns like these?"

"Yes, I do--"

The Protector's Ring

"Although," Omar interrupted, "I see you managed not to show Jonah your own."

Omar's mouth curved into a smile, but Marcus frowned at him.

"As I was about to say, Emily has them."

Emily pulled down the neck of her shirt to show him the very tip of the pattern on her collarbone.

Jonah turned to Omar. "What about you?"

"I've always been human."

Jonah considered that answer as he continued to scrutinize the elegant, thin lines of Kevin's patterns. "So, if Fallen Reapers want to use power, they have to cut themselves like this?"

"Yes." Marcus didn't elaborate as he motioned for Kevin to put on his shirt.

Jonah thought back to his father. He'd seen him shirtless when they went to the beach. His father didn't have the patterns on his body, yet his father had used power in the dream.

"Why didn't my dad have patterns?"

"Your father became human under… different circumstances."

"What circumstances?"

"That story can wait for later." Marcus came over to the sofa. "It's important that you understand what I've already told you." Marcus nodded to Kevin, who scooped up Jonah's book bag.

"Come on," he said.

Jonah stood in a tidy three-piece bathroom, staring at his shirtless reflection in the mirror. *I'm a half-Reaper.* He ran his fingers over his chest and shoulders, trying to imagine having patterns like Kevin.

A knock came on the closed bathroom door, breaking his thoughts.

"Are you all right, little man?" Kevin called through the door.

Jonah's hands dropped from his chest. He felt a little embarrassed because he'd been thinking about Kevin. "Go away."

"We don't have all night."

After a few seconds of silence, Jonah assumed Kevin had walked off. He picked at the debris still in his hair as he studied his smudged face. When he had pulled off his stained shirt earlier and sniffed it, he nearly gagged from the reek of smoke. He finished stripping and climbed into the shower.

Refreshed from a long shower, Jonah returned to the bedroom, that was directly across the hall. Kevin sat in the little chair by the desk, holding one of his deactivated blades. The strange markings on the blade's cylinder fascinated Jonah.

"Can I hold it?" He held out a hand.

Kevin shook his head, and Jonah huffed as he got in bed and pulled the covers up to his neck. He wondered if Kevin was angry because he had taken so much time in the bathroom. The older boy laid the cylinder on the desk and nudged the door partially closed with his foot. When he took off the shades and rubbed his eyes, Jonah was surprised because Kevin didn't look any older than Tyrone Garrett.

Jonah's eyes narrowed as he watched Kevin. "How old are you?"

"Fifteen."

"I thought you were like eighteen or nineteen."

Kevin gave him a tired smile. "No."

"You work with Marcus?"

"Yes, I do." Kevin folded his shades with hard movements of his hand. Jonah thought he'd snap them in two. "Marcus still treats me like a kid even though I have to deal with the same things they do."

"You don't like him."

"No, I don't. I can't wait until I'm finished with his stupid--" Kevin stopped and shook his head. "I'm stuck with him for eighteen more months. Longer if I keep screwing up like I did tonight."

"You didn't screw up tonight."

"Yeah, I did. I disobeyed an order when Marcus told me to get you out of the house. Your safety was the most important thing."

"Why? Those strange dogs weren't after me."

The Protector's Ring

Kevin leaned forward in the chair and rested his elbows on his knees. "They're called Grim Hounds."

"Grim Hounds?" Jonah's eyes widened as he recalled the creature's double row of teeth. "Are they anything like Hell Hounds? I read about Hell Hounds."

"I guess you can call them that."

Jonah's eyebrows drew together. "What were they doing in our empty house?"

Kevin avoided answering as he checked his watch.

When he stood, Jonah sat up in bed. "Where are you going?"

"They need me in the meeting."

"Can't you stay a little longer? It's cool talking to someone my age."

"I'm not your age. I'm fifteen. Besides, you need to sleep." Kevin held up a closed fist. "It's been interesting meeting you, little man."

"Don't call me that."

"Sorry. It's been interesting meeting you, Jonah."

Jonah tapped Kevin's fist with his own. "I'll see you tomorrow, right?"

"You're going to Georgia in the morning. I doubt I'll see you again for a long time." Kevin hesitated before grabbing his shades and the cylinder off the desk. Jonah had hoped the older boy would forget the blade so he could inspect it, but Kevin slipped it in the pocket of his black jeans.

"Wait," Jonah called out.

"I gotta roll."

"Marcus used his blades on those Grim Hounds."

"The blades are really old and made to fight supernatural creatures." Kevin reached for the doorknob and Jonah stopped him again.

"Are you sure I won't see you tomorrow?" Jonah suspected he sounded like a little kid, but he didn't want Kevin to leave—and Kevin didn't seem too happy about attending a meeting with Marcus. Jonah was sure of that when Kevin came back and knelt down beside the bed. Jonah rolled onto his side. Kevin stared back for so long that Jonah wondered if…

"Are you trying the Marcus stare?"

"No." Kevin finally blinked. "It's called the Reaper stare, and I wasn't trying it on you. It's just that, well, you have cool eyes. Gray."

"Oh. Thanks." Jonah experienced a funny, excited sensation. What should he say now? Should he tell Kevin that his brown eyes were nice? Would he believe that? Kevin looked at his watch again and Jonah mentioned the next thing that popped into his mind. "You have a little brother?"

"Yeah."

"Do I look like him?"

"In a way, you remind me of him."

"Is he here?"

Kevin shook his head. "He lives with a family in Chicago."

Jonah propped himself up on an elbow. "You're adopted? Is Marcus your step-father?"

Kevin laughed. "No. He's more like a legal guardian. Just don't let him know I told you that." Kevin gently pushed Jonah's head back onto the pillow. "Lay down."

"Do you ever see your brother?"

"It's been a long time. Go to sleep, little man."

"Maybe you could go visit him in Chicago." Jonah started to raise his head again, but Kevin pushed it back down on the pillow. He pinched Jonah's nose and released it.

"I used to do that to my brother. The little crumb snatcher."

Kevin stared off into space for a moment. Whenever he talked, Kevin seemed like any other fifteen-year-old to Jonah. When Kevin grew quiet, Jonah could sense the difference, the strange otherness in the boy. *Was that his Reaper side?*

Jonah hesitated, then tapped Kevin's hand to get the boy's attention. "Crumb snatcher?"

"My little brother always wanted part of whatever I had."

"I don't have a brother or a sister."

The Protector's Ring

"I know." Kevin smiled and started to slip on his shades. "I'll see you again sometime."

"You promise?"

Kevin paused, his shades halfway to his face, and stared at Jonah for a long moment. He smirked and raised his hand as if making a solemn oath. "I promise you, Jonah Blackstone, that I will see you again."

Jonah thought he heard a pop. Along with the strange sound came a set of goosebumps racing all along his arms and legs, like a cool wind blowing across his bare skin.

"Whoa! What happened?"

Kevin dropped his shades on the floor. His brief playful mood evaporated.

"Jonah! How old are you?"

"I turned thirteen this past week."

Kevin swore softly to himself. "Marcus never told me that." He plucked the shades off the floor and headed for the door.

"What happened?" Jonah called out. "Why's it important that I'm thirteen?"

"Bye, Jonah."

"Kevin?"

This time, Kevin didn't allow Jonah to stop him. He flicked the light off and closed the door.

Jonah lay back in the darkness and reached up to touch his nose.

"Bye," he said in a soft voice.

He wasn't angry with older boy for not explaining that weird sensation. Kevin had made a promise to him and the certainty of it pulsed inside Jonah like a warm glow.

CHAPTER THIRTEEN
STRANGER IN A STRANGE LAND

Marcus sat alone at the dinning table, the end nearest the kitchen, sipping coffee and reading the newspaper. He paused when Jonah shuffled into view.

"Good morning," Marcus smiled. "Did you sleep well?"

"Yes, sir." Jonah's eyes widened when he saw the stack of pancakes, sausages, eggs, and toast on the breakfast counter.

"Please don't call me sir. Marcus will do." Jonah nodded, and Marcus glanced at the counter behind him. "I take it you're hungry?"

"Yeah."

"Good." Marcus nodded at Jonah's bags. "Place those in the foyer."

Jonah did as he was asked, returned to the breakfast counter and grabbed a plate. "Thanks for letting me stay here."

"You don't have to thank me." Marcus glanced at the food. "Go ahead."

Jonah's mouth began to water, blanking out all other thoughts as he helped himself to a heaping breakfast.

"Did you cook all this for me?"

Marcus choked on his coffee just as Omar came around the corner from the hallway on the other side of the kitchen.

He finished buttoning a light green shirt and said, "Marcus can't boil water." He gave Jonah a pat on the shoulder as he walked into the kitchen. "I made a little of everything. We have cereal, if you'd prefer that."

The Protector's Ring

"All this is cool." Jonah sat down with his plate and paused, watching Omar set a plate of food in front of Marcus. The action reminded Jonah of Kevin's comment about the men last night. "I saw your pictures on the bookshelf."

Omar gave Jonah a piercing look as he placed his own plate opposite Jonah's and sat down.

But it was Marcus who answered. "Yes, about the photos," Marcus placed his coffee cup on the saucer. "Jonah, I don't know if you realized it--"

"Oh, I know about you and Omar."

Omar seemed to relax, but he arched one of his eyebrows. "Really?"

"Yeah." Jonah swallowed. "Kevin said you're dating."

"We're partners, Jonah. And, we don't want you to feel uncomfortable…"

"I don't."

Omar smiled and hurried into the kitchen to fetch glasses out of a cabinet. Marcus continued watching Jonah, who dug into his breakfast to prove how cool he was. Of course, it also helped that he was hungry. He devoured the first plate of food and made a second. As he sat down, he paused to gaze out the window, reminded of Kevin standing at that spot the night before. The boy's comment about his eyes popped into Jonah's mind. Was that the same thing as Marcus and Omar?

"Jonah," Marcus asked. "Are you okay?"

"Leave him alone." Omar tapped Marcus on a hand as he took his seat. "I think he's daydreaming."

"But--" Marcus's eyes widened

Jonah's face grew warm. "I'm fine."

As breakfast continued, Jonah snuck glances at Omar and Marcus without being too obvious.

Omar was friendlier than Marcus, asking Jonah questions about school, the types of music he liked, and even drawing Marcus into the conversation. Jonah wondered if Omar and his mom had been friends. They were so much alike.

Marcus reminded Jonah of his dad. He bet the only people his godfather knew were the people from work. As he gazed around the condo, a new thought occurred to him.

"Did my parents ever come here?"

"Yes." Marcus set his coffee cup down, one finger tracing the rim. "They came here from time to time." He traded a glance with Omar. "Why?"

"I just wondered." *Maybe they sat at this table and talked about me.*

Jonah became so lost in his own thoughts at that point, he didn't realize he had cleaned his plate until he tapped it with his fork several times. Omar noticed.

"You want more breakfast?"

Jonah shook his head no. Omar stood, collected the empty plates, and took them to the sink. When he came back, Omar patted Marcus's shoulders. "I'll see you at the airport, Jonah."

Omar gave Marcus a hug and patted Jonah's shoulder with his big hand before leaving the condo.

Jonah leaned forward in his chair as a question exploded in his mind, one he hadn't asked Marcus yet. "My parents didn't die in an accident, did they?"

"No, they didn't." Marcus subjected Jonah to his intense stare, waiting.

"How did they die?"

"Jonah," Marcus blinked, breaking eye contact. "Your parents were real archeologists. They searched for and recovered powerful objects for our organization."

"What kinds of powerful objects?"

"Oh, all types. There were medallions, rings, pendants, talismans, among other things. All were imbued with magical or supernatural power."

"Wow."

"There are people who would use these objects to do great harm. That's why our organization takes them and keeps them safe. It's a constant race, at times a very dangerous and even fatal undertaking."

Jonah caught the reference to his parents and let out a breath, the pang of loss feeling like he'd just been sucker punched.

"So one of these bad people killed my parents?" Jonah could picture that Deyanira woman again. She'd attacked his parents; she had to be one of the bad people who'd use the artifacts for harm.

Marcus, who had hesitated before answering, nodded. "I'm afraid so."

Jonah was relieved that Marcus admitted that much without asking why he knew his parents were attacked. Again, he thought about the dream. The bad guys wanted a ring. Clearly, that was one of those artifacts. Despite the pain of loss, Jonah couldn't deny an intense curiosity about his parents' job.

He thought about all the objects they brought home and wondered if any had magical powers. Even though most of his parents' belongings were destroyed in the fire, he still had one object. He had the paperweight, a copy of a medallion. So many things about his parents began to take on new meaning. Jonah put that aside to jump to another topic.

"Kevin said I could learn to change my position when I phase." Marcus nodded, and Jonah glanced down at his hands. "Can I be a trainee, like Kevin?" As Marcus opened his mouth, Jonah rushed on. "He's fifteen and a trainee. Why can't I do it when I'm fifteen?"

"I didn't say you couldn't train."

"You mean I can?"

"Yes, Jonah." Marcus smiled. "In fact, your parents wanted you to train."

Jonah sensed the truth coming from his godfather. He'd get to train. The thought filled his mind.

Marcus cleared his throat. "I give you my word. You can start training when you turn fifteen."

Jonah's arms and legs tingled with the same odd sensation he had experienced when Kevin made him a promise the night before. It felt less strange this time and just as certain to come true.

If his godfather felt anything, he didn't show it. He didn't seem to notice anything in Jonah, either, as he cleared his throat to continue talking.

"Your parents were heroes in the true sense of the word, Jonah. They dedicated their lives to protecting the world from bad people. It can be dangerous, so don't rush it."

Jonah nodded. "Why do I have to wait? Can't I train now?"

"There are certain things you'll learn now, but more formal training won't start until later, Jonah." Marcus raised his hand to stop Jonah's next question. "Be patient. Wait until you've settled in Georgia. For now, we'll watch over you. Okay?"

Jonah didn't want to wait, but just like the promise from Kevin, he had an inner sense that Marcus would keep the promise to train him.

Marcus watched Jonah with that unblinking stare. When he seemed satisfied, he glanced at his watch. "We better get to the airport."

"Ladies and gentlemen, we will begin boarding Delta flight 403 from Reagan National to Atlanta in twenty minutes. Please have your boarding passes ready."

Jonah peeked at Marcus, curious how his godfather could remain as still as a statue. As if sensing his thoughts, Marcus stirred, glanced at his watch, and pulled a large brown envelope out of his briefcase. He tapped the edge of the envelope on the briefcase's shell as he watched the main concourse.

At last, without looking at him, Marcus handed the envelope to Jonah, who immediately opened it and shook the contents onto his lap. A small black wallet slid out along with a new cell phone, some printed sheets of paper, and a blue envelope. Jonah picked up the wallet and opened it. Inside were twenty-dollar bills and a bankcard. He counted the money: two hundred dollars in all.

"Wow."

"I assumed you'd need cash for the trip." Marcus raised an eyebrow. "Is that too much?" When Jonah smiled without answering, Marcus frowned but continued, "The bankcard accesses the account I set up for you. A small allowance will be deposited in it every two weeks."

"You're giving me an allowance?"

"Your parents are, in a way. You already know they made me the executor of their estate. I'm also responsible for the trust that has been set up for you."

"Trust? My mom and dad left me money?"

"Yes, they did."

The Protector's Ring

"How much?"

"Enough. When you turn eighteen, you can decide what to do with the remaining funds." Marcus picked up the business card and handed it to him before Jonah could ask another question. "My emergency number is on the back. If you ever need me or need something from me, call."

"Okay."

"If I don't answer, leave a message, no matter the subject. It's a safe number. Understand?"

Marcus stared right into Jonah's eyes—and Jonah, understanding, stared right back. "Yes."

"The bus ticket is for the trip from Atlanta to Mount Vernon," Marcus said, tapping the blue envelope. "When you get to Atlanta's airport, just take the airport shuttle to the bus terminal. Your plane should arrive in plenty of time to make the connection."

The flight attendant raised the mic to her mouth and announced, "At this time, we will began boarding flight 403 to Atlanta. First Class passengers can come forward for boarding."

In quick order, the groups disappeared down the gangway to the plane. Finally, Jonah's group was announced. He stuffed the wallet in his back pocket and took his place in the forming line. He got a pleasant shock when he saw Omar striding down the concourse toward them. People stared at him, and one woman hurried over. Omar stopped, spoke to her, then took a pen and magazine she held out. After signing it, he smiled and hurried on.

Marcus let out a snort, causing Jonah to glance up at his godfather. He wondered if Marcus hated that Omar drew attention. Even the flight attendant, an older woman, halted before announcing the next boarding group in order to stare. Omar seemed oblivious to it as he came over to stand beside Marcus, giving Jonah a quick wave.

Jonah lowered his gaze to the envelope in his hands as he moved toward the flight attendant checking the passes. If he boarded the plane, he would leave everything he knew, and that scared him. He'd been comfortable with Omar and Marcus this morning. They knew his parents. They knew about his abilities. They could even train him.

Jonah stepped out of line and hurried back to Omar and Marcus.

"Do I have to go?" He looked up at Omar. "Why can't I stay with you and Marcus?"

"Your parents made arrangements," Omar answered. "These are your mother's people, Jonah."

"But I've only seen them once."

"You've been there more than that." Omar leaned down to stare into Jonah's eyes. "You just don't remember right now." He motioned toward the gate. When Jonah refused to move, Omar stood straight, crossed his arms, and said, "What would your father tell you if he were here?"

Jonah swallowed. "He'd tell me not to be afraid."

"Then don't be afraid."

Jonah continued to stall as the attendant made another announcement for the rest of the passengers to board.

"How about this?" Omar smiled. "See how it goes over the summer, and we'll talk about it later." Marcus stirred, but he didn't say anything. Omar gave Jonah a one-armed hug. "Now hurry before you miss the flight."

When Omar released him, Jonah hurried to the gate. He flashed his boarding pass to the checker. Glancing back, he waved to Marcus and Omar before walking down the gangway.

Jonah's plane touched down at the Hartsfield International Airport in Atlanta, Georgia an hour and a half later. He entered the main airport terminal, expecting to hear a lot of deep Southern accents in the airport. However, most of the travelers spoke in accents as varied as those in Washington.

Jonah followed the other passengers to the designated luggage carousel. As the luggage from his flight began to arrive, Jonah wondered if he could leave the duffel bag. The clothes in it weren't his in the first place. He didn't want them. And he really didn't want the reminder of what he'd left behind.

A mother and two young kids waited nearby. When their bag slid down the chute, the kids yelled and rushed forward. The mom laughed as they struggled to pull it free of the conveyor belt.

The scene reminded Jonah of Mrs. Garrett, Kim, and Little Tim. She'd packed the duffel bag for him as a way to help and he would be wrong to abandon it. After a few more minutes, it arrived. Jonah glanced at digital clock on the wall as he scooped the duffel bag off the luggage carousel. He had just enough time to find his airport shuttle to the bus station.

The Atlanta cityscape soon gave way to the surrounding suburban malls, then scattered rural developments, and finally wooded areas and pastures. As the bus rolled down the highway, Jonah thought about his parents and the burned house. Everything he knew seemed far away. *Don't be afraid of the new and unknown.*

Jonah tried to cheer himself up with his dad's favorite quote. Marcus had said his parents were heroes, and they were. They had faced the dangerous and unknown. His dad stood up to that strange woman named Deyanira. He hadn't backed down or run. Jonah released a breath and fogged up a small patch of his window. Could he do the same thing? He didn't think so. Maybe it would be different when he turned fifteen and could train like Kevin.

Soon, Jonah's own fear returned. To take his mind off of that, he lost himself in a video game until the bus stopped in a small town. A man in military fatigues grabbed a carry-on bag and walked down the aisle. Jonah pressed his nose against the window as the man exited the bus. Two young kids, a girl and boy with flaming red hair, raced into their father's outstretched arms. The man's wife gave him a hug as the man ruffled his son's curly hair with his hand.

Jonah's vision blurred and he sucked in a breath. His dad would do the same thing to him. As he watched the family walk off, his tears obscured the scene. He let them flow as he imagined the moving, blurred shapes were the taxis dropping off passengers at Dulles, the day his parents left on their final trip.

"You need to get a haircut, mister." Jonah's mom had run her fingers over his tightly curled black hair. "It's bushy."

Jonah squirmed and ducked. "Mom, don't do that. It's embarrassing." He looked around, hoping no one saw them.

"My little boy is growing. At least an inch in the last year, and you look more like your father all the time."

Jonah stuffed his hands in his pockets and watched his dad make his way through the airport crowd. With two tall parents, Jonah knew he'd eventually grow. He just hoped he turned out big like his dad and not slender like his mom.

Once his dad rejoined them at the curbside drop-off, he took out his wallet and counted out several bills. "Don't spend all of the money at once. It should last you until we get back."

"What about my birthday?" Jonah took the money and slid it in his jeans pocket.

"We'll make it." His mom placed a hand on his shoulder. "We promise, sweetheart."

His dad held up a silver house key next. "I don't want you hanging out at home the entire time."

"I won't." Jonah frowned and slipped it on his blue Lanier Middle School key chain.

His mom raised an eyebrow. "Remember, Jonah, you're staying with the Garretts."

"Do I have to stay with them? Tyrone hates me."

"Tyrone does not hate you, Jonah."

"I guess he hides from me because he likes me?"

Jonah knew he went too far when his dad gripped his shoulder.

"Have you tried talking to Tyrone?" Jonah shook his head. "You make the first move. If he doesn't respond, at least you know you tried. Don't assume someone hates you."

"Yes, sir."

Jonah looked down at his feet. His dad lifted Jonah's chin so that they looked directly into each other's eyes.

"Never be afraid to try something new. Hear me?"

Jonah nodded.

"We better get inside." His mom checked her watch before glancing at Jonah. "Will you be okay on the metro, Jonah? Maybe we should call Mrs. Garrett to get you."

The Protector's Ring

"He'll be fine, Janice." Jonah's dad flashed him a smile. "Won't you, young man?"

"Yes, sir."

"We'll call you as much as we can." His mother gave him a hug.

Jonah's dad started to shake his hand, then suddenly pulled Jonah into a hug. He ruffled Jonah's bushy hair with a big hand. "Take care, son."

Jonah watched as his parents gathered their carry-on bags and disappeared into the busy airport terminal. The images blurred and shook and he raised his head, hastily wiping his eyes as the bus moved down the highway. He put the game aside and leaned his head against the window again. Soon, he'd be in Mount Vernon. The anticipation about what lay ahead began to build and intrude on his memories of his parents.

What would Mount Vernon look like? Would it be a sleepy little Southern town? How would the people treat me, a young black kid from Washington? Tyrone had joked that Georgians still flew the rebel flag. Was that true? Jonah hated that he never got a chance to do some research. He had planned to look the place up before the fire ruined everything.

Mount Vernon must be okay. My cousins live here, and my parents wouldn't send me if it weren't safe.

CHAPTER FOURTEEN
THE HIGHTOWERS

Slipping on his book bag, Jonah stepped off the Greyhound bus and into the oven of late-June Central Georgia. By the time the bus driver handed over his duffel bag, beads of sweat already trickled down the middle of his back. He squirmed in his hand-me-down clothes as he followed the other passengers into the comparative coolness of the bus terminal.

Jonah paused, realizing he wouldn't recognize his aunt and uncle if they were standing in right in front of him. That's when he noticed a short, solidly built woman near the front doors with two lanky teenagers beside her. She waved frantically at him.

"Jonah! Over here!"

Jonah grabbed the duffel bag and quickly threaded his way across the crowded area, toward his relatives. As soon as he came within reach, Jonah's aunt pulled him into a warm embrace.

"Oh, Jonah! You've grown so much! And you're the spitting image of your mother." She released him and stood back to look him up and down. "I'm so sorry about your parents. The news devastated James when he heard." Jonah needed a second to remember that she meant his uncle on his mother's side of the family.

"We're sorry we couldn't make their memorial service. And then we got the news about the fire. Everything destroyed! Oh my Lord—I couldn't believe it. How are you holding up?"

"I'm doing okay."

The Protector's Ring **101**

Aunt Imma fussed with his clothes, which embarrassed Jonah. She wore a white blouse, black pants, and comfortable-looking black shoes. Jonah remembered seeing waitresses wearing the same kind of shoes. He wondered if his aunt had taken off work to come here.

"That Marcus fellow told us your neighbor gave you these clothes," Aunt Imma continued. "It's obvious her son's bigger than you, Jonah. We'll need to get you more clothes, unless you like them baggy. That seems to be the thing nowadays." She finished pulling and tucking and then stood back, shaking her head.

"Robert and Lynn, say hello to your cousin. What's wrong with you two?" She waved the twins forward.

"Hey, little cousin." Robert spoke with a mild Southern accent as he shook Jonah's hand first.

"Hi," Lynn said. She had a high-pitched accent like her mom. Lynn stepped forward and tried to shake Jonah's hand, but Aunt Imma nudged her in the back.

"Give your cousin a hug."

Lynn obeyed with a quick hug, then stepped back and crossed her arms.

The twins were slender and taller than their mother. Like Jonah, they had vanilla-wafer complexions and medium gray eyes.

Robert wore a simple black t-shirt, cargo shorts, and black sneakers. He had angular eyebrows, and the edges of his bushy Afro were neatly trimmed.

Lynn, on the other hand, could have stepped off a basketball court with her jersey, trunks, and high-top sneakers. Her thin braids fell to her shoulders. She tossed them with a graceful flick of her head.

Aunt Imma poked Robert in the arm. "Help your cousin with his bag." Robert sighed and took the duffel bag from Jonah. She nodded and said, "Let's get you home."

Thirteen thirty-eight Morningside Drive turned out to be a tidy, one-story brick house with a two-car garage and neatly trimmed yard. It also had a matching brick mailbox with *The Hightowers* on the side.

Jonah followed his relatives to the front door, which opened with a wave of cool air. He stopped, reminded of the dream about his parents. Robert noticed his expression.

"You okay, little cousin?"

"I'm fine." Jonah blinked.

Robert continued on inside as Lynn bumped Jonah in the back with the duffel bag.

"Well, get going. You're letting out all the cool air."

Jonah stepped into the Hightowers' foyer. There was a living room on his right and a neat dining room on the left. Robert continued down the hallway to a large, open room. The L-shaped sofa and two well-worn armchairs looked extremely comfortable. All were positioned to face a big-screen TV above a fireplace and mantel. Game consoles sat on a TV stand beside it. A breakfast bar, on the left, separated the family room from an open kitchen. A set of sliding doors led out to a patio and a fenced-in backyard.

Aunt Imma stood in the narrow hallway that ran the entire length of the family room. A bathroom was at the end of the hallway, but she pointed at a closed door to the right of it. "That's Lynn's bedroom."

She indicated the next door, also closed, with a *keep out* sign on it. "That's Robert's bedroom. And this," she motioned to the first door off the hallway, "is your room. I'm afraid it isn't too large. It used to be your uncle's office."

Jonah suspected that meant his was the smallest room. He entered and dropped his book bag on the twin-sized bed positioned beneath a window. Jonah knew with a glance that the bed wouldn't be as comfortable as his old one. He went over and peeked out the window. It faced a narrow side yard. He turned, noting that the off-white room smelled of new paint.

Aunt Imma hovered in the doorway. "I'm sorry about the fumes. We painted a few days ago. I know it's different from your old room."

"It's nice."

Lynn slipped past her mother, dropped his duffel bag on the bed, and said, "Fantastic."

Aunt Imma frowned and brushed her hand along the top of the dresser. "I've put some of Robert's old clothes in the drawers and the closet. They should fit you."

The Protector's Ring

"Thanks." Jonah slid his hands in the pockets of his oversized jeans and looked around. Compared to his old room, this looked like an empty shoebox. "Really, it's okay. And I'm sorry that Uncle James lost his office."

"He's happy you're here, Jonah." Aunt Imma smiled at him and went back into the family room.

Lynn stood in the hallway, her arms crossed and foot tapping on the floor. "Mom, I have a game. Let's go."

"Okay, okay."

Lynn caught Jonah staring at her from his bedroom doorway. "Are you into sports?"

"I played sometimes with the other kids--"

"Oh Lord, not another geek!"

"Lynn! Be nice to your cousin."

Robert came to stand beside Jonah. "Just because he likes to read doesn't mean there's anything wrong with it."

"He'll fit right in with you, Sci-Fi Boy."

Aunt Imma swatted Lynn on the arm with a fistful of letters. "Lynn, be nice."

"Robert calls me *jarhead* all the time."

"Fine impression you two are giving your cousin." Aunt Imma grabbed her purse and keys. "Robert, you entertain your cousin until I get home."

"But I have something to do at the rec center."

"Then take Jonah with you. Don't leave this house without your cousin."

Robert hung his head. "Yes ma'am."

His aunt gave Jonah another hug, then left. Lynn shot her brother a quick glance before following her mom out the front door.

Jonah turned to his cousin as soon as the door closed. "You don't have to stay."

Robert couldn't hide the relief on his face. "I really need to do something."

"Then do it. I'm okay on my own."

"Don't mention this to Mom."

"I won't."

Robert crossed through the family room and went out the kitchen door. Jonah followed, pausing in the doorway to watch as his cousin rolled a bike from a large utility shed out back. After Robert waved and rode off, Jonah went back to his new bedroom. Once he finished unpacking, Jonah lay on the new bed, gazing at the ceiling. Being here in his relatives' house made all those strange things about himself seem a little less real. He liked that.

Robert came home an hour later, and Aunt Imma soon afterward. Jonah laughed and enjoyed playing his cousin in a video game so much that Aunt Imma's return caught him by surprise.

She paused on her way to the kitchen, a grocery bag in hand, and shook her head at the mayhem on the TV screen. Jonah thought she looked happy. Maybe she assumed Robert had stayed here with him all afternoon.

Aunt Imma continued on into the kitchen to put away the groceries. Jonah's concentration was shattered when he heard his uncle call from the garage doorway.

"I'm home." Uncle James came into the family room carrying a worn brown satchel. His eyebrows shot up when he saw Jonah sitting on the sofa. "Jonah?" He bounded over and gave him a vigorous handshake. "My God, you look like Janice."

Jonah thought that his uncle also looked like his mom with his thin face, pecan tan skin, and brown eyes. Actually, Jonah's uncle reminded him of a professor with his sport coat, goatee, and round eyeglasses.

"How are you doing?" Uncle James leaned back, holding Jonah at arm's length. "Did the flight go well?"

"The flight was cool." Jonah gave up the video game and let his cousin win.

"Sorry we couldn't come up to Atlanta and get you from the airport," Uncle James said. "The memorial service took place so soon, and the news about your parents' house shocked us."

"James..." Aunt Imma had leaned over the breakfast bar. Jonah saw his uncle fighting to keep himself together as he waved to her. When he turned back to Jonah, he wore a sad expression.

The Protector's Ring **105**

"It still doesn't seem real to me. I expect your mom to call and…" He took a handkerchief from the inner pocket of his sports coat, removed his glasses, and dabbed at his eyes.

Jonah understood. Sometimes, he found himself waiting for his mom or dad to call and say they were on the way home.

"We're happy to have you here." Uncle James put his glasses back on and sat his satchel beside the armchair. Then he went into the kitchen to wash his hands before pulling salad greens, tomatoes, carrots, and other items out of the refrigerator.

Before Jonah could ask to help, Robert, who had also gone into the kitchen, reached over the breakfast bar to hand him the forks, then yanked them away.

"Wash your hands and follow me." Jonah copied his uncle and rinsed his hands at the kitchen sink. He had to duck around Uncle James to follow Robert, who had pulled a stack of plates out of the cabinet, placed the silverware on top, and marched into the dining room. They began setting the table. Lynn came home a short time later and helped them finish.

As everyone gathered around the table, Uncle James went to the china cabinet and took out a plate. A folded napkin and silverware lay on top. Uncle James placed it on the table beside Jonah and noticed the confusion on his face.

"You're wondering about the extra place setting?"

Jonah nodded.

"It's a custom in my family. We do it to honor the memory of someone who has gone home, as we say." Uncle James reached over and straightened the folded napkin. "This is for your mother."

Jonah stared at the plate for a long time. He had never heard of this before. It did remind him of the remembrance ceremony for his parents. The tightness in his chest loosened a bit. Everyone stared at him, waiting for him to say something.

"How long do you …"

"Oh, we set the place for thirty days from the time of the funeral or, in your mother's case, the memorial service."

The more Jonah talked about it, the more he thought it the type of thing his mom would have done. He looked at his uncle. "Can I set it tomorrow?"

His uncle smiled. "Of course you can."

Three hours later, Jonah slipped into bed, listening to the sounds of the Hightower house. Robert moved around in the next bedroom, the low thump of music vibrating the wall. Someone watched TV in the family room, probably his uncle, Jonah thought. He wondered if he would ever get used to the newness. Jonah yawned and in no time, he descended into sleep.

Jonah dreamed that he ran along a steep dirt road on four feet. *I have paws!* Jonah realized with a start. The paws looked like something on a dog or bear. *No, I'm a Grim Hound.*

The Grim Hound's body stumbled and lost speed. The creature shook its head from side to side, and Jonah realized it heard his thoughts. He calmed himself and the creature set off again, quickly gaining speed.

Jonah had never experienced anything like this. He wasn't the Grim Hound itself. He was a passenger in the creature's body. He swore his own hands mauled the hard ground as the creature's paws kicked up dirt. His lungs burned each time the Grim Hound drew in the hot, dry air.

He concentrated on being with the Grim Hound and began to sense the creature's thoughts. As it darted around boulders and leapt over bushes, a single idea repeated itself.

Have to find it! Have to find it!

The urgency grew inside Jonah. He needed to find it. His own heart thumped with anticipation and a little fear. The creature's master would be angry if it didn't find it.

What do I have to find? Immediately, the answer came to him: The Ring.

The Grim Hound reached the top of the hill and rushed around the clearing, digging up the dirt. Something gleamed in the sunlight, catching its attention. The creature jumped and sailed several feet. Growling with eagerness, it attacked the dirt with its massive paws.

The object turned out to be the back of a plain watch. The Grim Hound let out a frustrated sound. It gripped the watch fragment in its jaws and tossed it away with a flick of its head. The Ring wasn't here.

The beast howled in irritation, and an unpleasant ringing hurt Jonah's ear as a woman's voice spoke directly in his mind.

Come to me! Now!

A ball of smoke blossomed in midair like a dirty, time-lapse flower. The Grim Hound raced forward and dived into the swirling mass. Jonah sucked in a breath as the damp wetness of the mist touched the creature's body. He was just thinking it didn't feel that bad when a moment later, darkness exploded around them. Clinging strings of vapor blurred his vision, and as they dissipated, a cul-de-sac came into view. Stars twinkled above in the velvet-black sky.

The Grim Hound padded over to a woman in a black dress. Jonah's heart beat faster as the creature looked up. The woman's pale skin glowed in the dimness. She wore square glasses and her red hair was in a tight bun.

When she peered down into the Grim Hound's eyes, the weak streetlight revealed faint lines crisscrossing her face. The creature whined as it looked away and scratched restlessly at the asphalt road beneath its paws.

The woman pointed, and Jonah heard the unspoken command. *Go!*

The Grim Hound hunched its muscles and sprang down the darkened street. Again, Jonah let the animal move in its own way. The Hound rounded a corner, leapt over a parked car, and landed with a heavy, muffled thud behind a tall bush. When it raised its head to watch a house directly across the street, Jonah's heart stopped.

That's my aunt and uncle's house!

Something tugged on Jonah and, suddenly, he wasn't part of the Grim Hound anymore. As he shrank away from the creature, the angry, red eyes seemed to watch him.

Across that very same street, in his own bed, Jonah's eyes flew open. His heart pounded furiously as he sat up and looked at his hands. They weren't large paws anymore.

I'm out of the Grim Hound's body!

Jonah whirled around in bed and looked out his window. The darkened yard outside was empty. He caught himself. Wait. *The Grim Hound watched the front of the house.*

Jonah tried to leap out of bed, but he fell to the floor with a solid bang; his blanket had wrapped around his foot. He untangled himself and rubbed his sore elbow as he walked to the door. He looked out into the silent house and waited. No one came out of their room to investigate, so he tiptoed down the hallway toward the front door.

Just as he reached out to grip the doorknob, he thought of a better idea: the dining room had a large bay window. He slipped into the room, pulled back the curtains, and pressed his face to the glass. That was a mistake because his rapid breathing quickly fogged it and obscured his view. Jonah wiped the glass, clamped his hand over his mouth and nose, and peeked through again.

He spotted the tall bush across the street and let his eyes move to the shadows. He gasped when he saw two glowing red eyes staring back at him. The Grim Hound watched the house from the exact spot as the dream! How could that be? How could he dream about the creature?

The Grim Hound leapt into motion, shocking Jonah out of his thoughts. He threw himself back from the window, cracking his head against a dining room chair. Fortunately, he still held the hand over his mouth; otherwise, someone would have heard him scream.

After seconds of pure terror, Jonah's mind registered the fact that the Grim Hound hadn't charged the house. Even though his entire body shook, Jonah stumbled back to the window and looked out. Far down the street, the creature passed below a streetlight and disappeared into the darkness.

Jonah slumped to the floor. It took a while for him to get his racing heart under control. Slowly, the shock of seeing a real Grim Hound on Morningside Drive began to fade.

How did the Grim Hound find me in Georgia?

Jonah already knew the answer. That mysterious woman in the black dress had called the beast, and she knew exactly where he lived.

The Protector's Ring

CHAPTER FIFTEEN
TEEN CENTER

"Good morning, Jonah!" Aunt Imma hummed as he shuffled into the kitchen table. She paused her stirring of a skillet full of fluffy scrambled eggs and glanced over her shoulder. "I guess you're not used to the new bed."

Jonah nodded as he sat at the kitchen table. His problem wasn't with the bed. He was tired because he had tossed and turned for two hours after seeing the Grim Hound. A real Grim Hound! That thought still scared him. Of course, he couldn't tell his aunt. He couldn't tell anyone—except Marcus.

Aunt Imma set a plate stacked with buttered toast on the table. "Lynn's gone already, so it'll just be you boys this morning. I hope you like scrambled eggs."

"Uh, scrambled is fine." The smell of eggs, toast, and bacon began to push out thoughts of the Grim Hound.

Aunt Imma pointed to the refrigerator with her spatula. "Why don't you get the orange juice?"

Jonah fetched the carton of juice and sat down as his aunt placed a dish piled with eggs and bacon in front of him.

"Robert! Come and eat your breakfast!" Aunt Imma took in Jonah's baggy shirt and shook her head. "We'll get you some new clothes this afternoon, okay? I have to get to work. Robert promised to take you around this morning. You two stay out of trouble." She winked at Jonah, grabbed her bag, and headed for the garage door.

Jonah thought about waiting for his cousin, but the smell of the food made his stomach grumble, so he ate alone. He was halfway through his breakfast when Robert emerged from his room. Within minutes, the shower was running. Afterward, Robert went back to his room without pausing to say good morning.

Maybe he's trying to avoid me.

Jonah finished breakfast and started back to his room, but changed his mind. He walked up to Robert's closed door, ready to knock, and paused when he heard his cousin's voice inside. Should he knock or just leave it alone?

The door opened, and Robert, seeing Jonah, stumbled back. "Hey, little cousin. " He snapped the cell phone closed. "You weren't listening to my conversation, were you?"

"No. I wouldn't do that." He saw the smirk on Robert's face. His cousin was just kidding. "Breakfast is still on the table…" He looked over Robert's shoulder. "Wow!"

Robert stepped back, swinging his door wide. "Come on in."

Jonah entered another world, a very fantastic one.

Overlapping posters from fantasy and sci-fi movies covered every square inch of one wall. Charcoal and pen drawings of other worldly landscapes and ships hid the opposite wall.

One of Robert's drawings caught Jonah's attention, a perspective drawing of a tear-drop-shaped vehicle soaring above a flat plane. Robert had drawn a huge building in the background, its upper portion shrouded in clouds. Jonah reached out a finger, tracing the complicated lines of the ship.

Something about it pulled at him. He could almost feel himself inside the scene. "This is really good."

"Thanks." Robert looked at the floor and absently tugged at his ear. "My mom doesn't like them. That's why I keep my door closed most of the time."

Jonah turned and tripped over a long, black case. "Whoa."

"Careful." Robert scooped up the case and leaned it against the side of his dresser. "That's my trombone. I'm in the symphonic and marching

The Protector's Ring **111**

bands at school. In fact, camp starts soon." Robert sat down on the bed again. "You play an instrument?"

Jonah shook his head and noticed the floor-to-ceiling shelving unit on the other side of the dresser. DVD movies filled the top shelf while hundreds of neatly displayed CDs filled the rest.

It reminded Jonah of his own lost mp3 collection. He began pulling random CDs from the wall. Robert had a wide variety of styles, including some of Jonah's favorite soundtracks. He put them back, suddenly sober. "I've never seen anyone with this many CDs," he said softly. "I have everything loaded on my iPod."

"You can borrow mine, if you want. With a really good pair of headphones, it'll sound better."

"Thanks." Jonah looked around Robert's room again, noting a one-fourth scale Predator model, still in the box. "You're really into the fantasy stuff."

"Yeah. You should meet my friend Wick. He's into magic."

"Magic?"

Robert laughed and ran his hand over his bushy hair. "My mom would have a fit if she heard some of the things Wick talks about. We're working on a supernatural computer game together. He does the heavy research. I'm the artist and programmer." His cousin nodded to the pictures. "Most of those are designs for the game."

Jonah stood back, taking in the entire wall of drawings. Robert pulled a pair of white sneakers from underneath a pile of shoes. He paused before putting them on.

"Sorry about your parents. I can't imagine what it feels like." He stared at his sneakers. "My dad took off work for three days. I've never seen him like that." Robert finished putting on his shoes and leaned back on his unmade bed. "We liked your mom. She was cool and used to tell me and Lynn about the places she went."

"I guess it was long time ago."

"A year isn't that long."

"A year?"

"Your mom visited just before school started."

Jonah rubbed his head, trying to remember his parents coming here without him. "I didn't know my parents came down to visit."

Robert sat up. "No, just your mom. We haven't seen your dad since, well you know, when you were a baby. I think there's a picture in the den with my dad, your mom, and Aunt Ruby." Robert grinned. "Your mom has Little Jonah in her arms."

Jonah nodded. He had seen the picture the day before, but he hadn't recognized the woman beside his mom. Aunt Ruby? He couldn't recall her, yet that dread he experienced when Marcus told him about Georgia returned. Jonah rubbed his head. "A lot of things have happened to me. Sometimes, it's like a bad dream."

Robert leaned forward, watching him. Images of Grim Hounds and his strange dream popped into Jonah's mind. He relived the shock and weirdness of running through the streets of Morningside Drive. Could he tell Robert about the strange people in black or the woman with the faint scars on her face? His cousin waited with an intense expression on his face.

Jonah bit down on the urge to say anything. He hoped that Robert would take the hint. After another uncomfortable minute, his cousin leaned back on his bed.

"You'll be okay, little cousin."

"Yeah." Jonah glanced at the wall of drawings and the large artist desk that sat in one corner of the room. Pens, charcoals, rulers, erasers, colored pencils, and several unfinished drawings littered its surface. A thought struck him. "Are all of you artistic?"

"No!" Robert laughed. "My dad is the editor of the local black newspaper. Lynn is into all things sports, as I'm sure you guessed. Now, my mom always has an artsy project going on." Robert snapped his fingers. "You know, she got a commission to do an art piece for the teen center."

Robert hopped to his feet and walked over to a wall-mounted shelf that contained several red wire magazine holders. Each had the word SUMMIT on the spine. Robert tipped back a holder and thumbed through the papers inside.

"Here we go." Robert slipped out a thin newsletter and gave it to Jonah. It had a small picture of a mountain at the center top and the words *The*

The Protector's Ring **113**

Summit in large blue letters. The most surprising thing was Lynn's name as editor and Robert as assistant editor. Jonah's jaw dropped.

"Is this yours?"

Robert nodded. "We do it for older kids, like us. There's an article about my mom in there. She registered for one of those art classes at the community college. A bunch of the art students submitted original works for the new center and the city picked three entries, including my mom's piece. Now we can't get her to stop talking about her latest idea."

Jonah quickly scanned through the newsletter. "This is cool."

"My buddy Wick helps out sometimes. We also do an online version as a blog." Robert's stomach grumbled, cutting off his words. He patted it.

Jonah laughed. "Maybe you should eat something."

Robert grinned and said, "Yeah. Then we head to the center."

Jonah followed Robert to a large shed in the backyard. He peeked around Robert's shoulder and saw a wheelbarrow and other gardening tools inside. Then he saw two older 12-speed bikes chained to the vertical struts.

"We're riding bikes to the Recreation Center?"

"Sure. We ride most places we have to go, unless we need to go to the County mall or downtown." Robert gave Jonah a sly smile. "You do know how to ride?"

"I rode my bike to the metro all the time."

"Is that what you call the subway in Washington?"

Jonah nodded.

Robert unhooked the first bike and rolled it out to Jonah. Then he unchained the second bike.

"I wish my mom would let me drive." Robert took the chain from the strut and wrapped it around the bar on his bike. He nodded to Jonah to do the same thing. "Mom barely lets me practice even though I have my learner's permit. I already know how to drive."

Jonah remembered Robert telling his mom that yesterday. He finished hooking his chain on his bike and gave his cousin a curious look.

"How did you learn to drive?"

"Wick's big brother lets us practice in his old pickup truck." Robert gave Jonah a serious stare and closed the shed.

"I know. I won't tell your mom. Maybe you should give me a list of all the secrets I need to keep."

Robert laughed and easily straddled his bike. Jonah sized up his bike before carefully straddling it. The bike was a little larger than his old bike and Jonah had to stand on his tiptoes to keep from hurting himself.

"Is this Lynn's?"

"Lynn has her bike. Wick gave us that one for you. I guess it's a little too large."

"You think?"

Robert laughed. "Ready to go?"

Jonah nodded and they set off.

The first several blocks on the way to the teen center were relatively flat, so they rode along with no difficulty. Then Robert began to climb a series of hills. He resorted to a switchback pattern on a particularly steep hill, and Jonah followed his lead. Robert paused when they reached the top and sounded a little short of breath when he spoke. "That's the steepest hill. And that is the Cedar Hill Recreation Center."

Jonah couldn't believe his eyes. The recreation center was an old Southern mansion with a commanding view of the surrounding neighborhoods.

"The county bought and renovated the old mansion about ten years ago," Robert continued. "The east and west wings of the original house were extended about a year ago. As you can see, we have basketball courts, four tennis courts, and a swimming pool on the other side."

The boys rode up to the center and chained their bikes to the racks near the basketball courts. Jonah followed Robert up the sidewalk, pausing when he came even with the recreation center's sign. Although the sign read *Cedar*, Jonah noticed that Robert pronounced it *Ceda* with no *r*.

Jonah hurried to follow his cousin into the main atrium of the building. He stood beside Jonah and pointed out a starburst sphere made out of thin metal rods and glittering rings. It, and two other art features, was suspended from the atrium ceiling.

The Protector's Ring

"My mom did that one."

"Wow. Where'd Aunt Imma find all those rings?"

"People donated them. I think there are about two hundred and fifty. It's on the plaques." Robert nodded toward three plaques attached to the far wall.

In addition to Aunt Imma's piece, there was a hanging tangle of real children's bicycles. Most of the bikes were metallic blue, green, or red. Beside that hung the third piece, a collection of old wooden tennis rackets. They were cut so that each racket actually intertwined with the others.

"They're interesting the first few times you see them," Robert whispered. "Then you get used to them."

Jonah lowered his gaze and let out a low, "Whoa!"

Directly ahead, kids sat around colorful café tables, talking or texting their friends. A few typed away on laptops. A deli counter sold sandwiches, bottled drinks, candies, and as Jonah watched, a couple of kids got fresh, hot pizzas. He drew closer and noticed the bright blue neon cursive letters above the counter. They spelled out *Cyber Café*.

Robert tugged Jonah back toward one of the arched openings off the atrium.

"This is the East wing. You have all of the recreation game rooms with pool, ping-pong, video games, and board games. On the other side is the West wing. Through there, you have study rooms, a small library, and study tables with built-in Internet access. Administrative offices and meetings rooms are upstairs. I guess you'll want to go in the library first, huh?"

It so amazed Jonah that something like this existed in Mount Vernon that he didn't even pay attention to Robert's picking at him. He didn't want to explore only the library, he wanted to explore every inch of the place.

"So, I can hang out until we leave?"

"Sure. Don't forget we're heading to the mall later."

"Okay."

"Stay out of trouble."

Jonah frowned. "I won't get in trouble."

"I'm just kidding you, little cousin." Robert laughed, but Jonah saw the strange look in his cousin's eyes before Robert headed for the main stairs.

Once again, Jonah wondered if his cousins sensed the difference in him.

CHAPTER SIXTEEN
FRIEND AND BULLY

As Jonah approached the Recreation Center library, he slowed. Three boys about his age stood at the entrance, laughing and talking. A light-complexioned boy with curly hair snatched a cell phone from a shorter, pudgy kid, held it up, and started laughing.

"For real, Drew? No one uses this old phone anymore." He threw the phone back to Drew, who fumbled and caught it.

"What do you use, Brandon?"

"Man, please." Brandon puffed out his chest. "My dad buys me the new models as soon as they come out. And I don't stand in no dang lines, either. It's shipped right to my house. Tell your old man to come off that money he makes. Right, Antwan?"

"Yeah." Antwan, the third boy, answered with a distinct African accent. He was the tallest of the three, with dark skin and a long neck.

Brandon went quiet when he saw Jonah and openly stared, sizing him up. When Brandon didn't bother to say hello or nod, Jonah decided not to bother, either. He slipped by the boys and caught a glimpse of Drew's phone. It was just like the one Marcus had given him.

As Jonah stepped into the library, all three boys laughed, causing him to wonder if they were making fun of him. Probably, he decided and turned down the first aisle of books so he wouldn't be in their line of sight.

Instead of books, Jonah faced a tall display of popular magazines. He peeked around the display, spotted a Young Adult fiction section, and headed straight for it. A few kids were around, including a boy his age who sat in one of the brightly colored chairs along the wall. The only reason Jonah noticed him was because the boy raised his book when Jonah glanced in that direction.

Jonah paused, pretending to check out the books on the shelf. The boy kept the book held high, covering his face. At least he's quiet, Jonah thought, scanning the titles on the shelves. He chose one, began reading the back cover, and almost dropped it when the boy spoke.

"There's not much of a selection." The boy stood at the end of the aisle, peering at Jonah through black-rimmed square glasses. He wore jeans and a pale blue shirt, and his hair was in a small jet-black Afro that set off his pale skin. "I'm sorry. You're new here, right? I haven't seen you before." He clutched the book to his chest as he approached. "I'm Mike."

"Hi, I'm Jonah."

Mike's eyes widened. "You're not from here."

"How did you know?"

"You sound different."

"I'm from Washington, DC."

Mike bounced on his feet with excitement. "Wow! I've always wanted to visit Washington, DC. What's it like living in the capital?"

"Well, I lived across the river in Virginia--"

"Did you ever see the President?"

"Well, the--"

"What about the Capitol building?"

"I never--"

"Or the Washington Monument!"

"Sometimes, but--"

"I bet the museums and libraries are much better than what we have here." Mike waved at the bookshelves. "Do you like to read a lot?"

Jonah blinked several times, waiting for Mike to bombard him with another question. Instead, Mike pushed up his glasses and stared back at him. Jonah opened his mouth to speak just as Brandon loomed behind Mike.

He snatched the book from the other kid's hands. "Hey nerd!"

Mike gave a little yell and stumbled back into Jonah.

Brandon glanced at the cover and made a face. "A romance novel? You wish."

"It's not a romance…"

Brandon puckered his lips and made loud kissing sounds, causing Antwan and Drew to laugh like demented henchmen.

Jonah could feel Mike shaking with fear. He stepped in front of Mike to face Brandon. "Give it back to him."

Brandon looked Jonah up and down, a sneer on his face. Jonah grew self-conscious, his eyes catching the designer logos on the other boy's clothes. Suddenly, he couldn't wait to get to the mall and buy his own things. Brandon stepped closer; he was taller than Jonah expected.

"So you're from DC?"

Jonah blinked. "Yeah. Who're you?"

"Brandon M. Warner, the third." Jonah noticed that Brandon's snide-sounding voice didn't have a heavy Southern accent. When Brandon offered to shake hands, the light reflected off a gold watch on his wrist. "My parents built this place."

"No they didn't, Brandon," Mike spoke right over Jonah's shoulder, causing him to jump. "They gave money like everyone else."

"Yeah, that's right. They gave more than anyone else, especially your folks. So be quiet, nerd." Brandon glanced over his own shoulder. "These are my friends, Drew and Antwan."

Antwan didn't even bother to nod. He stared at Jonah with his chin held high.

Drew at least waved before stuffing his hands in his pockets. All the while, he avoided looking anyone directly in the eye. Both boys wore gold watches like Brandon's. Jonah wondered if the watches were a club thing.

"So DC," Brandon continued. "What do your parents do? Are they FBI agents, or do they work on Capitol Hill? Antwan's uncle is an ambassador. We're always in Washington visiting."

Jonah hesitated. He wasn't going to tell Brandon his parents were dead. However, Mike saved him from having to answer. "Drew! Why do you hang out with him? You're better than that."

Drew glanced up at Mike before averting his eyes.

Brandon caught the quick look between them and turned on Mike. "I told you to shut up, nerd."

Jonah had heard enough. "Give Mike his book."

"Or what?"

Jonah didn't know what he would do. He'd spoken without thinking. It seemed that Brandon didn't know what to do next, either. They stood toe-to-toe, neither one willing to throw the first punch, and neither willing to be the first to back down. Jonah thought they'd have to stand there forever until he heard Lynn's voice.

"What's going on?" Lynn stood behind Brandon and his friends, arms crossed. Mike moved out from behind Jonah.

"Brandon has my book."

"Here," Brandon said. He shoved the book into Mike's hands. "I was just playing."

Lynn tossed her long braids behind her shoulder. "I suggest you go to the East wing if you want to play." Her voice let the bully know she meant business.

Jonah was impressed by his cousin because Brandon backed away and motioned to his friends. He bumped Jonah's shoulder as he walked by. "See you later, DC."

As the three boys walked off, Brandon glanced back at Jonah and whispered to his friends. When all three laughed, Jonah had no doubt they were making fun of him this time.

Lynn waited until they were out of the library. "Robert's leaving soon. Maybe you should wait in the café so you don't miss him."

Even though she made it a suggestion, Jonah didn't think it was one. "Okay."

He waved to Mike and followed Lynn out of the library.

The Protector's Ring

"Stay out of trouble this time," Lynn said, pausing by the atrium staircase.

Jonah puffed out his chest, ready to defend himself until he saw the hint of a smile tweaking the corners of Lynn's mouth before she turned and walked off.

"I should have known," Mike said from right behind Jonah. "You look like Robert."

"Yeah, they're my cousins. I'm staying with them over the summer."

"Wow." Mike glanced around the atrium. "Over here." Mike claimed an empty café table and sat down. He slipped off his glasses as he waited for Jonah to take a seat. "Thanks for standing up to that bully Brandon. He's a total jerk."

"Was he bragging about his parents?"

"Not really. His dad is a big shot doctor, and his grandfather is an important attorney in Atlanta." Mike made a sour face. "And, of course, all the girls think Brandon's light skin and soft, curly hair are so cute."

Jonah resisted the urge to smile as he wondered exactly how Mike knew Brandon's hair was soft.

Mike slammed his fist on the table top. "Did you see him back away from Lynn? I wish I were tall like Lynn. I'd kick Brandon's butt." As suddenly as it came, the fire leaked out of Mike and the boy slumped back in his chair with arms crossed. He looked miserable.

All at once, Jonah wondered if Mike thought Brandon was cute, just like all the girls did. Maybe that's why his bullying got him so angry. Jonah didn't know why he thought that. Maybe it was a slight prissiness in Mike. Or maybe it was the guilty glance that Drew gave Mike.

Mike huffed. "I get enough pranks at home from my big brother. I don't need it here."

"Why does he pick on you?"

"He thinks reading sci-fi and fantasy is… "

Jonah understood. He'd been accused of being weird because he carried those types of books. Some kids were just plain stupid, he thought.

"What about your parents?"

"My dad agrees and my mom, well…" Mike lowered his gaze but his voice grew angry. "She never sticks up for me."

Jonah couldn't imagine a more horrible position in which to be. Except to have dead parents.

"So," Mike reached across the table and poked Jonah's forearm. "Do your parents work on Capitol Hill?"

A flash of annoyance hit Jonah. Why did everyone want to know about his parents when they heard he was from DC? He wondered how many times he'd have to dodge the question.

The irritation must have shown on his face because Mike leaned back. "I'm sorry. You don't have to tell me." Mike stood.

"No, wait. I don't mind." Jonah smiled, hoping it would cover his earlier annoyance. "My parents are researchers, so they read a lot. My dad even has a library at home."

"Wow! It must be really nice to have parents like that." Mike's brow wrinkled. "Why are you here instead of Washington?"

Jonah swallowed, not wanting to lie, but he also didn't want to reveal the awful truth about his parents.

"My parents are traveling overseas, for work. They sent me to stay with my aunt and uncle over the summer. I haven't been here in years."

"It's like you're getting to know them all over again."

Jonah nodded. "Yeah, it's strange."

"Robert and Lynn are so cool, and they do a lot of stuff. You already know about the newsletter and blog? In fact, they're probably working on them right now."

It took Jonah a moment to catch up with Mike's rapid Southern delivery, wondering if he always talked fast whenever he got excited about something.

"Do my cousins have an office here?"

"It's upstairs in the attic." Mike pointed toward the stairs.

"Attic?"

The Protector's Ring

"Yes. They didn't tell you?" Jonah shook his head. "Well, I bet they're under a tight deadline."

Mike went quiet and glanced down at his hands as he wrung them together. "You know, I thought about showing them something that I wrote, you know, for the blog." He glanced at Jonah, waiting for him to say something.

"That's a good idea."

Mike's hunched shoulders relaxed a bit. "Hey! Have you met their friend Wick? He does stories about strange and weird stuff." Mike lowered her voice. "I think he's a witch."

"A witch?"

"Well, he uses a different name for it, but yes. I think he's a witch."

Jonah laughed, causing Mike to cross his arms and glare back. "What's so funny?"

"Nothing." Jonah couldn't shake the sudden image of a kid dancing around a black cauldron with a pointy hat on top of his head. The words Wick the Witch bounced around his mind. Why should that be so funny, Jonah wondered. He was a half-Reaper!

Mike narrowed his eyes as he watched Jonah. "If you don't believe me, just ask him. He hangs out with your cousin Robert all the time."

"I believe you."

Jonah honestly did believe him. Grim Hounds existed, he was a half-Reaper, so why couldn't other things exist?

Robert and Jonah returned home just moments before Aunt Imma drove up to the house and honked the horn. Jonah paused on the Hightowers' front walkway, staring at the champagne-colored vehicle.

"You have a minivan?"

Robert pushed Jonah toward the sliding passenger door.

"My dad took the van in for a checkup yesterday. Mom drove his car to get you from the bus station."

"I didn't know that."

Robert closed the side door and hopped in the front. "You caused a lot of fuss, little cousin."

Aunt Imma swatted him on the arm. "Robert, that's not true."

"You picked dad up from the repair shop and took him to work almost two hours earlier than normal!"

"Your father didn't mind at all. He was able to get some extra work done." Aunt Imma backed out of the driveway and set off for the mall.

Jonah didn't know if his cousin exaggerated. Frankly, the whole situation made him uncomfortable. He didn't like his uncle giving up his office or changing his schedule.

He knew what his mom would tell him to do. He leaned forward between the front seats. "Thank you for taking me to get new clothes, Aunt Imma."

His aunt smiled back at him. "It's not a problem, Jonah. You're part of the family now."

Green Oaks Mall was located near the Mount Vernon city limits and was a small town in itself. In addition to the mall, there were numerous chain restaurants, supermarkets, and car dealerships all within easy walking distance.

Aunt Imma pulled into a multi-level parking garage and hustled Jonah into the boy's section of the nearest department store. Although she allowed Robert to help Jonah pick out his clothes, she insisted on approving all purchases. When Jonah exited the store an hour later, he had two bulging shopping bags.

"I'll put those to the van." Aunt Imma took Jonah's bags. "I have to pick up supplies for the salon."

"No problem Mom," Robert said, leaning on Jonah's shoulder. "I'll show him the mall."

"Remember you need some shoes, Jonah."

The Protector's Ring   125

"Yes, ma'am."

Robert watched his mom head off across the pedestrian bridge to the parking garage. Then he tweaked Jonah's ear. "Yes ma'am?"

Jonah shrugged as he batted Robert's hand away. They headed straight to the food court to get lunch. Afterward, they rummaged through the discount bins in a music store, toured the new titles in the video game shop, and then stopped at a computer store so Robert could buy parts. Jonah found it cool to hang out with his cousin.

As soon as Jonah bought a pair of new sneakers, Robert headed out of the mall's ground floor entrance. Jonah followed, taking two steps for each of Robert's longer ones.

"I need to check out the art store," Robert explained. "It's a cool place and has the biggest selection of supplies in the county."

Once they reached the store, Robert held the door open for Jonah. However, Jonah's attention was drawn to a flashing sign two doors down. It read Mystic Worlds. Jonah gave his cousin a sheepish look and hurried down to peer in the store's window. The display featured books on all kinds of supernatural, spiritual, and religious topics.

"Wick told me about this store." Robert stood beside him and tapped the display window. "It opened a few days before you got here." He nudged Jonah with his arm. "You want to go in, don't you?"

"Yeah."

"I don't know." Robert gave the display a worried look.

His attitude bothered Jonah. Robert had all kinds of supernatural pictures on his wall at home and he worked on a paranormal computer game. So why did his cousin think he shouldn't go inside the store?

"It's just a book store, Robert. What's the problem?"

"Wick told me the owner is strange."

Jonah turned back to the window. "I'll be okay. You go to the art store. I can meet you back here in thirty minutes."

"Just be careful, little cousin."

CHAPTER SEVENTEEN
MYSTIC WORLDS

Jonah didn't like Mystic Worlds from the moment he stepped through the entrance. For one thing, it didn't smell like a real bookstore—not the kind with plenty of interesting old books. This store smelled new, and the burning incense couldn't quite hide it.

Maybe it was the statuettes of dragons, winged demons, goblins, reapers, bats, and other strange things that lined the shelves along the dark walls. Or maybe it was the black counter in the back of the store that set Jonah's nerves on edge.

He tried to ignore the sensation and the nagging feeling that his cousin may have been right. Jonah walked between the short bookshelves that covered most of the floor space, glancing at various titles as he went. *Understanding the Real Matrix, Behold the Horsemen of the Apocalypse, 1000 Myths about Modern Science, Beyond the Third Eye,* and *The Wiccan Way*, just to name a few. A store clerk stepped from a back room, slid around the counter, and came up to him.

"May I help you find something?" The clerk talked with a deep voice that didn't fit his very thin appearance. What drew Jonah's attention was a cross hanging from a chain around his neck. No, Jonah corrected himself. The cross had a loop at the top and a brilliant blue stone just below that. Jonah had seen this before, in one of his parents' books. It was an Egyptian Ankh, not a cross. The clerk noticed his stare and fingered the amulet.

Jonah felt a slight tremor in his Death Sense, and he thought the clerk's eyes clouded over for just a second.

"Huh… I wanted to look around." Jonah moved down an aisle on ancient religions. The clerk followed him.

"You're a little young to be interested in these books."

Jonah deliberately turned his back on the clerk, though the hairs on the back of his neck stood on end. "I'm doing research."

"Research? School's out, you know."

Jonah's irritation with the clerk peaked. Pushing aside his uneasiness, he whirled to face the man. "It's personal research. I'm looking for information on Death Sense."

Jonah smirked at the look of surprise that transformed the clerk's face. A shiver ran down his spine when he heard a cool woman's voice. "What does such a young boy know about Death Sense?"

A tall, severe-looking woman in a dark lace turtleneck and a long black chiffon skirt stood behind him. Jonah sucked in a breath. *It's her! It's the woman from my dream.*

Unlike the dream, her hair fell to her shoulders in fiery red curls. She didn't look any older than his mom, Jonah thought. And her eyes never blinked behind her black-rimmed, rectangular glasses as she continued to study him.

Her lips curled into a sneer. "Well?"

"I don't know about it. That's why I'm doing research." Jonah emphasized the last word in an obnoxious way that would have gotten him in trouble with his parents. It had the desired effect, as the woman suddenly stiffened.

"I'm not sure I like your tone."

"I don't like being treated like a kid."

"Indeed. What's your name?"

"Why?"

"Well, if I'm going to help you find what you're looking for, Mr. –"

"Hightower."

"Thank you, Mr. Hightower. It's polite to be able to refer to my customers by name, and some of us do value politeness." Jonah's face warmed at the rebuke. The sneer returned to the woman's face. "Randy, please show *Mr. Hightower* to the appropriate section. I think we have a couple of books on Death Omens."

128 *John Darr*

Randy nodded and led Jonah to the other side of the store. Despite the weird vibe he got from the clerk, Jonah was relieved to move away from the strange woman. He didn't like the way she kept emphasizing his last name as if she knew it wasn't real.

He glanced over his shoulder at her, and his Death Sense gave a funny twinge. It wasn't like the time he saw that mysterious man at the memorial service or the strangers on the Garretts' front lawn. This time, the sensation was sharper.

Jonah suspected the difference had to do with the level of danger. The strangers on the Garretts' lawn meant him no harm. This woman was dangerous and could hurt him, yet she didn't want to do that at the moment. Jonah nodded. *That's it. She's curious about me.*

The clerk made an impatient sound to get Jonah's attention. He grabbed a book off the shelf without really looking. Then he stared at the clerk until the man got the message and moved away. Jonah thought about putting the book back and leaving the store. However, when he glanced at the cover, his heart jumped into his throat.

The Death Omens book featured a hooded figure in a blood-red robe. The robe's hood was drawn forward, hiding the face except for two shining points of light where the eyes would have been. Large Grim Hounds crouched on either side of the robed person. Their mouths were open, showing off double rows of razor-sharp teeth.

Without warning, memories flooded into Jonah's mind. He saw his burning house and tasted the acrid smoke again. He remembered the raw fear the first time he encountered a Grim Hound. The light from the roaring flames had reflected off the creature's double row of teeth as it snarled at him.

Jonah shook his head to dispel the awful memories. The bookstore owner watched him with a smirk on her face, and the temptation to run from the store increased, but Jonah resisted the urge. He wouldn't let the woman scare him away. He selected another book with a shaky hand and carried them to the counter.

"I'll take these."

The owner glanced at the titles of the books before refocusing her intense gaze on him. Jonah wouldn't be intimidated. If he could deal with Marcus's Reaper stare, he could certainly deal with this woman.

The Protector's Ring

Jonah stood straight and glared back at her. The clerk paused ringing up the books to watch the silent battle.

Finally, the woman frowned. Instead of looking away, she leaned forward over the counter. "You don't sound like the locals. You're not from around here."

Jonah made sure to avoid her gaze as he pulled out cash and not his bank card. He didn't want the woman to see his real name. The clerk took the money and wasted time slowly counting it. When he started to count it a second time, Jonah knew he'd have to respond to the woman. "What about you?"

"Oh, I'm new in town. I'm from the Northern Virginia area. Aren't you?" Jonah couldn't shake the feeling that he'd seen her somewhere other than the Grim Hound dream. And her voice sounded familiar, too.

"Small world, isn't it?" She smirked as she watched his expression.

"I don't know what you mean. I'm from Atlanta. I'm staying for the summer."

"Really?" She moved around the counter to stand in front of him and flicked out a hand without warning. Despite his determination not to allow the woman to scare him, Jonah stumbled backward. The woman laughed with a low chuckle that sounded like someone who'd proven a point. "It's just a business card."

When she laughed again, the faint lines across her cheeks and side of her nose seemed to move strangely in the light. The owner noticed the direction of his stare and shook the card.

"Are you afraid?"

"No."

Jonah snatched the card from her hand. She raised an eyebrow at him. "Manners, Mr. Hightower."

Jonah kept his mouth shut. Anything he said would make him sound scared. Instead, he examined the business card. A stylized image of a Grim Hound glared out at him. The name of the store was embossed in red letters across the creature's body. Below that was the store owner's name: Neera Bledsole.

Jonah stared at the name and flinched when a hand gripped his shoulder.

Robert stood behind him. "You ready to go?"

"Yeah." Jonah grabbed his bag from the clerk and followed his cousin to the front door.

Neera called after him, "Have a nice day, Mr. Hightower."

Robert turned, a confused look on his face. Jonah pushed him out the front door. "I'll explain outside."

"Are you alright?" Robert frowned as Jonah wiped his forehead.

"I'm fine."

"You look sick."

"It's the owner. She's weird." Jonah wanted to say she was evil, but he thought that sounded over the top. At least, he did until Robert answered him.

"She's probably a witch."

"A witch?"

"Yep. I shouldn't have let you go in the store all alone."

Jonah stared at the store again. Could Neera be a witch? Was that the reason he felt strange the moment he entered the store? The other times he felt that sensation was when he saw the people in black, but they had been Reapers. Neera wasn't unDead; she walked around, talked with him, even gave him her business card.

Jonah nudged Robert's arm. "Do you believe in that kind of thing? You know, witches, Reapers, supernatural stuff?"

"Yeah, I do. A little." Robert lowered his voice. "Wick's more into it than I am."

"Is he a witch?"

Robert grinned. "He calls himself a practitioner."

"What's the difference?"

"A practitioner can do small things and is sensitive to magic. A witch is very powerful and often very evil."

"Can Wick really do magic?"

Robert looked down at his feet. "I've seen him do a few things."

"Wow."

"He told me the bookstore owner gave off a magic vibe. He could sense it."

Jonah nodded. "Well, she's creepy."

Robert didn't say anything else for a while as he stared at the passing cars. Then he glanced back at the Mystic Worlds bookstore. "If Wick could feel it, then she must be into serious magic."

Jonah thought back to the encounter at the memorial service. Omar could also sense the Reaper even though the man had disappeared. Omar said he was a Memory Charmer, but Jonah wondered if he could be a practitioner. He toyed with the idea of asking Robert about Death Sense and Reapers but chickened out and showed his cousin the book and card.

"That's the best drawing I've seen of Grim Hounds." Robert whistled as he turned the book over in his hands. "They even got the double rows of teeth. She's definitely into the weird." Robert paused, his eyebrows drew together as he ran a finger over the author's name. Hackett. "It can't be…"

"What? Do you know the author?"

"No. It's nothing." Robert shook his head and began flipping through the Death Omen book, but his hands shook a bit. Jonah stuck a finger between the pages to get his cousin's attention.

"How do you know about Grim Hounds?"

"I told you." Robert snapped the book closed, almost catching Jonah's finger. "Wick and I are working on a computer game about the supernatural. It includes Grim Hounds and other creatures." He handed the book back to Jonah, who slipped it in his shopping bag.

"I know that. You called it a Grim Hound and not a Hell Hound."

"Well…" Robert held Neera's business card in his hand. He tapped it on a finger, refusing to look directly at Jonah. "Wick found a really old book, and it had that name for them. We use the book as source material for the game's mythos."

Robert's confession was interesting to Jonah. Clearly, his aunt would consider all supernatural things witchcraft. Robert didn't hold that view, not if his best friend was a practitioner of magic. Not if they were reading old books with accurate information about the supernatural world and making a game about it.

Jonah had never even considered such things until the day he heard his dad mention Death Sense. Since then, he'd seen Grim Hounds and people who could disappear. He found out his dad was a Fallen Reaper and he was half-Reaper himself. Jonah's knowledge about the world around him continued to change in strange ways. And his cousin appeared to know more about it than he let on.

Jonah took Neera's business card from Robert and slid it in his back pocket. "Can I ask you a question?"

"Not so fast, little cousin. How do you know the name for Grim Hounds?"

"My godfather told me."

"He did?"

"I guess he's into strange stuff like you and Wick."

Jonah tried to smile, and Robert crossed his arms and glared at him. "I told you the truth about how we found out. Why did your godfather tell you about Grim Hounds?"

"I asked him," Jonah paused before plunging on, "because I saw one."

Robert's jaw dropped. "You saw a real Grim Hound?"

"I saw two inside my house the night it burned to the ground. I think they caused the fire." Jonah went on before Robert could interrupt. "And that woman in the store knows I'm from Washington. She gave me that business card to see my reaction to it."

"No way," Robert said. He let out a slow breath and ruffled his Afro as he stared at Jonah. "We thought we'd find out something interesting when you came, but this-"

"We?"

"Lynn and I." Robert snapped his fingers. "That's why you bought the Death Omen book. You thought you saw…"

The Protector's Ring

"You believe me, right?"

"I don't know."

"What do you mean you don't know? You're working on that computer game. You know the real name for the Grim Hounds."

"Books and games are one thing, Jonah. Seeing real Grim Hounds in real life is another." Robert looked around. "I know you've been through a lot of things…"

"I'm not crazy." Jonah began to think he'd been a fool to tell Robert about the Grim Hounds.

"I'm not saying that, little cousin. Maybe you saw a large dog or a bear."

"A bear in a burning house?"

Robert shrugged, and the corners of his mouth twitched.

"You're not going to tell Lynn or Wick, are you?" A knot formed in Jonah's stomach when Robert smiled. "Robert!"

"Okay." His cousin held up both hands. "I won't tell Lynn."

"Or Wick."

"Come on, Wick's a cool guy. He'll believe you."

"No, Robert. I'm serious."

"I won't tell Lynn or Wick. Let's get back to the Mall. My mom is probably waiting for us."

As Jonah fell into step beside Robert, his mind swirled. Grim Hounds were real. He had confronted one. Marcus had fought them. Yet Robert couldn't accept that Grim Hounds were more than fantasy creatures.

Jonah decided to never mention the dreams, transformable blades, or the fact that he was half-Reaper. He glanced back at Mystic Worlds as the heaviness weighed on him. The strangeness had followed him to Mount Vernon after all, and he would have to face it on his own.

CHAPTER EIGHTEEN
GRIM CHASE

"Eighty-two degrees." Jonah let out a sigh as he double-checked the weather report the next morning. He glanced at his book bag and decided it would be better to travel light. He set the bag down beside the bed and pulled out a small notepad and pencil. Stuffing those into the back pocket of his cargo shorts, he set out for the teen center.

No sooner had Jonah reached the teen center when his Death Sense spiked, forcing him to wince and grip his head. A second later, he heard the familiar growl. Jonah looked around and nearly fell off his bike because a Grim Hound perched like an oversized house cat on the teen center sign.

The creature's jet black body resembled a living shadow in the late morning sun. The glowing red eyes narrowed and it opened its massive mouth to reveal the double set of razor-sharp teeth. No one else paid any attention to the creature as if it wasn't there. But Jonah noticed people shifted, not walking too close. He wondered if mortals could sense the danger even though they couldn't see it.

He locked eyes with the Grim Hound as he lifted his bike, his movements slow as to avoid triggering an attack, although he knew that was impossible, given the way his head ached. Throwing caution to the wind, Jonah slung a leg over his bike and took off.

When shouts and grunts erupted behind him, Jonah glanced back. The Grim Hound had knocked a group of unsuspecting kids aside as it launched itself off the sign. Fear surged through Jonah as the creature bounded after him. His legs pumped the pedals frantically, scrambling to pick up speed. He risked another glance behind him. The Grim Hound brushed against cars and people, creating havoc.

The Protector's Ring

He couldn't worry about that as he darted into an adjacent neighborhood. The Grim Hound let out a growl, sounding much closer than it had been when he'd last looked. His heart pounded with terror and he tensed his back, expecting to feel the creature's teeth bite into him.

The panic became unbearable, and Jonah suddenly veered through a front yard. The Grim Hound leapt at the same time, missed him, and slammed into a parked car. Shattered glass flew everywhere and the car's alarm blared.

Jonah sped through the home's backyard, into an adjacent yard, and out onto another street. He made turn after turn, occasionally skidding as he fled through the unknown neighborhood of two-story homes. Finally, he reached a steep hill, and the downhill descent brought him more speed.

The houses were little more than blurs on either side of him now. For one bright moment, Jonah thought he might actually get away from the Grim Hound. That hope died as he realized the street emptied at the bottom of the hill onto a busy roadway.

He couldn't stop nor safely turn without crashing. As he neared the roadway, a gap appeared in the passing cars. Jonah plunged ahead. Horns blared and tires screeched as he dodged between the cars and into an apartment complex on the other side. He heard the impact and the Grim Hound's howl of pain as the creature tumbled into a row of parked cars. Jonah paused to catch his breath and hoped the Grim Hound was dead.

He wasn't that lucky. The beast regained its feet, shook itself, and oriented on him.

By now, the commotion had caused people from the complex to gather outside. Jonah paused. If he went toward them, the Grim Hound would hurt somebody. He turned and plunged through the shrubbery bordering the complex. The bushes poked and scratched as he fought his way through and came out in a trailer park.

Each time the Grim Hound appeared behind him, Jonah would dodge around a trailer before it could pounce. That worked until he miscalculated and came around a trailer directly in front of the Grim Hound. He dodged as the beast slashed at him. Its claws ripped the back of his shirt.

Pain exploded across Jonah's upper back and he tumbled off the bike. The only thing that saved him was the fact that the Grim Hound's momentum took it clear past him. It smashed into the wooden steps of a trailer. Someone inside screamed as the impact rocked the entire trailer.

Even though his shoulder burned with pain, Jonah hopped on his bike and raced for the trailer park's exit. He managed to reach it without the Grim Hound catching him. Crossing the road right outside the park, he sped into the empty lot of an adjacent shipping building. The black surface of the lot was like a red-hot grill. Jonah's breaths started to come in gasps, and the hot air burned his nose and throat.

He didn't know how much longer he could continue. Sweat poured down his face, and the salt from it stung his eyes. His ripped shirt stuck to the drying blood on his shoulder. Whenever it pulled free, Jonah would suck in a painful breath. Stopping or turning around wasn't an option. The rain of small pebbles as the creature's huge paws ripped into the surface of the lot came from close behind.

So he raced on. And when he reached the end of the vacant building and rounded the corner, his hope faltered. A high metal fence enclosed that end of the parking lot. Cars zoomed down the busy road on the other side, and beyond that sat an abandoned gas station.

I need to get to the other side.

Jonah's fear infused the thought. For a second, he imagined heat distortions caused the ripple in front of him. Then a familiar sensation rolled along every inch of his body. With a jerk, the black parking lot disappeared, replaced by the broken concrete and gravel lot of the abandoned gas station on the other side of the busy roadway.

Jonah skidded, lost control, and went down. His bike flipped and slammed into an old gas pump. Jonah landed next to it, smacking his injured right shoulder on the pump's concrete base.

He screamed in pain and his vision blurred with tears. A wave of dizziness prompted Jonah to roll over and throw up. Once the spasms passed, he struggled to a seated position and watched in fascination as the Grim Hound pulled itself from the mangled fence. A few cars slowed and the drivers gaped as the fence buckled without an obvious reason for its collapse.

The Grim Hound shook its head, spotted Jonah, and let out a frightening bark. Even though people couldn't see it, they hugged themselves as if a chilled wind had reached them. Jonah's own body froze with fright. He forced his memory to cough up what it had learned about Grim Hounds. They could use their snarls and barks to paralyze a victim with fear. All at once, Jonah's fear lifted and he sucked in a breath.

By that time, the Grim Hound had backed away from the fence and was charging toward it. It didn't matter if the supernatural beast couldn't paralyze him with fear; Jonah didn't have the energy to move. The Grim Hound leapt the fence in a high arc, leaped over two stalled cars, and continued on toward him. Jonah's Death Sense screamed, the pain nearly causing him to faint. There was no hope of dodging this time.

As he braced himself for the Hound's attack, the air rippled and Kevin appeared between Jonah and the Grim Hound. Unfortunately, he phased with his back to the action.

"Kevin! Behind you."

The boy whirled, his blades out. The Grim Hound leapt for him, and Kevin blurred into motion as he dodged to the left. The Grim Hound landed and turned to swap a massive paw at Kevin. He phased, reappearing behind the beast. The creature sensed him, whirled around, and snapped its jaws at Kevin's head, but the boy moved almost too fast to see as he dodged the razor-sharp teeth.

He charged the creature. When it tried to claw him, Kevin cut the paw. This deadly dance continued. Each time the creature lunged, trying to grab him with massive paws so it could use its jaws, Kevin would blur into motion or phase. When he reappeared, he'd cut the Grim Hound again along its body, causing the beast to whirl or roll away.

The Grim Hound had a body like a dog and was a large as a Kodiak bear. Jonah felt the vibrations each time its paws slammed on the ground. He began to worry for Kevin, but Marcus's apprentice held his own.

The older boy crossed his arms and dodged underneath the Grim Hound's snout. When Kevin brought his arm up and out, he sliced the creature's head off its body. Dark liquid splattered his black shirt and jeans. He delivered a blurred kick to the decapitated Grim Hound, sending the headless body into the roadway.

The severed head landed a few feet from Jonah. He stood on wobbly legs and stared in shock as the remains of the Grim Hound's head began to sizzle and melt.

Kevin turned around, covered in goo. "Jonah? Are you alright?"

Before Jonah could say anything, a horrible crunching sound came from the road. It was followed by another loud bump and screeching tires. Cars rammed into the Grim Hound's body before it started to melt. The drivers exited their cars, scratching their heads.

"Oh no." Kevin's shoulders slumped as he watched the mayhem.

Any other time, Jonah might have laughed, but not today. He had never ached this bad in his life, not even when his Death Sense spiked. His shoulder was a big mass of pain, the dizziness made him light-headed, and his bike was a mess.

Jonah willed himself to walk slowly to Kevin. His energy failed him and he started to collapse. Kevin was at his side in a blur, catching him.

"Take it easy." Kevin lowered him to the ground. "You're hurt."

Jonah's rapid breathing slowed and his legs began to ache with fatigue. Kevin hovered over him with a concerned look on his face. "I need to get you somewhere so you can heal."

"How did you find me?"

"Marcus knew you were in danger."

"Then why didn't he come?"

"You were moving, so it was hard to be accurate." Kevin wouldn't meet his eyes.

"But you came to help me."

"Yeah, well, I didn't want to wait." Kevin locked eyes with Jonah before sliding one arm under his back and the other under his legs. Jonah screamed as Kevin lifted him.

"Sorry, little man," Kevin said in a soft voice.

"Don't call me that."

Kevin turned toward the rear of the station. "You're half-Reaper, so your body can heal itself. You know that right?"

"No."

"Oh. Well, you need to rest." Kevin had almost reached the cover of the ramshackle building when someone called out.

"Hey!"

The Protector's Ring **139**

Jonah grunted at the flare of pain in his shoulder caused by Kevin whirling around. A kid with short twists in his hair, a black muscle shirt, and Army fatigue pants ran over to them.

"What happened to you?" He had a slight Jamaican accent, not Southern, Jonah noted. The curious boy offered to shake hands, then thought better of it and settled on a quick wave. "I'm Wick, by the way. I'm friends with Bobby and Lynn. And you must be their little cousin from DC." Wick's eyes narrowed as he shifted his gaze to Kevin. "Who are you?"

Jonah was caught between going somewhere to heal or finally meeting Wick. He tapped Kevin's shoulder. "Put me down."

"You're bleeding, dude." Wick's eyebrows shot up as he pointed at Jonah's shoulder.

"Can you take me home?" Jonah asked.

"Maybe we should wait for someone to look at you."

"That's not a good idea," Kevin said.

"Who's he?" Wick nodded at Kevin.

"He saw me fall off my bike and came to help," Jonah offered because Kevin had opened his mouth to respond. "I need to talk to Robert and Lynn first."

Behind them, drivers shouted to the police as they pointed at ruined cars and the mangled fence. Other cops searched up and down the street. Since the Grim Hound's remains had melted, the dents in the cars presented a big mystery.

Wick turned back to Jonah, and his eyes widened. "They were right about you, huh?"

"Who?"

"Robert and Lynn. They knew things would change with you here."

Jonah wanted to ask Wick about that, but his shoulder flared with pain again. "Help me."

"Oh, yeah." Wick pointed to a small pickup at the edge of the lot. "We need to get you in the truck."

When Kevin didn't move, Jonah whispered, "You have a better idea?"

Kevin grunted and helped Jonah to the truck. An older version of Wick hopped out of the driver's side and opened the passenger door while Wick ran back to get the damaged bike.

Kevin was extremely gentle as he set Jonah inside. He could tell the boy wasn't happy about letting him go. He didn't like it either, but Wick was already curious and the last thing Jonah needed was Robert and Lynn asking even more questions.

Jonah started to lean back, but his shoulder touched the seat and the pain returned. He rested his hands on the dashboard, leaned his head against them, and closed his eyes. "Thanks."

"No problem," Wick answered.

The driver's side door opened and the truck rocked as someone got behind the wheel.

"Oh, by the way, this is my brother, Desmond," Wick said.

Desmond nodded as he started the truck. Jonah noticed that Desmond wore jeans and a t-shirt and his hair was in dreads instead of twists like his brother. He spoke with a more pronounced island accent than Wick. "Shouldn't we get him to a hospital?"

"Just take me home," Jonah said.

"You heard the man, Desmond."

"If anything happens to him, I'll swear I be mud-ridin' when this happened, man."

Jonah didn't know anything about mud riding and didn't care. He just wanted to get home. His thoughts returned to the Grim Hound and why someone would send it in the middle of the day with so many people around.

The little voice in his mind supplied the answer. *Somebody wants me dead.*

The Protector's Ring **141**

CHAPTER NINETEEN
HEALING FACTOR

"What happened to him?" Lynn rushed to help Wick place Jonah on a kitchen chair, then leaned back with a frown. "Well?"

Wick shrugged and ruffled his twists. "He claims he fell off his bike."

Lynn pushed Jonah forward in the chair. He screamed, "Hey that hurts!"

"Oh my God. You're cut." Lynn rounded on her brother. "Get the med kit. Wick, you hold up his shirt until I can get it off."

Wick hissed when he saw the injury. "Looks like you were mauled by something, dude."

Lynn nodded in agreement. "You're gonna need stitches, Jonah."

"I can't." Jonah didn't know how to explain his cuts to a doctor, nor to his aunt, who would have to take him to the hospital.

Robert returned a few minutes later with the kit. Lynn cleaned and bandaged the cuts with practiced ease. Robert handed Jonah a glass of water and a pain tablet.

Lynn crossed her arms and tossed her braids behind her back with an angry flick of her head. She waited for him to swallow the pill before asking, "Why can't you go to the hospital? What happened?"

"A Grim Hound attacked me."

"I knew you saw it!" Wick slapped his hand on the table, causing everyone to jump. "A Grim Hound, huh?"

Lynn shushed him. "Start from the beginning, Jonah."

He began with arriving at the teen center and told them everything that had happened. When he reached the part about his escape from the creature, he felt a little light-headed and realized the pain pill must have been working. Jonah claimed he managed to weave through the traffic and the creature wasn't so lucky. A shocked silence settled over the group when he finished.

Lynn, Wick, and Robert traded serious looks.

"Why are you looking at each other like that?" Jonah asked.

Wick elbowed Robert. "Show him the drawings, Bobby."

"No," Lynn interjected. She held up her hand. "We don't have time for that now. Jonah should go to the hospital. Wick, call your brother."

"Lynn, I can't," Jonah protested. "What am I supposed to say happened to me?"

"We'll think of something. I can't let you bleed to death."

Jonah shook his head, which made his shoulder ache. "Just give me some time."

"What will that do?"

The answer was on the tip of Jonah's tongue when he stopped himself. He didn't understand it all. Kevin had been sure that he could heal if he had time to rest, and Jonah wanted to trust the boy. He wanted to know if his body could heal from more than a simple cut.

"Jonah? What's going on?"

"Let me take a nap."

Lynn shook her head, causing her thin braids to flip around. She reached for Jonah's arm, but Wick stopped her.

"I think he'll be alright."

"Wick..."

"Come on, Lynn. You need time to come up with something to tell your mom and dad. Jonah's a minor, so they'll have to know."

"You two are being weird. Well, in your case, Wick, weirder than usual."

"Gee, thanks." He winked at Jonah. "If I'm wrong, you can remind me about it forever."

The Protector's Ring   143

Lynn crossed her arms, but Jonah thought she looked less defiant. "He could be in worse shape by then."

"I doubt it. Support me, Bobby."

Robert stirred at the mention of his name and nodded. "Let him sleep, Lynn."

"You guys are crazy." She frowned for a second, then took Jonah by the arm. Jonah feared she planned to make him go to the hospital anyway. Instead, she helped him stand. "You go lay down."

Robert helped Jonah into his room and pointed at his dirt-stained clothes.

"Time to change, little cousin."

Jonah slipped off the ruined shirt and winced, but not from the pain. The shirt was the first one his aunt had picked out. How would he explain it being destroyed in just a day? He quickly handed Robert the rest of his dirty clothes and got in bed.

"Thanks, Robert." He pulled his cover up.

"No problem."

Robert closed the door and Jonah let the pain pills do their job. His shoulder throbbed and tingled a bit. When he wiggled it, real pain made him grimace. He took a deep breath and told himself to be still and rest. Just as he settled down, he felt a pressure on his ears.

"Jonah?"

Jonah sat up and yelled as much from the surprise as the pain in his shoulder. Kevin stood beside the dresser, but he blurred into motion as he caught Jonah and covered his mouth.

"Sorry. I didn't mean to scare you."

"Whm amhfn?" Jonah smacked Kevin's hand, and he pulled it away. "What are you doing here?"

"I'm making sure you're alright." Kevin smirked at him. "You're not gonna scream like a girl again, are you?"

Jonah shoved Kevin and said, "Where did you go?"

"Around. I had to keep an eye on you." Kevin glanced at the door. "Don't tell your cousins about me."

"I won't."

"Good. I'm in enough trouble. I don't need your cousins knowing all about us."

"What did you do this time?"

"I saved you, again. Marcus is pissed with me, again."

"You mean he wanted to let the Grim Hound finish me?"

"No. It's not like that." By the way Kevin studied his hands, Jonah knew the boy was holding back details. "Like I said, you kept moving…"

"That Grim Hound chased me from the teen center."

"I know. Marcus wanted you to run away from trouble and call from someplace he could phase without being seen."

"I couldn't stop and make a phone call! The Grim Hound would have killed me."

"I know."

"And you're telling me Marcus wasn't going to help?"

"I didn't say that. As soon as you stopped, I phased before Marcus could do anything."

"Thanks. I'm glad you did it."

"You don't understand." Kevin shook his head, a worried expression on his face. "It's dangerous and against the rules to phase somewhere with other people around. I didn't even have a memory charmer to deal with any witnesses. And you saw what I did with the Grim Hound's body."

"You didn't mean to cause that accident."

"Marcus won't see it that way."

Kevin looked miserable as he toyed with the edge of the top sheet. Jonah didn't know what to do. Besides, the pill was making him sleepy and he still hurt all over. Without thinking about it, Jonah touched Kevin's hand. He didn't know what the boy would do, but Kevin opened his fingers, allowing Jonah to slide his hand over the palm, and then Kevin closed his fingers.

The Protector's Ring **145**

"Little Jonah is causing all kinds of problems," he whispered.

At first, Jonah bristled at the comment, but he noticed Kevin was smiling and relaxed. It wasn't his fault. These people and creatures kept coming for him.

That reminded Jonah of Neera. "Kevin, there's a woman in town with scars-"

"We know about Neera."

"You do?" Jonah blinked in surprise. "We think she's a witch."

"She's a sorceress, or was a sorceress." Kevin shook his head. "It can get complicated."

"Why did she send a Grim Hound after me?"

"She didn't."

"What do you mean? You fought the thing."

"Marcus tracks Neera whenever she leaves Mount Vernon. She was nowhere near here when the attack happened. I think that's the reason he hesitated. He didn't want to lose Neera unless it was needed. Plus, he hoped a Memory Charmer would arrive before one of us phased, or you would at least find a more private place to call."

Jonah started to sit up despite his injured shoulder. Kevin placed a hand on his chest and held him down. "You need to get some rest."

"Kevin. She's looking for that ring, isn't she?"

"I'm not telling you any more. Marcus is right about keeping you out of this mess."

"They killed my parents because of a ring."

"That's why you need to stay out of it, Jonah."

He didn't struggle as he considered everything Kevin told him. He had Marcus on speed dial, but had he really had the chance to call? When he was in that parking lot, no one was around. Maybe he could have called then. Kevin or Marcus could have shown up before the Grim Hound reached him.

"I'm sorry I didn't call."

"Don't apologize." Kevin leaned back in surprise. "You were great. Everyone was impressed. You're not the one in trouble."

As if to underscore Kevin's statement, his cell phone beeped. He pulled it out of his pocket, glanced at the message, and stood. "I have to go. Marcus is ready to kill me now."

"Don't leave."

"Jonah, not this again."

Kevin knelt by the bed, reminding Jonah of that time at Marcus's. He noticed the embossed symbol on Kevin's black t-shirt, the same symbol on the Reaper long coats. He touched it. Kevin stared at his hand without saying anything. Then he puffed out his chest. Jonah let his hand rest against Kevin's chest, sensing the steady heartbeat beneath his touch.

"What does that symbol mean?"

"It's the group we work for."

"Monarch? Marcus works for Monarch?"

Kevin laughed, the sound vibrating Jonah's hand, still resting on his chest. "No, it's called the Alliance. It's the real company behind Monarch."

"Oh."

Kevin took Jonah's hand and intertwined their fingers. "If you're done feeling me up, get some rest, little man. It'll help your body heal itself."

Jonah gave him a lazy smirk and didn't let go of Kevin's hand as he closed his eyes. When Kevin remained still, Jonah allowed his mind to relax, and soon he was asleep.

Jonah's eyes snapped open when someone shook his good shoulder.

"Kevin?" he said, thinking that only a short time had passed. He rubbed his eyes and saw that Lynn stood beside his bed.

"Who's Kevin? Is he the boy that Wick saw holding you?"

Oh no, Jonah thought. Clearly Wick and his cousins had a talk after he fell asleep.

"He's no one."

The Protector's Ring

Lynn folded her arms, staring down at him, causing Jonah's irritation to bubble up.

"What do you want, Lynn?"

"I need to change the dressing." She held up the fresh bandage. "Now, sit up."

Jonah threw off the cover and sat obediently on the side of the bed. He yawned and looked for his watch until Lynn pinched his good shoulder. "Keep still."

"How long have I been asleep?"

"Almost five hours." Lynn placed the new bandage on the bed and started to remove Jonah's old one. "So who's Kevin? Were you dreaming about him?"

"Just drop it."

Lynn gave him a sly smile. Her expression changed when she finished peeling off the old bandage. "Oh my God! The cuts have sealed themselves."

She touched Jonah's shoulder. Pain flared, but it wasn't sharp like it had been.

"There's barely a scar. Jonah, how is that possible?"

"Well, I always healed fast." He thought back to the times he had cut himself. The injuries were always gone the next morning. The first time that happened, he had shown his mom. *That's so wonderful, sweetheart. Now, let's keep the bandage on a little longer. Okay?* In the end, she always made him wear bandages for a couple days after he knew his cuts were healed.

This situation was something else. He'd never been hurt this bad, yet his body had managed to heal, just like Kevin had told him it would.

"It tingled and itched just before I fell asleep." Jonah reached over to feel the partially healed scar. "I just ignored it."

Lynn quietly prepared a new bandage. She kept her gaze focused on her hands as she worked.

Jonah tried to look her in the eyes. "Lynn?"

"Yeah." She finished and sat back.

"I've never been sick before."

Lynn finally looked directly at him. "Never?"

"Never. People always called me extra healthy. My best friend…" Jonah paused when he thought about Oliver. "My best friend used to joke and call me Superman." Jonah laughed to himself and relaxed a bit when Lynn smiled. "I guess I'm really different, huh?"

"Jonah…" Lynn stopped and looked away. "We'll see about this later." She stood and helped him up. "Dinner's ready."

Near the end of dinner, Uncle James turned on the local news. Robert, Lynn, and Jonah listened to the anchor talk about a bizarre series of property damages and accidents in the Hightowers' part of town. Police concluded that a stray animal went on a rampage. Authorities urged residents to be on the lookout for any large animals.

CHAPTER TWENTY
THE SUMMIT

"Can I see it?" Wick asked. He had arrived in time for breakfast, but his focus was entirely on Jonah as he sat down at the kitchen table.

"See what?" Jonah paused with a spoonful of cereal an inch from his mouth.

"The scar."

"He's not a sideshow freak." Lynn poked Wick in the head as she crossed by to sit at the breakfast bar.

"But I was the only one to believe him." Wick caught Jonah's look and shrugged. "I'm sorry. This is just so cool. How can you heal like that?"

"I don't know."

Wick sat back as Robert entered the kitchen with his sketchbook. He set it on the table and announced, "Wick wanted me to show you this yesterday."

Robert flipped the sketchbook open. Jonah's insides froze when he saw the first picture of a Grim Hound. He dropped his spoon in his bowl and tried to point at the picture but regretted it when his shoulder throbbed. "That's what I saw!"

Robert flipped through the rest of the pictures, then closed the sketchbook and sat down at the table. "I'm sorry, Jonah."

Lynn slipped off her stool and gave her twin brother's head a little shove. "Why are you apologizing to him?"

"Jonah told me that he saw a Grim Hound the night his parents' house burned. I didn't believe him."

Jonah thought Lynn looked uncertain as she glared at her brother.

Wick patted Jonah on his uninjured shoulder. "I would have believed you, Padawan."

Jonah smiled at him. Robert's friend seemed to be the only one excited about his healing ability and the fact that Grim Hounds were real. On the other hand, Robert and Lynn acted careful around him, like he was a time bomb.

Wick leaned forward. "So there were Grim Hounds in your parents' house?"

"Yeah."

"You know Grim Hounds hunt for things, right?"

"Marcus told me." Jonah noticed Wick's curious look and explained, "He's my godfather, and he said Grim Hounds can show up where something bad happened."

Wick rubbed his chin as he considered that. "I don't know, Jonah. From what we've read, Grim Hounds go where they are sent. My guess is they were sent to look for something in your house."

Lynn eyes narrowed as she watched Jonah. "Do you know what they were searching for?"

Jonah squirmed in his chair; Wick was correct. And the mention of his parents' house reminded him of the dream. That strange woman had obviously sent the Grim Hounds to search for a ring. Jonah had heard it in the creature's own thoughts, in a dream he didn't want to mention to his cousins. They were on the verge of freaking out already.

"My parents found a lot of objects for their company," he answered, refusing to meet any of their eyes as he spoke. "But they didn't tell me anything."

"Grim Hounds are serious." Wick tapped the sketchbook. "They must have been looking for something related to the supernatural. You never saw anything like that?"

Lynn crossed her arms, tapping her foot on the floor. Wick toyed with the pages of the sketchbook while staring Jonah, clearly expecting

The Protector's Ring **151**

him to reveal some kind of deep secret. When Jonah met Robert's oddly intense gaze, images of the silver blades flashed into his mind. Memories of holding the medallion paperweight came to him next. He even recalled the strange portal from his dream about his parents.

A chill ran down his spine. His own memories were on display, like someone else was picking through them, looking for information.

"No," Jonah said. He shook his head. "I-I don't know." The slight pressure on his mind lessened and disappeared.

Robert slumped back in his chair. Lynn stalked to the kitchen window.

"Sorry." Jonah watched his cousins, sensing their disappointment. "What do you want me to say?"

"Don't worry about them," Wick answered. Lynn whirled around with her mouth open to speak, and Wick plunged ahead in a louder voice. "Somebody sent this Grim Hound straight after him. They have to be summoned and then given their mission." He turned to Jonah. "Who did you piss off?"

Robert smacked his own forehead. "It must have been that Neera woman in the bookstore. I knew I shouldn't have let you go in there."

"Although my doubting buddy didn't mention that you saw Grim Hounds," Wick spared Robert a glance, "he did tell me about Neera. She has a cool name, by the way. Did you know that in some forms, it means creator of chaos?"

Lynn nudged him in the back of his head. "Wick, stay on the subject."

"That is on subject," Wick objected. Lynn raised a fist. "Okay, sorry." He focused on Jonah. "She gave you a business card. Can I see it?"

Jonah tried to take out his wallet, but his shoulder throbbed again. Lynn had told him the cuts may have sealed themselves, but the shoulder would probably hurt for a day or two as the deep tissue healed. Jonah thought she'd been correct, as he winced once more from the unexpected pain.

"I'll get it, little cousin." Robert pulled out the wallet and passed the business card to Wick, who held the card up with a flourish. The action reminded Jonah of a magician performing a trick.

Wick closed his eyes and began to mumble under his breath. As soon as Jonah opened his mouth, Robert motioned him to keep quiet. A second later, a glowing symbol appeared on the back of the card.

"Just as I thought," Wick announced. "Neera marked the card so she could use a tracking spell on you."

Jonah's jaw dropped as Wick held the card closer, allowing him to see the symbol. Jonah was caught between awe at Wick's skill and a lack of understanding of what the boy meant. "A tracking spell?"

Wick smiled at Jonah's confused expression and explained, "Yeah, a tracking spell is like using a locator or transmitter. She planted this card on you as a locator. The tracking spell allowed her to find you whenever she wanted. That is, as long as you keep the card with you."

Wick pulled a lighter from one of his pants pockets. His unlaced black boots clacked on Aunt Imma's linoleum floor as he rose and then walked to the kitchen sink. Pausing to glance inside the sink, he set the card on fire.

"Why are you burning it?" Jonah struggled to his feet.

"It's the only way to destroy the locator."

"Otherwise," Lynn cut in, gently pushing him back down into the kitchen chair, "Neera could use it to track you down again."

Wick let the burning card drop into the sink. Once the card was reduced to ashes, he turned on the water and rinsed the sooty pile down the drain. "Then again, we could have set up a trap."

"That would be too dangerous." Lynn frowned as she watched him. "She plays seriously."

A silence fell over the group again until Robert glanced at his sister and said, "The Summit?"

"Are you sure, Robert?"

"He's seen real Grim Hounds. We can't hold out on him, not if we want information."

The twins shared a look between them that only ended when Robert turned to Wick. "What do you think?"

Wick's twists shook as he nodded. He absentmindedly opened and closed his lighter in his right hand, watching Jonah with a thoughtful expression.

Jonah shifted his gaze away and found Robert and Lynn also watching him.

"What are you three talking about? What's the Summit? Isn't that the name of the newsletter and blog you do?"

Lynn and Wick shot Robert curious looks.

"I showed him the article about Mom." He turned to Jonah. "It's more than just a newsletter and blog, Jonah. It's a place. Well, it's all three."

Jonah followed his cousins and Wick through the recreation center atrium and up the stairs to the second floor. Adults buzzed in and out of offices. Jonah thought they would go into one of those areas, but Robert paused in front of an old wooden attic door. It had *The Summit* printed in bold black letters on a piece of plain white paper.

Jonah's cousins unlocked the door, flicked a wall switch just inside, and stood back. Lynn slipped by and up a narrow staircase. Robert, waving Jonah and Wick forward, followed behind.

The Summit turned out to be a spacious attic. The exposed wood rafters were high enough for lanky Robert and Lynn to stand without bending. The dark hardwood floor creaked slightly in places, and the stairs divided the attic into two areas. The area to the right contained two computer monitors on a large fold-up table. Stray papers and computer parts littered the top of a smaller worktable situated just beyond the computers.

"We do the newsletter and blog here." Lynn gestured at the computers. "It's our own little office." She walked around the computers to lean against a grey metal desk in the back corner. The only things on it were a small lamp, an old rotary telephone, and a black nameplate with the word EDITOR in white letters. "This used to be my father's desk, from his home office. He gave it to us when we found out you were coming."

"That's our clubhouse over there," Robert said.

He pulled Jonah into the left side of the attic and to an old, slightly sunken yet comfortable-looking sofa. Two mismatched armchairs with numerous rips in the fabric faced the sofa with a battered brown steamer trunk in between. The trunk was large, with brass rivets in the corners and metal handles on the sides. Several dog-eared magazines and a few crumpled soda cans littered it.

Just beyond the sitting area was a square card table with three folding chairs positioned around it. Jonah wondered if his cousins used it to play board games or cards, but before he could ask, he noticed the wire-frame bookcase to one side of a bricked-in fireplace. He walked over and pulled a book off a shelf. The entire thing swayed.

Wick grabbed hold of the bookcase. "I'm supposed to fix that."

"And clean up, you slob." Robert picked up the soda cans and tossed them in a metal wastebasket.

Lynn spread her arms wide. "Welcome to the Summit. What do you think, Geek boy?"

"It's totally cool," Jonah gushed before pausing and frowning. "Why do you call it the Summit?"

Lynn pulled back the makeshift curtain made from a blue bed sheet and revealed a rather large, multi-paned window.

"The rec center is located at the top of one of the largest hills in Mount Vernon, and this attic is at the top of the center."

"We also have a great view," Robert added as he steered Jonah to the window. The land behind the building sloped downhill into a wooded ravine. Beyond that, Jonah could see rooftops through the trees on the other side.

"There's a creek at the bottom of the hill," Robert whispered right over Jonah's shoulder. "It's a nice getaway area."

"Yes, Robert gets a lot of use out of that place." Lynn smirked at her brother.

Wick laughed and Robert grinned as he patted Jonah on the shoulder. "I'll show you one day, little cousin."

Jonah peered over the back of a computer monitor while running a finger along the top. "Is this what you were doing the other day?"

"We were on a deadline to finish the last blog." Robert walked around into the office section and sat at one of the computers. "Lynn does most of the reporting and story gathering. I do the layouts and any artwork." Robert leaned back and pointed to the computer cases underneath the tables. "I built these computers from parts the rec center gave us. I even run our own web server and maintain the center's website."

"That's so cool."

Wick, who lounged on the sofa, his unlaced black boots hanging over the side, lifted his head into view and smiled. "I met Bobby and Lynn three years ago when they interviewed me for a Halloween piece. Lynn doubted my ability."

"I still do sometimes."

Robert glanced at his sister. "Wick's done a Halloween story ever since."

"And they use me as a source on the unexplained and weird." He winked at Jonah. "Go ahead. Ask me the million-dollar question."

Jonah knew exactly which question Wick meant. He decided to have some fun and snatched a little notepad from beside Robert's computer, being careful to use his good arm. When he crossed over to the sofa, Wick slid his black boots off the puffy armrest so Jonah could sit there.

"Sources tell us that you are a witch?" Jonah said in an exaggerated news anchor tone. "Any comments?"

"Unfortunately, people can be cruel and judgmental." Wick sat up and screwed his face into a hurt look as he gave a dramatic sigh. "I'm just a normal guy who's sensitive to magic. I don't have a cauldron or a black cat or any of that stuff."

Jonah struggled to stay in character, even though a smile threatened to break through. "What about Neera's business card?"

"I used a little spell to reveal recently performed magic." Wick shook his head and ruffled his twists as he frowned. "I'm a practitioner, and I can do things like that."

"You two stop, please," Robert groaned.

Wick sat up straight on the sofa and gave Jonah an excited look. "My big project is a working shield."

"A shield?" Jonah slipped down onto the sofa beside him.

"It's a barrier made out of magical energy."

The more Wick talked, the greater Jonah's fascination with him and the subject of magic. Until a few days ago, he wouldn't have given it much thought.

"What does a shield do?"

"A shield protects you from other magical energy and physical objects. It could also protect you from supernatural creatures if they aren't really powerful."

"Could a shield stop a Grim Hound?"

"Well, my shield couldn't stop one, but one day, I'll be able to do it."

Jonah's mind raced with the idea of having something that could protect him from a Grim Hound. He almost told Wick about the time his neighbors accused him of being a witch, but he would have to tell them about his Death Sense, and he wasn't ready for that yet. Instead, Jonah glanced over the back of the sofa at Lynn.

She balled up a piece of paper and bounced it off her brother's head. "Show him, Robert. You made the suggestion."

Robert hopped to his feet and started across the attic, then whirled around and threw the balled-up piece of paper at his sister. Lynn caught it with a quick movement of her hand and stuck out her tongue. Robert grumbled as he continued to the rusted filing cabinet on the opposite side of the fireplace.

Lynn's reflexes amazed Jonah. She had barely moved her arm as she caught the piece of paper. Jonah must have stared at her too long because she narrowed her eyes. Without warning, she threw the ball of paper at him. He didn't even have time to think about it as his right hand shot up and caught it. His shoulder throbbed because of the effort.

"Whoa, dude. You're almost faster than Lynn." Wick whooped and patted Jonah's good shoulder. He met her gaze, pleased with himself, and she finally smiled.

"There may be some hope for you, Geek Boy."

Robert cleared his throat to get their attention. He held up a thick, rectangular box, placed it on the card table, and motioned everyone over. The ornate, golden box had two locks and strange symbols covering the top and sides. When Robert touched the small knob between the locks, recesses appeared that Jonah swore hadn't been there before. The locks clicked open and folded in on themselves, setting into the recesses so that the box's surface was seamless again.

"Wow!" Jonah said.

The Protector's Ring

"Cool, eh?" Robert smiled. "It scared the crap out of me the first time it happened." He touched the knob, and the locks slid out of the recesses and snapped into place with a click.

"Can I try it?"

Robert nodded.

Jonah pressed the knob, but nothing happened. He tried a few more times, but still nothing.

"Am I doing it wrong?"

"You're doing it right."

"Then why doesn't it work?"

"The box will only lock and unlock for me." Robert pressed the knob and the locks slid away. "I found that out by mistake. I didn't even know about the locks when I first got it." Instead of pressing the knob and making the locks appear again, Robert pushed it to the right this time, Jonah observed. A release clicked and the box opened.

Robert closed the lid. "That's how I used it until the day the locks appeared."

"Why did they appear?"

"Well," Robert glanced at Wick, "I cut my finger on my art knife. A drop of blood fell on the box and before I could wipe it off, the blood disappeared."

"The box absorbed it. Blood sacrifice," Wick said, his voice an exaggerated spooky whisper. "Very cool, if you ask me."

"Anyway," Lynn interrupted, "the locks appeared and snapped into place a few seconds later." Lynn smirked at her brother. "He wouldn't touch the box after that. Too scared."

"No, I wasn't. I just wanted to be careful, that's all." Robert frowned at his sister. "I tried the knob again and discovered that when I pressed button, the locks slid into the recesses."

"Robert asked me try to it next, and nothing happened." Lynn peeked over her brother's shoulder and tapped the box. "That's how we knew that only he could lock and unlock it."

158 *John Darr*

Jonah examined the box, pressing his fingers against the symbols etched into the surface. "Do you know what these mean?"

Robert shook his head. "We haven't been able to figure that out yet."

"Where'd you find it?" Jonah realized that his parents would have loved to see something like this. He had continued to study the symbols, so it took him a moment before he noticed that Lynn and Robert were staring at him. "What's wrong?"

"Jonah," Robert glanced nervously at Lynn before he continued, "Your mom and dad sent the box to me as a birthday gift, two years ago."

CHAPTER TWENTY-ONE
BIRTHDAY GIFTS

Jonah's anger and shock warred with each other. His parents had given Robert a special gift on his thirteenth birthday. Yet they had refused to even discuss his abilities with him. It seemed they trusted his cousin more than they trusted their own son.

"We're sorry, Jonah," Lynn finally added. "We thought you knew about the gifts. I mean, you're thirteen now. We decided that meant something."

"Turning thirteen is often an important event when it comes to powers." Wick patted his own chest. "That's about the age I first noticed mine. And you obviously have abilities. Didn't you get something?"

"Wick!" Lynn gave him a hard look.

Jonah ignored them as he went over to his book bag, rummaged around inside, and pulled out his old cell phone. He didn't want to get rid of this one even though Marcus had given him a new one; it reminded him of his parents—and their old voice messages were on the memory card. He found the last one from his mom and played it.

Hi sweetheart. Our flight plans have changed again. I'll send you the updated times as soon as we know. But don't worry, your father and I will be home in time for your birthday. This is an important time for you and we wouldn't miss it for the world.

Oh! Your father found the perfect gift for you and we both look forward to seeing your reaction.

Take care. We love you.

By the time it finished, Lynn stared out the attic window. Robert and Wick looked totally stunned. Jonah slowly turned the phone over in his hands. "I guess they did have something special for my birthday. They just never made it back." He sat down on the edge of the sofa, feeling ashamed for doubting his parents.

"Dude. I'm sorry." Wick sat down on the steamer trunk. "I didn't know."

Jonah shook his head. He didn't want Wick or his cousins feeling sorry for him. "It's strange to discover so many things about my parents that I never knew. And now I can't ask them anything because they're gone."

"This wasn't a good idea." Lynn frowned at her brother.

"I want to know everything." Jonah jumped to his feet and leaned over the box, looking at Lynn. "Did my parents send you something?"

In answer, Robert opened the box. Lynn took out two silver palm-sized cylinders and stood away from the table with one in each hand. She activated the cylinders and, with distinctive metallic *swish* sounds, they transformed into two silver blades.

It was actually cool seeing someone transform them up close, Jonah thought. His parents had used cylinders like those in the dream. Marcus and Kevin had also used the silver blades when they rescued him.

Jonah's heartbeat sped up as he watched Lynn. She twirled and pivoted with the blades, her moves graceful and practiced. And the blades hummed as they sliced through the air. Lynn ended her demonstration with the blades crossed in front of her. In one smooth movement, she brought herself to an upright position and collapsed the blades.

Everyone clapped as Lynn took a mock bow. Then she, Robert, and Wick stared at Jonah. He knew why. He hadn't shown any obvious surprise when Lynn activated the blades.

"My mom and dad used silver blades like those. They were really good…" Talking about his parents brought back the memory of their last fight. Jonah could feel the heat of the explosions and the sounds of his parents as they fought for their lives. He slumped down on the sofa again and buried his head in his hands. Lynn sat beside him and patted his back.

"Stop trying to hide it. If this is too much for you, tell us."

The Protector's Ring

"No! It's not, and I want to know." Jonah wiped at his eyes and blinked the moisture out of them. "I'm serious." He held out a hand and Lynn gave him one of the cylinders. He ran his fingers over the strange symbols, but his eye caught a thin line of topaz inlaid along one side of the handle.

He glanced at Lynn. "How did you learn to use the blades like that?"

"I've been practicing. You know, your mom and dad didn't tell us how to activate the gifts, not directly."

"What do you mean?"

"They gave us riddles to solve," Robert explained as he tapped the archive box. "But we figured out the gifts without solving the riddles."

"I nearly lost a finger when I activated one of the blades by accident." Lynn held up the other cylinder and rotated it around in her hand. "I started taking lessons. Then my mom found out about the real blades and she locked them away. She wasn't happy with your parents about that."

Jonah was careful not to activate the cylinder himself as he handed it back to Lynn. "But how did you get the blades here if your mom took them away from you?"

"I picked the lock on the storage trunk and put some practice swords in their place, just in case Mom ever checked."

"So," Robert continued, "you can see why we keep these things a secret. Our parents would never understand them." He took the cylinders from his sister and placed them in the box. "It's kind of cool your parents owned blades."

"Yeah. I just wonder why they sent a pair to you, Lynn."

"I don't know." Lynn shrugged and gave Robert a quick glance.

During their little discussion, Wick had pulled a couple of large black books from the wobbly bookshelves. "Hey, maybe that's what they planned for you, Jonah."

"Maybe. You'd think Marcus would tell me. He has a pair of blades, and he used them on the Grim Hounds."

"No way!" Wick dropped the books on the card table.

"They're meant to fight supernatural things."

Everyone went back to staring at him until Robert moved the archive box out of the way so Wick could sit the books side by side.

"What's in those?" Jonah pointed at the books, glad for a distraction.

"My brother drove me way out to an estate sale in Ellaville." Wick opened one of the books and flipped through the pages. "The old guy who sold me the books called himself a Prophet. Local folks just thought him a nut case or a Satanist." Every page in the book contained at least one picture surrounded by tiny writing. Jonah tried to read it as Wick continued, "Bobby and I have been using the books to do research for the computer game."

"Yep," Robert added. "This is where I got the idea for the drawings of Grim Hounds."

Robert pointed to a realistic drawing of the creature, complete with the double rows of teeth. Jonah stepped back from the table before he could stop himself. He could hear the angry growls of the real creature, and his heart pounded in his chest.

Lynn watched him. "That thing must have really scared you."

"Yeah, it did. You try having a Grim Hound chase you down in the street." Jonah couldn't explain to his cousins the awful dread and fear that had come over him when he had seen it.

He shifted his eyes to the writing to avoid looking at the picture. Robert tapped the page. "See? Wick was right. It says here that people thought the Grim Hound, or Hell Hound, hunted doomed individuals. In reality, the Grim Hound hunts for objects a doomed person possesses." Robert shot Jonah a worried glance. "Sorry. I didn't mean that."

Doomed. Jonah rolled that word around in his mind. Were his parents doomed? Was he also doomed? Somebody was sending creatures after him now. Once again, Jonah caught the quick glances from the others. He had told Lynn this wasn't too much for him, and he meant it.

He found where Robert had stopped reading and continued, even though his voice shook a little. "The Grim Hound is not a dog. It is a supernatural being that assumes a canine shape when summoned. Maintaining the form requires a great deal of energy. Therefore, Grim Hounds can only stay in the mortal realm for limited periods of time."

"So," Lynn leaned against the table, eyeing Jonah. "The woman in the bookstore-"

The Protector's Ring   163

"Neera," Wick interjected.

"This Neera woman called that Grim Hound and sent it after you. She used the card to pinpoint your location. She has to be powerful."

"Maybe she's responsible for the first ones you saw, Jonah," Robert answered before Jonah could. He snapped his fingers. "You were convinced she knew you were from DC."

"Mystic Worlds opened a couple of weeks before Jonah arrived in town," Lynn said, her lips pursed as she thought about it.

"It all adds up," Robert offered.

"We can't know for sure until we do some investigating, Robert."

"But we can't go near that store again. There's no telling what she'd do the next time. Plus, Jonah looked sick after that first visit."

"Is that true?" Lynn looked at him like she just remembered his presence.

"Well, yeah. I did feel strange being around her."

"Have you ever experienced this feeling before?"

Jonah didn't want to mention his Death Sense to her. However, he realized they needed to know more than he had revealed so far. His cousins had invited him into their inner circle and trusted him with their secrets. And, of course, he hated it when someone kept information from him. How could he do the same?

He held up his hands. "I don't want you freaking out or anything."

Wick raised his own hand immediately. "I promise you, Jonah, that I won't freak out by anything you tell me."

Goosebumps rose along Jonah's arms. Wick also blinked, looked down at his arms, and said, "Whoa."

Robert stared at his friend. "Are you okay?"

"Yeah, that was just freaky. It's like..." Wick paused and stared at Jonah.

"What?" Robert pressed, watching Wick and Jonah.

"Nothing, Bobby."

"You felt that?" Jonah asked. Wick nodded. "Why does it happen to me?"

"I want to look up something first, then I'll let you know."

"But…"

"I prom-" Wick stopped himself and offered Jonah a weak smile.

Lynn cleared her throat. "Well, if you two are done being even weirder than usual, I also promise not to freak out."

"So do I," Robert added. He and Lynn sucked in breaths, staring at the goosebumps along their arms.

Jonah took a deep breath and told them all about his Death Sense and the first times he experienced it. Lynn and Robert couldn't hide their shocked reactions.

Jonah was heartened by Wick's outrage at his old neighbors. Even Lynn's nostrils flared with anger.

"There's something else I need to tell you." Jonah paused to swallow past his nervousness. "The night of the fire, I tried to run back to my house and my neighbor grabbed me. I remembered thinking I needed to get past him and suddenly, I was in the next yard."

"What do you mean?" Lynn asked. "You slipped out of his hands?"

"No. I disappeared and then reappeared in my neighbor's yard."

Lynn was too shocked to reply. Robert leaned down to look Jonah directly in the eyes. "You can teleport, little cousin?"

Jonah smiled and shook his head. "It's called phasing, Robert."

He wanted to explain more about his rescue from the house and the trip to Marcus's apartment. The problem was Kevin. Jonah had promised the boy he wouldn't mention his name. Thankfully, his cousins were more concerned with the fact he could phase rather than the details of the house.

Robert ruffled his Afro for a moment, then gave Jonah a sly look. "You can disappear from one spot and reappear in another spot?" Jonah nodded. Robert glanced around the attic. "You can look at the bay window and…"

"I would appear there."

"Show us."

Jonah looked at the ground. "I can only do it when I'm in trouble."

"What do you think, Wick?" Lynn said, shifting her gaze from Jonah to Wick. "Is it magic?"

"It's not any kind of magic I've seen or read about. I mean, some powerful mages can make a vortex." Wick pointed at Jonah. "This is something else."

Jonah stared at Wick. "What's a vortex?"

"It's like a tunnel between two locations," Wick explained. "Real Mages are supposed to be able to do it."

"Can a witch or sorceress do it?"

"Yeah, if she's powerful enough. You worried about Neera?"

"No," Jonah lied and looked away. He was still freaked out about the dreams and feeling a bit guilty about not telling everyone he was half-Reaper. "I don't understand how I can use my power without training."

"Well, your power could be tied to your emotions." Wick held up a hand to tick off his points. "You were running away from bullies that day at school, and then your house burnt down. Those events involve powerful emotions." Wick gasped, causing everyone to look at him. "That's how you got away from the Grim Hound, isn't it?"

Jonah nodded as he experienced a surge of gratitude toward Wick. The older boy had already told him far more about his powers than anyone else, except maybe Kevin. Wick and his cousins weren't freaking out as much as he feared. In fact, as they continued to talk about his abilities and who might want to hurt him, Jonah was glad he had opened up to his cousins. They, and Wick, were trying to help him.

Jonah was nervous going outside, in the open, so he stuck with Robert and Wick for the rest of the day. Just before dinner, his phone started vibrating on the bedside table. Jonah fumbled to pick it up even though he didn't recognize the ID. But when he opened the phone, he saw he had a text, from Marcus.

Sorry to contact you so late, Jonah. Things have been extremely hectic here. Kevin told me all about the Grim Hound. I'm relieved that you are okay. I wished you'd ran in the opposite direction and called me. You know that one of us can be there in seconds.

Jonah stared at the message, wondering what else had happened that kept Marcus so busy that he couldn't call. Then a second text came in.

You shouldn't have to worry about anyone else bothering you. They know we're watching. And as much as I want you to get to know your relatives and settle into your new surroundings, you need to be prepared.

Jonah's eye's widened when he read that. *Prepare? How?* The next text came in.

I've made the decision to start teaching you to use your power. I think we should start with phasing. One of us will call you later to make arrangements. - Marcus.

Jonah tossed the phone on the bedside table with a mixture of emotions. Marcus didn't answer any of his questions—like who was after him. Why did they want to hurt him? At least Marcus promised to start training him to phase. That thought filled Jonah's mind as his Aunt Imma called him out to dinner.

CHAPTER TWENTY-TWO
PHASING LESSONS

Jonah had just finished clearing the table after dinner when his phone rang. He glanced at Aunt Imma, who was preparing the leftovers for the refrigerator, then slipped outside onto the patio and answered the call.

"What's up, little man?"

"Kevin? Why are you calling?"

"You talked to Marcus. He assigned me to train you."

"For real?"

"Yeah. Will you be alone, at home around eleven on Saturday?"

"I guess so, why?"

"I'm gonna phase down. Be ready at eleven. Backyard."

"Cool." Jonah nervously swallowed and said, "Kevin?"

"Yeah?"

Jonah just wanted to talk to Kevin. Yet his nerves failed him and the words wouldn't come out. Finally he muttered, "Nothing."

"See you then, little man."

Jonah had to admit that he was excited about seeing Kevin again, but nervous about learning to phase, too. Plus, he wasn't sure what to wear to

John Darr

a phasing lesson. *It's not a date*, he told himself and pulled on some athletic shorts and a plain tee.

The house seemed strangely quiet as he exited his bedroom. Lynn was off helping Uncle James at the newspaper, Robert worked on the blog at the teen center, and Saturday mornings were always the busiest times for Aunt Imma at the salon. Feeling a bit restless and alone, Jonah went outside and began pacing around the patio.

A change in air pressure alerted Jonah and he glanced at his watch. Kevin appeared right on time in the backyard, near the shed. He wore an off-white, short-sleeved workout shirt, dark blue athletic shorts, and black high top sneakers. He looked ready to go running or to a workout, Jonah thought. He began to wonder exactly what learning to phase would include.

The Fallen Reaper slowly looked around the yard before focusing on Jonah. When their eyes met, Jonah's heart fluttered a little. He felt a bit light on his feet as he approached the older boy.

Kevin raised his chin in a *whatsup* greeting. "You ready to learn phasing, little man?"

"Don't call me that."

Kevin grinned and held out his arm.

Jonah locked his arm in Kevin's while glancing toward the backyard fence. The neighbors weren't out and despite standing beside the shed and under the largest tree, someone could be watching. That raised a question for Jonah. "Why did you phase to the backyard and not inside the house? No one's here."

Kevin cocked an eyebrow, watching Jonah. "Your house is protected from that kind of thing. Marcus didn't tell you?"

"No." Before Jonah could fully digest that bit of news or ask another question, the world around him shifted and disappeared as Kevin phased them.

The first thing Jonah noticed when they reappeared was that the temperature was slightly cooler and the air less humid than it had been in Mount Vernon. The sun was just as bright, though, and he heard the lapping of water. Jonah turned to find a large, glittering lake behind them.

"Wow."

He released Kevin's arm and walked closer. They stood on a deck done in light wooden tiles, arranged on the diagonal to the building behind them. That structure and the other buildings on the opposite side of the lake all had Asian-inspired roofs. Jonah experienced a moment of dislocation when he saw that. "Where are we? We didn't phase to another country, did we?"

Kevin laughed. "No, we're still in Georgia. Come on." He crossed a little white stone bridge that connected the deck to a bamboo-covered pathway. Once there, he took the left branch in the pathway that cut across a grassy field. "This place is called Camp Alliance," he continued.

Jonah's mouth hung open as he took in his surroundings. The pathway led toward four large fields, each about half the size of a football field. A sturdy looking lean-to was set at the far end of each, with waist high shrubbery separating one from the next.

"This is a camp?"

"Yep, a training camp."

Jonah scanned the area, his face a confused mask. "Where is everyone?"

"It's Saturday. They have the day off."

Kevin entered the closest field. Jonah moved to the edge to peek over the shrubs into the next field. There were rocks and other objects of all sizes piled near the front of that one. But the one he and Kevin entered was bare except for the cut grass.

The Fallen Reaper stood near the center, arms folded behind his back. "These are ranges and we use them to train new members of the Alliance."

"Really? Who?"

Kevin nodded. "Gifted mortals, like Omar and Mages."

"Mages?"

"Spell casters, people who can use magic."

Jonah's eyes widened. "My friend Wick can use magic. Could he be a Mage?"

"You mean that kid at the old gas station? Interesting."

The idea of Wick coming here to train was cool to Jonah. And what about Lynn, he wondered. She had real Reaper's blades and could use them. Shouldn't she come here and train? Jonah started to ask about that when it occurred to him that Kevin was still an apprentice. "Are you training at this camp?"

Kevin hesitated before saying, "Yeah."

"You have to teach me phasing on your day off?"

The boy shrugged. "I'm working for the Alliance already. Besides, training you is worth a lot of credits. So let's get to it." He squared his shoulders and assumed an authoritative air. "Your state of mind is extremely important when phasing."

"Okay." Jonah blinked, thrown off by the sudden shift in Kevin's tone.

"I know you've phased before," Kevin continued, "but only when you panicked. If you want to phase without being freaked out, you have to learn to clear your mind. Watch me."

Kevin closed his eyes. The air rippled around him and he phased to the other side of the range, near the lean-to. He called out to Jonah, "Think about where you want to go. See it in your mind."

On his last word, Kevin phased to the opposite end of the range. "It only takes a split second to focus." Again, he phased. Jonah sensed the change in air pressure right before Kevin appeared beside him.

"It's like riding a bike," Kevin continued as if disappearing and reappearing was the most normal thing in the world. Jonah supposed it was, for a Fallen Reaper. Even a young one.

"Picking where you want to go and phasing can happen as fast as a thought." Kevin stepped away from Jonah. "We'll go slow today. Think about a spot in the clearing. Now, close your eyes."

Jonah closed his eyes and relaxed his body.

"Good. When you're ready, I want you to phase."

Jonah pictured a small bush beside the lean-to. He thought about it and imagined standing next to it, but nothing happened. No ripple of air or the sensation along his skin. He knew before he opened his eyes that he stood in the same exact spot.

He let out a moan. "It's not working."

Kevin crossed his arms as he watched Jonah. "You're letting the doubt get in the way, aren't you?"

"Well, I did it before. Why can't I do it now?"

"Like I said, you were in a panic, Jonah. That panic cut through the doubt, and you phased."

Jonah's frustration kicked in and he balled his hands into tight fists. "So I can't do it now?"

"It's okay for you to doubt, at first, but don't stop there." Kevin waited for him to nod and relax again. He gently tapped Jonah on the chest with his fist. "You have to believe you can do it, inside, and you'll do it." He stepped back. "Try again."

Jonah closed his eyes and willed himself to phase several more times, and each time, nothing happened. Why would he doubt his abilities? He had done it before. He believed, he knew deep inside that he could do it. He even knew how his body responded to a phase. Could that be the key, Jonah wondered?

He thought about the small tree again. This time, he imagined the sensation along his skin and slight increase of pressure on his body. Then he told himself to phase.

When he opened his eyes, the small bush was directly in front of his face.

Kevin clapped from the other side of the clearing. Jonah started to cross to him and Kevin held up a hand.

"Hold up. I want you to phase back."

Jonah closed his eyes, thought about the spot beside Kevin, and then willed himself to phase. A moment later, strong hands gripped his arms to steady him.

"I knew you could do it." Kevin patted Jonah's shoulder.

"Yeah. It's cool!" The very idea that this would be natural was exciting to Jonah. Maybe being a half-Reaper wasn't so bad after all.

Kevin made him phase two more times. After his third successful phase, Jonah paused to rub his arms. "Why does phasing make my skin feel funny?"

"You're traveling through the Afterworld when you phase. It happens so fast that you don't realize that for a split second, your body doesn't exist in the mortal side at all."

"Whoa! That's like Night Crawler. He goes through part of Hell when he teleports."

Kevin cocked an eyebrow. "You would find a geeky way to describe it. Gee whiz."

"So the funny feeling on my skin is my body disappearing? Does it break down?"

"Not exactly. Your soul travels through the Afterworld for that split second. You carry the blueprint for your body with you and it comes out on the other side."

"Wow." Jonah thought this was the coolest thing he ever heard. Then he remembered his mom and Omar, and another question occurred to him. "Why can regular people travel with us?"

"While their own souls keep their blueprint, our power allows them to travel through to the other side with us. It can only happen for a few seconds."

Jonah sucked in a breath. "Can someone like me or you cross over for longer than that?"

Kevin stared at him for several seconds, long enough for his stare to turn into one of the uncomfortable, unblinking variety. Jonah had learned, though: he calmly waited for Kevin to answer.

Now that he finally had a teacher, Jonah couldn't wait to ask everything he'd been wondering since he'd first phased, back in Virginia. His question had been sparked by the info Wick gave him on the Grim Hound. They could be summoned into the mortal realm for certain periods of time, far more than a few seconds. Why couldn't it work the other way, with Fallen Reapers?

Kevin blinked and broke the Reaper stare. "That's a deep question for a little kid."

Jonah shoved Kevin, and the boy reacted by grabbing him into a headlock.

"You can save that talk for Marcus," Kevin said, ruffling Jonah's hair. "Today, you're learning to phase on command. Got it?"

The Protector's Ring

Jonah mumbled his answer, and Kevin released him. As they continued with the phasing lessons, Jonah began to see a different side of the Fallen Reaper. The older boy took his job seriously. Each time Jonah phased, Kevin wanted him to pick another spot and phase faster.

"Try four phases in a row."

Jonah succeeded in doing four, but he paused before the final phase.

Kevin shouted, "Don't hesitate between each one. Start over, at the beginning."

Jonah grumbled but eventually, he managed to do four in a row without pausing. By that time, he swayed on his feet from dizziness.

Kevin gripped his shoulder. "Careful."

"Why do I feel so dizzy?"

"Doing multiple phases takes a lot out of you. Here, try this." Kevin handed him a piece of butterscotch candy.

At the first taste of the buttery candy, a pleasant jolt of energy ran through Jonah. He glanced up at Kevin. "Does the candy work for you?"

"It makes me feel better, but I still have to recharge. I bet you just need a little down time and you're as good as new."

"Yeah, I feel better after a nap."

"Lucky you." Kevin paused as he gazed around the range. Jonah expected the Fallen Reaper to have him perform something else, but Kevin clapped his hands together once. "That's enough for today."

Jonah glanced in the boy's face, trying to judge how the session had gone. After a few moments, he gave up and simply asked, "How was I?"

"You were great."

A knot in Jonah's stomach released itself. Kevin looked sincere, and he hadn't used that stupid nickname. Jonah's excitement about having Kevin here returned now that the lesson was over. "You want to hang out? Maybe I can see the rest of the camp."

Kevin blinked in surprise and Jonah felt his own face warm. The older boy had said before that he thought Jonah was a kid. *Surely he wouldn't want to hang out with me*, Jonah decided. He'd been stupid to even ask.

Instead of making fun of him, Kevin smiled. "You have to get back before someone misses you. I have work to do."

"Oh. Same time tomorrow?"

"No. Marcus thought you should practice doing short phases on your own."

Doubt nibbled at Jonah's insides. "Can't we do both?"

"Sorry. Marcus has me working on other things." Kevin gestured around him. "And I have camp."

Jonah gaze down the line of ranges as he thought about trying to phase alone. He'd hoped Kevin would be there because he'd feel more confident.

Kevin leaned down to look him in the eyes. "The whole point of the lesson is so you can phase on your own. A little private practice won't hurt."

Jonah nodded, and Kevin continued to stare at him. "Go hang out with your friends when you get back. Have fun and clear your mind." He tapped Jonah's chest. "Your body needs to recharge anyway." He held out an arm to Jonah. "And don't look so sad. We'll meet up again."

CHAPTER TWENTY-THREE
BASEMENT AMBUSH

After the phasing lesson from Kevin—and the fact that no more raging Grim Hounds appeared—Jonah was confident enough to go out on his own. He'd decided to check out the creek side clearing behind the Teen Center. Following the well-worn path through the grass and down the hillside, Jonah reached the clearing with little problem.

Someone, probably the older kids, had moved several large rocks and a couple of moss-covered logs around the clearing. Discarded soda cans, bottles, and wrappers littered the area. At the dead center was a shallow depression with burned sticks and matches in it.

Jonah didn't try to figure that one out. All that mattered was that the stream ran clear and the place was quiet. For now, it was the perfect place to think. He breathed in deeply, listening to the gurgling creek. Branches rustled high overhead, punctuated by occasional bird calls. He let out a slow breath, enjoying the cooler air under the thick tree cover.

Of course, his mind went straight to his incident with the Grim Hound. Despite what his godfather said, Jonah wanted to know who sent that creature. He needed someone who could give him answers and he longed to talk to Kevin again. The problem was he didn't know how to contact the boy.

At least telling his cousins and Wick about himself had lifted a weight from his shoulders. He didn't have to lie anymore and could bounce ideas off them. However, they couldn't give him all the answers he needed. In fact, his cousins hoped that he would give them information.

He closed his eyes and breathed in deeply, yet again, to clear his mind. He tried to let the sounds carry him away, but someone laughed close by in the woods.

Jonah hoped whoever it was would stay away. No luck. The laugh was much closer the second time it came, followed by the sounds of shuffling feet sliding through leaves.

An older girl and boy came around a bend further up the creek and paused when they saw him. The boy waved, and Jonah noticed the tattoos covering his entire arm. "Excuse us, little dude."

Jonah frowned as he glanced back the way they had come. The river turned sharply several yards upstream and disappeared around a hill full of the moss-covered tree stumps.

Jonah originally thought the boy was thin because the oversize shirt had fooled him. The older boy had broad shoulders and biceps that bulged when he clapped his hands. Numerous tattoos covered both forearms and he had a scar on his left arm, like someone had pressed a hot iron against the skin.

The boy coughed into his fist. "Yo, are you meeting someone down here?"

"No."

"You mind if we use the spot?"

The girl watched Jonah with a curious expression. She finally jumped and said, "You're Lynn's cousin, the one from DC."

"Huh, yeah."

The boy gave Jonah an appraising stare, like knowing he was related to Lynn made a difference somehow. "Cool. Well, if you meeting your girl or something, we can go somewhere else."

Jonah stood so quickly, he actually startled the boy and girl. "I'm not meeting anyone."

With that, he ran up the hill. The girl laughed and, for a second, Jonah thought she laughed at him. He paused to look back. The boy and girl sat side by side on a boulder, their heads very close together as they talked. Jonah shook his head. He couldn't imagine ever coming down here to make out with anyone.

The Protector's Ring **177**

He entered the recreation center, intent on playing ping-pong to let off some tension. Jonah had started toward the East wing area when a girl in a staff shirt called out to him.

"Are you Jonah?"

Fear gripped him. Had he done something wrong? "Yeah, why?"

"You know Wick?"

Jonah relaxed a bit and nodded.

"Well," the girl continued. "He wanted you to meet him in the basement."

"In the basement?"

"Ah, he works here part-time in the summer, with the custodian. The office is in the basement."

"Oh, okay."

"Follow me."

She led Jonah back through the main lobby to the elevator. He couldn't imagine why Wick needed to see him. *Maybe it has to do with magic*, Jonah thought.

When the doors opened, the girl inserted a key into a lock above the button marked *basement*. She continued to worry her lower lip as the elevator descended.

"Are you okay?" Jonah asked.

"I heard there are rats in the basement."

She made a face, but when the doors opened, she didn't hesitate to lead Jonah to a storeroom.

"There you go. He's in there." She turned and hurried off.

Jonah stepped into the room, looking around. The basement storeroom only had one light working, and it flickered. Jonah was reminded of the mausoleum crypt and the memorial service for his parents. He paused just inside the door, concentrating on his Death Sense. His stomach was calm and he didn't have a headache, so none of the strange people were around. The flickering light began to bother him, and he started down the aisles of cleaning and office supplies and old books.

John Darr

He peeked through the gaps in the items on the shelves, trying to spot Wick. No one seemed to be here. He returned to the front area, by the door. Maybe he should call Wick's name, he thought. Then he heard someone behind him.

"It's about time…" Jonah turned around and paused.

Mike stood panting in the doorway, his eyes wide. "Jonah! You have to get out, now. I know what they're up to."

"What…"

"It's a trap!"

Jonah's uneasy feeling morphed into a sharp prickle from his Death Sense.

"Well, well, well. It's DC." Brandon, Drew, and Antwan stepped into view. Mike bolted into the room to stand beside Jonah.

Brandon grinned at them as he entered the storeroom. "I caught you and your boyfriend in the basement." Brandon's friends laughed, but he sneered at Jonah. "You don't have your cousin to hide behind this time, DC."

"My name's Jonah." He kept cool as his mind caught up with Mike's warning. "What are you doing down here?"

Brandon's buddies stepped into the room and moved to either side of Jonah.

"So tell me, DC," Brandon continued, ignoring Jonah's question. "Is it true what I hear? You're not visiting your cousins for the summer. You're staying here for good."

Jonah's shock must have shown on his face because Brandon laughed and took a step closer.

Mike spoke in his ear. "I'm sorry, Jonah."

"I heard your parents are dead. No one wanted you, so you came here." Brandon smirked. "Poor baby. What's it like not having a momma and daddy?"

Jonah's heart hammered in his chest as he lunged at Brandon. Drew and Antwan were prepared, grabbing and pushing him back against the shelves. Without thinking, Jonah snatched a plastic bottle of cleaner off the shelf and slammed it against Antwan's head. The boy howled and leapt back.

The Protector's Ring **179**

Mike yelled, which caused Drew to hesitate. Brandon took advantage of the confusion and punched Jonah in the stomach. He collapsed to the floor, unable to catch his breath.

Mike jumped between him and Brandon. "Leave him alone."

Jonah struggled to his feet and Antwan and Drew moved in, grabbing his arms and holding him while Brandon shoved Mike out of the way. That done, Brandon punched Jonah two more times, then drew back his fist to smack Jonah in the face.

Mike launched himself at Brandon, grabbing the bully's arm and yelling, "Stop!"

Antwan shoved Jonah roughly into another row of shelves while Brandon struggled with Mike, who wouldn't let go. He managed to free his arm, then pushed him into Jonah. Both lost their balance as they toppled over with the shelves. That section crashed into the others, causing all of them to wobble. Cleaning supplies, boxes, and all kinds of debris rained down on them. Brandon and his buddies scrambled back toward the safety of the door.

Jonah looked up in time to see an entire upper section of shelving falling toward him. Mike saw it too and let out a real scream. Jonah grabbed his arm, wishing with all his might that they were anywhere except here.

In a flash, he recalled Kevin's lesson about picking a destination. The first place that came to his mind was the last place he had visited: the clearing beside the creek. He felt the ripple along his skin and in the blink of an eye, the basement room was gone.

The soft ground near the creek replaced the hard basement floor. Jonah rolled over, saw no one else around, and let out a breath. A second later, a wave of dizziness hit him, and he scrambled to the nearest rock and sat down before he collapsed.

"Oh my God! Oh my God!" Mike shouted and crossed to the rock furthest from Jonah, sat down, and watched him with wide eyes.

Jonah took a few breaths. The cooler air and sound of the water helped the light-headed feeling pass.

Mike's voice shook when he finally spoke. "Are you a witch?"

"No."

"Then how did you do it, Jonah? One minute, we're in the basement, then we're outside." Mike stood, turning around on the spot as he rubbed his arms. Jonah noticed that he took care to keep the distance between them. "My skin felt all funny and…" Mike looked down at his chest and hugged himself. "Oh my God."

Jonah understood what he meant. Phasing was like having goosebumps all over your body, all over, even the private places. It still made him feel weird.

Mike sat down and took several deep breaths. "How did you do it?"

"When I'm in trouble, I just think about being somewhere and it happens."

"But… is it magic?"

Jonah shrugged. "All I know is it's called phasing. The first time it happened, I thought I just imagined it."

Mike's eyes went wide and out of focus, as if he remembered something. Jonah knew Mike couldn't really believe what happened even though he had experienced the phase.

They sat in silence for a while, listening to the sounds of the nearby creek. When Jonah moved, Mike jumped to his feet, pointing at him.

"I know what you are!"

Jonah's insides froze. He had expected Mike to be afraid; now he was the one fearful of what Mike would say.

"What do you mean?"

"You're a Fallen Reaper, aren't you?"

Jonah's mouth hung open. He didn't know how to respond except to deny, but Mike went on first.

"I'm right!" Mike pumped his fist in the air. "My uncle has all kinds of secret books locked away. I know where he keeps the key." He settled down, looking doubtful for the first time. "I didn't know Fallen Reapers could be my age."

Jonah shook his head, trying to get his own head around the sudden change. "I'm sorry. I never meant for this to happen."

The Protector's Ring

"Are you kidding," Mike breathed. "This... is... so... cool!"

Jonah blinked in surprise. "Mike, I'm not a Fallen Reaper."

"Yes you are. I know about this stuff, Jonah. You called it phasing. Fallen Reapers do that!"

"How?"

"I told you, my uncle has all kinds of books about supernatural stuff. He owns a bookstore."

"Really?" Jonah blinked in surprise again, trying to catch up to Mike's reaction. "That's awesome."

Mike subsided, looking amused. "That's the first time anyone's said that about my uncle having a bookstore." He sat on a closer rock, peering into Jonah's eyes. "You really are into books. You're a nerd like me?" He cracked a nervous smile.

"Yeah. I guess." Jonah lowered his gaze. "Okay. You're right."

"I knew it."

"Mike!"

"Sorry."

"I'm not a Fallen Reaper."

"But--"

Jonah held up a hand. "I'm half-Reaper." Mike's jaw dropped. "My dad was a Fallen Reaper."

"I never knew about half-Reapers." Mike paused. "This is so awesome."

Jonah realized that his own fear and agitation had subsided. He was comfortable talking with Mike. "You promise not to tell anyone?"

"I wouldn't do that. You stood up for me and even saved my life just now." Mike's voice shook a little. "I promise."

Jonah glanced up the hill and around the clearing. He took a deep breath and began to tell Mike everything he knew about himself.

CHAPTER TWENTY-FOUR
RESEARCH PARTNERS

Jonah rolled his bike up Morningside drive, still thinking about Mike. All he did was go to the recreation center. He never meant to use his powers. Once he did, he had assumed Mike would accuse him of being strange, weird, or even evil. That didn't happen.

He kicked a stray rock as he pushed his bike up the Hightowers' driveway and stowed it beside Lynn's in the backyard shed. When he reached the kitchen door, he paused to peek through its little window. He may have saved himself and Mike, but Jonah had scratches and a few cuts.

He didn't see Lynn in the kitchen or den, and that was good, he decided. She would blow a fuse if she saw him like this. Screwing up his nerves, Jonah entered the house.

Music blared from Lynn's room. Excellent, Jonah thought as he hurried through the kitchen and into the den. He was just a few feet from the safety of his bedroom—and a quick nap to let his body heal—when Lynn called his name.

"Jonah, why are you sneaking through the house?"

"I'm not sneaking through the house."

She carried a basket of clean laundry. When she saw his cuts, she dropped the basket on the floor. "Can't you go one day without getting into trouble?" She went for the med kit.

"It wasn't my fault. Things just keep happening to me!"

Lynn came back, grabbed him by the arm, and sat him down at the kitchen table. He winced and moved each time she tried to clean his cuts.

The Protector's Ring

"Hold still and tell me what you did this time."

"Brandon and his buddies ambushed me." He recounted the entire story, being careful to leave Mike out. By the end, Lynn's nostrils flared with anger.

"I'll break his rich little neck. You could have been seriously hurt."

"I just wish I could protect myself." Jonah sat back and rubbed his side where Brandon had punched him. "It's bad enough with the supernatural stuff happening. Now, regular kids are beating me up."

She threw away the bloody swabs. "I'll take care of that arrogant punk."

"No! You can't fight for me." If Lynn got involved again, Brandon would do something even crazier to get even. He needed another idea.

Jonah decided to avoid the teen center over the next couple of days. He didn't want to see Brandon, not that he was afraid of the bully. Jonah feared that something else would happen and he'd use his power, maybe in front of more people. He hadn't lied to Lynn. He needed a way to control himself.

He talked his aunt into dropping him off at the Twiggs County library. He was impressed at his first glimpse of the modern, three-story library, and then he stepped through the center set of double glass doors and into a spacious atrium. A light, tiled marble covered the floor, creating hard echoes as people walked across it. Jonah craned his head back to see the domed ceiling of the atrium three floors above.

Ignoring the daily newspapers and Juvenile sections directly ahead through the atrium, Jonah headed for the wide staircase to the second floor. He'd looked up the library on the Internet and knew it had a large, second-floor study section. Once at the top of the stairs, he took his time walking past the periodicals and computer rooms before entering the main study section. Floor-to-ceiling wood bookcases covered every wall. Numerous large study tables filled the center of the open space. Each one contained a raised center portion with two stubby reading lamps on top and electrical outlets and data ports on each side.

Golden afternoon sunlight streamed through the massive windows, giving the adjacent reading nooks and low-slung reading chairs an inviting quality. Jonah paused to get his bearings. Not only were there nooks spaced around the outer edge of the study area, but there were also four study alcoves.

Those were his target, and Jonah hurried over to one, placing his bag on the table. This was perfect, he thought. The alcoves had three walls of floor-to-ceiling bookshelves. The fourth side was open to the study room.

Once he settled in, and he began to pull books on Reapers, Jonah's worries about Brandon, and whether or not to tell his cousins he was a half-Reaper, receded. Jonah sunk into the familiar routine of a library. Even if it was a different building, Jonah was reminded of his own lonely, yet comforting, hours in the Arlington Central Library.

He spent the rest of that afternoon pouring over information on mythology, visions, premonitions, and Reapers. Jonah found that much of his research on Reapers never touched on the things he could do. Marcus told him that the real information had been kept from mortals, and Jonah began to see the truth of that. Putting those books aside, he focused on the ring instead. He didn't know where to begin, so he delved into everything he could find. Time slipped away, turning into the early evening hours before he went home.

Jonah's cellphone rang as he stepped out of the bathroom, body damp from a morning shower. He sprinted down the hallway and into his room, glad that everyone was gone. His aunt would go crazy if she saw his wet feet on her hardwood floors. Jonah entered his room and dived across the bed to scoop up the phone from the bedside table.

"Hello?"

There was a long pause. "Hi, Jonah."

"Mike?" Jonah tossed his towel aside. "Are you okay?"

"Yeah. I've been looking for you."

"Oh, sorry."

"Can we talk?"

"Yeah." Jonah waited for him to continue, but Mike remained silent. "I thought you wanted to talk."

The Protector's Ring

"I do, just not on the phone. Let's meet."

"Sure. Where?"

Mike paused again. "Are your cousins home?"

"They're gone. Why?"

"I'll come over. We can talk on your patio."

"Okay."

Jonah wasn't sure how to read Mike's tone as he dressed and headed outside to the patio. It was only after he sat down at the wooden table that he wondered how Mike knew about the patio.

The Hightowers' backyard wasn't visible from the street because of the high fence and shrubbery. Maybe he'd been over to the house before, Jonah thought just as Mike rode his bike into the backyard. Jonah relaxed a little when Mike gave him shy smile, leaning his bike against the tree.

Once Mike had plopped down into a chair on the opposite side of the table he said, "I've been thinking and I have a question." Jonah nodded. "Can Lynn and Robert do it?"

"No."

"Do they know about you?"

"Yeah." Mike went quiet. Jonah had done some thinking of his own over the past few days. Once the panic and fear of Mike revealing his secret subsided, he had begun to go over the events of that day. "Mike, how did you know about the ambush?" Jonah waited as Mike gazed out across the backyard. "Mike?"

"Drew told me."

"Why would Drew tell you anything?"

"He didn't mean to tell me. He let it slip out while we talked."

"Why were you talking to him?"

"We used to be friends--"

"He tried to hurt us. How can you take his side?"

"I'm not taking his side. I told Drew he's stupid to hang out with Brandon."

186 *John Darr*

Jonah rose from his patio chair. "Is that how Brandon found out about my parents? Did you tell Drew?"

Mike pushed himself to his own feet, facing off. It was only then that Jonah realized he leaned over the patio table with his fists clenched. He took a deep breath and sat down, pressing his hands flat against the table top.

"Sorry." Jonah glanced down at his splayed hands. "I didn't mean to yell at you."

Mike's shoulders slumped a bit. "I understand, Jonah. I didn't know about your parents, so I couldn't tell Drew anything. Besides, I would never do that."

"I wonder how Drew found out?"

Mike gulped and slumped into his chair. "It was your aunt."

"My aunt wouldn't tell Drew anything about me."

"She didn't, directly."

"Then I don't understand."

"Jonah, Mount Vernon isn't a big place, and our community is even smaller. A lot of moms go to the beauty salon where your aunt works. Drew's mom goes."

Jonah stared at him. "Does your mom go?"

Mike nodded. "Yeah, but Drew told me that your aunt mentioned you at work. She talked about your parents dying and you coming to live with them. Knowing your aunt, she probably asked people to pray for you. Drew's mom heard about it."

"And she told Drew?"

"She told him to be nice to you, maybe try to be friends and make things easy on you."

Jonah snorted. "He screwed that up."

"Parents can be stupid when it comes to their kids. Did you tell your--" Mike stopped and covered his mouth. "I'm sorry."

"It's okay. I know what you mean. My aunt and uncle don't know half the things we do," Jonah admitted, thinking about all the secrets he and

The Protector's Ring

his cousins kept to themselves. When Mike refused to say anything, Jonah continued, "So she wanted Drew to be my friend?"

"I told you. His father's a dentist and they have as much money as Brandon's family, but they stay on this side of town. They aren't snobs like Brandon and Antwan's folks."

Jonah shook his head. He was certainly starting to understand more and more about Mount Vernon. "How did you know where to go?"

"I saw that rec center girl talking to Brandon and I ran to the library to find you."

"I went to play ping-pong."

"Oh. Well anyway, when I saw her coming off the elevator, I made her tell me what she did and take me down there."

Jonah was amazed. He never thought Mike could scare anyone. "How did you do that?"

"I told her that my big brother would beat her up if she didn't."

Jonah couldn't stop himself from laughing. "What?"

Mike bit his lip and lowered his gaze. "My brother goes to the same high school."

"Would he do that?"

"No, but she didn't know that." Mike flashed Jonah a mischievous silver grin, showing off his braces. Jonah whooped with laughter.

"That was brilliant, Mike." Jonah laughed again until a sobering thought struck him. "Do you think they saw me phase?"

Mike stuck out his lower lip as he considered it. "I don't think they saw anything. They were running toward the door when it happened."

Mike leaned forward, scanning Jonah's face, hair, hands, and arms. He held out a hand.

Jonah hesitated at first, but not because another boy wanted to see his hand. He knew Mike wanted to see the cut. He reached across the table, letting Mike grip his hand and turn it over. Mike's eyes widened when he saw the healed cuts.

"I heal fast," Jonah explained.

After a few moments in which Mike brushed his fingers across Jonah's hand, he took a deep breath and looked Jonah directly in the eyes. "Never, ever phase me again."

Jonah burst out laughing. Mike joined him after a few moments.

"Did you hear what happened to Brandon?" he said, voice full of excitement.

"No."

Mike switched to a closer chair. "Brandon, Antwan, and Drew were caught running from the storage room. The rec center demanded their parents pay for the damage. Of course, Brandon's father refused."

"What happened?"

"He and Antwan are banned from the center," Mike said, "for the rest of the summer."

"What about Drew?"

"His father agreed to pay, so Drew's okay. Can you believe it?"

Jonah enjoyed listening to Mike talk as much as he liked hearing about Brandon's troubles. When the temperatures started to rise, they went inside to play videos. Jonah enjoyed the break from his research, so when Mike suggested they head up to the teen center, Jonah was ready to return. They spent time going through the fiction section of the small library.

Around midday, Jonah had his first real chance to try out the Cyber Café. Mike chose a table in the back and Jonah ordered them burgers at the counter. Despite enjoying himself, Jonah began watching the other kids who laughed, talked, and made plans for the evening or weekend with their friends. He glanced at Mike, who had been watching a boy two tables over until he saw Jonah watching.

"We were in the same homeroom."

Jonah nodded at the explanation, even if he didn't totally believe it. He also didn't care. He liked hanging out with Mike, and he guessed they were becoming friends. So why did he feel different, like he missed something?

I'm half-Reaper.

That's it, Jonah thought. He couldn't imagine any of the other kids ever talking about Grim Hounds or Death or Reapers. How many of them lost both parents and a home? The heaviness from his first day returned and not knowing so many answers caused Jonah to slump in his chair.

Mike watched him as he slurped the last of his milkshake. "Jonah?"

"What?"

"Are you bored?"

"No."

"What's wrong? You're frowning."

"I don't know." That was true. He didn't know how to explain that he needed information. Jonah tapped the tabletop with his fingers. "I want to find out about rings."

"Rings?"

"Yeah. Ones with power."

Mike dropped the empty cup on the table, his mouth hanging open. "This has to do with your..." he glanced around, "...your power?"

"Yeah. My parents used to find powerful artifacts like rings, medallions, talismans."

"That's so cool."

Jonah met Mike's gaze. "It was dangerous." He paused at the spasm of pain from the loss. "I tried the county library, but that didn't help. The only store I know with books on things like this is Mystic Worlds, and I can't go back in there."

"Why not?"

Jonah caught himself on the verge of telling Mike about his last bookstore visit. It wasn't that he expected Mike to freak out when he mentioned the Grim Hound, but he didn't know how Mike would respond to knowing the creatures were real. Maybe he'd save that part for later.

He smiled and lowered his voice to a whisper. "We think the owner is a witch and she doesn't like me."

"Are you serious?"

Jonah nodded and Mike squared his shoulders. "Mystic Worlds isn't the only store to have those kinds of books. My uncle owns a bookstore, remember. It's called Hackett's Emporium, and I bet he has the books you need."

Jonah sat up in his own chair. "You mean I can see the secret books about supernatural stuff?"

A shadow of doubt flashed across Mike's face. "I don't know about that. I was able to see those because my uncle went out of town one time. He has a lot of regular books on the occult."

"This is about the real things, my power."

"I know, but let's see if the regular books have anything on the rings, okay?"

Jonah agreed. This was a better option than Mystic Worlds. Maybe he'd find out what he needed. That thought cheered Jonah as they headed out of the teen center.

CHAPTER TWENTY-FIVE
THE LITTLE BOOKSTORE

Hackett's Book Emporium wasn't like Mystic Worlds at all. The bookstore was located in a small, one-story house that the county had rezoned for commercial use. It was situated on a small plot of land between a hunting supply store and a propane store. A large wooden sign was nailed above the old front porch and featured the store name in painted lettering.

Mike and Jonah locked their bikes to a metal rail out front.

"My uncle can get cranky," he whispered to Jonah as they mounted the creaky steps. "And he can be strange at times. I know he doesn't like young people in the occult section, but he's my uncle and I work here part-time, so…"

"You think he'll let us see the books?"

"Yes."

"Okay." He didn't know if Mike was sure or if he was being optimistic. He decided not to press as Mike opened the old front door, causing an overhead bell to tinkle.

Jonah stopped just inside the front door to breathe in deeply. It smelled like a real bookstore, which meant it smelled like old, used books. He knew he would find slightly abused first editions of novels the mall stores would never keep in stock.

He was reminded of all the times his mom had taken him to out-of-the-way secondhand bookstores like this. He would lose himself in the mountain of books, looking for old paperback adventures and sci-fi novels.

He'd always leave with a stack of them in his hands and spend the next week being transported to strange worlds.

"Mike," he breathed, "this is fantastic."

"It's larger than it looked from outside because my uncle has two trailers attached to the back of the house. The occult section is back there."

Jonah craned his neck to see the back of the store as an old man stepped out of a side aisle. He wore blue jean coveralls and a grungy, paint-splattered cap over his curly, silver-grey hair. The bushy silver-grey mustache seemed to accent the man's frown. As he approached, Jonah could understand why Mike didn't want to cross his uncle. The man never smiled as he pulled a small paintbrush from a back pocket and started chipping dried paint off the handle with a fingernail. He didn't quite have Mike's pale oatmeal complexion, but Jonah could see the resemblance as the man eyed him.

"You related to Robert Hightower?"

"Yes, sir."

"I knew it. You got those same grey eyes. Robert never mentioned a younger brother."

Jonah opened his mouth and Mike spoke over him. "Jonah's not his brother. He's a cousin."

The old man glanced briefly at his nephew, then back at Jonah. "That so?"

Jonah nodded. "You know my cousin?"

"I used to be his art teacher. I won't hold that against ya. Business is business, I say. How can I help ya?"

Mike traded a glance with Jonah, then smiled at his uncle. "We wanted to look in the Occult section."

"I've been in enough trouble with your parents, Mike. You two a little young to be involved in that kind of stuff."

Jonah wanted to sigh because Mr. Hackett sounded just like the clerk from Mystic Worlds.

Mike didn't seem put off. "We just want to look up stuff like special rings, you know…"

The Protector's Ring 193

Mike trailed off because his uncle's hazel eyes narrowed. Most surprising to Jonah was that his Death Sense tingled. Hackett held the paint brush in a tight grip, he noticed.

Without having to think about it, he moved in front of Mike. Only after he moved did it occur to him that Mr. Hackett would never threaten his nephew. *It's me*, Jonah thought to himself.

Mike gave Jonah a curious glance but kept silent.

Hackett also noticed his move and blinked. "You said you're Robert's cousin?"

Jonah nodded, but he didn't relax, not with his Death Sense still vibrating.

"Are you a Hightower?" The man asked.

"No. My last name is Blackstone."

Hackett blinked wildly again. "Your daddy was…"

"My dad was Isaiah Blackstone."

Hackett mouthed the name *Isaiah* as he watched them for a moment longer. The man's posture relaxed, and Jonah's Death Sense quieted, but that made Jonah suspicious.

"Did you know my dad?"

"No, I never met him."

Jonah caught the way the man refused to meet his gaze and could sense that Hackett didn't tell the whole truth. Maybe Hackett never met his dad, but he had heard the name. For some unknown reason, that made the difference to this man.

Hackett nodded once, then pointed toward the front door. "Go."

"Uncle?" Mike's shocked expression matched Jonah's.

"Come back after I clear the store."

Mike glanced around at the scattered customers and nodded. He motioned Jonah to follow.

The boys hung out at the teen center until Mike's uncle called. He'd closed up a few hours earlier than normal. That made Jonah feel a bit guilty until they arrived at the bookstore and saw the *We'll Return* sign on the front door. Judging from the position of the clock hands, Mike's uncle was giving them an hour of his time. Mike gave Jonah an embarrassed shrug as he knocked on the windowpane.

As soon as they stepped through the front door of the deserted store, Hackett led them around tottering stacks of paperback books and through the narrow aisles to the very back of the store. He paused in front of a door that Jonah knew would have been a bedroom a long time ago.

Hackett moved aside and pointed them through the opening. "Go on."

Jonah stepped into the next room and gasped. The room was bulging with paintings of dragons, knights, elves, and other kinds of fantastical things, and books crowded the space just like the rest of the store. Hackett dropped his paintbrush in a jar of turpentine to soak and then motioned them to two folding chairs in front of a cluttered wooden desk. Jonah sucked in a breath because he saw a full-sized painting of the cover from the Death Omen book.

"Your uncle wrote that book?" Jonah whispered. "I bought a copy at Mystic Worlds."

Mike leaned closer and grinned. "I could have gotten it for you at half-price, and with an autograph."

Mike's uncle cleared his throat as he squeezed behind the desk, taking care not to bang his head on a large, multicolored lamp hanging overhead. Jonah thought it looked like the type of light over a pool table in a movie.

Mr. Hackett clicked on the lamp, which Jonah thought odd. Although thick dark curtains covered the room's only window, the overhead light was on as well as a couple of lamps around the room. Then Jonah noticed that the painted lacquered sides of the multicolored lamp served to focus all its light directly on the desktop, like an elaborate reading lamp.

Hackett had turned to unlock a large black safe behind his desk, and he pulled out a very old book with burnished brass clasps. He dropped it on the desk with a surprisingly heavy thud, unhooked the clasps, and began turning through the pages, which made crinkly sounds.

When Mr. Hackett found a page he looked for, he rotated the book so Jonah and Mike could see. The page contained several drawings of rings, each with different markings, but all similar.

Mr. Hackett pressed a boney finger to the illustrations and leaned over the desk to peer at them. The lamplight cast deep shadows under his eyes, making his wrinkled face even more ominous. "Only Fallen Reapers and their allies know about these things."

Jonah had expected this as soon as Hackett reacted to his real name. "You knew my dad." Jonah didn't make it a question.

Hackett nodded. "I knew about him. Fallen Reaper. I thought they couldn't have kids."

"My mom was a mortal." Jonah shrugged. "They had me."

Hackett shook his head. "Well, I'll be…" His mouth continued to move though no words came out. He cleared his throat after a moment and said, "If you want any information from me, you'll tell me how you know about the rings?"

"My godfather told me." Mr. Hackett raised an eyebrow and Jonah rushed on, "He's executor of my parents' estate."

"Estate? You mean your parents are…"

Jonah nodded.

"How long?"

"It's been a month," Jonah answered.

Hackett sat down in the squeaky desk chair and lifted the paint-splattered cap to wipe his forehead. "They didn't tell me…" Hackett shook himself and glanced at Jonah. "I'm sorry to hear that about your parents."

"Thank you." Jonah paused until Mike nudged him in the arm. "How do you know about Fallen Reapers, Mr. Hackett?"

Mr. Hackett gazed at his nephew. "I suppose you two have been talking?"

"Yes, sir. Jonah told me all about it." Mike flashed a silvery smile.

"If your momma ever finds out…" Mr. Hackett pulled out his handkerchief and wiped his forehead again. "So be it. I've seen a Fallen Reaper before, and I know all about these rings." The old man shook his head and laid his cap on the desk. He watched them for a long time. Just when Jonah decided the man was never going to answer, Mr. Hackett leaned back in his chair.

"People called me a crackpot," he shot a glance at Mike, "because I believed in a larger truth about Angels, Demons, Reapers, and other supernatural beings. I found books that talked about these powerful rings made for human beings to balance the scales between us and the supernatural." Hackett paused, his eyes slightly out of focus as if he saw the information in his head.

"The Fallen Reaper I met confirmed my research. He told me the rings existed and one of his kind could use a ring to draw in power."

Jonah's stomach bunched into a knot.

Mike looked between Jonah and Mr. Hackett. "You said the rings were meant for humans. Fallen Reapers aren't exactly human anymore, are they? Not if they still use power."

"The Fallen Reapers are human," Mr. Hackett continued. "Even more important, they existed on the supernatural plane."

Mike shook his head. "Does that make a difference?"

Mr. Hackett snorted. "It makes a heck of a difference. Once they experienced that, they're always in tune to the supernatural. That's why they can work the binding spell to draw power." Hackett paused, raising a questioning eyebrow at Jonah. "You know about the binding patterns they use?"

"Yeah. My godfather told me about that, too."

Mike gaped at his uncle and Jonah. "Really? I didn't read about that in ─" His voice trailed off at the scathing look from his uncle. "Sorry."

"I see I'll need to find a better place to hide my spare key." The sour expression remained as Hackett focused on Jonah. "Anyway, a Fallen Reaper may be able to use one of them rings."

Jonah's mind replayed the conversation between his dad and Deyanira, when he had refused to give her the ring. In fact, his dad hadn't seemed to have it at all. Jonah sat up in his chair. "Have you ever seen a real ring?"

"Not in person." Hackett waved at the books. "Only the drawings."

Once again, Jonah sensed the half-truth in Hackett's comment. Finally, he got it. Hackett knew about the supernatural world, but not everything. He heard about his dad, but never met him. He could write the book on

The Protector's Ring   197

Death Omens because he knew a Fallen Reaper. But clearly, the Fallen Reaper hadn't told Hackett everything.

Jonah leaned on the desk and pointed to the ring on the page. "Do you know what the symbols say?"

Mr. Hackett shook his head. "The writing is called Angel script."

Jonah lapsed into silence as Mr. Hackett continued, "You ever heard of the Ring of Solomon? It allowed King Solomon to command and control the demons. Well, I figure it was one of these rings."

"How many rings are there?" Mike ran his finger down the page, scanning through the text.

"As far as I could tell, there were thirty-five. They were given to chosen humans so they would have the power to serve as protectors of the secret."

Jonah sat forward in his chair. "What secret?"

"Legend says that in times of great need, a group of special humans called the Children of Light would appear and balance things out. The guardians would protect and watch over them. After the Children of Light did their thing and everything is right with the world again, the Protectors would remain behind like sentinels."

Hackett paused, scratching his head. "The problem is the Protectors have been missing for nearly two thousand years—or rather, their rings have been missing."

The words *protect* and *protectors* finally connected for Jonah. His dad had underlined a passage about Protectors and rings in the little gray book.

Did my dad actually find a ring that belonged to the Protectors? Is that why my parents were killed? They died to protect me!

He couldn't hide the pain in his voice when he asked, "What happened to the Protectors?"

"They were all hunted down and killed. I'm talking about whole families and bloodlines being ruthlessly destroyed. The rings were lost."

Mike gave Jonah a worried glance before he asked, "The rings weren't destroyed?"

"Of course the rings weren't destroyed. Supernatural beings can't even touch them, let alone destroy them."

"What about the people?" Jonah cut in. He balled his hands into fists. "You're saying all the Protectors were killed?"

Mr. Hackett nodded. "There are still groups out there dedicated to finding the rings. Foolish, if you ask me. Who wants that kind of trouble?"

"What do you mean?"

"Whenever someone has claimed to have found one of the rings, they've always disappeared a short time later. You don't need a college degree to know what happened to them."

"My dad worked for one of those groups," Jonah shouted, his anger flaring. "He found a ring!"

Mr. Hackett jumped out of his chair and cracked his head on the low-hanging lamp. Mike sprang to his feet to reach up and stop its erratic swinging.

"Your father found a ring?" Hackett managed through clenched teeth, still clutching his injured head.

"Yes."

"You said your parents died?"

"Yes."

"What happened to the ring?"

Jonah shrugged. "Nobody knows."

Mr. Hackett stared at the drawing of the rings. "Your godfather is looking for the ring, isn't he?"

"Well, I guess he wants to do the same thing my parents did." The man's blatant interest in the ring rather than his dead parents began to bother Jonah. "He wants to keep it from the…"

When Jonah paused, Mr. Hackett leaned forward under the harsh lamp light. "Who's after the ring?"

Jonah glanced at Mike as he answered, "A strange woman named Deyanira."

Mr. Hackett's light face went pale and his eyes bugged out. "Deyanira!"

"Yeah." A strange thought came to Jonah, one he never considered. "I think she's a Fallen Reaper."

The Protector's Ring

"Deyanira ain't no Fallen Reaper. She's a true Reaper, young man. She's a member of the KIN!" Hackett swore under his breath.

"What's the KIN?"

Hackett stared at Jonah like he didn't recognize him. Then his expression turned to one of surprise. "Your godfather never told you?" Jonah shook his head no. "Son, the KIN are a very dangerous and evil sect of Reapers. They have totally shunned the human lives they once lived and despise mortals." Mr. Hackett sighed. "You know, they're the ones who inspired the stereotypes about Reapers. And they personally serve the Grim Reaper."

"Th-there's a Grim Reaper?" Mike stammered.

"Of course, and he's the oldest of all Reapers."

"How's that?" Jonah's dread began to grow, but he had to know more.

"Your godfather should be ashamed of himself." Hackett drew in a breath. "As I hear it, most Reapers serve their term and, they, too, move on. However, long ago, an arrogant Reaper refused to follow the rules. He's remained a Reaper for over two thousand years, gaining power and knowledge about Life and Death.

"He made himself into the Grim Reaper, a deliberate evil image, meant to strike terror in the hearts of mortals. He hated his own former human life so much that he cut up his face and always hides beneath the hood of a red robe. Many of the KIN did the same thing to their faces. They ain't a pleasant bunch. And if Deyanira's involved, that means the Grim Reaper's involved."

Jonah was stunned. He had seen the cuts on Deyanira's face. Now he understood.

Hackett surprised Jonah when he slammed the books shut. "Listen to me, both of you: get out of this and stay out of it." He held up a boney hand as Mike and Jonah both opened their mouths to protest. "No, listen to me. Your parents got killed because of what they found. That's the way it's always gone down. Didn't you listen? Those rings are dangerous because they can control the very power of the universe."

Jonah slumped in his chair.

Mr. Hackett spoke in a calmer voice. "Look, son, you're the same age as my nephew?" Jonah nodded. "You're still too young to be caught up in these things. The legend of the rings is over two thousand years old.

Waiting until you're older won't make any difference. Come and see me then and we'll talk."

"But--" Jonah jerked upright in his chair when Mike kicked him. "Ow!"

They glared at each other. Mr. Hackett didn't seem to notice as he stood and waved them to the doorway. "Remember what I said. Stay away from this stuff."

Mr. Hackett rushed them out of his store, locking the door behind them. Jonah glanced at the front window as he unlocked his bike. Then he rubbed his leg and glared up at Mike. "Hey! Why'd you kick me?"

"I'm sorry, Jonah. I didn't want you to argue with my uncle." Mike glanced back at the store. "Besides, my uncle says he knows a Fallen Reaper."

"Well, so do I. Actually, I know three."

"Jonah, you trust your godfather and his friends."

"And?"

"What if Fallen Reapers aren't the same? Couldn't one be a bad person? You heard what he said about the KIN."

Jonah hadn't considered that. He just assumed that all Fallen Reapers worked with Marcus and the company. In truth, he couldn't know that for sure. As always, the more information he got, the more questions he found.

"You're right," he admitted. "Do you think we should listen to your uncle?"

Mike frowned at him. "Your parents were killed because they found the ring?" Jonah nodded. "You're lucky no one came after you. I mean, if whole families were killed."

Jonah felt a stab of guilt because Mike didn't know they had tried to kill him. Wasn't that why they'd sent the Grim Hound?

"I don't have it, Mike."

"Good."

Jonah sighed and thought about it for a long moment as Mike unlocked his bike. If all the bad guys thought he knew something about the ring, they would eventually show up again. There was only one thing he could do, something he could sense inside.

"I need to find that ring."

CHAPTER TWENTY-SIX
PRACTICE CLUB

Jonah lay out on his bed, thinking about the Protector's Tale. It occupied his mind all during dinner and afterward. It was awesome, in a way, that the ring existed. And his dad had found it. His parents had died to keep it away from Deyanira. *And to protect me.* Jonah pushed that thought away. The question was, where did his parents hide the ring? He was sure they hid it; otherwise, why would someone send Grim Hounds to search their house?

Jonah had just reached for his book bag when someone knocked on his door.

"Yeah?"

Lynn opened the door and leaned against the frame. She had something blue rolled up in one hand as she folded her arms. "You're serious about wanting to learn to protect yourself?"

Jonah had to refocus his mind before he could remember their earlier conversation. "I have to do something," he answered. "If I keep phasing, someone will catch me."

"Why don't you come with me on Saturday? I have a meeting with some friends."

"What kind of meeting?"

"You'll see." Lynn stepped into the room and held the rolled-up bundle right under his nose. "Wear this on Saturday."

Jonah took it and discovered a shirt and a pair of dark blue athletic pants. He held up the shirt. It had the recreation center logo on the left chest with the words *Practice Club* underneath.

He glanced at Lynn. "What's this?"

"It's a uniform."

"What?"

"Just do it, Geek boy." Lynn paused before closing his door. "Be ready to go at noon."

Jonah stared after her, wondering what he needed to be ready to do. *Well*, he thought. *I'll find out soon enough.*

Jonah followed Lynn for several blocks as they cruised through the neighborhoods on the Hightowers' side of town. The afternoon bike ride was easy, yet Jonah fidgeted and looked around, hoping that no one noticed that he and Lynn wore the same thing. His cousin didn't seem bothered at all.

When they reached the elementary school, Lynn led the way through the playground and down a rough incline that ended at the base of a larger, tree-covered hill. A well-worn path angled up the hillside. Lynn started up, and Jonah followed. The thick bushes and shrubs made the climb rough. Lynn made it without getting off her bike. Jonah tried, but he had to hop off his bike halfway up the hill.

He expected Lynn to say something as she waited quietly for him. When Jonah reached her, she got off her own bike and started walking toward a gap in a screen of small trees. A burly Hispanic boy with spiky black hair stepped into view, blocking their path. He wore the same light blue shirt with the logo, and darker athletic shorts.

"What's up, Lynn?"

"Hey Rico."

Rico held up his hands as he came over, exposing tattoos on his arm. "Whoa, nena. Who's this?"

"This is my cousin, Jonah."

"Cousin?" Rico stroked his thin goatee as he eyed Jonah. "I don't know about this. It's gonna cost you to get him in."

"Really?" Lynn crossed her arms and let her bike lean against a hip.

Rico flashed a devilish grin. "You have to go out with me."

"What if I promise not to rub your face in the dirt if you let him in?"

Rico placed his hands over his heart. "You wound me, nena."

Jonah thought Lynn smiled as she edged by Rico and headed for the opening in the trees. Rico watched Lynn walk away with a grin on his face. "We're destined to be together, Lynn," he said. "You'll see."

"Whatever." She motioned to Jonah. "Come on."

Jonah waved and hurried to follow his cousin. Within a few steps, they entered a large circular clearing with a hard red clay surface. The trees shielded the entire area from the view of anyone passing by on the road near the school.

At least twenty teens were scattered around the clearing, talking in loose groups. All wore the same clothing. A few kids were Jonah's age, while others were clearly older than Lynn.

Jonah grew nervous because people were pausing to stare at him. He whispered to Lynn, "What is this place?"

"It's a practice club." Lynn tapped the logo on his shirt. "Everyone here takes some form of martial arts or martial weapons classes sponsored by the rec center. We come here to practice and share what we know with each other."

Lynn placed her bag on a metal wire bench and began wrapping her wrists. "One of the counselors at the rec center started the group a while back. They thought it would give us kids something creative to do during the summer.

"We even have a few former gang members here. I'll admit the practice club keeps the guys out of trouble. Plus, we compete with other practice clubs from other towns." She finished wrapping her wrists, closed her bag, and sat it beside other bags along a strip of grass.

"We do car washes and yard sales at the center to raise money for the trips. It's not a bad way to spend your time." She nodded to a muscular older teen. "I see you're not the only newbie today." Lynn waved to the older boy. "Hey Alex."

Jonah's eye's widened when he saw the skinny kid standing beside Alex. It was Mike. He stood with his head down and hands at his sides. When Mike noticed Jonah, he perked up.

"Good to see you, Lynn." Alex waved and pointed at Jonah. "Who's this?"

"My cousin Jonah. I told you about him."

"Right." Alex and two other boys wore white-collared polo shirts. Alex had his shirt neatly tucked into his dark blue athletic shorts. He stood tall and straight with an important air about himself. A silver whistle hung from a bright silver chain around his neck.

He pulled a folded sheet of paper from his pocket. "Should I add him to the official list?"

"Yeah, I guess so." Lynn pointed to a group of the youngest kids: two boys and one girl.

"You're in the beginning group, over there." She paused to tie her braids behind her head. "Remember, I didn't bring you here to learn to beat up anyone. I just think you'd feel more confident if you learned some basic moves."

When Alex blew his whistle, everyone gathered in what were clearly pre-assigned teams.

Jonah lingered, watching another group of kids take out the practice swords. He turned to join his group and walked straight into someone.

"Yo." Jonah stumbled back and looked up to see the tough looking boy he had met at the creekside behind the teen center. His dark skin appeared to shine in the sunlight. And to Jonah's surprise, he wore a white shirt, like Alex's.

The boy crossed his muscular arms and rubbed his square chin for a moment. "Lynn told me you were coming. You're Jonah, right? My name's Vincent." He didn't offer to shake hands. Instead, he glanced over Jonah's head. "You must be Alex's little brother."

Jonah turned just as Mike came over. Vincent gave the boy the same crossed-arm scrutiny.

The Protector's Ring 205

Mike lowered his gaze and hunched his shoulders. "My name's Mike."

Vincent's somber face broke into a smile. He motioned them toward the rest of the group as he stepped aside. "Go and introduce yourselves, and I'll be back in a sec." Vincent ran off to talk with one of the other group leaders.

As soon as Jonah and Mike joined their group, the tallest boy, with a picky brown Afro and a long thin nose, thrust out his hand.

"Hi. I'm Anthony." He pointed to a shorter, mixed boy standing next to him. "This is Rodney, but we call him Ming, because he's Asian."

Rodney screwed up his face. "I'm not Asian. I'm from Guam."

Jonah blinked at Rodney. "You're Chamorro, right?"

"How did you know?"

"My parents went to Guam on a research project."

Rodney laughed and elbowed Anthony. "I try to tell this hick about my mom's home country all the time, but he won't listen."

Anthony shrugged and began to go through warm-up exercises.

The girl stepped forward. "My name's Lorraine." After that, she whirled away and started doing her own warm-up exercises.

Anthony did a rather impressive series of hand thrusts. Jonah wondered if he showed off for his benefit. Rodney shook his head and started his own warm-up routine.

That left Jonah and Mike with no clue what to do. They exchanged glances. Just then, Alex's voice reached their group. Jonah turned and watched as Lynn and Rico sparred with each other. Lynn's blades moved almost too fast to follow with the eye. She countered every thrust and jab from Rico's practice sword.

"I could never do that," Mike observed.

"It just takes practice."

Mike didn't look sure about that. Jonah shifted his gaze to Alex, who fingered his whistle as he prowled around Lynn and Rico. "Why does your brother have a whistle?"

"He's a drum major. Band camp started last week. I think he uses it for that."

Vincent surprised both boys by clapping his hands right over their heads. "You, new guys. Eyes over here."

He waited as Rodney, Lorraine, and Anthony stood side by side at a sort of attention and bowed. Once that was done, Vincent gave them instructions. Then he focused on Jonah and Mike. He pulled Mike's hands out of his pockets.

"Hands are at your side, in a fist, like this." Vincent demonstrated. "Feet apart, even with your shoulders. This is your ready stance."

Vincent stuck his foot between Jonah's feet to knock them further apart. When Jonah started to look down, Vincent pocked him in the forehead with two fingers and pushed his head back. "Keep your eyes focused straight ahead."

Vincent moved back to Mike and repeated the same actions, spacing his feet apart. Jonah and Mike repeated the ready stance over and over until Vincent was satisfied. Only then did he show them the basic fighting stance.

The time flew, and before Jonah knew it, his first lesson ended. He bowed to Vincent and the others and made his way over to Lynn.

"How did it go?" she asked.

"Vincent's cool." Jonah watched Lynn zip her bag closed before he asked the question that nagged him. "I saw a couple of kids with blades like yours. How can they have Reaper blades?"

Lynn smiled. "They don't. Those blades are regular ones. Like a traditional sai weapon except without the hand guards."

"You mean like Elektra uses?"

"Yes." Lynn hefted her bag, avoiding his gaze. "Come on."

Jonah followed. "You like Elektra." When Lynn blushed, he laughed. "I never thought you'd be into fantasy."

Lynn huffed. "At least she's a woman."

As they reached their bikes and got on, Jonah held back. "Wait. I wanted to ask you something. Can I learn to use the blades?"

"You came here to learn defensive moves."

"Can't I do both?"

The Protector's Ring

"Maybe." Lynn paused, adjusting the straps so her bag lay snuggling against her back. "I thought you'd want to do the sword. A lot of little geeks like you want to pretend they're a Jedi or something."

Jonah didn't say anything because he had considered doing that. However, when he saw Lynn in real action, the choice became obvious. It was personal. His parents had used blades in his dream the last time he had ever seen them alive.

"I want to learn the blades," Jonah repeated.

Lynn watched him for a long time before she nodded. "Okay, but you do it my way. Understand? No complaining, and you have to keep up the lessons with Vincent."

"Deal."

Jonah's personal training with Lynn began Sunday morning when she woke him up just before dawn.

"What?" He blinked the sleep out of his eyes as she pulled his covers off.

"Up. We're going for a morning run. Well, maybe more of a walk for you."

"But..."

"You agreed no complaining." Lynn placed her hands on her hips. "We have to do this early, before church."

Jonah pulled on his socks and sneakers and stumbled out of the kitchen door behind his cousin.

She gave him the once over as she stretched outside. "You're slender, and I bet you don't have any stamina. So we're going to start with building up your endurance."

It didn't take long for him to wake up. True to her word, Lynn started with a run but alternated with walking the first day. She did the same thing on the second day.

By the third morning, Jonah waited for Lynn's knock with his shoes on. As she had done the past two days, she spent the morning building his endurance, followed by a short karate lesson in the backyard. Robert found it amusing until Lynn threatened to use him as a demonstration dummy.

Jonah understood Lynn's method. Even though he itched to try the blades, he also wouldn't give her the satisfaction of complaining. Besides, he needed a better way to deal with kids like Brandon without fear of using his abilities, and this was it. He hoped.

Normally Jonah and Lynn fought each other for the shower after their morning run. But one morning, Lynn went into the kitchen first to make a bit of breakfast. When Jonah shrugged and started for the bathroom, Lynn grabbed his shoulder.

"You've done okay over the past four days. I'm gonna start teaching you the basic blade."

Jonah let out a whoop and pumped his hand in the air. Lynn crossed her arms and waited for him to calm himself and give her a decent bow.

"That's better," she said while pulling a banana off a bundle on the counter. "I want to eat something first."

As Jonah calmed down, Lynn's comment reminded him of how much time had passed. Today was the twentieth of July. He'd been in Mount Vernon for over three weeks. So much had happened that it felt longer to him.

Lynn tapped his forehead. "What's wrong?"

"Nothing. It's just… we only have less than a month before school starts."

Lynn glanced at the kitchen calendar on the wall beside the refrigerator. "Yeah, so? If you're worried you won't have enough time to learn…"

"No. I didn't mean that." He caught the grin on her face and relaxed. "Where are you gonna teach me the blades?"

"Where do you think?" She handed Jonah a banana. "We're going to the practice field."

Robert had come out of his room when Jonah yelled. He wrinkled up his nose as he entered the kitchen and took out the cereal. "You know, we have plenty of hot water if you two want to take showers."

Robert started pouring cereal in a bowl. Lynn threw her banana peel away, then leaned on her brother's shoulder.

The Protector's Ring

"Can't, dear brother. I'm teaching Jonah to use the blades today."

"Really?" Robert forgot about the cereal. "Can I come?"

Jonah opened his mouth to tell Robert he could come along.

Lynn stopped him. "I don't think Jonah needs a crowd his first time out." She grabbed her brother's hand to stop the cereal from spilling on the table. "You're making a mess." She motioned Jonah to the kitchen door. "I'll catch up with you at the Summit."

"Just make sure you take a shower," Robert said as he scooped up the extra cereal.

Lynn stuck her tongue out at her brother.

Jonah waited eagerly as Lynn pulled a pair of practice blades out of the carry case. He pointed at them. "Where's your blades?"

"I'm not letting you use the real thing. Not yet."

"Oh. Sorry."

"I guess I should start with how to handle the blades." She demonstrated, holding the blades in a reverse grip with the blades pointed back along her forearm. "Make sure you position them like this, with your arm rotated." Lynn shifted her arm so the blade faced out, along the outside of her forearm rather than turned underneath.

"The blades are primarily defensive weapons. With your arms rotated like this, the blades can block an attack. Otherwise, your enemy would be able to cut your arms. Understand?" Lynn slipped the blades down into her hands, the hilts out toward Jonah. "You try it."

The blades are heavier than I expected, Jonah thought as he lifted them.

Lynn picked up a practice baton that leaned against a tree. "Now, get into the start position."

Jonah mimicked Lynn's hold on the blades. He thought he did it right until Lynn stepped forward, swung the baton, and smacked it against his right forearm.

He cried out, dropping the blade. "Ow! Why did you do that?"

Lynn wagged a finger at him. "No complaining." She waited for Jonah to nod. "What did I tell you? Rotate the arm. Do it again."

Jonah picked up the blade and got into position again. He concentrated on his right blade and noticed too late that his left blade wasn't in proper alignment. Lynn switched her aim and landed a blow on his left forearm. He grunted, but he didn't drop the blade this time.

In quick succession Lynn went for his right arm, the left, and then the left again. *Crack, crack, crack.* Jonah dropped the blade and rubbed his forearm. Although Lynn's strikes weren't hard, his arms were beginning to ache.

After several more successful whacks on his arms, Lynn stopped and held the baton out to him. "Here. You try it on me." She took the blades and readied herself. Jonah tried one arm, then the next. Lynn blocked each strike and made sure to hold her arms in place for a brief moment before sliding them back into a perfect ready position.

"In time, it'll become second nature to you. Now, try it again."

They switched and worked for another hour.

The Protector's Ring

CHAPTER TWENTY-SEVEN
THE CHALLENGE

When Jonah set out for the recreation center later that afternoon, his forearms were still sore from the blade practice. Maybe he'd take it easy and play some board games, he thought. He locked his bike in the bike rack just as his Death Sense buzzed. For one horrifying moment, Jonah thought another Grim Hound had been sent after him. Then he heard a familiar, snide voice.

"Hey, freak." Brandon strode up to him with Drew and Antwan trailing behind. "I've been looking for you."

Jonah tried to walk around the boy.

Brandon moved to block his path. "I'm talking to you." Jonah stepped right up to him, forcing the other boy to back up before he spoke again. "My parents paid for the mess in the basement."

"That's a lie. Drew's father paid for it." Jonah looked at Drew. "Mike's right. Why do you hang out with him?"

He brushed past Brandon. When the boy reached out, Jonah blocked the other's hand.

Antwan stepped in the way, and Jonah's Death Sense spiked. Brandon repositioned himself in front of Jonah again, and Drew came up behind, boxing him in.

Brandon puffed out his chest. "I don't know how you and your boyfriend got out, but you're gonna pay."

"Ooooh, I'm really scared now."

"I hear you're part of that little practice club."

"So what if I am?"

Antwan tapped Brandon on the shoulder and said, "Challenge him."

"Yeah," Brandon nodded. "I challenge you to a blade duel."

Jonah opened his mouth to accept, but paused. Lynn would be furious with him if he accepted.

Brandon laughed. "What's the matter? You scared to face me?"

Antwan and Drew snickered.

"Just like I thought, guys," Brandon sneered. "He's a chicken."

"I accept, jerk." The words were premature, but man, he wanted to wipe that sneer off Brandon's face. "Just tell me when and where."

"Meet me on Summer's End, at the practice field. Six o'clock. Be there, freak."

Jonah nodded as Brandon walked off, his mind racing. How horribly would Lynn kill him when she heard about the challenge?

"You did what?" Lynn shouted at the top of her lungs. Jonah tried to escape to his room, but she followed, knocking his door open to continue her tirade. "This is exactly what I didn't want to happen, Jonah! How could you accept a challenge from Brandon?"

"He made fun of me."

That statement got Lynn to calm down a little. "Jonah, you do realize that it isn't Brandon that you're angry about?"

"I think nearly being killed by falling junk is enough to make me angry with him."

"You're angry about all the things that happened to you." Lynn paused, took a breath, and plunged on. "You're angry about your parents and your old house and all the things you've lost. Brandon is just a convenient excuse."

"You don't know what you're talking about! You don't know what it's like to lose your parents." His anger had spilled out before he could stop it. He

The Protector's Ring

expected Lynn to hit him, but she watched him with a sad look on her face. It took him a second to see he'd just proven her point.

"See what I mean?" Lynn began. "Brandon is good at hitting people's buttons. He's got yours, and he knows it. Never let your enemies control you. That's the sure way to lose."

Jonah dropped onto the bed. Lynn sat next to him.

"I used to be like you, Jonah, two years ago. When Mom took the blades away from me, I got angry. I could have done something stupid. Well, I did, in a way. I broke into the locker and took the real blades. I think my mom saw the anger in me." Lynn toyed with the end of one of her braids. "Then I met Rico, Alex, and the others and I started working with them. I can hear Rico now. 'You have to stop letting people push your buttons, nena.'"

She smiled. "I listened to him, and I don't feel the anger anymore. It's what the practice club is all about. It's helped a lot of kids."

"But you wanted to break his neck the other day."

"I can lose my temper sometimes, but I wouldn't have hurt Brandon. At most, I would have had a few words with him." She nudged him. "You know that, right?"

"Yeah, I guess so."

"Anyway, I knew if Vincent and the others could change their attitudes, I could."

Jonah nodded as he stared down at his feet. "I'm sorry."

"It's okay. The next time Brandon tries to get to you, be ready for him."

"I can't back out now, can I?"

"Are you kidding? It'll be a cold day in hell before I let that snob beat up my little cousin."

"So you'll help me?"

"Yes, I'll help you." Lynn shook Jonah's head with her hand. "Geek boy."

They started the very next day. When he groaned at the increase in the training, she put her hands on her hips. "Falling down and panting for breath is a sure way to lose."

Jonah's face warmed and he conceded her point. As he started into the routine again, the desperate run from the Grim Hound popped into his mind. He'd been at the end of his endurance. If Kevin hadn't ignored Marcus and shown up, he would be dead.

Yet, if he learned to use the blades like Kevin, he wouldn't have to run. He could defend himself, no matter what his godfather said. Buoyed with that thought, Jonah didn't complain anymore.

After he and Lynn finished, Jonah lingered on the practice field, continuing to train. He was concentrating so completely that when he noticed movement near the clearing's opening, he figured Lynn had returned. Instead, Mike stood in the clearing. He laid his bike down and walked over, making sure to keep out of the way of the practice sword.

"Jonah, where have you been?"

"Busy." Jonah continued to move through the positions.

"So it's true?" Mike asked. "You're really going to duel with Brandon?"

Jonah stopped to face him. "Yes, I am."

"But Jonah, that's crazy!"

"I have to do it."

"No, you don't. Besides, will it be fair? You're--"

"I'm what?"

Mike refused to meet his gaze. "Nothing."

"If I don't stand up to Brandon, he'll keep trying to bully me."

"He's jealous of you. Beating him won't change that."

"Backing out of the duel now won't help, either. I'm in, and that's it."

Jonah started into another exercise. Mike watched him for a moment.

"Fighting's not the answer!"

"You're in the practice club."

"Yeah, to learn to protect myself. But you picked a fight with Brandon."

"So…"

"I bet Lynn wasn't happy."

The Protector's Ring **215**

Jonah paused again, his concentration gone. Mike had hit the mark.

"Brandon's a bully," Mike pressed. "When you fight, you're no better than people like him!"

"You didn't feel that way when I helped you in the library."

"You stood up to Brandon."

"I'm doing that now."

"No! You didn't fight him. You faced him. That took courage, Jonah. This is just--" Mike slapped his hands against his legs in frustration. "We should be looking for that ring, Jonah." Mike stepped closer. "Come on. Let's find that ring. I thought it was important to you."

"It is important."

"Then forget this duel. Please. You should concentrate on finding out about the ring."

"I'm not backing down." Jonah whirled away from Mike as doubt gnawed at him. "So get over it."

Mike stood on the spot for a stunned minute before he ran to his bike. He hurried out of the clearing without looking back. Jonah hated himself; Mike wasn't wrong. He had slacked off on searching for the ring. That was true. But once Brandon was no longer a threat, he'd go back to it. For now, he needed to be ready for the Summer's End Festival, which was only a week away.

CHAPTER TWENTY-EIGHT
MIDNIGHT MEETUP

Mike didn't speak to Jonah at the Saturday club practice and avoided him all the next week. That bothered Jonah, but he'd made his decision. Besides, with another week of extra training with Lynn completed, he was confident in his ability to beat Brandon. He often found himself mimicking his dad's style with the blades, when Lynn wasn't around.

All-in-all, Jonah went to bed feeling a bit better about the coming duel. He certainly didn't expect to dream of a wind-swept clearing in some far land. Just when Jonah wondered why he was there, Marcus phased into view. His godfather stood tall, waiting.

A second later, a vortex blossomed into life and Jonah gasped as Neera, the witch from the bookstore, stepped through. Her black dress looked even more ominous emerging from the swirling mass of vapor.

Marcus shouted over the howling wind, "Why do you persist? You'll never find it."

"I will have the ring, Marcus. It's only a matter of time. Perhaps the boy knows something."

"Jonah doesn't know anything."

The woman threw back her head and laughed. Then she began circling around Marcus. "The Wraiths are upset about the boy; they think he's dangerous."

"He's just a boy, that's all."

The Protector's Ring

"The son of Isaiah cannot be innocent. His very existence is a threat to everything we've built."

"You won't harm Jonah as long as I live."

Neera grinned at Marcus. "Have it your way, Fallen One."

Jonah watched in horror as the woman's features morphed into something more skeletal. He yelled as horrible scars erupted across her face. Her red hair fell away, carried on the wind until little more than a ponytail remained. The black dress changed into a long, blood-red hooded robe. She produced two glowing blades out of the folds.

Deyanira and Neera were the same person. Jonah couldn't believe he'd been face to face with the woman who helped kill his parents. He recalled Kevin's comment that Marcus followed Neera. Now he understood why.

Marcus activated his blades and dropped into a fighting stance. He and Deyanira shouted to each other and lunged. Light and pain exploded in Jonah's mind as their blades met.

He woke up in his bed with his heart racing. Somewhere out there, Marcus and Deyanira continued in a fierce battle.

The image of Marcus fighting a transformed Neera continued to haunt Jonah all the next day as he spent the afternoon, after the practice club, helping Wick research an article on the supernatural. Jonah's guilt over his fight with Mike didn't help matters. It seemed his friend was right. The ring continued to be important to everyone surrounding him.

Once or twice, Jonah felt the urge to tell Wick and his cousins about the dream, and each time, he decided against the idea. However, by that evening, he couldn't hold out any longer. At least they should know the bookstore woman's true identity.

Everyone gathered at the Hightowers' to play video games. Aunt Imma was in her art room and Uncle James had carried his stack of newspapers to his bedroom to read. That left Lynn, Robert, Wick, and Jonah free to talk as they played videos. Jonah had called Mike, but his friend had been frosty on the phone and refused to stop by.

That was just as well, Jonah thought. He'd never told his cousins that Mike knew his secret, so he could talk about Deyanira without bringing up that problem. Before Jonah could think better of the idea, he blurted it out.

"Neera's not a witch. She's a true Reaper named Deyanira." Only after he said it did he realize he hadn't given them any warning.

Robert and Wick stopped playing their video game and stared at him. They didn't even notice their players being killed on the screen. Lynn, as usual, seemed a little suspicious.

Wick sat down his controller and grinned at Jonah. "So, you're a psychic now? Did that just come in a vision?"

Lynn reached over and yanked on a couple of Wick's twists. "Be serious." She stood beside the sofa, arms folded. "How do you know that, Jonah?"

"Marcus told me. I forgot to mention it."

"How can Deyanira or Neera interact with us? Robert saw her. The store clerk works with her."

Jonah shrugged, regretting mentioning that much. "I don't know. Marcus didn't explain that to me."

Lynn scowled and Jonah gave her the best innocent look he could make. "When did you talk to Marcus?" she asked.

Jonah's mind raced and he grabbed his cell phone. "I got a text." He thought the excuse sounded lame and doubted it would fly.

"That doesn't sound like the Marcus you've told us about," Lynn offered, shaking her head.

He hopped off the sofa and headed for the patio. "I have to send him another message."

Lynn watched Jonah until he closed the patio door. He didn't lie to his cousin, and he set about typing the message that proved it. He wanted to meet with Marcus.

He didn't expect his phone to buzz in response five minutes into his video game. He gave up his turn and hurried into the kitchen to read the text.

Jonah, meet me by the backyard shed at midnight. Marcus

"Do you have more information to share?" Lynn asked as soon as Jonah came back and sat on the sofa.

"Nope."

At midnight, Jonah peeked out of his bedroom. The house was quiet. He snuck through the family room to the patio door and had almost opened it before he remembered to turn off the alarm. Once it was disarmed, he slipped outside into the hot July night. He nearly jumped out of his skin when he heard the rustle of cloth in the shadows beside the shed.

Marcus stepped into the moonlight, and Jonah noticed immediately that his godfather carried himself stiffly and leaned against a tree for support. Jonah moved to help him, but Marcus held up a hand.

"I'm fine. There's no need to worry."

The sight of Marcus's injuries brought the dream rushing back into Jonah's mind, and he forgot about his initial reason for contacting the Fallen Reaper.

"Why didn't you tell me about Neera?"

"What do you mean?"

"She's a Reaper called Deyanira and she…" Jonah choked back the rest, realizing he was about to mention the dream about his parents. "I know you fought her," Jonah admitted. "That's why you're hurt."

"How do you know that?" Marcus stepped away from the tree. "Who told you that?"

"No one told me. I saw it in a dream. You and Deyanira argued about the ring, and then you fought each other."

Even in the darkness, Jonah could see Marcus's eyes widen. "I shouldn't be surprised by your abilities." He let out a breath. "How long have you been dreaming like this?"

Jonah shuffled his feet on the soft grass and refused to meet Marcus's gaze. "I've been able to do it for a couple of years. It only happens when I'm worried about something."

"You were worried about me?"

Jonah nodded. "I know Deyanira wanted the ring my dad found." He watched Marcus as closely as he could in the dark.

Marcus shook his head. "I'm not getting you involved in that. Just keep your head down."

"Keeping my head down didn't stop a Grim Hound from attacking me."

"That's why I agreed to start your training." Marcus paused as if winded. "How did it go, with Kevin?"

"It was cool. I remembered what he said and phased to get away from a bully."

Marcus pushed himself into a standing position. "Jonah. We're not training you to use your powers on everyday… teen problems."

"I had to. Me and my friend Mike would have been hurt if I didn't."

"You phased someone with you?"

"It's cool." Jonah shouted. He cringed when his voice rang out across the quiet yard and he lowered his voice. "Mike knew about Fallen Reapers. His uncle owns a bookstore and he told us about the Protector's Ring."

Marcus stood at his full height. "Obviously you've been busy." He wiped a hand over his forehead. "I'm serious, Jonah. Phasing Mike could have been disastrous. We have ways of cleaning up or hiding our true selves from others."

Jonah sucked in a breath. "Kevin mentioned Memory Charmers, like Omar. Is that what he does?"

"Sometimes, yes. You have to be careful."

"I'm know."

"Are you practicing?"

Jonah nodded. "I'm tired of only doing it when I'm scared. It's going to get me in trouble sooner or later."

Marcus paused, gazing at Jonah. "Being able to control your phasing ability was supposed to make my job easier." Marcus gave him a tired smile, then winced in obvious pain. "We can discuss these things at another date. I need time to think about your ability to eavesdrop."

"Wait. When can I have another lesson?"

"Give me the week to regain my strength. Let's say Saturday morning?"

Jonah nodded.

"Keep practicing on your own. Good night." Marcus stepped into the shadows and vanished.

CHAPTER TWENTY-NINE
DREAM WALKING

Marcus arrived at the Hightowers' home on Saturday morning. After a brief conference in the dining room with Uncle James and Aunt Imma, he led Jonah outside to the car.

When Marcus got into the driver's seat, Jonah gave in to his curiosity. "What did you tell my aunt and uncle?"

Marcus started the car and let it idle as he answered. "I told them I wanted to spend a little time with you so we could talk about how you're adjusting."

"Oh."

"In addition to that," Marcus went on, "today, I want to take you for a little drive. I deemed it appropriate to let your aunt and uncle know you were with me."

Marcus drove them north out of Mount Vernon. Thirty minutes later, he reached a wide entrance to an open pasture. He pulled to the side and motioned for Jonah to get out. They stood beside the car, looking out over the fields.

"Observe your surroundings," Marcus began, "and remember what you see. As Kevin should have mentioned in the first lesson, phasing is about clearly picturing where you want to go in your mind."

Jonah followed his godfather's instructions and noted his surroundings. There were tree-covered hills in the distance and wide pastures on either side of the highway. This was pretty easy to picture, Jonah decided.

He frowned and turned back to Marcus. "Kevin phased to me at the old gas station. How could he picture that if he'd never been there?"

Marcus gave Jonah a big smile.

"I hoped you would notice that. When a Reaper is given an assignment, a bond is created between the Reaper and the mortal. They use that bond to locate the mortal. I'm able to perform a similar action with you."

Jonah's eyes widened. "That's how you knew I was in trouble with the Grim Hound?"

Marcus nodded.

"But Kevin showed up, not you. He doesn't have a connection to me, does he?"

"No, he doesn't." Marcus took Jonah's arm in a light grip before he could ask another question. "Are you ready?"

"Yes. What are we--"

A moment later, he and Marcus stood on a tree-covered hillside overlooking a valley below.

Marcus released Jonah. "How far do you think we've come?"

"I don't know."

"Think about it."

Jonah didn't have any idea how to do that. Marcus tapped him on the forehead. "A Reaper can feel the distance."

"But I'm not a Reaper."

Marcus smiled. "Close your eyes."

"Why?"

"Close your eyes and think about it."

Jonah obeyed. He concentrated, and to his surprise, he did feel something that he couldn't translate into words. "I can't tell for sure. I'm sorry."

"That's understandable, Jonah. You'll be able to tell when you've gained more experience." Marcus gestured around them. "We're about three miles away. I know that's farther than you've ever phased. Now, all you have to do is phase back to the car. It's simple." He gave Jonah a small wave and vanished.

The Protector's Ring

"Marcus!" Jonah looked around and waited for Marcus to reappear. *Maybe he's playing a trick*, Jonah thought.

As the seconds turned into minutes, Jonah realized that Marcus had abandoned him on the hillside. At that moment, panic and doubt began to fill his mind. How could Marcus do this to him?

Jonah's heart raced and his breathing quickened. "Take me back, take me back." He said it over and over until the air rippled around him and suddenly, he stood several feet away from Marcus and the car.

Jonah ran over, shouting, "Why did you leave me there? I could have been lost!"

Marcus, who had leaned against the car when Jonah first appeared, stood tall, facing the boy for several tense seconds. At last, his shoulders relaxed and he folded his arms as he leaned against the car again. "You're supposed to be learning to phase with a clear head."

"But you left me!"

"Yes. I wanted to know if you would keep a cool head and remember all that you've learned. Clearly, you panicked and then phased here."

Shame began to slowly replace Jonah's anger. He had asked Marcus to teach him how to phase, and now he acted paranoid. Jonah shook off that sad thought, not willing to let go of all his anger.

"What if I couldn't have done it?"

"I knew you could do it. You just needed a little push."

"But what if I couldn't?"

"Jonah, I wouldn't leave you out there alone." Marcus's eyes widened and he stepped forward, gripping Jonah by the shoulders. "I'm sorry. I should have known you'd be sensitive to people leaving you."

"I'm not sensitive." Jonah shrugged out of Marcus's grip and refused to meet the Fallen Reaper's gaze.

Marcus motioned for Jonah to follow. "Come here."

He walked around to the back of the car and opened the trunk. Inside was a backpack and bottled water.

"I would have phased back to you," Marcus explained. "And if I didn't have enough power to bring us both here, we could have taken a nice hike back to the car."

"But, but what if I phased short and got lost?"

"I can sense where you are, Jonah. When I agreed to your parents' request it created a special bond between you and I." Marcus looked Jonah straight in the eye. "I'm connected to you, Jonah. I'll always be able to find you."

"Always?"

"Yes. Well, at least until you're eighteen."

Jonah's eyes went out of focus as he thought about it. "Why? Is that important in the Supernatural world?"

"No. Thirteen is the age when a supernatural being gains his or her powers. I'll always be your godfather, but you'll be an adult at eighteen, and the bond ends." Marcus paused. "It was your parents' decision." He closed the trunk. "Do you believe me?" Jonah nodded. "Now, can you do it again, with a clear head?"

Jonah turned and looked around. *Why not?* With Marcus standing behind him, assuring him he'd be there, Jonah knew he could phase back to the hillside. He stepped away from Marcus and stood in a perfect ready stance.

In a Yoda-type voice, he said, "Size matters not. Distance matters not."

Marcus cocked an eyebrow, and Jonah laughed to himself. At least Wick would have appreciated it. And with that thought, he closed his eyes, took a breath, and phased.

Marcus and Jonah rode back to Mount Vernon in an uncomfortable silence. His godfather told him he did well today, but his face didn't match his words.

After several more quiet minutes, Jonah couldn't hold back. "What's bothering you?"

"Why do you think something's bothering me?"

"You have that look."

The Protector's Ring

Marcus glanced at him in surprise and laughed. "Omar always says the same thing about me."

"So what's wrong?"

"Your dreams concern me, Jonah. I've been thinking about it, and I've concluded that they must be a form of phasing. You said that when you're really worried about something, you tend to have the dreams. My guess is you're sensing the person involved and phasing to their location."

"But how can it be phasing when the people never see me? It's like I'm not really there. I'm like a ghost."

Marcus flinched when Jonah said that, then quickly spoke to cover it. "I'm not saying it's exactly like phasing. I'm suggesting that it's similar. In fact, I think…"

"What?"

"I think your soul is traveling or phasing to these locations. If not for the fact that you see things as they happen, I would call them visions. It's more like an out-of-body experience."

Jonah's jaw dropped as he considered that. He'd come across out-of-body and astral projection in his research after his first dream. He glanced at his godfather. "How about dream-walking?"

Marcus nodded. "You have to understand, Jonah, you're the first half-Reaper, so anything is possible." Marcus looked at him. "If it is your soul, that takes on a different meaning because you're half-Reaper. And nobody understands what you'll become as you mature."

"That's why Deyanira wants me dead." The statement didn't scare him as much anymore.

"For what it's worth, I don't believe Deyanira wants you dead."

"Why not? She helped kill my parents." Even as Jonah said it, he knew that wasn't totally true. Deyanira had offered his dad an exchange. She wanted the ring.

"I know it sounds unbelievable, Jonah, but no one knows what would happen if you…"

"If I what? If I die?"

Marcus stared at the road ahead and didn't meet Jonah's eyes. "I didn't want to say that."

"What could happen to me if I die?"

Marcus's hands gripped the steering wheel tightly. "The decision to turn someone into a Reaper is made at the highest levels. You're only a half-Reaper, yet you have the powers of a full Reaper, and more. You could become even more powerful."

Jonah couldn't believe it. Was everyone afraid that he could become some kind of super Reaper if he died? Could he really become dangerous?

He glanced at Marcus. "Deyanira or someone else is going to come after me, aren't they?"

"Deyanira's focus for the last year has been on the object your father found."

"You mean the ring."

Marcus let out a low breath. "Yes, I mean the ring. She meant those comments she made as a taunt for me. It's what she does."

"What about the other Reapers?"

"Despite that spat of sightings around the time of your birthday, I don't think most Reapers really know about you." Marcus glanced sideways at Jonah. "You have to stop worrying about all this."

"Why?"

"It's dangerous, Jonah. Eventually, the beings you spy on may be able to sense your presence. If that happens, they could hurt you. Just promise me you'll try."

"Okay." Jonah tapped his knuckle against the window. *Keep from worrying?* He was learning to use the blades and phase. And he had the duel with Brandon in five days. Plus his best friend wouldn't talk to him which reminded Jonah he still didn't know where to find the Protector's Ring. After all of that, he would start a new school. As he saw it, he had more than enough to worry about.

CHAPTER THIRTY
REAPERS

Jonah changed into his practice clothes and rushed to the practice field after Marcus dropped him off. Anthony, Lorraine, and Rodney were stunned when he worked out with the blade group at practice. Mike, who ignored his own training to watch Jonah, received ten laps around the clearing from Vincent. When practice ended for the day, Rodney was the only one of Jonah's original group to wave goodbye. Mike slipped out of the clearing with his brother Alex without speaking.

Jonah frowned, wondering if he should have listened to Mike and backed out of the duel. Finding the ring was important and Jonah told himself he could do both, but in reality, he couldn't. He stood, gazing at the exit and not moving to put his things away when Lynn tapped his shoulder.

"What's up?"

"Huh?" Jonah focused on her. "Nothing. You didn't tell me what I did wrong?"

"That's because you're getting better."

"Really?"

"Yeah." Lynn closed up her bag. Rico and Vincent motioned to her, and she ran over to talk with them.

Jonah gathered his things, feeling happier than he had in days, despite his trouble with Mike. But he also couldn't shake the feeling that something was up with Lynn. Even on his best days, she always found something for him to improve. Mike wasn't the only one unfocused today, Jonah decided.

His waning happiness shifted to confusion when Robert and Wick waltzed into the clearing.

"What are you two doing here?"

Robert stood right beside Jonah and glanced at Lynn.

"We're betting on you killing Brandon in five days." Robert lowered his voice. "Thought we'd come by and watch practice."

Wick slapped Jonah on the back, coming around to his other side. "We wanted to make sure we're not gonna lose our money, Padawan."

Jonah didn't know whether to laugh or not. "Are you guys serious?"

Robert nodded. "The odds are on the home team to beat the kid from DC. Sorry, little cousin."

"You're betting against me?"

Wick squeezed his shoulder. "Of course we aren't betting against you. We know you have powers."

"I can't use my powers."

"Well, you can't phase in front of everyone, little cousin." Robert glanced in Lynn's direction again. "When you beat Brandon, we'll make a ton of money. It should be a great Summer's End."

"Why's it called Summer's End?"

Robert traded a disbelieving look with Wick. "It marks the last week of summer vacation, so it's called…"

"…Summer's End," Wick concluded.

"Back to business, little cousin. You need to beat Brandon."

"It couldn't hurt to use a little power, either," Wick added, giving him a wink.

Jonah opened his mouth to protest and Robert held up a finger. "Not too loud."

Jonah pushed his cousin's hand aside. "How will people know who won? You're not gonna record it, are you?"

Robert smiled. "We have that handled. You just beat Brandon. You didn't look too bad out there."

The Protector's Ring

"You saw the practice?"

"Yeah." Wick pointed to the treeline. "We sat out there."

Jonah laughed, but Wick and Robert's expression sobered. Jonah understood why when Lynn gripped his shoulder.

"Let's go to the Summit." Lynn pushed Jonah toward the exit.

All at once, Jonah suspected that whatever they had planned, this was the real reason Wick and Robert had come by the practice field and the reason why Lynn had seemed distracted all session. His insides begin to squirm. *At least my Death Sense isn't going off*, he thought.

Wick dropped his large black book down on the steamer trunk. Unfortunately, it sounded like a gunshot in the quiet attic clubhouse. Robert scowled at his friend.

Wick gave him a weak smile. "Sorry."

Lynn all but ordered Jonah to sit in the spongy arm chair. Now she stood over him, arms crossed. "You've been holding out on us."

"What do you mean?"

Lynn flicked her braids over a shoulder without answering. Instead, Wick cracked open the large book, opening it to a bookmarked page.

Jonah glanced at the heading at the top and his insides froze. It said *Reapers*.

Wick cleared his throat and began reading. "Reapers collect the souls of the dead and, wow, I never paid attention to this. They can't be seen by mortals." He paused, glancing at the others. Lynn gave him an impatient wave to keep reading. He leaned over the book again. "Here we go. Reapers are able to appear at the location of their next soul reap. The term for this ability varies and includes apparrating, tunneling, portaling, and phasing." Wick sighed. "I'm sorry, dude. You told us you can phase."

Lynn snapped her fingers. "What else does it say about Reapers?"

Wick hesitated before glancing down at the book again. "Let's see. Reapers are drawn to scenes of death as part of their job. They... can sense death in general."

Robert came to stand beside Wick. "Reapers have Death Sense."

"It doesn't actually say Death Sense." Jonah tried to hold down his panic, but he could see that his cousins and Wick weren't gonna accept that lame point. And having Lynn standing right over him made Jonah feel trapped.

Thankfully, Lynn sat down on the edge of the steamer trunk, facing him. "What I don't understand is how can you have Reaper powers?"

Anger built up inside Jonah and an irrational disregard for keeping his secret overcame him. "I'm a Reaper. Okay?"

Robert gripped Jonah's shoulder. "You can't be, little cousin."

"Why not?"

"Reapers are the Undead and exist on the other side."

Wick reached over and poked Jonah in the chest. "You aren't dead, let alone an undead being."

"There's a passage in the book about Fallen Ones. Are you one of those, little cousin?"

"No." Jonah slumped under the weight of the older kids' questions. "My dad was."

Wick's eyebrows shot up in excitement. Robert and Lynn carried identical, slightly out of focus gazes. Jonah wondered if they were replaying everything they remembered about his mom and dad. After several quiet, tense moments, Lynn nodded.

"This explains everything." She gazed at Jonah. "So, what are you?"

"I'm a half-Reaper. The only one, according to Marcus."

"What's Marcus? Is he…"

Jonah nodded. "He's a Fallen Reaper."

Wick let out a slow whistle as he ruffled his twists. He seemed pleased about this, but Robert looked a bit spooked, Jonah thought.

"We talked about it," Robert said. "Lynn and I agreed that you had to be something more than, you know, a normal person. I mean, you can see Grim Hounds, sense death, and even do that phase thing? No regular person can do that."

The Protector's Ring

"And we can't forget the gifts your parents sent us," Lynn added. "They aren't exactly normal. We've known for a while there was something different about your family, Jonah."

Robert nodded in agreement. "Can I ask you question?"

"Robert, don't…" Lynn shook her head.

Jonah found it odd to see his cousins disagree about something secret. That made him more curious to hear Robert's question. "Yeah, I guess."

"I'm warning you." Lynn raised her fist.

Robert blinked and looked between his sister's fist and Jonah. He swallowed and hunched his shoulder as if expecting to get hit. "Can you suck out our souls?"

"Robert!" Lynn shot to her feet and punched her brother in the bicep.

"Ow!" Robert clamped his hand over the injured arm, glaring back at his sister. "You and Wick wanted to know."

Jonah's moment of curiosity over his cousins' disagreement evaporated as the anger returned. He saw the fear in Robert's eyes and the way Lynn's hand shook as she toyed with one of her braids.

"No, I can't suck out your soul. I'm only a half-Reaper."

"That's good, little cousin."

Jonah shot to his feet, facing Robert and Lynn. "My dad never did anything like that. Marcus and Kevin didn't do that. Besides, Marcus told me that Reapers help souls, not suck them out like monsters." His voice bounced off the wooden attic ceiling.

Robert held up his hands. "Alright. I was just asking."

The anger continued to build and Jonah's pulse thudded in his ear. He started to pace back and forth until Lynn reached out for him.

"Jonah, listen--"

"No." Before Jonah knew it, he ran for the attic stairs, descending them two at a time.

Robert shouted from behind, "Stop him."

Jonah leaped down the last few steps and slammed into the attic door before he could open it. He recovered and started to pull it open as Lynn reached the top of the stairs. She was fast, but Jonah's thoughts were faster. He phased before Lynn could grab him.

Jonah appeared in the clearing by the creek behind the recreation center. *Why not use my Reaper power?* However, he took a wrong step and stumbled backward over one of the flat stones. Jonah landed hard on the ground and tumbled into the shallow water.

"Dang it!" The tepid water sloshed over him, soaking his clothes. He climbed out of the creek and sat down on the nearest flat rock. He took off his wet shoes and socks and sat there, seething with anger. He wanted to be normal, but he never was, and he never would be. That Seer back in Virginia had been right about him. He could see the fear on his cousins' faces.

It wasn't fair that all these things happened to him. He never did anything to anyone. He hated being here. He hated this place. He hated everything about his life.

Jonah wanted to scream and cry at the same time. In a fit of frustration, he took his wet sneakers and flung them away. He didn't even care when he heard them splash into the creek.

Lynn stepped into view and came over to stare down at Jonah with her hands on her hips. "If you're done feeling sorry for yourself, I have a question for you, genius."

"Lynn, I don't want to hear it…"

"Shut up and listen anyway."

Jonah shot to his feet, his hands balled into fists. For a wild second, he found himself wishing for power that would let him attack. Jonah shivered at the thought. Yet the anger over the unfairness of it all thundered in his ears.

Lynn dropped into a ready stance. "Go ahead, Geek boy."

Her nickname released a dam inside of Jonah. Before he knew it, he swung at her. His anger prevented him from concentrating and remembering everything he'd learned, and Lynn blocked all his swings and kicks but resisted pressing her advantage. Jonah grew even more frustrated. His technique suffered, causing him to overreach with a punch. Lynn easily slipped under his arm, came up behind, and pinned him in a head lock.

The Protector's Ring **233**

"Let me go!" Jonah screamed and struggled.

Lynn obliged and shoved him forward. She also hooked her foot between his feet, causing him to trip and land face-first in the muddy creek water. When he sputtered and tried to raise himself, Lynn planted a foot in the small of his back and pushed him down. He roared in frustration as he pulled his head out of the water for a second time. She caught him up in a tight hold, planting her feet to either side to keep him from flipping her over. He struggled, pushed, and screamed, and through it all, Lynn held on to him.

Jonah smacked the water over and over again with his fists, letting all the anger, frustration, and fear out. After what felt like forever, the fit subsided and he let go of the troubling impulse to lash out. He took gulping breaths as he tried to stop the tears that splashed into the water, only inches from his face. Lynn's hold on him turned into a gentle rocking motion until the sobs gave way to slow, shallow sniffles.

She never said anything. When Jonah relaxed, she changed her grip and helped him stand, wrapping her arms around his shoulders. "Are you done?"

He nodded and she helped him onto the bank and sit down on a stone. Then she knelt in front of him and peered into his eyes.

Jonah refused to look at her at first, but Lynn tapped his forehead until he met her gaze.

She spoke in a quiet voice. "Can I ask you my question now?" She waited for Jonah to nod. "Why did you run?"

"You all think I'm a freak, a monster."

"No we don't, and we never said that."

Jonah blinked at his cousin. "Then why did Robert ask if I could suck out his soul?"

"Robert's being an idiot, that's all."

"You thought the same thing."

"Well, fine. I won't lie to you." Lynn leaned back. "Everyone knows that Reapers take souls. So yeah, I wondered about that."

"See!"

"Jonah, I know you wouldn't do that, even if you could." Lynn waited, but Jonah didn't want to yell anymore. "If you had waited, Robert and I had something to tell you."

"What?"

"We aren't normal, either." Lynn swallowed and gazed off. "I have very strong intuition about things. It runs in the women on my dad's side. My Aunt Ruby has it and your mom had it, big time."

Jonah wiped his eyes, unable to believe what he was hearing. "I didn't know that."

"Obviously. Think about it, Jonah. That's why your parents knew they could send the gifts to us. Once we had them, your mom came to talk with us all the time. I bet she had the feeling that you should be here, with us."

"What about Robert?"

"Oh, he gets images in his head when he concentrates on what someone is thinking. It works best if he's drawing, and the person is really thinking about a particular thing." Lynn lowered her gaze, causing Jonah to think she was embarrassed. "We've developed a routine for getting information from people. We've gotten good stories that way."

Jonah's eyes widened. "That's… kind of cool." He sucked in a breath, remembering the times that images exploded in his head while talking to Robert. "He did it to me?"

"Yeah. We thought you knew more about where the gifts came from. Your mom promised to tell us when…" Lynn's own eyes widened and she stood.

"What?"

"I think she meant to tell us when you turned thirteen."

"Oh."

"We weren't making fun of you." She waited a minute before starting in again. "That brings me to my last point. Jonah, you're not alone. Robert, Wick, and I are part of this, so stop trying to handle it all by yourself."

Lynn's frown was a signal, Jonah knew, that she wanted to goad him into seeing the situation as she did. He didn't know what to say, so he sat there and stared into the little creek. But he thought Lynn was right.

The Protector's Ring

"Why did I get so angry?"

Lynn's expression grew serious. "You still have a lot of anger inside. I thought the practice club would help."

"I'm sorry I tried to attack you."

"Don't apologize. You need to get it out, otherwise it'll eat you up inside." She leaned forward, meeting his gaze. "We don't understand everything that's happening, so don't jump to hasty conclusions. Okay?"

Jonah nodded. "I won't."

Lynn tapped Jonah on the shoulder. "Come on."

Jonah stood up, holding his wet socks in one hand. Lynn's eyes widened as they moved from the sopping socks down to Jonah's bare feet. "Where are your shoes?"

Jonah pointed at the creek, his face growing warm with embarrassment.

"Why'd you throw them in the water?"

"I didn't mean to do it."

Lynn shook her head and muttered something about geeks as Jonah sloshed into the creek to fetch his shoes.

CHAPTER THIRTY-ONE
DEYANIRA'S CHAMBER

Jonah stood in a dank, torch-lit passageway with a low ceiling. Directly ahead, at the end of the passage, was a modern-looking steel door with a blinking display set into the stone wall. *Why am I here*, Jonah wondered, trying to puzzle out the mixture of old and new in this dream-walk. Voices and footsteps sounded behind him. He turned and saw a darkened stairway made of the same rough stone as the walls.

Marcus's warning about being detected in his dream-walks popped into Jonah's head. Before he could move, the bookstore clerk descended the stairs, followed by a young man and woman. They were engaged in an argument.

The woman voice's was an angry whisper. "You were right to attack the boy with that Grim Hound. He's dangerous."

The clerk made a sharp jerk of his head. "That wasn't my decision to make. I paid for that mistake."

"If the boy finds the ring, he'll condemn us to this plane forever." The young man pounded his own chest with a clenched fist. "The promises to our kind will mean nothing!"

The clerk whirled to face the man and woman. "You repeat the Grim Reaper's fears and propaganda. Even the most powerful of our Seers don't agree with him. As long as our king trusts the counsel of the Seers instead of the empty promises of the Reapers, none of us are to harm the boy."

The Protector's Ring

The argument took place less than half a dozen feet from Jonah, pressed against the wall. He thought it lucky that they argued with each other. All three acted as if he wasn't there, and he breathed easier.

The clerk stepped by Jonah, lifting a small, round object that he wore around his neck. It wasn't the Ankh amulet, which the man still wore. This object was smaller, made of a slender piece of carved wood, and with multi-colored beads attached to one end. The clerk held it high, and a distortion appeared in the air in front of him.

The strange barrier parted like curtains as the clerk stepped forward. He passed through three more similar distortions before reaching the metal door and typing a code into the wall-mounted keypad. Jonah edged forward. Just as he crossed the first distortion, it closed, touching him. Pain lanced Jonah's arm, and he gasped.

Oh no!

Jonah darted forward, racing through the rest of the openings before they snapped closed. He came to a halt, right behind the others, to catch his breath and rub his left arm, which was still a bit numb. Wick said a shield could protect against supernatural and magical things. *If I'm a ghost in this dream-walk, that includes me.*

The first distortion continued to undulate before going transparent again. That drew the clerk's attention, and he paused with his hand on the door, eyes narrowed. Jonah remained still, fearing the man would sense him.

The clerk scanned the tunnel for several tense moments before he pulled the thick metal door open and entered the chamber. When the young man and woman followed, the door began to swing shut. Jonah hurried through with less than an inch to spare before the door closed with a thud.

The interior of the chamber was circular, with high metal walls that tapered toward a much-smaller opening at the apex. Stars twinkled in the sky, visible through the grate covering the opening. Jonah glanced down and gulped. One large symbol covered the entire floor, and it looked as if someone had drawn it with blood.

The young man and woman positioned themselves to the left of the doorway, near a cot. A pair of ominous-looking black handcuffs hung on the wall above it. Jonah shivered when he saw those, and he shifted his gaze around the chamber again. Something on the far side caught his attention. He squinted into the shadows and gasped. A stone portal stood against the far side.

An image of a huge red fireball streaking out of a similar portal popped into his mind. He clenched his fists as sweat broke out on his forehead. *Could it be the same one from the dream about his parents?* He thought the symbols on its surface were the same, but he had no way to be sure.

The clerk moved, revealing a pedestal in the center of the room. It had a simple stone base that flared at the bottom and a circular flat surface on top. A pair of lights mounted high on the wall created overlapping cones of harsh light on the pedestal. The clerk ignored it as he waited, his attention on the stone portal.

Several symbols on the portal flared, casting an eerie glow. A small hole appeared at the very center and expanded out to the edges. A sudden gust of cold air washed over them as the opening reached its full size, revealing a dark, cavernous interior on the other side.

Deyanira stepped into view in her true form as a tall, red-robed, and menacing KIN member. The ritualistic slashes and cuts were clearly visible on her pale face. Pain flared in the pit of Jonah's stomach.

He shuddered as he watched the woman turn slightly to the assembled group and bow. Several more red-robed people stood behind her. Unlike Deyanira, their hoods were pulled forward over their heads. She completed her bow and walked toward the portal.

The air around the opening shimmered as Deyanira stepped through. Jonah's jaw dropped when her body rippled and transformed. The red robe became a black, thigh-length dress. Her skeletal face lost the scars and became severe and normal. Long red hair quickly grew down to her shoulders like some time-lapse movie.

By the time she stood on this side of the portal, she had transformed into the bookstore owner, all evidence of her true form hidden.

The clerk inclined his head and waited until the portal closed before he spoke. "Welcome back."

Deyanira sneered and looked over the clerk's shoulder. "What are they doing here?"

The young man stepped forward. "We're making sure things get done."

The Protector's Ring **239**

"You haven't found the ring yet." The young woman joined the young man. "Our king is concerned."

The man and woman blinked and in that instant, both sets of eyes turned milky white.

Deyanira never took her pale green eyes off the two people. "You aren't needed, Wraiths, and you certainly aren't welcomed."

"The Grim Reaper's day is coming," the young man sneered at Deyanira. "All Reapers will have to answer for the bad choices you've made."

He pushed the clerk aside and started around the pedestal. The young woman went around the opposite side.

Jonah would have been scared if two Wraiths, whatever they were, circled toward him from both sides. Deyanira's long fingers curled like talons as she tilted her head back and laughed. "Today is not that day, so either leave willingly or I'll be forced to make you leave. I'd hate to damage those poor, innocent bodies."

The young man let out a snide laugh. "You wouldn't--"

He didn't finish speaking because Deyanira blurred into motion, shoving the woman into the wall, grabbing him by the neck and slamming him against the pedestal. With her other hand, Deyanira activated one of her blades and hurled it into the young woman's shoulder, pinning her to the metal wall. The woman howled and tried to pull the weapon free. When she touched the blade, her hands began to smoke.

Meanwhile, Deyanira had raised her free hand over the young man's head. He craned his neck around in order to stare at the clerk. "Brother! Are you going to let her do this?"

The clerk shrugged, making no move to help.

Deyanira smiled. "You've forgotten yourself, spirit. Reapers command all of you."

She pressed her hand against the young man's forehead. He screamed as a translucent shape was sucked out of his body. Jonah's jaw dropped when he saw a human spirit dressed in colonial-era clothes. That was a Wraith, he thought. Deyanira released the human and gripped the Wraith around its ghostly neck before it could escape. The Wraith let out another agonized scream, flared brightly, and exploded into smoking threads.

Deyanira turned on the young woman, whose white eyes narrowed in pure hate.

"You haven't heard the last of this, Reaper." The young woman opened her mouth in a silent scream. The Wraith poured out of her, a female with curly hair, and flowed up and through the grate. The young woman's body sagged against the blade that still protruded from her shoulder.

Deyanira pulled the blade free. When the woman slumped to the floor and groaned, Deyanira motioned to the clerk. He slid a Taser out of his pocket and calmly zapped both people.

"Leave them in the woods near the crossroads," Deyanira ordered.

The clerk nodded. "You are sending a not-so-subtle message to my Wraith brethren."

"Of course."

Jonah stared at the two bodies and suddenly, he wanted out of this dream-walk. *Wake up,* Jonah told himself. Nothing happened. Maybe if he went back to the foot of the stairs, he could do it. Jonah took a step toward the door.

Deyanira tensed and looked around the room. "Who's there?"

The clerk watched her with a worried expression. "We're alone, Deyanira."

"No, we aren't." Her eyes narrowing to mere slits like a tiger that's spotted its prey, she stepped toward the door, never taking her eyes off it. "I can sense you."

Without warning, Deyanira's hand shot directly at Jonah's throat. He had discovered in practice sessions that he had excellent reflexes. They allowed him to avoid her first attempt. However, every movement on his part enabled Deyanira to sense him more.

Her head followed his progress as he scuttled around the chamber. Jonah tried to remain calm and think clearly about his bedroom. That proved difficult with Deyanira stalking him. It took all his willpower to stop himself from taking another step. Deyanira paused.

Come on. Come on. Don't panic. Think clearly.

Deyanira stepped toward him with her hand outstretched.

The Protector's Ring

"Who are you?" She looked over her shoulder at the clerk. "Is it one of your brethren?"

"I can't tell while in a human host. It's a limitation of human senses."

"Then come out of him now."

The conversation terrified Jonah. If Deyanira figured it out, she would kill him for sure, no matter what Marcus said.

Stay calm and think about the bedroom. I can do this.

Deyanira lunged forward and managed to wrap her thin fingers around Jonah's neck. She let out a wicked cackle as he twisted in her grip.

"Show yourself!"

The awful truth hit Jonah. Deyanira had said it earlier: Reapers controlled spirits. She had been able the grab the Wraith before it could escape. And if he was a ghost in these dream-walks, she could also hold on to him. Total panic suffused Jonah's body and he shuddered.

Behind Deyanira, the clerk's body collapsed to the floor as the Wraith released it. Jonah watched as an ancient Egyptian warrior floated into the air. He couldn't imagine why a being so dignified would possess a lowly clerk. The Wraith stared at Jonah.

"Who is it?" Deyanira demanded as she shook Jonah. "Answer me, Wraith!"

The Wraith shifted his gaze to her, disgust and loathing twisting his face for a brief moment, and then he smoothed his ghostly expression. "I can't be sure."

Deyanira roared in anger and activated a blade with her free hand. She couldn't see as the Wraith touched the ankh amulet, the same one the clerk wore. Light shot out from it and heat flared under Deyanira's hand. She screamed and released Jonah. Immediately, he felt the welcomed pull as he was ripped away from the dream-walk.

He awoke in his own bed and sat up, rubbing his throat. His heart raced at ninety miles an hour, and he could still feel Deyanira's hard fingers around his neck. He didn't care about the things he heard or the fact that he had watched Deyanira destroy a Wraith.

I never want that to happen again.

Jonah thought of sending Marcus a text, but he didn't want to worry him and Omar. So he tossed and turned, afraid to sleep. At last, the terror of the dream-walk faded enough for his mind to form questions. Why did the Wraith lie to Deyanira or use his amulet to help him escape?

That action bothered Jonah as much as anything else. Surely Deyanira would know what happened and punish the Wraith, maybe even kill him, like she did the other one. Jonah wondered at his concern for the ghostly warrior. He rolled that and all the other questions around in his head until he descended into a dreamless sleep.

CHAPTER THIRTY-TWO
CROSSROADS

Home from church and changed out of his Sunday best, Jonah sat at the Hightowers' kitchen table as Robert sketched. At least, his cousin tried to sketch. Robert had the sketchbook in his lap, and he slapped the pencil down on it. "You have to focus, Jonah."

"I'm sorry. I'm just thinking about that Wraith." Jonah still had to get used to his cousins knowing everything about him.

Robert arched one of his sharp eyebrows. "Lynn wants the sketches of the people as soon as possible."

"Okay." Jonah concentrated and eventually described the two young people from the dream-walk. As Robert put finishing touches on the sketches, Lynn came through the kitchen door. Wick was right on her heels.

"Excellent," Lynn said as she took the pages from her brother and left the house.

Meanwhile, Wick helped himself to a soda from the refrigerator and sat down at the kitchen table. "What's up, Padawan?"

Jonah shrugged, and Robert gave his best friend a serious look. "He had a dream-walk."

"Dream-walk?"

"Yeah. Jonah calls them dream-walks now."

Wick blinked at Jonah. "Oh, that's a cool name. It's like astral projection." Wick's eyes widened. "That means your soul is traveling around."

With that, Robert, looking a bit shocked at Wick's words, proceeded to tell his friend everything about it. Wick leaned back in the kitchen chair and plopped his black-booted feet on the table.

Robert scowled and knocked his friend's feet back onto the floor. "My mom would kill all of us if she saw you."

"Sorry." Wick took out his lighter and played with it as he leaned back in the chair again. "When you think about it, Reapers and Wraiths kind of go together."

"You mean disembodied, super-angry human spirits?" Robert asked, his eyes widening slightly. "I thought they just floated around, haunting places. I never heard of them having a king or working together."

"Me neither," Wick said, ruffling his twists, thinking.

Jonah waited for his friend to go on, but the boy looked like he was deep in thought. Jonah tapped the table to get Wick's attention. "Are they just ghosts?"

"Oh no. They're human spirits that were killed out of time or order and didn't move on for some reason. That's why they turn super-angry and tend to haunt places."

"What does *out of order* mean? Like what it says in the Bible, where everyone has a time to die?"

"Your guess is as good as mine, Jonah."

"But the people were possessed. Can Wraiths take over you?"

Wick laughed. "No. I'm guessing these people welcomed them in. It had to involve some ritual, probably a corruption of the ancient Voodoo Loa ritual. If you heard any music in the background, that would have been a clue."

Robert gave his friend a doubtful look. "You know, Lynn's right about you."

"I'm wounded, Bobby." Wick feigned being stabbed in the chest. Robert scowled, but Jonah noticed the beginnings of a smile on his face. Meanwhile, Wick turned back to Jonah. "I'm more interested in the bookstore clerk. You saw him hold something in his hand as he walked toward the security door."

The Protector's Ring

Jonah nodded, happy to be on another subject.

"Did he say anything in a strange language or do anything?"

"No. I saw the air shimmer like a force field. The clerk walked through it."

Wick snapped the lighter shut. "They have wards protecting the door."

"Wards?"

"They're basically shields, except they protect a fixed location. Wards are also stronger and more intricate. I'm sure the clerk held a talisman. It allows him to walk through the wards without having to take them down."

Jonah continued to be amazed by Wick's knowledge. A thought occurred to him. "Can you make a talisman?"

Wick's jaw dropped. "Wards are way above what I can do, Jonah. Besides, the person who made the barrier is the only one who can make the one to work on it. Talismans are individual things, like the signature of the person."

"But why use wards? Do they work on regular humans?"

"Oh yeah. They protect against anything mortal. My guess is Deyanira's more worried about something supernatural getting into that chamber."

"You mean Fallen Reapers and Wraiths?" Jonah lapsed into silence as his mind picked through the information.

Wick traded a glance with Robert. "You know, Jonah, if she has wards, I'm sure she has ways to prevent phasing into that chamber. Usually, it's a symbol called a sigil."

"She does. I saw a huge one on the floor. Deyanira used a portal to get in."

Robert startled Jonah when he jumped from his chair and hurried off to his room. He returned with a different sketchbook in hand.

"The first time you mentioned portals, I wanted to show you these." Robert placed the sketchbook on the kitchen table and showed Jonah detailed, hand-drawn images of a stone portal. Robert even included the strange symbols around its surface.

Jonah's eyes widened. "I saw this."

Robert nodded. "The portals are doorways between the mortal realm and the supernatural realm."

"You mean …."

Wick nodded. "Yep. The Afterworld. The domain of the Undead."

Jonah took the sketchbook and flipped through, his mind racing. Robert had drawings of the blades, graceful looking ships, and the irregular gaseous shape like the one Jonah had seen in the Grim Hound dream.

Robert looked over Jonah's shoulder and pointed at the gaseous drawing. "That's a vortex."

"Does it connect to the Afterworld, too?"

"It only works on this side. Have you seen one of those?"

"Deyanira can make one."

Robert's eyes widened at that and he turned on Wick. "I thought only humans could make those."

"True. Witches, sorcerers, mages, and magicians can open them."

"Then how can Deyanira do it?"

Wick clicked his lighter open and closed. After a minute, he gave it one final snap and stood, excited. "In one of your dream-walks, you said Deyanira stepped through a vortex in her human appearance." Jonah nodded, caught up in Wick's growing excitement as the boy paced back and forth. "But in the latest dream-walk, when she crossed through the portal, it transformed her from Reaper into a human disguise?"

"Yeah. Why are you smiling?"

"It's obvious. When she comes through the portal, it transforms her. My guess is that it allows her to interact with humans."

Jonah finally understood the taunt his dad had hurled at Deyanira. He said she needed to cross back over. It all made sense. "You, Robert, and everyone else could see Deyanira as the store owner because the portal makes her more human."

"Well, not exactly human," Wick corrected. "I think it's more like the Grim Hounds. They have a physical form wrapped around them. Because of the power needed to do that, they can only stay for a limited time."

The Protector's Ring 247

"That's why she crosses back to the Afterworld," Jonah concluded.

"Correct. And being in a human form also allows her to use her old abilities. She must have been a witch or sorceress in her former life."

Robert pumped the air with his fist. "That's why she can do wards!"

Wick stood up as he and Robert touched fists, smiling. Jonah shared their excitement as he recalled Kevin's comment about Deyanira. A knot grew in his stomach and he frowned.

Wick noticed. "What's troubling you, Padawan?"

"I think that we'll have to get inside that chamber."

Robert gave him a quizzical look. "Too bad we don't have a clue where she lives."

Jonah closed his eyes and thought about the chamber and then sitting here in the Hightowers' kitchen. He wished Marcus was here to help, but he gave it a try anyway. He imagined an invisible thread connecting both locations. And it worked. "It's outside Mount Vernon. I'd say about fifteen miles."

Wick let out a low whistle. "Dude, that is so cool." He blinked and looked at Robert. "It's probably an old house or mansion. Deyanira would need somewhere private to work her stuff."

"That's a start," Robert agreed. "I can go to the Summit tomorrow and run an Internet search of the county records."

Searching the county records turned out to be boring, Jonah thought. Robert simply created an automated search routine and let the computer do all the work, accessing various databases from surrounding counties.

Jonah peeked at the screen. "Can't you just do an Internet search?"

Robert raised an eyebrow. "Where's the fun in that? Besides, I'd have to go to each County's website. That's boring and tedious, especially when I can do it with a simple algorithm."

"Okay." Jonah set Lynn's bag down and pulled out the deactivated blades. "Here. Lynn cut my practice short to go investigate something. She wanted me to bring these to you."

Robert took the blades to the filing cabinet, took out the archive box, and locked them inside. That done, he returned to the work desk, where he opened an old laptop. He paused, glancing at Jonah. "You are ready to kick Brandon's butt in two days, right?"

"Yeah, I am." Jonah picked up a connector cable and turned it over in his hands. "What is all this stuff?"

"You got me thinking yesterday when you mentioned the keypad beside that metal door. If you're serious about getting into Deyanira's chamber, then I'll need to be able to break through the door's security." He took the connector from Jonah and placed it back on the desk. "This may look old, but it has more than enough power to get in."

"You can do that?"

"Well, I won't know until I actually see it. Still, it doesn't hurt to be prepared."

"Thanks. For listening to my hunch."

Robert paused his typing and gave Jonah an embarrassed grin. "Don't sweat it, little cousin. This is nothing. You should see Wick. He's busy trying out ways to take down a ward without getting himself killed."

"For real?"

Robert grinned. "And he has working shield bracelets. Can you believe it? He showed me. They stopped everything I threw at him. Too bad you can't use one against Brandon."

Jonah stared at his cousin in amazement, unable to think of anything to say. He sat with Robert, occasionally asking him questions. Lynn came up the stairs an hour later, humming and swinging a small bag from the café downstairs. She also had a satchel slung over her left shoulder. Without a word, she pulled out a large sub sandwich and divided it into three pieces, handing one section to Jonah and another to Robert.

"I have good news." Lynn dropped her satchel on the far end of the table and continued after taking a quick bite of her piece of the sub. "The two people you saw in your dream-walk are okay. The police picked up the woman for vagrancy. She remembered being at the roadhouse restaurant, and then nothing until the police found her."

Robert paused in his work and looked at his twin. "You know the name of the place?"

Lynn nodded, pulled a bunch of flyers out of her satchel, and placed them on the table.

"She's not the only one to have memory loss," Lynn continued. "Other people have reported waking up in strange places around town. None of them remembered how they got there. The one common element is the roadhouse."

Lynn shifted the ad for the roadhouse to the top of the pile of papers. Jonah read it.

"The Crossroads?"

"Yes. Interesting name, isn't it?"

"Wait a minute." Robert turned to his desktop computer, minimized the search window, and opened up a different file. "I knew it!"

Lynn peered over her brother's shoulder. "Knew what?"

"Wick's always going on about magic power lines." Robert clicked on an icon, and a color map of Twiggs County opened. "He made this map of Mount Vernon and the surrounding county. That roadhouse is built on a Ley line." Robert tapped the computer screen. "Wow. Looks like it's near an actual crossroads." He laughed. "That makes sense."

"Why?"

"It's an old Blues tale about selling your soul to the devil at the crossroads." When Jonah gave him a blank look, Robert continued. "My dad used to listen to this old song. I should have known it would be based on something real."

"Maybe the singer knew about Wraiths," Lynn offered.

"Could be."

Jonah pointed at the thick red lines forming the crossroads. "That's cool, but what are Ley lines?"

"Wick is better at explaining these things," Robert hedged. "Ley lines are supposed to be like magic power lines."

"We forget you're not from around here." Lynn looked up from the screen as she explained, "A lot of the newer businesses were built on the site of much older places. I bet that old roadhouse used to be something related to the supernatural."

250 *John Darr*

Jonah couldn't imagine why people would build on a site like that. He shook his head in confusion. "Why are they important to Wraiths?"

Lynn glanced at Robert, waiting for him to answer. He paused as if to gather his thoughts. "Wick said that it's easier for the Wraiths to cross over at those locations. They may not be in the Afterworld, but they are on the supernatural plane."

"I wondered why they've become so active." Lynn peered over her brother's shoulder again. "The number of missing people hasn't been this high since…" Lynn glanced at Jonah, then lowered her gaze back to the screen. "Well, never."

She didn't have to say it. Jonah knew what she thought because he had come to the same realization. "It's all because of me."

Lynn glanced at him. "Jonah, what did I tell you about jumping to conclusions?"

"I'm not jumping to conclusions. I know what everyone wants." Jonah looked his cousins squarely in the eyes, took a deep breath, and said, "They want the Protector's Ring."

CHAPTER THIRTY-THREE
KAYAKS AND RINGS

"The Protector's Ring?" Robert ruffled his Afro as if trying to remember. "What's that?"

Jonah experienced a surge of embarrassment. It was Mike who had urged him to look for the ring. After all, his parents were killed because they found the Protector's Ring. An evil Reaper—Deyanira—had injured Marcus in an attempt to find it. Whole families and bloodlines were destroyed because of the ring.

Lynn gave him a shrewd look. "I think the more interesting question, my dear brother, is why does Jonah think it's all about a ring?"

Robert caught on, and he, too, looked at Jonah with the same, shrewd stare.

Lynn quickly cleared a space on the work table and sat down. Robert turned all the way around in the computer chair and leaned forward. Jonah began with the information he had learned from Mr. Hackett.

Robert leapt out of his chair when Jonah mentioned his old art teacher. "Did he say anything about me?"

"No." Jonah looked away. Mr. Hackett had certainly seemed angry with Robert about something, but Jonah didn't want to get into that at the moment. He continued on, telling his cousins about Marcus's encounter with Deyanira.

"That's how you knew about the woman from the bookstore." Lynn flipped her braids behind a shoulder with an angry twist of her head. "Is there anything else?"

"I found those words written on a piece of paper in one of my dad's books. I remembered it after visiting Mr. Hackett."

Jonah grabbed his book bag off the sofa, pulled a small grey book out, and hurried back to Lynn.

She took the small volume, turning it over in her hands. "I thought your father's library burned to the ground."

"I had this book in my bag." He slipped the folded piece of paper from the book and showed it to her.

She read it out loud. "The Protector's Ring."

"My dad must have found it."

"Then why turn around and hide it?"

"Well, Mr. Hackett says it's always been too dangerous to keep a ring."

"But your dad was a researcher, Jonah. He would have known about the ring's history. He thought the risk of finding it was acceptable. I wonder why." Lynn curled a finger in one of her braids as Robert took the piece of paper from Jonah.

"What does H mean?"

"Mr. Hackett?" Jonah suggested. "He claimed he met a Fallen Reaper, but said he never met my dad. I think he lied about that."

Robert smacked his hand on his desktop. "Old Man Hackett never told me any of this while I took art lessons."

"Get over it, Robert." Lynn leaned on her brother's shoulder until he shrugged her off. Lynn ruffled his Afro as she turned to Jonah. "I don't know. Your dad only came here once."

"Really?"

"Yep, little cousin." Robert nodded. "I told you. He came with your mom right after you were born."

Jonah frowned as he considered that. If his cousins were right, either his dad never visited again, or he had phased down to see Mike's uncle without telling anyone.

Robert swiveled his chair around to his computer and started typing. "You said Hackett mentioned the Solomon Ring. I've seen something

The Protector's Ring   253

about that, something recent." He typed furiously for a few minutes before letting out a shout.

"Dr. Francis Halliwell, a renowned collector of ancient rings, risked his professional credibility after he claimed to have found a powerful yet obscure ring called King Solomon's Ring." He gave them a significant look. "Solomon's Ring supposedly endows the wearer with extraordinary powers. Dr. Halliwell disappeared from the public scene shortly after his claims were made, thus preventing authentication of his find."

Lynn nodded. "Your dad must have found out about Halliwell and tracked down his last known location."

"Look! I found a drawing of the ring." Jonah and Lynn huddled on either side of Robert.

The image on the computer screen was exactly like the one in Mr. Hackett's book. Jonah took in the details of the mysterious ring as he recalled Hackett's comments. "Mr. Hackett told me that the Solomon Ring was actually a Protector's Ring."

"So, you still think your dad meant Hackett in that note?" Lynn gave him a questioning look, and Jonah nodded.

"Why not? All he put was… wait a minute!" Jonah snatched the piece of notepaper from the desktop where Robert had dropped it, and stared at the *H*. "Halliwell was the one who had tracked down the ring. Maybe my dad meant Halliwell."

"That makes more sense than Hackett." Lynn noticed Robert's shocked expression. "What's wrong? You don't think so?"

"Lynn! We know that name from a certain sculpture made from rings."

"Halliwell's Sphere." Lynn's eyes went wide with understanding and she glanced down at the attic floor. "Does anyone think that's just a coincidence?"

Moments later, Jonah, Robert, and Lynn stood on the second floor landing, gazing at Aunt Imma's hanging art piece. The late afternoon sunlight streamed through the high skylights and glinted off hundreds of rings.

Jonah squinted at the brilliant points of lights. "You think it's one of those?"

"Your parents sent the blades and archive box to us." Robert's voice sounded awed. "It's possible they sent the ring to our mom. That means it's been right in front of us all this time."

Jonah gazed at the rings, feeling the same growing excitement as his cousin. "Too bad we can't tell from here."

"We don't have to." Robert smacked the railing with a hand. Jonah and Lynn looked at him in confusion. "Mom kept records of every ring donated. She wanted me to make a database. It's all at the house, in her art room. We can check."

Jonah shook his head. "My dad wouldn't have told her the real name of the ring."

"He didn't have to, Jonah. I took pictures of every ring submitted."

Lynn eyed her brother. "Can you access that from here?"

"I wish I could. Mom's computer isn't on the Net. She's afraid of viruses, so I planned to connect it anyway and just not tell her."

"We'll have to wait until tomorrow to check. I'm sure Mom's home by now."

"Wait." Robert smacked his forehead. "I have band practice all day. And you're working with Jonah on the duel." When Lynn threw up her arms, Robert added, "Why don't we just ask Mom?"

Aunt Imma wasn't at home when Jonah and his cousins arrived. So instead of waiting to ask her about the records, Robert changed his mind and decided to search the art room. After about fifteen minutes of frantic looking, he slammed the last drawer and leaned against his mom's desk in a huff.

"She used pre-printed submission forms. I helped her fill them out."

Lynn crossed her arms, leaning against the doorframe and smirking. "I thought you wanted to ask about them."

Robert gave her a frosty look. "They're supposed to be here." He cast a disgusted glare around his mom's art room.

Jonah sat on the sofa in the family room, listening to the argument. He had a practice stick in his hand, flipping back and forth between ready

The Protector's Ring **255**

positions. Lynn wanted it to be second nature to him by the time the duel arrived.

Wick, who reclined in the armchair, watched him until Lynn stalked out of the art room and plopped down on the sofa beside him. A moment later came the sound of the garage door closing.

Aunt Imma walked into the family room and stopped. "Goodness, I didn't expect to see all of you here." Aunt Imma started for the kitchen with her grocery bag when she noticed Robert standing in the entrance to the hallway leading to the art room. "Robert, what were you doing in there?"

Everyone froze, but Robert didn't miss a beat as he came over, took the grocery bag from his mom, and carried it into the kitchen. "Mom, what happened to all the records on the Halliwell Sphere?"

"Honey, I gave the records to the county library."

"Why'd you do that?" Robert started squeezing the box of cereal he'd just taken out of the grocery bag.

Aunt Imma smacked his hand to get him to release the box. "Well, they're going to do the database and make an interactive display for it. If you had started on it when I asked, you could have finished it. Why is it so important now?"

Robert sat down at the table and looked at his mother with a blank expression. Jonah knew his cousin didn't have a response, so he jumped to his feet.

"I wanted to know if my parents sent you a ring." His words prompted Lynn to shake her head, but he sent her a silent plea. He didn't have any intention of telling his aunt everything.

He walked into the kitchen. "I don't have many things left after the fire. I thought that if they sent you a ring, it would be cool to see it."

"Your parents did send a ring. It's part of the sculpture. I can show you if you want."

Wick gave Jonah a thumbs-up gesture as Aunt Imma began putting up the groceries. She stopped suddenly.

"You know, Jonah, your parents sent two rings: a family ring and another strange ring with a lot of funny writing on it. I never saw anything like it

before. Your mother told me the most interesting story about the art collector who owned it. That's where I got the name from—Halliwell's Sphere."

Robert leapt up from the table. "Mom, I thought you read about Halliwell in your art book from class."

"Oh Robert, what does it matter now?" Aunt Imma looked at her watch and started to take out pots and pans. "Your father will be home soon. Wick, you can stay for dinner if you'd like." She began cutting up vegetables and loading them into a pot. "I wasn't going to do rings. I wanted to do kayaks."

"Kayaks, Mom? Why kayaks?" Robert threw the folded grocery bags on top of a recycling stack in the corner.

Aunt Imma smiled at her son. "Exactly! No one would expect kayaks. It would have been spectacular, but Jonah's mom convinced me it may have been too large for the small space. She suggested that I do rings and even offered to donate the first ones."

Jonah couldn't believe it. Robert, Lynn, and Wick all stared at him.

"It turned out so well," Aunt Imma continued. "I meant to thank your mother personally and have her come down and see it..." His aunt's voice trailed off and she busied herself with preparing dinner.

Jonah knew he had to say something. "My mom would have liked it."

"Thank you, Jonah." Aunt Imma paused, holding a whole butternut squash in her hands. "Life is funny. No one asked about the sculpture in months and then twice in one day, people want to know all about it."

Lynn sprang off the sofa and joined them in the kitchen as Aunt Imma began cutting the squash.

"Mom, who else asked about the sculpture today?"

Jonah had a sinking feeling in his stomach as Aunt Imma paused to answer. "This odd woman came into the shop today with long red hair that felt strange to the touch. She probably uses a lot of chemicals on it."

"Mom, what did she ask?"

"She recognized my name from an article on the recreation center, and we started talking about the sculpture. She asked where I got the rings, and

The Protector's Ring

I told her about the donations." Aunt Imma paused and gazed at the grim looks on the faces around her. "Honestly, what's gotten into all of you? It's not a secret. It's in every article written about the center." She pointed at Robert and Lynn with the half-cut squash. "That includes your blog, if I'm not mistaken."

"Aunt Imma?" Jonah got her attention. "Did you tell the woman my parents sent rings?"

"She asked about any strange ones and I mentioned the one your mom sent. That's when she told me about her bookstore with the funny name."

Everyone spoke at the same time. "Mystic Worlds."

Aunt Imma blinked at them and nodded. "Yes, that's the name. Doesn't sound like any bookstore a good Christian would visit, does it? Anyway, she said she'd be interested in seeing a ring like that one. I told her she could see it anytime she wanted because it's still on display in the center." Aunt Imma turned her attention to the steaming pots on the stove.

Lynn motioned to the back patio. Everyone followed her outside and sat around the patio table.

Robert was the first to speak. "So what do we do?"

"We stop her, that's what we do." Jonah pounded lightly on the table with his fist. "We have to get the ring before Deyanira does."

Wick gave him a slight nod. "I agree with Jonah. We have to get it first."

"We will, but I think Deyanira will wait until Thursday." Lynn eyed Jonah. "She can't do anything while the place is set up for the Summer's End celebration."

"Oh, yeah. That's right." Robert nodded. "With the extra vendors in the parking lot, there are too many people around, even at night."

Jonah watched the others nodding, but he didn't get it. "Why wouldn't she try tomorrow night, after the celebration?"

"That's break down night, little cousin. The vendors won't clear out until late Thursday."

Wick tapped Jonah's fist with his own. "Plus the rec center goes into shut-down mode for a week. It'll be the perfect time for Deyanira to go for the ring."

Jonah looked off across the darkening backyard. He wanted to do something now, not in two days.

Lynn nudged his chair with her foot. "There's another very good reason for you to hope Deyanira waits." When Jonah didn't say anything, she continued, "Haven't you forgotten something, Jonah? The Summer's End duel is tomorrow evening."

"I know that." Jonah held up the practice stick.

Lynn nodded and leaned forward with a serious expression. "We go on Thursday night." Everyone nodded. "We'll have to wait until late. I think midnight should be late enough."

"Lynn!" Jonah lowered his voice when everyone waved for him to keep it down. "Deyanira could be there by then."

"Think about it." Lynn gave Jonah a thump on the head. "We have to wait until my parents are asleep. Otherwise they'd notice us leaving." She continued staring at him until Wick changed the subject.

"If Deyanira is back in town, shouldn't Marcus be nearby?"

"I don't know." Jonah hadn't had time to think that far ahead yet.

"Well, I hate to say it, Jonah." Lynn gave him a thin smile. "Marcus would be a big help. You haven't heard from him?"

"No." When everyone continued to watched him, Jonah held up his hands. "I'll give him a call."

Robert glanced through the patio doors. "Dad's home."

Jonah worried so much about Deyanira getting the ring that he barely ate any dinner. The twins were just as keyed up, and none of them asked for seconds.

After dinner, Jonah went outside on the patio to call Marcus.

"Hello, Jonah. I didn't expect to hear from you so soon."

"I know where the Protector's Ring is hidden."

Marcus let out a startled breath. After a moment, he asked, "How do you know?"

"My mom and dad sent it to Aunt Imma. It's in her Halliwell Sphere sculpture. Right in the rec center." Jonah spoke in a rush. "We think Deyanira will try to take it on Thursday night."

The Protector's Ring

Marcus muttered something under his breath. Jonah wondered if the Fallen Reaper would believe him.

He relaxed when Marcus said, "That explains things."

Jonah blinked. "What things?"

"Deyanira and her agents have become very active over the last few days. My people are spread far and wide. I see it was a diversion."

"What about the ring?"

"Have you seen it? This could have been a planted mis-direction by your parents. They did a lot of that, which is why we have to follow all the leads."

"I'm sure. This has to be it." Jonah heard the desperation in his own voice. He never knew his parents had set up an entire plan to fool everyone else.

"Well, either way, you leave that to us."

"But we need to watch it, in case she tries to take it. We can let you know."

"Jonah…"

"I know, keep my head down."

"It's too dangerous for you and your cousins to get involved."

"We're already involved."

"Jonah, please. I'll send a couple of people down there."

"That's all?"

"If we pulled everyone back, that would alert Deyanira that we think you're right about the location. In that case, Mount Vernon would become a battle zone. It's delicate, but we need to keep a low profile ourselves until we can confirm the ring is there. Understand?"

Jonah tightened his grip the phone. He knew he was right, but he could also see Marcus's point. They didn't want Deyanira to bring all her people. The idea of facing her alone was bad enough.

"The rest of us will be there as soon as we can," Marcus added.

"Okay." Jonah let all the bitterness come out in his voice. They were the ones to discover its location, not Marcus and his people. He could feel it in his bones. This is where his parents hid the ring.

CHAPTER THIRTY-FOUR
SUMMER'S END

The Summer's End Festival hummed with the atmosphere of a county fair. Carnival vendors set up rides and games in and around the parking lot of the recreation center. Because the parking lots were taken, cars lined the streets for several blocks into the surrounding neighborhoods. The town provided a couple of school buses as shuttles to make rounds through the neighborhoods. The rides were free.

Jonah was amazed at the transformation as he walked the outside crowds, handing out flyers for the various clubs. Even with the constant activity, he began to feel a little lonely and scanned the throngs of people in a vain attempt to find Mike. Jonah suspected he still worried about the duel and wanted to hide that fact. But Jonah would welcome an argument with Mike over not hanging out at all.

Both Robert and Lynn worked inside the recreation center. Robert helped out with the teen art show while Lynn worked a booth featuring the center's youth programs. After an hour and a half of walking through the outside attractions and handing out brochures, Jonah had enough and headed for the main building.

A Native American magician roamed the festival attracting a crowd wherever she stopped. She wore a tunic of light brown material with the darker shapes of animals woven into the fabric. As Jonah drew close, he picked out the story the woman weaved around each trick she performed. It was about the fabled phoenix. The cadence of her voice rose to a climax just as she produced a fist-sized version of the mythical bird in mid-air.

Jonah and the crowd gasped, spellbound as the fiery bird flared and burned out. Enthusiastic applause erupted, drawing even more attention. But the magician simply bowed and nodded as she folded her arms. Soon the crowd began to move away, and the woman turned to catch Jonah's gaze. She bowed to him, her two long braids nearly touching the ground.

Caught off guard by the formal greeting, Jonah returned the gesture with an awkward bow of his own. He straightened, and that's when he noticed the symbol stitched into the left front of her tunic. It was three circles with wings stretched over the center one. Even though it was done in golden thread, it was just like the symbol branded into his godfather's long coat. This woman was part of the Alliance.

Jonah opened his mouth, but the woman turned and slipped through the crowd. He considered following her until he realized that wasn't necessary. She worked with Marcus, which meant she was here to keep a watch on the ring. That thought relaxed Jonah as he changed direction and headed toward the center.

Long banners were strung from the atrium ceiling and hung down between the art pieces. In the East wing, the game rooms were being used as booths for civic and county organizations, most focused on teen-related activities.

Lynn sat at a long fold-up table with two other girls. She wore a teen center shirt and had her own stack of brochures beside her.

As Jonah approached, the girl to Lynn's left smiled up at him. She had neat black curls and large loop earrings that matched her deep green shirt. "You want to join a club?"

"He's with the Practice Club already, Tamara."

Tamara looked between Jonah and Lynn and her eyes widened. "Is he your little brother?"

"He's my cousin."

Tamara pulled a rainbow-colored ribbon out of a small box and stood to pin it on Jonah's chest. "I'm with the Rainbow Coalition."

"What's this for?" Jonah tweaked the little ribbon.

"We promote tolerance and anti-bullying efforts. We have a chapter at the High School. We call ourselves Upstanders. You want to join? You're a freshman, right?"

Lynn laughed. "He's still in middle school."

That news seemed to animate Tamara even more. "Oh, well, middle school is the perfect place to teach tolerance." She leaned over the table. "You can start a chapter there."

Jonah shrugged and stuffed his hands in his pockets. Thankfully, a couple of older kids came over, and Tamara busied herself with them.

Lynn reached out and straightened Jonah's rainbow ribbon. "Have you heard back from Marcus or his people yet?"

"He sent someone, a magician. She's walking around outside." Jonah glanced around. He had hoped to see Kevin again, but so far, nothing.

Lynn looked impressed with the news. "Really? Did you talk to her?"

"No." Jonah frowned. "I was going to when she moved off like she didn't want to talk to me."

Lynn shook her head. "Well then, I say we go ahead with our plan."

Tamara finished with the other kids and glanced at Jonah again.

Jonah knew she wanted him involved in her group, but he wasn't ready for something like that. Besides, Mike would make a better Upstander, he thought. "I think I'll go see what Robert's doing."

He waved to Tamara and hurried toward the atrium. Jonah paused inside the open space and glanced up at Aunt Imma's sphere. He couldn't believe that the Protector's Ring floated above his head, in plain sight, and none of the people walking by had any clue about any of these things.

He shook his head and continued on into the West wing. The library's transformation surprised Jonah. The bookshelves remained in place, but all the chairs and study carols were stacked along the back wall. Movable partitions stood in the space now, and all of them were covered with hundreds of pieces of art and photos.

Robert stood among other kids, talking about his own pieces. As Jonah approached, he saw a big blue first place ribbon on a stark watercolor piece. Jonah lingered, impressed with how confident Robert sounded when dealing with art and computers.

Soon, the press of people entering this section became too much, so he waved goodbye to Robert and went back to the atrium. He received a warning buzz in his head just as he spotted Deyanira standing in the center of the atrium, gazing up at the Halliwell Sphere. Her bright red hair stood out in the sunlight and in stark contrast to her black pants and shirt.

Even though Jonah stopped, she must have sensed his presence because she turned to look directly at him. Would she try something around all these people, Jonah wondered? Deyanira's attention was drawn to the magician, who had just entered the atrium. Even Jonah could sense power in her.

Deyanira flicked her hand. At first, Jonah thought that had been a fluke until the cables holding two of the heavy banners snapped. As they began to fall, the magician raised her own hand and the banners stopped in mid-air. Jonah doubted that anyone milling around realized the woman had just saved them from getting hurt.

Using the diversion as cover, Deyanira stalked through the front doors. Jonah caught the magician's eyes and the woman gave him a slight shake of her head. He only took a second to decide to follow Deyanira anyway. He couldn't let the sorceress get away.

Jonah ran outside and caught a glimpse of her slipping through the crowd and hurried to catch up. She weaved toward the row of radio trucks along the edge of the carnival and dodged around the front of a radio station van. Her movement startled a heavyset employee sitting beside the vehicle.

"Hey! You can't jump the rope!" He struggled to his feet to follow.

The large speakers mounted on the truck sparked and popped. The van's music broadcast filled with electronic squealing, causing everyone nearby to cover their ears. Technicians rushed over to help, and Jonah slipped by them, unnoticed.

Deyanira headed toward the trees behind the center, and he followed. Just as she entered the cover of the trees, she waved her hand, creating a vortex. Instead of entering, she whirled to face him.

The move shocked Jonah and he skidded to a stop. "I know who you are."

"You've been talking to Marcus."

"I won't let you have the ring."

"You're so much like your father." She stepped toward Jonah, a curious look in her eyes. A second later, her demeanor changed. Moving faster than Jonah could imagine, her right hand blurred into motion as she cast a spell, right at him.

Pain from his Death Sense threatened to split his skull at the same time something slammed into Jonah from behind, taking him down. He expected the spell to fly past. Instead, it splashed against an invisible barrier right where his head would have been if he hadn't been tackled. The sudden lessening of his Death Sense buzz let Jonah know that Deyanira must have slipped through the vortex.

Someone hauled him to his feet and turned him around. Kevin stood there, looking serious. The Native American magician stood behind him, her hand still raised as if expecting Deyanira to reappear and attack again.

Jonah pointed at her, but whispered to Kevin, "Is… is she a Mage?"

Kevin nodded while giving him the once over. "That was stupid to chase Deyanira by yourself."

"She was getting away."

"So?" Kevin shrugged. "She didn't have the ring."

Jonah wanted to argue *so what* when something else occurred to him. "Why didn't she try to take it?"

"Deyanira couldn't," the Mage answered. She had a calm, serious voice. "I put a protective ward around your aunt's sculpture."

Jonah thought back to image of Deyanira staring at the sculpture. "Can she get through?"

"Not without a lot of power and alerting us." The woman crossed her arms, watching him.

For a moment, he thought she was angry with him for not offering to help back in the atrium and his ears reddened. "I'm sorry about the banners."

"You didn't break the cables and I was able to fix it without the mortals noticing anything."

Unable to decipher the woman's neutral expression, Jonah had no choice but to accept her words.

The Protector's Ring

"Come on," Kevin said. He led the way back to the recreation center and inside, where they found Wick.

"Hey, Padawan."

Jonah hurried over to his friend. "Wick, she was here."

"Who?"

"Deyanira. I caught her looking at the sphere."

"Well, I doubt she could get it. There's a ward protecting the sculpture. I can sense it." Wick peeked over Jonah's shoulder, noticing the Mage for the first time. "You did it?" She nodded. "Whoa. Can we talk? Let's grab a table in the café."

Although the Summer's End had plenty of food vendors, the café tables were available to Festival goers if they needed to rest—or a table to sit at while they ate. Wick found a table close to the atrium and begin to ask the Mage all kinds of questions. The woman's cool expression softened into genuine interest as Wick talked.

After fifteen minutes, Jonah couldn't sit still anymore and hopped to his feet.

Kevin rose from his chair. "Where're you going?"

"I can't wait around."

"It won't do you any good getting all worked up." Kevin lowered his voice. "She's gone for now. The ring is safe."

Jonah flopped down in his chair and checked the time.

Kevin waved to get his attention. "This is Mage Trueblood, by the way."

The woman nodded to Jonah. "You shouldn't concern yourself. I'll check the ring on a regular basis."

"You're not gonna stay?"

"We have to report back to Marcus," Kevin answered.

"And I know my ward will alert me if Deyanira tries anything."

Wick patted Jonah on the shoulder. "Concentrate on the duel, Padawan."

Jonah tried, but that didn't help at all. In addition to worrying about Deyanira, his anxiety about the challenge also grew. After all that he'd been through, a duel with Brandon should be easy. Yet Jonah's stomach had developed a case of the butterflies by the time Robert and Lynn were ready to leave.

CHAPTER THIRTY-FIVE
THE DUEL

Jonah's butterflies turned into full-blown dismay when they arrived at the practice field. All of the club members turned out, along with extra kids Jonah didn't know. Lynn wore an *I told you* so expression on her face. Jonah tried to ignore her as he took out his practice blades and began warming up.

As duel time drew near, Lynn began muttering last-minute instructions to Jonah, which made him even more nervous. Wick came over and leaned close, speaking in a perfect Yoda voice. "Mind what you have learned. Save you it will."

"Wick!" Lynn punched him on the arm. "You're not helping!"

Jonah disagreed as he, Wick, and Robert all laughed. Lynn crossed her arms and muttered, "Geeks." Jonah didn't care. He needed to let off the tension.

Five minutes before six o'clock, Brandon, Drew, and Antwan arrived. Brandon had a large carry bag slung over his shoulder. He unzipped it, pulled out his own short blades, and strutted around, taking half-hearted swings and lunges.

Jonah fingered the edges of his practice blades as he watched. Brandon's blades looked sharp, whereas his tips and edges were blunt so as not to puncture clothes; however they could still deliver pain. Lynn had proven that more than once in practice.

At six, a hush fell over everyone. The sun hung low enough in the sky for the surrounding trees to cast shadows over the duel area. Jonah welcomed the shade. It would still be plenty hot during the challenge.

Alex broke away from the crowd and stepped into the center of the clearing. "If you're not here to see a practice duel, you're in the wrong place." He paused as a few kids laughed. "The duelers will use practice blades and the match will continue until someone submits." Alex glanced at Jonah and then Brandon. "Are you ready?"

Jonah moved immediately into the center of the clearing and stood in a ready stance. Brandon took his time entering. When he did, both boys bowed to Alex and then to each other. Despite the formal curtesy shown, Jonah's Death Sense buzzed at a continued low level.

His thoughts turned to Deyanira, and his anxiety about getting the ring increased. Maybe he could end this before it started.

"Brandon. You don't have to do this."

"Screw you, Jonah. You're not backing out."

"I just wanted to give you a chance to run home."

Brandon bared his teeth and nodded. Jonah returned the gesture. Both boys dropped into position. Brandon's blades were more or less in the correct positions as he bounced on his feet, ready to go. Jonah snorted; Lynn would crack his arms if she caught them like that.

Alex nodded to each boy, blew his whistle, and quickly moved back as they lunged.

Brandon pressed the attack, swinging his blades at Jonah's forearms and then his legs, forcing Jonah to defend himself repeatedly. He lost precious ground, but held the blades as Lynn had taught him, knocking each attack away. Brandon continued to concentrate on Jonah's legs. As soon as Jonah settled into the repetitive defensive moves, Brandon switched up. He whacked Jonah hard against the head with the butt of his blade. Jonah stumbled back, slightly dazed.

Brandon shot his friends a big smile. The crowd murmured because club members never openly gloated. Jonah prepared himself and waited as Brandon returned to the center.

At Alex's signal, they lunged. Brandon came on strong again, but Jonah stood his ground this time. When Brandon brought his blades around from either side, Jonah reared up and blocked each one. Then he reversed his own grip and struck out at Brandon, forcing the boy on the defensive.

The Protector's Ring

That's when Jonah noticed it: Brandon didn't bother to bring his blades back to protect his forearms. That gave him an idea.

When they lunged at each other for a third time, Jonah went in with both blades attacking Brandon's right side. As expected, Brandon moved to block that side, using both blades in a forward grip. In a flash, Jonah reversed the angle of his attack and struck Brandon's unprotected left side, scoring painful hits on the boy's left forearm. Brandon's face twisted into equal parts surprise and pain as he spun away from Jonah.

For a brief moment, Brandon left his back exposed, and Jonah considered taking advantage of it. The cheers of the practice club members registered and, remembering his training, Jonah dropped into the ready position. Brandon took his time coming back to the center. The smug look on his face was gone as he eyed Jonah.

Brandon pointed a blade at him and sneered. Without waiting for Alex's signal, he attacked. Jonah was ready, and he blocked Brandon even better than before. After a particularly messy flurry of thrusts that were easily countered, Jonah began to feel confident that he would win this duel. That proved to be a mistake, as he didn't account for Brandon's frustration. The boy's added height and longer arms allowed him to move in and elbow Jonah in the face.

Jonah heard, and felt, the sickening crunch a moment before pain exploded across his face. He fell hard to the ground, clutching his nose, blood running freely down his chin and onto his chest. He sucked in a startled, painful breath as the crowd roared its disapproval.

Robert and Wick's yells were the loudest among the shouts. When Brandon turned to face him, Jonah knew the boy was gonna ask him to yield. He struggled to his feet again, wiped his nose, and stared at the scarlet smear across the back of his hand.

The anger rose inside Jonah, but then his gaze fell on Lynn. Unlike the others, she remained quiet, her arms crossed, watching him. She hadn't run out to see if he was okay. This was his fight, and she couldn't help. No one could. He had to overcome Brandon's tactics on his own. Jonah sucked in a painful breath, causing his nose to throb.

Remembering her warning, he clamped down on the anger. As he dropped into his stance again, Jonah noticed something about Brandon, something he wouldn't have seen if he had allowed the anger to get the better of him.

Even though Brandon strutted back and forth, sneering at him, the boy breathed hard and took his time getting ready.

So Brandon cheats when he gets tired. It's time to change things up.

Jonah moved first, the tactic throwing Brandon off balance as he kept attacking the boy's arms and legs. He caught one of Brandon's blades and twisted it painfully from his grip. However, the move put Jonah too close. Brandon hit Jonah's arm with his own and then caught Jonah with an upward elbow in the stomach.

The force of it lifted Jonah off his feet and he toppled to the ground, clutching his stomach. The crowd booed and hissed. Fearful that Brandon would attack him while down, Jonah grabbed his blades and stumbled away from where he thought Brandon was. He didn't have to worry because Brandon stalked over to his bag, shaking his injured hand. Antwan grabbed Brandon's arm, and they argued. When Brandon yanked his arm free, he held a real sword.

An abrupt silence spread through the crowd.

Alex blew his whistle and hurried over to Brandon. "You can't use real weapons."

Many in the crowd voiced agreement. Jonah ignored the real sword in Brandon's hand and focused on Antwan. The boy didn't have his usual sneer on his face anymore. In fact, Antwan looked worried. His eyes met Jonah's for a moment. Then Antwan gave a slight shake of his head and pulled Drew back. Brandon didn't even notice the subtle distance his friends were putting around him.

Lynn called out from her spot beside Robert and Wick, "Practice weapons only, Brandon. You've cheated enough already."

Once again, more than one person offered agreement. Brandon ignored them all as he took a few practice swipes with the sword. Then he faced Lynn. "We didn't have that in writing. I won't cut him. I promise."

"No."

Lynn broke away from the crowd and marched over to stand beside Jonah. "Don't fall for it, Jonah." She tightened and loosened her fists.

Jonah knew his cousin wanted to teach Brandon a lesson. He touched her arm to get her attention. He sucked in a painful breath, his swollen nose making it harder to breathe. "It's cool, Lynn."

The Protector's Ring

She opened her mouth to protest, and Jonah tapped his forehead. "I'd know if he really threatened me." Lynn realized what he meant, but she folded her arms and didn't move. "Let me use them." Jonah held out his hand. "I know you have the real blades. Please."

Lynn glanced at the blood covering the front of his shirt and the smear of red on his open palm. Then she raised her gaze to Brandon, huffed, and marched back to her bag. Jonah noticed that she activated the blades inside the bag just before taking them out.

She held out the blades, hilts first. "You better be right."

Alex saw her and stomped over. "Lynn, you can't be serious."

"It's up to Jonah."

"But..."

Lynn whirled on him, her braids whipping around with her. She grabbed Alex by the hand holding the whistle and pulled him off to stand among the crowd. Jonah noticed Mike Littleton watching him with wide eyes. In fact, everyone in the crowd now watched him.

He pushed that out of his mind as he tested the blades. They felt lighter than the practice ones. He tried a move he'd seen the older kids do and twirled the blades. They seemed to hum and move of their own accord as they stopped in position. He could feel the warm metal against his skin.

Brandon stood in the center of the clearing with the sword held loosely in his right hand. Jonah moved forward, watching Brandon's stance. He could tell when the boy would move. Again, he decided to change things. As soon as he saw Brandon's leg tense, Jonah began to circle. Brandon's face showed momentary surprise as he moved to keep Jonah away.

Jonah grinned, and Brandon attacked. Jonah's hands moved swiftly into place as he blocked Brandon's sword jabs. When Brandon brought the sword around in a low arc toward his right leg, Jonah reversed his blade to block it.

Letting go of his semi-controlled attacks, Brandon just came at him. Jonah blocked every swipe, thrust, and poke of the sword. He anticipated Brandon's moves, and that made the boy more frustrated.

When Brandon pulled back, then rushed forward with an overhead strike, Jonah brought his crossed blades up and blocked the blow. He twisted and forced Brandon's sword off and down to one side. Jonah followed up by flipping one of his blades around and banging Brandon hard on the forehead. The boy stumbled back and fell on his butt, his face twisted in fury.

The crowd cheered, but Jonah didn't smile or acknowledge them. He simply dropped into the ready stance. Brandon didn't bother to ready himself. He grabbed the sword and charged as soon as he got up, and Jonah easily parried a low swing at his legs. Reversing a blade, Jonah scored a solid hit to Brandon's upper arm and the other to the side of his head. Brandon screamed in rage, on the verge of tears, and charged again. Jonah moved to parry when Brandon suddenly reared back and tried to ram him with the sword.

Jonah knew what to do. As Brandon came forward, he caught the sword at waist height with both of his own blades. He immediately applied a little twist and his blades locked around the sword like a vise. With a twist of his upper body, Jonah snapped the weapon in two.

He reversed his twisting motion and landed the hilts of both blades on Brandon's forehead, watching in satisfaction as the boy fell to the ground. The broken sword flew out of his hand.

In one smooth motion, Jonah reversed his blades again, leaned over Brandon, and put the point of the right blade against his neck, just below the Adam's apple.

"Submit." When Brandon hesitated, Jonah applied a little pressure.

"Okay! I submit!"

Jonah stood and whirled the blades so fast, they appeared as a bright blur. When he stopped, the blades were in perfect position. He slipped both into his left hand. It was only then that he registered the crowd had erupted in applause and wild cheering. Robert, Lynn, and Wick broke away from the throng and rushed up to him. Lynn hugged him while Robert and Wick patted him on the back.

"How did you do that, Jonah?" Lynn sounded amazed. "I never taught you all those moves."

"I just knew when I held them," Jonah said in a low voice. He handed the blades to Lynn.

She gasped. "They're hot!"

The Protector's Ring

Robert gave her a funny look. "He just used them. It has to be natural body heat." Lynn held the blade out and Robert touched it. He pulled his hand back. "Wow." They both looked at Jonah.

Wick reached out and touched the blades. "It's power."

Jonah heard someone yell his name. A split second later, Mike collided with him, giving Jonah a playful punch on the arm.

"That was so scary," he gushed. "But, oh my God, you were great!"

"Thanks," Jonah stammered. "I didn't think you would come to a duel."

"You stood up to Brandon." Mike gave an embarrassed smile. "I couldn't skip that."

Jonah's Death Sense gave a little twitch. He turned and saw Brandon glaring at him as Antwan helped him to his feet. Brandon shrugged off the help and yelled at Jonah, "Freak!"

Unlike all the other times, admirers surrounded Jonah now. That simple fact finally registered on Brandon. He looked nervously around at the crowd, then pushed past his friends toward his bike.

Lynn thumped Jonah on the shoulder. "He's just a bad loser. Don't worry about him."

Jonah wasn't worried about Brandon. He'd just beat him, and right now, he was on top of the world.

CHAPTER THIRTY-SIX
BUSTED

Jonah didn't like waiting, and it proved to be sheer torture, as expected. His nose had healed by the next morning, but it was still a bit swollen. He hid out in his room until Aunt Imma headed off to work, then dressed and hopped on his bike and rode to the center.

Vendors and county volunteers dismantled the booths and rides while center personnel cleaned up the surrounding area. Robert and Lynn were among the volunteers helping out. Jonah rode past the recreation center several times.

When Lynn caught him on his eighth trip around the parking lot, she recruited him, putting his nervous energy to better use. Every chance he got, Jonah would slip into the atrium to make sure his aunt's sculpture was still there. So far, he hadn't seen Mage Trueblood, but Deyanira never appeared again, either.

They came home that evening exhausted from the work and ate dinner in a hurry. Claiming they wanted to go to bed early, Jonah, Robert, and Lynn all went off to their rooms. Jonah was about to close his bedroom door when someone knocked.

Lynn poked her head in and whispered, "Black shorts, shirts, and sneakers. Got that covered?"

"Yeah."

"I suggest you get a few hours' sleep."

"Lynn? You think we should ask the Mage?"

The Protector's Ring 275

Lynn stepped inside the room. "We thought about that, but do you know how to contact her or Kevin?"

"No. And if I call Marcus, he'll tell us to stay out of it."

"Then it's settled. Wick's sure he can take down the ward."

"I bet Deyanira can do the same thing."

"That's why we need to get there first. Are you having doubts? It was your idea."

"I know. I'm in." Jonah sat down on the edge of his bed. "If Trueblood is right, they'll come as soon as Wick tries anything. My godfather's gonna be pissed."

Lynn twisted a finger in one of her braids as she gazed out the window. "We'll deal with that when it happens. At least we'll know about the ring." She opened the door. "See you in a few."

As soon as Lynn closed the door, Jonah pulled a bag from underneath his bed, took out his clothes, and quickly changed. Then he lay down, never expecting to sleep, yet the next thing he knew, Lynn crouched over him in his darkened room.

"Wake up, sleepyhead."

Jonah sat up. "Sorry." He rubbed his eyes and touched his nose, noting that it felt normal after the short sleep. Kevin was right. Resting did help the healing process. Jonah wondered about the Fallen Reaper as he shuffled out of the room behind Lynn. He wished that Kevin was here with them. At least the young Fallen Reaper had been trained to fight. They didn't want to face Deyanira, just beat her to the ring. But things seldom worked out as planned.

Robert waited by the kitchen door with a black backpack on. Another sat on the floor.

Lynn slipped that one on, caught Jonah's curious expression, and said, "Robert has his computer gear and I have my blades and a few things we might need."

Jonah nodded and glanced at the time on the game console; twenty minutes 'til midnight. They grabbed their bikes out of the shed and met Wick at the end of the street.

Riding through the neighborhoods this late at night was a little surreal. The only sounds Jonah could hear were the hum of their tires against the street top. Without warning, a shiver went down his spine as he recalled the Grim Hound chasing him through these very streets. Jonah shook off the memory and concentrated on the ring.

Everyone seemed charged with nervousness. Or was it excitement, Jonah wondered. He found it interesting that they were able to take every hill without slowing down.

When they reached the center, Jonah paused by the bike rack.

"What are you doing?" Lynn called out as she rode by. "We can't park our bikes out front."

Robert stopped beside him. "We're gonna lock them up on the other side of the tennis courts. That way, a security patrol won't see them."

As Jonah followed his cousins around to the far side of the tennis court, he agreed that it made sense. They were furthest from the main building, and the bikes would be invisible in the shadows.

Once they were done with that, Lynn and Robert led the way to a gray side door. Wick kept an eye on the main road while Robert positioned himself.

Lynn took out a key. "You ready?"

Robert nodded.

Jonah felt the change in air pressure right before Kevin appeared. He held onto Trueblood's arm, giving her a ride.

Lynn paused with the key ready to unlock the door, her mouth hanging open. Robert and Wick looked just as stunned.

Kevin crossed his arms, ignoring the others while glaring at Jonah. "What are you doing?"

Jonah's moment of shock and then embarrassment over getting caught evaporated. "We're gonna prove the Protector's Ring is inside."

Trueblood stepped forward. "How were you planning to get around my ward?"

"I planned to short it out with my shield bracelets," Wick answered.

The Protector's Ring

Trueblood whirled to him, her face showing surprise. "You have shield bracelets?"

"Yeah," Wick hunched his shoulders. "I made them." He held out his right arm toward Trueblood.

"That's impressive." The woman inspected the bracelet, running her fingers over the pieces of polished wood. She gazed into Wick's face. "Why aren't you in training to be a full Mage?"

Wick gaped at the woman until Lynn cleared her throat.

"I'm glad you're impressed." She motioned to the door. "Move out of the way, or you could just take the ward down for us."

"We have to know," Jonah added. He faced Kevin. "My parents died because of the ring."

Kevin didn't answer for a long moment. "Fine. I'll take you and Trueblood inside and--"

Everyone spoke at the same time. Lynn succeeded in voicing her concern the loudest. "You don't know the code and will set off the alarm."

"Tell us the code."

Lynn crossed her arms, refusing to give the information to Kevin. Robert and Wick stood with her. After a moment, Jonah joined them.

"We go inside, too," Lynn said. She made a point of holding up her watch. "Time's wasting. Deyanira could be here any minute."

Kevin exchanged a quick glance with Trueblood before stepping away from the door. Lynn unlocked it and opened it wide so Robert could duck inside. She held up her hand when Jonah started to follow.

"Robert has to turn off the alarm at the other end of the hall, and he only has thirty seconds to reach it."

The door opened a minute later and Robert stuck his head out. "All done."

Trueblood slipped inside the building first. Kevin motioned Jonah next, but he held back, staring at his cousins.

"How did you get the key and code?" Jonah asked Lynn.

"A while ago," Lynn whispered. "Wick swiped the director's keys." She held up the key so it reflected in the weak security light over the door. "We made a copy and use it sometimes when we have a tight deadline."

"And I pulled the code from the director's computer about a month ago." Robert gave him a smug grin. "She kept a whole list of codes on there."

Lynn crossed her arms. "Anything else you want to know, Jonah?"

"No, ma'am."

Lynn balled a fist and held it under Jonah's chin, causing Wick to laugh.

Robert gave his sister a mock bow. "After you, ma'am."

Kevin snorted. "You guys are such geeks."

Lynn gave him an appraising stare as she pushed Robert and Jonah ahead of her and into the darkened building.

CHAPTER THIRTY-SEVEN
HALLIWELL'S SPHERE

Jonah watched as Lynn and Wick positioned a fifteen-foot ladder under Aunt Imma's art piece. Robert stood off to the side, clutching his archive box in his hands. Trueblood stood in the entrance to the East wing. Kevin covered the West wing entrance, his Reaper blades activated.

Wick got everyone's attention by tapping on the ladder. "Who wants to go?"

Everyone turned to Jonah. He gulped and gripped the ladder while Lynn and Wick positioned themselves to either side to hold it in place.

When Jonah reached the top, he paused to stare at the sphere. Recessed lighting gave the atrium a soft nighttime illumination, and pale blue moonlight shone through the skylights. The angled display lights caused many of the rings to glitter. Even with that, Jonah knew it wasn't enough.

He glanced down at Lynn. "I'll need a light."

Lynn took a flashlight out of her backpack and tossed it up to him. Jonah flicked it on and tilted the light so just a little of it touched the rings. And then he heard a growl. Jonah froze in place and listened.

Robert noticed his hesitation first. "What's wrong, little cousin?"

Jonah peered into the darkened café below and the corridors leading off the atrium. He met Kevin's gaze. "Did you hear that?"

The Fallen Reaper nodded and started to prowl back and forth, his eyes darting everywhere. Robert clutched the archive box to his chest, staring around him. Lynn moved away from the ladder to stand at the entrance to the café.

Finally, she came back to the ladder and shook her head. "I don't hear anything."

Wick gulped. "I don't either, but it's the Witching Hour. Midnight."

"Wick. This is creepy enough." She glanced at Jonah. "Keep going."

Jonah moved the light back and forth over the rings. "It's gonna take forever."

"I have an idea." Wick glanced at Lynn before he continued. "Do you think you can sense the ring?" Everyone, including Jonah, stared at Wick. "Your father owned it for a time, right?"

"Sometimes," Trueblood said, "that creates a connection with an object. The young Mage has a point."

Lynn looked around the atrium again. "Well, do something. We're wasting time."

Jonah closed his eyes and thought about his dad wearing the ring. He pictured it clearly in his mind. And then he thought of all the power and good the ring represented. Jonah held on to those images and concentrated. He sensed something, like a pulsing heartbeat.

Gasps came from below him. When Jonah opened his eyes, he understood why. A single ring, high on the opposite side of the sphere, glowed with a pulsing amber light.

"You did it!" Lynn thumped the ladder.

"Very cool." Wick smiled up Jonah, but he wasn't listening. The pulsing of the ring echoed his racing heartbeat. He deliberately calmed himself, and the ring's pulsing slowed to match.

"Jonah?" Lynn peered up at him. "Should we move the ladder?"

"Huh—oh. Yeah." Jonah climbed down.

"Maybe I should get it," Lynn offered after they repositioned the ladder. She placed a foot on the bottom step.

Wick stopped her. "I think Jonah should be the one to do it."

The Protector's Ring

Jonah glanced up at the pulsing ring and thought Lynn might have a point. He would have to really stretch; the ring was near the top of the sphere.

I made the ring glow, not Lynn. The pulses matched my heartbeat. I should be the one to get it.

Wick gave him an encouraging tap on the shoulder, and Jonah climbed the ladder again.

Once he reached the top, he stretched out a hand. As his fingers brushed against the ring, it pulsed brighter. A surge of satisfaction shot through him. At long last, after the attempt on his life and the half-truths, he had found the Protector's Ring. Jonah stretched further.

As soon as he'd enclosed the ring in his fist, the atrium skylights exploded inward and two huge Grim Hounds crashed through. They barreled straight at Jonah from two directions, leaving him no time to move out of the way.

I need a shield.

The thought was instant, and the ring pulsed brighter as a sharp prickling sensation rolled up Jonah's arm and away from his body. A pale blue circle of distortion snapped into existence around him a split second before the Grim Hounds hit.

The barrier flared where the creatures struck it and deflected them in opposite directions. One smacked into the far wall and slid to the ground. The other tumbled into the hanging tennis racket sculpture, causing rackets to explode in all directions.

Jonah grabbed onto the sphere to keep from falling to the floor. His shoelace got tangled in the top step of the ladder, which yanked hard on his leg as it toppled sideways. Jonah's hands slipped along the sphere's metal rods for a few terrifying seconds. He managed to grab onto the ends where the rings were welded in place, groaning in pain as they cut into his palms. "Help!"

But no one could help him at the moment. Wick held his right arm up, and Lynn and Robert huddled beside him. Broken glass smashed against Wick's own activated shield, falling in a circle around them.

Kevin and Trueblood were busy because a vortex formed just inside the front doors. Four men in grey tunics and with glowing white eyes stormed out of the opening. Each carried a jet-black scythe. Kevin blurred into motion, snatched a side table, and hurled it across the atrium into the new arrivals. Trueblood began casting spells at the men. These actions served to hold the attackers away from Jonah and his cousins.

One of the Grim Hounds had rolled to its feet and ran toward the stairs, getting in position to jump on the sphere from the second floor landing. "Help!" Jonah shouted.

Robert grabbed the ladder and stood it under him. Wick took a fistful of glittery powder from a small brown sack and blew on it. A huge cloud of sparkly silvery dust blossomed into the air. The second Grim Hound, which had slammed into the far wall, ran straight through it.

The dust acted like metal drawn to a magnet as it attached itself to the hound's body. The creature stumbled and rolled around, knocking café tables and chairs in every direction. After a few frenzied moments, it gave up trying to dislodge the dust. Its claws slid on the smooth marble as it regained its feet and charged for the stairway.

By that time, Lynn stood in its path, her silver blades in hand. She whirled and struck the now-visible Grim Hound across its snout. It growled furiously, baring its doubled row of teeth as it scrambled backward.

Lynn tossed her braids over her shoulder. "Thanks, Wick, but I kind of wish I couldn't see it."

Wick didn't answer because he and Robert stared in shock at a real Grim Hound.

"Get down." Kevin's shout stirred the boys into action. The Fallen Reaper charged past them to take on more attackers, who came out of a new vortex near the West entrance.

Jonah lowered his weight onto the ladder and sucked in a breath as his injured hands gripped the top. He watched, amazed at Kevin's skills. But he only had a second to catch his breath before the first Grim Hound launched itself from the second floor landing.

Jonah gazed at it in morbid fascination as the creature sailed through the air, hit the sphere and scrambled for a hold. The impact snapped two of the holding cables, allowing the entire sphere to swing away.

Jonah sprang into motion and made it halfway down the ladder before the sphere swung back toward him. The Grim Hound slipped, its

The Protector's Ring

hindquarters smacking into the top of the ladder, sending it spinning in one direction and Jonah in the other. He landed on the polished marble floor and grunted as pain blossomed along his shoulder and arm.

Wick overcame his shock and ran to help. "Lucky you were halfway down."

"Yeah, just great."

A snapping sound came from above as the Grim Hound tried to claw its way around to the still-glowing ring.

Oh no! He had created a beacon for the creature to follow.

The mounting plates couldn't support the added weight and the remaining cables tore themselves from the ceiling. The entire sphere fell like a meteor and hit with a huge, ground-shaking bang.

Hundreds of pieces of sphere, rings, and metal rods flew everywhere. Several pieces of debris nicked Jonah's arms as he shielded his head from the worst of it. Silence rolled across the atrium, and only Kevin moved. He turned to kill the Grim Hound.

As he lunged for it, a bright sphere appeared in front of him. He impacted and bounced back, dazed. A tall man with dark curly hair, black tunic, and pants had stepped out of another vortex, his thin fingers raised like claws. "Don't touch Deyanira's pets." His mouth curved into a devilish grin. He waved his hands to cast another spell at Kevin. Trueblood dodged between them, deflecting the attack.

She stood straight, looking dignified and unruffled. "I'll deal with him." And she did, casting a series of spells at the sorcerer. His smile faded as he had to defend himself. They circled around each other, but Trueblood managed to maneuver the sorcerer into the West wing. Their continued fight shook the floors.

Jonah had never seen anything like it. Even the silvery-dust-covered Grim Hound paused in its attempts to reach the stairs. Kevin, though, was engaged again with another set of attackers who had followed the sorcerer through the vortex.

Robert made use of the general confusion to edge around the distracted silvery-dust-covered Grim Hound to crouch near a tangle of parts. He put something in the archive box, and the locks clicked shut.

The second Grim Hound turned at the sound and stepped toward Robert. Lynn jumped between them and nicked the Grim Hound across the jaw with a blade. The creature growled in pain as the cut sparked.

"Stay behind me, Robert."

The Grim Hound growled in frustration but didn't approach her. Jonah sensed and understood its basic desire. It needed that ring or Deyanira would punish it.

Robert took a step toward the stairs, drawing Lynn's attention. "Don't move!"

"We can't stay here all night, Lynn." Robert held up the box. "I want to put this in the safe. We drew protective sigils on it. The Grim Hound won't be able to touch it."

Lynn huffed. "Fine. You stay right behind me."

They edged toward the stairs together, with Lynn carefully keeping her body between the Grim Hound and Robert at all times, her blades ready. When they reached the foot of the stairs, Robert sprinted up them. The Grim Hound let out a fierce snarl and Lynn poked it on the nose, forcing it back.

Robert and Wick's planning impressed Jonah. It also helped that Lynn had real Reaper blades, which could hurt anything supernatural, including Grim Hounds. Something would have to give soon; Jonah could sense it. He opened his mouth to warn Lynn when the Grim Hound crouched and leapt.

It soared over Lynn's head and grabbed hold of the second floor railing, which sagged under the weight. Jonah prayed the creature might crash back down to the atrium. Instead, the Grim Hound managed to pull itself onto the landing. Lynn screamed in frustration as she ran up the stairs.

The Grim Hound wasted no time in smashing through the door to the attic and bounded in after Robert.

The Protector's Ring

CHAPTER THIRTY-EIGHT
THROUGH THE VORTEX

Lynn reached the broken attic door and charged inside. Knowing he'd never get up the stairs in time, Jonah gripped Wick's shoulder and phased.

When they reappeared in the attic, Wick stumbled away, rubbing his arms. "Whoa! That's wicked, dude."

Jonah shook off the slight dizziness and scanned the attic. His jaw dropped. Lynn had the Grim Hound backed into the office section of the attic amidst destroyed computers and overturned desks.

Jonah couldn't understand her actions until he heard a moan. Looking up, he saw Robert holding onto a rafter over the club area. He still held the archive box, even though his arm dripped blood onto the ground. "Finish it, Lynn."

The sounds of heavy thumps drew closer. Jonah's Death Sense screamed just before the second Grim Hound bounded into view. It bulldozed Wick in the back and sent him flying into Lynn. Before Jonah could dodge to the side, the creature knocked him into the wall.

Jonah slid to the floor and watched in horror as the Grim Hound leapt up and swatted at Robert with a massive paw. His cousin yelled, dropped from the rafter, and landed on the old sofa.

The archive box fell right in front of the Grim Hound and was scooped up in its powerful jaws. The silver Grim Hound leapt over Wick and Lynn and tried to help its mate tear the box apart. The creatures acted like real dogs fighting over a bone, but the archive box defied their efforts.

Robert moaned from the other side of the sofa. "Stop them. Get the box."

Lynn untangled herself from Wick and rose to her feet. The first Grim Hound, with the box in its jaws, turned and crashed through the attic window, ripping the blue curtain. The silver Grim Hound leapt out of the opening behind its mate.

Lynn ran to the window. "Dang it!"

Jonah stepped past a dazed Wick to look out the shattered window. "We have to go after them."

"Won't they phase?"

"They can't. They need a vortex, and Deyanira hasn't opened one yet." Jonah closed his eyes. "I can feel the ring." He ran for the staircase.

"Jonah, wait!" Lynn wrapped her arms around his shoulders just before he phased. A second later, they both reappeared beside their bikes. Lynn released him and stared at her arms. "That was freaky."

"You grabbed onto me," Jonah said, unlocking his bike. Lynn didn't hesitate to unlock her own and they set off after the Grim Hounds.

Speeding down the moonlit hillside on his bike seemed stupid and suicidal to Jonah, who couldn't see anything until he was on top of it. He sensed Lynn right behind him and knew she focused on the silver-dust-covered Grim Hound, which seemed to glow in the moonlight. He tried to weave faster through the trees and smacked his head against a low-hanging branch for his efforts.

The second Grim Hound had paused to bang the box against the trees in an attempt to get it open. That gave Jonah an idea. He concentrated on that Grim Hound, waiting for it to throw the box against the tree. When it did, he phased.

A moment later, he reappeared beside the Grim Hound and caught the box just as it bounced off the tree. The silver Grim Hound responded faster than he had expected. It raked a paw across his back, ripping his shirt and almost knocking him from the bike. Jonah screamed as he kept pedaling.

"Go, Jonah!" Lynn shouted from behind him. The Grim Hounds howled as if to answer her.

The Protector's Ring

Seconds later, he burst into the creek-side clearing. Before he could adjust, his wheel hit one of the large rocks and sent him flying into the water. His bike tumbled across the creek and onto the opposite side. The archive box splashed into the water several feet away.

Jonah pushed himself toward the half-submerged box, but a huge, silver paw splashed down in the water right in front of him. Jonah stumbled back and fell on his butt.

The silver Grim Hound stepped toward him, ignoring the archive box. The red eyes glowed eerily bright in the dimness as it stalked closer. Jonah expected the creature to attack. When the Grim Hound hesitated, he waved to it.

"Hi, ugly."

The Grim Hound bared its double row of razor-sharp teeth. Jonah knew he should have been more frightened, but he wasn't. The creature appeared to recognize him, making Jonah wonder about the beast's intelligence.

"Sorry about the silver dust."

The Grim Hound cocked its head to the side like a real dog, as if watching something interesting. Or listening to something, Jonah thought. Was Deyanira communicating with it? She could do that. He'd seen that for himself in his strange dream-walk the first night here in Mount Vernon. Then Jonah sucked in a startled breath. *Could this be the same Grim Hound?*

He had thought Kevin decapitated that one. Or had the Fallen Reaper? As Jonah concentrated on the beast, he knew it wasn't the same one that had chased him from the Teen Center. This one felt different, familiar to him. It had to be the one from the dream-walk. Did riding along inside the hound's mind create a connection? Almost like the one with the ring?

The creature shook its head, let out a whine, and pawed at the ground. *It doesn't want to attack me.* Jonah suspected that Deyanira shouted her attack command into the creature's mind. As if confirming his thoughts, the Grim Hound focused on him, and Jonah inched backward. It crouched low, muscles tensed to spring, and Jonah's Death Sense spiked.

Lynn burst into the clearing, rolled off her bike, and came up slicing at the silver Grim Hound. The creature leapt aside, its huge paws dripping mud and water all over Jonah. Lynn positioned herself in front of him.

"Forget about me." Jonah smacked his hand down in the muddy water. "Get the box."

"Don't be crazy, Jonah." Lynn reached down and hauled him to his feet.

The first Grim Hound scooped up the box. Both creatures became rigid as statues, focusing on the same spot on the opposite side of the creek.

Jonah thought he could feel a change in the air. "Deyanira's opening a vortex."

A moment later, it blossomed into view, giving off its own shimmering, greenish light.

Lynn let out a frustrated scream. Her blades flashed as she rushed the Grim Hounds. The silver one leapt first through the vortex. The second, with the box in its jaws, turned to follow.

"No!" Jonah reached out for the ring with his mind. He could feel it, and he refused to let it go. The Second Grim Hound leapt for the vortex, then twisted around almost comically in midair. Its body disappeared in the vaporous opening of the vortex while its head stayed on this side. It tugged furiously at the box, trying to yank it through.

Jonah called on the ring. "You won't take it!" He could feel it pressing against the inside of the archive box, trying to come to him.

"Keep it there!" Lynn shouted to Jonah. She readied herself to strike the creature just as Jonah's Death Sense spiked.

"Lynn, look out!"

A ball of green supernatural fire spewed out of the vortex, singeing the Grim Hound. Lynn ducked as soon as Jonah warned her, but he hesitated and barely made it out of the way in time.

The fireball hit the stream, and a fog enveloped the clearing. Jonah lost sight of the Grim Hound, and his concentration faltered. He could feel it go as the Grim Hound took the ring through the vortex. "Dang it!"

The vortex snapped closed, plunging the area into moonlit dimness. Jonah slumped in muddy creek water. Lynn seemed to materialize out of the fog. Several braids were loose, giving her an impressive silhouette as she stood over him. Jonah glanced up at her. "I'm sorry I couldn't hold on longer."

"Don't apologize, Jonah. You were awesome. Sorry I took so long. I got tangled in vines."

Jonah lowered his head, feeling defeated. "Deyanira has the ring."

"That's not a problem."

"But we don't know where Deyanira is hiding."

"Yes we do. Robert searched the county records." At the mention of her brother, Lynn grew serious. "Let's head back."

As they turned, Jonah felt the change in the air that told of someone phasing. He tensed and Lynn drew her blades. Kevin stepped through the fading fog with Trueblood, Robert, and Wick trailing behind.

He searched the clearing before turning to Jonah. "What happened?"

"Deyanira opened a vortex and the Grim Hounds ran through."

Kevin nodded to Trueblood. "Can you detect it?"

The Mage, with one of her braids unraveling and hanging loose, stepped to the water's edge and raised a hand. "Yes, I can. She's opened so many that I can follow the magic back to the source."

Jonah was impressed with the quiet, powerful woman. As he caught Kevin's look, something occurred to him. "What took you so long?"

"We had to clean up and get out of the center. We couldn't leave injured mortals laying around."

"It's part of what we have to do," Trueblood explained, "to keep mortals oblivious to the supernatural world around them."

Robert, his arm bandaged with a torn piece of his shirt, stepped around Kevin.

Lynn gasped and rushed over to look over the bandage. "How is he, Wick?"

"He's okay. We turned on the alarm and then cleared out." Wick gave Trueblood an awed look. "She opened a vortex so Kevin could carry the… mortals through. It was wikid awesome." Jonah opened his mouth to ask a question, but Wick beat him to the answer. "When someone sees that damage, they're going to wonder why the alarms didn't go off. We don't want any of the workers getting blamed for it not setting it."

Lynn finished checking Robert's arm. "Did you clean up everything?"

Robert surprised everyone when he answered, like he'd been turned on. "We wiped off the doors and security locks." Robert shook his head and continued in a numb voice, "The Summit is a total loss."

"It's time to get even, Robert," Lynn said. "Tell me you have Deyanira's location."

"Of course I do."

Lynn thumped Robert's backpack. "Do you have what you need?"

"I can deal with the door."

"And I can deal with the wards." Wick held up his arm to show more than one bracelet on it. He handed Lynn her backpack.

She slipped it on just as Kevin raised his hands.

"You guys aren't going anywhere."

Jonah had been expecting this from the moment Kevin and Trueblood showed up. "We have to go after the ring."

"Deyanira could have taken the ring to the Grim Reaper by now," Kevin countered.

"I don't think she'll go anywhere," Lynn cut in. "She has to make sure the ring is in the archive box."

Jonah's eyes widened. "She won't be able to open it." He glanced back at Robert, who smiled at him.

"Hey, I have good ideas sometimes."

Trueblood gave him a curious look. "You have a Seeker's box?"

Robert shrugged. "Jonah's parents gave it to me."

Jonah smiled at the Mage's astonished expression, but a problem presented itself. "Deyanira lives fifteen miles away. That's too far out for bikes."

"That won't be a problem." Kevin glanced at Trueblood. "Open a vortex."

"Are you sure? Maybe we should wait for the others."

"They're right. Deyanira won't take the box over, not until she's sure. This is the best chance."

"This is also dangerous, Kevin."

He shrugged. "I think Deyanira sent most of her people already. If not, well, I'll be with them. You bring Marcus when you can."

The Protector's Ring

Jonah felt a wave of appreciation toward the older boy for standing with them. He was sure Marcus wouldn't agree if he were here. But at least now, they had a fighting chance to get the ring.

Trueblood raised her hand, her brow furrowed. Within seconds, a large bluish vortex opened. She raised an eyebrow to Kevin. "Be careful."

Kevin faced the group and activated his blades. They shone a pale blue in the vibrant light of the vortex. "I'll go first. Jonah, you come behind me. Wick and Robert come next. Lynn, you bring up the rear, blades ready."

Lynn slipped out her blades and activated them.

With a final glance at Trueblood, Kevin stepped into the vortex. Jonah's fear and excitement built to a crescendo as he moved forward. He didn't know what he'd face on the other end, but he felt ready with Kevin, his cousins, and Wick with him. Taking a deep breath, he stepped into the swirling mass of magical vapor and left the clearing behind.

CHAPTER THIRTY-NINE
STATUES, WARDS, AND STEEL

Going through a vortex was similar, yet different, to phasing. It was different because the trip took longer since you had to walk or run. However, the vapor was like a dense fog or mist touching every inch of your body, just like a phase.

Seconds after entering the vortex, Jonah exited onto a dirt road outside an old rusted gate directly in front of the house. Vapor from the vortex clung to him for a few moments, causing him to shiver.

Wick didn't seem bothered at all as he exited and leaned against the gate. "No lights on inside."

Lynn started through the gate, but Wick blocked her path. "Before we attempt the house, I have an idea." He turned to Jonah. "Can you still sense the ring?"

"I can't feel it."

"Maybe because it's in the box."

"More likely Deyanira has it in a warded location," Kevin concluded. He opened the gate. "Let's go."

The paint peeled off the walls of the deteriorated plantation house, exposing crumbling masonry underneath. The shutters were rotten and hung at severe angles to most of the windows, which were all shattered.

But it wasn't the depressing appearance of the old house that made Jonah and the others edgy. Without warning, fear gripped Jonah's stomach. As they drew closer to the house, the fear became an intense urge to turn back.

"Do you feel that?" Wick's voice caused everyone to jump. He didn't seem to notice their reactions as he faced the eerie mansion. "Deyanira set up a deflection charm. It's designed to keep curious people away." Wick started to walk on, following Kevin but had to pause when he realized no one else followed. "Don't worry. It'll stop affecting us once we're inside."

Kevin snorted and continued toward the house, Wick right behind. Robert, Lynn, and Jonah traded dubious glances and kept going.

When they mounted the porch, Jonah followed Wick to one window while Lynn and Robert chose another. Each step was accompanied by a growing sense of dread. The urge to run away intensified. Wick scrambled through their window without any apparent problem, but Jonah required an act of pure will to place a leg through the opening. Voices kept shouting in his head that his parents were in trouble and would die. Above it all, he heard a cold, inhuman laugh. The fear morphed to dismay until a small voice spoke in his mind. *Don't be afraid.*

Halfway through the window, Jonah felt a jerk on his inside leg, as if someone had given him a yank. Suddenly, he was falling. As he made contact with something hard, the huge pressure lifted from his shoulders. He blinked and tried to focus as Wick helped him off the floor.

"See?" Wick patted him on the shoulder.

Jonah rubbed his sore arms and looked around. Kevin had a haunted expression and his shoulders shook as if he was in pain. When he saw Jonah watching, he stood tall and moved off, searching the room.

Lynn was across the room, gripping the window frame to keep from falling.

Robert held out a steadying hand to his sister. "Are you okay?"

"I'm fine. Just give me a minute." She wandered a short distance away.

Wick hurried over and tugged Robert in the opposite direction. Robert whirled on his friend. "First we find out about wards and now deflection charms?"

"I know, Bobby. Deyanira was a sorceress in her first life." Wick gave Jonah a troubled look. "We should be ready for more magic."

Robert threw his hands up as he looked around the decaying house. "Where to now?"

Lynn came up and leaned on her brother's shoulder. "Look for a door to the basement, genius. Right, Kevin?"

The Fallen Reaper motioned to a door down a narrow hallway. It showed signs of recent use. The dust on the floor in front of it had been swept away in a long curve. Several sets of footprints were visible, too.

Lynn eyed the door. "Do you sense anything, Wick?"

"No."

"What about you, Jonah?"

"I can't tell."

Kevin opened the door and grimaced when it creaked loudly in the silence. "Here goes." He took a breath and stepped into the darkened stairway.

Jonah felt like he was swallowed by the pitch darkness; the only sound was their footsteps. He thought they had descended three floors before they reached the bottom. Lynn entered a wide, torch-lit hallway with an arched ceiling and a broken stone floor. Jonah thought the dark recesses halfway down the hallway might be the entrances to side tunnels.

Lynn spoke from the back of the line. "Does any of this look familiar, Jonah?"

"No, it doesn't. There must be another stairway at the other end."

"Great," Kevin muttered. "Everybody stay alert." He started forward.

Jonah sensed the heightened tension around him, but nothing happened as they continued down the tunnel. Still, Jonah was certain that something was wrong, besides being in Deyanira's hidden tunnel.

Jonah tugged on Kevin's shirt as they reached the bottom of the next stairway. "This is the hallway I saw in the dream-walk."

Kevin nodded and looked over Jonah's head at Wick. "It's your turn to do your thing."

Wick raised his hand and took one step forward, and then another. After the third step, he paused. "Just as I thought. These wards are designed to stun, not kill."

Jonah inched his way forward until he stood beside Wick. "Can you get through them?"

Wick held out his wrist, showing Jonah the bracelets. "That's why I have these."

"But these wards are different from Trueblood's," Robert objected, directly behind Jonah.

"Calm yourself, Bobby. I'll be able to set them off."

Even Lynn tossed an unsure look over her shoulder before she went back to watching the stairway. "Isn't that dangerous?"

"There's only one way to find out."

Robert tried to step in front of his friend, but Wick pulled him away from the invisible ward.

"Whoa, dude. Don't get to close or you'll set it off. And you don't have a shield. I'll be all right." He looked at Jonah. "I think everyone should step back."

When Robert hesitated, Jonah tugged on his cousin's backpack to get him to move. Wick raised his hand to activate his shield. The telltale blue haze surrounded him, making the hairs on Jonah's arm rise. He shivered from anticipation or anxiety; he wasn't sure which.

When Wick stepped forward, a bolt of energy hit him. The air popped and sizzled. After a few more seconds, the fireworks abruptly died out. Wick lowered his arm and sniffed the air. "That one's down. I tripped it."

Jonah released a breath he hadn't realized he held. Wick's plan was like deliberately exploding mines to clear a path.

"Jonah, how many did you say there were?"

"Four."

Wick prepared himself and started the whole thing all over again. He set off two more wards in the same fashion as the first. Jonah noticed that each time, the boy's expression grew more concerned. Wick's arm begun to tremble, and the bracelet blackened and smoked.

Wick held up the bracelet afterward and inspected it. "It's about done. It may take one more."

He stepped forward and tripped the fourth ward. This time, his bracelet sparked and started to burn. Wick ripped it off and threw it to the ground before the ward completely dissipated. The remaining power zapped him, and he fell to his knees.

Robert didn't wait for the okay. He rushed forward and helped his buddy to his feet. Wick flashed him a lopsided grin. "I'm cool. Truth is, those bracelets lasted longer than I expected." He nodded toward the metal door. "Your turn, Bobby."

Wick reached out and Jonah's Death Sense spiked through his persistent headache. Before Jonah could open his mouth, Wick brushed his hand along the door. Jonah thought he saw a shocked expression on Wick's face a second before another ward went off with a loud bang.

Energy raced up and down Wick's arms and legs and even made his twists crackle with energy. He collapsed to the ground, shook violently for a few terrifying moments, and then didn't move.

Lynn and Robert screamed his name in unison and ran to his side. Lynn turned him over, pressed her ear against his chest, and let out a sigh of relief. "He's still breathing. Thank God."

Robert whirled on Jonah. "Why didn't you warn him?"

"I'm sorry, Robert."

Jonah looked at Lynn for help. She stepped forward, grabbed Robert's shoulder, and shook him. "Robert."

"What?" He rounded on his sister but Lynn didn't back off.

"Robert, you need to open the door. Wick told us the wards only stun. He'll be fine." Lynn leaned so close, their foreheads nearly touched. She looked directly into her twin brother's eyes. "I'll stay with him. You unlock the door. Okay?"

Robert nodded and stalked to the door without looking at Jonah.

"I'm sorry I couldn't warn him in time. My Death Sense is on overload."

Lynn pulled Jonah back and lowered her voice so Robert wouldn't hear. "He doesn't blame you." She glanced at her brother. "Is your Death Sense really that bad now?"

"I just have a huge buzz in my head and a blinding headache. I'm fighting to keep things straight."

"We better finish this and get out of here." Lynn knelt beside Wick.

Robert had his backpack off and his small laptop on the floor in front of him. He detached the door's colored keypad from the mounting and connected his computer to the exposed wires underneath.

"This may take a few minutes," Robert explained as he worked. "I have to find the combination while keeping the security system from issuing an alert." Robert typed on the small keyboard. Jonah peeked over his shoulder but couldn't understand the code that scrolled up the computer screen.

One of the lights on the dangling color keypad lit up.

"That's one. Five more lights to go." Robert glanced up at Jonah. "You didn't see the code in your dream?"

"The clerk moved too fast. I'm sorry."

"That's okay. I'll have this door opened in no time."

Jonah relaxed; his cousin didn't sound angry anymore. Talking about these things seemed to keep Robert from worrying about Wick.

Three more lights on the panel lit up. Robert frowned, speaking as he typed. "I'll have to stay here to keep the system from sounding the alarm."

Wick surprised everyone and mumbled something. Robert didn't miss a beat. "What did he say?"

Lynn lowered her ear to Wick's mouth which still moved. "It sounds like he's saying, 'Too late.'"

Robert glanced at her while his fingers flew over the laptop keys. "Oh, boy. I've heard him say that wards can be like security alarms. You set one off, and the person who made it gets a warning."

Lynn stood. "Then I should stay here, too. In case someone comes. Wick can't be moved until he's awake, anyway."

"But–" Jonah began but he stopped when the final two lights lit up. The lock mechanism in the door clicked and it swung open. Kevin pulled Jonah back and stood ready with his blades activated. Nothing happened. Clearly visible inside the chamber, Robert's archive box sat on the center pedestal, well lit and inviting.

"I don't like this," Kevin said. "It's a trap."

"At least Deyanira doesn't want to kill me." Jonah knew that wasn't totally true. Deyanira had commanded the silver Grim Hound to attack, he was sure of it. He kept that information to himself as he moved around Kevin to face the open metal door. As he did, they heard a distant growl from the direction of the stairs.

Lynn drew out her blades and positioned herself between the stairway and Wick. "You and Kevin should go, Jonah."

"No," Kevin said. "We should take care of whatever they send first, then we can check out the chamber."

Jonah agreed with Lynn. This was the reason they had come here, and he didn't want to stop now. The sudden spike of his Death Sense caused Jonah to wince. Before he could warn the others, a pair of hands gripped him from behind and yanked him into the chamber. The metal door slammed shut.

The Protector's Ring

CHAPTER FORTY
THE PROTECTOR'S RING

Jonah experienced a moment of pure fear as he sprawled on the floor just inside the chamber. His reflexes were ready and waiting for the person to attack. Nothing happened. The room remained silent. He strained to see into the room's few shadows.

"Who's there?"

In answer, a shape moved, causing Jonah's heart to leap into his throat. The store clerk, or rather the Wraith, stepped into the light and gazed down on him. Dull thuds came from the metal door, breaking the eerie silence in the chamber.

Jonah expected that was Kevin and Lynn trying to get in. He bet that Robert wouldn't be able to override the lock this time. This had been a trap, set just for him. The most unnerving thing was the continued silence from the store clerk, as if he waited for something.

He's waiting for Deyanira, Jonah decided.

As the initial panic receded, he took the opportunity to scan the chamber. It appeared exactly as he remembered it from the dream-walk. The curved metal walls arched high overhead toward a much smaller circle at the apex. The stone portal Deyanira would use stood opposite the metal door.

Robert's archive box sat atop the stone pedestal in the center of the room. Spotlights high on the wall shone down on it. Crossing the chamber, Jonah reached out to touch it with his right hand. He sensed the ring inside and relaxed, running his fingers along the edges. As he did, a familiar rush of coldness reached him and Deyanira's stony voice floated through the chamber.

"Jonah Blackstone."

Deyanira stood in front of the portal, which showed a dark cavern on the other side. The former sorceress wore a red dress this time, her hair pulled so tightly back against her head that her square black glasses seemed to pop off her face.

She strode slowly toward the pedestal, watching Jonah intently. When she reached the pedestal, she, too, touched the archive box with a finger. Jonah pulled his hand away, fearing she would discover his connection to the ring.

Deyanira smiled and started to circle around the pedestal toward him. He moved away, maintaining their distance.

"You've caused a lot of trouble for one so young." Her voice was mild. "Why, you're just a little boy."

Jonah's tempered flared at her mocking tone. At the same time, he remembered Lynn's warning: Don't let her get to you.

"Hmmm. Someone has been learning self-control. Admirable." She made a full circle around the pedestal and stopped. "Tell me, Jonah Blackstone, why have you broken into my house and caused so much damage?"

"I want the ring."

Deyanira frowned for a second and narrowed her eyes. "I could have you and your cousins arrested for breaking and entering. You wantonly set off my security alarms and broke into a secured chamber. Isaiah Blackstone would have been shocked that his son turned out to be such a delinquent."

"You don't know anything about my dad." Jonah spoke before he could stop himself.

Deyanira laughed. "Child, I spent decades with your father. He became one of us, one of the KIN. I will admit that he proved very good at his job. All the mayhem, all the pitiful souls he reaped from worthless mortal bodies. It was glorious!"

"Shut up!" Deyanira's gloating made him sick. "Shut up!"

"Watch your tone with me, Jonah Blackstone." Deyanira's voice carried an icy tone. "I know things about your father that would give you nightmares."

Jonah shivered. *Nightmares? Could she know about his dream-walks?* That thought scared him, and he decided to do something: he darted forward and grabbed the box. He strained and pulled, but it wouldn't budge.

Deyanira laughed again. "The box can't be moved."

Jonah gave up and stared at the dangerous Reaper. "Why don't you just take it to your master?"

Deyanira's smile disappeared instantly. "Don't insult my intelligence! We both know the box can't be opened except by the person who locked it."

"You want to make sure the ring is inside."

"Of course. Open the box for me, Jonah Blackstone, and I'll let you and your cousins go. I have no interest in hurting you."

For a wild second, Jonah played with the idea that Deyanira would let them go, but he realized that would never happen. She belonged to the KIN and wasn't into doing kind things for mortals.

"Sorry I can't help you."

"You're going to force me to get nasty, I see." Jonah stared at her. "I know what you're thinking. I have other options besides hurting you, Jonah Blackstone."

He heard a sound behind him and turned around. His heart sank. The clerk led Lynn and Robert into the room. Behind him were two more goons in the grey robes with white skulls on the chests. Their green-edged, black scythes hung from clips on their sashes. Jonah understood now. They were Wraith possessed. Deyanira had been working with them all along, even when she attacked his parents.

One of the Wraiths carried Wick over his shoulder and dumped him onto the cot. Robert and Lynn were stopped a few feet away. Behind the goons came the two Grim Hounds from the rec center. Kevin shuffled along between the beasts, his hands in a pair of heavy cuffs. The silver Grim Hound continued to shake its head, trying to dislodge the glittering dust while the other nipped at Kevin.

Jonah's Death Sense spiked, and he thought his head would split open. He turned back to Deyanira as he tried to keep from vomiting. "I can't open it."

Deyanira held up a hand and let her index finger point at Lynn, then Robert, and back as if playing a game in her head. Finally, her finger stopped on Lynn.

"I'll ask you one last time, Jonah Blackstone. Open the box."

"He can't open the box!" Robert moved forward. The clerk grabbed his arm and jerked him back.

Deyanira shook her head. "Pity."

She flicked her hand in a quick, fluid motion and shot a bolt of supernatural lightning at Lynn. It hit her square in the chest. She let out a strangled huff as if punched and then began screaming in pain. Robert and Jonah screamed at the same time. The clerk held Robert tightly, and one of the goons grabbed Jonah when he moved to help. The man took his scythe and pressed it against Jonah's neck.

A tear rolled down Jonah's cheek as he was forced to watch Lynn convulse. The energy played up and down the length of her body. It took several horrible seconds for the effect to dissipate.

When it finally did, Lynn curled up in a ball and began to sob. Tears streaked Robert's face, and Jonah's breath came fast. He couldn't believe it.

Deyanira turned on him. "If you don't want your cousin to suffer more pain, then open the box."

"I–I can't open it."

She gave a dramatic sigh and shot Lynn with another lightning bolt. Her screams were even more anguished this time. Jonah couldn't do anything. The Wraith-possessed goon wisely pinned his arm behind his back and pressed the scythe into his neck, drawing blood.

When the second bolt faded, Lynn's screams abruptly died away. She didn't move.

Robert's voice was raw from shouting and crying. "Stop it! He's telling the truth. He can't open the box because it's mine!"

"Robert."

"No, Jonah! I can't let her hurt my sister anymore! First Wick and now Lynn." Robert spoke with so much pain that Jonah thought his own heart would burst.

The Protector's Ring

Deyanira advanced on Robert, looking him up and down. "So." She let the word drag out. "The Seeker's box is yours? Where did you get it?"

"It doesn't matter. I'll open it. Just don't hurt my sister anymore. Please!"

Deyanira watched Robert for a moment until he pleaded with her again. She gestured to the clerk, who let Robert go. Jonah struggled in the Wraith's grip when his cousin hesitated, looking at his sister. Deyanira pointed sharply at the box.

"Open it."

Robert wiped the tears from his face and walked to the pedestal. He touched the lock mechanism, causing the locks to click and slide back into their recesses. Robert's hands shook as he activated the release on the lid and opened the box. Faint, pulsing amber light reflected off his skin.

He dropped his hands to his sides and looked around, but Deyanira's attention remained on the opened box. He took one step, and when no one stopped him, ran to Lynn's side and sat beside her. Placing Lynn's head in his lap, he began rocking back and forth, muttering to her.

Deyanira gazed into the opened archive box.

"The Protector's Ring. All this trouble over one ring." Despite her clear fascination, she didn't reach in and take the ring. Instead, she snapped at Jonah, "You. Come here and take the ring out of the box."

"Why don't you do it?"

Deyanira sneered and raised a hand toward Robert and Lynn.

"Wait! I'll do it." At a nod from Deyanira, the Goon lowered his scythe. Jonah yanked his arm free and walked over to the box.

Deyanira gave him plenty of room as he reached in and gripped the ring. It was warm to the touch and the pulsing was like an actual heartbeat. Jonah held the ring up. "It's beautiful."

"Here!" Deyanira held a small sack in her hands. "Put it in here, now!" She raised a hand toward Robert and Lynn to back up her command.

Jonah's rebellious side wanted to do something, but that would cause his cousins more pain. He reached out to drop the ring in the bag when he sensed the increase of pressure a second before he heard a familiar metallic swishing sound. Jonah thought someone had activated Lynn's blades until he heard Marcus's voice.

"I told you, Deyanira. You will never have the ring."

Jonah's heart leapt as he saw Marcus, Omar, Trueblood, and Emily standing around the edge of the chamber. He couldn't understand how they had managed to phase inside.

Wick hissed at Jonah to get his attention and pointed down at the symbol on the floor. He had rubbed out a small portion of it.

The Grim Hounds attacked. Emily blurred into motion and sliced one of the creature's head cleanly off. A spray of blood splattered the floor, but it and the creature soon dissolved into puddles of ecto goo. Emily turned and cut Kevin's cuffs with follow-up slices of her blades.

Trueblood had attacked the second Grim Hound with supernatural lightning. The creature was bathed in the glow of it, howling in pain. Kevin, with a pair of blades in hand, took down the second hound just as Emily had taken out the first.

Jonah ducked and rolled toward Lynn's backpack and drew out her blades. He whirled and managed to block first one swipe of a scythe, and then another. When the man prepared to strike a third time, Jonah dodge forward and stabbed him in the arm holding the weapon. The man screamed as he flailed backward, the scythe dropping to the floor. Marcus didn't miss a beat and sliced him across the back. Sparks flared out of the guy's mouth and eyes as the Wraith inside died.

Marcus whirled around to face the second goon, blocking swipes of his scythe. Marcus blurred into motion, cutting him across the chest with both blades and leaving a blood-stained X in the grey tunic. The goon's eyes flashed as one more Wraith was killed.

Meanwhile, Omar and Wick helped Robert and Lynn to the door. They had to duck aside when a third goon charged inside the chamber.

The man lunged straight at Jonah. The Wraith was so focused on the blade in Jonah's left hand, gripping it with both of his and trying to crush it, that he didn't give Jonah's free hand any mind. Jonah grabbed the man's head just as he had seen Deyanira do in the dream-vision.

He didn't know if he could suck out a human soul. He just hoped he could suck out a Wraith, hopefully before the man broke his wrist. He held on to the Wraith's head, digging his fingers into the skin, unsure of what to do next. Just as he feared he'd made a mistake, he sensed something, like a burning flame.

The Protector's Ring

It was the person's soul, but the flame was wrapped in what looked like a spiky dark vine. *That's the Wraith!*

Jonah pushed against the angry spirit. The Wraith resisted and howled in response. Jonah's Reaper side swelled with authority and he shouted, "Out!"

The Wraith howled again, in obvious pain as it was sucked from the man's body. For a second, Jonah wondered if it was painful for a Wraith to be wrenched out of a mortal. He didn't care, but that thought stopped him from grabbing the Wraith as it broke free and soared up through the grate at the top of the chamber.

Jonah stared at his trembling hand. *I forced a Wraith out of a body.*

He only had seconds to exult in his accomplishment because the man's body sagged onto him. Jonah thought he would hit the ground under the added weight, but Marcus grabbed the man's collar and lifted him away. He gave Jonah an intense stare before barking orders to the others. "Get these people out of here, now."

Emily grabbed hold of the man's body and phased. Trueblood already grasped the one Marcus had cut down, and she opened a vortex to drag the man from the chamber. Kevin and Robert held up Lynn, and all three phased a second later. Only Jonah, Wick, Omar, and the third unconscious goon remained behind.

"Move back." Marcus positioned himself between Deyanira and the others. Just like the dream, they readied themselves and blurred into motion. The fighting style alternated between blinding-fast movements and short pauses. Jonah thought that Marcus had to use an incredible amount of his stored energy to keep up with Deyanira.

Marcus's black long coat whipped around as he attacked with slashes and precise thrusts of the blades. For a moment, Deyanira fought defensively. Then she did what Jonah hoped she wouldn't do: she began to morph into her true form. She became at least a foot taller, more skeletal, and she wore the blood-red robe.

Wick sat up on the cot. "Whoa!"

Jonah would have thought fighting in a robe would hamper Deyanira. However, she seemed to get even stronger and faster. *Of course*, Jonah thought. The portal had been opened during the initial confusion. Deyanira was drawing power from her Master.

Jonah didn't know what he could do because Deyanira and Marcus continued to move with an odd fighting cadence. He thought about keeping the clerk at bay. Yet when he turned, he found the Wraith calmly watching the fight. His milky white eyes missed nothing.

Marcus made a desperate attempt to slash Deyanira and over reached. She delivered a devastating blow to his midsection. Jonah heard loud cracks, and Marcus fell to the ground. Blood seeped from the side of his mouth.

"Marcus!" Omar ran forward. Deyanira hit him with a blast of supernatural lightning, sending the man to his knees. Omar raised his head, pain etched in his face as he tried to crawl forward.

Deyanira stepped over Marcus and kicked his blades across the chamber. She planted her foot on Marcus's neck. "Stay where you are, Omar." She turned to Jonah. "Now, young Blackstone, bring me the ring or I'll snap this pathetic fool's neck!" She gave her foot a little twist. Marcus gagged and reached feebly for her foot.

The ring pulsed furiously in Jonah's pocket. He took it out but paused when he heard Wick whisper to him.

"Don't do it."

"Silence!" Deyanira glared at Wick, but he ignored her.

"She can't touch it, Jonah. She's a Reaper and afraid of it."

Deyanira roared in frustration.

Jonah feared she would snap Marcus's neck at any moment out of sheer rage. He couldn't stall any longer. He took a quick step toward Deyanira as she snapped her fingers. The clerk scurried over to pick up the discarded sack near the overturned pedestal and brought it to her.

Jonah held the ring up and Deyanira's eyes widened with triumph. "Put it in the sack, child."

Jonah's rebellious side won out, and he tightened his grip. The Protector's Ring was supposed to give the wearer power, and it had responded to him. Didn't that mean he was a Protector?

At that moment, Jonah made his decision. He didn't know if it would work, but he wanted to wipe that smirk off Deyanira's face. Too many people had died to keep the ring out of her hands. He wouldn't let her win.

The Protector's Ring

Jonah held up the pulsing ring and slowly put it on the index finger of his right hand.

Time stopped.

CHAPTER FORTY-ONE
GRIM FINALE

Did time stop or did I speed up?

Jonah didn't know which as he looked around the chamber. Everyone appeared frozen in place. Omar wore a terrified expression as he watched Marcus suffer. Deyanira looked shocked. Marcus grimaced as she pressed her foot against his throat. Wick sported a suspended relieved expression as he watched Jonah put on the ring. The clerk's eyebrows were high on his forehead in amazement. Everyone was fixed in place and unmoving.

Then the familiar sensation rolled along Jonah's skin and Deyanira's chamber disappeared. In the next moment, he stood on a mountainside overlook. Across the valley, on another mountain, was an immense building. *Is this a dream-walk?* He jumped when his thought echoed across the valley as if spoken aloud.

Something appeared at the corner of the platform. Jonah whirled toward it, and his breath caught in his throat.

"Dad?"

His dad didn't respond. In fact, his dad's body was semi-transparent, and he wore the ring. Jonah looked down and saw the ring on his own finger. He took a step toward his dad, and the image wavered and disappeared, replaced by an old man in classic hiking clothing. He held the same ring in his hands as if holding a precious treasure. *Mr. Halliwell.*

Jonah recognized the reclusive artist from a picture Robert had found. Halliwell disappeared and another person appeared. In fact, a whole series of people came and went in faster and faster succession. Jonah understood they represented every person who had ever worn the ring. The parade of

The Protector's Ring **309**

people finally ended with a tall, strong-looking man with rich, ebony skin who wore a royal blue, toga-like garment.

Unlike all the others, this man turned and mounted the platform. He raised an imposing arm and waved his hand in the air. *Behold.* His voice boomed across the hilltop, even though his mouth never moved.

A glowing symbol appeared, hovering about ten feet away.

Jonah stepped onto the platform and walked to the rail. His eyes widened as he took in the symbol. It was a bird of some kind, its long neck turned so that the beak faced backward. Deep down, he knew this symbol, something his mom or dad had shown him once. But he couldn't pull the fragment of memory into focus.

The man regarded Jonah. *Do you know the term* Sankofa?

Jonah sucked in a breath as that word ignited the memory. His parents had returned from one of their trips abroad. The symbol had been one of about fifty on a tablet from Ghana.

"Yeah. I've seen it before." He recalled his dad's rich voice explaining that the bird's beak was turned backward so it could see as well as get something from behind. "It means to learn from our past."

The man nodded, then pointed down into the valley. *Behold and learn.*

Jonah leaned over the railing, and his jaw dropped at what he saw far below. Instead of a true valley floor, he gazed upon an impossibly large crystal viewing surface divided into football-field-sized segments. Varying images of a magnificent city were displayed across many of them. The man's words seemed to form in Jonah's mind.

Sumer, the first civilization on the planet.

When it was destroyed, more images of other civilizations appeared. Again and again, the humans were destroyed until they were given powerful objects.

Watching the history lesson was like viewing bits of several shows at the same time. Jonah focused on an image of ring bearers, and the large screens obeyed. All switched to images of the people with rings. This allowed Jonah to catch the flow of the story. The humans with the powerful rings rallied mortals and restored the balance. Again, speaking directly into Jonah's mind, the voice floated to the surface.

Children of Light.

The images turned grim as the ring bearers were hunted down and killed. In the final images, the rings were gathered and hidden by the being who stood beside Jonah. The final image showed the same man with a powerful woman wearing a gleaming medallion and surrounded by four sons, all wearing rings.

Destiny.

The scenes changed again, this time to images of the Grim Reaper and another being in a grey robe standing on this very platform, looking out at the building across the valley. Jonah lifted his own gaze to the building. It was impossibly large, the upper portions hidden in the clouds. Understanding seeped into his mind. That was the Central Archives, storehouse of the recorded lives of all human beings who ever lived, and of all mortal knowledge.

Like a dam breaking, the entire history of the ring and its purpose rushed forward, downloading into Jonah's mind. Fearing he'd lose himself and his own memories, he staggered under the information assault. *Help,* his very soul pleaded. In answer, a part of him surged forward and lifted him away. As the tidal wave of knowledge flowed by, a cool remoteness descended over Jonah, allowing him to watch and learn without fear.

He relaxed into the cool yet strange power until the scenes changed again. A gasp escaped his lips and he leaned against the railing. He saw his mom and dad fighting their way through grey-robed attackers and into an amphitheater. As they reached the stage, a young guy wearing the Protector's Ring caused it to explode, killing all the attackers. Jonah's parents hid under his dad's long Reaper's coat, somehow protected from the blast.

Deyanira was there, and his dad refused to give her the ring. The next scene showed Marcus taking the oath of the Alliance Council and finally his mom and dad embracing while discussing hiding the ring. Jonah knew the rest of the story because he and his cousins found the ring.

Tears ran down his cheeks as he watched the super-sized image of his mom and dad together. And he understood their last message in the dream-walk. They did everything to protect him for as long as they could.

He soaked it up like a dry sponge and experienced a pang of regret as he sensed most of the specifics fading. But he would hold on to that last image of his parents for the rest of his life.

As the screens turned a pearlescent color, the being next to him answered the unspoken question. *You may not be able to access the information now. Yet someday, you will be able to recall it all.* He pointed to the ring on Jonah's finger.

Jonah held up his hand and asked, "Am I a Protector?"

No.

"Then what am I?"

You're something much more. That is the reason the ring has responded to you.

The man stood tall, his expression blank. He waited, still as a statue.

Jonah was at a loss until the ring pulsed. Untold numbers of voices began to echo through his mind, all making the same pledge in different languages, but Jonah understood them. *Forever standing in between, I maintain the balance. I am a Protector.*

The urge to repeat the pledge was strong, but Jonah reminded himself he wasn't a Protector. There was something else he needed to do. He gazed at the ring, sensing the increased pulse that didn't match his own heartbeat for once. It was if the ring anticipated something. *What?* He asked himself.

An image of what he did in the chamber came back to him. He'd been able to expel a Wraith from a mortal body. His Reaper side did that. *Of course!* The answer flooded into his mind. Covering the ring with his left hand, Jonah summoned his Reaper power. "Come out," he commanded. "I set you free."

When he spoke the last word, a pulse of energy shot out of the ring, up his arm, and over his entire body. The ring bucked, causing Jonah's arm to twitch. A ghostly shape detached itself from the ring and floated into the air.

Jonah's jaw dropped. It looked just like the quiet man standing beside him. The ghost swooped down and entered the man. He sucked in a startled breath and his skin seemed to glow with life as his chest heaved up and down.

It seemed like his body had been awakened from a long sleep. When he turned and leaned closer, the distant look was gone from his dark features, and Jonah sensed the first real emotion: sadness.

The man opened his mouth and spoke with a rich, deep voice. "You're so young to have this responsibility." He blinked. "I was older than you when I was chosen."

"Are you a Wraith?"

"No. I bound my spirit to that ring. For two thousand years, I waited for you to come. Now, I can move on and rest."

Jonah didn't understand. He pointed down at the display screens. "What about the last guy who wore the ring? He was a Protector. Why didn't he release you?"

"As you said, he was a protector, a mortal. They can't cross over to the Afterworld as you did. So I had to wait for you." The man patted his own chest. "I was never a Protector, either. My destiny was greater, to gather the rings and medallions in order to hide them from the darkness covering the world."

Jonah's eyes went out of focus as he recalled the Seer's words. "I'll change everything…"

"You'll restore the order."

"What are you?"

"I've had many names: The One, The Repairer of the Breech, and The Deliverer."

"And that's what I am?"

The man nodded. "If you believe in yourself."

That answer caused all kinds of questions to surface. But the image of his dead parents popped into his mind, overriding all the rest. "Were your parents… like mine?"

"My mother was a fallen one. My father was a mortal."

"Did they die?"

"Yes. It's a terrible burden, but it's your destiny." The man raised his strong chin to look off into the sky as it opened to shine a bright light on his body. He turned back to Jonah. "Remember that you're special, young Blackstone. This is just the beginning for you. Someday, you'll understand what you are and all that you can accomplish." The man rose into the air, his arms spreading wide, welcoming the light. He paused in mid-air, gazing at Jonah. "Listen to the ring. It will protect you and guide your actions."

With that, he soared off into the midst of the light. The opening, or whatever it was, snapped closed.

The Protector's Ring

Jonah imagined he'd feel alone with the stranger gone, but power and confidence swelled inside, and he knew what to do. He held the ring close to his mouth and whispered, "Take me back."

Jonah phased back to the dark chamber. Everyone remained frozen in time, but Jonah knew that would change in a second. With the ring's encouragement humming in his mind, Jonah raised his hand, thought *Sakoto*, and a torrent of wind rushed through the opening in the ceiling. Jonah sent the blast of wind directly into Deyanira.

Everything snapped into motion as she tumbled across the chamber. She was quick to roll back to her feet. When she saw the Protector's Ring on his finger, she screamed. "You can't use the ring!"

Deyanira's blades were in her hand in a flash. Jonah merely thought, and two flaming blades appeared in his hands. He met Deyanira midway. As they fought and whirled, Jonah allowed the ring to guide his hands. Each time their blades connected, brilliant flashes of light erupted and the sounds shook the chamber.

Jonah matched Deyanira, blow for blow. She might have been fast, but she wasn't adaptable, and before long, he began to outmaneuver her.

Enough of this, he thought. He swept his blades up and out, slicing through Deyanira's. The move nearly took her hands with the weapons. Before she could recover, Jonah used another blast of wind to pin her against the wall. Deyanira's scream of frustration was cut short as a petrified look transformed her face.

The Grim Reaper, taller and more massive than Deyanira, stood on the other side of the portal. His crimson robe writhed and moved like a living thing. Coldness, hatred, and anger emanated directly from him.

Deyanira crawled to the portal opening.

"He shouldn't have been able to use the ring. He's not a Protector."

The Grim Reaper ignored her, raised a skeletal red hand, and pointed at Jonah. When he spoke, his gravelly voice grated on Jonah's nerves. "Give me the ring and I'll let you live."

Jonah's eyes were drawn to the Grim Guards standing behind their Master. Each wore what Jonah hoped was a bone-white skeleton mask clearly visible underneath their hoods. They held large black scythes in their hands. Fear bit down on Jonah, and doubt nibbled at his mind.

The Grim Reaper's voice sliced through the air. "Yes. Yes. This is too much for you. You're just a boy. Take off the ring."

Jonah's rebellious circuits fired, and the fear receded a bit. Hackett's comments about the Grim Reaper bubbled to the surface. The Scythes were just symbols of fear. And the Grim Reaper fed off fear and misery.

Jonah grunted as the mental assault intensified, forcing him to his knees. He raised the ring close to his mouth with a trembling hand. "Help me. Please."

An energizing warmth sprang up around him. The horrible headache and pressure subsided. He could think clearly as confidence surged back into his body. Standing, he positioned himself to protect his friends.

The Grim Reaper raised his hands and held them still. A huge red ball of supernatural fire appeared and shot at Jonah.

A sudden rage took hold of Jonah's body as he deflected the fireball up and into the chamber. It exploded against the upper portion, dislodging a piece of metal and warping the others. Jonah ignored that as rage built inside him. He'd only seen red fireballs once: the day his parents died. He knew, at that moment, that the Grim Reaper had personally killed his mom and dad.

Jonah screamed, conjured his own green fireballs, and sent them through the portal. The Grim Reaper deflected them back through and into the chamber.

Omar pushed Wick out of the way of one of the fireballs. "Jonah!"

Jonah spared a glance around the chamber and realized he had been tricked into destroying it himself.

The Grim Reaper chuckled, and a shiver went down Jonah's spine when he spoke. "Embrace Death, young Blackstone, as your father did. Who knows, maybe you'll be reunited with your parents when you die."

Jonah grew even angrier. He didn't care if he brought down the chamber; he would make the Grim Reaper pay.

Marcus's weak voice penetrated Jonah's fog of rage. "Resist him, Jonah. He can use anger as well as fear and doubt." Marcus coughed. "Remember your father…"

Jonah gasped. If Marcus was right, why didn't the ring block the Grim Reaper's mental attack? The answer rang out in Jonah's mind like a bell on a clear day. He had allowed the anger to goad him. He had opened the door.

But how could he overcome the anger that still burned inside of him? His mind latched onto memories of his parents' bravery. Pride in their ability to face their enemies surged through him, displacing the anger. Once again, the pressure ebbed and Jonah could think clearly.

He shouted at the Grim Reaper, "My dad resisted you!"

The Grim Reaper roared in response and shot balls of red-tinged, sizzling lightning through the portal.

Jonah was prepared. Instead of deflecting the balls of lightning, he created a powerful shield directly in front of the portal. That surprised the Grim Reaper and forced him to dodge his own attack as it rebounded.

Jonah took advantage of the distraction to pour a burst of fire through the portal. The Grim Reaper staggered backward under the assault, totally enraged.

In a moment of clarity, Jonah understood that the Grim Reaper reminded him of Brandon, only a hundred times worse. He also pushed people's buttons and fed off the anger and misery he caused.

As the Grim Reaper retaliated with another fireball, Jonah reached out and shouted in a voice deeper than his own and much more like his dad's voice, "*Sakoto!*"

The fireball stopped in midair. Jonah started to weave his hands in a circular motion above his head, and the fireball went into a graceful spinning orbit around the interior of the chamber.

Wick stared at it. "Unbelievable. You've got to teach me that trick." He and the clerk huddled to avoid the intense heat of the fireball.

Once again, the Grim Reaper fired. Jonah increased the speed of his hand movements, and the second fireball joined the first as they coalesced into one ball. It streaked around the chamber in a perfect, tight circle like an angry red comet.

Jonah added his own power to it. He let his anger, frustration, and hatred bleed out. He didn't stop until he had drained himself of the hurtful emotions. By then, the fireball was twice its original size.

As it completed the last circuit around the chamber and neared the portal, Jonah prepared himself. "You may have killed my parents, but you won't kill me or my friends."

At precisely the right moment, he released the fireball and scored a perfect three-pointer through the open portal. The fireball exploded like a bomb on the other side.

Jonah watched in satisfaction as red-robed beings and Grim Guards dove for cover and the structure on the other side shook and began to fall apart. A thick smoke rose up, obscuring his view.

Somehow, through all the noise, he heard Marcus's voice again. "Jonah, shut the portal. This is too dangerous, even with the ring on."

Marcus coughed up more blood. Omar cradled Marcus's head gently in his lap and spoke softly to him.

Jonah wondered how to close a portal, and the answer came to him. He raised his hands, and after a second, he could feel the power around the opening. He imagined himself gripping the edges of it and brought his hands together. The portal resisted as the Grim Reaper fought to keep it open.

"Jonah!" Omar warned.

"I'm trying, Omar."

The Grim Reaper rose to his feet and raised a hand. Supernatural electricity crackled as he conjured a ball of lightning. Jonah concentrated with all his might and, just before the Grim Reaper attacked, slapped his hands together. The portal closed.

Jonah staggered a bit as the oppressive coldness and evil vanished. He took deep breaths and glanced around just as the chamber begin to collapse on their heads.

CHAPTER FORTY-TWO
HEALING POWER

"We have to get out of here." Wick pointed at the opening. "The door is toast."

Jonah saw the scorched and melted door and wondered if he had deflected a fireball right into it. More and more pieces of the chamber began to fall, and the entire thing began to vibrate.

"We need a shield, Wick."

"I don't have another bracelet. Besides, you made a shield at the rec center."

Jonah knew that, and he was sure he could do one now. However, he was very aware of the silent store clerk watching everything he did. He wanted to confront the Wraith within, before it could get away. He doubted that, even with the ring, he could do both.

"You can do it without one."

Wick shook his head. "I'm not powerful enough."

Jonah grabbed Wick's wrist. The boy gave him a funny look.

"Huh, Jonah?"

"Shut up."

Jonah concentrated, causing the ring to flare in response. Energy flowed from the ring, through Jonah, and into Wick, who let out a startled gasp.

"Dude!" Wick closed his eyes and a moment later, the blue distortion of a shield snapped into place around them. Debris began to bounce off it. Wick opened his eyes, amazed. "I'm not even straining! This is too cool."

Jonah turned and faced the clerk, who huddled against the wall, watching him. As soon as Jonah took a step toward him, the clerk fell onto his knees.

"Please, don't hurt me. That evil spirit left my body."

Jonah gave him a slow smile as he lightly tapped his temple. "I know you're still in there."

The man's shaking stopped, and he stood tall and straight. His eyes changed from their natural green color to milky white. Despite being in the body of a clerk, the dignity of the ancient Egyptian warrior came through. The Wraith raised his hand to stop Jonah and spoke in a deeper voice. "You've beaten the Grim Reaper with the power of the Protector's Ring. My king will want to know what happened here today."

"Is that why you helped me escape from Deyanira?"

The Wraith inclined his head. "Yes. Your actions change everything."

Jonah paused in mid-step, bathed in the sudden memory of the Seer he'd sat beside on the bus. She had prophesied he would change everything. "I spoke to a woman. A Seer. Is she one of you?"

The Wraith shook his head. "The woman is a priestess, one who can summon our Seers, allowing them to communicate through her."

"She said the same thing you did, about me changing things."

"The prophecy." The Wraith smiled. "Wraiths possess far more knowledge than mortals."

Jonah had opened his mouth to ask about the prophecy when a huge piece of the upper chamber broke free and slammed into the shield. Wick's arm bent in response to the force of the blow. Jonah stepped toward the Wraith again, and the man gave him a genuine salute.

"We will meet again, Jonah Blackstone." With that, the clerk fell to the ground and the Wraith exited his body.

Wick let out a snort. "Wow. He literally gave up the ghost."

The Wraith didn't fly away or disappear. Instead, the ghostly warrior hovered inside the shield. Jonah understood and turned to his friend. "Wick, it can't get out. You'll have to lower the shield."

Wick nodded, and his brow drew together as he concentrated. A second later, the blue, hazy distortion of the shield winked out of sight. The Wraith

The Protector's Ring

saluted Jonah, then flew up and out of the enlarged hole in the ceiling. When pieces of the chamber thudded to the ground near his feet, Jonah whirled to find Wick had moved.

He knelt beside the overturned pedestal. Jonah hadn't noticed until he saw it from this angle that the top was made of a clear crystal. Inside was a pulsing dome, undamaged by the fighting. The setup reminded Jonah of a computer desk he'd seen once, the kind with sunken monitors, leaving the entire desk's surface free for work.

Jonah's attention was snapped back to reality as Wick stood, holding Robert's archive box under one arm. He hurried back and activated his shield just as a large warped section of the upper wall crashed down.

He noticed Jonah's exasperated frown and shook the box. "You heard Deyanira: it's a real Seeker's box. Even she couldn't open it. That means it'll come in handy later."

"Whatever," Jonah said and turned to Marcus and Omar. His irritation dissolved, replaced by fear.

Omar stared up at him, perhaps sensing his unspoken thought. "He's still alive, Jonah. We should go now." His African accent was strained with worry. "You have to phase us."

"But I never phased this many people."

"You have the power of a Protector. Remember everything Marcus taught you and you'll be able to do it."

Jonah closed his eyes and thought about the clearing on the plantation grounds. The ring pulsed brighter. Jonah sensed when Omar stood and lifted Marcus. He kept his eyes closed. "Don't worry about touching me. I can get us all out."

His could do this. His Reaper side could touch their souls, which burned bright like stars. He raised his hands. Energy flowed from the ring, through him, and connected with every soul under the shield.

Jonah willed himself to phase. Cool predawn air touched Jonah's skin a moment later. He lowered his arms and opened his eyes. He knew without looking that everyone had made it out with him.

A low rumbling vibrated the ground. Someone yelled, and everyone watched as the earth buckled and collapsed in an expanding fissure that headed straight for the plantation house. The decayed Antebellum columns wobbled and fell into the fissure, along with half the house. A thick layer of dust rolled over the clearing, causing everyone to cough. As the dust began to settle, the sun broke over the horizon. The first morning rays allowed Jonah to see the devastation.

The house looked like someone had cut it in half and scooped it away, leaving the insides exposed. The sound of loose earth tumbling into the fissure punctuated the otherwise quiet morning.

Emily let out a startled gasp and pointed at Omar, who lowered a bruised and battered Marcus to the soft ground.

The Fallen Reaper's hand moved, beckoning Jonah to his side.

Omar knelt over Marcus, gripping his hand. "Don't try to talk."

Marcus shook his head, in a movement that was little more than a jerk. He reached out his free hand, and Jonah didn't hesitate to take it. "Well done, Jonah." Marcus paused to take a painful breath. "You saved us all."

He tried to say more, but it turned into coughs. His head drooped and his eyes closed. Omar touched his head to Marcus's, and his shoulders shook with quiet sobs.

Marcus's patterns, visible through the ripped and blooded-shirt, turned a lighter shade of red. They were nearly gone, and Jonah thought it strange that Marcus would become fully human again at his death.

Without warning, something deep inside Jonah roared out in anger at the very notion. He had lost his parents to the Grim Reaper. And now the man who had pledged to protect him and train him would die because of the same being. The anger over the unfairness of it all boiled up inside Jonah and a single word tore its way out of his mouth.

"No!"

Jonah's shout shook the ground, causing everyone in the clearing to jump and stumble about. He pressed his palms flat against his godfather's chest.

Omar looked on, dazed. "Jonah. It's too late."

"I can save him!"

The ring started to pulse brighter and brighter. Jonah closed his eyes, willing it to draw in more power. He would save Marcus. He would not

The Protector's Ring **321**

lose another person. The ring pulsed so bright, no one could even look at it. When Jonah could no longer hold the energy, he let go. Power flowed out of him and into his godfather.

Marcus's body jerked and his back arched. Omar stared in open shock as the cuts and bruises began to heal. Jonah could feel the broken bones knitting together beneath his hands. After what seemed like an eternity, the patterns began to return. First, they grew deep red, then brown, and finally black. Once they had fully returned, to Jonah's amazement, they began to glow with light.

Jonah pushed the last bit of power into Marcus and let go. Marcus sucked in a deep breath and his eyes snapped open. He took several more breaths before he was able to sit up. His hands fumbled around, slipping off his long coat and then ripping the mangled shirt off. He stared down at his glowing patterns.

"Marcus!" Omar's deep voice boomed across the clearing in relief. The two men embraced, rocking each other back and forth for several minutes.

"Whoa!" Wick's jaw dropped.

Robert sounded just as shocked as his friend. "You mean they're together?"

Jonah had begun to smile when the world tipped sideways and an intense rush of dizziness hit him. He swayed and pitched forward. The ground, rushing toward his face, stopped less than an inch from his nose.

Kevin spoke softly, in his ear. "I got you." He pulled Jonah back to his feet and wrapped a protective arm around him.

Jonah tried to pull the ring off his finger but missed; his right hand trembled too much. Kevin gripped the hand and held it steady until Jonah could slip it off.

Relieved at having the ring off, Jonah shook his head to clear it, which only made him dizzier.

"Take it easy, Jonah." Kevin held up a butterscotch candy. Jonah smiled up at him as he took it.

Omar and Marcus were on their feet now. Marcus moved his arms around, testing them out. He ran his hands along his healed ribs and only stopped when he realized everyone watched him with awed expressions.

Omar motioned to Jonah. When he tried to move, Kevin refused to let go.

"I'm alright."

Kevin slowly released his hold and Jonah walked, a little unsteadily, up to Omar.

The big African pulled Jonah into a bear hug and lifted him off the ground.

"Thank you, Jonah. I owe you so much." Omar set Jonah down and added, "I just hope you'll forgive me someday for what I've done."

"What did you do?"

He tapped Jonah on the forehead in response before turning back to Marcus, who was still checking over his mended body.

When Marcus finished, he nodded to Emily. "You, Kevin, and Trueblood, take care of Deyanira's people. Omar, you go with them."

"I'm staying with you, Marcus." Omar crossed his arms.

Marcus gripped the man's muscled forearm and smiled. "I'll be fine. I have to get the kids home."

Omar let out a deep laugh that seemed to relax everyone.

Kevin turned and raised a closed fist to Jonah. "See you later, little man." He helped Emily march two of the groggy people out of the clearing.

Omar lingered, pointing at Marcus, who stood bare-chested. "At least put on your long coat. You look like a walking neon sign." Omar smiled and hurried to follow Kevin and Emily.

Through it all, Jonah remained in a kind of daze. He appreciated Kevin saying goodbye to him, but frankly, Omar's apology still rolled around in his mind. Had Omar really suppressed one of his memories? Jonah didn't know how to respond at the moment, and he didn't get a chance to consider it because Lynn called to him.

"Jonah, please tell me you kicked in Deyanira's teeth."

"Yeah." Jonah gave her a smile.

Lynn nodded as the energy seemed to flood out of her, and she settled against her brother.

The Protector's Ring

Robert frowned. "We need to get her home."

Marcus buttoned up the long coat, the glow from his Fallen Reaper patterns unable to seep through the dark fabric. After that he motioned to Trueblood, who had stayed behind.

The Mage opened a vortex and everyone piled through without being told. Jonah wasn't surprised to find the vortex opened into his relatives' backyard, near the shed. Robert had already helped his sister into the house by the time Jonah arrived. Wick had followed.

However, Jonah stopped at the kitchen door to watch the vortex snap closed. That's when he noticed that his godfather had paused to stand in a ray of morning sunlight that peeked its way between the houses.

Marcus tilted his chin up toward the rising sun, his eyes closed. "Thank you, Jonah."

"You're welcome." He glanced inside the house. "I need to get inside before my aunt or uncle…" When he turned back, Marcus was gone.

Jonah stumbled out of his bedroom late in the afternoon. Robert and Wick were already up and playing video games. They glanced at him and nodded without stopping play. Jonah went into the kitchen to get a bowl of cereal and noticed the blinking message light on the phone.

"Anyone checked the messages?"

"We figured they were all from Mom calling to tell us about the rec center." Robert looked a little uneasy. "Lynn called her."

"And?"

"Mom asked if we knew anything about it. Lynn convinced her we didn't, but Mom's not stupid. We asked about the sphere, then, two days later, someone destroys it. She'll keep an eye on us from now on."

Jonah didn't argue as he sat down on the sofa with his bowl of cereal and watched Robert and Wick battle each other on the screen. It took him a minute before he noticed Lynn's opened bedroom door. He tapped Robert's shoulder.

"Where's Lynn?"

"She went for a walk."

"I thought she should get some more rest." Wick blasted one of Robert's men and snorted. "She told me what I could do with my suggestion."

Jonah laughed and, of course, Lynn walked through the kitchen door at that moment.

"What's so funny, geek boy?"

"Uh, nothing." Jonah slipped into the kitchen to rinse out his breakfast bowl while Lynn took his seat on the sofa.

Jonah thought his cousin looked tired, and he couldn't stop the wave of guilt that threatened to overwhelm him. He also wanted to apologize. When Lynn saw the look on his face, she gave him a slight shake of her head.

After a few minutes of watching her brother and Wick play their video game, Lynn sat forward. "You two are pathetic."

Robert held the controller out to his sister. "Can you do better?"

"Easily. Let's do teams. Jonah's with me."

"Deal."

CHAPTER FORTY-THREE
BULLY TAMED

Jonah, his cousins, and Wick spent the weekend cleaning debris out of the Summit clubhouse. Even Robert, with all his computer skills, couldn't salvage the equipment. The center's director promised to consider buying new computers once she had the insurance estimates.

By Monday, most of the heavy lifting was done. The remaining furniture was pushed to the center of the clubhouse so the walls could be repainted. After that, there was nothing left to do except clear out.

Robert and Lynn decided to head over to Wick's house while Jonah stayed at the center. He couldn't believe the damage to the atrium. A large section of the marble floor had been removed to make way for replacement tiles. The overhead skylights were covered in heavy plastic. The center of the atrium was roped off and had an extendable construction crane parked there.

Jonah edged around the obstructions and walked into the café.

"Jonah, over here!"

Mike sat at a blue-topped table. As soon as Jonah took a seat, he started in. "What happened?"

"Huh?"

"Don't play dumb with me." Mike lowered his voice. "I know you have something to do with that mess in atrium."

"Can't I get a soda first?" Mike crossed his arms and waited. When Jonah returned, he told Mike everything that had happened.

Mike leaned across the table and punched Jonah in the shoulder.

"Ow!" Jonah said, shooting Mike a scandalous look as he rubbed his shoulder. "What's up with you?"

"Why didn't you tell me any of this earlier?"

Jonah blinked at him. "Everything happened so fast. Besides, you didn't want to go with us, did you?"

"Maybe." Mike slumped in his chair, crossing his arms. "I guess not. I don't want to see the Grim Reaper or anything like that."

"So what's the problem?"

"I wish I could have helped you, Jonah. The discussions with your cousins and Wick sound so interesting."

Jonah stared at his friend and thought he understood. Mike was smart and knew a lot about everyone else. Aside from his broken friendship with Drew, Mike didn't seem to have that many friends of his own. In fact, Mike reminded Jonah of himself.

"I'm sorry. I'll tell you more the next time."

Mike's eyes grew wide. "Do you think there will be a next time?"

"Yeah, I do." Jonah nodded. "Deyanira and the Grim Reaper are still out there. You heard your uncle. There are thirty-five rings, not just one." Jonah glanced around the café, having a hard time believing that just a couple days ago, they had fought Grim Hounds in here.

"I think this is just the start." He gave Mike a smirk. "You sure you want to be my friend?"

Mike blew out an exasperated breath. "Are you kidding? I never had this much fun."

When school started on Wednesday, Jonah wondered if his cousins would use that as an excuse to put the destroyed clubhouse out of their minds. Robert and Lynn would continue to collect stories, but the blog was on hold for the week.

As for the police, they concluded their investigation into the bizarre break-in at the recreation center and labeled it an act of random vandalism. So far, they hadn't been able to explain how the vandals managed to get through the skylights without any gear. The only evidence found were strange gouges on the roof's surface.

The police detective in charge never questioned Aunt Imma. Jonah thought that very fortunate because his aunt took her Christian faith very seriously, and she would have felt honor-bound to mention her conversations with the kids. Just for good measure, Robert managed to hack into the county computer system and release a virus into the donation database. They'd have to work out a way to get the hard copies.

The center requested Aunt Imma and the other artists resubmit pieces for the atrium. Aunt Imma announced she would go with her original idea and use kayaks.

Marcus, Emily, and Kevin remained silent. Jonah didn't expect his godfather to call. He imagined Marcus off somewhere with Omar, enjoying his power boost. Even though Kevin had helped in their rescue, Jonah still felt the warm glow from his promise, deep inside. Did that mean that Kevin would return? Jonah hoped so because he wanted to see the young Fallen Reaper again.

Jonah entered the attic clubhouse after school on Thursday and grimaced. A painter's cloth covered the old sofa, conference table, and rusted filing cabinet. The center had chosen to repaint the attic walls a light grey. They also replaced the busted attic window and frame.

Jonah's footsteps echoed off the dark wood floors and exposed rafters as he crossed to the new window. The painters had left it open to air out the paint fumes. Jonah enjoyed the fresh breeze as he looked out onto the ravine below him. This was all his fault. He had brought this danger and destruction into his cousins' lives.

A sudden change in air pressure surprised Jonah as much as the voice behind him. "A penny for your thoughts."

Marcus stood near the top of the attic stairs. Instead of wearing his trademark black long coat or even a suit, he wore a long-sleeved black shirt and tan pants. He looked rested, Jonah thought.

"Where have you been?"

Marcus spread his long arms, revealing a black onyx and ivory bracelet around his right wrist. He also held a small gift bag in his left hand.

"I've been using the power you gave me. I feel like my old self." Marcus smiled as he lowered his arms. "Actually, Omar made us take a mini-vacation." He strode over to Jonah. "You look worried."

"I'm just thinking how all of this is my fault. Lynn and Robert don't even come in here anymore."

"Don't blame yourself, Jonah. In fact, I'm the one who should apologize to you."

"Why?"

"I never told you the whole truth about the ring. I thought if I could find it, I could use it--"

"You wanted to use the ring to give yourself power without the binding spell. I know. I understand."

"I appreciate you understanding." Marcus looked out the window. "But the ring would not have worked. In fact, I don't think the ring has worked for anyone in a while, not even your father."

"It worked for me."

"You're half-human, so the ring responded to your human side. That's incredible, when you consider it."

"I don't feel incredible. I almost got us buried alive."

Marcus turned Jonah so he could look him in the eyes. "You faced the Grim Reaper, Jonah, and prevented him from winning. Because of you, the Protector's Ring remains here in the mortal world, where it belongs. You've no idea how much can be changed. Don't ever underestimate what you've accomplished."

Once again, Jonah was reminded of the Seer's prediction that he would change things. He gazed out the window until Marcus cleared his throat and handed him the gift bag. As soon as Jonah took it, Marcus held a hand over the top to keep him from looking inside. "We recovered a fireproof safe from your old home."

Jonah's eyes widened. "Really? What did you find?"

"We found copies of legal documents, and this."

Jonah tried to peek around Marcus's hand. "What's in the bag?"

"I hope you'll forgive me, Jonah. I kept this from you because I thought it might be too much for you. After seeing all the things you've faced, I realize that you're far stronger than I would have imagined."

Marcus removed his hand and Jonah peeked inside. A jeweler's box sat at the bottom.

"It's from your parents, Jonah," Marcus whispered,

Jonah's stomach clinched. "My parents sent this? But…"

Marcus leaned down to peer into his eyes again. "It's the birthday present they meant to give you."

Jonah couldn't speak and his hands shook as he reached in the bag and lifted out the box. Inside was a gold-and-silver compass. It appeared ordinary except for a strange dial around the face.

It's beautiful, Jonah thought as he removed the compass from the box. A folded piece of paper slipped free. Marcus caught the paper before it hit the ground and handed it to Jonah.

When he opened the note, he couldn't believe his eyes. It was a riddle in his father's handwriting. Both his parents had signed *Happy Birthday* at the bottom.

Jonah's eyes blurred, and he hastily wiped them with the back of his hand. "Thank you." When Marcus didn't respond, Jonah looked up and saw an awed expression on his godfather's face. "You know what it does?"

"Yes."

"Can you tell me?"

"You should discover that for yourself, Jonah." Marcus took his eyes off the compass. "I'm sorry I held on to it. Omar was livid with me when he found out. He said it was yours, and I was wrong to keep it from you. I hope you'll accept my apology."

As Jonah turned the compass over in his hands, he realized he wasn't angry with Marcus. "I accept it."

Marcus let out a breath and looked at his watch again, but he didn't seem ready to leave.

Jonah decided to take advantage of that. "Can I ask you a personal question?"

Marcus cocked an eyebrow and nodded.

Jonah hesitated a moment, then asked, "Why did you become a human if you miss your power so much?"

Marcus abruptly turned to look out the window again. "Your father asked piercing questions like that."

Jonah nodded and waited.

"I was convinced of the error of our ways. After that, I felt compelled to change, even though I didn't like the idea of becoming mortal again." Marcus stared down at his hands, his brow furrowed. "Sometimes, Jonah, you'll find that staying where you are is impossible and you have to move, even if you don't like the options available to you. Most people require a lifetime to learn that. I suspect the things you've been through have already taught you that lesson."

Jonah considered that. He'd lost everything he knew and been sent here to Georgia. He had never wanted to come here, but now that he was, he wouldn't give up his relationship with his cousins or his new friend for anything.

"I've gotten used to it." He leaned against the window. "I feel like this is home now."

"You see? You've learned a lesson that even I haven't." Marcus crossed over to the old sofa and sat down on the cloth-covered arm. This allowed the Fallen Reaper's eyes to be level with Jonah's. Marcus gave him the Reaper stare, but only for a brief moment before he lowered his gaze.

"Jonah, do you remember the day you left for Georgia? You asked why Omar and I didn't take you in. I wasn't totally honest with you." Marcus laughed softly. "I seem to do that often." A worried expression returned to his face. "Your parents asked me to be executor of their estate instead of your aunt and uncle because they knew I would become like a surrogate father to you."

"I don't understand."

"Think about it, Jonah. You are half-Reaper. When you needed phasing lessons, you called me. When you experienced the dream-walks and needed help with Deyanira, you called me. There's going to be more and more things in which your mortal relatives can't help you. Each time, you'll turn to me. Your parents knew this."

"Are you saying you don't want to help me?"

The Protector's Ring

"Of course I want to help you. I'm attempting to explain my thoughts on the night I realized your parents would…" Marcus paused. "When I realized they would die and leave me to watch over you. They were my best friends, and I lost them. My promise to your father required me to do something I never anticipated doing: help raise a teenager."

Marcus allowed Jonah to absorb everything he said before going on. "Jonah, you're going to elevate the whole angst-ridden teenager thing to a new level. You're not just a teenage boy; you're also a teenage Reaper. As your mortal side grows and develops, your Reaper side will also grow and develop. If anyone needs a father to guide him through the coming changes, it's you. And who will you call on in the future?"

"I'll call you."

"Yes, you will, and I'll always help you. I do that because it's the right thing to do and because I admire you. Never doubt that."

"I won't." Jonah held the compass up to the window, watching the light reflect off its surface as he thought about everything Marcus said. "Hey, if you're going to teach me a lot of things, will you teach me to drive?"

"No." Marcus sounded so serious about it that Jonah actually laughed. Marcus cocked an eyebrow at him, and that made it even funnier.

"You have a cool car."

"My car will continue to be cool and stay in one piece because I will not have an underaged driver behind the wheel. That is one thing your relatives can teach you."

Jonah cocked his head to the side. "Maybe I'll ask Omar."

"You will not ask Omar, and that reminds me. These little conversations are just between you and I. Attorney-client privilege. You understand that?"

Jonah nodded and couldn't hide the smile that tweaked the corners of his mouth. He could already detect the differences in Marcus's voice. One day, he just might persuade his godfather to let him drive his car.

Someone cleared their throat. Marcus and Jonah looked up to see a delivery driver at the top of the stairs, holding an electronic notepad.

Marcus stood and brushed a bit of lint off his pants. "Finally." He waved the man forward and signed the pad. The deliveryman looked around the attic.

"Where should I put the boxes?"

"I'd say over there, on the other side of the stairs."

Jonah watched as the delivery guy and a helper carried several large boxes into the attic. When they left, he hurried over to look at the labels.

"What are these?" For a wild moment, he thought Marcus had found a hidden stash of books that belonged to his parents.

"I felt responsible for what happened to the Summit, so I asked the company to purchase new computers and work desks for you."

"Wow! Thank you."

"You're welcome." Marcus clapped his hands together. "Well, my work is done here. Tell your cousins I said hello."

"Wait. Where are you going?"

"I have to get back to Washington."

Jonah hurried to his book bag and pulled out a small used jewelry box. "Take this. It's the ring."

Marcus stared at the box. "Are you sure?"

Jonah nodded. "I'm not a Protector. Find the real ones and give it to them. I'm sure the company can keep it safe."

"We can certainly do that." Marcus took the box from Jonah and turned it over in his hands. "There's a legend that says any one of the rings can be used to find the others."

"That's great. Use it to find the others."

Marcus subjected Jonah to a long stare—but Jonah realized it wasn't a Reaper stare this time. It was all human, and unless Jonah was wrong, Marcus looked impressed.

"You are a special young man, Jonah."

"Maybe." Jonah lowered his head and stuffed his hands in his pockets. Marcus laughed and patted him on the shoulder.

"Take care, Jonah, and enjoy the school year."

With that, Marcus waved and vanished.

Jonah made it to the end of his first week at Eddie Middle School before he came across his least favorite classmates: Brandon, Antwan, and Drew.

Brandon spoke loudly as he approached Jonah and Mike in the hallway. "Hey, freaks."

Jonah stood his ground, more than ready to face Brandon and his buddies. The boys seemed insignificant compared to raging Grim Hounds, a mad sorceress, and the Grim Reaper. However, Jonah didn't need to deal with Brandon alone.

Mike stood tall next to him, along with their practice club friends Rodney, Lorraine, and Anthony. Rodney had made the football team and had a couple of his football buddies with him. In short order, Brandon, Antwan, and Drew were surrounded.

Brandon looked wildly around, realizing his mistake. Antwan and Drew took a step back, leaving space around their friend. A month ago, Jonah would have liked to kick Brandon's butt; however, he didn't feel the need to do that anymore. Jonah didn't have any buttons for Brandon to push. Yet, he did want something from the would-be bully.

Jonah smiled. "My name isn't freak or DC. My name is Jonah."

Although Brandon looked as though he had swallowed something sour, he nodded and said, "Jonah," in a very low voice. As soon as the word passed his lips, he whirled on the spot and pushed his way through the crowd. A few students gave Brandon grief as he passed out of sight. Drew and Antwan slouched after their friend.

"That was brilliant, Jonah." Mike punched him on the arm. "Can I call you DC?"

Jonah laughed. Having the other kids standing with him was something he'd never imagined could happen. In that moment, he understood exactly what his mom had meant. The connections he made in life are the really important things. Jonah wasn't a loner anymore. Despite being a half-Reaper, he had made friends in Mount Vernon, Georgia.

BOOK TWO
THE SEEKER'S COMPASS

CHAPTER ONE
GRIM GUARDS

Trevor Deriba's First Death happened at age fifteen. Now he was one of the UnDead, serving as a low-level courier in the Afterworld. He began to wonder if he would experience Second Death soon. The Grim Guards were storming his rebel hideout, no doubt, with orders to kill him and his visitor.

Sitting across from Trevor, the Alliance representative, a mortal who made the dangerous journey to the Afterworld, glared at him in obvious distrust.

As a leader among the rebels, Trevor managed to earn their respect despite his appearance, which was that of a kid. Whatever your age and the way you looked at your First Death was the way you remained in the Afterworld.

However, the mortal didn't seem to understand that point. The twitchy man winced at the sudden shouts and booms of distant fighting. "Are we safe?"

"No," the third member of the meeting said. He was an older rebel, a Spire Guardian from the Central Archives. "The Grim Guards are working their way here." Rankled at the mortal's attitude, he made a show of respectfully waiting for Trevor's orders.

Trevor gave his mentor a curt nod. "We should go. Lead the way."

The Guardian moved in the quick, fluid steps of a trained fighter, gripping the Alliance man by the arm and hustling him to the door.

The Alliance visitor regained some of his earlier arrogance as he yanked his arm free and whirled on Trevor. "How did they know about our meeting?"

"It wasn't me," Trevor hissed in annoyance. "Someone on your side sold us out to the Grim Reaper."

"But… but…" The man's sputtering was cut short when the Guardian opened the door to reveal a squad of grim-faced rebels. They snapped to attention. Each had their blades activated. Trevor slipped past his visitor and into the corridor, allowing the Guardian and his men to form a protective circle around him.

A sudden shout of pain echoed through the hallways. It abruptly ended. An eerie silence settled on the base.

"Where are we going?" the Alliance man asked with a shaky and too loud voice.

All the rebels glared at him.

Trevor sighed and said in a hushed tone, "We're headed to the portal chamber to send you back." Secretly, however, he began to fear they wouldn't make it that far.

His doubts were proven out when his group rounded a corner to find two Reapers, a man and a woman, blocking the hallway. They wore the signature, flowing blood-red robes of the Grim Reaper's inner circle: the Kin.

Both had the same dark features and curly, black hair. Trevor recognized them from the Alliance's intel. Fabian and Thera Rasmussen. Siblings. And deadly adversaries, if the blood on their blades were any indication. The doorway to the portal chamber was just beyond the Reapers.

Trevor had never seen a real Reaper in person. As an archivist and courier, he didn't associate with such beings who roamed the mortal realm, reaping souls. And the Reapers, in turn, showed open disdain for the work of the archivists. They shared a mutual distrust that went back eons.

Naturally, there were exceptions, but most rebels from the Grim Reaper's side chose to fall back to the mortal realm. Only within the human-Fallen Alliance did rebels from both groups work together in true harmony. That made this failed meeting all the sadder for Trevor.

Thera tilted her narrow chin upward. When she spoke, her smug voice vibrated the walls. "Heretics and a mortal." Her lip twisted in disgust as she added, "Pathetic."

"Prepare to die," Fabian announced as he brandished his Reaper's blades.

Trevor activated his blades. Like all the others', his were gleaming, double-sided, fifteen-inch weapons with flowing Angel script covering every surface.

When Trevor prepared to defend himself, the Guardian pressed his arm down. "You have to get out."

"I want to stay and fight."

The man gave his shaggy, red head one violent shake. "You're more important than any of us. You heard the Elder."

Trevor realized, for the first time, his friends expected him to cross to the mortal world to escape. He deactivated his blades and huddled with the Alliance visitor. The Guardian faced the Reapers, holding up his own blades, and shouting a challenge. The others in his group joined in as they rushed forward.

The Reapers were fierce, enhancing the use of their own blades with spells. Thera sliced a rebel across the abdomen. He screamed as the hot flames consumed his body in seconds. Fabian plunged his blade through the heart of a second rebel whose body was also instantly consumed by white-hot flames.

But the remaining rebels fought on with conviction and eventually forced the siblings back, clearing the way for Trevor and the Alliance man to reach the door.

"Go!" Trevor's mentor shouted.

At that moment, darkness and cold swept through the corridor as three tall figures in black robes rounded the far corner. Everyone, including the Reapers, froze. The Grim Guards approached the melee.

Their bone-white skull masks hid their faces, except for the glowing-red eye slits. They carried seven-foot long, wooden poles with jet-black scythes on the ends. The edges of the weapons glowed a sickly, green color.

One Grim Guard already had his weapon in motion, sending it whirling through the air. The weapon slipped in and out of sight, making it hard to follow. That's why Trevor and the other rebels were totally unprepared when the scythe reappeared right in front of the startled Alliance man, severing his head with a clean swipe.

Since he was a mortal in the Afterworld, his body didn't erupt into white-hot flames. Instead, it, and the now free head, dropped onto the polished floor amid an expanding pool of blood collecting at Trevor's feet. The attack was so swift, he never had a chance to react.

The Grim Guard summoned its scythe back to his hand. The blood that stained the weapon's blade sizzled, sickening Trevor.

The lead Guardian gripped Trevor's forearm and pointed at the door. "Go, now. Deliverer's speed to you, my young friend."

"May the Deliverer quicken your steps," Trevor replied. His hands shook, but he managed to type in the code before the door whooshed open. His anger boiled when his mentor shoved him into the portal room. One final glance as the door closed showed something that would stay with Trevor for a long time: his mentor placing protective wards over the opening.

His body ached with the knowledge that his friends would die in their efforts to protect him. *It wasn't fair*, he fumed, but he kept quiet. He had to stick to the hasty plan.

The portal dominated the center of the space. A few feet away stood the dialing pedestal. It had a simple stone base that flared at the bottom and a circular, flat surface on top. The Angel script symbols were etched into the surface.

He rushed to the pedestal and pressed the combination for the mortal realm. Several matching symbols on the portal flared, casting an eerie glow. A small hole appeared at the very center and expanded outwards to the edges. The opening reached its full size, revealing a well-lit, cavernous room on the other side.

A horrible screech came from the door, and Trevor spared a fleeting glance. A scythe sliced through the right side of the door, followed by a second one on the left. The metal continued to emit the ear-splitting screeches as both scythes cut, moving toward each other.

Using a small, watch-like device on his wrist, Trevor beamed his courier code through the portal just as the door behind him was ripped away. Corridor light flooded the room. The Grim Guards had to stoop to enter, but they were quick. Both charged Trevor, their lethal scythes already slicing through the air in order to decapitate as well as disembowel him.

Trevor dived through the portal and into the mortal world. He rolled to his feet inside a subterranean chamber. Against the far wall was an observation room and guard station. At the center of the space was the portal. Thick, plexiglass walls were erected around this precious device.

The only way out of the enclosure was the open doorway where the two guards stood. Their mortal guns were raised because of his unorthodox entry.

Before they could question him, Trevor felt the hair rising on the back of his neck.

"Look out!" He shot forward between the guards just as he heard the distinct sound of a scythe choosing through the air.

The guards began firing on the Grim Reaper's minions instead of heeding his warning. The scythe sliced through the abdomen of one guard, cutting the unfortunate man in half. His fellow guard blanched at the sight as he fumbled before hitting the button that sealed the inner chamber.

As soon as the door swung close, the Grim Guards went into a frenzy, plowing into the glass partition repeatedly. More security rushed into the outer room, weapons drawn and ready, but all were unsure what to do.

When cracks began appearing in the plexiglass, an electrical current was sent through the enclosed chamber. It was a practiced precaution used to dissipate magical and supernatural energy. In response, the Grim Guards released unearthly screeches of anger, freezing everyone in the basement.

Trevor had been warned, but it took him a few horrible moments to force his immobile muscles into action. He inched around the guards and toward the exit. The electrical discharges began to work, forcing the Grim Guards toward the portal's opening. Eventually, with one last, bone chilling howl, they soared back through to the Afterworld.

Relieved, Trevor slipped out of the nearest door. He ducked into an alcove and shed his Afterworld robes. Underneath, he wore a stolen guard's uniform.

With his job as courier, he managed to prepare rather well for this worst case scenario. He used a stolen security key card to open a maintenance hatch. Metal rungs were bolted to the inner wall of the narrow passageway. Making sure no one spotted him, Trevor clambered inside and started his long climb.

Several nerve-wracking minutes later, he pushed open the exit grate and thankfully inhaled the rich, hot air of the mortal world. It was night here. *Good*, he thought. That would help in his escape. In the distance, the alarms still blared from the unremarkable building that hid the portal.

A shudder hit Trevor. *Grim Guards. Gods below!* Even worse, his alias as a courier was blown. His former master would know he had defected and certainly hunt him down. He calmed his racing thoughts as he summoned all of his courage.

But he couldn't prevent the pang of regret that overcame him. *Was his mentor even alive? Would he ever see the Elder again?* He shook his head, striving to push aside the distracting thoughts in order to focus on his current situation. He couldn't go to the Alliance. They had a mole in their midst.

No, he needed another way back home. Trevor unhooked an amulet from the chain around his neck and broke it open. Inside was a small, slightly curved, rectangular piece of metal. He pressed it to his temple, where it remained. With a tap on the device's notch, he activated it, washing the side of his head in a soft glow while transmitting mission information directly into his mind.

What it revealed shocked Trevor. His way back to the Afterworld was located in a small town in Georgia, several states away. Trevor detached the device and dropped it onto the ground where it sparked and turned to slag within seconds.

He moved away from the facility and soon reached a lonely stretch of highway. Keeping to the high grass and scrubs, Trevor plodded along on a path parallel to the road. The going was rough, but his mind stayed focused on replaying the final, shocking information downloaded from the device.

It was about a boy, who, at age thirteen, had put on a Protector's Ring and fought the Grim Reaper. *Unbelievable!* Of course, every rebel was aware of the Elder's prophecies, which stoked the fires of rebellion against the evil Rulers of the Afterworld.

But to have a thirteen-year-old… Trevor stopped himself. People often doubted him because of his age. He wouldn't do the same to someone else. *Still, the kid must be something special.*

With that encouraging thought in mind, Trevor set out to find this amazing boy.

CHAPTER TWO
HORUS

Jonah Blackstone didn't feel special at the moment. It wasn't his fault he couldn't activate a magical shield bracelet. He wasn't a mage or a wizard. He was a half-Reaper, darn it!

Or rather, he couldn't activate the bracelet on command. Instead, he'd triggered it by accident, creating a protective bubble around himself. The natural sounds were dulled and his view of the trees became blurred and wavy.

He glanced at the connected polished pieces of darkened wood that made up the bracelet, thinking. He had activated it by accident. No one else had to know that. Not even his best friend, Mike Littleton, and his cousin, Robert Hightower, who were both watching Robert's twin sister Lynn and their best friend Wick work with him.

They'd come to this barren field on the outskirts of Mount Vernon so he could practice his abilities, a subject Lynn had grown adamant about over the last week.

She was two years older than Jonah, lanky, and sported long, thin braids that fell just below the shoulders of her ever-present sports-themed t-shirt. Today, Jonah's cousin had a baseball bat slung over her left shoulder while tossing a baseball in her right hand.

Wick, the maker of the magical bracelet, stood beside Lynn in his trademark fatigue pants, muscle shirt, and unlaced combat boots despite the early summer temperatures.

He shook his head, causing his short dreads to wobble. "Drop the shield."

"What are you talking about?" Jonah hoped his voice sounded innocent, but doubted he succeeded.

"Don't try it, Padawan. As a budding mage, I can see the distortions. You're supposed to activate the shield before the baseball hits you."

"Duh!" Jonah waved his arms, his voice coming out close behind the magical barrier that surrounded him. "That's what I did."

Lynn let the heavy end of the bat drop to the ground in frustration. "That's not what he meant, and you know it."

Jonah scowled, concentrated, and deactivated the shield. Releasing the magic was easier than summoning it, particularly because he knew how badly it hurt when one of Lynn's line drives hit him. That was more distraction than he needed.

He pointed at the pile of baseballs, thinking it a little unfair. "Why use baseballs?"

"Motivation." Lynn readied herself, bat raised and ball ready to toss and hit.

Wick offered him an encouraging nod. "Remember what you've learned, young one. Magic is using controlled thoughts to produce a result. Don't try to activate the shield. Just see it already around you."

Lynn let out an exasperated breath. "Enough with the Yoda."

"That was Obi-Wan." Wick pulled a mock hurt expression.

"Whatever." Lynn didn't wait any longer. She tossed the ball up, reared back with the bat, and hit it.

The baseball streaked through the air and right for Jonah's chest. He had less than a second to try and activate the shield. Of course, it didn't work. At the last minute, he contorted his body so the ball whizzed by his abdomen.

"You're supposed to activate the shield." Wick sounded disappointed.

Mike's oatmeal complexion twisted into a frown, but Robert doubled over in laughter. Normally Lynn would punch her twin brother to stop him from being silly, but today she allowed it. Jonah suspected she meant for Robert's laughter to embarrass him, and it worked. His face warmed.

Lynn smacked two more balls in rapid fire succession at Jonah.

Caught by surprise, Jonah didn't have time to even focus his mind. He phased, allowing the balls to pass through where he'd been standing. The process had been so sudden that he didn't even visualize a destination. That's how phasing, his power to move from one place to another in the blink of an eye, worked.

He would envision his destination, someplace he'd either visited or seen at least once. And with a mental nudge, the ripples would play along his body and he would phase. Marcus, his godfather, explained that when he phased, Jonah passed through the Afterworld, the domain of the Undead, for a split second before reappearing at his destination.

Real Reapers used the power to travel around the world, reaping souls. Fallen Reapers like Marcus retained the power when they returned to the mortal realm. The key was having a destination. Only this time, Jonah didn't have one and when the world burst into existence around him, Jonah stood in the same spot.

Wick let out a whoop of approval. "That was wikid cool! Do it again."

"Wick!" Lynn shoved him. "He's supposed to be learning to activate the shield, not phase on one spot."

Despite her objection, Jonah noted that Lynn looked impressed. The problem was Jonah didn't know if he could repeat the unique phase either. It had been sudden, instinct. Maybe Lynn had a point and he needed more practice.

It also occurred to Jonah that the mental nudge to phase was an act of will he had learn to do on command. So why couldn't he activate the shield bracelet the same way?

He dropped his hands to his side, accepting the inevitable, and shook his arms as if releasing pent-up energy. Sweat beaded his forehead from the late June sun. "Okay. I'm ready."

"It's about time." Lynn frowned, tossed the next ball into the air, and hit it straight at Jonah.

He stood his ground and sent the act of will into the bracelet. To his surprise, he felt the tingle along his arms as the shield activated. As soon as the ball impacted the barrier, it collapsed with a pop and the ball continued forward to thump harmlessly against Jonah's chest.

Before he could congratulate himself on at least a partial success, a second baseball smacked him in the sternum. Jonah collapsed to the ground, clutching his mid-section.

Mike was at his side in a second, kneeling down and shaking Jonah's shoulder. "Are you alright?"

"No." Jonah raised his voice. "Lynn broke something."

"Your rib?"

Jonah peaked behind Mike. "Well, no. But don't tell Lynn, okay?" He winked at his buddy.

Mike frowned and shoved the side of Jonah's head. "I thought you were really hurt."

Lynn stood over Jonah. "Don't worry, Mike. I can fix that." She pressed her bat into Jonah's chest.

"Lynn." He struggled, but she had the advantage. Jonah held up the bracelet. "Activate. Activate!"

"Too late." Wick stepped into view with Robert right behind.

"Pathetic." Lynn removed the bat. "You're supposed to be learning to use your powers, Jonah."

"I practice my phasing."

"Not good enough."

Jonah pushed himself up on his elbows. "You sound like Marcus."

Wick and Robert backed away, giving Lynn space to hit him.

She arched an eyebrow at Jonah. "Your godfather's right. Maybe I should call him."

"No, don't do that. I'll get better."

Lynn shook her head. "I don't know. You act like you want to be normal, and you know that's not possible."

Mike leapt to his feet. "What's wrong with being normal?" His outburst surprised everyone.

Lynn blinked once, and the irritation sharpening her edges flashed away. She reached for Mike, who wore a pained reaction, but he whirled and stalked away.

348 *John Darr*

Jonah rolled to his feet to follow his buddy. When Robert blocked him, Jonah turned on his cousin. "Let me go."

Robert held on. "Give him some space, little cousin." He glanced at Lynn. "What gives? You do sound a bit like Marcus." He raised his hands. "Just sayin'." When Lynn didn't punch him, Robert leaned closer. "You sensed something's gonna happen?"

Lynn looked off over the field, avoiding their gazes. "Not really, but it's been quiet over the school year. I don't think that's gonna last much longer; that's all."

"Yeah, right." Robert rubbed his chin while frowning at his sister.

A loud horn interrupted the conversation as Wick's brother pulled his blue pickup to the edge of the field. Lynn moved off to collect the baseballs. Robert hesitated until Wick pulled him toward their bags.

Jonah was torn between seeing what was up with Mike and helping Lynn gather the scattered baseballs. He decided on the latter. By the time they finished and reached the pickup, Wick had hopped inside the truck with his brother. Mike reclined in the truck's bed, head down, looking low of spirit. Robert was across from him talking to Wick through the cab's little rear window.

After tossing the bag of balls in the back, Lynn climbed in and began toying with her Reaper blades, activating and deactivating them with a familiar swish.

Jonah sat beside Mike. As they started home, he tapped Mike on the leg with the back of a fist. "What's wrong?"

Mike worked his jaw while staring at the dandelion clutched in his hands. "It's all of you."

Lynn glanced up at the remark. "What about us?"

"Everyone has a power, except me. I just work the database for the Summit blog."

Lynn nudged Mike's foot with her own. "That's a big help to us."

"She's right," Jonah added.

Mike shook his head. "You're just trying to be nice. I can't do anything special, and you know it." Mike held up a hand to stop Jonah's protest.

"Lynn can use real Reaper blades. Wick can do magic, and Robert helps him." Mike glanced at Jonah. "And then there's you."

Jonah didn't bother to argue because Mike made a good point. Wick's ability with magic had grown stronger. Lynn was superb with the Reaper blades, and she had a strong intuition about things, hence Robert's earlier questions. And Jonah suspected Robert had some abilities that he hadn't revealed yet.

The task of Summit database keeper belonged to Mike. Jonah truly didn't think of the job as busy work. Mike was a marvel at organizing things as well as remembering dates, topics, and subjects.

Plus, Jonah delighted in having his best friend a member of the club. Robert, Lynn, and Wick remained a close trio, leaving Jonah feeling like an outsider. As a result, he grew weary of tagging along behind them and wanted to form his own group of friends. Mike was a logical choice to include in his club.

Wick leaned through the cab's window. "Don't worry about it, Mike. Everyone has a Haru in them. You need to find your purpose, that's all."

The others nodded, but Jonah scrunched up his face. "Haru? You mean hero?"

"No," Mike answered. "He means Haru, or Horus. The source of all hero myths."

Wick gave Mike a thumbs up.

Jonah leaned his head against the side of the truck bed, allowing the wind to buffet his face. He had heard the Horus stories before. As always happened, odd moments like this reminded Jonah of the wealth of information his mom and dad had taught him.

"You think so?" Mike asked Wick.

"Yeah, I do."

"You're part of the Mount Vernon Social Club for a reason," Robert seconded.

Mike's slouched posture straightened. A wan smile touched his lips as he raised the dandelion. The wind whipped the puffy white seed heads away, leaving Mike holding the bare stem.

He tossed it over the side and then elbowed Jonah. "It was easy for you."

"What do you mean?"

Mike smiled. "You're the one who beat the Grim Reaper and wore a Protector's ring. You're already a hero, Jonah."

"No, I'm not." Jonah crossed his arms. Yeah, he had faced the Grim Reaper and saved his friend's lives, including his godfather's. But Jonah still hated to be the center of attention. And being a hero demanded that he become the focus for everyone, including his enemies.

He was so caught up in his own worries that he didn't notice Lynn's gaze shifting to the cars behind them until her body and expression tensed. "Lynn? What's wrong?"

She met Jonah's curious gaze. "We're being followed."

CHAPTER THREE

THE TAIL

Jonah was speechless, forcing Lynn to repeat herself. "I said we're being followed." She tilted her head to the side. "Three cars back."

"How can you tell?" Robert leaned forward to see around his sister.

Lynn pushed him. "Don't everyone look. Geesh. Whenever there's not a car between us, they fall back."

Wick brightened despite the seriousness of the situation. "Should we check? There's a stop light coming up after we reach the four-lane section."

Lynn nodded, pulled her cell phone out, and opened the photo app. She tossed the phone to Jonah. Sure enough, the traffic grew thicker as the group entered the city proper of Mount Vernon and the two lanes switched to four.

Wick, who had a better vantage considering he faced the rear, whispered to Jonah, "There's a semi truck in the lane beside the target car."

Jonah nodded, glanced behind at the semi, and fixed a mental image of the truck in his mind.

"Are you sure it's a good idea?" Mike interrupted.

"It'll be cool." Jonah crouched low, making sure his head wasn't visible to cars around them. As soon as the traffic slowed and stopped, Jonah began to rise from his crouch. Before his head would have come into view of other motorists, he disappeared.

Another thing about phasing is that any motion you start before the phase continues on the other side. So when Jonah reappeared next to the overheated grill of the semi, he also continued the movement of raising from his crouch.

The phase had been perfect. From this angle, he could see through the side back window of the dark government sedan following them. Jonah raised the phone and snapped two quick pictures of the man in the driver's seat.

The stranger spoke into a radio mic while scanning the area. A chill traveled down Jonah's spine at the same moment it occurred to him the man suspected he wasn't in the back of Wick's truck anymore.

Jonah phased just as the guy twisted in his direction, and reappeared right behind the car. He tried to snap a picture of the license plate but was too close and couldn't get the phone to focus.

He reared back, smacking into the bumper of the car behind.

Come on. Jonah's hands shook, but he snapped a photo of the plate just as the traffic moved. He phased and returned to the bed of the pickup. The sudden forward motion of the truck pitched him sideways.

Lynn reached out to steady him. "Did you get it?"

"Yeah." Jonah handed over the phone. "It's a government car."

Lynn showed Robert the image. "Can your girlfriend's dad tell us which agency?"

"Aw Lynn." Robert frowned and ran a hand over his picky afro "I'd have to listen to all his conspiracy theories."

"Hey Bobby," Wick interrupted, "think about the points you'll score with Jennifer. That outweighs the inconvenience." He leaned out the window to hi-five Robert.

"Cut it, you two." Lynn smirked at Jonah. "There're kids present."

Jonah scowled and crossed his arms.

Mike looked just as pissed. "I've dated and..." His oatmeal complexion darkened in embarrassment.

Wick hooted at that. Lynn gave Mike a shrewd once over.

Robert leaned forward to tap Mike's foot. "Good for you, Mike. That means Jonah's the only one not getting–"

The Seeker's Compass

Lynn elbowed her brother but spoke to Wick. "Have your brother take us to the teen center."

Jonah sat in silence as the others went on talking. His thoughts were on the government car, wondering why anyone would follow his group, and fearing all the possible answers.

*

The actual name for the teen center was the Cedar Hill Recreation Center, and it was a renovated old southern mansion that still sported the majestic white columns. If Jonah stood at the central glass doors and faced out, he'd have a commanding view of the hilly surrounding neighborhoods.

The vista didn't draw Jonah's attention as he and the others hopped out of the truck and headed inside. Their destination was the attic, where Lynn edited a teen blog and Robert maintained a website for the center.

Mike seemed much happier as he peppered Lynn with all kinds of insightful questions about upcoming blogs. Jonah listened to the conversation without comment as they mounted the curved central staircase from the atrium to the second floor.

The group halted in front of an old attic door. A black sign with white letters adorned the entrance and said *The Summit*. A second sign below that read *The Mount Vernon Social Club*.

Robert pulled out his key to unlock the door. Instead of opening it, he yanked his hand away from the handle, confused. "It's unlocked."

Wick reached past him to pull open the door and inspect the staircase. "The director comes in sometimes."

"Yeah," Robert admitted, "but she usually tells us ahead of time."

"One way to find out." Wick entered the narrow doorway and started up. Robert exchanged a glance with his sister before following.

Jonah went next, with Lynn and Mike behind him. Within seconds, he knew something was wrong because Robert and Wick had stopped at the top of the stairs that divided the attic into two areas.

Squeezing past Jonah to join her brother, Lynn asked, "What's wrong?"

Robert lowered his voice to a whisper. "Someone's in the attic."

Lynn slipped between him and Wick and up into the attic space. Everyone else followed. Robert was wrong, Jonah discovered. There were two people in the attic.

The first was a tall black guy in tan slacks and a royal blue jacket. He stood with his back to the kids, gazing out the large, multi-paned window. His jacket had *GBI* stylized on the back in big yellow letters.

Lynn positioned herself in front of the rest of the gang. "What are you doing in here?"

The agent turned. "I'm Special Agent Ramsey, of the Georgia Bureau of Investigation." He spoke in a clipped baritone voice as he withdrew a black leather wallet from his jacket and flipped it open to show off a light bronze badge. "We have questions for you."

Lynn examined the ID the longest before focusing on the second guy. He was shorter, olive-skinned, and dressed in a black sport coat, pants, and tie.

Ramsey flipped the wallet closed and motioned to the black-clad guy standing beside him. A small white skull pin glimmered on the man's lapel. "This is a consultant with the department."

The guy's eyes narrowed when he saw Jonah. The quick flare of milky brightness in the pupils was a sure sign of Wraith possession.

As if to underscore that, Jonah's Death Sense gave a painful twinge of warning.

The Seeker's Compass 355

CHAPTER FOUR
GBI

Agent Ramsey's lean mocha face reminded Jonah of a hawk. His steely light-brown eyes seemed to look through a person. Jonah didn't like this agent nor the consultant guy, who caused his Death Sense to throb.

The GBI agent smiled. "The director of this center let me into the office."

Robert yelped and hurried over to the computers with Mike in tow.

This area of the attic, called the Summit, included printers and desks where Jonah's cousins worked on the blog. Everyone watched as Robert checked his servers and Mike typed away at a keyboard. After a while, and a relieved look from Mike, Robert's hunched shoulders relaxed and he gave Lynn a slight nod.

Agent Ramsey took a few steps toward Robert and placed a hand on the computer monitor. "I understand you do a teen blog. That's a noble pastime for young people. But I guess you get that from your father."

"What do you know about our dad?" Lynn asked.

Agent Ramsey turned to her. "You're Lynn Hightower and this is your twin brother Robert. Your parents are James, a local newspaper publisher, and Imma, a hair stylist." Agent Ramsey focused on Wick, "You are–"

"I'm Wick," the young mage proclaimed.

Ramsey raised an eyebrow and said, "Mr. Jean-Baptiste." He continued on to Mike, who had slipped behind the old gun-metal grey editor's desk in the back corner. "You are Michael Littleton." The agent ended with a dramatic show of turning and looking at Jonah. "And you are Jonah Blackstone."

"Yeah, glad you know all our names," Jonah said. He didn't like the agent's strange way of making statements sound like questions, like the man was challenging them.

Ramsey continued to scrutinize Jonah until Lynn stepped between them, arms folded. "You didn't answer my question."

Agent Ramsey took a notepad and pen out of his pocket. "I'm looking into the events that happened here in Mount Vernon last summer. The Bureau believes they may be connected to other crimes around the state." He paused and consulted his pad. "Despite a large amount of damage in the center's atrium, the vandals ignored the other offices and burglarized your space."

"Yeah, and we took a week to clean up the mess," Robert said. He didn't move away from the computers.

Ramsey turned to him. "You replaced all your computer equipment in a short period. The center's director told me she didn't use insurance proceeds for that. How did you manage it on your own?"

"Our parents paid for it," Lynn answered.

The agent smiled. "That information is also easy to verify."

"It was a gift from my dad's old company," Jonah volunteered.

Lynn glared at him, but Jonah didn't think telling obvious lies to a GBI agent was a good idea.

"And the name of this company would be..." Agent Ramsey had his pen poised over his notepad.

"Monarch Associates. They're in Atlanta and Washington, D.C." Jonah didn't look at Lynn. As long as Ramsey focused on this, the agent wouldn't ask more dangerous questions.

"My godfather works for Monarch. When he heard about the damage, he helped. I guess he thought doing a news blog was a noble thing for teenagers to do."

Lynn gave Jonah a thumbs up gesture.

If Agent Ramsey took issue with the implied dig, he didn't show it. "Why would the vandals break into your office and trash it?" he continued. "Were you working on a story that was damaging or embarrassing to someone?"

"No," Robert answered.

The Seeker's Compass **357**

"It's also curious the vandals destroyed your mother's sculpture." With his eyes, Agent Ramsey searched every corner of the attic as he walked to the window. He tapped the frame with his pen.

"The Recreation Center replaced the window and frame. It was an egress point. Also interesting, don't you think, considering it's on the third floor?"

No one bothered to answer as Agent Ramsey continued to look around. "The local police were too quick to rule it simple vandalism."

Jonah couldn't resist asking, "Why do you think it's more than that?"

"There are other things that happened in this town at the same time. People found dead."

The goon snorted at that remark, drawing a sharp glare from Agent Ramsey before he continued. "Others complained of being drugged. The owner of a bookstore went missing and her home was destroyed." He closed his notepad and put it in his pocket.

As much as Jonah feared a GBI agent investigating Deyanira's attack on the center, he didn't believe the agent. He stepped forward, ignoring Lynn's warning glance. "Why are you here?"

Agent Ramsey refocused on Jonah like a laser beam. "I told you-"

"If someone stole a ring," Jonah barked at the man, "go find them and leave us alone."

Ramsey's jaw muscles worked as he loomed over Jonah. "Have you seen any strangers lurking around town?"

"You mean besides you?" Robert asked. "No, we haven't."

The consultant roared, breaking his silence. "You're wasting time." He glared at Jonah. "Where's the courier, half-breed?"

Jonah had never heard the term *half-breed*, but the goon's tone left no doubt the name was derogatory.

Jonah met the fool's gaze. "No one was talking to you," he paused before ending with, "...Wraith."

The consultant dropped all pretenses of hiding. His eyes shifted to pale white again, with that unearthly glow. He pulled a scythe from a scabbard attached to his belt. Before Jonah could blink, the wraith hurled it.

John Darr

Lynn's fast reflexes—and intuition, Jonah suspected—allowed her to activate a blade and knock the weapon away. The scythe embedded itself into the wall beside the attic window. Lynn positioned herself in front of Jonah, and Mike who had come around the computers to stand with them.

Light flared to their left as Wick ignited two balls of supernatural fire.

Robert cursed and called the consultant names while pointing at the scythe. He finished with, "You lost your freakin' mind!"

Agent Ramsey ignored the comment as he stared at Wick's supernatural fire and Lynn's Reaper blades with smug satisfaction.

If Jonah hadn't seen the moment of panic on Ramsey's face, he would have believed the man planned the attack to tip their hands.

Hurried footsteps sounded from the attic stairs. Two adults charged into the room, a Native-American woman and a tall blond man. Jonah recognized the woman. Her name was Mage Trueblood, and she was the wizard who'd helped them fight Deyanira. The other person, a tall, stocky white guy with a mop of blond hair, was unknown to Jonah.

Trueblood's long black hair was done in twin, elaborate braids that fell below her shoulders. She wore a pale grey tunic reminiscent of her heritage, but beneath were jeans and hiking boots. When the accomplished mage raised her hands, magical energy infused her voice with power. "What's going on?"

Ramsey raised an eyebrow and stood taller. "Who are you?"

"I'm a youth counselor, working with the center," Trueblood answered, not missing a beat. "I came to talk to the young man about his blog."

Ramsey glanced between Robert and Trueblood, his eyes narrowed. After a long pause, he slipped a hand inside his jacket. The butt of a standard-issue gun showed, but Ramsey's hand reached beneath that, ready to pull out a different weapon.

Jonah wondered if the man had his own blades.

There were more hurried footsteps and then a second GBI agent pushed his way into the attic. It was the guy from the government car, Jonah noted. He was as tall as agent Ramsey and his black hair was cut neat.

The new agent froze, his pale blue eyes taking in the tableau until Agent Ramsey called out to him, "Harris. Take this fool out of here."

The Seeker's Compass

Agent Harris grabbed the Wraith-possessed guy and hustled him out of the attic.

Ramsey held both hands away from his body. "I apologize for my associate."

"Leave," Trueblood ordered.

Anger flashed across Ramsey's face as he assessed the situation. Trueblood never relaxed her stance. Lynn held her blades ready. Wick's green balls of flame showed no signs of fading, and the big blond guy stood ready to launch into action.

The agent relaxed his own posture and his hand moved in a non-threatening way as he pulled a card from his pocket. He strode to the attic stairs and dropped the card on the railing. "I'll have more questions for all of you." With that, he descended the steps.

Robert waited for the click of the attic door closing before yelling, "That guy tried to kill Jonah!" He jabbed a finger at the scythe.

The big blond man yanked the weapon free. Chipped paint and plaster rained down on the floor. "I'll be. A grown man trying to cut up a bunch of kids." The guy stammered, "Sorry. No offense."

Jonah moved from behind Lynn to face the man. "Who are you?"

"Oh, don't mind my bad manners." He extended a beefy hand. "I'm Rexford Montgomery. Everyone calls me Rex," he announced in his booming Southern drawl. "I work with Marcus."

"You're a Fallen Reaper?"

"Yeah, buddy." Rex patted his barrel chest. Then he jumped liked he'd been shocked and offered to shake hands with the others.

"Are you okay?" Trueblood asked Jonah in a calm voice.

"Yeah." Jonah nodded and poked Lynn's arm. "Thanks."

Lynn shrugged and deactivated her blades.

After greeting Rex and Trueblood, Mike said, "We're lucky you showed up."

Rex laughed. "It wasn't luck, young man."

Trueblood frowned at him. "Marcus sent us to warn you about the GBI."

Robert, still agitated by the attack, waved his arms around in frustration. "You're a little late for that."

"Relax, Bobby." Wick made calming motions with his hands. "It's not their fault."

Trueblood nodded, but her expression remained serious. "We'll have a talk with the director about allowing people inside the attic. And we should develop better protection."

Wick brightened at that idea. "I want to help."

Trueblood inclined her head. "That can wait. What did the agent ask?"

"He wanted to know about a courier," Jonah answered.

Mike raised his hand. "Who's this courier and why are the GBI following us?"

Trueblood shifted her gaze to the window. Rex glanced down at his big feet, refusing to meet anyone's gaze.

Jonah knew the answer before the adults responded. "You can't tell us."

"Someone tried to kill Jonah," Lynn shouted, just like her brother had done moments before. "You're not gonna tell him why?"

Rex rubbed the side of his nose with a finger. "It's Alliance Council business."

"Jonah's godfather's on the council," Mike pointed out.

"Yeah," Robert said. "Where is he?"

Trueblood raised her hands and motioned for them to calm down. "Marcus is in an emergency Council meeting at this moment." She crossed her hands behind her back as she came to stand in front of Jonah. "He is asking for permission to tell you everything."

Jonah gulped. He never imagined his godfather would fight to tell him something. Marcus had always been the one to hold back information.

"You can't give us anything?" he urged the mage.

Trueblood exchanged a nervous glance with Rex. "We've lost all contact with our allies in the Afterworld because of a mole inside the Alliance."

Jonah nodded, wondering how much more the adults would reveal. Better to try, he reasoned and asked, "What about this courier guy?"

The Seeker's Compass

"He was our Afterworld contact," Trueblood said. "When the Grim Reaper's minions attacked, he fled into the mortal realm to escape."

Robert's jaw dropped. "Wow." He scratched his head. "We call them Grimnions, by the way."

Trueblood didn't bat an eye. Rex chuckled.

Lynn frowned, remaining serious. "They're using the GBI to find the courier?"

"And Wraith-possessed goons," Wick added.

Trueblood nodded. "These agents were corrupted into working for the Grim Reaper."

"Plus," Rex held up a finger to make his point, "we've suspected infiltration of law enforcement. This confirms it."

Jonah could see the unspoken reality on the adults' faces. "The GBI agents already know all about us and the supernatural world, don't they?"

"Yes, they do," Trueblood admitted.

After that, Mage Trueblood and Rex refused to reveal more about the Alliance and the courier. Jonah tried, but the serious mage grew impatient and went off to discuss attic precautions with Wick.

Rex ruffled his shaggy blond hair as he watched Jonah. "We told you, can't say anything else because we don't know anything else. Just wait for your godfather to get here."

Jonah decided he'd go crazy waiting for Marcus to arrive.

Mike, who had been watching Jonah, motioned toward the stairs. "Let's go downstairs and get something to eat or play games."

Jonah agreed, but his intention to clear his mind came to an abrupt end as they descended the main staircase.

Today, Brandon Warner, the Third, stood at the entrance to the east wing. The tall man in the dark grey suit beside the bully had to be Mr. Warner, Jonah decided. The man had the same arrogant look as his son, the chin tilted up, and a knowing frown on his light caramel face.

The sight that troubled Jonah the most was that Brandon's father talked with Agent Ramsey.

CHAPTER FIVE
REAPER'S GIFT

Jonah and Mike were stunned, watching as Mr. Warner, as if he owned the place, pointed out various features of the center to Agent Ramsey and an older gentleman wearing a black suit and shades.

Meanwhile, Brandon, looking bored with the conversation, scanned the atrium and spotted Jonah. He scowled and muttered something, drawing his father's attention. The older Warner's hazel eyes narrowed as he too focused on Jonah.

Within seconds, Agent Ramsey and the man in the shades paused in whatever they'd been saying to look in Jonah's direction. The combined scrutiny caused Jonah's Death Sense to throb.

Mike intervened and pulled him into the café. They found a table in the back corner and out of sight of Agent Ramsey.

Jonah peeked over his buddy's shoulder and toward the atrium. "Why's Brandon's dad talking to the GBI?"

"Hold that thought," Mike replied. He made his way to the food counter and bought them both a strawberry smoothie. He returned and plopped the smoothies on the table before answering Jonah's question.

"That guy in the black suit owns a security company," Mike explained. He took a big slurp of his smoothie. "My guess is they're talking about new security for this place. They upgraded nothing after the break-in last summer."

"I can see that, but why the GBI?"

"Well, it's obvious the security guy has contacts in law enforcement."

That made sense to Jonah, and he nodded. Brandon and his father moved out of the atrium and into the east wing. Only then did an obvious question occur to Jonah and he reached across the table to tap Mike's arm. "Hey. How did you find out this stuff?"

Mike lowered his smoothie and looked away. "Drew told me."

"Drew?" Jonah snorted. "He hangs around with that bully Brandon."

"Jonah." Mike shoved Jonah's hand and then stage-whispered, "You don't understand. Me and Drew grew up together."

"Wait." Jonah lowered his own voice as a group of kids walked by, chattering to each other. "Drew didn't always hang with Brandon?"

"He started that after Brandon's family moved here. Before then, well..." Mike shrugged and crushed his empty smoothie cup in his slender hands.

Jonah worried he had touched a sore spot with Mike. He began to apologize when his cell phone buzzed with a text message from Lynn. Marcus and Omar had arrived. "Time to get some answers." He showed the message to Mike.

*

"Jonah." Omar's deep African-accented greeting filled the attic space. He pulled Jonah into a one-armed hug while ruffling Jonah's picky hair with his other hand. "I swear you're taller each time I see you."

The muscular model-by-day, Alliance member in secret, released Jonah and treated Mike to a vigorous handshake.

Marcus stood beside his partner, watching with a speculative expression.

Jonah noted that his godfather wasn't wearing his usual suit and tie for work, nor did he wear the dressy casual look he and Omar wore for special occasions.

Today, Marcus wore his long Reaper coat, a knee-length black coat with a distinctive Mandarin collar. And on the left chest, the Alliance symbol had been branded into the leather.

Even more unusual, a smile tweaked the corners of his mouth. "Trueblood told me you persisted in finding out what's going on."

Jonah glanced at the mage and felt his face warm. "Sorry about that."

Trueblood graced him with a nod.

Jonah wondered if the mage would complain about him later in private as he turned to his godfather. "How'd the meeting go?"

"Well enough." Marcus stood tall and spoke to the others. "I need to talk with Jonah alone."

Wick, Robert, Mike, and Lynn all protested at the same time.

Marcus waved them silent. "The Council gave me permission to share details with Jonah." Marcus focused on Lynn and raised an eyebrow.

Her mutinous expression morphed at once into understanding. "You need us to clear out?"

"Lynn!" Robert protested.

"He can't tell us," Lynn explained and smiled at Marcus. "My guess is Jonah can tell anyone he likes."

Rex guffawed. "How'd you work that one, Marcus?"

Marcus arched an eyebrow. "I'm a lawyer. As long as Jonah is alone when we talk…"

"He's not bound by the same oath," Rex finished and laughed even louder.

"You never heard me say that," Marcus added with a smile. "And to address Lynn's first question, no, I don't want to inconvenience everyone else." Marcus placed a hand on Jonah's right elbow. "I know a secure place we can talk."

Jonah had a few seconds to prepare himself. The sensation of phasing, when it occurred this time, was harsher and the transition longer than normal.

When the world reappeared, a moment of pure disorientation hit Jonah. He was outside and, judging from the high-angle view of the surrounding suburbs, up in the air. Jonah glanced at his feet to confirm he stood on something solid, a rooftop.

Marcus released his hold and entered a landscaped section of the roof that featured a dome-covered, seven-column portico at the center. Low flames flickered in tapers attached to each column.

Jonah fought down his disorientation and asked, "Where are we?"

Marcus glanced back. "We're on top of the Monarch Associates Building in northern Atlanta."

HQ. "The phase took longer," Jonah observed.

"This building is protected by strong magical wards and spells." Marcus gestured around himself. "The entire roof is covered in a protective shield, but I have a talisman." He pulled a black beaded chain from his long coat. "Being a partner has its privileges."

Marcus turned and mounted the shallow marble steps to the portico. Jonah followed. When he reached the top and moved between the columns of the structure, the sounds of the outside world dropped away.

"Oh." Jonah's jaw dropped.

The portico had a seven-sided stone slab, at least five feet wide, positioned in the middle of the columns. Jonah focused on the large black box with a bright lime green bow someone had placed on the slab's cushion.

Marcus lifted the box and handed it to his godson. "Happy Birthday."

Jonah accepted the gift. "What's this?"

Marcus smiled. "Open it."

"Aren't you gonna tell me about the courier?" Jonah asked.

Marcus gestured to the box, and Jonah peeked inside to find a leather coat. His irritation evaporated, replaced with disbelief.

"Is it...?" He lifted the coat from the box and let the garment hang free. "It's a Reaper long coat!"

"Yes." Marcus' mouth twitched with amusement. "Omar and I decided it best to give this to you away from the others." When Jonah gave him a curious expression, Marcus added, "It's enchanted."

"To do what?"

"Put it on and you'll see." When Jonah hesitated, Marcus added, "I'll tell you about the courier."

That was all Jonah needed to hear. He slipped the coat on. His first impression was the coat was too long and he'd have to grow into it. But no sooner than he thought that, a sharp tingle traveled over his body and the coat adjusted itself.

The hem shortened until it hung just below Jonah's knees. The arms shrank, fitting more snugly, but not tight. And the cuffs retreated, revealing Jonah's hands.

"This is so cool!"

Marcus didn't bother to hide his genuine smile. "The enchantments do more than resize the coat. You'll be protected from a wide range of spells and attacks." He grew serious as he watched Jonah turning on the spot, admiring the coat. "You know about portals?"

"Yeah, Deyanira used one to cross over."

"Correct," Marcus said. "Portals allow us to cross between the mortal and Afterworld. But what you may not have known is two portals are required to make a crossing. One in the mortal world and a corresponding one in the Afterworld."

Jonah's jaw dropped. "They're like subway stations."

Marcus nodded. "Through a mutual agreement, the Grim Reaper and his people control the main portal here in the mortal world. Another Afterworld faction called the Archivists controls the Afterworld portal."

Jonah paused the tweaking of his coat. "Archivists? Are they record keepers?"

"Yes. They maintain data on every mortal who's ever lived. A segment act as a police force of the Afterworld. They're called Guardians."

"Okay," Jonah said, trying to imagine archivists and Guardians.

When his godfather moved, Jonah glimpsed something shiny under his long coat and held out his hand. "Can I hold your blades?"

Marcus arched an eyebrow, but after a moment, let out a breath and withdrew his blades. He retreated a few steps as Jonah activated the weapons and went through the standard defensive postures.

The new Reaper's coat was like a dream to Jonah. It didn't hinder him at all as he moved.

"Not bad," Marcus observed. "It's well you're keeping up your blade skills."

The compliment focused Jonah. He asked his next question while testing the weapons. "What about the courier?"

"The Rulers of the Afterworld use special archivists called couriers to send and receive information through the portal." Marcus gazed out over the northern part of the city. "We did the same thing with our Afterworld allies. An undercover courier delivered messages to us by way of a secret drop not far from the portal."

Jonah stopped performing practice swipes with Marcus's blades. He sensed the sadness from his godfather. "What happened?"

"Three days ago, the Alliance smuggled an agent into the Afterworld for a face-to-face meeting. Our contacts had their own portal, so we thought the mission would succeed. But the Grim Reaper's people were waiting."

Marcus turned to face Jonah. "We lost our Alliance agent. The courier had to flee into the mortal world to avoid being captured by the enemy."

Jonah lowered the blades to his sides. "The GBI Agents are looking for him."

"We were surprised to learn the Grim Reaper has agents in the GBI," Marcus admitted. "The courier's afraid to trust anyone and is in hiding."

"What'll happen if he's caught?"

Marcus took a deep breath. "He would be tortured for information and then executed." When Jonah winced, Marcus patted his arm. "I'm sorry to be so blunt, but you're old enough to understand about our enemies."

"But why would those GBI agents come after me?"

"I'm part of the Alliance and your godfather..."

"They think I know something." Jonah deactivated the blades and handed them to his godfather. He pulled his new long coat closed as if warding off a chill. "Thanks, for the birthday gift."

"You're welcome." Marcus put his blades away. "Jonah, if you see the courier, please tell me. It's vital we find him."

"Why wouldn't I tell you? I don't want him to be tortured." That was true, even though he'd never met the man.

"Of course you don't." Marcus perched on the edge of the padded seat. "I'm worried about the courier for another reason. When a being travels through a portal, the change they undergo is temporary. If he doesn't cross back, well, he'll die."

Jonah gulped as a pit formed in his stomach. "How long does he have?"

"We estimate less than a week."

Jonah toyed with the clasps on his long coat as his mind raced with the sad information. "What about the mole? This is all his fault."

Marcus met Jonah's gaze, which was easier now that he sat on the slab. "I can't reveal anything else about that subject." Marcus paused. "I'm sorry."

The apology rung true for Jonah, even without using a partial Reaper stare. He nodded, letting his godfather know that he understood and wouldn't pester for more details.

Marcus's tense expression relaxed as he collected the empty gift box.

Jonah watched his godfather, feeling anything but relaxed. An invisible weight settled on him, and it wasn't the Reaper coat. One way or another, Jonah told himself, his quiet summer was over.

CHAPTER SIX
STRANGE VISITOR

Jonah covered his eyes as he squinted into the blazing summer sun. Mike, who hated getting baked in the sun, didn't even seem to notice today. He was too shocked by Jonah's recounting of the previous evening's visitation and dream-walk.

They were riding their bikes through the neighborhoods and to the teen center.

Mike overcame his shocked silence. "Telling your godfather was a smart move. It would be bad if the courier was caught by the agents."

Jonah was glad Mike sounded just as worried about Trevor as he. While Jonah trusted his godfather to keep the boy's appearance from the Alliance mole, he doubted he could convince Trevor of that, if he ever saw the boy again. "What do I do now?" Jonah glanced at Mike. "Wait?"

"Oh." Mike went silent as they did a switchback pattern up the steepest hill. "Figure out the compass."

Jonah shook his head. "Working out the compass in front of Rex or Trueblood would cause too many questions."

"But your godfather wouldn't have sent them if he couldn't trust them." Mike paused before crossing the street in front of the teen center. "We can go to the library."

Jonah brightened at that idea until he checked his watch. "The library doesn't open for another hour."

"Well, how about Ping-Pong or pool until then?"

Jonah agreed. They locked their bikes in the racks, went inside and were in luck. Lorraine Hughes, Anthony Freeman, Rodney Elkins, and Stephanie Brown, all younger members of the Practice Club, had gathered to play Ping-Pong.

Anthony, still a type of show off, assumed the lead in organizing an impromptu tournament. Jonah didn't mind as he and Mike joined the others. He realized the group accepted him into their loose circle because of his friendship with Mike.

As usual, Jonah and Anthony were in a friendly competition, each having lost only one game and in a tie for the lead. As Jonah stepped to the table, ready to square off with Anthony, he didn't see Brandon and Antwan enter the room.

The bully hurried over and shoved Jonah to the side. "Out of the way, DC."

Antwan tried to shove Anthony aside, but the boy was prepared and stood his ground. At least three other beefy guys had followed Brandon into the room. By this time, other kids had wandered into the room to watch, but the Practice Club members, including Lorraine and Stephanie, were on alert and unafraid as they faced Brandon and his crew.

Jonah nodded with pride at the others as he glared at Brandon, who was still inches taller. "Wait your turn, jerk."

"Yeah," Mike added.

Brandon laughed. "What are you gonna do, Brianiac?"

Mike's face flushed, causing Jonah's anger to build. He smirked into Brandon's arrogant face. "I'll school you again, in front of a crowd."

Brandon's light brown complexion grew darker as he swelled with anger. Just when Jonah thought the idiot would throw the first punch, someone grabbed Brandon by the forearm.

Wick stood behind him. Today he had on dark blue custodian pants and a shirt. He worked part time in the summer with the custodians at the center as part of his summer community hours. "Wait for the next tournament, Brandon."

Brandon tried to knock Wick's hand away, but Wick was too fast for that and let go.

"Mind your own business and don't touch me again, freak."

Everyone froze, waiting to see how Wick would react. He stepped right up to Brandon, looming over the boy. No one had ever seen Wick fight, but Jonah suspected the young mage could break Brandon in two.

Wick stared down at the bully. "You know, there's a reason they call me Wick."

He whirled his hands, causing Brandon to cower and cover his head. But instead of hitting the boy, Wick produced purple flames in his palms. Jonah thought they were beautiful. Everyone else let out startled gasps.

Wick leaned into Brandon's scared face. "I'd watch your mouth." He whirled his hands over Brandon's head. The boy yelled and ran for the door, Antwan right behind him.

The rest of Brandon's group seemed unsure what to do with their leader heading for the door. Wick threw the flames at the boys, scattering them. The flames didn't burn anything, they just splattered into nothingness upon impact.

Even so, Brandon's crew sprinted for the doors as the room exploded in laughter.

When everyone continued to gawk at him, Wick opened a hand and revealed an ornate silver lighter. "Just a little trick."

Kids laughed. Anthony grunted and motioned for Jonah to play him in Ping-Pong.

Jonah wanted to talk to Wick. "I'll be there in a second. " He had a bad feeling about Brandon. When Anthony let the others play, Jonah whispered to Wick, "He'll tell."

"I don't care about Brandon and his dad."

"Wick," Jonah glanced around. "I don't mean his dad. I mean the GBI."

Wick's face went slack. "Good point, Padawan. I forgot about that." He ruffled his twist and gave Jonah a lopsided smile. "They already know about us. That reminds me." He steered Jonah off to the side of the room and away from the other kids. Wick had to beckon to Mike twice to get him away from an intense conversation with Stephanie, who kept gazing at Wick with interest.

When Mike finally came over, Wick said, "Tell Stephanie that I already have a girlfriend."

Mike's eyes widened. "How'd you know she asked about that?"

Wick didn't bother to answer. Instead, he reached in his pocket and pulled out two of his polished, octagonal tokens. "These are for you guys. One each."

Jonah and Mike took the small tokens, both boys wearing matching confused expressions.

Wick beamed at them. "I helped Trueblood come up with a warning system. These are talismans. If you enter the attic without one, all the others grow hot and warn us."

"Whoa," Mike breathed, examining the token. "You did that?"

"Well," Wick hedged. "Trueblood put the spell on them, but she let me place the ward on the attic door. Also, if you hold the token up to the door, it'll get warm to remind you that some unauthorized person has been inside."

"That's cool," Jonah said. "But shouldn't the ward keep someone out?"

"Trueblood wanted to do that, but Marcus disagreed." Wick frowned. "He says we can't lock out the director. Anyway, that's why I came in here. See you later."

Jonah turned and found Anthony waiting impatiently for him to finish the tournament. Mike, however, headed for the door with Lorraine, Rodney, and Stephanie.

Jonah called out to his buddy, "Where're you going?"

Mike glanced at the others. "We're headed down to the creek side."

"Oh, okay." Jonah returned to the Ping-Pong game. During his decisive match to win the tournament, he felt a sudden pinpoint spike of heat against his thigh. He lost his concentration and the tournament went to Anthony Freeman.

When Jonah reached in his pocket, he found the source of the heat. The talisman was hot to the touch.

Jonah hurried from the game room and upstairs to the second floor. He paused at the attic door and held up the talisman. Sure enough, it warmed in his hand. That scared Jonah now. Should he go in or call his cousins?

The Seeker's Compass

Deciding to be brave, Jonah opened the door and mounted the narrow staircase. By now, he knew which steps creaked and avoided them. He reached the top attic step and peeked over the railing.

The attic was quiet and empty. But Jonah's Death Sense stirred. Something was off. He took another moment to make sure someone wasn't hiding behind the desk or the sofa and then headed down stairs.

He had pulled out his phone to call Mike, but he stopped in mid-motion. Harris approached the front doors with two hulking men in tow.

Jonah hurried into the west wing before the agent spotted him and then ducked into the community room on his left. He jumped when his cell phone rang, echoing in the empty space. "Mike?"

"Yeah." Mike sounded concerned. "Did you get the alarm?"

"Yeah. I bet Ramsey broke into the attic." Jonah cracked the door open and peeked outside. After a group of kids passed, he leaned out far enough to see Ramsey had joined Harris and the two goons standing in the atrium. When the agent turned in his direction, Jonah ducked back inside and closed the door.

"What should we do?" Mike asked.

"Well, I'm sure Wick and the others know. They'll call Trueblood." Jonah backed away from the door and bumped into a nearby table. He sucked in a breath when he turned around because someone had draped a large *Happy Birthday Jonah* banner over a pile of party supplies. "Wow."

"What's wrong? Is it Ramsey?"

"I forgot it's my birthday."

Mike laughed. "You want me to come back there?"

"No. Let's go to the library. Now's a good time to figure out the compass and get away from Ramsey and his goons. You still at the creek?"

"Yeah, by the old bridge."

Jonah used an exit door in the back corner of the hall and hopped over the railing along the rear sidewalk. He pulled out his compass as he started along one of the well-worn paths.

His thoughts had turned to Trevor and how the compass would figure into all of this. The spike from his Death Sense interrupted his musings.

Before he could fully turn around, Brandon grappled with him and snatched the compass out of his hands.

"What's this, DC?"

"Give it back!" Jonah lunged for the device.

Brandon used his height advantage to hold the compass high with one hand and push Jonah back with the other.

"You want me to throw it in the woods?" Brandon reared back as if to make good on his threat.

"No." Jonah waved his hands in a pleading gesture until the obvious occurred to him. "Go ahead." He suspected he could sense wherever the compass might end up and retrieve it.

Brandon blinked at his change in attitude. Then a nasty smile played across the boy's face. "Maybe Agent Ramsey would like to see it?"

Jonah experienced a moment of panic as Brandon poked at the compass face.

The bully frowned after several moments of useless prodding. "What the heck? This ain't even real gold? This sucks."

"Then give it back."

"Nope. You want it too bad." Brandon smirked. "Yeah. I think I'll give it to Agent Ramsey."

Fury surged through Jonah as he thought about a way to get the compass. The problem was he couldn't use any of his abilities. Then again, he was dealing with Brandon. Jonah had beat him in a duel last Summer's End. All he had to do was surprise the boy. Without giving it another thought, Jonah charged, ramming into Brandon dead center and knocking the taller boy to the ground.

Brandon was so shocked that Jonah almost clawed the compass out of his hand. But the bully proved he could also do the unexpected and shouted, "Help!"

Jonah's Death Sense prickled a moment before Antwan grabbed him from behind. Jonah kicked and struggled at first, then chided himself and called on what he had learned in his self-defense sessions. He planted his feet, gripped Antwan's arms, and bent forward at the waist. Antwan tumbled over Jonah's lowered head, landing flat on his back with a loud *oomph*.

Brandon took advantage of the distraction and sprinted for the tennis courts with the compass in hand. Jonah charged after him. By the time he reached the courts, Brandon had circled around them and started for the front of the Center.

Oh no. Agent Ramsey. Jonah decided to cut through the open gates to the tennis courts. That's when his Death Sense spiked.

Antwan tried to tackle him, but Jonah let out a frustrated roar as he pivoted and landed two solid punches to the boy's chest. As soon as he did so, Jonah knew something was wrong. He had hit Antwan with too much power, more than he could deliver.

The bully grunted in pain, stumbled backward, and hit the bike rack. The next moment, Antwan's feet shot up into the air as his head fell toward the pavement. Jonah didn't think twice about it as he leapt forward. *I'm too far away.* But the world around Jonah blurred for a dizzying moment and then he was right on top of Antwan.

In fact, Jonah was moving so fast he threatened to overshoot the boy. Without any time to puzzle it out, he grabbed Antwan's ankle and phased.

CHAPTER SEVEN
BULLY'S GAMBIT

Jonah and Antwan smacked head-first into the creek water.

Antwan let out a startled cry, rolled over in the water, and scrambled away. At a safe distance, he raised a shaky finger to point at Jonah. "That's how you got away from the basement last summer. But… but…" He looked around with terrified eyes.

Jonah sat up in the water. "Antwan, listen to me…"

"You're a freak."

"Antwan…"

The frightened boy stood and wiped the water out of his eyes. His clothes sagged against his thin body, making him look pathetic as he shook in fright. Antwan pointed at Jonah again. "Is that why Agent Ramsey's interested in you?"

Jonah began to tremble with fear as he stood.

Antwan sloshed out of the water and onto the bank. "Stay away from me. I'm gonna tell everyone about you!"

"Don't. I can explain."

"Jonah, what's going on?" Mike stepped into view. He'd come from upstream, along the creek. Jonah was worried that the practice club members were with Mike, but his buddy seemed to be alone.

Antwan stared between the two boys. "I knew you were involved, Mike." He only made it two more steps before he ran straight into Rex, who had just appeared. Antwan saw his buddy Brandon lying on the ground behind the big Fallen Reaper and opened his mouth to scream.

Rex blurred into motion, clamped a hand over Antwan's mouth and whispered, "Be still. I won't hurt you. Your friend is asleep. That's all."

Antwan must not have believed that because he continued to struggle in Rex's iron grip. That's when a vortex appeared and Trueblood and Omar stepped through.

The Mage took in the scene, including Antwan squirming in Rex's grip. She stepped over to the duo and pressed the spread fingers of her right hand along the base of Antwan's thin neck. Jonah saw her lips move with a silent spell. Antwan's body went rigid and then he slumped, unconscious.

Rex let out a relieved breath. "Thanks, Eleanor." He laid Antwan on the ground beside Brandon.

Jonah scrambled onto the edge of the creek and pointed at the downed boys. "How did you know about Brandon and Antwan?"

Trueblood held up her talisman. "I got the warning and asked Omar and Rex to come with me. We had just arrived in the attic when Rex glanced out the window, saw the mishap on the back lawn, and followed you."

Jonah pointed at Antwan. "He's gonna tell people about me. He'll tell Brandon's dad." He sucked in a shaky breath. "I'm sorry I phased, but Antwan would have hurt himself. What could I do?"

Rex responded with a tolerant smile. "Not to worry, son. Omar's here. He'll fix everything. You just watch."

Jonah turned to Omar with a start. "You will?" Usually, his godfather's partner was always the first to greet him, but today, he stood there quietly, watching.

"Omar?" Jonah asked.

Finally he smiled. "Rex's right. I'll handle this."

"How?"

In answer, Trueblood knelt over Antwan and muttered under her breath. Antwan's eyes snapped open and he rolled to his feet with surprising energy. Rex gripped the boy by the arms when he stood and tried to run.

Omar positioned himself in front of Antwan. In contrast to how Antwan had reacted before, the boy seemed relieved to have a fellow African here.

378 *John Darr*

"Relax, brother." Omar's deep African voice was surprisingly soothing. "I won't hurt you."

Antwan's Adam's apple bobbed up and down as he swallowed. "Who are you?"

"I'm gonna remove those memories." Despite Antwan's constant squirming, Omar never broke eye contact. "You don't want those memories. You should not be burdened with them. Let them go."

Antwan's struggling subsided a little.

"Yes. Let them go. That's it." Omar held a hand to the side of Antwan's head. A faint glow surrounded his outstretched fingers. "Yes. Let them go, Antwan."

Omar continued to encourage the boy to let go. As he said it once more, something strange came over Jonah. His own body stiffened and everything went dark.

The next moment, Jonah stood on a busy street in Paris. At first, he thought he had phased until he recognized this from a snatch of dream he'd had once. It hadn't been a dream-walk, either. It had been a normal dream, as far as that went.

Then he remembered the Pale Man with the black clothes, top hat, and a shiny cane. As he watched, the man appeared in the midst of the pedestrians. The people parted for him, like a ship's bow cutting through the water as he strode in measured steps toward an upscale Parisian restaurant.

The sudden urge to warn the people inside that restaurant became unbearable. In fact, he needed to warn a particular person about the Pale Man. *My dad?*

He tried to move at the same time a strong, deep African-accented voice spoke to him. "Let go, Jonah. Let go of the memory."

It was Omar's voice. Jonah resisted because he needed to be inside the restaurant. Again, Omar's disembodied voice called to him.

"No, Jonah. Let it go."

"Jonah please." His mom spoke now. Jonah responded to her, relaxed, and everything went dark again.

The Seeker's Compass

When he opened his eyes, he stared at the treetops high above. The sound of gurgling water came from somewhere nearby. He remembered that he was at the creek with Mike, Omar, Rex, and Trueblood.

Mike's face moved into his field of vision, twisted with worry.

Rex loomed into view next. "You alright, son?"

"Yeah." Jonah sat up, rubbing his forehead.

"You went limp," Mike said. "Rex had to keep you from cracking your head on a rock."

Jonah stood. He was a little unsteady, and Mike propped him up. Rex also hovered nearby, ready to help. Antwan and Brandon lay out on the higher ground, apparently asleep.

Omar stood beside Trueblood with a worried expression on his face.

"I'm okay, Omar." When that didn't soften Omar's expression, Jonah pointed at Antwan. "Did it work?"

Omar spread his arms. "I know my job."

Afraid he'd offended the man, Jonah fumbled for something else to ask as his mind shook off its sluggishness. "How long will the block last?"

"For a lifetime." Omar shifted his gaze from Jonah to Antwan. "That is, if another Memory Charmer doesn't open the wall."

Jonah latched onto that, thinking back to the night he had defeated the Grim Reaper and saved Marcus's life. Omar had been so grateful that he admitted to blocking off some of Jonah's memories and apologized for doing it.

Since that evening, Jonah had given the matter some thought. He liked Omar and he couldn't imagine being angry with his godfather's partner. But maybe the time had come to find out what was blocked. He suspected it had to do with the strange dream that also had the unsettling feeling of being real.

Jonah met Omar's gaze. "Can you unblock my memories?"

A pained look returned to Omar's face. "I'm afraid I can't make that decision. Our jobs often require suppressing memories and events that could expose our world to regular mortals. And at other times, we're called in to suppress traumatic experiences."

Jonah understood. Someone must have called Omar to wall off a traumatic event that had happened to him. Jonah heard his mom's voice in the dream. Could she have ordered the block? The thought of experiencing something bad enough that his mom sought out protection scared him.

Rex squeezed his shoulder. It was gentle considering the man's size. "He's not saying it can't be done, just that maybe you should hold off."

Jonah stared at the adults. "Does everyone know what happened to me?"

"Nah. We don't know what happened. Only your parents, Marcus, and…"

"Rex!" Omar raised his voice.

Rex shook his shaggy blond head. "He should know that much. You think so, too."

"Yes I do, but…" Omar sighed and turned to Jonah. "There's so much else happening right now. Let this rest for now. We can talk to Marcus about it after this mess with the courier is done."

Omar was so unlike Marcus because he didn't hide his emotions, like now, when Jonah could feel the other man's concern flowing off him. He wondered if Omar had been afraid all along that something would happen. *Like I might remember?*

Jonah met Omar's troubled gaze and nodded. "Alright. But I wanna know someday."

Rex cleared his throat and held out the compass. "I took this from Brandon."

Jonah stared at the device, shocked that he'd forgotten about it. "What about Antwan and Brandon?"

"We'll leave them here," Trueblood said. "The pretty boy didn't see anything, and Antwan is safely blocked. Agent Ramsey won't get anything out of either of them."

Mike snorted and poked Brandon's foot with his own.

Omar stroked his clean-shaven chin, watching Mike and Jonah. "Why were you two meeting down here?"

Mike blushed. "We were gonna go to the library and…" his voice trailed off.

The Seeker's Compass **381**

Jonah never told Mike about his godfather and Omar's relationship, but it seemed his buddy had caught on to the jist of Omar's question. Jonah had a different worry. After what just happened, he didn't think he could face seeing his dad's handwriting, not right now.

Omar seemed to understand his feelings. "Take it easy today, Jonah. It's your birthday."

"Why don't you help the others get the hall ready?" Trueblood offered. "I think doing something normal would frustrate Agent Ramsey."

Jonah glanced at Brandon and Antwan once more and thought Trueblood had a good point.

CHAPTER EIGHT
MEMORY CHARMER

Jonah and Antwan smacked head-first into the creek water.

Antwan let out a startled cry, rolled over in the water, and scrambled away. At a safe distance, he raised a shaky finger to point at Jonah. "That's how you got away from the basement last summer. But… but…" He looked around with terrified eyes.

Jonah sat up in the water. "Antwan, listen to me…"

"You're a freak."

"Antwan…"

The frightened boy stood and wiped the water out of his eyes. His clothes sagged against his thin body, making him look pathetic as he shook in fright. Antwan pointed at Jonah again. "Is that why Agent Ramsey's interested in you?"

Jonah began to tremble with fear as he stood.

Antwan sloshed out of the water and onto the bank. "Stay away from me. I'm gonna tell everyone about you!"

"Don't. I can explain."

"Jonah, what's going on?" Mike stepped into view. He'd come from upstream, along the creek. Jonah was worried that the practice club members were with Mike, but his buddy seemed to be alone.

Antwan stared between the two boys. "I knew you were involved, Mike." He only made it two more steps before he ran straight into Rex, who had just appeared. Antwan saw his buddy Brandon lying on the ground behind the big Fallen Reaper and opened his mouth to scream.

The Seeker's Compass **383**

Rex blurred into motion, clamped a hand over Antwan's mouth and whispered, "Be still. I won't hurt you. Your friend is asleep. That's all."

Antwan must not have believed that because he continued to struggle in Rex's iron grip. That's when a vortex appeared and Trueblood and Omar stepped through.

The Mage took in the scene, including Antwan squirming in Rex's grip. She stepped over to the duo and pressed the spread fingers of her right hand along the base of Antwan's thin neck. Jonah saw her lips move with a silent spell. Antwan's body went rigid and then he slumped, unconscious.

Rex let out a relieved breath. "Thanks, Eleanor." He laid Antwan on the ground beside Brandon.

Jonah scrambled onto the edge of the creek and pointed at the downed boys. "How did you know about Brandon and Antwan?"

Trueblood held up her talisman. "I got the warning and asked Omar and Rex to come with me. We had just arrived in the attic when Rex glanced out the window, saw the mishap on the back lawn, and followed you."

Jonah pointed at Antwan. "He's gonna tell people about me. He'll tell Brandon's dad." He sucked in a shaky breath. "I'm sorry I phased, but Antwan would have hurt himself. What could I do?"

Rex responded with a tolerant smile. "Not to worry, son. Omar's here. He'll fix everything. You just watch."

Jonah turned to Omar with a start. "You will?" Usually, his godfather's partner was always the first to greet him, but today, he stood there quietly, watching.

"Omar?" Jonah asked.

Finally he smiled. "Rex's right. I'll handle this."

"How?"

In answer, Trueblood knelt over Antwan and muttered under her breath. Antwan's eyes snapped open and he rolled to his feet with surprising energy. Rex gripped the boy by the arms when he stood and tried to run.

Omar positioned himself in front of Antwan. In contrast to how Antwan had reacted before, the boy seemed relieved to have a fellow African here.

"Relax, brother." Omar's deep African voice was surprisingly soothing. "I won't hurt you."

Antwan's Adam's apple bobbed up and down as he swallowed. "Who are you?"

"I'm gonna remove those memories." Despite Antwan's constant squirming, Omar never broke eye contact. "You don't want those memories. You should not be burdened with them. Let them go."

Antwan's struggling subsided a little.

"Yes. Let them go. That's it." Omar held a hand to the side of Antwan's head. A faint glow surrounded his outstretched fingers. "Yes. Let them go, Antwan."

Omar continued to encourage the boy to let go. As he said it once more, something strange came over Jonah. His own body stiffened and everything went dark.

The next moment, Jonah stood on a busy street in Paris. At first, he thought he had phased until he recognized this from a snatch of dream he'd had once. It hadn't been a dream-walk, either. It had been a normal dream, as far as that went.

Then he remembered the Pale Man with the black clothes, top hat, and a shiny cane. As he watched, the man appeared in the midst of the pedestrians. The people parted for him, like a ship's bow cutting through the water as he strode in measured steps toward an upscale Parisian restaurant.

The sudden urge to warn the people inside that restaurant became unbearable. In fact, he needed to warn a particular person about the Pale Man. *My dad?*

He tried to move at the same time a strong, deep African-accented voice spoke to him. "Let go, Jonah. Let go of the memory."

It was Omar's voice. Jonah resisted because he needed to be inside the restaurant. Again, Omar's disembodied voice called to him.

"No, Jonah. Let it go."

"Jonah please." His mom spoke now. Jonah responded to her, relaxed, and everything went dark again.

The Seeker's Compass 385

When he opened his eyes, he stared at the treetops high above. The sound of gurgling water came from somewhere nearby. He remembered that he was at the creek with Mike, Omar, Rex, and Trueblood.

Mike's face moved into his field of vision, twisted with worry.

Rex loomed into view next. "You alright, son?"

"Yeah." Jonah sat up, rubbing his forehead.

"You went limp," Mike said. "Rex had to keep you from cracking your head on a rock."

Jonah stood. He was a little unsteady, and Mike propped him up. Rex also hovered nearby, ready to help. Antwan and Brandon lay out on the higher ground, apparently asleep.

Omar stood beside Trueblood with a worried expression on his face.

"I'm okay, Omar." When that didn't soften Omar's expression, Jonah pointed at Antwan. "Did it work?"

Omar spread his arms. "I know my job."

Afraid he'd offended the man, Jonah fumbled for something else to ask as his mind shook off its sluggishness. "How long will the block last?"

"For a lifetime." Omar shifted his gaze from Jonah to Antwan. "That is, if another Memory Charmer doesn't open the wall."

Jonah latched onto that, thinking back to the night he had defeated the Grim Reaper and saved Marcus's life. Omar had been so grateful that he admitted to blocking off some of Jonah's memories and apologized for doing it.

Since that evening, Jonah had given the matter some thought. He liked Omar and he couldn't imagine being angry with his godfather's partner. But maybe the time had come to find out what was blocked. He suspected it had to do with the strange dream that also had the unsettling feeling of being real.

Jonah met Omar's gaze. "Can you unblock my memories?"

A pained look returned to Omar's face. "I'm afraid I can't make that decision. Our jobs often require suppressing memories and events that could expose our world to regular mortals. And at other times, we're called in to suppress traumatic experiences."

Jonah understood. Someone must have called Omar to wall off a traumatic event that had happened to him. Jonah heard his mom's voice in the dream. Could she have ordered the block? The thought of experiencing something bad enough that his mom sought out protection scared him.

Rex squeezed his shoulder. It was gentle considering the man's size. "He's not saying it can't be done, just that maybe you should hold off."

Jonah stared at the adults. "Does everyone know what happened to me?"

"Nah. We don't know what happened. Only your parents, Marcus, and…"

"Rex!" Omar raised his voice.

Rex shook his shaggy blond head. "He should know that much. You think so, too."

"Yes I do, but…" Omar sighed and turned to Jonah. "There's so much else happening right now. Let this rest for now. We can talk to Marcus about it after this mess with the courier is done."

Omar was so unlike Marcus because he didn't hide his emotions, like now, when Jonah could feel the other man's concern flowing off him. He wondered if Omar had been afraid all along that something would happen. *Like I might remember?*

Jonah met Omar's troubled gaze and nodded. "Alright. But I wanna know someday."

Rex cleared his throat and held out the compass. "I took this from Brandon."

Jonah stared at the device, shocked that he'd forgotten about it. "What about Antwan and Brandon?"

"We'll leave them here," Trueblood said. "The pretty boy didn't see anything, and Antwan is safely blocked. Agent Ramsey won't get anything out of either of them."

Mike snorted and poked Brandon's foot with his own.

Omar stroked his clean-shaven chin, watching Mike and Jonah. "Why were you two meeting down here?"

Mike blushed. "We were gonna go to the library and…" his voice trailed off.

The Seeker's Compass

Jonah never told Mike about his godfather and Omar's relationship, but it seemed his buddy had caught on to the jist of Omar's question. Jonah had a different worry. After what just happened, he didn't think he could face seeing his dad's handwriting, not right now.

Omar seemed to understand his feelings. "Take it easy today, Jonah. It's your birthday."

"Why don't you help the others get the hall ready?" Trueblood offered. "I think doing something normal would frustrate Agent Ramsey."

Jonah glanced at Brandon and Antwan once more and thought Trueblood had a good point.

CHAPTER NINE
MIKE'S SECRET

Wick stood in front of the large attic window, legs apart and right arm held up while Robert tossed empty soda cans at him. Every can hit an invisible barrier, that flared at the point of impact.

"Wow," Mike, who stood beside Jonah, breathed.

Jonah agreed as he and Mike clapped.

The noise caused Lynn to frown at them. "Will you guys give it a rest?"

"Sorry Lynn," Wick grinned at her. "Last-minute practice for Jonah's party." Wick planned to do a magic show and to dress like a traditional magician. The clothes hung from a hook on the south attic wall: a white dress shirt, black slacks, and black shoes.

Wick rubbed his hands together, smiling at Jonah. "That's only part of the act. Robert's gonna do his thing."

"Really?" Jonah had discovered his cousin was more than a computer wiz and a fantastic traditional artist. Robert could draw whatever someone concentrated on as long as he maintained eye contact with the person.

Wick hustled a startled Mike over to the old sofa and pushed him down on a cushion. Jonah followed, eager to see Mike's reaction to Robert's ability.

Robert retrieved his sketch pad from the computer desk, plopped into an armchair, and opened the pad as he focused on Mike.

Lynn came over and waved Jonah into the second armchair. "You'll want to see this." Once Jonah sat down, she perched on the arm of the chair, arms crossed and waiting.

Wick waltzed around and behind Robert's armchair like he was already on stage. "Now, Mike, I want you to clear your mind and concentrate on one thing. It doesn't matter what it is."

Mike's eyes narrowed with suspicion. "Why?"

"Robert's gonna sketch it."

Mike's jaw dropped, but he nodded after a minute. When his eyes went out of focus, Jonah suspected his friend had decided on something. A quiet scratching sound drew everyone's attention to Robert.

Jonah's cousin never lost eye contact with Mike, but his hand moved in quick, sure motions across the sketch pad's surface. A slight furrow and wrinkle to Robert's brow was the only other sign that he, too, concentrated.

After several minutes, Robert's hand stopped. He closed his eyes while leaning back in the armchair.

Wick peeked at the drawing and whistled. Then he tapped Robert's head and pointed at Mike. "Show him."

Robert held up a very accurate drawing of a single-prop airplane.

"That's amazing!" Mike took the drawing from Robert. "I was thinking about the plane they use for my flying lessons."

Jonah was equally shocked at Mike's revelation of the flying lessons and at Robert's talent. He wanted to ask his cousin about the ability when Mike dropped the sketch pad on the steamer trunk and stood.

"You read my mind?" He trembled slightly.

"No." Robert gestured for Mike to sit down. "I didn't read your mind. I can't see anything unless I draw it and even then, the thought has to be focused." He shrugged. "My power's weird that way. I won't know what I'm getting until I finish drawing."

"Whoa." Mike leaned forward staring at Robert, at a loss for words.

Jonah sympathized, remembering his first session.

Lynn leaned on her brother's shoulder. "We use it sometimes while interviewing people." She raised an eyebrow at Jonah and Mike. "Don't tell anyone."

The boys agreed at once.

"So," Wick said, giving Jonah a lopsided grin. "You okay with us doing the tricks? It's your party."

"Yeah, I'm fine." The reality of the party caught up to Jonah. He glanced at his feet.

"What's wrong now?" Wick asked.

Mike laughed. "He's afraid no one will show up."

"No," Jonah objected. "I'm scared a lot of kids will show up."

Robert shook his head. "I don't get it. What's wrong with people coming?"

"I've never had a real party before." The confession spilled out of Jonah. "And it's gonna be here in the teen center, where everyone can come."

Lynn gave him the once over. For a moment, Jonah feared she'd make fun of him. Instead, she nodded as if finally understanding something else about him.

"Don't worry," she said. "You'll know everyone there."

"But, what if something goes wrong? What if... what if the courier shows up?"

Lynn's eyes widened slightly before she caught herself. Jonah noticed anyway.

Robert snapped his sketchbook closed and stood. "I doubt he'd do that, little cousin."

"Yeah," Wick agreed. "Too risky."

Jonah didn't think so, and he wanted to know what Lynn sensed.

She met his gaze. "Everything will be fine." She gestured to her brother and Wick. "We have a party to prepare."

Jonah and Mike trailed behind the others to the atrium. As they reached the west side hall, Lynn whirled on them. "You two go and do something else."

"Why?" Jonah gaped at his cousin.

"I want the final decorations to be a surprise for you." She crossed her arms, barring their way into the side hall.

Mike pulled Jonah toward the front doors "Don't worry. I have to watch the store for my uncle. Jonah can come with me."

The Seeker's Compass

CHAPTER TEN
PARTY CRASHERS

The transformation of the teen center atrium amazed Jonah and took his mind off his trouble with Mike. Black and white balloons hung in long streamers from the ceiling. The *Happy Birthday* banner was attached high between two of the streamers.

Given the height of the central dome, Jonah imagined Wick had talked the custodians into mounting the balloons. A DJ spun the latest tunes from a low stage in the west wing entrance. On the opposite side of the atrium, another low stage had been set up for the birthday cake and Wick's show.

The café was open and serving catered food for the kids. Perhaps the thing that shocked Jonah most was the number of kids crowded into the Atrium talking, shouting, and dancing.

The music dimmed in volume, alerting the crowd. The DJ grabbed his mic and said, "Ladies and gentlemen, the birthday boy has arrived. Give it up for Jonah!"

Jonah's face reddened as everyone turned to clap and cheer for him. Danita, the leader of their reading group, materialized at Jonah's side and pulled him into the crowd of kids. It was bewildering. He knew a lot of kids from his practice group or from hanging out at the teen center. But many others had come on their own.

Except for the owner of the café, the only other adult was Mr. Varnadore, the middle school assistant principal. Although he was cool with the kids, Mr. Varnadore was a former football player and none of the guys gave him lip.

The man prowled the edges of the gathering, preventing kids from sneaking off into the darkened hallways and side rooms of the center. He paused to wave a greeting.

Jonah acknowledged it and then busied himself searching the crowd of faces, looking for the courier. Danita had other plans. She pulled Jonah into the middle of the crowd of kids to dance.

Just a year before, he would have never done this. He had confessed to Lynn that he wasn't a good dancer. She took pity on him and, without telling her brother or Wick, taught Jonah the latest moves. As with the blades, Jonah was a quick learner.

"You just need someone to challenge you, that's all," Lynn had said, looking impressed.

He thought about that now as he danced with Danita, who also surprised Jonah. He thought of her as even more of a nerd than he and Mike. She devoured books of all genres. That, the straight A's, and the thick glasses she used to wear landed her on the geek and nerd lists. But tonight, her trademark ponytails were gone, she wore her contacts, and she held her own for three songs.

Someone tapped Jonah's arm at the start of the fourth song. He spun around and found Mike standing behind him. Jonah smirked at his buddy. "You wanna dance?"

Mike looked stunned and uncertain for a moment. "Not with you." He cracked a smile as Danita pulled him toward her, then paused long enough to point past Jonah and toward the front doors. "You're not gonna like who just arrived."

Jonah's stomach knotted when he looked. Brandon, Antwan, Drew, and a beefy crew of four boys stood in the entrance. He began to get a bad feeling about this because all the boys wore black polo shirts with the teen center logo on the left chest.

"No way." Jonah slipped through the crowd. Lynn moved to the doorway from the direction of the café, but Jonah arrived first and confronted Brandon. "You're not invited."

"The center hired us as security tonight." Brandon puffed out his chest to show off the word *Security* under the teen center logo.

The Seeker's Compass

"No they didn't." Lynn reached the doors. "My parents didn't order any security. And they wouldn't have hired you."

Brandon crossed his arms, but Jonah noted he stepped closer to his crew. "The director assigned us tonight. Either we stay or the party's over." Brandon smiled and pointed to Mr. Varnadore. "Ask him."

"I will." Lynn pushed through the crowd and to the assistant principal. A moment later, she crossed her arms, her nostrils flaring with anger.

"Told you." Brandon smirked at Jonah and stood right in front of him. "You step out of line, freak, and we'll close you down." He leaned closer. "You never know who'll show up."

Brandon bumped into Jonah as he pressed into the crowd. His guys didn't bother to avoid elbowing people out of their way, creating a ruckus and drawing irritated glares from the other kids. It was clear to Jonah the bullies were trying to start a fight.

That wasn't Jonah's biggest worry. He waved Lynn closer. "He's looking for the courier."

Lynn made a hand signal to Rico. He nodded in return and within seconds, the oldest boys from the Practice Club stood in a loose circle around him. After a few whispered words, the guys spread out through the crowd in order to check Brandon's crew.

The burning in Jonah's stomach worsened. "This isn't gonna end well."

Perhaps Wick noticed the tension in the crowd because he stepped onto the stage. With a cue to the DJ, who changed up the song to a Reggae tune, Wick began dancing around the stage while calling out to the crowd.

As the kids focused on him, Wick began his magic act, pausing between each gag to dance and strut around. The crowd loved it. Jonah had to give the young mage credit. Wick could dance, and he had a smooth and funny way with the crowd.

Then Robert hopped on stage, and more than a few of the girls whistled and called out to him. Once he started into his routine, the kids began to clamor for him to draw their thoughts. Wick handled that, too, and actually goaded one of Brandon's goons into having his thought drawn.

Throughout the entire routine, Jonah clapped like wild with everyone else. About the time the music started again, Jonah caught Brandon and

Antwan talking to each other while watching him. Making sure Mr. Varnadore faced the opposite direction, Jonah headed for the stairs to the second floor balcony.

Once there, he placed his hands on the railing and watched the crowd below. The bass of the popular song vibrated the metal.

There was something primal about the whole scene that penetrated to his very soul. The energy in the room was almost suffocating. As Jonah grew in touch with his Reaper side, he wondered if that was the reason he preferred smaller groups of people.

Jonah shook his head and started to scan the tops of heads below again until he sensed the person behind him and to the side. He froze, trying not to alert the individual. Whoever it was must have already been up here, lurking in the shadows.

Think, Jonah told himself. His Death Sense wasn't buzzing, so the person wasn't dangerous. At least that was a good sign.

Then a familiar voice said, "Why aren't you down there enjoying the party?"

Jonah turned. Trevor stood in the shadows, watching him. The courier moved forward, but not close enough to the balcony that people below would see him. "You don't like crowds, do you?"

"I..." Jonah had to adjust his thinking to the question and away from his fear for this boy. "How do you know?"

Trevor shrugged, looking like a normal kid. "I wondered if it was your nature."

Jonah glanced over the railing at the crowd again to hide his reaction to Trevor's comment. His Reaper side could touch the other kids' souls. He let himself slip into a Reaper stare. Brilliant hues and colors of fun and joy swirled around the kids' auras. The brightness of the young, vibrant souls nearly blinded him. So much energy and potential.

"I can sense every soul," Jonah admitted. "It's..."

"Suffocating?"

Jonah nodded, wondering at his willingness to be so open with this strange boy. He never told his cousins and friends about this side of his nature. "It's like the physical bodies and souls double the pressure on me

The Seeker's Compass

and I just need to get away sometimes and breathe." He glanced at Trevor. "But I don't get it. I've been to theme parks with my cousins. This doesn't happen."

"Maybe it's like telepaths in your movies. They have to learn to block out the other thoughts. When you're at a park, your mind is on having fun." Trevor gestured over the railing. "Tonight, you're worried about other things."

"Yeah, I am. Like you getting caught."

Trevor held a finger to his lips. "Not so loud."

"It's not funny."

"I know. This was the only way to see you. My time's running out. Have you activated the compass?"

"No."

Trevor's eyes narrowed. "Why not?"

Jonah blinked at the sudden intensity in the boy's question. "It's a long story."

"You're not at all what I expected," Trevor said, disappointment clear in his tone.

"Tough," Jonah shot back. He bristled at the feeling the boy expected more from him.

Before either one could respond, Jonah's Death Sense spiked.

He turned toward the stairs, but no one was there. That's when the elevator to the far left of the second floor dinged. Jonah wanted to kick himself. The elevator was locked after hours, so Jonah had expected danger to come by way of the stairs. He should have known the director would have given Brandon a key to the elevator.

As the doors opened to reveal Brandon, two of his bogus security team sprinted up the stairs. A third had distracted Mr. Varnadore near the front of the atrium.

Brandon signaled to Drew and the remaining guy below, and that's when things got crazy. The boys began to shove and push people, creating a ruckus.

Jonah knew why. Brandon wanted to take the courier without anyone noticing. Jonah wasn't going to allow that, not without a fight. He couched, ready to face the bully.

Trevor turned in the opposite direction as Brandon's crew rushed them from behind. The first boy swung at Trevor, who grabbed him by the arm, pivoted, and slung him into the second boy.

Meanwhile, Jonah ducked Antwan's punch and took the bully's feet from under him. Antwan landed on his butt. Brandon was right on his heels, using his friend to cover his advance.

He would have caught Jonah if Trevor hadn't whirled around just in time. He blocked Brandon's precise punches and kicked the bully, sending him tumbling over the second floor railing.

For one horrid moment, Jonah feared Brandon would smash into the kids in the atrium below. That didn't happened because Trevor was at the railing in an instant and grabbed Brandon's hand. He heaved Brandon upward, showing more strength than Jonah would have expected. "Hold on to the railing," Trevor said through clenched teeth.

Once Brandon gripped the rail, Trevor let go and backed away. He motioned for Jonah to follow. "Come on." He dashed into the elevator.

As soon as Jonah entered, Trevor flashed the key he stole from Brandon, slipped it into place, and pressed the down button. The last thing Jonah saw was Antwan helping Brandon over the railing.

Jonah stared at Trevor as the doors closed. He was impressed the courier wasn't even breathing hard. "Where'd you learn to fight like that?"

"Long story," Trevor deadpanned.

The elevator reached ground level and the door opened onto pandemonium. The Practice Club boys were wrestling with Brandon's crew. A couple of the would-be security guards were already down, with their hands tied behind their backs. The balloon streamers had been torn loose. Loud pops went off like gunshots as people stepped on the balloons in their dash for the doors.

The DJ's table and equipment had been turned over. At least one speaker emitted loud squealing noises, causing Jonah to wince and cover his ears. The birthday cake had toppled over and smashed against the wall.

Robert and Mike helped kids through the doors. Flashes went off like crazy, and not from the strobes. Kids were taking pictures and recording videos. Jonah had little doubt that this fiasco would be all over the Internet within minutes.

Brandon and Antwan raced down the stairs, only to get swallowed up in the mess they had created. Jonah met Brandon's furious gaze for a moment before Trevor pulled him into the darkness of the west wing.

"We can't go out the front," Trevor breathed. "We need a place to phase out of here unseen."

Jonah had an idea. He cut in front of the boy and ducked into a side hall, headed for the nearest exit door. "We can head out back." He burst through the door and was in the process of vaulting over the back railing when Trevor grabbed his arm.

It was too late. Jonah's momentum took him over the railing, and Trevor with him. The boys sprawled on the darkened grass. At the same time, an unpleasant tingling sensation traveled over Jonah's entire body.

Only then did he notice that they were surrounded by at least six people, and all of their eyes glowed a pale white. Each also held a scythe, the edges glowing with a sickly green color in the dimness.

Trevor ignored them while pointing at the spikes stuck in the ground in a loose circle. Each emitted blinking lights.

"What's that?" Jonah asked.

Trevor frowned. "It's a nullifying circle. You won't be able to phase." Trevor's voice shook with anger as he stood and helped Jonah to his feet.

Jonah wanted to kick himself for falling into the trap. It was obvious now that Brandon's group had been meant to lure him out of the teen center. Away from the chaos and witnesses, these Wraith-possessed goons could capture Trevor using whatever powers they needed.

"Sorry," Jonah said.

"It wasn't your fault," Trevor answered. "I should have seen this."

The silence of the group unnerved Jonah. Why didn't they attack, he wondered.

Then one of the Grimnions held a phone up and spoke into it. "Tell the agents we have the courier."

CHAPTER ELEVEN
REUNION

The group of Wraith-possessed goons tightened their circle while taking menacing swipes with their scythes. At least four more stepped into view behind these.

Trevor snorted. "They're just trying to scare us."

"It's working," Jonah whispered. He had to admit he was impressed with Trevor. But Jonah thought he should point out the obvious. "Ah, we don't have any weapons and I can't phase us out of here."

Trevor turned his head slightly, allowing Jonah to see the smirk there. "What do you mean?" He pointed at the guy on his right, in the two o'clock position. "I'll use his weapon."

Jonah gulped, not knowing if Trevor was joking or dead serious. When the boy shifted his weight in preparation, Jonah decided Trevor wasn't joking. Calling on his own training, he relaxed into the ready stance and prepared himself to snap into sudden motion.

He had discovered another burgeoning power. He could be pretty fast. It was something Lynn had first noticed. Since then, Jonah had tried slipping into the ability, but it was hit and miss. Tonight, he was sure he could do it.

Copying Trevor's confident demeanor, Jonah chose an opponent.

Trevor bumped his elbow against Jonah's and whispered, "Now."

That was it. Jonah summoned all of his will and pushed himself. Just like with Antwan earlier that day, the outside world blurred for a fraction of a second. That was all he needed to get inside the goon's safety zone and strike. Even before the guy could adjust, Jonah delivered well-placed blows to the man's arm and wrist.

The scythe flew free. Jonah snatched it out of the air as his Death Sense spiked. He rolled away, back toward the center of the circle. When he came up, he saw Trevor also had a scythe, but his guy was on the ground.

Jonah knew he and Trevor had shocked their attackers. He sensed fear in the air as they charged. Jonah went into defensive mode, using the scythe to block the attacks of at least two guys and cut back in return.

Trevor grabbed the striking arm of his assailant and flipped the guy over. He cut the man across the chest with a practiced flourish. The goon's eyes sparked and the Wraith within died.

"Kill the boy," their leader shouted. "We only need the courier."

Jonah's inside went cold at that. With the element of surprise gone, he had to flail with all of his might to defend against the renewed determination of his attackers. And Trevor was busy with his own Grimnions and couldn't help.

After one of the goons nicked him on an arm, Jonah began to grow desperate. That's when something black and whirling appeared behind the enemies.

One attacker's eyes sparked from a cut Jonah didn't see delivered. A split second later, he was hauled up into the air and thrown several feet away. Another goon faltered in his attack as a Reaper's blade protruded from his chest. He crumbled to the ground, dead.

Jonah thought Marcus had arrived as he watched the long-coated figure rip up three of the blinking spikes in a blurred move, breaking the nullifying trap.

When their rescuer stopped and moved closer to retrieve his blade from the downed Grimnion, Jonah gasped. "Kevin?"

The young Fallen Reaper nodded without his usual smirk. "That's right, little man."

Rex and Trueblood had also appeared. The adult mage used a spell to stun another attacker. Rex wasn't so kind and cut yet another with his blade, killing the Wraith inside. The mortal lay on the ground, moaning. The rest retreated.

All of this happened in the span of minutes. Jonah's brain attempted to process the sudden change of fortune. He also wanted to ask Kevin a thousand questions, but the boy was all business, helping Rex lay the dead and injured in a line.

Once he was done, Kevin pulled up and destroyed the rest of the phase-blocking spikes. At once, a new group of people arrived and began to retrieve the fallen. Jonah had never seen this side of the hidden fight among the supernatural. It shocked him.

"It's a clean-up crew," Trevor whispered to him.

Trueblood must have heard because she detached herself from the work and pointed at Trevor.

Rex nodded and grabbed the boy with his big hands. Trevor struggled until Rex shook him like a rag doll. "Be still."

"Get him to the safe house, now," Trueblood ordered.

Rex nodded and phased them away.

"Wait!" Jonah shouted. "I wanna go."

"You can't," Kevin told him.

Jonah whirled on the older boy. "Why not?"

"Because you have to go back inside. This is your party. People will notice you missing." He hustled Jonah through the back entrance and into the west wing of the teen center.

Jonah stopped just short of the atrium, forcing the older boy to halt. But Jonah lost his train of thought because Kevin had shed his long Reaper's coat. He wore a nice black tee, fitted to his developed upper body, and a pair of jeans. The young Fallen Reaper could have walked in to the party like anyone else.

With that thought, Jonah realized that was exactly the point. The clean-up crew out back, Omar's memory charm earlier today, and Kevin losing the long coat; it was all about keeping what they did secret. "Ah," Jonah stammered, trying to recall his earlier questions, "where did you come from? Where have you been all school year?"

"Training." Kevin prodded Jonah in the back. "Keep moving."

"I thought you weren't working with Marcus anymore."

"I'm not. I had to go out on my own missions to complete my training." Kevin motioned toward the atrium and the commotion, but Jonah stood his ground. Kevin sighed. "I'm a full member of the Alliance now."

"Oh." Jonah allowed Kevin to steer him into the atrium.

The place was a mess, and then there was Brandon's crew sitting on the ground, hands still tied behind their backs. Rico and the other boys stood over the group.

While Lynn and Wick worked with the other kids in cleaning up the atrium and café, Robert helped the DJ, who complained in a loud voice about someone paying for his ruined speaker.

Lynn broke away and hurried over to Jonah. "Where were you?"

"Ah, upstairs." Jonah knew that sounded lame. He raised his eyebrows and glanced at Brandon.

Lynn nodded and motioned to Rico. "Let them go."

Rico didn't look happy about that, but he did it. Brandon shot to his feet and poked out his chest until Rico loomed over him.

The bully backed toward the front doors. Once he had space between himself and the Practice Club guys, his snobbish air returned. "You're all gonna get in trouble. You can't tie us up."

"You were causing a problem at the party," Lynn said. "People took plenty of pictures and video."

They were interrupted when flashing lights arrived outside the center. Jonah's heart sank. If someone had called the police, they would be in trouble.

Lynn motioned for the other kids to keep cleaning. She stood beside Jonah and waited. It wasn't the local cops. Agent Ramsey charged through the doors, looking wild.

"What happened?" he asked the group in general, but Brandon started talking.

Jonah stirred when Brandon accused Rico and his guys of attacking. Lynn gripped his hand and squeezed.

Once Brandon finished, looking smug, Ramsey turned to Jonah's group.

Lynn met the agent's angry gaze. "He's lying. We're cleaning up after they started a riot." She gazed down her nose at Brandon. "Besides, they look fine to me."

Ramsey squared his shoulders. "Where is he?"

"Who?" Lynn adopted a confused expression.

Ramsey's hand flicked toward his belt. "I'm searching for a fugitive."

Lynn made a grand show of gesturing around. "Well, he isn't here. Now, if you and Brandon want to help us clean up, start with the café."

Agent Ramsey vibrated with repressed anger. But what could he do, Jonah wondered. There were too many witnesses. He wanted to smile, but feared that would send the guy over the edge.

Ramsey lowered his voice to a whisper and hissed at Jonah and Lynn, "You two won't get away with this."

In response, Lynn reached over and took a broom from Mike and offered it to the agent. The look of fury on Ramsey's face was frightening to see up close.

Rico stood beside Lynn. He was as tall as Ramsey and returned the agent's glare, measure for measure. Lynn never flinched.

Mr. Varnadore entered the atrium. At his arrival, Agent Harris grabbed his partner's arm and pulled him toward the door.

Ramsey continued to glare at them all as he went outside. Harris motioned to Brandon and his crew to leave and followed them out.

Once they were all gone, Lynn let out a breath and leaned against Rico for support.

"What the hell was that about, nena?" Rico asked.

"Just a crazy GBI agent. That's all," she whispered.

Mr. Varnadore clapped his hands. "Let's get this place cleaned up."

Lynn took both Rico's hands in hers. "Come on. We'll be here all night." She pulled her boyfriend into the café.

Jonah glanced up at Kevin. "Where's Trevor?"

"Safe for tonight."

"Trevor? He was here?" Mike winced and lowered his voice. "That's what this was all about? Why didn't you tell me?"

"It all happened so fast. And now the Alliance took him," Jonah explained. "And Kevin won't tell me where."

Mike cornered the taller boy. "I want to see Trevor."

Kevin frowned. "You can see him tomorrow. Right now, both of you have to stay here." Rico caught Kevin's attention and waved him toward the stage.

Jonah tugged on Kevin's shirt before he could move away. "How long are you gonna stay?"

Kevin smiled for the first time that night. "You're my new assignment." He went to help Rico break down the stage before Jonah could ask any more questions.

The cleanup process went fine until the real police arrived. The assistant principal intercepted the officers with Wick's girlfriend, Lynn, and Danita in tow. It wasn't lost on Jonah that Mr. Varnadore kept the cops' focus on him and not the others.

The teen center director's arrival was the only thing to defuse the situation. She was a woman of medium height who wore her hair cut short but stylish. During the day, she sported large earrings, a lot of makeup, and dressed business professional. Tonight, she clutched at a wrinkled coat she had pulled over a printed t-shirt and rumpled jeans.

And she was livid, at Jonah's group and the police, who she succeeded in sending away. Even so, a squad car parked itself within obvious view of the front doors with lights flashing the whole time.

Lynn had a quick conversation with the director.

"We'll have it out in the morning," the director announced and stormed out the front door.

The head custodian had also arrived and assessed the damaged as he scratched his uncombed hair. "Don't worry about her. Just clean up everything best you can. I'll get the rest in the morning," he told Wick before stepping outside to pick up stray trash that had been left out there.

Meanwhile, Lorraine and Rodney had rescued what remained of the cake. Anthony stepped over to gaze at the partially smashed creation. Jonah expected the arrogant boy to make a snide remark.

Instead, Anthony surprised him and shrugged. "The bottom layer never touched the floor. I think it's still good." He turned to Jonah, waiting.

When everyone else also stared at him, Jonah nodded. Plates and forks were passed around and soon all the kids found spots to sit and eat his ruined cake. The tension seemed to leak out of the group and kids began to joke and laugh.

Wick moved to an overturned smaller table and yelped when he lifted it. "Jonah! Your presents."

With Rico's help, the older boys grabbed the presents that had toppled out of sight behind the stage. They dumped them at Jonah's feet.

One by one, he opened the gifts and showed his friends. The whole thing was a bit surreal considering everything that had happened, but Jonah enjoyed it. The final gift was a small bracelet made of polished wooden pieces. "Thanks, Wick."

"You're welcome, Padawan."

Jonah slipped it on his wrist, feeling the power stored inside. *My own shield bracelet.*

After that, people gobbled down the rest of the cake at an alarming rate. Someone suggested they take a piece outside to the custodian and Mr. Varnadore. The two men were still out front. At the last minute, Danita also suggested a slice for the police officer. Rico didn't care for that idea, even though Lynn agreed.

Kevin sat next to Jonah in a brooding silence, watching the others. When people began to toss their plates in the trash and leave, Jonah stood.

He watched Lorraine fold the cardboard cake box. He thought the ruined cake represented his first real party. Smashed but still okay.

When Kevin rose and gently bumped against him, Jonah sighed. "I'm never gonna live this down, am I?"

Kevin snorted and said, "Nope."

The Seeker's Compass

CHAPTER TWELVE
OUTCASTS

Jonah blinked the bright morning sunlight out of his eyes and tried to focus on the bedside clock. When his eyes cooperated, he groaned in surprise. It was half past nine in the morning. *Dang!*

He lay his head on the pillow, thinking about sleeping a little longer, when he heard Aunt Imma's raised voice. Jonah's drowsiness evaporated as he listened. Was his aunt yelling at someone?

He had his answer when both Robert and Lynn yelled in reply. Jonah sat bolt upright in bed and threw his covers off. Today was a weekday. Aunt Imma should be at work by now.

This wasn't a good sign. Well, the yelling made that obvious, Jonah guessed.

He slipped on a pair of basketball trunks and exited his room.

Aunt Imma's angry voice became crystal clear as she bellowed, "You should have told us about the fight."

Jonah stopped, hoping no one would notice him. But it was too late. Aunt Imma turned in his direction. She was dressed in her pastel shirt, black slacks, and black comfortable work shoes.

"Oh, Jonah." She cast an angry glance at Robert and Lynn, who both looked just as heated yet carefully defiant. "I don't blame you for last night," Aunt Imma continued. "I'm just disappointed your party was ruined."

Robert gave him a pleading look and Jonah gulped as he moved into the family room. "It wasn't their fault. Brandon and his gang crashed the party."

"See, Mom?" Robert said. "That's what we've been trying to tell you."

Aunt Imma placed her hands on her hips. "That's not what Brandon's father is saying, nor the director of the teen center."

"She's covering her..." Lynn stopped herself in a huff and stared out the sliding door to the backyard.

Jonah's worst fear was coming true. Brandon had lied and now his powerful dad was interfering. "It's true, Aunt Imma. Brandon did crash the party. Lynn and Robert helped the other kids."

"You don't understand, Jonah." Aunt Imma paused, collecting her thoughts. "With people like the Warners, it's best not to get into anything with them." Aunt Imma seemed stuck between wanting to yell and fearful of doing that to Jonah. "Couldn't you let them patrol the party?"

"No!" Robert and Lynn shouted in perfect unison.

It would have been funny to Jonah in any other situation. "They started the fights," he added. "They did it on purpose to cause trouble." As he recalled the events, his own anger began to leak out. "What was I supposed to do, tell everyone to go home just to keep them from ruining it? How was that fair to me? It was supposed to be my party."

Aunt Imma's eyes widened and she didn't seem to know what to say for several long moments. Eventually, she crossed to Jonah and gave him a hug. As much as Jonah wanted to be a big kid, the hugs always got to him.

He was glad when the front door opened and Aunt Imma released him.

But Jonah's relief changed as soon as he saw Uncle James' face. Not only wasn't his uncle at work when he should have been by this time, but Uncle James also looked worn out. The man's collar was open and his tie was loosened and flopping against his chest as he strode down the hall.

Jonah's insides burned because he could guess why.

"Well?" Aunt Imma asked as soon as her husband reached the family room.

Uncle James threw his wrinkled sports coat over the back of his favorite armchair, pulled his glasses off, and took out his handkerchief. Jonah knew that was his uncle's way of processing what to say.

The Seeker's Compass

"I had it out with the director," Uncle James began. "She wanted to side with Brandon's father."

Aunt Imma swelled with anger. "She never said anything about having security."

"I know, Imma." Uncle James put his glasses on and blinked around at the group. "Brandon's father threatened to file a police report."

Everyone shouted at the same time, forcing Uncle James to wave them silent. "Please."

Aunt Imma wouldn't be quieted. "I hope, James, that you told that woman you'll pull her free ads from your paper."

Jonah wanted to cheer for his aunt. It seemed she was finally on their side despite the earlier yelling.

"Yes, I did." Uncle James eyed Jonah. "I also reminded her that Jonah's godfather is our attorney. I gave her Mr. Armstrong's card to pass along to Brandon's father."

Aunt Imma blinked in surprise.

Robert whooped, "Way to go, Dad."

"Did that work?" Lynn asked.

"Well, judging by the change in her expression, I don't think any charges will be filed. It's one thing to mess with the locals, but Marcus' firm is worldwide."

That was the best news Jonah had heard, but his uncle's face remained solemn. Jonah opened himself to a partial Reaper stare and sensed the dread leaking off his uncle.

"That being said," Uncle James continued in a low voice, "I suggest you three stay clear of the teen center for a few days."

Lynn's arms dropped to the sides and she stared at her father. "Why? We didn't do anything."

"I know that, Lynn."

"Then why can't we go around the center, Dad?"

Uncle James closed his eyes. Jonah suspected he was counting to ten or something like that. His voice was measured when he continued. "The director's still angry, plus Brandon's father is working with the firm adding in the security cameras. So, I think it's best if we let things cool down."

"That's not fair." Robert sounded as bummed as his sister. "It's like we're outcasts from our own space!"

"Oh Robert, don't be so dramatic," Aunt Imma said.

"I'm not being dramatic, Mom." The veins on Robert's thin neck stood out as he yelled. "What about the website and blog?"

Uncle James' eyes gleamed as he said, "You can work on the blog from one of my offices. The teen center website will have to wait. In fact, without you doing updates, maybe they'll see how important you are." He offered Robert an encouraging smile.

Robert shook his head in dismay. "It still isn't right."

"Well, don't forget the break-in last summer," Uncle James added. "This makes two incidents in about a year."

Jonah was numb. In one night, their clubhouse was off limits. But Uncle James' comment about the break-in sparked something else in Jonah's mind. "It's those GBI agents."

Lynn nodded. "I bet Agent Ramsey is egging things on."

"That's another reason to stay away." Uncle James met Lynn's gaze. "Why don't you and Robert come with me today?"

Robert stormed off to his bedroom, looking defeated, but Lynn didn't move. "I have some things to do with Rico."

Aunt Imma made a disapproving sound under her breath and looked away. Jonah had discovered that his aunt didn't care for Rico. It was the tattoos that covered his arms. She thought that proof positive the boy was in a gang or something like that.

"Don't go near the teen center, Lynn." Uncle James' voice had a rare edge to it.

"I won't." Lynn stalked off to her room, leaving Jonah alone with his aunt and uncle.

When Uncle James turned to him, Jonah said, "I'm hanging out with Mike. We're going to the library."

"Good."

The Seeker's Compass **409**

Aunt Imma grabbed her purse and kissed Mr. Hightower on the cheek. "I have to go. You sure it'll be okay?"

"Yes," he assured her.

Robert came out of his room, dressed to go. Uncle James called out to Aunt Imma, "Hold the door. We're coming."

"See you around, little cousin." Robert followed his dad and mom out of the house.

The buzz in Jonah's head from everything that had happened began to irritate him. It was as if every time he made plans, something else happened. Jonah retreated to his room and grabbed his clothes for the day.

By the time he finished with his shower, he was less bummed with the situation and ready to find Mike and hang out. As he walked down the hall to his room, shirtless, Jonah received an unpleasant surprise. Lynn, Mike, and Kevin sat talking in the kitchen.

Mike waved at him.

Kevin smirked and said, "Show off."

Jonah gazed at his bare chest, so much less developed than Kevin's, and hurried to pull on his shirt. "What's going on?" he asked, moving through the family room and into the kitchen.

"Marcus wants me to bring you to the safe house," Kevin said.

Lynn wore a defiant look on her face. "I've already told him I'm going."

"Me too," Mike chimed in.

"I thought you were meeting up with Rico?" Jonah thought to point out.

Lynn shrugged. "I was just saying that to bug Mom."

Jonah smiled at that, then he focused on the central question. "Is Trevor all right?"

"Yep." Kevin glanced at Jonah's bare feet. "You gonna put on some shoes?"

Jonah experienced that quick annoyance at Kevin's poking fun. At the same time, he liked sparring with the boy. "I thought I'd go barefoot." He raised his foot to wiggle his toes at Kevin.

Mike giggled while Lynn rose from her chair and shoved Jonah toward his bedroom. "Get real. You have one minute."

Jonah only needed half that time to grab his favorite pair of red sneakers and return to the kitchen. "We can't phase from in here," he said while slipping on his socks and then shoes.

"I didn't intend to." Kevin rose from the table and opened the back door. "Come on." He stepped outside and crossed the backyard to the shed.

"You also can't create vortices, either," Kevin added.

"Wow," Mike breathed. "That's cool."

"No it's not." Jonah said it before he could stop himself.

Kevin laughed. "You must have been trying to sneak out of your room at night."

"No." Jonah's face warmed, causing Mike to laugh. Jonah scowled at Kevin. "We can't phase in the daylight, either. Someone could see us."

"He knows that too, Jonah." Lynn unlocked the shed's door and stood back to let everyone else inside.

It occurred to Jonah that Lynn, Mike, and Kevin had talked things through while he showered. He stepped into the darkened shed. With the lawnmower, gardening tools, and all three bikes still chained inside, the fit was tight.

Lynn came in last and closed the door, leaving them in almost pitch black except for where sunlight leaked through gaps in the wall joints. With the door closed, the overpowering smell of grass cuttings, oil, and a faint whiff of gas from the gas can became more pronounced.

"Everyone hold onto me," Kevin said.

"You can handle three people?" Lynn sounded impressed.

"Of course he can. He's an alliance member now." Jonah let some of his irritation come through.

Even in the darkness, Lynn's aim was true as she smacked him across the back of the head. Mike stifled his giggles.

Jonah fumed. An awkward shuffling happened when Lynn and Mike fumbled to grip Kevin's hands. Jonah started to grab onto Kevin's arm when he remembered the last time they did this sort of thing.

Today, Kevin wore a light blue t-shirt and dark cargo pants without a belt. Jonah decided to slip a finger through a belt loop on the boy's pants. But when he tried, his aim was off and he poked Kevin in the hip.

"Excuse me," the older boy said, sounding amused. "That's not my hand."

"What?" Lynn asked.

"Nothing," Jonah said, glad that the darkness hid his embarrassed face. He succeeded in threading his finger through a loop on the second attempt. When Kevin shifted, Jonah wondered if the boy was smirking at him in the darkness.

A second later, the familiar ripples traveled over every inch of Jonah's body. Lynn didn't utter a sound, but Mike gasped. The sensation only lasted seconds. One moment, they were in the darkened shed. The next moment, muted light flared around them as they reappeared on a large, shaded patio.

A lush manicured yard and garden stretched out to their right. The smell of late summer plants filled the air. And on their left was a huge mansion.

"This is nice," Lynn gushed. "When you said safe house, I was thinking something smaller."

Kevin motioned for them to follow him to the upper landing and then to a back door. "We only called it a safe house because of the courier, but it's really a guest house."

He opened the back door and entered a large pantry and then a restaurant-grade kitchen. Rows of silver pots hung from hooks overhead. The stove contained numerous burners, some with bubbling pots on them.

The aroma of cooking sauces hit Jonah's nose and his mouth watered, reminding him he hadn't eaten breakfast. Plates were stacked to the side on a large wooden worktop. And beyond the kitchen and in a side nook was a round wooden table.

Trevor sat there, eating and talking to a stout woman whose hair was a bright cinnamon color. The courier dropped his fork when he saw Jonah and shot to his feet. That caused the woman to whirl around. She rose from the chair and, despite her size, moved rather quick to enfold Kevin in a bone-crushing hug.

"Kevin!" she mumbled into his chest because that's as far as her face reached.

Kevin returned the hug, wrapping his long arms around her. "Hey Mom."

Jonah's jaw dropped. He, Lynn, and Mike exchanged similar shocked expressions.

CHAPTER THIRTEEN
SAFE HOUSE

All Fallen Reapers had first lives. That's the period of time from their original birth to their moment of death as mortals. Once they became one of the Undead, if they rebelled and became mortal again, all contact with former families was forbidden. At least, that's the way Marcus explained it to Jonah.

In most cases, such as Jonah's godfather and his dad, they had been Reapers for decades and their immediate mortal family members were long gone. But Kevin was different. He confessed to Jonah last summer that he had only been a Reaper for a few years and still had a family and little brother alive and well.

For obvious reasons, Kevin could never show up on their doorstep and say, "Hi." And there was the fact that Kevin's family lived in Chicago and not Georgia. For all those reasons, Jonah was confused when Kevin called the woman...

"Mom?" Jonah repeated while gaping at the older boy.

He didn't get it for another basic reason. Not only was the woman's oatmeal complexion as light as Mike's, whereas Kevin's skin was a deep chocolate, they also didn't favor each other at all.

The woman smiled at Jonah's confused expression. "I'm not really his mom." She held out a hand. "Hi, my name is Mabel," she said with a hint of a Creole accent. "You're Jonah." Mabel gently ran her hands down Jonah's cheeks. "My God, you were just a bundle in your parent's arms when I last saw you. Now, you're all grown and look so much like your father."

"You knew him?" Jonah asked.

"Of course. I took him in when he came back. He wasn't much older than Kevin is now. Well, in human years." She winked at Kevin.

"She runs a foster home in D.C. for special people," Kevin explained.

"And all the kids call me Mom," Mabel finished.

Jonah's eyes widened. "Kids? You mean Fallen Reapers?"

"Oh no, *mon cheri*. Most are mortals like your friend here." She graced Mike with a smile. "Except they have a talent like Omar, who can do memory charms." Mabel stroked her double chin, peering at Mike. "I'm sure you have a gift too."

Mike shrugged. "I don't think so."

Mabel chuckled. "Give it time, *mon cheri*. Give it time. Humans are capable of a lot of things. The Alliance tries to find and recruit them."

She took Lynn's right hand in her own. "I hear you have the Sight, like all the women in your family." Lynn nodded. "Jonah's mom, your aunt, was strong in it. Don't you be afraid to use the talent, girl." Mabel released Lynn's hand and gazed around at the group. "It's often young people about your ages who show up. Their powers and gifts suddenly come out and they tend to do something big. It's easy to find them at that point."

"They need a safe place away from their families," Kevin added. As he looked around the kitchen, Jonah thought the boy was remembering his time there. "The Alliance teaches them to deal with their abilities."

Mabel patted Kevin's bicep, like a true proud mother. "Kevin was so young-minded when he came back that he fit right in with the rest of the young people."

Kevin frowned. "Marcus said I needed someone watching over me."

Jonah thought his friend was a little embarrassed. So he decided to help and bring the talk back to Mabel. "Where's your house? Here in Atlanta?"

"Oh, no. I still live in Washington. I just come down from time to time." Mabel smiled at Kevin and Jonah. "I'm lucky I did. I have my chance to see you," she continued. "Your parents kept you away. And when they died, Marcus bundled you up and shipped you to Georgia. I know they made arrangements, but..." Mabel sniffled, and Trevor handed her a Kleenex.

The Seeker's Compass **415**

"Thank you. I'm so sorry about your parents, Jonah." She gave his hand a gentle squeeze. "At least now you're on the right track."

She touched Trevor's cheek. "Now there's a new one to help." She gently turned Trevor and prodded him toward the opposite door. "Move along. Marcus will want to talk to you."

True to Mabel's words, Marcus waited for the group in the large living room. He stood by a fireplace and nodded to Jonah as he entered. Overstuffed comfortable furniture filled the space. Trevor sat down on a tartan-colored love seat, and Mike hurried to sit beside him.

Kevin and Jonah took the large sofa opposite them while Lynn picked a high-backed armchair. Jonah thought the chair fit her like a regal queen when she lifted her chin, surveying the room. He averted his gaze before Lynn could catch him.

Mike peppered Trevor with questions. "Why didn't you tell me you were the courier? What's it like?" Mike took a breath. "What's your cover job?"

Trevor laughed. "I'm just a glorified record keeper, and a real courier."

The answer seemed to animate Mike even more. "But what's it like, keeping records on the other side? I do the records for our blog."

A shy smile transformed Trevor's face as he regarded Mike. "What's a blog?"

"Well, it's a series of chronological articles, like written records."

Jonah smiled as Mike explained. His buddy suddenly showed more enthusiasm for a job he had called lame two days ago.

"Do you use Seeker archive boxes?" Mike pressed.

"You know about those?" Trevor turned to face Mike, ready to ignore everyone else.

"We can talk about his job later." Marcus had finished his quiet conversation with Mabel and waited as everyone settled down. "We know about the party and the aftermath. The law firm made it clear that if Brandon's father tries to make an issue of it, we'd counter."

Jonah wanted to ask about the bodies behind the teen center but decided he really didn't want to know the details. He chose something safe to comment on. "I bet Brandon loved that."

"Well," Marcus hedged, "I can't speak for Brandon, but his father isn't a fool. It's more important they keep their true aim undercover. So we expect him to back down."

Jonah welcomed that news, but they still had another problem. "We can't go in to the teen center."

"I know." Marcus crossed to the second armchair and sat down. "This is Agent Hunter's doing. It's an old tactic. Apply pressure to draw out the target. He's shutting you off from the places you can call a refuge."

Marcus's blunt statement confirmed Jonah's hunch, but he had never thought of it in that way. Lynn's expression also worried him. She looked spooked. Jonah begin to think she'd sense this would happen all along.

"What do we do?" Mike asked.

Kevin rapped the coffee table with a knuckle. "We keep moving forward. Don't let the enemy win." He glanced at Marcus. "Right?"

"Yes. And to do that, you need information." Marcus gestured to Trevor. "It's time to share everything you told me last night."

Trevor sat forward, resting his elbows on his knees and clasping his hands together. The posture and worry lines on the boy's forehead exuded the air of someone who'd been through a lot. Even his short dreads seemed to droop under the invisible pressure.

At that moment, Trevor struck Jonah as older than he appeared. But the effect was gone within seconds, leaving Jonah puzzled.

Trevor stared at his hands while he began. "My job was to meet with the Alliance rep and smuggle him through the portal and to the other side. We thought a face-to-face meeting was the next step in moving our common cause forward."

"You mean fighting the Grim Reaper?" Mike interjected.

"He means the Rulers of the Afterworld." Marcus gestured to Trevor to continue.

"The Grim Reaper shares power with the supreme record keeper, the Grand Oracle," Trevor explained. "While your Alliance works on this side to stop the Grim Reaper's plans, my people have their own quiet rebellion against the Grand Oracle."

The Seeker's Compass **417**

"You already know that someone inside the Alliance betrayed us and told both sides about the meeting," Marcus interjected to the group. "Now they're after Trevor."

Lynn asked the more probing question. "What do you know?"

Trevor met her determined gaze. "No one has ever seen our leader in person. We call him The Elder. As a safety measure, he transmits instructions and speeches in separate dispatches to one cell at a time."

Lynn's eyes widened and then she smiled. "You're the only one to ever see his face?"

"Yes. He's very high in Archivist administration. That's how he's able to help the dissidents."

"As you can imagine," Marcus added, "the Grand Oracle wants Trevor. With his knowledge, they could destroy the Afterworld rebels from the top."

Mike touched Trevor's arm. "But what about the Grim Reaper?"

Trevor shrugged. "He wants the leverage, I think. He'd use my information to end the power sharing arrangement. That's why I have to return. Not only am I running out of time, but the longer I stay, the greater the chance they'll catch me." He pointed at Jonah. "Ramsey will continue to come after you."

"Yeah, I know, but your cover is blown on the other side."

"I'll have to work directly with the Elder from now on." Trevor closed his eyes. "He can protect me."

Jonah was moved by the conviction in the boy's voice. "How can I help?"

"It's your compass."

Jonah pulled the compass from his pocket. He'd been planning to go with Mike to the library and try to figure it out.

Trevor stretched out his hand, and Jonah placed the compass on the boy's palm. "This is called a Seeker's compass." He held the device close to his face, examining the surface. "It's one of a kind, Jonah. Special."

"How will it help you get back?"

When Trevor hesitated, Jonah suspected the boy of filtering what he would reveal. He'd seen his godfather do it often enough.

Trevor glanced around. "This compass can open a back door to the Afterworld. I'll be able to cross over. But to do that," he looked at Jonah, "you have to uncover the true compass face."

Marcus stood. "Are you sure?"

"The Elder told me himself." Trevor handed the compass back to Jonah. "Only Jonah can do it."

"What happens when I open this true face?" Jonah glanced at the device and the normal face displayed at the moment. "Will it activate a vortex or something to the Afterworld?"

"No." Trevor sucked in a breath to continue. "Opening the doorway is a two-step process. First you have to find a Cognitive Enhancer. That's what the true compass face will reveal. A code or location where you can find it."

"Cognitive Enhancer?" Mike asked. "You mean a mind booster?"

Trevor gave him a wan smile. "I didn't name it, but mind booster is better."

Mike nodded. "And the second step?"

"There's a cavern with a special pedestal. If you set the compass inside the pedestal, you'll open a second set of special codes, each one a different location in the Afterworld. With the Enhancer, or mind booster, Jonah can decipher those codes, enter one into the compass, and open the doorway to that chosen location."

The implication staggered Jonah. At the moment, he didn't see a way to enter codes in the compass. He began to wonder what the true compass face would look like.

Lynn held up her hands. "Wait. In order to decipher the special codes, you need an Enhancer? But in order to find that device, you need a different code from the compass." She eyed Trevor. "Did I miss something?"

"No." Trevor seemed at a loss to explain further.

Jonah got it. "It's like our computers at the clubhouse, Lynn." He paused at the stab of pain at not being able to even go into their sanctuary. "We're the only ones who can log into the system and access the files."

Mike nodded and sat forward, excited. "Jonah's right. You can get into the system with a club password. That's like the first code when Jonah opens the true face of the compass. But to access your encrypted background files for stories, you need a second code, the encryption key."

Jonah snapped his fingers. "It's added protection to make sure the person using the compass is the right one."

Lynn frowned. "Sounds like a geek came up with this process."

Kevin snorted and clapped his hands. "Now that we figured that out, where's this Enhancer?" He looked ready to go right now.

Trevor pointed at the compass. "That initial code is locked inside."

Lynn stared at Jonah. "You need to figure out that riddle and open the compass, hero."

Jonah's annoyance flared. "I planned to do that twice already, but things keep happening."

"Well, you're in luck today. No interruptions. Get busy; we have a mission." Lynn pulled Jonah to his feet. "The County Library?"

With a graceful move, Marcus rose and blocked the doorway. "Given the importance of the compass, I think Jonah should figure it out here."

"But–" Jonah started.

"I'm afraid that's an order." Marcus arched an eyebrow.

Mike stood beside Jonah. "We can do it."

"I guess, but it would have been nice to use the library."

Kevin snorted. "There's a library here."

"Really?" Jonah thought the boy was joking.

Marcus moved aside and Kevin led the way down a wide hallway to a well-stocked library. Mike and Jonah moved into the large room of dark wood and earth tones. A huge table was situated in the center, with books of all kinds already placed on it. Some were opened. A few smaller tables were scattered around with study-type chairs beside them.

The room had the feel of the older college libraries Jonah had visited in Washington. Kevin's comment about this being a Guest House for young people made more sense.

Jonah turned to Marcus, who stood in the doorway. "The other kids use this?"

"Yes."

"Where is everyone?"

"They'll arrive next month for the summer session."

Jonah nodded.

Mike grinned. "It's like Xavier's school in the X-Men." He and Jonah laughed.

Kevin exchanged a glance with Lynn. "I see they haven't changed."

"Nope." Lynn thumped them on the heads. "Get busy, geek boys."

Jonah sat the compass on the center table and pulled the riddle from his other pocket. As the others headed for the doorway, Jonah called out to Kevin, "What are you gonna do?"

"I'm taking Lynn and Trevor down to the bat cave."

When Kevin grinned, Jonah wanted to punch him. The older boy knew the name would pique his and Mike's curiosity.

Mike beat Jonah to the next question. "What's the bat cave?"

Kevin lingered in the doorway. "That's the basement with the pool and Ping-Pong tables, the latest game consoles, big-screen TV, and all the movies you ever want to watch." He grinned. "Plus it has the best sofas and chairs, and a refrigerator full of sodas and snacks." He pointed at the compass. "Get to work."

CHAPTER FOURTEEN
THE RIDDLE

Jonah spent his first moments in the Guest House library thinking of all kinds of choice names for Kevin.

Mike pulled the thick curtains back to allow brilliant sunlight to stream through the massive window. "You think Kevin's telling the truth?"

Jonah blinked at the interruption to his pleasant thoughts of revenge. "Yeah."

Mike peered at Jonah as he returned to the table. "Why does he tease you?"

"Don't know." Jonah had to use two hands to pull out one of the heavy wooden chairs. He sat down.

Mike went around to the opposite side and pulled out the other chair. He had to hop on his knees in order to lean across the table. "Maybe you're like a brother he never had, or..."

Jonah hadn't intended to respond until Mike said that last bit. He paused, the riddle still unfolded. "Or?"

Mike met his gaze and then shrugged. "Maybe he likes you or something. I don't know."

Jonah thought his buddy tried to sound offhanded with the comment. But he caught the quick, nervous glance that Mike gave him.

The truth was, the idea didn't bother Jonah at all. He had wondered the same thing. Since Mike brought up the subject, Jonah figured it'd be safe to kick around the idea and ask about Trevor.

Mike tapped the riddle with a finger. "Hurry up and read it."

"But…"

"What?" Mike looked genuinely lost. "This is important. Trevor's waiting."

"I know that." Jonah tried to hide the irritation in his voice.

When Mike let out an impatient sigh, Jonah swallowed any comebacks and began to read the riddle out loud.

Who am I?
I always start at the beginning
But rarely end at the ending.
I am ruled by War and find comfort in Fire.
Freedom is my greatest desire.

Who am I?
I control the balance and tip the scales.
I'm driven by love and beauty's heroic tales.
My self-expression is done with style and flair
You'll find I repose in the air.

Who am I?
I am the bringer of old age and Time is my friend
Security is my cloak and on the earth I depend.
I'm extremely hard to open, my secrets reveal
Once naked and exposed I rarely conceal.

If you can answer these questions and unlock my true face
I will ever point you to the right and proper place.

Jonah's voice ended on a strong note. He was impressed with himself and relieved. Rereading the note hadn't made him lose it.

Mike took out his glasses and perched them on his thin nose. As soon as Jonah gave him the riddle, he settled into the mystery, his eyes darting back and forth as he read over the page several times.

The silence in the library stretched into minutes. Jonah grew impatient and tapped his fingers on the table. Mike ignored him, too engrossed in the riddle.

Jonah huffed and began spinning the compass on the table between them.

Mike broke off reading and leaned close. "Can I touch it?"

"Yeah."

Mike lifted the compass. "Wow. I never saw it up close until today. It looks normal except for the button on the side and this dial around the face. These are Zodiac symbols, Jonah."

"I figured out that much. I even tried turning the dial to my sign and pressing the button, but nothing happened."

"You had the right idea, but…" Mike paused, running his hand down the note while cupping the compass in the other. "I think you need three zodiac signs."

"Are you sure?"

"The riddle's divided into three sections, so I figure that means three signs, not one. That has to be it." Mike set the compass aside and used both hands to press the riddle flat. "Notice how each stanza mentions one of the four elements? Fire, air, earth, or water." Mike snapped his fingers. "We need an astrology book."

Without another word, Mike jumped out of his chair and began to search among the books. Jonah checked the shelf closest to him. The books covered all kinds of subjects, but most were on mythology, fairy creatures, folktales, and obscure histories.

Mike dropped two books on the table with loud thuds, drawing Jonah's attention.

When he saw the title of the book on top, Jonah smiled. "*Astrology and You?*"

Mike shrugged. "You have a better idea?"

Actually, Jonah thought Mike's idea was brilliant. He opened the book and found a section for Astrological Signs. "What should we start with?"

"Try fire."

"Okay." Jonah read down the list of zodiac signs. "I see three fire signs: Aries, Leo, and Sagittarius."

Mike gasped, "What are their characteristics?"

"That may take too long. What does the riddle say?"

"I always start at the beginning but rarely end at the end."

"Gee wiz, that could be anything."

"Well the second line says the symbol is ruled by war."

Jonah flipped the page. "Aries is ruled by Mars. That's the god of War. And it says that all Fire signs like freedom." He sat the book on the table. "Freedom is my greatest desire. That's what the last line of that first stanza says."

"The sign has to be Aries. It's the only sign to fit all the clues." Mike pulled out a sheet of paper and wrote *Aries* on it in a small, precise print.

The excitement begin to build inside Jonah as he lifted the book and read through the Aries characteristics. "Cool."

"What?" Mike tried to peer over the top of the book.

"Aries are quick to initiate new things but often don't follow through."

Mike laughed. "They are rarely at the end because they leave early. Your parents were interesting."

"Yeah, they were." Fresh pain spiked inside Jonah at the sad realization that his birthday would always bring pain because his parents had died the same day. Mike apologized, but Jonah tapped the riddle. "Let's keep going."

Now that they had the flow, figuring out the second sign, Libra, and third, Capricorn, was a snap. Afterward, Mike sat back in his chair, staring at the names of the three Zodiac symbols. "I wonder if we have to figure out the right order?"

The Seeker's Compass

Jonah shook his head. "My dad wouldn't make it that hard. He wanted me to be able to use it."

He rotated the dial to the first sign and pressed the button. He thought the compass vibrated in his hand, but couldn't be sure. When he rotated the dial to the second sign and pressed the button again, he was certain of it. He looked at Mike. "It's vibrating."

"You wanna keep going?"

Jonah nodded, turned the dial to the third sign, and pressed the button. The compass didn't exactly vibrate, but it hummed with power, growing warmer in his hand. The face began to waver and suddenly folded in on itself.

"Wow!" Mike said, then hurried around the table to peer over Jonah's shoulder.

A new, far more ornate face appeared on the compass, one made of a smooth, polished material. Its circular dials contained strange, yet beautiful, raised symbols.

Jonah pointed at the markings. "Those are the same symbols on Robert's archive box and Lynn's blades."

In addition to the double rows of symbols, the compass had two hands like an expensive clock. The longer hand resembled the engraved nib of an old-style fountain pen. The smaller hand looked like a short dagger. And at the very center of the face, a red button pulsed.

"Do you know what they mean?" Mike asked.

"We never figured them out."

"Maybe Trevor knows."

Jonah thought that a good possibility. He and Mike jumped when the longer clock-like hand jerked into motion on its own. When the hand stopped, the symbol directly above its pointed end began to glow a bright yellow.

The hand snapped into motion again. When it paused beneath another symbol, it too began to glow. The hand rotated again and again until six symbols in all glowed. The red button in the center of the compass's face switched to a pulsing green color.

Jonah moved his own finger over the compass face and the symbol directly beneath his finger glowed brighter. He paused, then brought his finger back to the edge of the dial. The symbol not only glowed brighter, but it also expanded. As his finger moved away, the symbol contracted to its original size.

"Cool!"

He wiggled his finger left, then right, watching as each symbol expanded and contracted. The fluid magnifying effect allowed him to easily see each symbol. That gave Jonah an idea and he moved his finger over the long hand of the compass, and it followed his movement.

He jerked a finger back and forth and the hand wavered, trying to follow the quick action. When he swiped a finger all the way around the compass, the long hand whirled around. Jonah laughed.

Mike shoved him. "Stop that."

"Sorry," Jonah said. "This is so cool."

"It's obvious you can change the combination of symbols. But we don't want to do that. Trevor said this was the code to the mind booster."

"Then what does the green button do?"

Mike hunched his shoulders. "Well, green usually means *go*."

Jonah considered that for a moment. "So you think it'll take me to the mind booster?"

"Yeah, I do. And that could be dangerous."

"Dangerous?" That had never occurred to Jonah, but considering it now, he didn't think it possible. "My parents meant for me to figure this out on my own and press the button. I'm sure they visited the place, which means it can't be dangerous."

Mike nodded. "I can see that."

"We should try the code." The recklessness nagged Jonah. He hated to wait after being pushed into doing something.

Mike tapped the table to get his attention. "Jonah..."

"You said this was important." Jonah pressed the green button, drawing a scathing look from Mike. His moment of rebellion was short lived. "Mike? I feel funny."

The Seeker's Compass

Mike slugged him in the arm. "Listen to me the next time, idiot."

"I'm serious. The compass is doing something to me."

Mike's mouth dropped open. "Oh. Well, let go of it!"

"I can't." Jonah's skin began tingling. "It feels like the times I phased. The compass is causing me to phase."

Mike started for the door. "I'll get Kevin."

"There's no time!" Jonah heard the fear in his own voice and hated it. The mocking voice in his head was ruthless and sounded a lot like Lynn. *Oh no, hero, you wanted to press the button. Now deal with it.*

Mike hurried back to Jonah's side and reached out.

"Don't touch me," Jonah said, realizing too late what his friend was doing.

Mike ignored the warning and slapped his hands over Jonah's hand and compass. "This may be stupid, but I'm going with you."

The air around them wobbled and distorted a second before a rippling sensation shot over Jonah's body. Mike let out a startled gasp. An instant later, the old library vanished.

CHAPTER FIFTEEN
PARENTS' HIDEAWAY

Jonah could usually shift his position while phasing, but the compass had thrown off his concentration. When the device transported the boys to a thickly wooded area, Jonah was still in a seated position.

"Oh no," he said and dropped to the hard ground, numbing his butt. Mike, who had been leaning over him, came down on top of him, crushing the air out of his lungs.

"Hey!" Jonah managed to scream.

Mike ignored Jonah's protests and scrambled for his glasses, which had clattered onto the leaf-covered ground. He succeeded in kneeing Jonah in the side.

"Get off me." Jonah heaved his friend off.

Mike whirled, his recovered glasses in one hand, and landed two punches to Jonah's chest with the other. "Don't you dare. This was your fault, not mine."

Jonah rolled away from his buddy. Mike didn't like to fight, but a year in the Practice Club had taught him to hit with power.

"You decided to come with me." Jonah climbed to his feet and winced. "And that hurt."

"Good." Mike dusted off his glasses, then folded them in angry motions. He shoved them in a pocket and began rubbing his arms. "Where are we?"

"Hold on." Jonah had already decided to try and sense how far they had traveled. Marcus said a Reaper could do it, and Jonah had been practicing.

The Seeker's Compass **429**

Once he was sure Mike wouldn't hit him again, Jonah closed his eyes and thought of the library. With that firmly in mind, he visualized this new location, creating an imaginary line connecting both points. The answer that materialized in his head shocked him.

"Well?" Mike asked.

"We're still in Georgia," Jonah answered, "but we're over two hundred miles from Atlanta."

"Wow." Mike gave him an awed look

Jonah began to explore the immediate surroundings, noting that the ground below them was higher than the rest of the immediate area. He stomped his foot, feeling the unexpected hard surface beneath. That gave Jonah an idea. He knelt down and brushed away the leaves, not caring about the dry dirt getting under his fingernails.

Mike knelt beside him. "Jonah? What are you doing?"

"Help me."

Mike frowned but joined in and together, they quickly uncovered a circular piece of concrete with large bricks bordering the edge. One brick in particular was larger and different from the rest. Years of hard-packed dirt covered it, falling away in dry flakes as Jonah began clearing the surface. Soon, he uncovered six symbols embedded in the brick's rough surface.

When Jonah sat back, Mike leaned closer to peer at the brick. "Those are the same symbols from the compass. Have you ever seen this place before?"

"No, but my parents went so many places that I never knew about."

Jonah brushed away as much dirt as he could from the edge of the concrete platform to reveal a connected walkway. It seemed to go directly under a thick wall of rhododendron bushes that was beside them. That's when he noticed a line of bricks beneath the bushes.

He stood, examining the bushes for a second before digging his hands into them and pulling the branches apart. "Look! It's a stairway, and it leads up a hill."

Mike squeezed beside him, pulling more branches out of the way. He gasped and pointed. "That looks like a brick wall at the top."

"Yeah." Portions of a brick wall were visible through the thick bushes and trees. "I say we go up."

"Are you sure? Maybe we should just go back."

"What about the Enhancer? My dad wanted me to come here." Jonah tested the first step.

Mike hesitated. "Jonah, you can get us back, can't you?"

"Yep," Jonah lied, keeping his face turned away from Mike. The truth was, he wasn't sure. He'd phased Mike or one of his cousins short distances on the practice field. But this was two hundred miles. "Let's look around first, okay?"

Mike crossed his arms.

Jonah sighed. "Come on. Don't you want to find the Enhancer?"

Mike let out a breath. "Of course."

"Well, what's wrong?"

"Why hide it in the middle of the woods?"

Mike's question stumped Jonah until he remembered how his dad thought. "Don't be afraid of the new and unexpected."

"What?"

"It's what my dad always told me. Don't be afraid. I think it's part test." When Mike refused to move, Jonah grinned at him. "You were the one who said my parents were interesting."

"That was the riddle. I didn't mean anything like this."

Jonah's irritation flared as he gazed up the steps. "Fine. I'm going up. You can wait here for me."

Without another word, he slipped through the overgrown bushes and mounted the brick steps. Soon, he heard Mike huffing and following.

Trees were evenly spaced on either side of the staircase. He could appreciate that the whole effort would have been nice once, but it was obvious no one had trimmed these trees in a while. Errant branches hung at odd angles, including right over the staircase. Plus there were accumulations of dead leaves covering many of the steps. They were bone dry from the near drought this summer and crackled loudly underfoot.

The Seeker's Compass

Mike stepped on a moss-covered branch, causing it to snap. He kicked it away and frowned when Jonah paused to look back. "Why not hide it in plain sight? The Protector's Ring was in the teen center."

"I don't know," Jonah admitted. "But it would be something unexpected."

The more Jonah thought about it, the more excited he became. His parents had found the Protector's Ring. Why wouldn't they have the Mind Booster too? Maybe this stairway led to a hidden entrance to an ancient cave and the device.

Without realizing it, Jonah started to leap over the debris on the steps. But when he reached the top, he paused, confused. The stairs opened onto a flat, brick-paved courtyard. At the center of the space was a tree with extremely long branches twisting up into the air.

Mike made a disgusted sound. "They look like worms."

The tree trunk was covered in bark with a patchwork pattern of various greens. Jonah guessed the tree reached at least thirty feet into the air. The branches wavered slightly as if in a breeze.

Jonah leaned back to see the top. "It's different. I've never seen anything like it."

"Do you think it's magical?"

Jonah shrugged. "Too bad Wick isn't here. I'm sure he'd know." He walked slowly around the tree as the disappointment replaced the earlier excitement. The tree may look weird to him, but it seemed like just another tree. "Why would my parents want me to see this?"

Mike didn't respond. Instead, he continued around the courtyard. Besides the tree, old wooden benches had been placed on the north and south facing sides of the square space.

Jonah sat down on the nearer one. "I don't understand," he continued. "I thought I would find the Mind Booster. What's so important about this stupid tree? Why bring me here?"

Mike wrung his hands for a moment, then he knelt beside Jonah. "You thought this was a test. Maybe you're supposed to figure it out."

Jonah's irritation peaked. "There's nothing to figure out. My parents were archeologists, not park rangers."

Mike pointed at something behind Jonah. "Look! It's an arrow. Someone pressed the shape into the wood."

At first, Jonah thought the arrow pointed into the woods until he spotted another brick step covered with fallen branches.

He stood and moved toward the step while Mike ran around to the opposite bench and called out, "There's another arrow on this one."

"And there's a set of steps over here." Jonah beckoned to Mike. "Come on."

They found a smaller courtyard at the top of the second series of steps. An uneven brick-covered path led from the stairway straight to the far side, disappearing into the surrounding forest. A second path bisected this one, leading off into the trees. And a sculptured rhododendron bush in a large brick planter sat at the center of this courtyard.

The end of a gold-colored cylinder stuck out of the bush, near the top of the planter, and glimmered in the weak sunlight. Jonah ran over and gently pulled the cylinder free. It was tied with a bright green ribbon.

He glanced at Mike and raised an eyebrow. "Should I open it?"

Mike nodded.

Jonah slid the ribbon off and turned the cylinder over in his hands. It had a line down its longest length and two latches that were clearly locks. Could this cylinder have been coded for him? It was just like Robert's archive box, which Jonah's cousin had accidentally coded for himself when he dripped a bit of his own blood on the box. Not even Lynn could unlock it.

Did my parents use a bit of my own blood?

After a second of exploration, Jonah's finger touched a small knot. He took a breath, pressed the knot, and the latches retracted into hidden niches that sealed themselves.

Mike's mouth hung open. Jonah had expected the weird latches, but he didn't know what he'd find inside. He blinked in surprise when his trembling hand brushed the surface of a rolled piece of paper.

"I'll hold that." Mike took the cylinder.

"Thanks." Jonah lifted the paper free. It was heavy, expensive paper with subtle designs woven into its texture. And it was exactly like the paper his dad had used for the compass riddle. Excitement ignited in Jonah's chest as he unrolled the paper, revealing a message in his dad's handwriting.

Jonah, if you're reading this note, you've learned to control your fear of the unexpected. I'm proud of you, son. You've also figured out the riddle and discovered another power. The compass engaged your phase ability. That's the ability to move from one place to another in the blink of an eye.

You must have a million questions, son, but don't worry. The compass was programmed to send me a signal. Your mother and I will arrive shortly and explain everything. You've known for some time that you're different from other kids. It's time you understood everything about yourself.

Jonah stopped reading because his eyesight blurred. He wiped his eyes with the back of his hand and sucked in a breath.

"They were going to tell me everything on my thirteenth birthday." Jonah lowered the note. "I already know I'm half Reaper. I know I have Death Sense. And I know I can phase."

He leaned against the brick planter, allowing the little branches to poke him in the back and not caring when one poked especially hard.

Mike sat beside him, their arms touching. "Jonah you're forgetting the compass was supposed to be your gift a year ago, before all those things happened. Think about it. If your parents hadn't died, this would have been a big deal. You would have figured out the compass on your own and come here alone."

Jonah blinked away the tears. "Maybe."

"It's true. Your mom and dad would have taught you about your powers."

Jonah nodded, remembering the phasing lessons Kevin and Marcus had given him. His father would have been the one training him, if he had lived. As sad as the thought made him, Jonah became aware of something else.

He stared into Mike's eyes. "I wouldn't have known you, or my cousins."

"You can't be sure about that. I believe your parents planned for you to meet your cousins anyway. Why else give Robert and Lynn those gifts?" Mike glanced down at the note in Jonah's hand. "Can I see it?"

When Jonah didn't respond, Mike slipped the paper out of his slack grip. "You didn't finish it." He rolled out the note, found where Jonah had stopped, and began reading.

There's a whole world out there you've only just begun to sense. You've come of age and it's time to take your place in it. We show you this hideaway. It is our favorite place to get away, to think, or to meditate. We share it with you, son. Welcome to our world.

Mike's voice quivered on the last sentence. He stared at his own hands as he rolled up the note and slipped it in the cylinder. Eventually, Mike raised his head, looking around the courtyard. "Jonah, they never mentioned any code. I don't think the Enhancer is here."

"I know. Trevor was right. My parents didn't know about the mind booster or the back door to the Afterworld."

The frustration burned inside of Jonah. He yanked the compass out of his pocket and held it tightly in his hand. He wanted to hurl it into the woods, for all the good it did him now.

Mike gripped his hand. "Jonah, what if the other code is still in there?"

Jonah gaped at his friend, ashamed he'd been too angry to even think of that possibility. He open his hand, palm upward. Mike touched the compass with a forefinger. Unlike the last time when nothing happened, there was an audible pop and a flash of light raced across the device's surface.

"Ow!" Mike yanked his finger away.

"You alright?"

Mike shook his hand. "Yeah."

The compass began to vibrate as the long hand whirled around and stopped six times, in quick succession, setting six new symbols aglow. The center button pulsed with a green light. Jonah couldn't believe his eyes.

Mike sounded sure when he said, "It must have been on a time delay. Don't you think so?"

Jonah nodded for his friend but didn't think the code was on a time delay. The compass had reacted to Mike's touch. Jonah wondered that his friend didn't make the connection.

Like before, the device buzzed and pulled on Jonah's phasing ability. With the knowledge of how it operated, Jonah knew better than to press the green button.

Mike touched the compass again in a tentative manner. When he didn't receive a shock, he tried to place his whole hand over the device. Jonah drew it away, afraid his friend would activate it.

Mike frowned at him. "Why can't I touch it?"

"I…" Jonah was stumped for an answer until an idea occurred to him. " I think I should close it."

"Can you do that?"

Jonah didn't know. "Maybe if I reverse the Zodiac symbols?" He tried, rotating each into place and pressing the notch. To his relief, the normal compass face folded into view. He showed Mike. "Let's get back and show everyone." He hoped his voice didn't betray any of his suspicion about Mike's ability to control the compass.

If Mike had any doubts or suspicions of his own, he didn't show it. Instead, he smiled. "Things are never boring around you, huh?"

"Who wants boring?" Jonah asked. He motioned Mike to grab a belt loop. Then, summoning his courage, he phased them to Atlanta.

CHAPTER SIXTEEN
FIRST CODE

Marcus, Lynn, Trevor, Kevin, and Mabel had crowded into the library during their absence. All wore varying frantic looks that dissolved into expressions of relief when Jonah and Mike returned.

Marcus stalked over to the boys, breathing heavily. "Where have you two been?"

Jonah held up the compass. "We figured it out."

Marcus covered his face with a hand and breathed between his fingers. "You weren't supposed to activate the compass."

"Sorry..."

"Mr. Armstrong," Mike chimed in, "we didn't think it would hurt to–"

"That's right, you didn't think," Marcus snapped, then collected himself.

Kevin crossed his arms, frowning at Jonah. "You could have run into trouble."

"The code was from my parents," Jonah said. "They wouldn't give me something dangerous."

Marcus seemed ready to explode again. "Jonah..."

"It took me to their hideaway."

"Hideaway?" Lynn scrunched up her face.

Trevor pushed to the front. "You mean it didn't take you to the Enhancer?"

"No." Jonah exchanged a glance with Mike.

"Was the Enhancer there or not?" Kevin asked. Jonah noted that the Fallen Reaper had edged between him and Trevor and watched the boy with a guarded expression.

"No," Mike answered. "But we have the real code. We can go and get the Enhancer."

Jonah quickly opened the compass's true face and showed them the waiting code. Every eye scanned the device. It was strange to see each person take a different amount of time to come to the same conclusion.

"It was on a time delay," Mike continued.

"Way to go, geek boys," Lynn congratulated them.

Jonah turned to Marcus, who had been quiet ever since hearing of the hideaway. Judging from the look on his godfather's face, Jonah suspected Marcus knew about the place. He wanted to ask questions, but didn't think now was the time. They had a mission to plan.

Marcus gave him a slight chin nod. "At least you showed enough judgment to return here instead of pressing the button again."

"Well," Jonah's face warmed, "yeah. We aren't that stupid."

Kevin snorted. Lynn crossed her arms, a skeptical expression on her face.

Trevor was the only one intent on the compass. Jonah began to sense a strange urgency in the boy. Of course, he reasoned, that could have to do with the fact that Trevor's time was running out.

When Trevor reached for the device, Kevin blocked the attempt. "Not so fast."

Trevor blinked at him, but not in surprise. Jonah had stood next to the boy at the teen center and seen him prepare to fight. Trevor had that same look in his eyes now and his body had tensed.

Kevin wasn't a slouch either, Jonah soon realized. The Fallen Reaper balled his hands into fists. "Calm down or else," he warned Trevor.

Lynn had also moved closer to Mike and Jonah. The tension in the room was palpable for several moments.

Trevor raised his hands as he took a few steps backward. "We have the code and know what to do. Let's get the Enhancer."

Marcus cleared his throat, drawing everyone's attention. "I don't relish the idea of traveling blindly to an unknown location."

"Why not?" Trevor countered. "We know what's there."

"Well, not really," Mike said.

Trevor frowned at him. "I'm running out of time, Mike."

Mike's eyes widened. "I know that."

Kevin cracked his knuckles and glared at Trevor. "We have to decide who's going."

"Well, I am, of course." Trevor tapped his own chest.

Marcus shook his head. "No, you're not. You're too important to risk. You stay here and that's final."

Trevor pressed his hands flat against the top of the large table. He fumed in silence.

"I've called Trueblood," Marcus went on. "She'll be here soon." He motioned to Kevin. "I think you should go, to watch over Jonah."

Kevin nodded.

"Maybe I should stay and keep Trevor company," Mike offered.

"We'll do that," Robert announced as he and Wick entered the library. Trueblood stepped into view behind them.

"What are you doing here?" Lynn asked her twin brother.

"Are you kidding?" Robert grinned. "Trueblood told us what's happening. We couldn't miss out."

Lynn asked, "What about Mom and Dad?"

Robert's grin widened. "We got that covered." He pointed at Jonah. "Although I think you should call and tell them you and Mike are cool. Say you're staying at the library or something." He glanced around the room. "That's not a total lie."

Wick sidled up to Trevor and slipped an arm around the boy's shoulders. "So, you're the courier?"

The Seeker's Compass **439**

"Yeah. Who are you?"

Wick wasn't bothered by Trevor's surly tone. "My name's Wick."

Robert arched an eyebrow like his sister always did. "He's a mage."

Trevor lost some of his combative stance.

Wick steered the boy toward the door. "You can show us this bat cave."

Jonah caught Robert's arm when his cousin turned to leave the room. "That's why you want to stay behind."

"Not true, little cousin." Robert tapped his own forehead with a slender finger. "We want to pick Trevor's brain for details about the Afterworld. We're working on an upgrade to the video game."

"I thought you had to finish the game before you started upgrades," Lynn jeered.

Robert ignored the comment as he joined Trevor and Wick.

Kevin threw up his arms in frustration. "Are we doing this or not?"

A pained expression crossed Marcus's face. "I wish we could send a scout."

"Jonah's the only one who can work the compass," Kevin answered.

Once again, Jonah wanted to say that wasn't true. He was sure the compass would respond to Mike. But again, he kept the thought to himself.

Marcus motioned the group to gather around Jonah.

A grin spread across Lynn's face before she wrapped her arms around his neck. "We all have to hold on to you."

"Lynn." Jonah squirmed under her embrace, but she wouldn't let go.

"I think holding hands would suffice," Marcus said. Jonah saw his godfather trying not to smile.

Lynn had mercy and released her hold on Jonah's neck. She grabbed his right hand and Kevin held her other hand. Mike, who stood on Jonah's left side, gripped his left wrist since Jonah held the compass in that hand. And last, Trueblood held Mike's free hand.

"This isn't gonna work, guys," Jonah said. "I need a free hand to press the button."

"Fine." Lynn released his right hand and wrapped an arm around his waist.

At the same time, a flash went off from the doorway as Robert snapped a picture with his phone. "You guys are so cute."

"I'm warning you, dear brother," Lynn breathed. "If I see that posted anywhere…"

Robert laughed.

"Wait," Kevin shouted. He activated his blades, which required he hook his left arm around Lynn's arm instead of holding her hand. "You have your blades, Lynn?"

Lynn activated her right one and held the second deactivated blade in her left hand. "Don't want to stab you by mistake, geek boy," she whispered to Jonah.

"This is the picture I need," Robert said, holding up his phone again.

"Jonah, hit it." Lynn ordered.

Jonah pressed the green button a split second before Robert could snap another picture.

*

Lynn and Kevin released their grips as soon as the group reappeared. They whirled, in unconscious unison, scanning the darkened surroundings, their blades ready. The weapons seemed to hum and emit light in the dim interior.

Likewise, Trueblood had released Mike and took up a protective position with both arms raised. Jonah sensed the crackle of magic about the mage as she too scanned the area.

They had arrived in a large alcove. Judging from the rough rock walls, Jonah figured the entire structure was underground. A smooth dome had been carved out of the raw stone high above their heads.

Mike stirred and pointed at the ground. "Jonah, those look like the symbols at the hideaway."

Jonah knelt. This platform was made of marble instead of concrete. Bricks bordered it, one larger than the rest. And that brick was just like the one at his parents' hideaway.

What amazed Jonah was that the symbols not only matched those of the code, but they continued to glow for several more seconds before fading.

Mike knelt and ran his fingers over the smooth stone. "Do you think every location has a stone like this and a platform?"

"Yeah, that's a good guess," Jonah agreed. "Two locations, two platforms." He rose to his feet.

"What do you think?" Kevin asked.

Jonah turned on the spot and pointed at the only doorway out of the alcove. "That way?"

Kevin nodded and assumed the front position. Trueblood waved everyone else to follow and then took up the rear.

Kevin reached the opening and peeked both ways. "Clear." He stepped into the corridor.

It was narrow and dark. The air was stale but not suffocating despite some decayed vegetation seeping through gaps in the stone. The dead plants also hung from the ceiling and walls like weird cobwebs. The sight caused Jonah's skin to crawl.

"Interesting," Trueblood said in a low voice. "There's a weak current of air."

Kevin nodded. "Either there's a opening nearby or…"

"Or what?" Mike asked.

"Someone's using this place," Lynn answered.

Kevin pointed to his left. "There're doors at the end of the tunnel."

As they proceeded down the eerie passageway, Jonah's Death Sense throbbed but not with anything imminent.

Kevin reached the doors and stopped to examine them. "These were repaired not too long ago. Look." He pointed at the hinges and latch.

The wood looked ancient to Jonah, but the latch was shiny and new.

"What does that say?" Mike pointed at the words pressed into the wood.

Jonah recognized the writing but not the actual words. It was an ancient African dialect, he was sure. One his parents had shown him.

Kevin prodded the door with a blade. "I say we go in."

At that moment, Jonah's Death Sense screamed. He jerked and turned around to warn Trueblood.

She was already in motion and produced a shield that blocked a thrown scythe. The owner of the weapon was a black-garbed, glowing-eyed Grimnion who charged in with another weapon.

Lynn leapt to help the mage when the doors behind them swung open and another Grimnion attacked from that side. Kevin blurred into motion, blocked the man's attempt to cut him open, and punched the goon hard in the face.

The Grimnion grunted and stumbled back a foot. When he charged again, Kevin went low, caught the weapon arm, and twisted the guy into the wall. He delivered two high-speed blows to the man's head. The Grimnion dropped to his knees. Kevin followed with a third blow that finally put the man down.

He turned to Jonah. "These Wraith-goons are hard to knock out."

Meanwhile, Lynn had charged the first Grimnion. While she presented the more dangerous target, Trueblood was able to get past the man's defenses with a well-placed spell. The guy dropped like a stone and didn't move. His scythe clattered on the stone floor.

Within seconds, it was over. Jonah appreciated the cover the others provided, but he also felt useless without his own blades.

Trueblood nudged her attacker with a foot before saying, "I think we should get inside and look around."

"What about them?" With her blades, Lynn motioned at the downed men.

In answer, Trueblood used a spell on the guy that Kevin had knocked out. "That should keep them out long enough for us to search what lies beyond."

"Security patrol, keeping watch," Kevin said. He readied himself and stepped through the open doors first. He stopped a short distance inside.

Jonah didn't understand until the taller boy moved aside and he could see the full room. It was an indoor amphitheater complete with tiered rows of circular seating all facing a large stage. And on that stage stood a gleaming portal.

"What's that doing here?" Kevin asked.

Mike moved around Jonah and his jaw dropped. "I thought the main portal was somewhere else?"

"This isn't the main portal." Jonah proceeded down the center aisle, not even conscious of Lynn, who dogged his steps. As he drew closer to the stage, he begin to notice that the amphitheater looked like a bomb had gone off inside. Scores of stone benches had been blackened in a radial pattern, originating from the stage.

In a flash of recollection, Jonah recognized this place and started for the steps.

Lynn grabbed his arm. "Where are you going, hero?"

"I've seen this place before, when I put on the Protector's Ring." He hurried up the steps. Lynn followed while the others spread out to search the space.

"The last person to wear the Protector's Ring was killed here." Jonah glanced down at the stage floor and at the obvious signs of the explosion.

"I thought you were the only one to put on the ring in over two thousand years?" Lynn's eyes widened. "You're telling me this damage is that old?"

"No. My dad found someone who could wear a Protector's ring, but not control it. Deyanira's people discovered the location and they were gonna kill him so he..." Jonah waved at the floor and Lynn hissed.

"Wow."

Now that he was close enough to the portal, he was sure of something else. "That's the one Deyanira had in her underground chamber, remember? It has the same scorch marks." Jonah's voice hitched because some of the marks were seared into the device's surface when his parents died.

Trueblood came to the edge of the stage. "If that's Deyanira's portal, we should finish our search and leave."

"Amen," Lynn called out while moving to examine the far edge of the stage.

Mike remained near the center of the amphitheater, gazing at the ceiling. Kevin stood nearby, splitting his attention between watching the door and Mike.

"Well?" Trueblood urged.

"Okay." Jonah had turned to leave the stage when a squat pedestal to the side of the portal drew his attention. He stepped toward the device just as his Death Sense spiked.

Trueblood shouted to him, "Don't move!"

It was too late. As Jonah's foot came down on a certain spot, magic surged and within a second, an almost-transparent bubble popped into existence around Jonah, trapping him.

CHAPTER SEVENTEEN
POWER OF THE SORCERESS

Jonah was pinned inside the bubble, unable to move as it lifted into the air and floated four feet above the stage. Lynn attempted to reach him but smacked into a separate barrier and tumbled backward over the lip of the stage. Kevin blurred into motion and zipped down the center aisle to catch Lynn before she hurt herself on the stone seats below.

Trueblood hurled spells at the outer barrier, her face a determined mask of concentration and worry. But her attacks couldn't penetrate the second magical ward that extended the entire edge and length of the stage.

Jonah's shock at the suddenness of the trap gave way to panic when he heard the low, evil laugh. A vortex had blossomed a few feet from his bubble and Deyanira exited, in her mortal guise as Neera.

The Reaper's brilliant red hair fell to her shoulders in curls. Deyanira wore all black, as usual, but this time the black was in the form of a long, elegant gown and high heels. Jonah wondered if the sorceress had been at a party. The notion of Deyanira loose in the mortal world attending social events scared Jonah.

Deyanira was a real Reaper and could only navigate the mortal world in her Neera personae, a human sorceress, by using a portal. Like Trevor, she had to cross back within a certain time period. But Jonah had no clue how long that might be.

The Reaper laughed again in a relaxed way and stepped to within an inch of Jonah's trap. At this close range, the sheen of the woman's lip gloss reflected the muted glow of the bubble. Deyanira's cheeks crinkled and her emerald green eyes sparkled with triumph. "Well, well, well. Look what I caught in my stasis bubble. Young Jonah Blackstone."

The sound of the sorceress's voice produced an involuntary shudder in Jonah. She regarded him for a moment before walking around the stasis bubble. Jonah experienced a moment of pure panic when she moved out of sight behind him and only relaxed when she came into view on his other side. The sorceress trailed a single finger along the bubble's surface, creating a dissipating trail of magic.

"I grow tired of catching you stealing my possessions." A wicked grin tweaked the corners of her mouth. "Aren't you turning into a tired cliché? A young boy of color resorting to crime because he doesn't have a father at home?" She cackled at the very idea.

Jonah's fury surged at the taunt. "I didn't come to steal anything."

"Really?" Deyanira motioned toward the portal. "You didn't come to take this?"

"We didn't even know it was here." As soon as the words left his mouth, Jonah knew he made a mistake.

As a real Reaper, Deyanira had the Reaper Stare and could tell if someone was lying or being truthful. Jonah had no doubt she subjected him to it now.

Deyanira's eyes narrowed. "You're telling the truth." The disappointment in her voice was mixed with growing suspicion. "Why are you here, young one?"

Jonah closed his eyes. "Just looking around."

"Now you are lying, Jonah Blackstone. I can't have that." Deyanira flicked her hand and lightning hit the stasis bubble.

Jonah couldn't stop himself from flinching in fear, but the frightening display coursed along the outside of the bubble without harming him. *She's toying with me.*

Kevin responded by beating on the outer ward with his bare hands. Trueblood waved him back and then shot an impressive volley of magic at the barrier, to no apparent effect.

Deyanira ignored them. Her focus was on Lynn. When she turned back to Jonah, an evil grin worked her mouth. "Remember what I did to your cousin?"

Remember? Jonah would never forget Lynn's heart-rending screams as Deyanira tortured her. He glared at the evil woman.

"Now it's your turn to suffer while she can't help you." Deyanira raised her hand toward the stasis bubble.

Jonah's terror spiked. He needed to stall her, but how? Behind the Reaper, Trueblood continued to subject the ward to various spells, as if studying the barrier. Jonah had an idea. "Trueblood's gonna make it through."

Deyanira lowered her outstretched hand. "She's a capable mage, but honey, I'm better. Now," she held her hand toward the bubble again. "Why are you here?"

"I told you, I don't–"

Deyanira touched a finger to the bubble and it reduced in size, enough to send a wave of agony through Jonah's shoulder, which had been caught at an awkward angle behind him when the trap was sprung. He let out a muffled cry of pain as the smaller bubble threatened to dislocate his shoulder.

"I told you no more lies." Deyanira stroked the bubble and the pressure relented a bit.

Jonah sucked in ragged breaths.

"I wonder," Deyanira mused, "if your healing ability will try to repair your shoulder while it's being pressed out of the socket." Deyanira tapped a finger on her bottom lip and adopted a ridiculous thinking pose. "It would be perpetual torture for you."

"You're crazy."

Deyanira touched the bubble, and it contracted for several excruciating seconds. She relented and frowned at Jonah. "Show some respect, child. And answer my question."

Jonah sucked in deep breaths, which was hard considering he couldn't fully expand his lungs. He was too confined and in pain. What could he do? He could phase, but when he tried, sigils appeared all over the bubble.

Deyanira laughed. "It's designed to prevent you from phasing to freedom." She touched the bubble again.

Jonah lost himself in screaming until the pressure eased. He gasped, thinking. *Stall her.* "We're... looking for something."

"Obvious." Deyanira reached for the bubble again.

"It's a device!" Jonah hurried to add.

"And?" Deyanira prompted. Her finger hovered less than an inch from the bubble's surface. "What is it? What does it do?"

"I don't know everything," Jonah lied. When Deyanira's eyes narrowed, he admitted, "It's called an Enhancer."

A thoughtful expression transformed Deyanira's face.

Jonah used the brief respite to try and adjust his position. Any twitch on his part sent waves of agony through his body and stole his breath away. But he did feel something, around his wrist. Wick's gift, the bracelet.

Jonah wondered if he could activate it. The bubble kept out magic, but the bracelet had its own power stored inside. Jonah closed his eyes and tried to concentrate on Wick's lesson, despite the pain.

"What are you doing?" Deyanira's voice sounded closer.

Jonah refused to open his eyes as he spoke. "Thinking."

"Of more lies?"

"No." Once again, Jonah prepared himself for the stasis bubble to contract and send him into fresh agony. That didn't happen. After a few confused moments, Jonah opened his eyes and recoiled. Deyanira stood right beside the bubble, gazing at him.

"I've heard of Enhancers," she said. "The Archivists used them to elevate the minds of chosen mortals for short periods of time. But the devices have been forbidden for centuries."

Jonah found it curious to watch Deyanira's mind working through the limited information she had. At least she wasn't torturing him for the moment. Taking advantage of that, he focused on the bracelet, sensing its stored power again. He didn't have to collect it, just release the energy.

The Seeker's Compass **449**

"Why would the Alliance want an Enhancer?" Deyanira asked. "It's useless without something ancient to decipher. Where is the device?"

This is it, Jonah thought. She wanted an answer and would shrink the bubble when he couldn't give it. Jonah bared down, called on that inner will, and pushed it into the bracelet. The result was like being suffocated as the energy of the bracelet collided with the bubble and had nowhere to go.

Jonah feared he'd made a mistake and would kill himself until cracks begin to appear on the bubble.

Deyanira backed away. "Impossible!"

The next moment, her stasis bubble burst with a release of energy. Jonah had a split second before he dropped to the ground with an audible pop from his shoulder. White-hot pain lanced through his body and into his head and he screamed.

The bubble's explosion rammed into the outer shield, producing eddies and distortions across the surface. Trueblood succeeded in collapsing the damaged barrier with a well-placed spell. Deyanira, still reeling from the initial explosion, phased to the opposite side of the stage. Trueblood attacked anyway, keeping the dangerous sorceress at bay while Kevin, Lynn, and Mike rushed in to surround Jonah.

Kevin lifted him, causing Jonah to waver on the verge of fainting from the pain. "Sorry," Kevin said, "but we gotta leave."

Trueblood backpedaled to them so Kevin could grip the back of her tunic. Lynn understood and clamped a hand on Kevin's forearm, and Mike held onto her. A second later, ripples played across Jonah's body, making his injury ache more.

That pain was nothing compared to the agony he experienced when they smacked hard into something and the amphitheater appeared around them again. They tumbled to the stone floor in a painful huddle.

Kevin helped Jonah stand.

"What was that?" Lynn's voice sounded pained as she regained her feet.

"Sigils." Kevin growled and kicked open the doors. He supported Jonah under one arm as they hurried down the dismal corridor that looked even more foreboding than ever. Jonah realized why when the old dead vines trembled and begin to grow out of the cracks and crevasses at high speed.

"Look out!" Kevin activated a blade and sliced through vines that tried to wrap around his arms. "It's Deyanira."

Lynn's blades worked non-stop, fighting to keep herself and Mike free of the grasping vines. As they made their way toward the alcove, the passage ahead grew darker. The vines had grown into a dense knot to block their way.

Kevin glanced back at Trueblood, who kept their rear covered. "Trueblood!"

The mage turned, mouthed a silent spell, and shot the magical enchantment over their heads. When the spell hit the blockage, it turned a ghostly white.

Kevin moved in front of Jonah and ran headfirst into the mass. It shattered into a large puff of bone-dry vine fragments and choking dust. But they were through and rushed into the alcove.

More vines crawled out of the passage, but now they began to merge together. Jonah and the others were transfixed in horror as the mass took on the general shape of a four-legged creature. The bulbous head was made of an undulating mass of vines.

"Oh my God." Mike sounded terrified.

The vine creature reared up on its hind legs and prepared to launch itself at the group. Trueblood positioned herself in front of the creature. She raised a slender piece of dark wood, about fifteen inches long. Jonah gaped at her, never having seen the mage use a wand before. He didn't even know she had one.

"Help me, Ancestors. Show the evil one your power." The mage's long black hair became tinged with fire and her eyes glowed. "Caha-queene!" She waved her wand and a fiery shape shot out of the end. It grew in size, sprouting two wings and a head with a beak. The creature was a much larger version of the phoenix the mage had used in her magic show last summer.

The majestic phoenix let out an ear-piercing scream. It dove into the midst of the vine creature, flapping its huge wings and lighting the vines on fire. The magical creatures stumbled around, sending burning vine fragments all around the alcove.

The Seeker's Compass

Jonah and the others huddled close together as much from the heat of the phoenix's fire as from fear of being trampled. The phoenix proved stronger, and the vine creature's entire body erupted into flames. Its scream of agony hurt Jonah's ears. Both creatures flared like a bomb going off and then they were gone, leaving behind a trail of glowing embers.

"Not bad, Shaman." Deyanira had appeared at the alcove entrance and began firing a barrage of supernatural fire at them. "Not bad. Maybe you should join us."

Trueblood put up a shield just in time to stop the fire, but not the heat. It began to blister everyone's skin.

"She wasn't grandstanding," Trueblood said through clenched teeth, sweat beading her forehead. "I'm no match for her."

Jonah wanted to argue after seeing the mage produce the phoenix.

Kevin cursed under his breath. "No matter where I phase, she'll trace us."

"What about Alliance HQ?" Lynn suggested. "That way she'd be surrounded."

Kevin shook his head. "We need clearance first and don't have time."

Trueblood grunted and dropped to one knee. Her arms shook with the effort to push back Deyanira's onslaught.

Mike dug his hands in to Jonah's pocket. "Ow!" Jonah screamed.

"Sorry, but we need the compass." Mike freed it from Jonah's pocket and manipulated the dials.

Lynn's mouth dropped open. "I thought Jonah was the only one who could work it?"

Mike ignored the question until he finished. Then he grabbed Lynn's hand. She didn't argue as she gripped Kevin's forearm again.

Trueblood risked a glance at Mike and touched his arm. "You better go now!"

She released her shield at the same time Mike pressed the compass's activate button. The onrushing ball of supernatural flame disappeared as they vanished from the alcove and reappeared at the hideaway.

"We need to move," Kevin said while turning on the spot.

Mike reached into the bushes and pulled them open, revealing the stairs. Kevin squeezed through and ushered Jonah up to the first courtyard.

Lynn motioned Jonah to a nearby bench and huddled close, examining his arm. "The shoulder's out of the socket." She gripped his wrist with one hand and the side of his shoulder with the other. "Hold still."

"No!" Jonah protested. "I know how this works. You count to three but try it on..."

Lynn made a sudden motion and the next thing Jonah knew, his world dipped sideways and went dark.

CHAPTER EIGHTEEN
MEMORY WORK

Jonah awoke with a start. He lay on a bed in a darkened room with the only illumination slivers of brilliant sunlight that leaked around the edges of dark curtains. The faint scent of jasmine tickled his nose. Jonah groaned and turned over. That's when he saw Kevin, sitting crossed-legged on the floor.

The Young Fallen Reaper was shirtless, arms resting on his knees, palms upward. And he faced a small burning scented candle. It was a classic meditation setup.

What drew Jonah's attention was the graceful binding patterns spanning Kevin's muscular upper back. Jonah had seen him shirtless once, over a year ago in Marcus's condo. The older boy looked more muscled now.

Jonah swallowed, unsure what to do. He didn't want to disturb Kevin's ritual to restore energy. The binding patterns allowed Fallen Ones to retain some of their former powers, but they had to recharge at regular intervals.

Deep in the meditation, Kevin's back heaved up and down in a slow, regular rhythm. Jonah couldn't be sure, but the patterns looked black, meaning fully charged. That was good. He released a breath he didn't know he was holding.

"Stop checking me out, little man," Kevin said.

"I'm not checking you out," Jonah lied, his face warming. "I don't like that name. Remember?"

After several more breaths, Kevin hopped to his feet and blew out the candle. He took his time stretching his arms over his head and bending from side to side at the waist.

Jonah couldn't resist returning a taunt. "Show off."

Kevin's laugh was relaxed as he retrieved his black t-shirt from the chair. "You're just jealous." He didn't pull on the shirt. Instead, he playfully nudged Jonah's head and quipped, "About time you woke up. You've been asleep for over an hour."

"An hour?"

Kevin slumped in the chair and dropped the t-shirt over his lap. "Trueblood gave you something to keep you out. Your snoring messed with my concentration."

"Funny."

Kevin poked Jonah's good shoulder. "Remember, you heal faster when you sleep."

"I know." The reminder of his injury filled Jonah's mind with Deyanira's torture and he shuddered for a moment.

Kevin switched from the chair to sit on the bed beside Jonah. "You okay?"

"Yeah."

"Turn your side to me." When Jonah complied, Kevin took Jonah's right arm and touched the injured shoulder. He began to work the arm around.

Jonah sucked in a breath from the brief spike of pain and the forgotten warmth of Kevin's hands. He had discovered last summer that the boy had a higher than normal body temperature. But he didn't know if that were true for all Fallen Reapers.

Jonah let out an involuntary sigh and asked, "Why are you so hot?" When Kevin grinned, Jonah's face warmed. "You know what I mean."

The boy shrugged. "It's an effect of using the binding patterns. All Fallen Ones are like that."

Jonah marveled at the news, and the boy's gentle touch.

"How does it feel?" Kevin asked after a few minutes.

"Not bad." Kevin's manipulation did hurt some, but as he continued, the pain lessened.

The Seeker's Compass

"Deyanira's an evil witch," Kevin breathed, the anger radiating out with his exhale.

"Oh no." Jonah met Kevin's close gaze. "I told her about the Enhancer."

"Doesn't matter; it wasn't there anyway." Kevin continued to massage the shoulder. "Better?"

"Yeah," Jonah whispered. It was wonderful, in more ways than one. His aborted talk with Mike in the library popped into his head. Or maybe it was Kevin's closeness. Jonah's nervousness returned and he chickened out on asking the older boy the question he really wanted to ask.

The maddening thing was that Kevin watched and waited. Jonah wondered if the boy sensed he wanted to say something else. What would Mike do in this situation, Jonah asked himself. The answer wasn't reassuring because Jonah didn't know. He'd never been interested in anyone before. What if he was wrong about Kevin?

After a moment, Kevin let out an impatient breath, stood, and pulled on his shirt. "Let's go," he said. "Everyone's waiting for us."

*

Jonah's first sight of the bat cave made him groan in envy and almost forget his embarrassed shyness a few moments before with Kevin.

The basement boasted all the name-brand game consoles, regulation-sized pool and Ping-Pong tables, a huge smart TV with cable, a legal bar, and separate movie room. And the spacious sitting area had two large sofas, scattered comfortable chairs, and a low coffee table complete with cup holders along the edges.

Amidst all these wonderful things, Jonah expected to see his friends and cousins playing video games, not in a heated conversation. When they noticed Kevin and Jonah, everyone went quiet.

Judging from the embarrassed expressions, Jonah suspected he'd been the topic of discussion. He experienced a sudden stab of fear. What if the others were talking about him and Kevin being absent, and speculating why?

Jonah glanced at Kevin, to find the boy looking at him with brows furrowed. Once again, Jonah suspected their connection allowed Kevin to sense his rollercoaster emotions without doing a true Reaper stare.

Lynn hopped from the sofa she shared with Mike and hurried to Jonah. "How's the shoulder?" She aimed the question at Kevin as she too begin to rotate Jonah's arm around like he was a doll.

"He's says it's fine." Kevin's eyebrows weren't drawn together anymore, but he continued to cast quick glances at Jonah.

Lynn finished her inspection and hustled Jonah to the space she'd vacated. Once he was seated, she squeezed between Robert and Wick on the opposite sofa.

Jonah was a little afraid to ask, but he needed to get it out in the open. "What's the argument about?"

Mike gave him a guilty look and didn't answer.

Lynn let out an exasperated breath. "Trevor thinks we should go back. Mike says it's not necessary."

Jonah gaped at the others. "Why not?" He elbowed Mike to get his buddy talking.

"I told them I saw an opened nook and it was empty," Mike explained. "I think someone took the Enhancer."

"Wick and I bet it was Deyanira," Robert added. Wick nodded in agreement.

"Trevor's saying we should go back and check to be sure." Mike cast a disappointed look at the boy. "I know what I saw."

Trevor turned in his chair to face away from Mike. Jonah couldn't believe his eyes.

Lynn gestured at the fuming boys. "That's where it stands. Do we go back like Trevor suggests—"

"No," Kevin interjected.

"Or," Lynn continued, "do we trust Mike?"

Every eye turned to Jonah and waited for his answer. He gulped, not really wanting to step into the middle of the fight but relieved they weren't talking about him and Kevin. "Well, I trust my buddy. If Mike saw the empty nook and thinks the Enhancer's gone, I believe him."

Mike was pleased, but Trevor frowned at Jonah's words.

"Besides, Deyanira doesn't have it," Jonah thought to add.

Trevor sat forward in his chair. "How do you know?"

"Because," Jonah paused, not sure how the next bit would go down with everyone, "Deyanira wanted to know why we were there. I told her about it."

Trevor hissed and covered his face with both hands as he slumped back.

Wick and Robert were stunned. Lynn tapped her bottom lip while staring off into space.

Kevin leaned on the back of the sofa, speaking right over Jonah's head. "As I told Jonah, that doesn't matter because I think Mike's right. It was gone."

"Where does that leave us?" Trevor blurted out. "We don't have the Enhancer and we don't have the next code."

Jonah patted his pockets, looking for the compass until Mike held it up. "You used it?"

Mike smiled and lowered the device to his own lap. "Yeah."

Trevor's eyes widened. "You can use the compass?" Mike nodded. Trevor stood, still marveling at Mike. "How did you know it would work?"

Mike's face reddened and he shrugged. "It just made sense."

"But you had to put in the code, dude." Wick looked impressed with Mike. "That was wikid cool."

"I think that's how we got away," Kevin explained. "Deyanira couldn't follow us when we used it."

Trueblood shook her head. "We can't be sure of that."

Marcus looked thoughtful. "We have to sense the person in order to follow. Maybe the compass obscured the scent." He met Kevin's gaze. "We'll have to test that theory, but that can wait." He turned to Mike. "Has the compass given another code?"

"No. I don't think it will." Mike cut a glance at Jonah before explaining. "The first code was a test. Jonah had to figure out how to activate the compass to access it." He looked around the room. "The next one will be somewhere at the location."

Mike sounded so sure and reasonable, no one bothered to argue with him.

Trevor banged his hand on the armrest. "Then we have to go back."

"I said no," Kevin growled. "It's too dangerous. Marcus will back me up."

"Did you see a code?" Trevor challenged the Fallen Reaper.

Kevin made a show of cracking his knuckles. Trevor didn't look intimidated and half-rose from his chair. Jonah didn't know whether to be impressed with the boy or not.

Mike stood and held up his hands to stop the boys. "Please. I think the answer was on the ceiling. It had a lot of design work."

"I guess you can remember all that in detail?" Trevor snapped at him.

The boy's harsh words caused Mike to redden again.

Jonah had enough. "Hey!" he snapped. "Be cool with my friend."

Lynn tapped the coffee table to get their attention. "Did you get a good look at the ceiling?" she asked Mike. When he nodded, Lynn gestured to Robert. "Do your thing."

Robert's confused look morphed into a knowing grin. "Yeah, right. I'll need some paper."

Wick, Lynn, and Robert jumped from the sofa and began to rummage through all the drawers in the basement. Wick found a ream of printer paper, pulled out a few sheets, and hurried back to the coffee table. By that time, Jonah understood their plan.

Kevin was at a loss.

Trevor, having seen the act at the party, scowled. "Magic tricks?"

"You know," Lynn crossed to Trevor and towered over the boy, "we can lock you in a room."

Trevor slumped back in his chair and remained quiet.

Meanwhile, Robert produced a pen and had it poised over the blank sheet of paper while staring at Mike.

Mike tore his troubled gaze from the brooding Trevor and sat forward. Focused now, he exuded a confidence Jonah had never seen in his buddy. Mike rested his slender hands on his lap as he returned Robert's gaze.

The Seeker's Compass

"Relax" Robert began, "and picture the ceiling of the amphitheater in your mind."

After a few quiet, yet tense moments, Robert's hand begin to move and the scratching sounds of his pen filled the quiet basement. Over the next half hour, Robert fast-sketched a rather detailed rendering of the amphitheater ceiling.

No one had to tell Trevor to keep quiet because the boy was amazed. Once Robert finished, everyone crowded close, scrutinizing the drawing. The drawing resembled a starry sky with repeated patterns of stars.

It was Robert who spotted the symbols. "Here, and here. Look, there's another one. They're worked into the design. Unless you knew about the symbols, you'd never notice them."

Mike sucked in a breath. "All of those are on the compass."

"Yeah," Jonah nodded, impressed that Mike had memorized the compass symbols. "Which order?"

"Go by the quadrants," Robert suggested. "Start in the North and work clockwise."

"Good call." Wick exchanged an excited glance with Robert. "This could go in the game. A player has to find the symbols in order to reach the next level."

Robert whooped and high-fived his friend. "Yeah, before the evil sorceress fries you."

Mike ignored the older boys as he entered the symbols into the compass. The green button activated and he raised it for all to see. "We got the code."

Clapping commenced as people congratulated each other, except Trevor, who sank into his chair again.

"What's wrong with you?" Jonah asked.

"We have the last code, but it's useless without the Enhancer. And we don't know where that's been taken."

"Or by whom," Mike added.

"Wow," Robert said. "You two are definitely the glass is half-full types."

Lynn threatened him with a knuckle punch.

460 *John Darr*

"I think my parents took it," Jonah announced. He'd been mulling that over all along. They were the last ones to use the compass. His dad found a way to put in a code. Maybe they did know about the Enhancer and the back door into the Afterworld.

"Okay. Let's go with that," Lynn offered. "But where would they take it? You and Mike said it wasn't at the hideaway."

"We may have to search it to be sure," Trevor said. "Please tell me you're not gonna shoot that idea down." He glared at Kevin.

Lynn glanced at Trevor. "I hate to admit it, but he's right. Unless you can think of anywhere else, Jonah."

A final piece of the puzzle snapped into place in Jonah's mind. It was something that had been nagging him ever since they arrived at the alcove and discovered the circular platform identical to the one at his parents' hideaway.

Jonah had seen a third stone and brick platform in a dream-walk. He met everyone's expectant gaze and said, "I think I know where the Enhancer may be."

The moment of elation was quickly overshadowed by severe dread. The location from the dream-walk was also the location where his parents had died.

CHAPTER NINETEEN
DREAM REVISITED

"This is it," Jonah said in a hushed voice. He stood facing the building from the fateful dream-walk. The crumbling stone façade had the same words carved into the face: Free Public Library. He, Lynn, and Kevin had appeared outside the abandoned brick building.

Lynn tapped his arm. "Jonah? What is it?"

Jonah ignored his cousin as the rush of memories roared through his head, more vivid than he would have expected.

His parents had appeared on this exact spot and he'd called to them, even though they couldn't hear him. At the time, Jonah didn't know how the dream-walks worked. He didn't know a lot of things back then, including that his parents would die here.

Kevin patted him on the back. "Are you okay? We can go back if you want to."

Jonah stared at the library and wiped the beads of sweat off his forehead. The day was still hot, in the low nineties. And the heat added to his sudden misgivings. Maybe coming here wasn't such a good idea, but they had a mission.

Jonah pushed aside his doubts and shook his head. "I'm okay."

Lynn examined a second drawing Robert had done before they left. "Looks just like it."

Jonah had asked Robert to pull details of this platform from the dream-walk memory. He'd been sure he noticed it and was relieved when Robert's drawing confirmed it.

The symbols on this platform's designation stone still glowed a bright yellow. Jonah knelt down to touch the stone. The symbols were hotter than the rest of the warm stones.

Lynn and Kevin stepped off the platform and moved toward the library, leaving Jonah behind. He finished his inspection of the stone and hurried to follow.

Kevin reached the building first and paused, frowning at the structure. "Are you sure we should go inside? It doesn't look like anyone's been there in ages."

Jonah slipped between him and Lynn. "Someone came here a year ago."

"How do you know that?" Kevin insisted.

"I just do." Jonah kept the real significance of the place to himself. "Come on."

Jonah ascended the cracked stone steps to the weather-beaten front doors. He pushed them open and crossed into the relative darkness. The old counters and railings of the main lobby were still in place. Everything looked just as it did in the dream-walk.

Kevin and Lynn lingered just inside the front doors, but Jonah continued on. He was on auto-pilot as he replayed his parents' movements in his mind. They had gone straight through this larger room to a back hallway, and Jonah did the same.

Lynn called after him, "Jonah, where are you going?"

"Follow me."

"Maybe I should go first," Kevin suggested, his long legs allowing him to easily catch up to Jonah. "In case there's danger."

"You don't know where to go. I do."

Kevin narrowed his eyes. "What aren't you telling us?"

Lynn nodded in agreement as they trailed behind. Jonah reached an open stairwell door, which his dad had kicked open in the dream. The splintered wood showed a large boot print. *This is the way.*

Kevin gripped the back of Jonah's shirt when he started forward. "Hold on."

"Let go!" Jonah whirled, trying to get free, but the Fallen Reaper refused to release him.

"It's my job to protect you. Unless you tell me what's going on, I'm taking you back to the safe house." Kevin shook Jonah to emphasize his point.

Jonah admitted to himself the Fallen Reaper could literally carry him back. He gave up squirming and said, "There's a basement. That's where we need to go."

"You think the Enhancer's down there?" Kevin peered into the gloom.

"Yeah."

Kevin crossed his muscular arms and didn't move. "Why?"

"That's where my parents came to meet the Elder."

"Hold on, hero." Lynn positioned herself in front of Jonah, blocking his path. "I thought Trevor was the only one to see the Elder's face?"

Jonah swallowed, his throat dry now. "The only one still alive."

Lynn's hand dropped to her side. "I'm sorry."

"So," Kevin said, looking around, "they came here and met the Elder?"

"No. He never showed up." Jonah knew if Kevin believed the half-truth, they could continue on. And he needed to know if he was right about this place.

Kevin sized him up with plain, human eyes before nodding. "Let me go first. You can follow me. Lynn's in back. Got it?"

Jonah relaxed and nodded. He and Lynn waited on the landing as Kevin activated his blades and descended the stairs. He let out a curse when he reached the bottom. Jonah knew why. The hallway had been musty and rat infested in the dream. Kevin muttered under his breath and one of the blades flared with light.

Lynn bumped against Jonah. "What's that sound?"

"Rats."

"I hate rats, Jonah." She didn't sound frightened as much as disgusted.

"It'll be okay," Kevin called up the stairs. He stomped around and Jonah heard the little patter of rat feet dwindle. The glow of his Reaper blade gave Kevin's dark skin an odd, ghostly look. "Better?"

Lynn peered into the dimness below. "Not really."

She nudged Jonah forward and they descended.

Kevin waited. "Where to now?"

Jonah followed his father's actions and stood in front of a blank section of the dingy wall. This level was dark, making Jonah glad for the light from Kevin's Reaper blade. It reflected off the light-colored walls, adding a soft haze of illumination.

He glanced at Kevin. "Can you move closer to the wall?" Kevin held the blade to Jonah's right. "Hold it up about here." Jonah pointed to a section.

Kevin adjusted the position of the blade and Jonah ran his hand over the spot. After a few seconds, his hand brushed over a slight impression in the old plaster. Jonah let his fingers trace the circular pattern of raised bumps. He pulled the compass out and held it against the spot, just like his dad did in the dream-walk.

Jonah began to feel a little foolish when nothing happened. What if it didn't work for him like it worked for his dad? Maybe he had to say a spell?

Kevin leaned over Jonah's shoulder, examining the wall. "Is something supposed to happen, little man?"

"Yeah," Jonah answered. "It's supposed to..."

A low rumble started underneath their feet, and the wall wavered. Jonah pulled the compass away just as a small opening appeared. The cinderblocks melted away, creating a hole. The opening grew and stabilized into a perfect circle large enough for a single person to step through.

Jonah was also relieved to see the faint glow of light that came from inside. What he didn't expect was the strong whiff of stale smoke, as if something had burned.

"What the ..." Kevin coughed. "What happened down there?"

Jonah motioned to Kevin. "There are stairs leading down to a hidden chamber."

Kevin hesitated before stepping through the opening and starting down.

Lynn paused next to Jonah. "You saw this in a dream-walk about your parents, didn't you?"

The Seeker's Compass **465**

Jonah nodded.

"That must have been over a year ago."

He swallowed. They were about to find out anyway. "I saw my parents here the night they died."

Even in the dimness of the hallway, Jonah could see the shocked expression on his cousin's face.

"Jonah…" Lynn shook her head. "That's what you meant by this place being personal."

"You two coming down?" Kevin called.

"Yeah, here we come." Lynn nudged Jonah. "Go on."

Kevin stood before two high metal doors, running his hand over the gold symbol spanning both: three interlocking circles with a pair of wings spread out above. "This is the Alliance's symbol." He turned to Jonah. "What is this place?"

"You'll see." Jonah placed the compass in the depression at the center of the symbol. It rotated ninety degrees, followed by a loud click. When he removed the compass, the massive doors opened. The overpowering smell of burnt things rolled over them.

Jonah raised his hand to cough, reminded of the night his family home in Virginia had burned. He had smelled of soot and smoke for hours.

Lynn covered her nose. Kevin mumbled a curse under his breath and inched forward into the room.

A strange tightness developed in Jonah's chest and the dread increased as he entered the chamber. It was all the same, and so different, like walking in the nightmare version of the original dream.

The ceiling high above was scorched and blackened from the intense smoke and fire. The shelves that covered three walls used to be full of ancient books. Now, they were reduced to patches of blackened boards and piles of ashes.

The loss of all those ancient books staggered Jonah.

Kevin picked his way to the fourth wall to study the large stone base, also blackened by smoke damage.

He called to Jonah, "A portal used to be here."

"It's the one Deyanira took," Jonah answered.

Kevin whirled around. "You mean this is where she got it? How?"

Jonah scanned the ground. Dust, dirt, ashes, and other debris had accumulated over the past year. Pain gripped his heart when he saw the large scorch marks. His knees buckled and he knelt down, pressing his hands against the charred stone.

"Jonah!" Lynn rushed to him and wrapped an arm around his shoulders. "His parents were here, Kevin."

Jonah nodded, aware that he would cry soon. "Deyanira attacked them in this chamber and the Grim Reaper killed them here!" Jonah's shout reverberated through the space.

Kevin swore under his breath.

Lynn pressed her forehead against Jonah's, whispering to him. She gently rocked him until he stopped crying.

"Jonah," Kevin whispered in an urgent tone, "you should have told us about this place."

"Kevin, this is personal and painful," Lynn said. "I'm sure he didn't like talking about it."

"I get that, Lynn, but we've already crossed Deyanira in a place she fought Jonah's mom and dad."

Jonah felt the sudden tightening of Lynn's hold.

"Oh my God." Lynn released him and stood. She took out and activated her blades. "You're right. She probably had some kind of alarm set."

"I'm sorry," Jonah began as he regained his feet. When he opened his mouth to continue, Lynn patted his arm.

"We don't blame you, Jonah," Lynn said, "but we should leave."

"What about the Enhancer?"

Kevin turned his ear toward the opened entrance. He activated his own blades. "Too late. Someone's here." He sprinted for the door at the same time a whistling sound filled the air.

The Seeker's Compass

A whirling scythe flew through the open door and headed straight for Kevin. The boy simply phased, allowing the scythe to continued through empty air. Kevin reappeared inside the doorway in time to duck and tackled the Grimnion who tried to enter.

Kevin heaved the guy back through the door and into a second henchman just outside.

"Lynn!" Kevin shouted as he gripped the heavy doors and pushed them closed with a loud clang.

Lynn joined Kevin and they leaned against the doors, keeping them closed despite the heavy blows from the other side.

Kevin had extra-human strength as a Fallen Reaper, but Wraith-possessed mortals also had above average strength. Jonah cringed when the banging against the door became frenzied.

Pressing his back against the door, Kevin dug in his heels while shouting to Jonah, "Find the Enhancer!"

"Yeah, yeah." Jonah began a frantic search around the chamber.

"I think it's more than just two Grimnions," Lynn gritted through clinched teeth as the door bucked inward again.

"I'm worried Deyanira will show up," Kevin said. "Too bad the lock is only on one side."

Thoughts of Deyanira subjecting him to more pain galvanized Jonah. He spun on the spot, searching. If Deyanira and her gang never found the Enhancer, it had to be out of the way.

Almost out of pure frustration, he focused on the dust and soot-strewn floor. That's when he noticed the stonework. It actually made a pattern in the relatively clear patches he could see.

A muted shout came from the other side of the door at the same time it bucked. Lynn was thrown forward. Kevin shoved the door back into place, his muscles straining the entire time.

"Jonah, hurry up!"

"I am." He used his foot to smear away dirt from a large concentric design of circular rows of stone. Each layer got smaller and smaller.

He dropped to his knees and brushed away the dirt to reveal a soot-filled hole at the center of the chamber's floor. Jonah shoved his hands into the crevice and scooped out the mess. That done, he pressed the compass into the hole.

A second later, Jonah leapt backward. A round section of the floor sank at least a foot before sliding sideways into a new crevice. Jonah gawked at the octagonal space beneath and the crystal half-globe inside. A dull gold object floated around inside the globe. It was thin with a slight curve to it, and the edges contained intricate details as well as angel script.

Jonah lifted the half-globe out of its hiding place. "Cool!"

"You can be awed later," Lynn shouted.

Kevin caught Lynn's attention and used his chin to indicate a warped iron candle stand.

Lynn darted to the piece and brought it back. In between shoves of the door, Kevin pressed one end against the doorknob and gouged the other end of the stand into the stone floor.

"That won't hold for more than a second," Kevin grunted. He slipped his blade in a pocket as he bounded over to Jonah. Lynn was right behind him, but her blades were out and ready.

The attackers hit the door again. For a second, the stand held. But the next blow knocked it free and sent it flying through the air.

Kevin ducked under it as he slid through the ash and soot to grab Jonah's hand. Lynn dived and gripped Kevin's foot a second before the Fallen Reaper phased them away from the chamber.

CHAPTER TWENTY
COGNITIVE DISSONANCE

The hot water pummeled Jonah's shoulder, forcing a sigh of relief from his lips. The others would have to wait, he decided, taking his time in the shower as the water washed away aches as well as the grit. The moment of quiet bliss didn't last long before his mind began replaying events.

Visions of the scorch marks on the chamber floor popped into his head. Jonah sucked in a ragged breath, fighting back tears. At the same time, he had a strange thought. His parents had been buried in urns. Yet the chamber had been locked, so the Alliance couldn't have retrieved his parents' bodies…

Jonah shook his head, not finishing the morbid thought. Back then, he had been in shock over their deaths. The idea of empty urns never entered his mind, but as he accepted the reality, his anger at Deyanira and the Grim Reaper spiked. He smacked wet fists against the tiled wall of the shower several times.

All the memories of his parents played out, every emotion and feeling he'd been holding off and not facing over the past year. At times, he smiled while remembering his dad's laugh or his mom getting angry at both him and his dad.

And just as quick, the grief, pain, and loss would surface. Jonah didn't hold any of it inside, allowing his tears to mix with the shower water.

"I miss you." The words caught in Jonah's throat. He smacked his hands against the shower wall again.

Somewhere in all the mashup of emotions, he decided that next year, he'd place roses on the alcove bench at the hideaway. Jonah didn't think he was ready to visit the actual tomb in D.C.

The decision fortified his resolve to get on with their mission. He toweled off and slipped into the clothes Mabel had given him: a pair of tan pants and sky blue shirt with *Camp Monarch* on the upper left front. Jonah checked himself in the mirror, shrugged at the fit of the slightly over-sized clothes, and headed for the bat cave.

*

Kevin stood outside the basement entrance with Lynn. He had changed into a clean pair of dark jeans and a pale green shirt. Jonah suspected the Fallen Reaper had phased to wherever he stayed to fetch fresh clothes.

Lynn was dressed like Jonah, since she didn't have a change of clothes either.

She pulled him close before he could enter the basement. "Marcus is gone."

Jonah glanced through the doorway and noticed Omar was there in his godfather's place.

"Where's Marcus?"

Omar heard and motioned them into the room. "He's been called to Alliance HQ, Jonah."

"Why?" Jonah asked as he entered. "What's happened?"

"The Council knows about Trevor. Marcus is trying to head them off, but he fears they'll take the courier into custody." Omar patted the globe. "At least the Alliance doesn't know about the compass and the Enhancer. Before that changes, I think Trevor should explain it to us."

Mabel waved her hands in frustration. "They need to eat, Omar."

"I'm sorry, Mabel. They'll have to do it while Trevor talks."

Mabel made a disapproving sound as she beckoned Jonah, Lynn, and Kevin to a high-top bar in the kitchenette area. "Kevin and Lynn wouldn't touch a thing until you got here."

Jonah didn't know what to say, so he kept quiet. Once Mabel had them seated, the motherly woman placed three full plates of thick, real turkey

The Seeker's Compass 471

sandwiches and potato salad in front of them. She added bottled water and a bowl of fruit to the feast.

Jonah began wolfing down his sandwiches but paused long enough to glance around the room. Robert and Wick stood beside Mage Trueblood. Rex hovered near Omar, who held the Enhancer globe.

Mike sat beside Trevor, compass in his hands, prodding the device.

Omar cleared his throat. "Trevor. We don't have a lot of time."

The courier rose from the couch. "We should use the compass and go to the cavern right now."

Rex chuckled. "That's not gonna happen, young man."

Omar favored the courier with a tolerant expression. "We've been over this before. Jonah and the others have to return home before they're missed."

Trevor's mouth opened and closed without words and his body spasmed.

Omar's immaculate eyebrows drew together in concern. "We can have a healer come and check you out."

"I don't want a healer poking me." Trevor drew in a deep breath to calm himself. "A healer can't stop what's happening."

Jonah wondered if that was the reason Trevor's mood seemed to shift. Maybe the effects of staying in the mortal world were starting to get to the boy. He did act more agitated and, Jonah noted, beads of sweat continually broke out on his forehead.

Omar patted the half globe. "Hurry."

"Please," Mike added.

Trevor glanced at Mike and placed his hands on either side of the half-globe, down near the base, and twisted the top with practiced ease.

There was a hiss of escaping air as Trevor lifted the globe free and then detached the Enhancer from its stand.

Jonah hopped off his stool and hurried closer to peek at the device. It was made out of the same strange metal as the compass. "So this is the Enhancer?" he asked.

"It's *an* Enhancer," Trevor corrected. "There are others. Most have been locked away by the Grand Oracle." The boy's voice was low and angry. "They are forbidden devices because Enhancers allowed a mortal to read angel script and the ancient texts for a short period of time."

"Awesome," Jonah breathed.

Mike also scanned the small device. "This is the only one not locked away?"

"We have a few others in our possession," Trevor confessed as he turned the device, showing Mike and Jonah all the angles. "It's another reason we're called heretics."

Mike's eyes widened.

Jonah sensed a punchline coming. "Why did the Elder want us to get this one? Why not use another?"

"This is the only one that can decipher the compass data." Trevor held out the device to Jonah. "It's meant for you."

Jonah thought this sounded like the Legend of the Guardians. Mortals were given the Rings to reset or maintain the balance. He took the device and inspected it.

Trevor mimed placing the Enhancer against the side of his head. "When you need to activate it, just place it against your temple and press the notch on the side." He waited while Jonah found the notch.

"Be careful." Trevor reached out to keep Jonah from actually pressing it. "You can activate the Enhancer without it being against your temple."

Jonah pulled his finger away.

"And never activate the Enhancer more than once on the same person," Trevor continued, "until the effect has worn off."

"What happens if I do?"

Trevor gulped and said, "You'll risk permanent brain damage."

Jonah held the device away, not sure if he wanted to have something that could damage his brain.

Mike wasn't afraid and lifted the Enhancer from Jonah's grip.

The Seeker's Compass

The young courier watched Mike. "It and the compass belonged to the last Deliverer. It was said only he could work both."

Mike almost dropped the Enhancer. "Jonah's the special one, not me."

Trevor's gaze turned calculating. "I know. Odd isn't it that you can also work the compass?"

Mike shoved the device into Jonah's hand like it was red hot. "What does that mean?"

For once, Trevor's expression seemed genuine and concerned. "I don't know. It's something we can ask the Elder when we cross over."

Trueblood frowned and pulled a small token from her tunic pocket. She held it up for all to see. Jonah thought it was one of Wick's pieces. "They've arrived," she said.

Omar motioned to Mabel. "Go and stall for as long as you can."

"I'll offer them some sweet tea." Mabel hurried from the room.

"Wick?" Omar nodded at a gym bag on the floor near Robert and Wick.

Jonah recognized it as the one the young mage used to carry his magical paraphernalia around. Wick knelt and unzipped his bag.

"What's this?" Trevor asked, frowning.

Omar ignored the question as he placed the compass and the Enhancer inside the bag. Wick zipped that closed and stood straight as Marcus stepped through the basement entrance. Jonah knew that guarded look on his godfather's face. Marcus wasn't alone.

A short, plump woman came through the door next. She bobbed on her feet as she took in everyone in the room. Marcus gestured to Trevor, and the woman wobbled to him.

"Let the healer check you out," a sharp voice commanded.

The last person to enter was a barrel-chested man with a deep tan complexion who was wearing a royal blue, knee-length tunic over his blue dress shirt and dark slacks. The Alliance Symbol was done in gold thread on the left tunic breast. The man's haircut matched his voice, military in style.

Marcus gestured to the man and said, "This is Mage Rubio, a member of the Alliance Council."

Mage Rubio noted everyone's position like a soldier scouting the location of the enemy before attacking. Once satisfied, he marched over to Trevor, who the healer had forced to sit.

Mike hovered nearby until Rubio turned his formidable gaze on Jonah's buddy. Mike paled and retreated to the sofa. While the healer poked and prodded Trevor, Rubio barked hushed questions at the boy.

At one point, the healer moved to lift Trevor's shirt, but the boy yanked it back into place. "You're not helping me," he shouted.

The healer stood back and frowned at him. Rubio stroked his chin before snapping his fingers at Rex. "Montgomery, take this young man to Alliance Headquarters."

"You can't do that," Jonah and Mike shouted at the same time. Lynn looked just has mutinous.

Marcus and Kevin maintained a resigned silence.

Rubio whirled to face the kids. He let his eyes linger on Jonah. "So much like your father, young man." He waved to Rex, who moved to obey.

"You can't take him," Mike insisted. He stepped right up to Rubio.

The mage's eyebrows rose. "I'm afraid we can."

Jonah turned to his godfather for help, but Marcus held up his hands. "The Council wants to question Trevor."

Even Kevin acted subdued in front of this new mage, although Jonah could feel the anger rolling off him.

"Montgomery," Rubio barked. Rex nodded, gripped Trevor's arm, and marched him out of the basement. Rubio turned on the spot, taking in the rest of the group. "Send them all home, Marcus. And join the rest of the Council at headquarters. It's gonna be a long night."

Rubio turned for the door and paused when he noted Mabel standing there. "Another time for the sweet tea, Mabel?" After a respectful nod, the mage slipped by Mabel and out of the basement.

Marcus clapped his hands to cut through the barrage of questions and shouts. "We don't have time for this." He met everyone's indignant gaze. "We will finish this mission."

"How?" Robert asked. "They jacked Trevor."

The Seeker's Compass

"And what about the mole?" Lynn added. "I bet that's how the Council found out you had Trevor."

Omar raised one of his precise eyebrows at Lynn's comment. "She's right, Marcus. Agent Ramsey will be on the alert for their return."

Jonah hadn't considered that angle. "Should we leave the gym bag here?"

"No," Marcus answered. "The Alliance has access to this place. It's better you keep it out of sight." He checked his watch. "Eleanor, can you and Kevin make sure everyone gets home?"

Mage Trueblood nodded. "Of course." She motioned for Robert, Wick, and Mike to join Lynn and Jonah.

Marcus surveyed the assembled group of young people. He drew in a deep breath, let it out, and said, "You've accomplished a lot today."

When Marcus paused, Omar took over. "What Marcus is trying to say is he's proud of you."

Jonah gulped, never expecting that from his godfather. "What'll happen to you?"

"Don't worry about us," Marcus answered. "We'll be back as soon as we can. Until then, be careful."

"Okay," Jonah replied for everyone. He didn't have Lynn's Sight, but deep inside, he knew things were going to get worse.

CHAPTER TWENTY-ONE
DISBANDED

"I don't like it," Jonah said, pausing in his manipulation of the compass.

Lynn nodded her agreement as she leaned against the breakfast bar. The warm morning sunlight making a counterpoint to her sour expression.

Kevin, along with Trueblood, stood in the middle of the Hightowers' family room. He frowned. "We were ordered onto other projects by the Council. We can't stay in Mount Vernon today."

Robert, who sat on the opposite side of the bar, dropped his spoon in his cereal bowl. "That's bull."

"It's the mole," Jonah insisted.

"We know that." Kevin looked just as angry as Jonah and his cousins. The young Fallen Reaper's hands were balled into fists. "The mole has fixed things to keep us away from you all."

"Then why do it?" Lynn raised an eyebrow.

"Because it's our job." Trueblood's serious tone cut through any further objections. "Marcus will sort it out and we'll be back."

Jonah thought the mage was missing the real point. "I'm worried about Ramsey."

"There's no reason for him to bother you. We have the courier." Trueblood crossed to the sofa and stared at the compass in Jonah's hands. "Even so, I think you should put that in your cousin's archive box." She motioned to Mike. "The Enhancer, too. For safekeeping."

The Seeker's Compass

While Jonah agreed placing the compass in the Seeker's box was a safe option, he also had doubts. In a pinch, the compass could transport everyone to safety, so he'd rather hold on to it. As for the Enhancer, Jonah noted Mike kept the device in his shirt pocket and didn't seem inclined to give it up.

Trueblood glanced at her watch and headed for the hallway and front door.

Kevin lingered. "If Ramsey does show up, little man, phase, no matter who's around. The Alliance can deal with the consequences."

"Kevin..." Trueblood warned from the hallway and stepped into view. "That's not wise."

"I don't care." Kevin turned to Lynn. "Keep your blades ready to use. The agent may have more of his goons with him."

Lynn nodded. Kevin waved and followed Trueblood out of the house.

Once they were gone, Lynn retrieved her blades from her room. When she returned, she waved to Jonah. "Let's go. We need to put the compass and mind booster in Robert's archive box."

Robert's cell phone rang. He answered and then held it away from his ear. Wick's voice rolled out of the speaker, sounding agitated.

"We're on the way." Robert hung up. "Wick says to get our butts to the teen center."

*

Wick waited in the teen center atrium, his face a mask of fury. "She has people in the attic." He pointed toward the second floor. "They're talking about taking over our clubhouse."

Lynn and Robert sprinted for the stairs at top speed without asking any questions.

"Who's in the attic?" Mike inquired, trailing behind Jonah and Wick.

The young mage growled before saying, "The director has county people measuring the space."

Mike reached into his pocket and pulled out his talisman. "Why didn't the token warn us?"

478 *John Darr*

Wick grimaced. "I took it down so they wouldn't keep setting it off."

Robert and Lynn's longer legs allowed the twins to reach the attic first and they stormed inside. By the time Jonah and the others caught up, the twins had already barreled out and down the second-floor hallway to the administration section.

"Hey," a startled secretary called out, "you need an appointment!"

Jonah, Mike, and Wick stumbled into the main office just in time to see Robert and Lynn crashing through the director's open door. They rushed by the agitated secretary and crowded into the office behind the twins.

The director's office was large, but overly stuffed with paper, books, and other official documents that littered every available surface, including the large desk.

The director shot to her feet. "I beg your pardon! You can't barge into my office."

"And you can't take our attic space," Lynn countered.

The shorter woman arched her eyebrows. "The attic belongs to the county."

"You made a deal with us!" Robert yelled. "If we cleaned it out and I ran the website, you agreed to let us use the attic for our clubhouse."

"Things have changed." The short woman held up a hand. "As for the website and servers, you can administer those from the offices on this floor."

Robert and Lynn started yelling at the same time, causing the director to march around her desk and past the group before slamming her office door.

She whirled to face the twins. "First of all, no final decision has been made. The Director of Public Facilities, my supervisor, wants to know the square footage, just in case."

"We know why he's doing it." Robert's voice was a little calmer but still full of outrage. "Brandon's dad."

The director averted her gaze for a moment. Jonah caught the look of guilt on her face and his insides began to burn.

Jonah knew the only reason she hadn't thrown the twins out was because she liked Lynn. Jonah's cousin belonged to a group of the older girls who

The Seeker's Compass **479**

were working in a teen center mentoring program. They helped younger girls that were suffering from troubled home lives.

"You might as well know this now." The director stopped when someone knocked at the door. She took a moment to smooth her brow with her hands. "Come in."

A police officer stepped inside the room, causing Jonah to instantly fear the secretary might've called for help. But the officer smiled at them as he hooked his thumbs into his leather belt. Stocky, with obvious muscle underneath his uniform, he nodded his bald head at the stunned kids.

The director gestured to the man. "This is Lieutenant Cook. He's the resource officer assigned to the teen center."

"Why's he here?" Lynn asked, her voice cool.

Cook smiled and said, "I'll be working with the new youth group."

"What group?" Jonah countered suspiciously.

The director met their angry gazes. "We're disbanding the Practice Club and rolling it into a new club."

Once again, Robert and Lynn started yelling. Jonah joined them this time. "You can't do that!"

"It's already been decided. The police department is going to work with the restructured group," the director continued.

"All of you are welcomed to sign on," Lieutenant Cook added. "Just come to me or see the group's leader."

"Who's that?" Jonah asked.

The officer turned to the director. "I believe his name is Brandon Warner?"

The director nodded.

Jonah couldn't take any more; plus the office was growing very stuffy with so many people crammed inside. He slipped past Lieutenant Cook and into the fresher air of the reception area. He didn't realize Mike and Wick had followed him until he reached the second-floor railing and stopped.

Mike stood beside him. "What are we gonna do?"

"I don't know." Jonah smacked a hand on the metal railing. "Brandon! That weasel!"

"It was Brandon's dad," Wick said. "Marcus trumped him, so he attacked you guys. He's a punk, just like his son." Wick eyed Mike. "Where're you going?"

"I need to use the bathroom." Mike paused at the top of the staircase and pointed toward the east wing.

Wick frowned at him. "We need to stay together."

"I'll go with him," Jonah volunteered. He looked around and lowered his voice. "If anything happens, we'll jump to the creekside and make our way around to the front parking lot."

Wick hesitated before exhaling a breath and ruffling his short dreads. "Okay. But hurry back. Lynn's already in a foul mood."

"Right." Jonah followed Mike to the bathrooms in the east wing. While Mike went inside, Jonah leaned against the alcove wall and waited. His Death Sense spiked within seconds.

"Mr. Blackstone?" Ramsey stood behind Jonah with a cup of coffee in his hand. The man's sharp eyebrows were drawn together, giving his mocha-colored face even more of a hawkish look. "I need to talk with you."

"Actually," Jonah replied as he moved away from the bathroom alcove while taking out his phone, "I was about to leave." He swiftly sent a text to Mike, telling his friend to stay in the bathroom for now. Jonah reached the staircase and hesitated because Agent Harris was standing there.

Thinking he could lose Ramsey in the small library and then phase to safety, Jonah headed for the west wing. But as he started past the café, Ramsey edged in front of Jonah, forcing him to stop.

"This won't take long." The agent stepped into the café and flashed his badge to clear the nearer table. The kids grumbled as they gathered their things and shifted to another table in the back. Ramsey placed his coffee cup on the table and waved Jonah over.

With Agent Harris hovering in the background, Jonah was torn. He couldn't leave Mike all alone in the bathroom. He also couldn't run to the second floor to get help; at least, not with Harris blocking his way.

The Seeker's Compass

Jonah had to get rid of the agents. He took out his phone and texted Wick. That's when he realized he'd become the subject of Ramsey's full-on stare. The intensity of the man's attention sent another warning throb to Jonah's Death Sense.

He sauntered over, pulled out a chair and sat. "What do you want?"

Agent Ramsey signaled to Harris and then took the chair opposite Jonah. He slowly sipped his coffee, contemplating Jonah before leaning over the steaming cup. "Where is the courier, Mr. Blackstone?"

Jonah jumped when his phone buzzed in his pocket. It had to be Mike or Wick, no doubt, wondering what was happening. Jonah tried to act casually, shrugging as he peeked at his phone's screen. Drawing on the honest truth, since he had no clue where the Alliance held Trevor, he replied, "I don't know."

Out of habit, he filled his mind with the truth of his answer. *I don't know. I don't know.* Ramsey couldn't do a Reaper Stare, Jonah reasoned. Only Reapers and Fallen Reapers could manage to do that. And Ramsey wasn't a Fallen one. But the previous signal from his Death Sense made Jonah curious about the agent.

When Ramsey lowered his gaze and sipped his coffee, a look of disappointment was on his face. "It's understandable; the Alliance wouldn't tell a child that bit." He smiled when Jonah struggled to keep from reacting to the insult.

A commotion from above, drew Jonah's gaze toward the balcony. His heart sank because Agent Harris had cornered Wick and his cousins. The agent also seemed to have drawn the resource officer into what looked like a spirited discussion.

Ramsey's gaze shifted between Jonah and the second-floor argument. He smirked. "First, Deyanira came to this out-of-the-way town," the agent began while leaning closer, "now the traitorous courier comes here. Why is everyone so interested in a half-breed like you?" Ramsey's eyes narrowed as he studied Jonah. "Perhaps you can discover the location of the courier, and tell me? I'll leave this place if you do. Otherwise…"

Jonah narrowed his own eyes. "Otherwise what?"

"You'll lose much more than just your pathetic fighting club and the attic hideout."

Jonah heard the blatant threat in the man's voice, but his own anger peaked. He shot to his feet.

The move startled Agent Ramsey, who instantly reached for that hidden weapon underneath his jacket while simultaneously rising to his feet.

Jonah's Death Sense spiked as he prepared to phase to the bathroom, no longer caring if anyone saw him. He intended to grab Mike, get to the creekside, and hope the Alliance could sort everything out. He concentrated hard, and was about to make the mental nudge and phase when a nearby cell phone went off with a loud, obnoxious ring-tone.

Ramsey's gaze flickered to the closest table and then around the crowded café. The agent frowned while withdrawing his hand from inside his jacket. Jonah nearly sighed with relief to see it empty.

Ramsey scowled at him. "I'm watching you, Blackstone."

"Fine! You do that," Jonah spat back at the man. After briefly pausing to make eye contact with Wick, who was still stuck with Agent Harris on the second floor, Jonah exited the café. He and Mike would wait for Lynn and the others outside the teen center. There were too many enemies inside today.

As if proving his point, Brandon's snobbish laugh cut through the air just as Jonah stepped into the atrium. The bully and Antwan had four girls gathered around them. Brandon's eyes narrowed when he saw Jonah.

Before anything else could happen, Jonah veered into the east wing and straight to the bathrooms. He peeked around the alcove's corner and toward the atrium. Ramsey had left the café and was beckoning to Brandon and Antwan to approach him. After a brief conversation, Brandon pointed toward the alcove.

Jonah shrank out of sight and slipped into the boys' bathroom.

Mike jumped and waved his phone around. "What's going on?"

"Agent Ramsey's in the teen center. He knows the Alliance has Trevor and he threatened all of us."

Brandon's snide voice sounded from right outside the bathroom. "I saw the freak come this way."

When someone pushed on the door from the other side, Jonah grabbed Mike's arm and phased.

The Seeker's Compass

CHAPTER TWENTY-TWO
THE CHASE

Mike shivered, rubbing his arms as soon as they reappeared at the creek side. He moved off along the bank. Jonah lurched into motion, following his friend until they reached the bend in the water's course.

Moss-covered stumps littered this area of the creek. Mike chose one, sat, and clasped his hands together. "He threatened us?"

"More than that," Jonah said. "Ramsey wanted to attack me." He surveyed the woods. Wick and the others had to be free of agent Harris by now, he decided, and motioned to Mike. "We should go–"

He paused because he sensed the tell-tale increase of pressure. Leaves crunched from the direction where they had first appeared in.

Jonah pulled Mike away from the stream side and into the trees where they both huddled, watching.

"Someone followed me."

Mike shook slightly. "Do you think it's Kevin?"

"No," Jonah whispered. "Kevin wouldn't know we're here."

"But who else could follow you?"

Jonah's first thought was Agent Ramsey. His fear was confirmed when he made out the agent's blue shirt and tan pants through the gaps in the trees.

Ramsey stepped into view, using his boot to shift aside the remains of an old fire. As Jonah watched, all the clues snapped into place. His initial suspicion that Ramsey wanted to pull a blade in the first encounter had been dead on. And the stare the Agent used in the café had been a true Reaper Stare. "He's a fallen one."

"Oh my God," Mike breathed in a horrified voice. "Jonah, this is bad."

"Tell me about it."

Mike punched Jonah's arm. "No, I mean we still have the compass and Enhancer. If he catches us with those…"

Jonah pushed aside his mounting panic and focused on his idea. "We have to phase."

"Ramsey'll follow you again," Mike said.

"I don't have a choice."

Mike nodded, looking grim. "I'm ready."

Ramsey moved along the creek's edge and in their direction, his attention on the ground. Jonah realized the agent was tracking them by their foot prints in the soft soil. Ramsey's gaze lifted to the tree line and settled on their hiding spot.

Now or never, Jonah told himself. He pictured his destination and phased.

When they reappeared, Jonah gritted his teeth until the dizziness passed. They stood atop his favorite grassy hillside, well outside the city limits of Mount Vernon. The distance and double phasing had taken a little out of Jonah and he regretted not bringing any candy. He leaned forward, resting his hands on his knees for a second before tugging Mike along behind him.

He hoped the extra distance would delay Agent Ramsey long enough for them to hide in the trees and make an escape. However, Agent Ramsey appeared a few seconds later.

"Halt!" Ramsey's order rolled down the hillside.

The command had the opposite effect on the boys. Jonah and Mike sprinted off through the nearby trees. Mike was careful to keep hold of Jonah's shirt, and that made it rough to get away. Plus, Jonah struggled with his mounting desperation in order to think about the next location to phase.

The Seeker's Compass **485**

He certainly didn't want to lead the agent to his parents' hideaway. But he had to do something because Agent Ramsey drew closer with each second they remained on the hillside. Finally, a less than perfect option occurred to Jonah.

He hesitated before phasing and warned Mike, "Here we go."

Jonah had his hands up and ready to break his forward momentum when he reappeared in the cramped stairwell of the Oak Hill Mall parking garage. He succeeded in not smacking the wall, but Mike rammed into his back.

Jonah slumped against the cold concrete, the air knocked out of him. The disorientation was worse.

Mike was on point and pulled Jonah to his feet. "Come on, Jonah. You know he'll be here any second!" Mike hustled him up the stairs.

They burst through the stairwell doors, startling a mother and her three kids.

"This way." Mike wanted to go deeper into the parking structure.

Jonah had a better idea and yanked Mike in the opposite direction. "No. This way."

Adrenaline surged through Jonah as they ran across the pedestrian walkway that connected the parking garage to level three of the shopping mall. A stairwell door banged open behind them just as the boys entered the building.

Mike slowed his pace at once to a fast walk and glanced at Jonah. "Why are you so dizzy now? You weren't like that before."

Jonah wondered the same thing. When he had phased himself and Mike from his parents' hideaway, he barely felt any dizziness. And that had been two hundred miles.

"I think," he began, working through the problem, "it was the compass. It used my power, but maybe it also charged me." The more Jonah thought about it, the more it made sense. Plus, something else niggled at the back of his mind. He pushed that aside when he spotted what he needed.

"There!" Jonah pointed at a candy shop.

They swerved inside the brightly lit store, nearly knocking over a little kid picking candy from a bin. Jonah crouched behind a large display of jelly beans of all colors and flavors. Mike fumbled with the dispenser. His hands shook, but he managed to scoop jelly beans into a cellophane bag. Mike paused and drew out several to hand to Jonah, who glanced around before popping them in his mouth.

"Thanks," Jonah mumbled around the mouthful of beans.

"You're the only kid who has to eat candy." Mike cracked a smile and added, "Stay down."

Jonah watched the front doors as Mike went to the counter. He jerked when Agent Ramsey paused just outside. Then the agent turned to peer inside the candy store. Jonah kept his head down, hoping that no one would notice his strange behavior.

"Jonah…" Mike whispered and waved to him. He had hid behind a large woman looking at a display of lollipops when Ramsey appeared. "Come on." He peeked outside, the small bag of candy clutched in his right hand. "Ramsey just went inside a game store. Let's go."

Jonah felt exposed as he and Mike exited and retraced their path to the pedestrian bridge. They needed a place to hide and call for help. Before they could reach the exit, a security guard came out of those doors. The man glanced in their direction and reached for a radio on his belt. Jonah had the sinking feeling that the startled mom had called security or maybe the candy store owner had reported them. He didn't wait to find out which and changed direction, heading for the down escalators.

The boys received an unpleasant surprise when they spotted Agent Ramsey talking to another mall guard. The agent pointed in their direction. Knowing it was impossible to go unnoticed anymore, the boys sprinted down the escalator, apologizing to all the people they bumped and pushed along the way.

"What's the plan?" Mike panted just behind Jonah as they reached the bottom and hopped the next escalator down to the first floor. "You can't phase in public."

The statement made Jonah look up as they neared the bottom of the last escalator. The security guard hurried after them, but Agent Ramsey stood at the railing on the third floor, watching. Jonah knew that had they not been in public, Ramsey would have simply phased right on top of him and Mike.

The Seeker's Compass **487**

Just as they turned for the main mall doors, a third guard jumped them. Jonah pushed Mike forward while he dropped to his knees to avoid the guard's outstretched arms. The man stumbled past and over. Jonah scrambled after Mike and out the front doors.

The situation became trickier as a black SUV screeched to a halt right in front of them. Mike faltered, but Jonah nudged his friend to the right.

"Go around, into the parking lot."

Jonah dodged to the left as a beefy guy in all black hopped out of the truck. The man only paused for a moment before moving toward him.

Jonah kicked the truck's door, sending it flying into the man's arms. Then he dodged around and into the parking lot. He expected to catch up to Mike, but the guy recovered quicker than expected and snagged the back of his shirt. Jonah twisted out of the man's grip and nearly froze.

The small white skull clipped to the man's lapel reflected the bright sunlight. *Grimnion*. Fear propelled Jonah in the opposite direction from Mike and down a different row of cars.

The goon kept right on Jonah as he dodged between vehicles.

"Let go," Mike called out.

Jonah phased without thinking about it. He appeared right behind another Grimnion, who held Mike by the arm. In his other hand was a scythe.

"Hey!" Jonah yelled.

The man spun around, slicing the air with the weapon. Jonah ducked under the swing and Mike used the distraction to stomp on the man's foot. Then he ran around one end of the car and Jonah went the other way. They met up on the opposite side and scurried between adjacent cars until they were at least two rows away.

Jonah dropped to the ground and waved Mike to follow as he rolled under a van. Mike bumped into him a second later, and they watched the black shoes of men crossing back and forth.

"Jonah, why didn't you phase us?"

"I have to be careful where we go."

Mike's eyes widened. "Oh. But won't he sense what you just did?"

At that moment Jonah noticed a different pair of shoes walking closer to their spot. Once again, something began to nag Jonah, but he didn't know what.

Mike elbowed him. "Jonah…"

"I see him."

The boys heard Agent Hunter's angry voice shouting over his radio. "I don't care about the mall security. Put a nullifying net over the entire parking lot. Do it now before Blackstone can phase."

The muffled thump of the nullifying poles hitting the surface of the heated parking lot and sinking into place reached their ears.

Mike's eyes were as wide as his own, Jonah imagined. Time was up. They were so close to each other, it was easier for Jonah to slide an arm across Mike's back. Just as Jonah phased, he felt the trap snapping into place over the parking lot. But it was too late to stop. The ripples from the phase already played over his and Mike's bodies.

The next second, he experienced a wrenching pull. It was so unexpected that Mike slipped free of Jonah's grip in the middle of the phase.

"No!"

The Seeker's Compass

CHAPTER TWENTY-THREE
REVELATIONS

Jonah's fear for his buddy overshadowed his own terror at being sucked back to the parking lot and Agent Ramsey. He focused on his destination, not knowing how or if he could get away from the trap's pull.

He strained, his muscles aching as he reached out, willing himself to go forward. His Reaper powers obeyed, moving him toward his destination. As he did so, he felt another presence, familiar and frightened. *Mike!* Jonah latched onto his buddy's soul.

"Come on!" He pressed all of his will into the struggle to free himself. Just when Jonah thought he'd split in half from the opposing forces, the real world returned and he slammed onto the smooth cold concrete surface of the parking garage ramp. Mike slumped beside him.

The shock of the close escape, combined with the change from the broiling hot pavement of the parking lot, caused Jonah to suck in a startled breath.

Mike groaned, rubbing his head. "I hate phasing."

A horn blared and tires screeched. Jonah glanced up in time to see a large SUV bearing down on them. He grabbed Mike and rolled to the side. The SUV drove over the exact spot where they had been.

Jonah helped Mike to his feet and they dodged between a row of cars. The change in air pressure came just as they ran into the nearest stairwell. Jonah's exhaustion increased, making his frustration more unbearable. When they reached the top level of the garage, he turned to Mike. "Ready?"

"Yes!"

This time, they reappeared at the ravine near the practice field. It was the only deserted place Jonah could think to go. He led the way along a fallen log which lay across the gap. The drop to the bottom of the ravine was maybe twenty feet.

Jonah thought it significant that neither he nor Mike even hesitated to run across the log in an attempt to reach the thicket of woods on the other side. Agent Ramsey appeared behind them, as Jonah expected, and then the agent did what Jonah didn't expect. Ramsey phased to a spot on the opposite site of the ravine, blocking their escape path.

Jonah stopped.

Mike bumped into him and then screamed at Ramsey. "We didn't do anything wrong."

Agent Ramsey didn't respond as he stalked toward them.

Jonah pushed Mike in the opposite direction, and they ran back the way they came. But Jonah already knew what the agent would do. But it was Agent Harris who appeared in front of them on that side of the ravine. And Harris brought along two Wraith-possessed goons.

Jonah's nagging warning became a cold reality. He had focused on Ramsey and forgot about his partner. With Ramsey a Fallen One, it only made sense that Harris would also be one.

The henchmen withdrew their weapons and started for the log. They planned to box Jonah and Mike between themselves and Agent Ramsey, who remained at the edge of the ravine

Ramsey smirked at Jonah. "Give up, young Blackstone."

"Use the compass," Mike whispered. "Remember what your godfather said about Deyanira not being able to follow us."

"He also said they weren't sure that's why Deyanira didn't follow."

Mike pointed at Ramsey. "It's time to test that."

Jonah didn't see any other options. He pulled the compass from his pocket but held it behind his back, hiding it from Ramsey's view. Mike caught on and activated the device.

The Seeker's Compass

As the first Grimnion stepped onto the log, Trevor appeared behind the goons. In one motion, he knocked the closer man over the edge and into the ravine.

"Trevor?" Jonah and Mike gaped at the boy.

Trevor grabbed the second Grimnion and hurled the man backward toward Agent Harris. But Harris dodged. At the same time, the agent pulled out two gleaming Reaper blades and attacked Trevor.

Jonah's heart rate spiked with fear for the boy, but Trevor was full of surprises. He too had blades. He blocked Harris's blows and scored a quick cut on the agent's left arm.

Ramsey's shout shocked Jonah and Mike out of their stupor. "No!" He activated his own blades and started across the ravine.

Jonah prepared to activate the compass just as a small object whistled up from the ravine below at high speed. His Death Sense spiked and he moved to push Mike aside. He was too late. The scythe struck Mike in the chest.

Mike collapsed forward with an explosive exhale of breath. The next moment, his entire upper body and head were engulfed in a brilliant light.

"Mike!" Jonah grabbed hold of his buddy. But he wasn't ready for the added weight and lost his own footing. Both boys tumbled off the log.

As they fell, Jonah only had seconds to concentrate and phase before they crashed into the broken limbs and branches below. He pictured the small section of grass near the center of the practice area and phased.

The softer earth cushioned the impact but, Jonah still let out a painful *oomph*. Mike flopped beside him and didn't move. The light engulfing his upper body and head was gone.

Jonah shook his friend by the shoulders. "Mike. Mike."

When Ramsey appeared, Jonah roared at the man in anger, dived for two practice batons the club kept nearby, and threw both weapons at the agent.

Ramsey knocked the batons aside and pointed a blade at Mike. "That was your fault, young Blackstone. How many more of your friends and family will have to die?"

Tears streamed down Jonah's face. His first impulse was to attack Ramsey again. A voice in his head said, *No. Get Mike's body away.* Jonah held up his compass in a shaking hand just as Trevor appeared.

The courier grabbed Jonah's hand and pressed it against the green activate button before Jonah could reach out for Mike.

"Wait!"

The compass activated and the clearing was gone in a second. He and Trevor reappeared at his parents' hideaway.

Jonah struggled in the courier's grip. "Let me go."

In answer, Trevor zapped Jonah in the neck with a small device.

Blinding pain shot into Jonah's head. His legs buckled and he dropped to his knees, cradling his head in his hands. The sharp pain from the jolt subsided, but his head was left buzzing.

"You bastard," Jonah managed through clenched teeth.

Trevor stood back, shocked. "I'm… I'm sorry. I thought you had Mike. I wouldn't have…" The boy swallowed. "It's too late."

"No it isn't. " Jonah lurched to his feet but when he tried to phase, his fuzzy mind refused to cooperate. He roared in anger at Trevor, "What did you do to me?"

Trevor moved away from Jonah's grasping hands. "You can't, Jonah. They'll catch you."

"But Mike," Jonah's jaw quivered. "He's dead."

"He's not dead," Trevor shot back.

Jonah sensed the raw despair in the courier and it shocked him.

Trevor took a deep breath to calm himself. "The Enhancer activated. I'm sure Mike's just unconscious from the shock of it."

Two conflicting emotions warred inside Jonah. He wanted to believe Mike would be fine. At the same time, Jonah hated Trevor for ruining his chance to get his best friend to safety. "I have to go back."

Trevor moved fast and pinned Jonah's arms behind his back. "I'm sorry, Jonah, but I can't let you do that."

"They'll hurt my friend."

"No they won't." Trevor shook him. "Listen to me. Ramsey will want to trade Mike for me. That's their way."

Jonah struggled but Trevor's grip was too strong, and his head still buzzed. "Whose way? Fallen Reapers?"

"No," Trevor answered, "something a lot worse. Hunters."

CHAPTER TWENTY-FOUR
RAMSEY'S DEMAND

Kevin's powerful upper cut struck Trevor below the chin. The boy landed on his butt and slid backward into Robert and Lynn's desks. The twins scrambled to keep their computer monitors from toppling onto the ground.

"You lying punk." Kevin stalked toward Trevor, his fist balled and ready to strike again.

"Hold on." Rex stepped between Kevin and Trevor. "Let the boy speak, then you can clobber him."

"You're not helping, Rex." Marcus frowned at Kevin until the young Fallen Reaper retreated to the sofa and sat beside Jonah.

"I understand your anger," Marcus continued, "And Jonah's."

"And ours," Lynn seconded from her spot behind the computer desks. She and Robert stared daggers at Trevor as Rex pulled the boy to his feet.

The thought of Rex helping the courier angered Jonah even more. He stabbed a finger at Trevor. "He let Agent Ramsey take Mike."

"He would have caught you–" Trevor began.

"Shut up!" Jonah didn't want to hear anything Trevor had to say. The last few hours had been the worst of Jonah's life as his terror over Mike's fate worsened.

Marcus stood in front of Jonah, blocking his view of Trevor. "We sent people to the clearing. Ramsey set up a nullifying trap and had four of his henchmen waiting."

The Seeker's Compass

Jonah hung his head low. He didn't want to see Trevor's decision as smart.

"Listen to your godfather," Rex urged. "They left Mike's candy bag in the open, right where you'd see it. They would have played your emotions to catch you."

"And," Marcus added, "Ramsey would possess the compass and Enhancer." He let out a breath. "The agents will offer to trade Mike, which means he'll keep your friend alive."

Kevin snorted and leaned against Jonah. "If anything happens to Mike, I'll take care of Ramsey and Trevor."

Jonah welcomed the comment but it didn't matter, not with his friend out there. And Trevor's genuine sorrow over Mike's situation also bothered Jonah. He wanted to hate Trevor, accuse the boy of not caring, but he couldn't.

When Jonah noticed his godfather watching his reaction, he covered by asking, "Why didn't you know about Ramsey and Harris?"

Marcus' eyebrows shot up and he exchanged a glance with Trueblood and Rex before answering. "This is our first time dealing with Hunters in the mortal world."

"But, what are they?" Lynn asked. She and Robert moved closer to Jonah and Kevin.

"They are former archivists who've been placed in the mortal realm for special assignments," Marcus explained. "Until they are activated, they lead normal mortal lives."

"So they're sleeper agents," Jonah said.

Marcus nodded. "In a way. A Hunter can stay undercover for years before he's activated."

All the talk of being activated reminded Jonah of Kevin's meditation. "If they have patterns like yours, that means they have to recharge or lose power?"

Marcus stroked his chin. "We energize our patterns on a frequent basis because we continually use our power. The Hunters go inactive for years, so their binding patterns retain their charge far longer."

Robert pointed at Trevor. "What about him?"

"I'm not a Hunter." The boy threw up his hands in a normal human gesture. "I crossed through the portal."

Kevin glared at him. "So what? That just means you're like Deyanira."

Trevor clutched the bottom of his shirt and twisted it in his hands. Jonah sat straighter, remembering the boy didn't want the healer to look at him. He nudged Kevin and pointed at Trevor's shirt.

Kevin's face went slack. "Do you have binding patterns?"

Trevor hesitated before answering. "The Elder put me through the trial." He winced.

According to Jonah's godfather, the patterns were a painful part of the falling process. Jonah couldn't miss the look of understanding passing between Rex, his godfather, and Kevin. For once, he felt outside a closed circle and understood why.

Unlike the others, Jonah was born to his powers. He didn't have nor need the patterns.

Kevin nodded to Trevor in sympathy, and the fire in the Fallen Reaper's attitude lessened as he crossed his arms. Jonah was about to ask Kevin if he was alright when something in Jonah's pocket spiked with heat.

It was like pressing a sun-heated coin on his bare arm. Jonah dug out Wick's talisman, recalling that after clearing the county people out of the attic space, Marcus had instructed Wick and Trueblood to restore the protections.

Jonah wasn't the only one to react. Lynn, Robert, and Trueblood did the same thing, each gaping at the coin.

Wick jumped up. "Someone's messing with the door."

Kevin pulled a blade and bounded down the stairs. The attic door opened and then closed with a soft thud. Kevin returned, holding a small white envelope in his hands. "I found this taped to the door." He handed it to Marcus. "I also saw Brandon running down the stairs to the atrium."

Wick ruffled his dreads while trying to peek at the note. "I bet Ramsey doesn't want to show his face right now, the jerk."

The Seeker's Compass

Marcus read the note once and then passed the piece of paper to Kevin. "Just as I said. Agent Ramsey wants to trade Mike in exchange for Trevor."

"How long do we have?" Trueblood asked.

"The meet is set for seven-thirty." Marcus glanced at his watch. "We have just over three hours to prepare. The exchange takes place at this location." He held up a picture that had been inside the folded message.

Kevin's jaw tightened. Rex grunted and Trueblood shook her head.

"What's special about that place?" Jonah asked. As far as he could see, it was a simple field of sparse wild grass and red clay.

Kevin handed the note to Wick and then told Jonah, "It's where I fell."

Jonah noted the older boy's haunted expression. "That place?"

"Yes." Kevin leaned against the back of the sofa next to Jonah again. He gazed at his large hands as he spoke. "The Alliance used that field a lot. Ramsey's letting us know that he's on to us."

Lynn took the picture and examined it. "Where is this?"

Kevin lifted his gaze to the photo. "North Georgia."

"It's not in Mount Vernon." Lynn furrowed her brow. "That's strange."

"Why?" Kevin slipped his hands in his pockets and shrugged. "You know distance isn't a problem for us."

"Yeah, I do." Lynn handed the photo to Robert and Wick, who huddled close to examine it. "It's almost like Ramsey wants to pull you away from here and..." Her eyes flickered to Jonah for a split second.

Rex nodded. "The little lady makes a good point. The mole did the same thing; why not try it again? Perhaps he wants Jonah after all."

"But that doesn't make sense," Jonah objected. "The mole ordered Ramsey to leave me alone."

"Then Ramsey is acting on his own, which makes it even more dangerous," Trueblood said.

"We can't give him Trevor." Jonah was shocked to hear himself defend the boy he wanted to punch a short while ago.

"Thanks, Jonah." Trevor gave him a tired smile. "You save Mike. He's more important than me."

Jonah wanted to object when a tiny light flared in mid-air, drawing his attention. He dismissed it as a lightning bug that had made its way into the attic. Then something larger zipped out of the pinpoint of light and expanded.

Everyone gasped except Kevin and the adults. The glittering shape formed into an undulating Alliance symbol, three interlocking circles with a pair of wings above. The symbol wasn't much bigger than a large butterfly. Adding to the effect, the symbol's wings flapped as it floated in the air.

Wick was ecstatic. "That is so freakin' cool!" He rushed over to peer at the beacon.

Marcus pulled Wick back as the beacon flared and faded away and a real vortex formed in the air.

Rubio exited the magical doorway. After a brief nod to Marcus, the intimidating mage turned to Trevor, held up his hand, and muttered, "Nishati," in his military voice. A beam of energy shot from his raised hand and enveloped Trevor. The boy let out an involuntary gasp.

"Hold out your arm," Rubio ordered. Trevor complied.

Lines appeared on Trevor's forearm and flared, leaving behind a sundial-type impression near the wrist.

Rubio drew in a deep breath. "That should help, for now."

Jonah grabbed Trevor's forearm to get a closer look at the tattoo. "You can't recharge his patterns with a spell, can you?"

Rubio chuckled. "That was for his mortal body." He rubbed his square chin while watching Trevor. "I'm guessing your patterns carried one charge?"

Trevor nodded.

Rubio crossed his hands behind his back. "Well, the Alliance would never think of giving you to Ramsey."

Jonah's relief over Trevor's fate only lasted for a millisecond. "What about Mike?" He had a growing sense of dread that worried him sick. The last time he experienced that had been…

The Seeker's Compass

All at once, Jonah's head split open with pain. His Death Sense was off the scale. Before he could stop himself, he bent forward and vomited on the floor. Everyone cleared a space out of reflex. But in seconds, Lynn and Kevin rushed forward to help him.

"It's Mike." Jonah paused to wipe his mouth. "Ramsey's hurting Mike!"

Trevor produced the device he had used to stun Jonah before. When Jonah saw it, he roared at the boy, "Stay away from me!"

Kevin whirled on Trevor and his face went slack when he saw the device. He grabbed Jonah's forearm. "Don't try to help Mike."

Marcus stepped forward. "Kevin's right. Ramsey may be laying a trap for you."

Jonah gave them a feeble nod. His head hurt too much to do anything else. Lynn pulled him to the sofa. She sat down and had Jonah stretch out with his head on her lap.

Robert was at their side with a bottle of water. Jonah took it, sat up and gulped it down. He gagged when his Death Sense spiked once more, then stopped.

Lynn forced him to lay back again and cradled his head in her hands. "It'll be alright."

When Jonah could trust his voice, he said, "He's not being hurt anymore."

Rubio stroked his big chin, eyeing Jonah. "So the boy can phase to someone's aid on instinct. Interesting."

Jonah's godfather's expression went stony. "That's something we shouldn't share with the whole council. Not with the mole around." Rubio looked ready to argue, but Marcus turned to Jonah. "Don't worry. We won't let Ramsey keep Mike." He paused as Rubio created another vortex. "I'm sorry, but we have an emergency meeting."

Rubio pulled Trevor in front of the vortex. "You won't be able to phase away again."

Trevor nodded, looking shocked and haunted, Jonah thought.

"We'll be back. Just stay safe," Marcus urged.

"What about the clubhouse?" Lynn gestured around the space.

Marcus's reaction intrigued Jonah. He glared at Rex as he said, "Ask him." With that, he stepped through the vortex with Trevor and Rubio.

Once the magical opening sealed itself, everyone turned on the Fallen Reaper.

Rex scratched the side of his big nose. His face had gone scarlet red with embarrassment. "Well, it seems the facilities manager's boat appeared several miles from his summer cottage and up a tree." Rex sucked in a breath. "He's taking his vacation early to sort it out. So no final decision on the attic for at least two weeks."

Wick, Lynn, and Robert whooped and clapped.

Jonah eyed Rex. "Marcus is pissed with you?"

"That's an understatement, buddy." Rex let out a low whistle. "But seriously, we'll get your friend back. Don't worry."

The last thing Jonah could do was not worry, considering his best friend was being tortured by a deranged GBI agent. One way or another, he knew he had to rescue Mike.

CHAPTER TWENTY-FIVE
BATTLE PLANS

The late afternoon turned into early evening before Rubio returned with additional Alliance personnel. They commandeered the clubhouse conference table and sitting area, and a hornet's nest of activity ensued.

Jonah and his cousins were left alone and out of the action. They debated among themselves whether the people traveled back and forth from Alliance HQ, the trade-off spot, or both. At one point Lynn followed Kevin to the conference table as plans for the trade were discussed.

Fifteen minutes in, Lynn slipped away and waved for Jonah, Robert, and Wick to follow her to the attic stairs. Jonah wanted to stay in the clubhouse.

Lynn twisted his ear and whispered, "Come on, hero."

Only when Kevin joined their group did Jonah relent and follow his cousin. Lynn didn't explain until they entered one of the smaller game rooms on the first floor.

Kevin stationed himself near the entrance to keep other kids from interfering. Robert and Wick took two of the chairs around the game table. Lynn forced Jonah into the third and took the fourth chair, opposite him.

"What's happening, Lynn?" Jonah raised an impatient eyebrow at his cousin.

Lynn waited for Kevin's nod before answering. "They're gonna use Trevor as a decoy."

"That's not gonna work," Jonah blurted out.

Lynn waved him silent. "He'll have extra protections and a lot of Alliance members ready to go. They want Ramsey to believe the Alliance is serious about the trade."

"But," Jonah stammered, "what about Mike?"

"They don't expect Ramsey to actually release Mike, which is why the Alliance plans to rescue him. It'll happen at the same time the fake trade is taking place."

Jonah couldn't believe what he was hearing. He glanced at Kevin for confirmation.

The young Fallen Reaper leaned against the doorframe and gave Jonah a sad nod. "Rubio's gonna lead that attack. He's pretty good in a fight."

Jonah couldn't relax, not with the tension he sensed in Lynn and Kevin. "What's worrying you, Lynn? Do you sense something?"

"No, but," she paused to swallow, "they got the location from a human agent they caught. And it's outside of Mount Vernon."

"You still think it's suspicious that the locations are always far from here?"

"Yes, I do." Lynn's tone left no doubt.

Kevin abandoned his perch in the doorway in order to kneel beside Jonah's chair. "Marcus said the same thing, but he was overruled. That's why he wants you to stay at the Guest House."

Jonah appreciated Kevin's idea, never truly considering that he was in any danger.

Kevin tapped Jonah's knee with his fist. "We'll all go. Robert, Lynn, and Wick."

Wick perked up at that news.

Robert smiled. "At least you'd have the video games to keep your mind off things, little cousin."

When Jonah continued to frown, Kevin leaned back. "What's the problem?"

Jonah threw up his hands, angry that the others didn't get it. "Kevin, if Mike isn't where they think, he'll still be in danger. We have to do something."

Kevin let out a breath. "Listen…"

Jonah leapt to his feet. "Lynn, you agree with me, don't you? If Ramsey's leading everyone out of Mount Vernon, then… then I bet Mike's here somewhere."

Lynn toyed with one of her braids. She did it whenever she was seriously considering an idea. Jonah silently urged his cousin to agree.

She leaned forward, her hands resting on the game table. "My intuition says Jonah's right. God forbid."

Kevin closed his eyes. "Where?"

Jonah traded a glance with Lynn. "The Crossroads?"

"No go," Kevin countered. "After you told us about the dream-walk, and seeing as Ramsey's using Wraiths, Marcus had the place checked out. We saw signs the agents had been there, but now it's empty."

A couple of younger kids appeared in the doorway, chess box in hand. Kevin caught their eye. "Use the next room." The kids gulped and hurried off. Kevin turned back to the others. "Lynn's on the right track. Ramsey and Harris needed a place empty of people and Wraiths."

Robert snapped his fingers. "I know where they could be. The old mill."

"Cool idea, Bobby," Wick agreed. "It's only a mile away from the Crossroads and it's been abandoned for over a decade."

"Huh, guys." Jonah waved his arms around. "Won't Ramsey have his own people there?"

"I'm sure he will." Lynn stood and turned to Kevin. "Are we gonna do this?"

Kevin's shoulders slumped. "You guys are trying to get me fired."

"You can claim it was all part of Rubio's plan," Wick laughed and plopped his boots on the table. "In fact, you can say he created the diversion just for you." He high-fived Robert.

Kevin scowled at the boys.

Jonah crossed his arms and stuck out his chin. "I'm saving my friend."

"We'll need protection." Lynn kicked Wick's boots off the table. "You got more shields, young mage?"

Wick exchanged an excited glance with Robert. "You bet I do. I've been working on a couple of them since, well," he looked at Jonah, "since Jonah gave me that power boost last summer."

Lynn crossed her arms. "Why didn't I know you worked on this?"

"You spent all your time working on your boyfriend," Robert said and wiggled his eyebrows at her.

When Lynn dipped her chin and narrowed her eyes, Robert hurried to explain. "Wick used Jonah's power boost to experiment with a couple of special shield bracelets."

Kevin's earlier scowl transformed into one of intense anticipation. "How powerful are they?"

Wick raised his eyebrows. "Really, really powerful."

Kevin shook his head in wonder. "Why aren't you guys working for the Alliance?"

"I told Trueblood a lot of stuff."

Lynn scoffed at Wick. "I bet you never told her about the bracelets."

"Well, not exactly ..."

Lynn yanked one of Wick's short dreads. "I thought so."

Kevin glanced at his watch. "We better go. I'll have to actually take all of you to the Guest House."

"We'll be able to leave, right?" Lynn asked. "What about Mabel?"

"No problem." When Lynn raised a skeptical eyebrow, Kevin held up his hands. "She's in Washington for the day."

Lynn smirked. "For someone who didn't want to do this, you sound like you had a plan already in place."

Kevin hooked a thumb at Jonah. "Things always go sideways when he's involved."

The Seeker's Compass

Jonah punched the boy's arm and regretted it. Kevin's bicep was hard as steel.

"One of these days..." Kevin flexed his muscles.

"You guys can fight later." Lynn wrapped an arm around her brother's neck. "Robert needs to get the bracelet from the Seeker's box."

The group was in luck. Rex was the only Alliance member still in the attic when they returned. Jonah breathed easier. The big Fallen Reaper was cool, and not as suspicious of them as his godfather or Trueblood.

Robert conferred with Wick in front of the old file cabinet where he kept the archive box. Lynn went to the old editor's desk and rummaged around in a drawer. She pulled out a county map and handed it to Kevin. When Lynn noticed Jonah just standing there, she nodded toward the clubhouse section where Rex sat in an armchair, an opened report on his lap.

Jonah got his cousin's meaning and crossed to the sofa, wondering how to distract the Fallen Reaper. He needn't have worried.

Rex looked up from his report to smile at him. "How're you doing?"

Jonah shrugged and sat. It occurred to him that he didn't need to hide his growing worry from the Fallen Reaper. It was real and he let it show.

Sure enough, Rex sensed his mood because he laid the report on the steamer trunk and leaned closer. "Don't worry about your buddy. We'll find him and bring him home."

"I know." Jonah's doubt about their little plan surfaced and for a moment, he almost came clean.

Rex shook his shaggy head. "It's no need to feel guilty about what happened. I'm sure Mike won't blame you."

Jonah nodded and took a deep breath to calm his raw emotions. Rex remained focused on him until a loud click caught the man's attention. Jonah recognized that sound. It was the locks on Robert's archive box. Rex started to turn around and would have caught Robert handing the bracelet to Wick if not for the sudden change in air pressure.

The Fallen Reaper's attention shifted at once to the attic window instead, where Marcus and Trueblood appeared. He jumped to his feet to greet his colleagues.

506 *John Darr*

Marcus paused to note everyone in the attic. Wick had shifted his body to hide the archive box from view. Jonah held his breath, waiting as his godfather started a quiet conversation with Rex and Trueblood.

As soon as that happened, Wick used the opportunity to snatch the bracelet from Robert and slip it in a pocket of his fatigue pants. Robert closed the box and put it back in the lowest drawer. That done, he and Wick sat at the card table and pretended to pour over one of their books on the supernatural.

Marcus disengaged from his conversation and stood back as Trueblood produced a vortex and left. By then Jonah and the others huddled in a group. "Innocent thoughts," he mouthed to everyone.

Marcus noticed and furrowed his brow before focusing on Jonah. "You've been to the Guest House before, so it should be easy. Back porch."

Jonah nodded. Lynn placed an arm around his shoulders. Kevin gripped Robert and Wick by the forearms.

Marcus glanced at his watch. "You better go."

Kevin phased first. Jonah followed a second later, and the attic disappeared.

Once they arrived at the Alliance Guest House, Kevin eyed Jonah. "How do you feel?"

Jonah took a moment to assess his strength. "Not bad." That was true. The journey didn't produce any dizziness.

"Good. That means you're building your phasing muscles."

Lynn shook Jonah's head with her hand. "That's about the only muscle he's working out."

Jonah ignored her quip, instead choosing to focus on Kevin's unexpected compliment.

Kevin motioned to everyone. "Wait here." He disappeared inside the house for about ten minutes. When he returned, he cracked a smile. "Making sure nobody's here and to get these." He held up a pair of binoculars. "I thought we could use them."

"Thanks." Lynn took them.

Kevin handed a set of keys to Wick. "It's all yours, young mage."

The Seeker's Compass

Wick flashed a lopsided grin while handing Kevin the shield bracelet.

Once Kevin slipped it around his wrist, Robert and Wick moved aside and waved.

Kevin gripped Jonah and Lynn's arms. "If this doesn't work, I'm out of a job. After Marcus kills me." He phased them away.

CHAPTER TWENTY-SIX
THE OLD MILL

Modern GPS, and a good Internet connection, allowed Kevin and Lynn to pull decent satellite images before leaving the attic. They'd chosen half a dozen pictures of a distribution building across from their goal: the old Iron Works mill. Jonah was impressed with the amount of work the two managed while he had distracted Rex.

But he also experienced a pang of guilt over fooling Rex and hoped the Fallen Reaper wouldn't get in trouble. If not for that worry, and the impending danger to Mike, Jonah would have found the whole operation cool.

Lynn held the binoculars to her eyes, gazing at the decrepit mill from their hiding place behind a stack of wooden pallets. "Why can't the bad guys ever set up shop in a luxury hotel?" She lowered the binoculars and frowned. "Last summer it was a creepy plantation house, and now this."

Kevin laughed. "You wouldn't believe some of the places I've had to go to."

Jonah found that bit of information interesting. He didn't know if Kevin meant his time with the Alliance or his time as a Reaper.

Lynn peered through the binoculars again. "I don't see anyone. We could be wrong, unless they used the river to approach the building."

"Let me borrow those." Kevin held out his hand. His attention seemed to be focused on the treetops to the right of the mill. The top of a rusted bridge rose above the trees where the highway crossed the river.

Lynn slapped the binoculars in Kevin's hand. "What's up?"

"I'm gonna see if you're right." Kevin phased without warning, drawing a startled breath from Lynn.

"You guys do that on purpose." She pinched Jonah's arm.

"Hey!" Jonah rubbed the painful spot. He jumped when Kevin returned less than two minutes later.

"They have boats docked at the old pier behind the mill," Kevin announced, causing Lynn to gape at him.

Her gaze shifted to the distant bridge. "You phased way up there?"

"Yep. Don't worry. I went to the top of the center pylon. None of the people in the cars passing below could have seen me." Kevin grinned. "What's the plan, Lynn?"

"You go in first."

He nodded while gazing across the lonely highway.

Jonah didn't understand. "That's the plan? He goes in first? What about the people inside?"

Lynn nodded. "Exactly. Kevin'll draw away any Grimnions inside."

"They'll hurt Mike if he tries that."

"I don't think so." Lynn crossed her arms. "My bet is they'll focus on catching Kevin."

"They'd have to hit me first." Kevin flexed his hands. "I'm fast."

Jonah gulped. "Maybe… maybe we should find another way."

Lynn tapped Jonah on the forehead. "This is the best plan. Kevin leads the Grimnions on a goose chase around the old mill."

Kevin held up his right wrist. "I use Wick's shield bracelet to hold off the bad guys."

"Jonah and I free Mike and get to safety." Lynn patted the compass Jonah wore clipped to a chain and under his shirt.

He caught on. "Oh, that's right. I can use the compass to take us to the hideaway. And Ramsey can't follow." Jonah began to like the simple plan more than he had at first.

"Kevin can get away once we're clear." Lynn held her chin high, waiting to see what the Fallen Reaper would say about the plan.

Kevin fingered the shield bracelet around his right wrist while gazing across the highway. For a second, Jonah feared he would suggest they tell the other Alliance members anyway.

A moment later, Kevin nodded. "Let's do it."

Lynn bumped fists with him. "I'm ready."

Kevin gripped Lynn and Jonah by an arm and phased.

They reappeared right outside a set of large wooden double doors that were painted a grayish-green color. Rusted metal bars ran horizontal at the top and bottom, and someone had cut through a large chain and left it on the ground for anyone to see.

Kevin grabbed the edge of the door and paused to give Jonah a playful shove on the head. "Find Mike and get out. Don't worry about me." He held up the wrist with the bracelet. "Okay?"

Jonah gulped and nodded. The seriousness of the whole thing left him feeling queasy. He took a deep breath to quell his stomach and prepared to do his part.

Kevin pulled the door open just enough to slip inside. Lynn and Jonah waited for several tense seconds. All at once, shouts and snapping sounds of what Jonah thought were stun weapons rolled from inside. His heart spasmed with worry over Kevin.

Lynn activated her blades and motioned with the right one for Jonah to follow.

He paused right inside the front doors in shock. Kevin zipped around the inside of the mill, with at least five guards trying to zap him. The Fallen Reaper mixed blinding-fast sprints across the floor with micro phases. At one point, he appeared right by a guard and knocked the man into a wall with one blow.

Kevin phased away right before the other guards fired on him. Jonah's mouth hung open in awe.

Deafening booms of discharges hitting the rusted metal walls rattled the entire building. Jonah's admiration for Kevin's bravery and skill went

The Seeker's Compass

up a notch. He would have stood there and ruined their own part of the plan except for Lynn, who kept her head.

She yanked Jonah behind a large piece of chipped concrete and out of sight. "Stay focused."

Jonah's face heated with embarrassment. "Sorry."

The building had been stripped of equipment. The only things remaining were reinforced foundations where the machines had been. The central part had a ceiling over four stories high. With most of the window panes busted out, Jonah thought the place looked like a weird cathedral.

Lynn indicated a walkway on the right with stairs leading up to an administrative level. The glass panes of the old offices were broken out and the metal walls rusted and dented. Lynn pointed one blade at that level and the other blade toward a stairway leading to a sub level. "Up or down?"

Jonah closed his eyes, thinking back to his escape with Mike from Agent Ramsey. When the Grimnion had grabbed Mike, Jonah felt his buddy's terror and had phased to him. Recalling the sensation, he reached out with his power. In response he received a vague sense of fear and confusion.

Jonah focused and pointed at the stair to the sub level. "The basement."

Kevin phased to the top floor of the office section, almost directly above their position. At once, the stun blast impacted the railings and walls around him. The Fallen Reaper activated Wick's shield to block most of it.

As soon as the blasts faded, Kevin dropped the shield and his arms blurred into motion as he shouted the deflection spell and batted aside several shots with his blades before phasing.

"Whoa," Jonah breathed.

Lynn's eyes were just as wide as his. "He wasn't kidding about being fast."

She recovered quicker than Jonah and waited for the sounds of battle to move far away before darting to the stairs. Jonah followed. He didn't know if Kevin sensed them or not, but the Fallen Reaper had all the guards occupied on the opposite side of the mill.

Jonah wished he could phase right to Mike, but that was a sure way to activate Ramsey's trap. They needed to check the situation below if they wanted to get Mike and escape. Forcing himself to stick to the plan, Jonah descended the steps and paused at the bottom to listen.

He closed his eyes and reached out with his Reaper side. He sensed Mike's soul straight ahead, but not Ramsey's. Either the agent wasn't here or he'd found a way to mask his soul. A serious case of doubt assailed Jonah at that thought.

Screwing up his nerves, he inched forward. The sunlight only reached this level through metal grates in the main floor. The effect created intense pools of light among the shadows.

Jonah heard something move up ahead, a soft scraping sound and low mumbling, just beyond a patch of light at the end of the corridor. Lynn pressed a small LED flashlight into his hand. Jonah lit it and moved forward. Within a few steps, his foot came down on something soft. Jonah shined the light at the floor and leapt back, heart racing because Agent Harris' lifeless face stared back at him.

Any other person would have been repulsed or scared at the sight. Jonah was, but he was also half Reaper. It was that side of himself that surged forward to touch the body while cushioning his mortal self from the initial shock.

There was little blood, except for the two large spots seeping through the fabric of the man's shirt. At the center of both spots was a large cut. The surprised expression remained frozen on Harris' face.

Jonah stood there, unmoving, until Lynn drew close.

She nudged him in the back. "Jonah, what's going on..." Her voice trailed off into a hiss of disgust. "He's been stabbed by blades."

Of course, Jonah said to himself. Ramsey must have killed his partner. But why?

Jonah squinted up into the brilliant sunlight just beyond Harris' body. That section of space appeared to be directly underneath a vertical shaft. Light poured in from windows far above and reflected off the pale, chipped walls.

The sound came again. Muttering, Jonah realized. Nonsense jumbles of words, rushed together. Jonah's eyes adjusted enough to make out a small shape in the relative darkness. That shape moved and Mike's face came into view. The sunlight made his eyes and his already light complexion glow.

Jonah dropped the flashlight, leapt over Harris and ran toward his buddy, forgetting any possible trap. Lynn covered his back, her blades held ready as she continually scanned the patches of darkness.

Mike's rocking back and forth stopped with a sudden jerk and his vacant expression cleared. "He's waiting for you to come and get me, Jonah. Go back!"

Jonah ignored the warning as he knelt beside his buddy. When he reached out, Mike recoiled. For the first time, Jonah realized that Mike's eyes did glow. It was obvious when his friend leaned back into the shadows.

"Mike, your eyes are glowing," Jonah said in a hushed voice.

"Really?" Mike's normal inquisitive tone asserted itself. He glanced up and over Jonah's head. "He's watching."

Jonah whirled, and that's when he noticed the tiny glint of light on a camera lens. He had to appreciate the agent's creativity. He couldn't sense Ramsey's soul because there was no soul present to sense. The agent was watching remotely, via camera.

Mike began to rock back and forth, shocking Jonah. Words tumbled out of his mouth. They were equations, calculations, and locations in English and occasionally in a dialect Jonah didn't recognize.

The sight horrified Jonah, but he reached out for his buddy again.

The motion focused Mike and he yelled, "Don't touch me. You'll get stuck here!" Mike shifted his leg so Jonah could see the strange lock around the ankle. "It'll keep you from…"

"That's enough!"

Agent Ramsey appeared on the other side of the bright sunlight. He stepped forward and clapped his hands. "I was beginning to think you wouldn't take the bait, Mr. Blackstone."

Jonah's wishful fantasy that they would succeed in getting Mike without facing Ramsey vanished. He and the others had known this was a trap and that Ramsey never intended to take Trevor. But they couldn't have anticipated the low rumble of arriving vehicles that filtered down to their level. No doubt more of Ramsey's men had arrived, Jonah decided, experiencing renewed fear for Kevin.

The Fallen Reaper had Wick's bracelet, but even with that, Kevin wouldn't be able to hold out forever. And he also wouldn't go anywhere until he knew Jonah and the others were safe.

Agent Ramsey's false smile morphed into a pure sneer. "Well, half-breed? Are you prepared to surrender or see your friends and family die?"

Jonah's breaths hitched in his lung as the awful weight of responsibility descended on him. Coming up with a plan and carrying it through were two different things. If this didn't work, Jonah would have to face another friend or family member being tortured or worse. He couldn't do that. Not again.

He rose to his feet. "I thought you wanted the courier?"

"His real value is that he sought you out." Ramsey pointed at Jonah. "I want to know why."

Mike whispered, pleading, "Don't let him get to you. Don't try to save me."

Jonah shifted until he pressed against Lynn. He readied himself to phase. "What'll the Grand Oracle say?"

Ramsey narrowed his eyes. Jonah couldn't tell if the man was going to yell or attack. The agent shook himself and plastered a sneer on his face. "That courier's out of time. With the portals closed, he's stuck here. Have you ever seen what happens to a supernatural who can't cross back?"

Jonah begin to see that the man was more than dangerous; he was sick. Despite the mole's order, this Hunter killed his own partner and gave up a chance to capture Trevor.

It's always about me.

Lynn met Jonah's sad gaze. "It's okay, Jonah."

Ramsey cackled like a madman. "No it isn't. My allies have arrived. That Fallen Reaper upstairs is capable, but even he can't win against the odds. Perhaps I can hurt him in order to convince you to submit." Ramsey cocked his head to the side. "Well young Blackstone, what will you do?"

The Seeker's Compass

Jonah didn't respond. Instead, he slipped a finger through a loop on Lynn's jeans. She nodded, the barest fraction, but enough to let him know she was ready.

Leaving Mike behind hurt Jonah like nothing else. He didn't want to, but he needed the agent to follow. It was the best option to save his friend. Jonah prepared himself and had to look away from Mike in order to nudge himself and phase.

CHAPTER TWENTY-SEVEN
HUNTER'S TRAP

Jonah and Lynn reappeared on the top floor, in the mill's old office section. He heard Agent Ramsey's laugh carry through the building.

Jonah tapped his cousin's hand. "Lynn-"

"I got it." She darted down the stairs to the level below.

Ramsey appeared on the landing. "I'm disappointed, Jonah Blackstone."

Jonah tried to ignore the taunt as he focused on the next location, this time the main floor. What he saw almost ruined his desperate idea. More of the agent's men had swarmed inside and converged on Kevin.

The idea of going for help himself entered Jonah's mind as he changed his destination and reappeared on a catwalk high above the mill's floor. He could get to Marcus and the others, but Jonah was afraid Ramsey could escape before the Alliance returned. Desperation began to mount and he forced himself to stay with the plan.

"Really, child." Ramsey scoffed as soon as he appeared on the catwalk. "Haven't we done this dance before? You can't escape me. Unless…"

Jonah didn't waste time listening to the rest of Ramsey's words. He began running and phased at the same time. He reappeared in the office section, already in a full sprint. He had just reached the stairs at the far end of that level when Agent Ramsey appeared behind him.

Ramsey lunged. Jonah dodged and leapt down the entire row of steps to avoid the agent's grasp. He slammed onto the lower landing harder than expected, but fear propelled him as he leapt down the next set of steps to the ground floor.

Agent Ramsey leaned over the railing and called after him, "I don't care if your cousin saves the boy. You are the trophy, Jonah Blackstone."

Jonah phased to the third level landing again. Only then did he realize the mistake. He'd settled into a pattern. Ramsey appeared right next to him and swung with a blurred punch. The power of the blow to Jonah's shoulder sent him sliding across the metal floor and smacking against the guardrail.

Ramsey blurred into motion and stopped right over him. "I'm going to enjoy cutting every bit of useful information out of you." He grabbed Jonah by the front of his shirt and hissed, "Now, I take you to my master."

Shoving Jonah against the stone wall, Ramsey turned him roughly around, and twisted his right arm back. The agent whispered right in Jonah's ear, "You and your cousin are nothing more than common criminals."

An explosion erupted from below, followed by several anguished grunts. The force of it rattled the ground. Jonah saw the flash of light reflected off the grimy walls, but couldn't see anything else.

The commotion drew Ramsey's attention. He dragged Jonah along with him to the railing to look over. Jonah twisted around in time to witness the fading effects of a blue wave of magical energy. At the center, Kevin knelt on hands and knees, breathing hard. Around him was a wide circle of downed Grimnions.

More rushed in and began using stun prods to shock Kevin into submission. Ramsey laughed so hard, his entire body shook. The movement caused pain to ripple up Jonah's twisted arm.

"The Fallen Reaper has fallen. Next we'll round up your cousin and that strange boy. Perhaps I'll make you watch as I kill them, hmm?"

Ramsey produced another pair of the strange cuffs and snapped them open. At that moment, Jonah felt the change in the air. It was different from someone phasing, which produced a slight pressure from displaced air. This was more of a pulling sensation, the same kind created by a vortex.

When the agent paused, Jonah thought he also sensed the coming vortex until vibrations rattled the metal floor. Something large bounded up the stairs. Within seconds, a huge Grim Hound sailed through the air, right at Ramsey. The beast succeeded in knocking the startled agent away from Jonah.

The cuffs clattered to the ground. With the pressure gone, Jonah whirled around and stared in awe as the Grim Hound snapped and ripped at the agent's arms. Ramsey phased before the beast could tear him apart. The Grim Hound let out a snarl of frustration and bounded down the steps. Jonah wondered if the hound could sense the trail a person left behind when they phased.

He peeked over the railing, hoping to see the beast tearing into Ramsey. Instead, he gaped in surprise as at least a dozen men in black pants and tunics streamed out of the supernatural gateway. The new arrivals engaged Ramsey's guards.

Jonah thought this development was the most welcoming sight at the moment. If not for the red skulls on the left breast, which seemed to be unnaturally bright, the two groups were indistinguishable.

As the men clashed, Jonah caught sight of Kevin on the far side of the mill floor. The young Fallen Reaper knocked out the guard covering him and phased away. When he didn't reappear inside the mill, Jonah knew Kevin went for help.

A sound to his right drew his attention. Jonah prepared himself to phase and only relaxed when Lynn reached the landing with Mike in tow.

The railing began to vibrate. Jonah backed away just as two of Ramsey's men vaulted over. They came at him, both slicing the air with handheld scythes.

"Jonah!" Lynn tossed him a blade just in time. He activated it and held off the first deadly swings from his attacker.

Lynn released Mike, whirled like a pro, and met the second goon. He scored a vicious slash across Lynn's right forearm.

She muffled her scream, ducked under his follow-up swing, and kicked him in the midsection. The man hit the railing and tumbled over.

Jonah blocked another slice from his attacker and dived to avoid two swings. He rolled to his feet and maneuvered himself around so the Grimnion's back was to Lynn. Only then did he noticed her cradling her injured arm.

Before Jonah could think of another move, the large Grim Hound roared up the stairs again, ignoring Lynn and Mike.

The Seeker's Compass **519**

Jonah's attacker sensed the danger and tried to turn, too late. The Hound managed to sink its teeth into his back and lift the man off the ground. With a violent twist of its large head, the Grim Hound snapped the henchman's back.

Mike's already pale face went paler as the beast dropped the dead man to the ground. Lynn looked equally as horrified. The Grim Hound snapped its massive jaws at them but didn't attack.

Jonah registered what bothered him from the moment he saw the beast. The Grim Hound had saved his life, like it had been commanded to do that. "Why'd you help me?"

The Grim Hound gazed at him with its red-in-red pupils. It opened its mouth, displaying the double row of sharp teeth only to let out a mournful growl.

Jonah stepped closer, not sensing menace, just curiosity. He understood in that moment. This was the same Grim Hound that had come to Morningside Drive. He had dreamt he was in the creature's head. *But how could it be the same one?*

Emily, one of his godfather's team members, had killed that Grim Hound by cutting off its head in the fight at Deyanira's chamber. Jonah concentrated on the beast. It stirred, keeping the eye contact and cocking its head sideways as if recognizing him.

Jonah was sure it was the same Grim Hound. Apparently chopping off its head just destroyed the physical body and sent the supernatural creature back across to the Afterworld. Probably until someone summoned it again, Jonah concluded. If that was true, then how did you kill a Grim Hound? He'd have to ask Marcus about this, if they survived.

He thought of reaching out to touch the beast, but the Grim Hound's snout lifted up into the air, sniffing, and then it whirled and thundered down the stairs.

Lynn overcame her shock first and pointed at Jonah while favoring her bleeding arm. "Get us out of here, hero."

Mike, who had moved closer to help Lynn, gasped and pointed below. "Look!"

Lynn and Jonah rushed to the railing.

Deyanira stood in front of her vortex in the personae of Neera. Today she wore a flowing black dress with sleeves that flared along the ends. Her red hair was curly and it cascaded to her shoulders.

She surveyed the continued fighting like a warrior queen. A stray shot from one of Ramsey's men zipped her way. Deyanira waved her hand and the shot flared against a protective barrier.

Meanwhile, the Grim Hound bounded across the plant floor and to her side. It made several strange growls, audible over the noise of the fighting.

Deyanira's gaze shifted at once up to the third floor landing, where Jonah stood. His knees began to shake, but his Death Sense was quiet. She meant him no harm.

"Jonah, do you think she sent the Grim Hound to help you?" Mike's quiet question shocked him.

At that moment, Agent Ramsey appeared in the midst of the fighting below, blades out and ready to engage Deyanira. It was if the sight of the KIN had pushed all other thoughts out of the man's deranged head.

Deyanira pointed a slender finger at Ramsey. "Where's the courier?"

"That's none of your business, witch."

"Hasn't anyone told you the Blackstone child is more trouble than he's worth?"

Jonah bristled at her comment at the same moment his Death Sense spiked.

Ramsey signaled, and stun blasts arched up from the floor and toward Jonah's position. He, Lynn, and Mike stumbled back, but the discharges exploded against a protective shield that shouldn't have been there.

Deyanira laughed. "I should have known."

When Ramsey risked a glance toward the third floor landing, Deyanira used his momentary distraction to attack.

She whirled her hands, conjuring two balls of green supernatural fire. The sudden flare of light blinded Jonah for a second.

Agent Ramsey weaved his blades in swiping motions as he shouted, "Kulinda!"

The Seeker's Compass

The balls of supernatural fire shattered into flaming fragments that drifted harmlessly to either side.

Jonah gawked at the display of power until someone nudged him in the back. Kevin stood right behind him with Marcus, Rubio, and Trueblood.

"Get Jonah and the others out of here." Marcus's voice and face shook with repressed anger and worry.

The adults positioned themselves at the railing, blocking Jonah's view of the battle. Despite wanting to object, Jonah also knew it was dangerous to disobey his godfather at this moment. He yanked the compass out of his shirt and waited as Mike and Lynn locked arms with him.

At the last minute, Kevin noticed what Jonah was doing. "Don't use the compass." He blurred into motion and gripped Jonah's arm a second before the compass activated and the mill disappeared.

CHAPTER TWENTY-EIGHT
THE LECTURE

Mike reached for Lynn's bloody arm as soon as they reached at the hideaway. "You're hurt."

Lynn jerked the arm away with a grunt of pain. "I'm fine," she managed through clenched teeth. She nodded toward Jonah. "Take my blades. I need to sit."

He pulled back the adjacent bushes to reveal the brick stairs to the hideaway. Lynn consented to Mike's help in order to remain on her feet. They maneuvered past Jonah and through the gap in the bushes.

"Hold up." Kevin blocked Jonah's way. "Why'd you use the compass?"

"That was the plan." Jonah grabbed Lynn's discarded blades.

Kevin scowled. "That was before things changed. We should have phased back to the clubhouse."

"I didn't know. Besides, it's better to be safe, right?" Jonah squeezed around the older boy and hurried to catch Mike and Lynn.

Kevin grumbled and followed to the courtyard above. "Has Marcus been here before?"

Lynn opened her mouth to say something at the same time her strength gave out. She collapsed on the edge of the closest bench. Mike hovered over her until she shook her head.

Mike recoiled. "I just wanted to help."

"I know, Mike. Thanks, but I'm fine." She waved him off.

The Seeker's Compass

Mike shoved his hands in his pockets as he plopped on the second bench beside Jonah.

Kevin stormed over to Lynn. "I don't care what you say to Mike. You're not okay." He ripped the bottom half of his shirt, leaving his abdomen exposed, and knelt in front of Lynn. "Hold still." Ignoring her protests, he wrapped Lynn's arm with the shirt and tied it with practiced motions.

Once he finished, Kevin whirled to look at Jonah. "She needs a doctor."

"No." Lynn shook her head. "I'm staying until this is over."

Kevin ripped off the remains of his shirt in frustration. "You're as bad as Jonah."

"Hey, we were in this together, remember?" Jonah's flare of irritation with Kevin subsided when he saw the way the boy balled the ruined shirt in his hands. He was nervous, and Jonah could guess why. They both knew Marcus well enough to dread the coming storm.

Meanwhile, Mike sucked in a breath and reached for Jonah's face. "You're hurt too."

Jonah wiped the dried blood off his mouth and wiggled his sore nose. "Ramsey threw me around."

"He's insane," Mike agreed while knocking dirt out of Jonah's picky hair.

Lynn watched with a pained smirk on her face. Jonah's own face warmed.

Mike didn't seem to care as he continued the inspection. When he finished, Jonah turned the tables. "Did he hurt you?"

"No." Mike hugged himself, rocking back and forth.

For a moment, Jonah feared his friend would start muttering to himself again. But Mike seemed over that now. "What about your ankle?"

Mike glanced down at his leg. "It's fine."

Jonah didn't believe his buddy. He could see two dark cuts on the right side of Mike's shirt. Both were stained red.

Jonah touched the shirt. "Don't lie to me."

Mike covered the cuts with his hand, keeping Jonah from prodding the spot. "He wanted to know how you got away and why he couldn't follow."

Jonah's insides froze. "Did you tell him about the compass?"

"I don't think so." Mike hugged himself again. "When the pain got too bad, I blacked out. But when I came around, Ramsey had a spooked look on his face." Mike winced. "He only did it twice."

Lynn cradled her arm, head cocked to the side. "I bet it was the eyes. They were glowing back in the mill."

"They were?" Mike touched his face. "What about now?"

Jonah peered at his buddy's eyes. "No. They're not anymore." He pointed at Mike's scorched left-side shirt pocket.

Mike reached inside the pocket and pulled out the Enhancer. "Oh no."

The device was blackened and ruined.

Jonah nodded, recalling Trevor's claim. "The Grimnion's scythe hit it. You took a jolt from the Enhancer."

"That's why my eyes were glowing?" Mike waved his hand in front of his own eyes, blinking. "I doubt it was supposed to work that way."

Kevin watched the entire exchange with a sour look on his face. "Are you three finished? Can we go now?"

The Fallen Reaper cursed under his breath when his cell phone rang. Kevin yanked it open while spearing Jonah with an irritated glare. "We're at the hideaway. Lynn's hurt."

Marcus, Trueblood, and Rex appeared in the courtyard before Kevin could even put away the phone. Jonah's godfather motioned at once to Lynn.

Rex hurried over. "I'll get you to a hospital." Lynn started to object, but that was cut short by a grimace of pain. "We have a plan in motion for this type of thing," Rex explained, helping her to her feet before they phased away.

Trueblood led Mike to the vacated bench and spoke to him in a quiet tone.

Marcus stood over Jonah like a storm cloud. "What am I going to do with you? Your actions were totally reckless! I know I'm not your father but…" He trailed off as he raised his balled fists and let out a frustrated growl.

The Seeker's Compass 525

"Mike's my best friend," Jonah began.

"Of course he is, but I'm supposed to protect you as best I can. You should have trusted me. Frankly Jonah, I think it shows a lack of respect."

Marcus turned on Kevin. "And you're a full member of the Alliance and should have known better." He took a deep breath. "The Council's waiting for you at Headquarters." Marcus handed Kevin a talisman. "I advise putting on a shirt."

Kevin's eyes widened in embarrassment. He met Jonah's worried gaze briefly, then nodded to Marcus and phased.

With Kevin gone, Marcus signaled Trueblood. She rose and motioned for Mike to stand beside her. "You should get home to your family."

Mike hesitated. "What about Jonah?"

"He'll be fine."

The look of doubt on Mike's face got to Jonah. "Go on. I'll catch up later."

Mike hugged himself and waited while Trueblood opened a vortex. He waved to Jonah as the mage urged him into the opening.

Marcus didn't say anything for several quiet moments after the vortex closed. When he spoke, his voice was calmer, but still tinged with anger. "You want to be treated like an adult, Jonah? You want to be treated as part of the team? Well, team members check in and let the rest know what's going on. We share information so we can all be prepared to help."

"I know about teamwork." It was dangerous to argue with his godfather, but Jonah couldn't stop himself. "You didn't tell the Alliance about Trevor."

Marcus reared back, surprised. "I had good reasons for it."

"So did we."

"Jonah…"

"You were impressed with us yesterday."

Marcus covered his face with his hands. He lowered them after a moment to reveal a tired expression. "I won't lie. I was impressed with you and the others." He raised his hand and ticked off his points. "But in this case, you failed to see the benefit of marshaling all resources to your advantage or accurately using the knowledge you have. That's a lack of experience. You and Lynn will make good leaders one day, if you two can learn that."

Jonah crossed his arms, considering his godfather's words.

"I know you have skills and can fight," Marcus continued. "Even so, you could have been overwhelmed and without backup. If we had known about the plan-"

"You would have said no." Jonah shrank away from the fury radiating off his godfather.

"You, young man, were lucky." Marcus's chest heaved up and down. "Perhaps luckier than most, but lucky nonetheless." He pointed to where Lynn had been sitting. Jonah was shocked at the blood-stained piece of shirt Kevin had left behind. A pit formed in his stomach.

"Lynn can't heal herself. You're going to get your cousins and friends in trouble one day and not be able to handle it." Marcus leaned over Jonah. "Do you understand me?"

"Yes, sir. I understand."

Marcus stood tall. "You have your father in you, that's for sure. He would go off and do things on his own." Marcus stopped to take deep breaths. "This whole affair has everyone acting strange. Rex messes with a mortal, you go off half-cocked, and Kevin risks his job."

The barb about his father stung Jonah. "I wasn't alone."

"That makes it even more dangerous. You owe it to those who follow you to make sure you've done everything you can to protect them from harm." He leaned down to force Jonah to look at him, the first time he'd done that in a while. "I thought after last year, we had an understanding."

Jonah's stomach turned itself into knots because of the disappointment on his godfather's face.

When he didn't keep yelling, Jonah began to see that his godfather was unsure what to do next. He glanced around, searching for something else to talk about. "My dad told you about this hideaway? Is that how you could phase here?"

"Actually, I've been here before. In fact," Marcus gestured around him, "I became a member of the Alliance Council about where you're sitting."

The Seeker's Compass **527**

His words pushed through Jonah's embarrassment from being fussed at, and a flood of memories opened. Jonah saw the moment to which Marcus referred. He had witnessed it the previous summer when the Protector's Ring took him to the Afterworld.

"My dad gave you his badge, and made you take his place on the Alliance Council." Jonah's voice caught and he stopped. He could read the unspoken question on Marcus' face. "I went to the Afterworld last summer. The Deliverer showed me records of my parents. I saw that moment."

Marcus swallowed and stared at his feet for several quiet moments. "Jonah, the Afterworld archivists can only store the records of mortals, in their first life. The lives of the Fallen Ones aren't recorded. It's one reason our kind is forbidden."

"Then how did I see those memories?"

"It was the Deliverer. He was here."

Jonah's eyes widened with understanding. "His spirit was in the Protector's Ring. But what about the mortals in the Alliance? Can their memories be accessed when they die?"

"No, they can't," Marcus answered. "When a mortal dies and moves on, their soul is intact and their memories go along with them. All the Archivists do is record the birth, type and means of death, and other dry facts about the life. They never have access to more personal memories unless a person chooses to share."

Marcus rubbed his hands together in a nervous motion. "That being said, there're rumors of a way for an individual's memories to be viewed without permission. It was whispered by those in the Afterworld that the Grim Reaper trapped and imprisoned certain souls. Through use of ancient magic, he's able to siphon off their memories and view them."

Jonah shivered despite the summer temperatures. "Couldn't he do that with any soul?"

Marcus shook his head. "Even the Rulers of the Afterworld have to follow some rules. The vast majority of mortal souls are beyond being tampered with. But in select cases, he can ensnare the soul if he personally kills the individual. It's a violation."

The more Marcus explained, the more Jonah wanted to be anywhere other than the darkening hideaway. This was downright creepy. The only up side was that his godfather didn't sound angry anymore.

Marcus peered at Jonah in the gathering gloom. "I think we've talked enough about this." He raised a questioning eyebrow. Jonah nodded. "If our story is to be told, it'll be written by someone else."

Jonah's godfather drew nearer and opened his long coat to reveal the golden Alliance badge clipped to an inside pocket. He unhooked it and held the badge in his palm.

Jonah's hand shook, as much from the recent excitement as from nervousness, as he gripped the badge. At once, a tingle of familiarity shot up his arm. "Wow."

Marcus nodded. "Your father owned that for many years. Being who you are, I'm not surprised you can sense his lingering touch on it." He looked off. "I considered having the Alliance make me a new one."

"Why?" The thought of his godfather discarding something that his dad entrusted to him made Jonah angry.

Marcus held up his hands. "You don't understand. I wanted to give the badge to you, Jonah, when you came of age."

The indignation leaked out of Jonah, replaced by a little shame. "I'm sorry." As soon as Jonah said it, the tense, raw concern over his friends and the crazy agent flowed out. A tear rolled down his face. "I'm sorry Lynn's hurt and Kevin's in trouble and..." Jonah let the rest go unsaid. Otherwise, he wouldn't be able to stop crying.

Marcus sat beside him on the bench and patted Jonah on the shoulder. "You're special. You're Reaper and human."

Jonah wiped his watery eyes to look into his godfather's face. "You mean a half-breed?"

Marcus frowned. "No, I mean in one being. As you grow older, more people will follow you. Most won't understand, and some will even fear." Marcus did something he rarely did: he allowed his own emotions to show.

Jonah sensed utter belief in his godfather. It was humbling. "You think I'm a hero."

The Seeker's Compass

"I know it. That's a powerful thing for a young man to accept and experience." Marcus tightened his grip on Jonah's shoulder. "Until then, I have to watch over and protect you. So do me a huge favor and stop making it so damn difficult."

The edge had returned to his godfather's voice. Once Marcus released the iron grip, Jonah leaned forward, resting his elbows on his knees, and gazing at his dad's Council badge.

He considered Trevor's sacrifice, coming here while knowing he might never get back. Jonah's throat tightened when he recalled his mom's last words to him. She and his dad did everything out of love for him.

Everything Marcus told him clicked into place and rocked Jonah. So much depended on what he did with his power.

His bottom lip trembled with the weight of that knowledge. "I'm sorry." He meant it with every bone in his body. Speaking those two simple words made him feel hollowed out.

Marcus sat straighter. "The fact that you said that means everything." He placed a hand over the badge. "Now is as good a time as any to have the replacement made." He lifted the badge from Jonah's slack grip. "I should hold on to this one for now."

Jonah didn't want to part with it, but he trusted Marcus to keep his word. After all, his godfather truly believed in his destiny.

CHAPTER TWENTY-NINE
LYNN'S ROOM

The hum of different, overlapping voices greeted Jonah when he and Marcus returned to the clubhouse. All the conversations came to an abrupt halt as Robert, Wick, and the Alliance members focused on Jonah.

He gulped, suspecting everyone was talking about him. He pushed that aside, realizing someone was missing. "Where's Mike?"

Rex chuckled and ruffled his untidy blond hair. "He put up a fuss, but I took him home. That kid has a lot of spunk."

Good, Jonah thought and then he met Robert's worried gaze. "What about Lynn?"

"She's at the hospital, getting stitches." Robert looked miserable.

Marcus gestured to Rex. "You should take Jonah and Robert home. I don't want them riding their bikes this evening. I'll escort Wick."

Rex nodded and motioned the boys to move closer.

But Jonah refused to budge. "Wait a minute. What happened after we left the mill?"

Marcus leaned against the back of the sofa. "Agent Ramsey ran off after a brief fight with Deyanira. We think he went through the portal and to the Afterworld."

"Chicken." Rex smacked his beefy fists together in disgust. "Big talk when it comes to hurting kids." He glanced at Robert and Wick. "No offense."

The Seeker's Compass

Jonah's eyes widened. "He'll tell the Grand Oracle about me."

"Probably," Marcus agreed. "But remember, he doesn't know anything about the back door. And he didn't get the compass."

"He'll be lucky to keep his head." Rex chuckled at the very idea.

Marcus frowned at his fellow Alliance member. "Take them home, Rex."

"I already called home." Robert waved his phone.

"Still..." Marcus stood.

"What else happened?" Jonah speared his godfather with a steady gaze. When Marcus looked as if he would refuse to answer, Jonah added, "You told me to come to you."

Marcus frowned. "You know that's not what I meant." He paused, noting everyone's curious expressions. "We had a little talk with Deyanira."

Robert and Wick were as shocked as Jonah.

He had a sick feeling what the sorceress asked. "She wanted Trevor and you told her no."

Marcus subjected Jonah to a Reaper Stare. "She says you owe her one. You care to explain?"

"I don't know why she helped us." That was true. Jonah didn't know why her Grim Hound saved his life. Twice.

Rex ignored the silent battle between Jonah and his godfather. "We suspect Deyanira was in a right state with the mole. Nothing like a little in-fighting with the enemies."

Jonah shifted his focus to Rex to prevent his godfather from looking him in the eye any longer. "But how do you know that?"

"Deyanira didn't know about the courier when you came across her." Marcus blinked, ending his Reaper Stare. "She's the Grim Reaper's main minion in the mortal world yet wasn't aware of what was happening, so..."

Jonah loved the conclusion. "She was out of the loop."

Marcus nodded. When Jonah and the others started to ask more questions, he held up a hand. "That's enough for tonight."

"But what'll we tell my mom and dad?" Robert asked.

Jonah perked up when he heard the question and nodded his head in agreement.

"We told your father that Lynn injured herself while exploring the old mill." Marcus fixed his gaze on Jonah and Robert. "And we're making sure there's no evidence of what really happened." He lifted his chin to look at Rex. "Take them home."

*

No one in the Hightower house was interested in sleeping, least of all Lynn. Aunt Imma alternated between talking with Uncle James and checking on her. Robert played Jonah in a lackluster video game. His thoughts clearly fixated on his sister's injury.

When Aunt Imma returned to the living room for the fifth time, complaining about Lynn not resting, Robert had enough. He threw the game controller aside and went to hover in his sister's doorway. Jonah joined him.

Lynn's room was generally off limits to the boys. So Jonah found it interesting whenever he got a peek inside. The soft touches were a surprise, like a small stuffed teddy on a shelf. But Lynn didn't go in for pinks and lavenders. Her room was in softer shades of red and orange.

Numerous posters were on the walls, a mix of music groups, athletic stars, and entertainers. And of course, Lynn had a shelf full of her sports trophies as well as academic awards. She lay propped up in bed, her bandage-wrapped arm cradled on a soft pillow.

Lynn motioned them both inside. Robert sat on the edge of the bed while Jonah leaned in the doorway. Her face was drained of color and her eyes closed to mere slits.

She was tired, Jonah decided, despite her refusal to rest. That got to him. "I'm sorry you're hurt."

Lynn waved away the apology. "What happened?"

Jonah wanted to tell her, but Robert was faster. "Mike went home and Deyanira said Jonah owed her a favor. Can you believed that?"

When Robert paused for a breath, Jonah added, "Oh, Kevin was called back to HQ to talk with the Council. He's in trouble."

The Seeker's Compass 533

Lynn blinked several times, forcing her drooping eyes to remain open. "They should give Kevin a medal."

Robert snorted.

But Lynn wasn't laughing. She watched Jonah with a tired, yet shrewd expression. "I wonder why she helped you, considering the pain she caused before?"

Jonah shrugged but began to seriously consider the possibility.

Robert laughed again. "Please, Lynn. She didn't help Jonah. Marcus said she was just pissed about being left out of the action."

"Not true, brother." Lynn lowered her voice when they heard a creak from the hallway.

Uncle James stepped into view and peeked inside Lynn's room. "Just checking."

"I'm fine, Dad." Lynn gave him a tired smile.

Uncle James motioned to Jonah and Robert. "You boys don't stay too long. She needs to rest. And that's an order."

As soon as he left, Lynn's face turned serious again. "As I was saying, Deyanira sent her Grim Hound to help Jonah."

Robert's jaw dropped. "No way."

"Yes. Weird, isn't it? I can almost believe she likes Jonah."

"Our little cousin, huh?"

"Funny, Lynn," Jonah frowned.

A little fire creeped into Lynn's face and posture. "You don't think she sees that as a favor?"

"No." The answer was immediate because Jonah didn't want to accept the truth. "Well, maybe."

"That's a scary thought." Robert shivered.

"Well, we can deal with that later." Lynn nudged her brother. "Did you two talk to Mike? I want to know why Ramsey killed his partner."

"Mike told me and Wick. The agents got in a big fight." Robert pointed at Jonah. "About him. Harris wanted to make the trade and take Trevor to the mole. Ramsey thought Jonah was more important and would help him get back his old position in the Afterworld."

"They fought and Ramsey killed him?" Jonah could imagine the deranged agent doing that.

"Yep." Robert cringed. "And Mike saw all that."

Lynn rotated her head on the overstuffed pillows to look at Jonah. "I'm sorry to say it, but everything revolves around you, Jonah."

"Tell me about it," he scowled, not liking his friend and family suffering because of him. His godfather's words made him feel even worse. "Marcus shouted that at me after you left the hideaway."

Lynn's eyes opened with interest and Robert turned on the bed to face him. Jonah didn't see any way to avoid telling his cousins about the lecture. He did omit the more embarrassing parts of the encounter.

"Ouch, little cousin." Robert leaned back on the bed, careful not to crush Lynn's leg.

"He's right, Jonah. I can sense that." Lynn nodded and settled into the pillows.

Robert grinned at his sister even though her eyes were closed. "You mean like your feeling that you, Jonah, and Kevin should rescue Mike?"

Lynn suddenly sat forward and shoved the side of her brother's head with enough strength to almost push him off the bed. "I was right, smart butt."

"You were lucky that Deyanira showed up. What if..." Robert's smug expression morphed into awe. "You didn't see that, did you?"

"No, but I knew it would work out, somehow." Lynn rubbed her forehead. "My intuition's gotten stronger since Jonah came here."

Robert made a cross with his index fingers. "You two are spooky."

Lynn bumped him with her leg. "Says the boy who can pick thoughts out of people's heads."

"I can't pick any thought, they have to concentrate and... I draw... it. Okay, I'm a freak, too."

"Say that a little louder." Lynn glared at her brother. "I don't think Mom and Dad heard you." She reached for his head and Robert batted her hand away.

The Seeker's Compass

Lynn closed her eyes and settled back. Jonah thought she was asleep until she spoke in a soft, drowsy voice. "You, me, Jonah, Kevin, Wick, and Mike are all important. I can just tell." She yawned. "And Trevor. Don't forget Trevor."

When she lapsed into silence and didn't move, Robert reached over her to pluck the empty water glass off the bedside table. "That took long enough."

Jonah smiled. "I'm gonna tell her you said that."

Robert shrugged as he turned out Lynn's light and ushered Jonah into the hallway. Once he closed the door, Robert headed to the kitchen to talk with his parents.

Jonah yawned again and decided to turn in. The exhaustion made his legs feel like rubber. Although he meant to stretch out on his bed, he collapsed on it in a wave of drowsiness. He didn't even care about undressing. Instead, he rolled onto his back, trying to think about everything that happened, but his mind refused to focus or cooperate.

Bowing to the inevitable, Jonah gave up and welcomed the buzz in his head until he fell asleep.

*

Cold.

That was the sensation Jonah experienced in his sleep. Then his eyes opened and he understood why. He stood in a dismal environment, overlooking an expanse of frozen tundra. Overhead, the bleak grey of an overcast sky added to the general gloominess. He turned on the spot, knowing he was in a dream-walk again.

Frigid cold began seeping through his socks, forcing Jonah to dance around on the spot. He stood on a solid piece of twisting rock that jutted out of the icy ground below like a tree root. He'd never seen anything like it. Other formations dotted the landscape, but this one was the largest. About twenty feet from Jonah, a portion of the rock had been sheered off, making a large, irregular platform.

Jonah shivered and blocked his face from a sudden spray of ice crystals carried on the wind. All the while, he tried to keep his feet in motion. It didn't help. The icy bits stung his exposed skin as he hugged himself, trying to keep warm. This was weird. In all the other dream-walks, he was more like a ghost, having the ability to float through walls but never feeling anything.

Why could he feel everything now? Before he could puzzle it out, he felt the change in air pressure behind him. Fear propelled Jonah as he scampered along the rough rock surface, ignoring the sharp jabs to his soles, and found a shallow crevice in which to hide.

He rose onto his knees to peek over the rim just as a short person appeared on the makeshift platform of the outcropping. Jonah squinted through the increased wind blasts to make out the features.

The newcomer was clothed in a reaper's long coat, black gloves and hat, and he wore a face mask. The eyes were the only part of the face visible.

Could this be a meeting place, Jonah wondered. As if in answer, he sensed the change in pressure again. Deyanira phased into view in her full Reaper form. Her hair was all but gone except for a lone straggly red braid on the back. The ritualistic scars that marked her as one of the KIN were visible. And her blood red robes bellowed behind in the wind as she stalked toward the waiting figure.

Jonah's knees quivered as the reality of his precarious situation became obvious. If Deyanira was in true form that meant he was in the Afterworld, the domain of the Undead. All the other dream-walks occurred in places on the mortal side. A ghost in the Afterworld was just another spirit. Not only could he feel things, this also meant he wasn't invisible, either.

Jonah went still because Deyanira had proved before that she could sense him if he moved. Well, this time she could also see him just fine. He prayed that wouldn't happen.

The short man jabbed a finger at the her. "You stupid witch!"

Deyanira's hands blurred as she conjured supernatural fire and flung it at the man.

He was ready, producing two Reaper blades. "Kulinda!" He batted the fire aside.

"Have a care, mole." Deyanira shot lightning at the man.

He used a shield to block the attack.

The Seeker's Compass **537**

Deyanira laughed.

That angered the man even more. "Why'd you save the boy?"

"I didn't save him." Deyanira pointed a slender finger at the mole. "I taught you a lesson."

"What lesson was that, witch?"

Deyanira raised her hands, energy playing around her fingertips. "You call me witch one more time and I'll kill you."

"The Grim Reaper won't like that." The mole thumped his chest with a gloved fist. "I'm valuable to him."

"You're a fool." Deyanira lowered her hands. "The idiocy of using Hunters should be evident to you by now. There's a reason they were banished to the mortal realm. They're all unstable."

"I had Ramsey under control." The short man began pacing back and forth, forcing Deyanira to turn and keep the distance between them. "If you hadn't interfered, we'd have the boy and the courier."

"As I said, you're a complete fool. Ramsey didn't care about the courier. He wanted the Blackstone child." Deyanira tapped the side of her bald, scarred head. "Think, mole. Why would he do that unless he wanted to impress his master?"

The short man stopped his constant movement. "Impossible. Ramsey hated the Grand Oracle for banishing him…"

"He's never abandoned the desire to return home in glory. What better achievement than to bring his master the boy who commanded a Protector's Ring?"

"But the courier–"

"He'll die in the mortal world soon enough. If the rebellion against the Grand Oracle continues, so much the better for my master. But at least the Alliance will have lost its Afterworld connection. That was your mission, nothing more."

The mole pointed a blade at Deyanira. "Don't lecture me. You failed the Grim Reaper last summer. There are others within the KIN who are on the rise."

Deyanira conjured more flame. "Who? The Rasmussen siblings? Eh? And you decided to go around me and work with them?" She launched the fire at the ground around the man's feet.

Caught by surprise, the mole yelled and stumbled back.

"Pathetic," Deyanira scoffed. "I warned the master you weren't a good choice to send into the midst of the Alliance."

She raised her hand and the mole prepared to defend himself with his blades. "Tell me," Deyanira continued, "where's Ramsey now?"

"I-I don't know," the mole admitted. "The Alliance thinks he crossed over."

"The Alliance thinks," Deyanira mocked the man. "Ramsey didn't cross through the portal."

"Well, I didn't know that. The Council is letting Marcus keep details secret. I'm being exposed here."

Deyanira threw back her head and laughed. Her red ponytail swayed with her amusement. "That's your own fault." She sobered. "I suggest you find a way to get the details before you're no longer useful to us."

"But..."

"Ramsey used you, mole. He's still in the mortal realm and his goal remains young Blackstone." Deyanira whirled and phased from the platform.

Jonah let out a relieved breath when he awoke in his own bedroom. He'd have to warn Marcus about Ramsey.

The Seeker's Compass

CHAPTER THIRTY
KEVIN'S STORY

Not again.

Lynn and Aunt Imma's raised voices awakened Jonah from a hard but sound morning sleep, the kind of slumber you slip into after staying awake most of the previous night.

Throwing off his covers, Jonah tried to rub the sleep out of his eyes as he entered the family room. Lynn sat on the sofa, her bad arm propped up by a couple of cushions. Her uninjured arm was raised in agitation as she argued with her mother.

"I don't have to sit around."

"Yes you do." Aunt Imma placed a bowl of chopped fruit on a cushion. "The doctor said you had to be careful not to pull out the stitches. That means taking it easy."

Lynn had to gulp down a mouthful of fruit in order to yell at her mom, who had gone back into the kitchen. "But I'll go crazy just sitting around the house."

"Robert and Jonah can keep you company."

"Mom!" Robert dropped his spoon in his cereal. He sat at the kitchen table, wearing his normal morning cut-offs and oversized t-shirt. "That's like a punishment for me."

Aunt Imma turned from the stove with her spatula raised, temporarily abandoning the scrambled eggs she was cooking. "Robert Hightower, you'll help your sister."

By then, Jonah had ducked into the family room. "Aunt Imma, I had plans with Mike this morning."

Aunt Imma shook her head as she slid Robert's eggs onto a plate. "Jonah, your cousin is hurt."

"Mom, I'll stay home until noon." Lynn caught Jonah's eyes and nodded. "I have research to do for Dad, anyway. Don't make Robert and Jonah stay. That's punishment for me."

"Oh, Lynn." Aunt Imma noticed Jonah's sad expression and gave in. "Fine. I'll call in to work. I can be a few hours late."

Lynn couldn't hide her dismay.

Jonah grinned as he hurried off to shower and dress.

Lynn stopped him just as he reached the back door. "Hey, we're having a Practice Club meeting late this afternoon. Rico's gonna come by and get me once mom goes to work."

"Okay. I'll let Mike know." Jonah slipped outside.

*

The Littletons lived in a cul-de-sac at the opposite end of Morningside Drive. Their split-level home was painted robin's egg blue and always reminded Jonah of a beautiful blue sky. It was one reason he had painted a wall in his room the same color.

Punctual Mike stood at the top of their sloping, U-shaped driveway with his bike in hand.

"How're you feeling?" Jonah asked as he brought his bike to a stop.

"Fine." Mike glanced back at his house. "You think someone from the Alliance watched the house all night?"

Jonah hadn't considered that before. "I doubt it." He debated mentioning Deyanira's revelations from the dream-walk until he caught the relief on Mike's face. "You weren't scared last night?"

"No." Mike toyed with the gear shifter on his bike. When he caught Jonah watching, he stopped. "Why'd you and Marcus take so long to come back?"

Jonah hesitated at the change of topic. "He fussed at me."

The Seeker's Compass **541**

"I knew it. That was a dangerous thing you guys did."

"You wish we didn't?"

"Of course not." Mike hopped on his own bike and started down the street. When Jonah caught up, he asked, "So, what did your godfather say?"

Jonah repeated the details of Marcus's lecture as they rode to the teen center. He included the parts he had skipped over with Lynn and Robert, grateful for a best friend who would keep these personal details private.

He began to rethink that, considering Mike apparently didn't feel the same way, not if he kept parts of his own life secret. As they paused at a stop sign, Jonah decided to broach the subject.

That's when he sensed the change in air pressure. An involuntary spike of fear shot through Jonah. He chided himself. It couldn't be Ramsey because his Death Sense didn't twinge. Whoever the person, they must be a member of the Alliance.

Mike noticed. "Something wrong?"

Jonah shook his head, reasoning that his godfather had acted on the news about Ramsey remaining in the mortal world. "Let's see what's up at the clubhouse."

*

Despite the chance of losing the attic, Jonah had never seen the space busier. Rex talked with yet another group of Alliance people near the attic window.

Jonah began to think their attic clubhouse was a weird sort of tourist attraction for the Alliance personnel. *Come and see where the boy who used the Protector's Ring hangs out! Just fifteen bucks.* He grinned, causing Mike to give him an inquisitive glance.

As he turned away, Jonah noticed Trueblood standing across the old card table from Wick and Robert, who must have arrived just before them. The Seeker's box was open, and Wick held his second bracelet in his hands. He was in the process of giving it to Trueblood.

Jonah hurried to them. "Why're you taking Wick's bracelet? It wasn't his fault we used the other one to rescue Mike. Don't blame him." He knew something was off when everyone stared at him in confusion.

Rex let out a hearty chortle in the background.

Trueblood's mouth tweaked with a suppressed smile.

Wick flashed Jonah a lopsided grin. "It's not about that. Trueblood and Rubio are impressed and want to examine it at HQ."

"Yeah, little cousin." Robert worked to hide his own grin. "They asked to borrow it."

"Oh." Jonah's building anger cooled in seconds, leaving him embarrassed. "Sorry."

Trueblood lifted the bracelet from Wick's hands and let out an appreciative sound. "This is very powerful. No wonder Kevin was able to hold out against Ramsey's people." She inclined her head toward Wick. "We'll take good care of this, young mage. You have our oath."

Wick stood tall and returned the respectful acknowledgement with a nod.

Ever mindful of her schedule, Trueblood checked her watch, moved to the attic window, and produced a vortex. With a final nod to Jonah, she entered the opening, leaving Rex and the others behind.

Seeing the vortex, and feeling its magical pull reminded Jonah of his ride to the center. "Rex, who followed us this morning?"

The big Fallen Reaper clapped his beefy hands. "Oh, that was Kevin. We needed to be more careful now that we know Ramsey didn't cross over."

"Ramsey?" Mike's eyes bugged out and he shoved Jonah. "You didn't tell me Ramsey was around and that someone followed us."

"Sorry." Jonah described the dream-walk to Mike. By the time he finished, Mike couldn't hide his anxiety.

"Don't worry, fella." Rex gestured to himself and the other Alliance people. "We won't let you and Jonah out of our sight."

Mike nodded.

"Where's Kevin?" Jonah asked.

Rex rubbed his square chin, thinking. "I reckon he's downstairs now that you're in the clubhouse."

The Seeker's Compass 543

"I'll be back." Jonah started for the attic stairs.

"Where're you going?" Rex asked.

"Down to talk with Kevin."

"I'm going too." Mike hurried to follow.

It was easy to find Kevin when they reached the atrium. He sat in the café, gazing out the windows, an island of calm in the general bedlam of the kid-filled café. In fact, Kevin was so still, Jonah began to worry. He and Mike approached the table but glanced at each other, neither wanting to be the first to interrupt.

Without warning, Kevin's eyes shifted to them. "You two geeks are weird."

Jonah cracked a smile at the Fallen Reaper's teasing tone. "You're the one staring into space." He pulled out a chair next to Kevin and sat down.

Mike took the one opposite the older boy, watching him with an avid expression.

Kevin went back to staring out the rear windows of the café. "I wasn't staring into space. I was listening."

Jonah gawked at the chattering kids all around them. "To what?"

"Conversations."

Jonah grinned. "Eavesdropping?"

Kevin sighed and threw up his hands. "No. I'm training my ears to separate streams of sounds."

Mike leaned over the table. "Do you have enhanced hearing?"

"Yeah."

"Cool! Is it like Superman? He had to train himself to isolate sounds."

Kevin glanced at the ceiling and shook his head in mock misery. "Well, not exactly."

"But similar, right?" Mike nodded in a thoughtful way.

Kevin shrugged. "It comes in handy on assignments."

"Oh. You're training for the Alliance." Mike stood. "We can leave you alone."

"Jonah would never do something that thoughtful." Kevin crossed his arms on the table and leaned forward, giving Jonah his full attention. "What's the problem, little man?"

Jonah hesitated, wondering if he should ask about the meeting with the Council.

Kevin guessed what was on his mind and frowned. "Yes, I got in trouble. Mandara, he's the lead Fallen Reaper, tore me a new one, after complimenting me."

"He did? Oh." Jonah could sympathize.

Kevin frowned and lowered his voice to a rich baritone. "I admire initiative and bravery, Mr. Brown. We need that in the Alliance."

Goosebumps ran up Jonah's arms. He hadn't heard this Mandara character before, nor could he guess if Kevin's impression of the man was accurate or not. What pained Jonah, and produced the goosebumps, was that Kevin's imitation sounded so much like Jonah's dad.

Mike dropped into his seat and tapped the table to get Kevin's attention. "That's a good thing, right?"

"No, it isn't." Kevin sighed. "You two don't understand Council politics yet."

"Politics?" The word snapped Jonah out of his moment of reverie.

"There are factions on the Council." Kevin placed his right hand flat against the table. "Mandara, Rubio, and others are part of a faction called the Hardliners. They believe we should fight the KIN and these Hunters." He placed his left hand on the table next, far apart from the right. "Marcus and the others are considered Moderates. They think we should be cautious. In the middle are the Centrist members, keeping the peace."

Mike's expression was serious as he held up three fingers. "Moderates, Centrists, and Hardliners. Got it."

Kevin shifted his gaze to Jonah. "Then there's you."

Jonah's eyes widened. "What do you mean?"

"Anytime you use your powers, the Hardliners like it. I bet they toast each other in private." Kevin scowled.

Jonah didn't know how to respond.

The Seeker's Compass

Mike hugged himself and began to rock back and forth. "You mean they want Jonah to be a weapon." His voice was flat and sure, like he had figured that out.

Kevin swallowed, watching Mike. "Yeah, exactly. Are you alright?" Mike glanced down at his crossed arms and stopped his rocking. Kevin gave him one last worried look before turning to Jonah. "You're not a weapon for anyone. Marcus has been saying it, too."

Jonah was dumbfounded by that news. He never knew about Alliance politics. But to find out Council members wanted him to do more worried Jonah. He also began to piece together why Kevin got in trouble. "You told Mandara that?"

Kevin nodded. "He expected me to support their position. I'm not Marcus's apprentice anymore, and I helped you rescue Mike. But when I disagreed with him, suddenly I was too close to you and Lynn and acting like a kid instead of an adult. And he decided someone older should watch over you for a while."

"Who?" A sinking feeling developed in Jonah's stomach. Marcus would be too easy a choice.

Kevin shook his head. "Don't know, but the Council can assign anyone they want to monitor you."

"I don't want anybody else," Jonah said, pounding the table. "I want you."

Kevin's eyebrows shot up. He leaned forward to play with Jonah's shield bracelet. "Well, when this assignment's done, I'm gone. Rex jokes they'll send me to Siberia."

Kevin tried to be flippant but Jonah heard and sensed the anger inside him. "That's not funny." Jonah let his raw emotion flow. It angered him that Kevin accepted the unfair situation, but what could he do?

Mike started rocking again. "It's not fair. You saved my life. I wonder if the mole is behind this." His eyes had gone unfocused, like he was referring to his own internal source of information.

"I told you. If I hadn't argued, Mandara would have been cool with everything. And I can't see the mole getting him to do anything. Mandara's too bullheaded." Kevin gazed directly into Jonah's eyes. "And I don't care what they think. You're not a weapon."

The sincerity rolling off the older boy staggered Jonah. It was even stronger than Marcus's belief from the previous evening.

Jonah swallowed. "Thanks."

"I know you don't get it yet. But you will, and soon." Kevin stood. "By the way, the Council agreed to have you open the back door into the Afterworld. Trevor's going home."

Mike's expression changed from slightly vacant to concerned. "How's Trevor?"

Kevin shrugged. "Fine, the last time I checked."

"We should open that door to the Afterworld as soon as possible."

"I'll make sure to tell the Council." Kevin grinned at Mike. "Relax. We're making the arrangements for everyone to stay at the Guest House during the mission." Kevin held out his fist. Jonah and Mike bumped it with their own. "See you two later."

With that, he strolled out and nodded to the Alliance guy hovering at the café entrance. More than a few of the girls watched him leave. Jonah envied Kevin. The boy was tall and carried himself with a confidence Jonah only wished he had.

The Seeker's Compass 547

CHAPTER THIRTY-ONE
THE AWAY TEAM

Jonah and Mike arrived for the emergency meeting of the Practice Club to find other kids already there. Anthony unloaded a cooler from his father's truck. Rodney helped him place it near the center of the field, on the grass plot. Lorraine hovered near, ready to drop bottled water and juices into the container.

"Whatsup, guys?" Anthony waved as he said goodbye to his dad.

Mike joined the others and helped stock the cooler. Jonah nodded in greeting but walked to the edge of the clearing. It wasn't that he didn't like the other kids. They'd been cool after his ruined birthday party.

It was the plot of grass. Seeing it caused a spasm of regret. He couldn't shake the image of Mike's unconscious body laying right where Ramsey had knocked him out. He didn't want to relive his own terror that his best friend had died.

And he had to add Kevin's situation to the worry load. In a way, Trevor had been perceptive about the feeling of being suffocated. Whenever Jonah grew anxious over things and was around a lot of people, their souls pressed on him. He gazed into the Georgia pines, listening to the sound of the others talking and laughing.

Eventually Mike came over and pressed a bottle of cranberry juice into Jonah's hand and then quietly sipped from his own while watching the surrounding trees. His buddy's willingness to hang with him, even when moody, got to Jonah.

He'd never said anything to Mike about recent events nor asked how he was really doing. Jonah opened the bottle and took a sip of juice before saying, "I'm sorry I left you behind with Ramsey."

Mike's eyes widened. "It's okay, Jonah. I don't blame you."

"Yeah, it was that Trevor. If he hadn't—"

Mike lowered his bottle. "I'm not mad at Trevor either."

"Why not?"

"He was right. And if you'd gone back, Ramsey would have taken you to the Afterworld. Even Deyanira admitted it." Mike poked Jonah's arm. "You see that, right?"

"Yeah, I guess, but…"

"I feel sorry for Trevor." Mike hugged himself, worry etching his face.

Jonah gagged on his own sip of juice. "He lied to us about having powers."

"I know." Mike shrugged. "He's put his life on the line, just like we did."

Jonah didn't know what to say to his friend. In the end, he didn't have the right to be angry in Mike's place. So he tried a different angle. "You and Lynn were hurt. I wouldn't blame you if you stayed behind and don't cross over."

"No. I'm going." The steel in Mike's voice surprised Jonah. "I helped you figure out the riddle and I used the compass."

Jonah leaned away at Mike's determined tone.

Mike continued, his voice raising. "And Trevor's brave." When Jonah couldn't hide his frown, Mike grew testy and shouted. "Has your Death Sense ever gone off around him? Well?"

"No." Jonah hated to admit that, but it was true. "And keep it down. The others are looking at us."

"Well then." Mike squeezed his empty bottle between his hands, looking defiant. "Trevor's one of the good guys."

Jonah watched his best friend's angry expression while recalling Mike's comments back in the bookstore. "You like Trevor, don't you."

The Seeker's Compass **549**

Mike crossed his arms, staring down at a rock he rolled beneath his right foot. "Yes, I do."

"Oh." Jonah blinked, not expecting Mike to be that honest. "Does he even like you back?"

Mike nodded and his jaw tightened. "We're alright?"

"Yeah." Jonah glanced behind them to make sure the others weren't trying to eavesdrop. "How can you know that about Trevor?"

Mike glanced at Jonah. "He called me."

"When?"

"Last night. He called to apologize for what happened. And, we–talked for a long time."

Jonah couldn't believe it. "How did he get a phone?"

"I didn't ask." Mike looked away. "The important thing is he called."

For a wild moment, Jonah imagined the slippery courier phasing down to Mike's room for a face-to-face talk last night. But that shouldn't have been possible. Rubio said Trevor wouldn't be able to phase from HQ again. But the guilty look on Mike's face said otherwise.

Jonah's eye's widened. "Mike?" When his buddy blushed, Jonah knew that Trevor had indeed found a way to visit. "How did he…"

"I don't know and don't care." Mike blushed even more.

Oh my God. Jonah experienced equal parts shock and envy. "What did you two do?" As soon as he asked, a wicked grin spread across Jonah's face.

Mike glared at him. "We *talked*!"

"Yeah, right." Jonah laughed and shoved his buddy. "How long did he stay and *talk*?"

Mike pulled a scandalized expression just as Lynn entered the clearing, arm in a sling and Rico hovering over her. Mike hurried over to talk with them, leaving Jonah alone with burning, unanswered questions.

He didn't have time to revisit the conversation because Practice Club members arrived in steady groups until the entire roster was present. Vincent, the leader for this year, began the meeting. Everyone had heard rumors about the Club's situation, but Lynn's detailed recounting of her conversation with the director shocked and angered the group.

"Yo!" Vincent's tough voice cut through the clamor Lynn's news produced. Everyone quieted in seconds, waiting. "Let Brandon and his friends meet at the Teen Center." He pointed at the ground at his feet. "We'll meet here." He pumped his fists in the air.

Everyone cheered. That soon gave way to chants of, "Boycott. Boycott. Boycott!" During the chanting that followed, Jonah glanced around the assembled crowd, noting the invited friends of members, including Wick's girlfriend Tamara.

Watching her holding Wick's hand and chanting along with the others brought his discussion with Mike to the forefront and the truly nagging aspect of it all. In the midst of everything happening, even Mike had found someone. Once again, Robert's quip from a few days ago stung Jonah. He was the odd boy out. Would he ever find anyone?

Kevin stepped into view at the entrance to the clearing, causing a stir. Jonah forgot that most of the club members had never met Kevin. Lynn was on point and whispered to Vincent.

Rico strode over to greet the Fallen Reaper. He turned to the Club. "Hey everyone. This is Kevin, and he's cool."

After exchanging greetings with Vincent, Kevin made his way to Jonah's side while drawing curious looks from several club members.

"What's up?" Jonah asked the older boy.

"Everything's set for ATL." Kevin lowered his voice to a whisper. "What's happening here? I heard the chanting. You gonna have a protest march?"

"Not really." Jonah smiled, glad to have Kevin standing beside him. As the gathering ended, he and Jonah trailed behind the rest of the club members, taking their time walking toward the nearby school.

Kevin used the opportunity to give him all the details of the plan. Along the way, Jonah came to realize he liked listening to Kevin talk. The boy was so sure of himself, even after getting in trouble. Jonah wished he could always be as confident.

The Seeker's Compass **551**

By the time they reached the building's gravel parking lot, most of the other kids were gone, either on foot, bikes, or in cars. Mike stood near the main road, waiting for Jonah.

Kevin stopped, shoved his hands in his pockets, and hunched his shoulders. "I have to get back to HQ."

"Oh." Jonah didn't want him to leave. When Kevin was around, he didn't feel like the odd person.

"Well, see you soon, little–" Kevin stopped when Jonah glared at him. "I need something to call you."

"How about my name?"

"Nah." Kevin stroked his chin. "I could use geek boy or hero."

Jonah glared at him. "Those belong to Lynn."

Kevin grinned. "How about the Deliverer or the One?" He snapped his fingers and treated Jonah to a mock bow. "Or Son of Isaiah."

"No way."

"Well, I guess it's little man." Kevin started for the woods behind the school.

"I hate that name." Jonah watched the older boy's retreating back, mindful of his own fervent wish for more muscles. "I'm gonna grow."

"I'll believe that when I see it." Kevin turned, his teasing grin giving way to an earnest expression. "Besides, you'll always be my little man." With that, Kevin stepped into the shadows of the tree line and phased.

The thrill Jonah experienced at Kevin's words lightened his footsteps as he rolled his bike to Mike, who was waiting.

"What did he say to you?" Mike peered into Jonah's face.

Jonah blinked. "Ah, the arrangements for the Guest House are ready."

"No." Mike shook his head. "That's not it."

"Why'd you think that?" When Mike grinned, Jonah grew irritated. "What?"

"You were smiling all the way over here and your expression was all dreamy."

This time, it was Jonah's turn to be embarrassed.

*

From the moment Jonah's group arrived at the Guest House, he and Mike were shuffled away from the others and made to endure several meetings in the library. Eventually they were released in order to prepare for departure. The boys headed straight to the bat cave.

"Trevor!" Mike shouted, hurrying to the courier's side. "How're you doing?"

"Weak." He offered Mike a tired smile. "It's good we're finally going. I'm running out of time."

Mike nodded his head in sympathy. His hands twitched as if he wanted to reach for Trevor. "Can't Rubio help?"

"He's done all he can. I have to cross over or..."

Mike shuddered.

Jonah was about to say he was sorry when Kevin entered the basement carrying a bundle of light grey tunics and pants. He tossed a pair to Jonah, Trevor, and Mike. "Get changed. We're leaving in a few minutes."

Trevor laughed at Jonah and Mike's confused expressions. "I suggested we should put on something so we blended in when we arrive in the Afterworld."

Jonah thought everyone made a strange sight after donning the baggy clothing. In the Afterworld, it might look normal but here, they were like extras in a fantasy movie.

Kevin handed Jonah and Mike standard survival backpacks.

Jonah held his up, a questioning look on his face.

Kevin took the pack and held it so Jonah could slide into it. "The doorway is on this side and we don't know the weather conditions or terrain. So we have the packs, just in case."

Jonah nodded. It made perfect sense. Plus, he might also need it on the other side.

Trevor fussed over Mike, making sure he was ready to go while carrying on a whispered conversation. Jonah was convinced the two boys had done

The Seeker's Compass

more than just talk. He frowned, feeling envious because he didn't have anyone to fuss over him like that. Well, except Aunt Imma. She didn't count.

Kevin cleared his throat to get Trevor and Mike's attention, then he led their group upstairs, through the den and kitchen, and outside to the large patio. Several more adults were present, including Rubio, Marcus, Trueblood, and Rex. All four of them were dressed in similar grey tunics and pants.

Jonah's attention was drawn to a large octagonal metal platform at the center of the patio. All the furniture had been moved aside to make room. He guessed the platform was about seven to ten feet in diameter.

A waist-high pole with a small hole near the top edge was attached to one end of the platform. Jonah pointed at the strange sight. "What's that?"

The Alliance adults grew quiet and waited as Marcus strode over to them. "We have a theory about the compass." He indicated the pole. "We think that if you attach the compass to a device, the entire piece can be moved."

Mike gasped. "Oh. That's a good idea."

"Maybe." Jonah frowned. "But why use it?"

Rubio's usual military tone carried a trace of humor today. "Because, young man, it's a little more dignified than everyone holding on to you."

Trevor and Mike stepped onto the platform in unison and began inspecting the short pole. Jonah hesitated when Lynn, Robert, and Wick exited the house.

Lynn didn't have her sling but held her arm close to her side and wore a solemn expression as she walked to Kevin. She activated a blade with her left hand and held it toward him, point first. Kevin nodded in understanding, activated his own, tapped the blades once, and then held still, blade against blade.

Everyone grew quiet, watching.

Lynn didn't seem to notice or care. "Keep Mike and Jonah safe."

Kevin nodded. "I promise."

Jonah was close enough to see the goose bumps race up Lynn's arms. Golden lines flickered in the air and settled onto the crossed blades as well as Lynn's and Kevin's forearms.

Wick pressed closer, reaching out to touch the blades, but stopping before doing so. "Very cool!"

Rubio let out an impressed grunt.

Lynn deactivated her blade and motioned Jonah and Mike to join them. Mike tried to bring Trevor along, but the boy held back, shaking his head. Lynn huffed, reached over, and pulled Jonah and Mike into a hug. Robert and Wick piled on, careful of Lynn's injured arm, and patted everyone on the back. After a long moment, which moved Jonah to his very core, they parted.

Lynn playfully nudged Mike with a fist. "Alex would be proud of his little brother."

Mike's face suffused with color at the compliment.

Lynn took both deactivated blades and held them out for Jonah. "Bring them back or else..."

Jonah didn't know what to say, so he accepted the cylinders in silence and nodded.

Rubio clapped his hands and motioned everyone onto the strange platform. Then the mage pointed to the pole. "Compass there please, Mr. Blackstone."

Jonah nodded and snapped the compass into place. The device pulsed with power when Jonah opened the true face and entered the code, creating a slight tug on his ability.

Rubio was the last to mount the platform. In all, eight people were part of what Jonah realized was a first group. *It's our own away team*, he thought, wishing he could whisper it to Mike and get a laugh. A second team of Alliance personnel waited at the edge of the patio.

"We're ready." Rubio nodded.

The reality of the situation finally registered. Jonah knew where they were going, but not until now did he truly face the prospect of crossing over. What would they find at the final location? Things had been so busy, he hadn't had a chance to consider it. Well, Jonah told himself, he'd find out in a few seconds.

After sucking in a breath, he activated the compass.

The Seeker's Compass

CHAPTER THIRTY-TWO
UNEARTHLY EARTH

The group reappeared inside a pitch black cavern. The only illumination was six large symbols at their feet. The air was close and bone dry. Jonah sucked in a startled breath at the lack of moisture.

"Keep still for a second." Marcus gripped Jonah's arm. "Let your bodies get used to it."

Jonah took shallow breaths, willing himself to relax.

Rubio and Trueblood ignited balls of blue flames in their palms and proceeded to drop them around the edge of the platform.

"Rex." Rubio's bark echoed off the walls, giving an idea of the cavern's size.

"Oh yeah." Rex sounded embarrassed.

The sudden change of air pressure let Jonah know the Fallen Reaper had phased away.

Marcus guided Jonah and Mike off the platform. Trevor stuck close to them as the group waited. Rex reappeared on the platform with two more Alliance guys in tow. They carried a large plastic container and a couple of flashlights.

In quick motions, the men opened the container and pulled out small, battery-powered LED lights. They moved around the cavern, activating and placing the lights against the wall. The extra illumination from the LEDs reflected off a smooth ceiling above, spilling soft, amber light into the space. The result was a cozy feeling.

Mike knelt down to touch the six large symbols etched in the cavern's version of a platform. There wasn't a designation stone here; each symbol was its own stone.

"Whoa." Mike traced the design in the air with his finger. "Jonah, it's three interlocking circles and wings."

Jonah knelt beside Mike to look at the cavern's dusty floor. "It's the Alliance symbol." Something about this version of the symbol, the circles, was familiar. He tapped his forehead, trying to remember, and then he had it. They were like the calendar circles he'd seen in photos his parents took of an excavation.

Jonah glanced at his godfather. "My mom and dad would have loved this place."

Marcus nodded and held out the compass.

Jonah rose to his feet, pulling a puzzled expression. "You won't need it anymore?"

"Now that we've been here, we can phase back and forth." He nodded at the compass, and Jonah took it.

As if proving Marcus's point, Rex phased into the cavern again, this time carrying a large trunk. He unpacked a compact table. As soon as it was unfolded, he unrolled a laminated map on the tabletop.

A mortal member of the crew affixed an LED to a portable light stand and pointed it at the table.

Marcus moved closer. "Let's see where we are." He allowed Jonah and Mike to scoot in front of him, since he could look over their heads.

Rex used a marker to draw a dot on the world map, in the Southern US. He drew a second dot in the area of the Eastern Sahara. In fact, the area was a vast desert near the borders of Libya and Sudan.

Laying a yardstick between the points, Rex drew a connecting line. That done, he started a second line, this time from a location in France, but it also ended on the same dot in the desert.

The nearest labeled regions were Gilf Kebir and Jebel Uwainat. The names seemed familiar to Jonah.

"I know those names." Mike tapped his finger on the map in excitement.

The Seeker's Compass **557**

"They're in the Eastern Sahara Desert."

Kevin snorted. "That's obvious."

"I know that, Kevin. I mean that's the most remote place on Earth." Mike leaned over the map to trace his finger along the outlines of the area. "I have a book about it."

Rex drew a circle around the area. "Well, we're hundreds of kilometers from those locations." He grinned at Mike. "You know your stuff, young man."

"That would explain the outside." Rubio paused to smack dust off his gloves. He had returned to the cavern through an opening Jonah hadn't noticed. A strong flinty smell accompanied the mage as he stepped closer to the table.

Mike jerked upright, staring at the mage. "What's outside?"

Rubio vibrated with suppressed enthusiasm. He placed his hands flat on the map. "Prepare yourself. The sight is something, even at night."

He led the way across the chamber and to the opening. Jonah glanced into the dim exit to see an ancient set of steps carved into the rock.

Regular flares had been spaced along the pathway. Jonah's sense of wonder increased as he followed his godfather out of the cavern. They ascended the steps toward a black opening. The closer he got, the more pinpoints of light Jonah saw.

Mike gasped, staring ahead. "Jonah. Those are–" His words caught in his throat as they exited the cavern and stars exploded into view above.

The starscape extended from horizon to horizon and was so bright and clear, Jonah imagined he could reach out and touch them. Even more interesting was the sudden cold wind that nipped at his face.

He huddled in his thin grey clothing and tried to find the horizon. It was easy to see because the stars abruptly ended in a thin line. There were no obstructions of the sky, just open desert.

Lifting his gaze overhead, Jonah's breath caught in his own chest because the stars began to move. The entire sky rotated like a time-lapse video. The effect was so jarring that Jonah almost lost his balance.

Kevin steadied him. "You okay?"

Jonah nodded, afraid to speak and break the spell, or whatever was happening. He tore his gaze from the rotating sky and focused on the ground. Ghostly images of people moved around on the leveled stretch of desert near the base where Jonah's group stood.

The people wore loose-fitting clothing and their skin was jet black. He could tell because they had lamps stationed all around the area, revealing a series of angular stones arranged in circular patterns.

That's it! The large circles were ancient calendar circles. A long succession of people used the stones, large and small to chart the stars in the sky.

The overwhelming sense of an immense span of time and history flowed over Jonah. This place had been a center of astronomical observations for thousands of years.

He marveled at what must be a weird sort of waking-dream. He'd always seen things happening in the present. He'd never seen things from the past. Certainly he'd never seen things happening over millennia.

A sense of connection to something greater awed Jonah. He was outside of his body, space and time, a traveler over the eons. The past and the future were just beyond his perception, but if he pushed, Jonah was sure those vistas would open to him. Is this what it meant to be a Deliverer?

Kevin's hold on Jonah's upper arm tightened a bit. "Jonah?"

The concern in the boy's voice grounded Jonah. He blinked, dispelling the vision. "This place is really old."

Mike gazed at him in the darkness. "It makes sense that the last Deliverer chose this site. Even today, satellites don't pass over and it's been ignored by explorers."

Jonah nodded. "I get that. But the place, it's..." He couldn't put it into words. The weight of history still pressed on his senses, his soul.

Marcus motioned toward the entrance. "Let's go down. We're here for a reason."

If Jonah thought returning to the cavern would help to dispel the pressure of history and time, he was wrong. The sensation grew more pronounced, and Jonah realized the source. "There's power in this place."

The Seeker's Compass **559**

Marcus faltered and turned to him. "Power?"

Jonah sucked in a breath. "Yes. It's getting stronger the closer we get to the cavern."

He was right. The power was almost alive now, and it focused on him. Fear gripped him and he sought out that safe place within himself. The haven opened and enveloped his mind. At the same time, the intrusive pressure turned questioning in nature.

Calmer now, Jonah assessed the nature of the power and understood. "This place wants to know something."

Everyone in the cavern stopped whatever they were doing and watched Jonah. He noted some awed expressions as well as suspicious ones.

Marcus dropped his voice to a whisper. "What does the cavern require?"

"It wants to know if I'm a Deliverer."

Marcus nodded. "Answer it."

Jonah wondered how to do that before deciding to answer the same way the cavern asked. He had to use his mind. *Yes. I am a Deliverer. Yes.*

In response, a rush of power seeped through the earth and into his feet and legs. "Whoa." Jonah sucked in a breath. The sensation was almost a violation of his body.

Rubio raised his right hand, palm toward Jonah. "I can sense the power. It's entering you."

Jonah pointed at the large Alliance symbol. Ghostly workmen floated in and out of his vision, carving the original design on the floor. "It's coming from below."

"A seal, perhaps?" Rubio looked skeptical.

Jonah agreed, but there was no obvious seal here. That's when faint lines appeared on the ground, elongating, spreading and connecting until they outlined shapes in the stone. The overall design was circular and the segments fit together like... like...

"Do you see them? The lines?" Jonah asked the group.

No one else seemed to have the same perspective, except Mike, who pointed at the ground. "I see them, Jonah."

The lines flared in Jonah's augmented vision and the name for the design came to him. "They're cover-stones." He raised his hand and concentrated. *Come on, show the others.* After a few tense moments, light flared along the lines and everyone gasped.

When the light abated, clear edges to the stones were revealed.

"I'll be." Rex's mouth hung open.

Rubio signaled to the mortal members of the group. They started to pry the stones loose with spades. With Kevin, Rex, and Marcus helping, the group was able to lift the heavy cover-stones away, one at a time, uncovering a smooth surface below.

"Stand back." Jonah raised his hand and concentrated, the power singing to him now and urging him on. A click sounded and the flat surface moved aside to reveal a golden seal.

An awed silence spread through the cavern.

Finally Rex said, "That's a seal."

Rubio frowned at him.

"Hey, someone had to say it. That's how it's done in the movies." Rex's smart comment broke the shocked tension. The big Fallen Reaper winked at Jonah. "I'd say you have the only key to open that, buddy."

Yeah, Jonah thought. At the very center of the seal was a round depression. It was like the one in the doorway to the underground chamber where his parents had died. At once, a sense of foreboding assailed Jonah and he wanted to step away.

Mike leaned against him. "Jonah, you have to do it."

"I know." He swallowed then stepped over the edge and onto the seal.

The metal was hard and solid beneath his feet as he moved to the center to place the compass in the depression. It fit perfectly, but nothing happened.

Mike knelt at the edge of the seal and whispered, "Maybe you have to rotate it."

Jonah lowered himself to his knees and tried turning the compass to the left. It wouldn't budge. But when he tried turning it right, it easily rotated ninety degrees, made a solid click and then came loose into his grip.

The Seeker's Compass **561**

Jonah stumbled back as a brilliant shaft of light erupted out of the opening where the compass had been. The entire seal bucked, heaving Jonah onto the cavern floor. The seal began to fold in on itself. A huge opening appeared, and a circular set of steps. The first ten were visible, but the rest were shrouded in shadows.

Mike pointed. "Oh my God."

Trevor and Kevin huddled in behind Jonah and Mike. The adults begun to whisper among themselves.

Jonah called out to them, "You want to check it out first, just in case?"

Rubio looked ready to do just that.

Marcus shook his head. "With that seal in place, I think it's safe. After all, you're the Deliverer." His godfather smiled. "And the cavern responded to you."

Kevin snorted. "That's lawyer double-talk for 'You go first.'"

Jonah exchanged an excited glance with Mike and Trevor. "Let's see what's down there."

CHAPTER THIRTY-THREE
THE BACK DOOR

Despite Marcus's comment, Kevin made it clear he had no intention of letting Jonah go first. He activated a blade and motioned Jonah to stay behind him as he took the initial tentative step onto the circular stairway.

Jonah was all too glad to let the Fallen Reaper lead, especially when blue flames roared to life, illuminating the entire length of the stairwell. A collective intake of breath went around the gathered people.

Kevin waved for Jonah, Mike, and Trevor to follow, and he began the descent. Jonah discovered the steps were shallow, forcing him to focus on what he was doing. There weren't any safety railings either. One slip and he'd tumble the entire way down.

The pale blue light reflected off the shiny obsidian of the steps and the curved wall. Unlike the worn, earthen steps leading up to the desert, these appeared smooth and well-maintained. Jonah couldn't shake the feeling that this place had awakened from a long sleep, one that had preserved whatever they would find below.

Mike huddled close behind, occasionally bumping into Jonah as they followed Kevin down and down. He whispered, "Wow. The lights are beautiful."

Jonah agreed, enjoying the cooler air inside the stairway. The change was comfortable after the bone dry cavern above.

When they finally reached the bottom, a row of purplish-blue flames erupted to life along the walls, illuminating a circular room. At the center was a crystal pedestal topped with a flat pinecone-shaped piece of smooth metal.

Kevin stopped beside the glowing pedestal, waving his hand over the device but never touching it.

Trevor gestured at it. "That has to be it."

Mimicking Kevin, Jonah stretched out his hand above the blank metal surface. The entire pinecone-shaped slab began to glow brighter.

The tremor rippling along the floor was the first warning. Then the far wall parted to expose a portal, larger and older than any Jonah had seen. This one had been made into the rock wall itself. The symbols around the opening were carved into the stone, much like the Alliance symbol in the cavern they had left behind

Jonah also noticed a depression had formed on the flat top surface of the pedestal.

Kevin nudged Jonah. "I think it likes you."

Mike huddled close, the pale light reflected in his wide pupils. "You gonna do it?"

In answer, Jonah placed the compass in the depression and held his breath. Like with the seal above, nothing happened. So he tried to turn it like he had before.

Still, nothing happened.

On a hunch, he tried to remove the compass, and it came away into his palm.

Jonah inserted the device two more times without any results or indications that the compass would activate anything. He became aware of the expectant silence of the others, and his face warmed with embarrassment.

After a fourth try, he took the compass in his hand. "It's not working." He turned to Trevor. "Are you sure about this?"

"Yes. It has to work." Trevor's voice shook and beads of sweat dripped off his forehead.

Jonah sympathized with the courier. If he couldn't open the doorway, Trevor would be stuck here to die.

Kevin tapped his arm. "You were able to open the seal. Why not this?"

Jonah thought he could read the unspoken truth on Kevin's face. Some hero he was turning out to be. He was the Deliverer, yet he couldn't open the doorway.

"Maybe you're doing it wrong." Mike brushed his finger along the edge of the depression. When the surface brightened even more, Mike snatched his hand away. He appeared unhurt, just stunned.

Mike's action reminded Jonah of the incident at his parents' hideaway, and a light went off in his mind. He stared at the compass as awareness dawned on him. All this time, he assumed it was about him, the Deliverer. But this was a *Seeker's* compass. And just as he wasn't a Protector nor meant to wear the ring, maybe he wasn't the one to own the compass either.

Shame hit Jonah like a punch to the stomach as he gazed at Mike. Jonah had assured Mike he was important to the group. But deep down, he saw his buddy as the weak link, the one without the power and in need of being protected.

But Wick had said everyone had a purpose. They just needed to find it.

Jonah gulped, ignoring the curious stares of the others. "I'm sorry, Mike. I really am."

"Sorry for what?"

Jonah held the compass out to his buddy. "You're the one who's supposed to use the compass, not me."

Trevor moved to stand right beside Mike, his face displaying awe. "You're a Seeker?"

Mike's gaze shifted back and forth between Trevor and Jonah, like a caged animal. "Are you sure, Jonah?"

"Yeah." The truth of the situation settled on him, and he smiled at Mike. "It's your purpose."

An ecstatic grin covered Mike's face as he cupped the compass in both hands, holding it high like a treasure. If Jonah wasn't mistaken, the device glowed in Mike's hands. When he faced the pedestal and lowered the compass into the niche, the entire structure began to hum with power.

Jonah's Death Sense spiked at the same time one of the Alliance men standing by the entrance screamed out in pain. A spray of blood splattered the wall as the man collapsed to the ground, dead.

A blurred shape roared into the chamber and toward the pedestal. Marcus and Kevin moved at once to intercept, their own bodies blurring.

The attacker stopped right beside Mike. It was Ramsey, and he grabbed Mike to use as a shield between Kevin and Marcus. The Fallen Reapers halted their blurred response, blades activated and ready to strike.

Kevin growled at Ramsey and moved forward, but Marcus pulled him back.

Rex yanked Jonah away from the agent.

But Jonah struggled in the big man's grip, terrified that his buddy was in Ramsey's clutches again. "Leave Mike alone. You can take me instead."

"Jonah!" Marcus shot him a warning glance.

Agent Ramsey tightened his hold on Mike's neck. "I don't want to take you, half-breed. I want to see what this boy can do with the compass."

"Liar."

Ramsey raised an eyebrow as he adjusted his grip. He nudged Mike. "I see the value of this boy now. He could be a true Seeker, the only one who can open the inner compass."

Marcus moved to block the agent's direct sight of Jonah. "How did you follow us?"

"Yeah." Jonah peeked around his godfather. "We used the compass. You can't trace that." But as Jonah said it, he recalled the agent's earlier use of modern technology rather than magic. That meant some kind of tracking device and… "The mole."

Ramsey grinned, looking smug. "Everyone was so worried about the supernatural that you didn't stop to consider everyday technology."

Jonah turned to his godfather, whose face had gone slack. Marcus began to pat his pants and then his grey tunic. His jaw slackened when he pulled out the new Alliance badge.

"That's right, traitor." Ramsey laughed.

Marcus's hand shook as he turned the badge over, found the embedded tracker, and yanked the tiny device free. He smashed it in his other hand and then threw it aside while glaring at Agent Ramsey.

"Now, move aside." Ramsey shook Mike for emphasis. "Let's see what the boy can do."

Marcus waved everyone back.

Jonah didn't like where this was going and yanked on his godfather's arm. "Don't let him do it."

"It's okay, Jonah," Mike said, sounding stronger than Jonah would have expected. "I wanna see if you're right about me." Mike shrugged in Ramsey's grip and the rogue agent relaxed enough for Mike to move to the pedestal.

He rested his slender hand atop the compass, fingers spread apart. For a moment, nothing happened. Then Mike gasped and his eyes began to glow a soft amber. The entire compass strobed with golden light, flashing patterns around the cavern walls.

Jonah shook his head because the patterns weren't on the walls. They had coalesced in mid-air, like a holographic image. He watched, mesmerized as a glowing, semi-transparent code floated before them. This one was composed of strange symbols that weren't on the compass.

It had to be the code into the Afterworld hideout, Jonah realized. He worried about Ramsey seeing it.

"Decrypt the code, boy," Ramsey ordered.

Rubio stepped forward. "Don't do it, young man."

"He has no choice." Marcus glared at his fellow Council member.

Mike manipulated the compass face while never taking his eyes off the code. It shifted into more recognizable symbols. Mike reached out and touched the decrypted code. Six symbols around the ancient portal flared with light, surprising everyone. The center portion of the rock face began to waver. When the turbulence stabilized, a scene appeared.

The cavern on the other side was so real, it was like looking out a window. Jonah took in the details of the room. It was similar to the cavern they were in, but much brighter with natural light. And there was an identical pedestal at the location. Jonah thought of the two caverns like terminals on either end of a secret route to and from the Afterworld.

Rubio shook his head in disgust, watching Ramsey study every detail of the room, no doubt so he could phase there later.

The agent nudged Mike. "Now, open the inner compass."

Mike pulled his hands from the compass and crossed his arms. He raised his chin in defiance.

Ramsey glared at him and activated a blade. He pressed it against Mike's chest, in the same spot he'd cut the boy before.

Marcus waved at the agent. "Don't hurt him. Mike, do it."

Rubio puffed out his chest in anger. "Marcus, we can't let that agent see that information."

Marcus whirled on the mage. "You want Ramsey to kill the boy?"

Rubio hesitated a fraction too long for Jonah. Eventually, the mage shook his head. But Jonah began to have a new, lower appreciation for Alliance Council politics. He didn't like what he saw.

Marcus raised his hands in a pleading gesture. "Mike, I appreciate your willingness to be brave, but I won't stand by and see you hurt." Marcus motioned to the compass.

Mike rested his hands on the device again. He closed his eyes and this time, a tidal wave of glowing, semi-transparent codes, numbers, and circles whirled through the air.

The much-larger display settled into a half-sphere above and in front of the pedestal.

"Amazing." Ramsey laughed in awe. "Those are designation codes for all the lost archives. They contain hidden knowledge that could change the balance of power."

Mike reached out and touched a close circle of seven glowing symbols. They revolved around each other in a cluster. As soon as his finger touched one of the codes, it enlarged at the same time six different symbols on the stone portal flared with light.

The vista shown was a forested area with strange colored trees and vegetation. Ramsey tensed when Mike pressed another code, but he didn't object. The scene shifted to a frozen, desolate tundra that elicited a startled moan from Marcus.

Rex swore under his breath. "I'll be. Never thought I see that place again."

Jonah recognized it as the same location of his last dream-walk.

The agent whispered to Mike, who selected another code. The view inside the portal changed to a scene of a bright, sunlit room with white walls, display shelves, numerous windows, and clear skylights overhead. The place was pristine and orderly, like a museum.

Marcus blinked in stunned silence. "Mike, choose another code."

"I don't think so." Ramsey ripped the compass from the niche in the pedestal while pulling Mike with him toward the portal.

Kevin, who had been watching the man all along, rushed forward in a blur of motion. Ramsey activated a shield and a blue distortion blossomed around the agent and Mike. Kevin hit the protective bubble and bounced sideways into the pedestal.

Ramsey dropped his shield and lunged for the opening. He would have made it through except Trevor shot forward and wrested Mike free of the agent's grasp. The courier paused for a split second to make sure Mike was okay before he plowed into Ramsey. He and the agent sailed through the opening and into the Afterworld.

When they hit the pristine floor on the other side, they slid along it for a few feet. Trevor grabbed the compass and tried to pry it from Ramsey's hands. The agent delivered two punches to Trevor's chest, sending the boy to the ground.

"Trevor!" Mike screamed.

The sight of the device in the agent's grasp angered Jonah. He sprinted for the opening. Someone shouted his name, but it was distorted as the chamber around him blurred.

Just before he crossed the portal's opening, something tugged on his tunic and yanked him back into real time. But his momentum couldn't be stopped and he tumbled through the opening and onto the marble floor of the pristine room.

Mike fell beside him.

The Seeker's Compass

Jonah rolled over just in time to see Trevor and Ramsey grappling with each other at the opposite end of the center aisle. Trevor tried to use the small stun device on Ramsey, but the man knocked it aside and the device skittered down a side aisle.

Jonah scrambled to his feet and rushed forward to help. His hands were mere inches from Ramsey when the slippery agent noticed and phased himself and Trevor from the chamber, leaving Jonah grasping empty air.

He collapsed to his knees and smacked a palm on the floor in frustration. "No!"

Mike joined him, looking stunned. "They're gone. With the compass."

Jonah whirled around. Instead of the open portal and his friends on the other side, he faced a blank, off-white wall. He gripped Mike's arm, thought about the chamber they had left behind, and tried to phase. A sudden, sharp headache made him gasp.

He couldn't phase out of this place. The awful realization settled on him. They were stranded in the Afterworld without the compass nor anyway to get home.

CHAPTER THIRTY-FOUR
THE REPOSITORY

"I'm sorry, Mike." Jonah continued to stare in dismay at the blank wall.

Mike elbowed him. "It wasn't your fault. We all wanted the compass."

"Yeah," Jonah answered, picturing the chamber in his mind. He tried to imagine the distance, but he couldn't. The chamber was on the mortal side, yet he did sense a faint power.

When he raised his hand, Mike stirred. "What are you doing?"

"I think I can sense the power in the chamber."

Mike placed his own hand on Jonah's shoulder. The effect was immediate and they sucked in identical breaths.

Jonah could clearly see the chamber in his mind's eye now. In fact, he could picture Rubio, Trueblood, Marcus, and Kevin. All stared in his direction, wide-eyed and shouting to them, almost as if they could see him and Mike.

That's odd. Was this another waking-dream, Jonah wondered. That's when Kevin darted forward, straight at them.

"Hey!" Jonah leapt backward on instinct, pushing Mike along just as Kevin walked through the wall. Unlike Jonah, Kevin remained on his feet and halted his forward momentum before he bowled over them.

"Leave it to you two geeks to jump right into the belly of the beast," Kevin scoffed.

Trueblood and Marcus stepped through the wall next. Like Kevin, they remained on their feet, and with more dignity.

Mike darted around Kevin and up to Marcus. "We're sorry."

Marcus raised a hand to calm him. "I understand."

Jonah joined his friend, looking for any clue that his godfather was actually furious with him. But he sensed a guarded curiosity from Marcus and relaxed. "How did you cross over?"

"I feared the portal had closed behind you and Mike," Marcus said. "Rubio used a series of spells to augment the fading power in the pedestal. His quick thinking kept the gate open. The problem was he couldn't open it enough to allow us through." He gestured to Trueblood, and she stepped forward.

"That's when it opened on its own and we saw both of you standing here." Trueblood turned and pressed her hand against the wall, frowning. "It's like you were helping Rubio reopen the doorway. We were able to cross over, but he had to remain behind to keep the connection open."

Jonah traded an awed look with Mike. "We were concentrating on the chamber, together."

Trueblood nodded. "It seems that worked. Perhaps the power from the pedestal was still connected to you?"

Jonah didn't know, but even if that was the case, the possibility seemed useless now. He frowned. "You're stuck here."

Marcus inspected the room with a tense expression on his face. "What happened? I suspect Ramsey and Trevor phased away."

Jonah nodded then snapped his fingers. "Hey! You can track them, right?" He glanced between Kevin and his godfather, feeling a surge of hope at that idea.

Kevin shrugged. "We could, but that would be a bad move."

"Why?" Jonah's face warmed at Kevin's rejection.

Marcus broke off his silent surveyal of the room. "Because you can be sure Ramsey phased to a secured location."

Mike paled at that answer. "You mean, Trevor's in trouble?"

"I'm afraid he is." Marcus frowned. "By now, the Grand Oracle has the compass and the courier."

"That's our worst nightmare." Kevin smacked his hand on a nearby shelf, causing the entire thing to rattle.

He whirled and walked down the center aisle, causing Jonah to wonder at the boy's increasing agitation.

Mike wore a stricken look on his own face. "We have to save Trevor and get the compass back."

"He's right." Jonah tore his gaze away from Kevin, who stopped near a window, head bowed. "And we have to get to the other location before Ramsey."

Marcus shook his head. "I wouldn't worry about that. It'll be protected against phasing, and Ramsey can't use the compass."

Mike nodded, but Jonah frowned. "Wait, my parents were able to use the compass. Maybe Ramsey can do it too."

"Jonah, you and Mike have proven the compass is special. I suspect your parents were never able to use it."

"What do you mean?"

"Your parents were good archeologists, but how did they find the Protector's Ring, the compass, and the Enhancer, all devices that had been missing for over two thousand years?" Marcus raised a questioning eyebrow. "I'm starting to believe they had help."

Jonah thought his godfather made a good point. But that didn't answer the pressing question. "Who would help them?"

"Perhaps this Elder we were supposed to meet."

Mike brightened at the thought. "Then Ramsey won't be able to get into the other location. Good."

"Exactly. That's our first piece of good news." Marcus turned to continue surveying the room.

The Seeker's Compass 573

Jonah decided to do something more than worry over Kevin's mood shift and copy his godfather. He took a deep breath and forced himself to notice the room for the first time. "What is this place?"

"A repository," Marcus stated in a sure tone.

When his godfather didn't offer more information, Jonah continued looking around. The space was a large oval with eight free-standing shelving units, four to each side of a center walkway. Each unit had numerous translucent displays, ten rows of ten cases each, or a hundred on each side.

The portion of the room near the wall where they had crossed over was open, with a large clear-top desk and sleek chair to the side. The space on the opposite end of the room had two slender benches built along the curving wall. The space between the benches was empty, or so Jonah thought. He had to stare at the wall a long time before he detected the outline of a door.

For no other reason than the presence of that door, Jonah decided that was the front of the repository. He would have asked Kevin about it, but he balked when he saw the frown on the boy's face.

Trueblood crossed to the window Kevin stood in front of and gave his forearm a gentle squeeze. "There won't be any Grim Guards here."

Kevin swallowed hard. "Just never expected to be back here… you know?"

Trueblood nodded. "We read the report."

Jonah exchanged a glance with Marcus when he heard that. "What report?"

"Kevin's report of his fall." Marcus watched the younger Fallen Reaper. "That's a story for later." Marcus lowered his voice. "So don't ask about it. Okay?"

Jonah gulped. "Yes sir."

Mike, gazing through one of the other large windows, beckoned to Jonah. "Come see this."

Jonah raced over and gawked at the spectacular view. They were so high that wispy clouds obscured a portion of the vista. But the flow of tear-drop ships, among other vehicles, could be seen through the gaps.

Pressing his face against the glass, Jonah peered into the clouds, and sucked in a breath. "Mike, do you see the lights through the haze? I think they're windows, like in an office building."

Mike darted between the display shelves and to an opposite window. "It's the same over here. I think it surrounds this tower."

The clouds cleared away as if blown on a sudden wind, giving Jonah an unobstructed view of a mammoth entry gate, far off in the outer wall of buildings. An entire glistening city was housed inside the larger outer building, reminding him of an immense fort.

"It's the Central Archive complex, gentlemen." Marcus stood behind Jonah, gazing out the window with a neutral expression. "You're standing near the apex of the Central Spire."

Jonah's jaw dropped. "You mean the Grand Oracle's somewhere in this building?"

Marcus nodded. "He has a suite of offices at the apex."

"And a killer view, no doubt." Kevin's voice was taut with suppressed emotion. "We should leave."

Marcus inclined his head. "I agree, but—"

Mike sucked in a quick, shocked breath, and Trueblood and Kevin were at his side in a flash.

Jonah followed his godfather to see what had startled Mike. He stood in front of a section where every case contained a single small carafe-shaped bottle. Each bottle was the same size, no more than six inches in height, and decorated in wild and mesmerizing colors and patterns.

The shapes seemed to be cut into the bottles themselves, allowing shimmering light to flare through the designs.

Marcus let out a low hiss of disgust.

"What do you think those are?" Jonah glanced up at his godfather.

Mike gestured at the small name tags with each bottle and said, "Those are names. For a second, I could decipher them."

Marcus spoked through a clenched jaw. "Reach out, with your Reaper side, Jonah."

The Seeker's Compass

Jonah closed his eyes and did as his godfather suggested. In an instant, he confirmed Mike's comment. "Those are human souls."

His insides burned. This proved the legend his godfather had mentioned at the hideaway.

"Those were the Grand Oracle's enemies," Marcus said. "All people important enough for him to kill in person."

That statement caused a ripple of pain to shoot through Jonah. *Like my parents.* The Grim Reaper had murdered them in person. A horrible thought occurred to Jonah. Did the evil being have his own morbid trophy case?

Mike backed away.

Marcus took a deep breath as he pointed toward a skylight. "Kevin? Can you phase outside the glass?"

"Don't," Jonah said.

Marcus frowned at him. "Why not?"

"I already tried it."

"Just as I remembered." Marcus lowered his gaze from the skylight. "The walls of the Spire are proofed against that sort of thing. Unless you break the glass and disrupt the pattern."

"Then we break it." Kevin balled his hands into fists.

Marcus shook his head. "It'll be protected and take a lot of force to punch through."

Trueblood raised an eyebrow. "Then we have no choice but to go through the front door."

Marcus shifted his gaze to the front. "I'm afraid so. Trevor's being held inside the Spire anyway."

A reddish light began to flash around the room along with an irritating buzzing, startling everyone. Mike grimaced as he covered his ears.

Jonah did the same, but it didn't help. "What's happening?"

Marcus seemed unaffected by the sound. "I think the Grand Oracle discovered how Ramsey returned to this place."

The distinct noise of approaching feet came from outside the room. Trueblood moved into the open area. Kevin went and stood at her side, blades drawn.

Marcus activated his own blades and stepped in front of Jonah and Mike. "When the door opens, blast them with a spell, Trueblood. We'll punch our way through and find a transport alcove."

Kevin and Trueblood nodded. Jonah had no clue what a transport alcove was, but he suspected it would get them away from anyone chasing. He didn't have any time to speculate because the door whooshed open to reveal grey-robed men with royal blue sashes. They were shocked to see Trueblood and Kevin.

In those crucial seconds, Trueblood hit the guards with a spell, knocking the front line backward into their companions. Kevin charged in and began fighting before the men could recover.

"Stay right behind me," Marcus ordered and followed Trueblood and Kevin out of the room and into the wide corridor beyond.

Jonah discovered he couldn't stay right behind because his godfather had to whirl and cut his way through the determined guards. Jonah activated Lynn's blades and stuck close to Mike as they tried to stay out of harm's way. When that proved futile, Jonah focused on defending Mike and himself.

More grey-robed men rushed in from their left, the direction they were trying to go. Kevin moved to counter, but there were too many. A few got around him and charged for the boys. Jonah waited until the last moment and instead of using the blades, he ducked and flipped the first attacker.

Mike dodged another, allowing Kevin to rush over and strike the man down.

Marcus and Trueblood had been separated from Jonah during the fight. They were attempting to fight their way back when a crystal partition dropped into place, blocking their way. Marcus hit and sliced at it with his blades, but only his muffled yells could get through.

Jonah sensed a powerful presence at the same moment Marcus's eyes widened. A regal man in a flowing grey robe approached from a side corridor, a full complement of guards with him.

The Seeker's Compass

The cowl of the newcomer's robe was folded back, revealing long, silver hair. He was very old, with deep lines etched into his thin cheeks. The corners of his mouth curved into a frown. His nose was long and pointed, and his dark grey eyes darted back and forth as he took in Jonah and the others.

Kevin let out a growl of anger, planted himself in front of Jonah and Mike, and whispered, "That's the Grand Oracle."

CHAPTER THIRTY-FIVE
JAILBREAK

The Grand Oracle's physical appearance may not have been as awful as the Grim Reaper's, but the evil intent around the being was just as strong and overpowering to Jonah. This ruler of the Afterworld sneered at Kevin in total arrogance and took his time to point out Marcus and Trueblood, still on the other side of the barrier. "Bring me those rebels. Now."

Jonah watched in mounting horror as Trueblood pulled Marcus away and down a side corridor just moments before the barrier opened, allowing the guards to swarm after them.

"Now, young Reaper." The Grand Oracle raised a boney hand and Jonah immediately clutched at his own throat. "If you don't want me to kill this one, drop your blades."

Kevin cursed and threw his weapons to the ground in disgust. Two guards rushed in to clamp him in semi-transparent stun-cuffs. All the while, Jonah continued struggling to breathe as the pressure increased to an unbearable point.

The Grand Oracle raised his hand and Jonah's feet left the ground. "Trying to rescue the courier scum?" The powerful being closed his hand and the pressure worsened, causing Jonah to gasp in agony. "You will tell me everything."

Jonah let out a strangled whimper and thought he'd pass out, but the Grand Oracle released him and let him drop to the ground. "They want to see the courier. Let them see their friend." The Grand Oracle strode

The Seeker's Compass **579**

past Jonah, who lay gasping for breath, and through the open door of his repository.

The guards rushed to Jonah. They were rough as they slapped stun-cuffs on his wrists and pulled him to his feet.

After placing cuffs on Mike, the boys were hustled down a side hallway. They arrived at a small rectangular alcove that didn't look wide enough to accommodate Jonah's group. The guards didn't hesitate to shove him inside and then press in behind. Jonah had no clue why until the familiar sensation played along his body and they phased.

The group reappeared in an identical, yet much darker, alcove. Jonah realized they had used a transport alcove and immediately thought of his godfather and Trueblood, and hoped they got away.

In addition to the low lighting, the place, with walls and floor of a deep, polished grey stone, had a sterile look to it. Jonah and Mike's sneakers made pitiful squeaking sounds as they stumbled along under the steel grip of the guards. Kevin's boots, on the other hand, were as quiet as the older boy himself.

After a short hallway, they turned a corner toward a checkpoint. Two powerful Guardians stood vigil on either side of a crystalline door. The hoods of their robes were drawn forward, hiding the faces in shadows.

Kevin went rigid beside Jonah, his jaw tight. "Just like Grim Guards. All they need are the scythes."

One checkpoint Guardian snapped to attention and pressed his hand to a glowing pad situated at chest height in the grey wall. The door whooshed upward to reveal a long, dark corridor with muted lighting.

Cell blocks lined the bleak corridor. As they stumbled forward, prodded in the backs by painful jabs, Jonah tried to glimpse what was behind the doors. All he saw were blurred darkened shapes through the opaque crystal.

A third of the way down, the guards yanked them to a standstill and opened a door on their right. After removing the stun-cuffs, the guards shoved the trio inside. Jonah bumped against the back wall before he could stop himself. Mike fell rather hard on a wafer-thin blue floor mat.

Kevin remained on his feet and whirled around, almost in a blur. The guards were ready, weapons raised.

One guard laughed at Kevin. "Filthy Reaper."

"I'm not a Reaper anymore." Kevin huffed out his words.

"That makes you even more pathetic." With that, the guard activated the cell door.

"They don't care for Reapers, I guess." Mike propped himself against the cell wall, watching Kevin.

"Not really." Kevin swore under his breath while circling his spot. "The Grand Oracle and Grim Reaper don't trust each other, and their people are even worse."

A muffled voice called out from an adjacent cell. "Mike? Is that you?"

"Trevor?" Mike scrambled toward the cell door.

Kevin gripped Mike's arm and stopped him. "Don't touch it. It'll shock you unconscious."

Mike gaped at the door. "Sorry." He moved to the wall and leaned his head against it. "Trevor, it's me."

"I guess Jonah and Kevin are with you?" Trevor's voice sounded clearer.

Jonah scanned the wall and spotted the slender vent near the floor.

Mike also spotted it because he sank to his knees against the wall. "We came after you, but Ramsey phased away. You okay?"

"I'm getting better." Trevor paused. "At least I'm in the Afterworld now."

Kevin snorted. "That's gonna do you a lot of good."

"What?" Jonah was shocked at the bitterness in Kevin's tone.

"He means," Trevor called out, "they're gonna interrogate and kill us."

Mike smacked his hand against the cell wall. "Don't say that, Trevor."

"It's the truth, Mike. I'm sorry."

Trevor sounded so sure and fatalistic to Jonah. He glanced at Kevin who, nodded in confirmation.

"You don't understand," Mike continued. "There's a chance Marcus and Trueblood can help us."

The Seeker's Compass

Trevor didn't respond immediately. When he did, Jonah thought his voice sounded guarded. "Explain."

Mike nodded and turned on Kevin. "Why did Ramsey call Marcus a traitor?"

Kevin blinked in surprise before furrowing his brow. "Duh! All Fallen Ones are traitors to them."

Mike shook his head. "But he didn't call you a traitor, just Marcus." Mike's light brown eyes sparkled with determination. "Marcus was a Archivist or a Guardian, wasn't he? Otherwise, Ramsey would have called him Reaper, like the guard just called you."

Kevin worked his jaw, refusing to answer.

Jonah realized where Mike's questions pointed and he rose to his feet and gripped the older boy's forearm. "Is Mike right?" Kevin gave him a hesitant nod, sending Jonah's mind racing back through everything he had assumed about Marcus. "But I always thought my godfather was a Reaper. He…"

Kevin let out a huff and threw his arms up. "None of that matters right now."

"I think it does." Mike lifted his chin, looking vindicated. "Marcus will know this building, and he'll find a way to free us."

"If Marcus knows his way around, he could find our operatives." Trevor sounded confident now.

Kevin gave Mike a skeptical look. "How do you two figure that?"

Mike's expression was sure. "It's a high probability."

Jonah cracked a smile despite the situation. "You're not gonna quote the probability like Spock, are you?"

The smile that touched Mike's face reassured Jonah. "No."

When Mike averted his gaze, Jonah knew his buddy was gonna do exactly that. The mind boost and touching the compass had changed his friend in more ways than Jonah expected. It was cool, but Jonah also worried about the long-term effects on his buddy.

Trevor called from the adjacent cell, "I trust Mike. Jonah's godfather must have been a rebel before he fell. That means he knows some of the safe…"

582 *John Darr*

"Don't." Kevin smacked his hand against the wall, blocking out the rest of what Trevor said. "The walls could have ears. So everyone just settle down and wait."

Kevin gestured for Jonah to sit down on one of the two mats and then joined him.

Mike leaned his head against the cell wall and started talking to Trevor in hushed tones.

Kevin grunted, watching the quiet conversation.

Jonah searched for something to say in order to keep the worry out of his mind. He really wanted to ask Kevin about the day the young Reaper fell, but he promised Marcus he would not do so. As he also watched Mike, Jonah wondered what his buddy and Trevor chatted about. They seemed to have no problems at all.

So, why did he and Kevin have such a hard time? Throwing caution to the wind, Jonah nudged the older boy in the side. "You think Trevor told Mike everything? You know, how he died the first time." Jonah regretted mentioning that personal subject when Kevin tensed. "I'm sorry. I didn't mean—"

Kevin glanced at him. "I doubt it. First Death is personal for a reason." Kevin's voice sounded hollow and a bit angry as he went back to watching Mike's conversation. After a long moment, he let out a breath. "Everyone didn't die doing something... noble." Kevin tapped his fist against the floor.

Sensing the boy's pain, Jonah said, "I'm sorry."

"Stop apologizing." Kevin sucked in a breath and met Jonah's gaze again. "I might tell you someday."

"Really? I mean, you don't have to."

Kevin bumped Jonah's leg with his fist and then let it rest there. "Who else am I gonna tell?" He shook his head and looked away.

Jonah understood in that moment that Kevin didn't have any friends. How could he, Jonah decided. He was a Fallen One and surrounded by adults. No wonder the boy liked to hang out with Jonah's cousins and friends.

The Seeker's Compass

And me. Even now, Kevin continued to playfully tap Jonah's knee with the back of his fist. And Jonah recalled the boy's parting comment after the Practice Club meeting.

Jonah pushed aside the shyness, not wanting to waste this chance. "You volunteered to watch over me, didn't you?"

Kevin shrugged. "Yeah, so?"

"You like being around… us." Jonah tripped over saying *me*. "We're your age and you can be yourself."

That caused Kevin to laugh. "I can be myself around the Alliance people, Jonah."

"No you can't. They're all older than you." Kevin started to shrug again and Jonah shoved the boy. "If the Alliance thought you were too close to our ages, why'd they let you come to Mount Vernon in the first place?"

Kevin's jaw worked for a moment. "That's a long story."

"We're connected." Jonah's voice cracked on the last word despite his intent to sound sure of himself. "I know it."

Kevin had been slouching against the wall. He pulled himself into a more upright position and leaned close to Jonah. "Does it bother you?"

"What? Being connected?"

"No." Kevin nodded toward Mike.

Jonah's eyes widened. "Mike's my buddy. I don't care who he dates."

Kevin laughed. "That's not what I mean. Mike's the one who took the mind boost and opened the doorway. He's the center of attention, not you."

Jonah glared at Kevin, knowing the boy hadn't meant that at all or had been vague on purpose, testing him. Either way, it irritated him. "I don't like being the center of attention."

"Yeah, but you are. Well, at least most of the time." Kevin laughed again.

Jonah decided to let that go and stay on topic. "I wasn't lying about the other thing. Mike's still my friend."

Kevin huffed, causing Jonah to wonder about the older boy's true feelings on the subject. He nudged Kevin's hand and asked, "Does it bother you?"

"Seriously? With all the things I've seen and we know." Kevin waved off the notion. "I'm cool."

Before Jonah could press Kevin more, the Fallen Reaper held up his hand and cocked his head to the side, listening. "Someone's coming." Kevin snapped his fingers to get Mike's attention. "You can talk to your boyfriend later."

Mike's oatmeal face went dark red. He cast an accusatory glare at Jonah.

Jonah held up his hands. "I didn't say anything."

"Quiet." Kevin motioned Mike to the back wall with Jonah. Once they were in place, Kevin positioned himself in front of the cell door, hands at his sides.

The quiet footsteps stopped right outside. A second later, the lock clicked and the door hissed open.

Marcus and Trueblood stood outside the cell with two guards, though not the same guards who had put the boys in the cell.

Jonah scrambled to his feet and ran to greet his godfather.

Marcus didn't even try to hide his relieved grin. "We thought you might need rescuing."

Jonah nodded and then pointed at the cell wall. "Trevor's in the next cell."

"We know."

At that moment, Trevor stepped into view. Mike gasped and moved past Jonah to see his friend. The courier had several cuts, a swollen black eye, and other bruises on his face as well as dark blood stains on his grey tunic.

"I thought they didn't …" Mike couldn't finish.

"This?" Trevor winced as he motioned at himself. "The Guardians were having a little fun with the traitor, that's all."

One of the new guards passed over a bundle that turned out to be tunics like the ones Jonah and the others already wore, except these had hoods.

Kevin glared at the man as he took one. "Why do we have to wear these?"

The Seeker's Compass 585

"You need to blend in." The guard motioned for them to change. Once they were done, the man turned to Trevor and said in a respectful tone, "Courier, we should leave now. Our diversion won't last forever."

The guards waited for Trevor's decision, impressing Jonah with the deference they showed the boy.

Trevor slipped on his tunic and then helped Mike. He gazed into Mike's eyes when he finished. "If anyone deserves to wear these garments, it's you."

Jonah resisted snorting, thinking the boy was trying to score points.

Trevor gave Mike a respectful nod and then turned to the guards. "He's a true Seeker. The first in over two thousand years."

The guards gazed at Mike in wonder and then executed respectful bows to him.

Trevor nodded. "Lead the way."

Mike grabbed Trevor's wrist. "Where?"

"To get your Seeker's compass."

CHAPTER THIRTY-SIX
HERETICS, HALF-BREED, MORTALS

The reality of the jail break began to settle over Jonah, putting his nerves on edge. He couldn't resist worrying they would be caught at every turn. However, they were able to reach the transport alcove without trouble.

The entire group was too large to fit inside. Marcus joined one of the guards, Trevor, and Mike on the platform. The guard pressed the appropriate button and the group disappeared.

The remaining guard presented Jonah and Kevin with their confiscated blades before stepping onto the platform.

"Thanks." Jonah nodded.

Kevin took his blades and motioned Jonah into the alcove. He and Trueblood positioned themselves so that Jonah was behind them and with the alcove wall at his back.

A second later, bright sunlight hit Jonah's eyes, forcing him to shield his face. The source of the illumination was a set of large windows just across the hallway. Marcus stood there, little more than a dark silhouette, looking out the window.

The striking image reminded Jonah that his godfather had been Archivist or Guardian. He wondered what emotions Marcus experienced now.

Trevor and Mike waited a few feet away. When Jonah and his group stepped from the alcove, Trevor made a hand signal to the guard. The man took the lead position and they started down the hallway.

The Seeker's Compass

Kevin remained at Jonah's side, and that reassured him as their group ventured further into the Spire. After negotiating the fourth hallway without trouble, Jonah grew impatient. "Where are we going?"

Marcus glanced back. "The Grand Oracle is moving his entire repository to a more secure location underground. We plan to intercept it and take the compass."

"Oh. Okay." Jonah could think of only one way to do that. "Are we gonna attack?"

"No." The lead guard spoke while keeping his attention on the way ahead. "You'll pose as low-level Inquirers who've come to inspect and record the items. It's part of my responsibilities to escort new Inquirers around the Spire, after all." The man paused at the next junction and tapped the blue sash that he'd slipped on. "I'm part of the Spire Guardian Corps."

Two grey-robed Archivists approached their group. The men bowed to them as they passed. When they were out of earshot, Trevor turned to Jonah. "You have to understand. Once we do this, my friends will be exposed." He motioned and the group continued on.

Jonah followed Trevor, growing more uncomfortable but keeping his thoughts to himself.

The lead guard glanced back and spoke in a quiet voice that wouldn't carry far in the hallway. "Do you understand, young one? We can never go back. Our ranks will be forfeited and we'll forever be traitors and heretics."

"That is until the Rulers of the Afterworld are overthrown." Trevor balled his right hand into a fist. "That's the whole point of the Rebellion."

Marcus spoke into the uncomfortable silence that enveloped the group. "I appreciate how difficult it must be for you. Accepting that everything you've prepared for is finally upon you is hard."

Glancing at Marcus, Trevor asked, "Is that how you felt, before you fell?"

Marcus stroked his own chin, thinking about his answer. "Yes. I was fearful."

Trevor bowed his head, deep in thought. But he spoke in a hushed voice. "When Jonah used the ring, the Elder knew he was the Deliverer. The rebellion couldn't hide behind cryptic comments and prophecies anymore."

The courier sucked in a deep breath and continued. "Our own fears and doubts had to be put aside in order to make the hard decisions." He paused by a window and peered out, forcing the others to stop.

Jonah saw a strange otherness come over the boy's features, the same thing that happened to Kevin at odd moments.

Mike slipped a hand into Trevor's. The courier glanced down at their clasped hands and smiled to Mike before turning to the others. "The Elder planned for nearly two thousand years. Today, we're required to take action." He gave Mike's hand a squeeze, collected himself, and started forward again.

Despite Trevor sounding surer of himself, Jonah could sense the increased apprehension in their group. He also thought the courier's little speech sounded too final.

The lead guard signaled for the group to halt while he inched forward to peer around the next corner. "The way is clear, Courier." The man wore a grim expression. "The halls are too quiet for my liking."

Trevor nodded. "What about the door?"

"Nothing. The security must be inside the chamber."

Trevor's own face was a somber mask now. He inclined his head to the rear guard. "I'll meet you and the others at the rally point."

Marcus gasped. "The rally point?"

"You've been there?"

Marcus pulled a frown. "Yes and we can't phase there. It's protected against that."

"Of course." The guard smiled. "You'll need a ship." He bowed to Trevor. "May the Deliverer quicken your steps, Courier."

Trevor raised his right hand, palm forward. "Deliverer's speed to you."

Jonah marveled at the formal parting, thinking it cool, but it also filled him with misgivings. He couldn't quicken anyone's steps, no matter how much they invoked his name. They made him out to be something special. Like he was godlike.

The Seeker's Compass **589**

The lead guard stood tall and gathered all the dignity his soon-to-be-forfeited rank provided him. The change in the man was amazing to witness and spoke of all he would lose within the next few minutes.

The further display of faith for their cause and the willingness to sacrifice their lives touched Jonah. A snatch of conversation between Marcus and Uncle James came back to him. Uncle James, while researching a book he wanted to write about the Civil Rights struggle, had engaged Marcus in a deep discussion.

The reason was obvious. Marcus displayed detailed knowledge about the historic era. Jonah suspected his godfather's first life had occurred back then. The discussion with Uncle James turned to the issue of an event versus a movement. Jonah recalled his godfather's total conviction when he described the difference.

An event, according to Marcus, was just that, a moment in time. But a movement was about sacrifice. Jonah stared at the backs of the Spire Guardian and Trevor. They represented a movement and were willing to sacrifice everything for the cause. They'd been at it for a long time, waiting for…

Me. Jonah swallowed past the sudden lump in his throat.

Kevin leaned against him. "You okay?"

Jonah nodded, afraid to say anything.

"Follow me and keep your hoods up." The Guardian strode around the corner as if he owned the place.

Jonah and the others did as he said and followed. When they reached the closed door, Trevor patted Mike's forearm and motioned him back. But Mike refused to leave his side.

Marcus gripped Mike by the arm and forced him to stand beside Jonah. "Trevor needs to be free to act. You and Jonah stay between us, got it?"

Mike's resistance wilted and his face reddened at Marcus's sharp tone. "Yes, sir."

Once Trevor nodded they were ready, the guard pressed his palm against the glowing panel beside the door. It hissed open.

Stacks of the square crystal containers from the Grand Oracle's repository had been loaded onto flat hover dollies and left in the middle of the space. There were other containers around the outer wall, all labeled and numbered. Other than that, the bay was empty.

A warning pricked Jonah's Death Sense as he searched the dollies, looking for the compass.

Mike tapped his arm. "It's on the second dolly."

"How do you know?"

Kevin hissed for them to keep quiet.

Trevor threw back his hood and scanned the deserted space. "This is odd."

"It's a trap," Marcus agreed. "We can't go back now." He gazed at the boxes. "I wonder if the compass is even here."

"It is." Mike rushed to the second dolly and opened a small container that reminded Jonah of Robert's Seeker's archive box. Mike reached inside and withdrew the compass.

Jonah's Death Sense spiked at the same time the door to the bay opened.

Everyone turned in that direction. The Grand Oracle marched through the door with confident, unhurried strides. At least twenty Spire Guardians fanned out behind him. The worst part for Jonah was Ramsey's smug smile as the man walked just behind and to the side of the Grand Oracle.

Shadows streaked across the floor, drawing Jonah's gaze toward the skylights. Four tear-drop ships hovered outside, weapons visible on the otherwise sleek hulls.

"It seems you were right, Hunter Ramsey." The Grand Oracle's voice was like sharp steel. It filled the space even though he didn't shout.

The dangerous being came to a stop and his Guardians fanned out in a semi-circle, blades drawn. The Grand Oracle's slate blue eyes narrowed as he peered at each member of Jonah's group.

"Heretics. Mortals." The Grand Oracle's gaze stopped on Jonah. "And the half-breed."

Jonah's stomach churned. The man's use of the term was a thousand times worst than Ramsey's.

Trevor activated his blades and stepped in front of Jonah's group. Kevin was only a second behind. When Marcus moved to join them, Ramsey detached himself from the Guardian's group and moved off to the side and activated his blades. Marcus adjusted his own position in order to block any attempt by Ramsey to get at Jonah.

A Spire Guardian with golden thread bordering his blue sash, tried to plant himself between Kevin, Trevor, and his Master.

The Grand Oracle barked at the man. "Move aside, Captain. Leave the traitors to me." The Grand Oracle had his own blades, ancient looking with a dull silver color and Angel script covering every inch.

As the Guardian Captain moved aside, the Grand Oracle raised his weapons in acknowledgement of Trevor and Kevin.

Trevor blurred into motion and attacked. The Grand Oracle wasn't flashy, but his movements were quick for an ancient-looking man. He blocked every tactic Trevor tried. When Kevin ran forward to help, the Grand Oracle raised one hand and shot a spell that smacked into Kevin's raised blades. The blocking spell that Jonah had seen others use had no effect and Kevin was knocked aside.

Ramsey blurred into his attack, but Marcus was ready. He and Ramsey whirled and fought in the common cadence of blurred motion and sudden stops that characterized the Fallen fighting style.

The rebel Guardian and Trueblood worked in a tandem, holding back the other Spire Guardians. Jonah pulled out Lynn's blades and motioned Mike back against the dollies.

Trueblood almost lost her concentration when she saw him step forward. "Jonah…"

"I can fight." As if to test Jonah's point, a Guardian slipped between the mage's barrage of supernatural fire and spells.

Jonah slipped into defensive moves, blocking every thrust and swipe of the Guardian's blades. He couldn't be sure, but the man seemed surprised that he was so capable. That shock proved the guard's undoing because Trueblood nailed him with a spell.

The man dropped to the ground and didn't move. Jonah whirled, blades ready to hold off any others. He wasn't prepared to see the Grand Oracle grab Trevor by the wrist and whirl the boy across the floor. Kevin regained his feet and charged the Grand Oracle while doing a better job of blocking spells with swipes of his blades.

Jonah thought his friend would actually succeed in reaching the Grand Oracle until the man lifted Kevin off the ground without touching him. Jonah winced in sympathy as Kevin struggled in the obviously painful grip.

"Guardians!" Trevor yelled.

Four of the enemy Spire Guardians reversed sides and attacked their own people. Using the momentary confusion to his advantage, the rebel Guardian in Jonah's group pulled two silver orbs from his tunic and heaved them into the air. The devices continued upward and attached to the ceiling high above.

Meanwhile, Trevor rushed the Grand Oracle, forcing the man to release Kevin and defend himself. At the same time, the silver orbs exploded overhead, sending huge sections of the bay ceiling crashing to the ground. Trevor blurred into motion and snatched Kevin to the side as the debris rained down on the Grand Oracle and a couple of his Guardians.

Ramsey lost his focus. "Master!"

Marcus scored two cuts across the man's chest before the agent phased to the opposite side of the pile of rubble and out of reach.

The debris pile moved and heaved upward to reveal the Grand Oracle. He was untouched and protected behind a powerful shield. He showed no concern for the broken bodies of his dead Spire Guardians in the rubble.

With a roar of anger, the Grand Oracle pushed his shield outward, sending the debris flying in every direction. A huge chunk headed straight for Jonah and Mike. The boys dived in different directions to avoid it. Trueblood used a charm at the last minute to turn the chunk of metal into a brittle material.

It impacted between Jonah and Mike and produced a cloud of fine dust. Mike staggered out of the cloud, clutching the compass.

The Grand Oracle noticed. "Never!" He shot a bolt of supernatural lightning at Mike.

Trevor shouted and charged forward, a blade in one hand and another silver orb in the other. He tried to deflect the lightning with the blade, but

The Seeker's Compass **593**

the volley was too powerful. The lightning struck the right side of Trevor's chest and heaved the boy up and across the floor.

He landed a few feet away from Kevin and Marcus. The silver orb tumbled free of Trevor's slack grip as the boy convulsed with painful spasms. Mike shouted and darted toward him.

Jonah did the same but his body blurred into motion and the next second, he knelt over the courier. He choked at the sight of the large burn mark on the boy's chest.

Trevor gripped Jonah's arm. "Where's Mike?" His voice was full of pain and his breathing labored.

Mike crowded in beside Jonah. "I'm here."

Trevor's gaze shifted. "I couldn't let you die. You have to… survive. Seeker."

"No, no, no." Mike repeated the word in a hushed voice.

The Grand Oracle watched with a sneer on his face. "Your Master, the so-called Elder, was foolish to trust in one so young." He raised his hands, gathering power to strike again. "You'll discover what happens to those who oppose the Rulers of the Afterworld."

CHAPTER THIRTY-SEVEN
SACRIFICE

Energy coursed around the Grand Oracle's fingertips as the powerful creature prepared to fry Jonah and his group. Trevor fastened onto his wrist and Jonah sucked in a startled breath as the shield bracelet activated, launching a blue distortion into existence around him and the others.

The Grand Oracle sneered. "That pathetic shield won't protect you heretics." He lit up the barrier with an impressive volley of supernatural lightning. The protective bubble held, despite several cracks that suddenly appeared. The force of the attack shook Jonah's arm.

Trevor pulled Jonah almost to the floor, forcing him to twist his body just to keep his left arm up and the shield activated

"The Elder..." Trevor's words were almost too low to hear and garbled because of the blood dripping from the corner of his mouth. "Get... to... him."

"I don't know where he is." Jonah faltered just as the world around them went crimson.

The Grand Oracle changed from lightning to red flames. The cracks in the shield widened even further under the new assault and the pressure shook Jonah's left arm even more mercilessly.

Trevor worked his mouth. "Take my power and knowledge."

Jonah tried to pull free. "I can't."

"What are you saying?" Mike looked appalled.

"It's the only way." Trevor pressed Jonah's right hand against his burned tunic, just above his heart. "Take it, Jonah."

"What about your soul?"

Trevor released his grip and fumbled with an intact portion of his tunic. His trembling hand pulled out one of the ornate, little bottles. "Hold it in here and take it to the Elder." When Jonah leaned back, cold steel entered Trevor's voice. "Do… it." The boy gestured to the silver orb bomb. It wobbled on the floor outside the shield, instantly forgotten by the Grand Oracle.

Trevor shook Jonah. "You don't have much time."

Jonah knew he didn't have any choice. His arm vibrated so much that his teeth began to clack together.

Trueblood pressed her hand over his, adding her own power to the shield. "Hurry, Jonah."

It was rare for the mage to use his first name and only highlighted her seriousness.

The heat of the assault had already warmed the inside of the shield, making their breaths ragged, and now threatened to suffocate them. If the shield did fail, the Grand Oracle would surely roast them all.

Jonah exchanged a frightened look with his godfather, then with Mike.

"Don't do it," Mike urged, his voice full of shock and hurt.

Jonah closed his eyes. Wetness touched his cheeks, but he ignored the tears and dug his hands into the fabric of Trevor's tunic, calling on his power.

At once, his Reaper half responded and Trevor's power and remaining life force flowed into his hands. Mike continued to yell behind him, but a sudden silence in the room caused Jonah to open his eyes.

The Grand Oracle looked appalled. His Guardians backed away, undisguised fear etched on each of their faces. The sight of them spurred Jonah on and he pulled every ounce of power from Trevor. Even near death, the boy retained a tremendous amount of energy.

Strength surged into Jonah and his mind opened up to a shocking truth as he touched the boy's soul. He could obtain knowledge from a person as well! At the same time, knowing that sickened Jonah; because it made him little better than the Grand Oracle.

The last of Trevor's life force flowed into Jonah and a golden light erupted around the boy's body, forcing Jonah to cover his eyes. The light felt warm and gentle against his skin. He peeked between his fingers and watched, becoming entranced as the glowing light collapsed on itself until all that remained was a brilliant pinpoint of soul energy.

Everyone watched the soul as it began to rise into the air. Jonah reached out a hand and the soul stopped and bobbed closer to him. He held out the bottle. Like a moth drawn to a flame, the soul jerked into motion and flowed into the container. The sigils carved into the sides flared with rich, golden light. Jonah replaced the stopper, mentally noting how warm the bottle was to the touch, along with its steady heartbeat.

After slipping the soul bottle into a pocket, Jonah stood.

The Grand Oracle's mouth twisted in disgust. "You're an abomination!"

Several of his Guardians dropped their blades to the ground in horror. Some began to mutter in shocked voices, "The Deliverer."

When a Guardian tried to flee, The Grand Oracle enveloped the man with a volley of lightning. Whirling on another who had also dropped his blades, he killed that guard on the spot with another bolt of lightning.

"The boy is not a god and therefore, he can't be a Deliverer." The Grand Oracle glared at his own men. "I'll prove it by killing him."

The dangerous being fired lightning, but Jonah reactivated the shield and used his augmented powers to strengthen it. He also sent the barrier surging forward. The Grand Oracle crossed his arms while muttering a spell. The barrier passed harmlessly over him, knocking his remaining Spire Guardians against the back wall, where they slumped to the floor, dazed.

The Grand Oracle retaliated with red flames. Jonah called on the wind, summoning it through the broken skylights to produce a blast. He succeeded in stopping the flames only a few feet away from his group. Gritting his teeth, he managed to push them back for a moment, but the flames still advanced.

"Jonah..." Marcus whispered.

"I know." Jonah never expected to hold out, even with the extra power. "Kevin."

He flicked his chin up. Kevin glanced that way and nodded. He gripped Jonah and Mike by their tunics. Marcus did the same for Trueblood, their helpful Guardian, and a surviving rebel.

The flames inched ever closer, coming to within a foot, where they began to blister Jonah's face. He shifted, using a gust of wind to push the flames into the remaining overhead skylights. Shards of crystal rained down. The blast of redirected fire caught one of the hovering crafts in the side. The ship spun away, trailing smoke as it slipped out of sight.

Jonah sucked in a breath, ignoring the chaos and clamor. "Now!"

The ripples played along his arms as Kevin phased them out of the chamber. They reappeared on top of one of the remaining armored craft that hovered outside the Central Spire. Marcus, Trueblood, and the rebel Guardians reappeared atop a second craft.

The movement alerted the pilot below Jonah, and the craft shifted into a tight spiral, moving away from the tower. The ships were large, but the hulls were curved and sleek, making it hard to stay in place. Mike yelped, lost his footing, and slipped. Kevin grabbed his arm and hauled him back.

"Sorry." Mike scrambled wrapped his arms around Jonah's arm.

Jonah was torn between his terror of sliding loose and dropping to his death, and the sheer wonder of the spectacular view of the Central Archives complex spinning below him. Mike let out a startled breath and clutched Jonah's arm even tighter.

The pilot's maneuver saved their lives because seconds later, a huge explosion blew a large hole in the Central Spire. Even so, the craft bucked hard when the pilot strove to establish more distance from the bellowing plume of smoke and debris.

Jonah lost his own grip and tumbled free, Mike with him. Kevin pushed off and grabbed both boys by the arm and phasing them safely to the huge public square far below.

Since phasing happened in a split second, they appeared in the square before the falling bits of Spire could even reach the ground. Jonah and the others stared in horror as debris smashed all around them, injuring several innocent people and creating panic and bedlam.

When Marcus appeared with Trueblood, the mage had the presence of mind to zap a huge chunk of wall with a spell before it slammed onto a huddled crowd of people. The spell transformed the debris into a powdery dust that merely coated the hapless bystanders. *At least they weren't killed*, Jonah thought.

Amid the screams of pain and shock, many people were pointing skyward at the huge plume of smoke now streaming from the windows of the upper section of the Central Spire.

Mike nudged Jonah. "Do you think the Grand Oracle is…?"

"Let's move," Marcus cut in. He motioned toward the nearer of two immense, curved colonnades.

Jonah was struck by how similar this space was to the pictures he once saw of St. Peter's Square. The colonnades all featured walls with three huge mosaics. He gasped because they were also very similar to the vistas they observed in the Deliverer's portal.

He opened his mouth to ask about the mosaics just as flashes of weaponry fire from a dogfight high overhead drew everyone's attention. One heavy-duty tear-ship fired on the others and led them away.

Kevin cheered. "Way to go!" He herded Jonah and Mike under the cover of the colonnade.

"What?" Jonah asked before registering that Marcus didn't bring the rebel Spire Guardians when he phased. He gazed at the retreating crafts. "They stole one of the ships?"

"Yep. A diversion," Kevin said, pushing through the bewildered crowd. "They'll try to come back and get us."

Jonah was about to point out that wasn't likely when Spire Guardians charged them from both directions, shoving people out of their way.

Marcus pointed at a large, two-tier craft with an open-air, upper deck. It was crowded with frantic people, each one trying to escape the chaos.

Jonah's godfather phased Trueblood and himself to the top deck of the vehicle as it rose into the air. Jonah, Mike, and Kevin followed. The upper deck was truly open. It didn't have seats, just guardrails around the sides and a central, waist-high rail to lean against.

The Seeker's Compass

The archivists on board were startled at their appearance, but soon cleared a space around Jonah's group. Ramsey's arrival, however, produced a stampede of citizens to the lower deck. The agent's grey robes were burnt away in places and the side of his face was dripping blood. Ramsey ignored the people streaming past him as he zeroed in on Jonah with slices of his blades. Jonah was able to dodge them easily until he lost his footing and landed on his butt in a sprawl.

Ramsey attempted to skewer him with a blade, but Kevin leapt over Jonah and stopped the agent. With his own blade locked against Ramsey's, Kevin twisted his weapon and succeeded in disarming the man. It thudded onto the vehicle's hull. Before Ramsey could regain his weapon, Kevin kicked the man in the chest and sent him tumbling over the railing.

Two more Guardians were engaging Marcus. He whirled and sliced at one. When he ducked a swing from the second, Trueblood hit the man dead center with a blast of green flame. The Guardian fell over the edge, his arms pinwheeling as he plummeted helplessly to the ground.

Marcus took down the remaining attacker with a cut across the man's chest. A third Guardian appeared right behind Mike and grabbed him in a bear hug. Mike crouched in a defensive move and flipped the surprised attacker over his head.

Jonah shouted, "Sakoto!" Calling on the wind was easier for him in this situation. All he had to do was augment the existing slipstream. The result was a hard blast that sent the last Guardian off the back of their craft.

Marcus winked at Jonah. "Good move, but we need to get clear and find our own ship. I don't think the rebels are coming back for us. Mike, do you remember any codes we can use?"

Mike nodded and yanked the compass free of a pocket just as another Guardian appeared almost on top of him. The attacker grabbed hold of Mike before Marcus or Kevin could react. The sudden action smashed Mike against the railing and knocked the compass free of his hand, sending the device over the side of the vehicle.

Trueblood raised her hand. "Duck!" Mike stomped on the Guardian's foot and slipped free. Trueblood nailed the man in the face with a stunning spell.

Jonah shot forward to grip Mike by the tunic and pull him away from the railing just as the stunned attacker tumbled over and out of sight.

Mike broke free of Jonah and hurried to the railing to look over the side. After a moment he dropped to his knees and exclaimed, "The compass is gone!"

CHAPTER THIRTY-EIGHT
SEEKER'S COMPASS

Jonah searched the Central Complex square below, but it was in vain, and he wanted to scream. The compass was gone. All their fighting and Trevor's sacrifice had been for nothing.

Marcus tapped his arm. "Watch, Jonah." He indicated Trueblood with a tilt of his chin.

The mage had her right hand extended as she muttered a spell. Her long ponytail whipped behind her in the wind. Marcus shook Jonah and pointed.

He blinked with surprise when something grew larger and began to approach their vehicle at a fast rate. He jumped to his feet when he realized it was the compass. Zooming past him and Mike, it landed on Trueblood's outstretched hand.

The mage handed it to Mike.

He took the compass, gazing into her face with awe. "Thanks."

"You're welcome."

Jonah's Death Sense, which had remained on constant throbbing warning, spiked when several heavy-duty ships set off in pursuit. They emerged from an opening high up in the outer wall. *A hangar bay*, Jonah thought. The knowledge from Trevor's mind produced images of the location in his head. *Ships! Just what we need.*

Jonah turned to his godfather. "Marcus–" The vehicle bucked beneath Jonah and slowed.

Mike had to clutch the compass with both hands so he didn't drop the device over the edge again.

Jonah's godfather reached out to steady Mike. "They must have ordered this craft to stop."

"Easier to shoot us." Kevin pointed toward the approaching craft. Pinpoints of light flashed on the lower hulls of the ships as they fired.

"Are you serous?" Jonah had his answer when the enemy shots peppered the top of the craft. Trueblood threw up a shield to protect them, but the muffled cries from below meant the rest of the passengers weren't so lucky. The enemy ships zoomed overhead and began to circle around like vultures.

The mage's normal solemn voice was tinged with fury when she rasped, "Those beasts! They'll kill everyone on board just to get us."

Jonah shared her outrage because he felt responsible. He was, after all, the target of all their shots. "We need to get off this thing."

"Unfortunately," Marcus said, his voice taut with anger, "most of the places I know are either shielded against phasing, or full of innocents." His jaw tightened, watching the ships approaching. "I won't endanger anymore people."

"I have an idea," Kevin and Jonah shouted at the same time. But Kevin was faster and gripped Jonah and Mike by their arms and phased before the ships could fire again. They appeared atop a curved building very near the base of the Central Spire. Marcus and Trueblood materialized beside them.

The vehicle they escaped from took a few more hits, but the attackers flew by, their crafts growing larger in size as they zeroed in on Jonah's group. He didn't know how the enemy pilots managed to guess where they were.

Then, a different craft, circling high overhead, zoomed downward and began firing at them. *A spotter*, Jonah decided as the rooftop exploded around them.

Kevin sprinted across the roof, keeping his grasp on Jonah and Mike. He phased again, just as the initial two attackers drew close enough to add their fire to the onslaught that was wreaking destruction on the building. Marcus matched his moves.

The Seeker's Compass **603**

They reappeared on the adjacent rooftop. It was one of six rows of curved buildings, *that were similar to the Pentagon's ring corridors,* Jonah thought. He didn't have any time for more sightseeing because they had to keep phasing to avoid enemy fire. Judging from the increasing damage to the buildings, the shooters didn't seem to care about the people inside there, either.

Perhaps Marcus came to the same conclusion because he called out to Jonah, "We need to use the compass."

Jonah didn't agree. For one thing, every time they tried, they had to phase again just to avoid the barrage of fire and explosions. Plus, he had a plan.

As if proving his point, Kevin growled in frustration and phase three more times in quick succession, and had to hop across five of the buildings. The enemy crafts broke off to circle around for another attack run.

Jonah knew they only had seconds to put his idea into motion. He shouted to his godfather, "I know where to get a ship! Follow me." He grabbed a handful of Mike's tunic and phased.

He and Mike reappeared in a hangar bay full of the tear-drop ships. Kevin, Marcus, and Trueblood also appeared within a second. The startled pilots and bay crew could only gape with astonishment at them.

Jonah knew the Guardians would follow once someone reported their location. He didn't waste any time and ducked under the nearest ships. Sure enough, he felt the telltale shift in air pressure as their pursuers instantly appeared in the bay.

"Where are you going?" Kevin's voice was curious as he followed close behind.

"Where do you think? The Guardian said we needed a ship." Jonah continued the mad dash under three more crafts before he stopped to clamber up the ladder of an open one.

Kevin grabbed the back of Jonah's tunic to stop him. "Yeah, but that's too small. And how did you know to come here?"

"I got some of Trevor's memories when I touched his soul."

Marcus frowned while Kevin looked unnerved.

Trueblood didn't say anything as she produced a shield to protect them from enemy fire.

Mike's face paled, but he remained focused and pointed to a bulkier craft off to the right. "Try that one."

Jonah maneuvered to the ship Mike selected. Unlike the sleek, tear-shaped ships, this craft had an oblong, flat-topped cargo hull, complete with side hatch. Kevin opened it like he'd done it a hundred times before and waved Jonah and Mike inside first.

The ship's cockpit contained only two seats while the forward cargo section had four facing seats. Rushing to the front, Jonah dropped into what he assumed was the pilot seat. Mike came in beside him, breathing hard and looking paler than normal.

Kevin crowded in behind. "Jonah, you don't know how to fly."

"No, but Mike does."

"That's a single-prop," Mike sputtered, sitting forward, "not something like this."

"Relax." Jonah cracked a smile at his friends. He felt unusually confident despite their situation. "Trevor knew how to fly."

As Mike and Kevin gawked at him, Jonah immersed himself in the strange new knowledge, allowing the information to guide his hands. He pressed a certain spot on the clear glass panel and the whole thing lit up with blinking, multicolored displays.

Touching a different glowing readout resulted in the ship sealing itself. Something thunked against the outside and clattered to the ground.

"It's the Guardians, trying to get in," Marcus said. "Stay focused, Jonah. We are safe, but don't dawdle."

More Guardians pounded on the hull, but Jonah followed his godfather's calm instructions. He concentrated, placing his hands over the touch-sensitive controls as he delved into Trevor's memories again. *That's it,* Jonah said to himself, activating the ship. It lifted off the deck, accompanied by startled yells and heavy thuds as the shocked people slid off the hull.

Pressing another control, Jonah sent the craft forward while activating its simple gun. In a way, it reminded him of one of the video games he often played with Robert. Jonah fingered the control, getting the feel of it while peering at the targeting display now splashed across the lower left of the viewport.

Two of the attack ships lumbered into view just outside the hangar bay doors.

Mike pressed himself back into his seat. "Jonah?"

"I see them." He targeted the engine of the enemy on the left and fired. Their own ship rumbled at the release of the brilliant orbs of plasma fire. Jonah's aim was true and the craft took a direct hit to its engine. The craft jerked sideways, opening the gap between the ships. Jonah angled skillfully between the attackers and out of the open hangar bay door.

Kevin gripped the backs of both chairs to keep from tumbling into the rear section. Jonah didn't have time to see if Marcus and Trueblood were strapped in.

His heart pounded like crazy in his chest. If he stopped to consider he shouldn't have known how to do that, they would surely have been in trouble. His hands shook, which was unfortunate owing to the sensitivity of the controls. The ship responded by almost flipping over in mid-air.

"Sorry about that." Jonah forced himself to relax as he sent the ship straight up, pressing everyone further into their seats. Distant thuds sounded, followed by a violent bucking.

Mike crossed his arms while scanning the console readouts.

Jonah began to wonder if his buddy could actually read the screens. "Mike?"

Mike shook his head, keeping his attention fastened on the controls.

Jonah turned to the front viewport, or rather, the portion of the hull that became transparent when the ship sealed itself. The craft was slipping through the wispy clouds toward, what Jonah assumed was, an opening at the top of the complex. He could see bright sky and clouds. In fact, he wondered why more ships weren't coming in and going out this way instead of using the massive entryway below.

"Jonah?" Kevin tapped him on the top of his head. "You can't get out that way because..."

Within seconds, projectiles impacted the invisible barrier above.

"There's a shield, smart guy."

"I didn't know."

Kevin shoved his head. "I thought you had Trevor's memories."

Jonah ignored the barb as he took the ship into a wrenching sideways turn. Mike gripped his armrests, and Kevin hung onto the seat for dear life.

The ship came around, and Jonah dived down along the central tower. When the hostile fire began to ping against the ship again, he leveled out, barreling toward the entryway. That wouldn't work either. Even from this distance, he could make out the rows of heavier ships waiting, and virtually blocking the exit.

"I understand the controls," Mike said. He tapped the console. A smaller window blossomed on the forward view screen, and Mike and Jonah sucked in simultaneous breaths. "He's alive and waiting."

The Grand Oracle stood on a floating platform, the ranks of Guardians behind him. His robes were frayed and blackened from the explosion and his silver-grey hair stuck like spikes out around his head. As they watched, he raised both hands and the air around him began to distort. Pinpoints of amber light appeared on the gun ports of the surrounding vessels.

Jonah pressed his eyes closed, shifting through Trevor's knowledge for a way to escape. "I know the location of the rally point."

Marcus crowded forward to see outside. "Jonah, I know the location too, but we can't get through the Grand Oracle's blockade."

"Yes, we can." Jonah smiled up at his godfather. "The rally point has a code. The Elder showed Trevor before he crossed over."

Mike held up the compass. "Tell me the code." He didn't look at Jonah and his voice sounded tight and tense.

Jonah nodded and did as Mike asked.

Kevin snorted. "You think the compass can move the whole ship?"

"Yes I do," Mike acknowledged. "Just like it moved that platform. But we need to attach it to something."

The Seeker's Compass **607**

Kevin activated his blade and plunged it into a thin air vent. He twisted the blade to widen the opening. Then he took the compass from Mike and wedged it into the space. "There you go."

Mike frowned. "That's crude."

Kevin shrugged. "Sue me."

Mike manipulated the compass dials. His eyes began to glow as a display appeared around the compass. The 3D versions of the symbols in Trevor's address were highlighted. The green *activate* button on the compass pulsed in readiness.

Marcus sighed a relieved breath. "Let's get out of here."

Mike stiffened in his seat and pointed at a readout that began flashing red. "Something's coming up behind us, and fast."

A second later, a dull thud vibrated the hull and their momentum dropped. It was so sudden that Kevin flew forward, crashing against the console. Marcus and Trueblood let out simultaneous, muffled cries. It was like someone was yanking them from behind.

Jonah glanced at his friend. "Mike, what's happening?"

Mike stared at the readouts in disbelief. "Someone hooked onto this ship."

"Look!" Kevin pointed out the hull as he heaved himself off the console.

The air distorted around the Grand Oracle as the man weaved a huge spell, something Jonah hadn't seen so far.

Trueblood's voice was still calm, but tinged with concern. "You should get us out of here, Jonah. That's a powerful spell he's conjuring."

A huge distortion wave rushed toward their craft when the Grand Oracle released the spell. The many ships arrayed behind him expelled volleys of energy from their weapon ports. As the supernatural firestorm sped toward him, Jonah reached for the *activate* button.

The spell traveled faster than Jonah could anticipate, appearing around them in less than a second. The ship bucked so hard that Jonah banged his head against his side of the hull. Mike let out a startled grunt before landing on the side of Jonah's seat.

Kevin slid to the deck while Marcus and Trueblood were thrown into the back of the craft. The vibrations and jerking were horrifying, but Mike managed to pull himself into his chair while staring out the front. His mouth hung open in horror.

Jonah braced himself to keep from being flung into the hull again. He dived forward and jabbed the green activate button just as the maelstrom of destruction engulfed their ship.

CHAPTER THIRTY-NINE
RAMSEY'S LAST RIDE

The ship continued to buck and gyrate around Jonah and the others. A horrific grinding sound of something being torn loose came from below their feet. To their right, a control panel sparked and exploded. Mike yelped, being the closest to the damage.

Jonah waved the resulting vapors away to glance out the front. Roiling fire and super-heated currents continued to obscure the view for several more terrified moments. Just as he began to worry, an azure sky appeared and the warm rays of the sun touched his face.

Jonah sighed in relief as he checked their location. The Central Archives complex and the Grand Oracle had been replaced by a semi-forested area and a meandering river below. Jonah leaned back in the pilot's chair.

It was only now that an incessant beeping attracted his attention. The display around the compass flashed what was clearly a warning signal. With his head still dizzy from the heavy bump against the hull, Jonah couldn't concentrate enough to understand what it meant.

Mike, leaning far to his left to avoid the sparking hull panel, began working the controls. Jonah turned around in his seat to find Kevin and Marcus helping Trueblood to stand. She favored her left foot, so Marcus held on as they moved to the back seats.

Kevin must have also heard the beeping because he returned to the cockpit and leaned over the back of Mike's seat. "What's wrong?"

"That ship came through with us and it's…"

A screeching sound drowned out the rest of Mike's comment. An accompanying heavy vibration began at the back of their ship and continued to the front. That's when a smaller tear ship tumbled by, trailing smoke and fire. And it was still attached to their ship by a burning cable.

Jonah glanced at Kevin. "Can't you phase outside to the hull and cut the cable?"

"It's too late for that. Hold on." Kevin gripped the back of Mike's seat. The cable reached its maximum length and yanked their ship hard to the right before snapping. The smaller Guardian craft tumbled end over end and exploded in a sudden ball of expanding gas and fire.

"Oh my God." Jonah couldn't believe his eyes.

Beads of sweat broke out on Mike's forehead as he worked at the controls. Their own craft continued to buck and wobble despite his efforts.

"One of the engines was damaged." The certainty in Mike's voice and manipulations of the controls impressed Jonah. Whatever Mike did worked because the vibrations in the hull finally subsided. "I'm pulling back on the power to compensate. That should level us off. I think."

With the mind boost from the Enhancer, Jonah realized it was quicker for Mike to read the display than it was for him to call up Trevor's memories. Plus, Mike had taken flying lessons and Jonah imagined that all ships had certain things in common after all .

Mike brought the ship around so it was facing where they had come from. He set it into a swaying hover so Jonah and everyone else could watch the remains of the guardian ship dissipate and its debris float away on the wind.

Jonah settled into his seat again, rubbing his bruised head. "Thanks." Mike nodded without taking his eyes off the controls.

Although the annoying beeping had stopped, other lights still blinked. Jonah pointed at a large yellow one. "What's that?"

"Oh." Mike touched a control and the alarm stopped blinking. "We overshot the rally point." He met Jonah's gaze. "Should we head back?"

"No." Marcus came forward again. "Jonah, did Trevor know the location of the hidden base?"

The Seeker's Compass **611**

Jonah closed his eyes, calling up Trevor's memories. "Yeah, but we need to change course a little." He told Mike the numbers that appeared in his head.

Mike frowned at him while entering the coordinates. "We should take it slow." He glanced at Marcus, who nodded. Mike sent their ship forward at a reduced speed. Finished with that detail, he leaned back in his seat and held out his left hand. "Give him to me."

Jonah needed a second to remember the soul bottle in his tunic pocket. With all their banging around, he was afraid the bottle might have been damaged. But when Jonah pulled the bottle from his pocket, it seemed fine. He handed over Trevor's spirit.

Mike pressed the bottle against his chest and closed his eyes. The spirit within flared brighter at the contact.

Jonah had the sudden feeling he was invading a private moment. So he turned to Kevin, who also averted his gaze to look out the front viewport.

Jonah tapped Kevin's hand. "Why not have the rally point at the hidden base?"

Kevin snorted. "That's too dangerous. What if the enemy discovered the location?"

Marcus nodded in agreement. "It's safer to have the rally point at a distance. That way the rebels have a checkpoint where they can clear anyone arriving. From there, they run people to the hidden base in ships. Only the pilots know the actual location."

"Oh." Jonah stared out the front viewport, thinking. "Hey. Wouldn't someone have seen us fly over?"

"Yes. That's why I told you to continue on." Marcus frowned. "I'm surprised they haven't–"

A dull thunk stopped Jonah's godfather in mid-sentence. The sound came from the rear compartment, followed by the screeching of metal. A warning light on the console began wailing.

Trueblood called out, "Marcus."

Jonah's godfather hurried into the back. Kevin followed, staring up at a blade sticking through the upper hull.

"What the…" Kevin muttered.

"It's a Guardian." Marcus drew his blades.

Jonah knew the real deal. "It's Ramsey." He hit Mike's armrest to get his attention. "Stop us."

Mike slipped Trevor's spirit bottle in a pocket and touched the ship's controls. The craft jerked and its forward momentum slowed to a bouncing hover. Something tumbled along the upper hull until two blades punctured the metal again, just behind the cockpit.

Jonah unstrapped himself and yanked the compass free of the air vent. He pulled out one of Lynn's blades and phased.

Despite the lack of forward movement, air buffeted Jonah's face as he appeared atop the bulky craft. Ramsey's burnt tunic flapped in the strong breeze. The agent pulled his blades from the hull and stood straight.

His face morphed into a rictus grin. "So, half-breed. You choose to face me instead of hiding behind the adults."

The frightful sight of Ramsey filled Jonah with rage instead of fear, and he charged the agent. Ramsey swung at him but Jonah expected that, blocked the man, and ducked under the blow.

The result was that Ramsey had his back to Kevin and Marcus, who had just phased outside the craft.

"Jonah, what are you doing?" Marcus called.

Jonah charged Ramsey again and shouted, "Sakoto!" The wind whipped at the man's feet and unbalanced him enough that Jonah tackled him. He had prepared for this moment. He was going to take Ramsey far away from the people he cared about. With that decision firmly in mind, he pressed the compass's activate button.

The next moment, Jonah and Ramsey reappeared at the rally point's destination platform, nestled inside a partial sandstone enclosure. The open side overlooked the base camp below.

Jonah had to focus on the immediate. He tried to dodge, but Ramsey's foot blurred into motion and caught him in the stomach.

Pain flared along Jonah's side as he flipped through the air and hit the ground outside the enclosure. He rolled to his feet to confront Ramsey, who was relentless and fast. Jonah called on his training and blocked most of the blows. That seemed to anger Ramsey, and he mixed in small phases, attacking from all sides and scoring more cuts and hits.

The cunning agent reappeared in a crouch to nick Jonah across the back of the leg. Jonah screamed and went down to one knee. He whirled, striking out with a blade, but Ramsey did another micro-phase. When he appeared behind Jonah, he lashed out with a boot to the back.

Jonah tumbled forward, losing a blade. He heaved and coughed up blood that splattered onto the light-colored stones beneath him. Ramsey attacked again before Jonah could regain his feet, scoring a stab to the left arm and numerous hits. The barrage ended with a power punch to the abdomen.

Jonah flew backward and landed in a heap, his remaining blade skittering across the stones and out of reach. The pain was unbearable, but Jonah was desperate now. In a last-ditch effort to escape, he clutched at the compass.

"No you don't, young Blackstone. You're not gonna use that compass." Ramsey lurched forward and yanked it away. A demented grin split the man's mangled face. "I will kill you and prove that you're not special. The entire Afterworld will know that Jonah Blackstone was not a Deliverer. He was just a pathetic half-breed."

Struggling to his knees, Jonah had to admit he didn't have any power left and he was physically done. And Lynn's blades were too far away. Despair threatened to overwhelm him, but he pushed it to the side. He'd successfully used the compass to keep the deranged agent away from the others. That's all that mattered now.

Ramsey nodded as if sensing Jonah's thoughts. "Yes, you're gonna die, young Blackstone. Don't worry; I'll take your broken body to your friends. And with me will be the full might of the Grand Oracle. This rally point and the hidden base will become smoking craters and all your friends here in the Afterworld will burn."

Ramsey loomed over Jonah, blade poised to strike. "When I return to the mortal world, I'll take care of the rest of your mortal family."

Jonah knew the man wasn't bragging. As the pain and mental anguish roared back with an oppressive zeal, something happened. Jonah's Reaper side surged forward and engulfed him in that calm inner space. Once that happened, the answer to his problem became clear.

He remained outwardly subdued as Ramsey stood behind him and grabbed a fistful of his hair. Bending Jonah's head back, the agent grinned in his face. "What are you gonna do, half-breed?"

Ramsey raised his blade, poised to drive it into Jonah's chest and through the heart.

But Jonah wasn't afraid. He was the Deliverer. His steady gaze met Ramsey's and in a moment of pure spite, Jonah mustered his best Obi-Wan voice. "If you strike me down, Darth, I shall become more powerful than you could possibly imagine."

Ramsey's confident stance faltered for the first time. "You are an abomination. Even a fool fears his own death." He scowled and brought his blade down, but it never connected.

Jonah had summoned his will and clamped his hands on Ramsey's blade-bearing hand to stop it. At first, the man tried to apply his full weight to drive the blade downward, but Jonah's Reaper powers surged forward, preventing that.

As soon as the Hunter's power begin to leak away, Ramsey understood the true danger and tried to release Jonah. "No. Impossible!"

Jonah held on, using the man's own power to strengthen himself. The blade slipped from Ramsey's hand and clattered on the stones. Jonah used the moment to flip Ramsey over and onto his back. Then he straddled the agent, pressed both hands against the man's chest, and began to suck every ounce of energy from him.

When Jonah spoke, the words that came to him weren't totally his own. They were the Deliverer's, as if the being spoke through him.

"You, the Grim Reaper, and the Grand Oracle have corrupted everything. It will end!" His last words shook the ground.

Ramsey gripped Jonah's hands, trying to pull free. But he was helpless as he aged before Jonah's eyes. "No!"

Ramsey's patterns, visible beneath the rips in the robe, vanished as the man aged twenty years. His normal chocolate complexion turned waxen in a few seconds. Jonah continued to pull until the spark of life that was the agent's soul began to flow toward his hands. His Reaper side wanted to take it.

A shadow zipped across the ground and stopped right overhead. Jonah dimly acknowledged that Mike had figured out where the compass had taken them. He remained focused on Ramsey even when Kevin and Marcus appeared on the platform and charged out of the partial enclosure.

The Fallen Reapers skidded to a halt half a dozen feet away, frozen in surprise.

"Jonah, stop!" Marcus inched closer but didn't move close enough to touch the boy. "You're not a killer like Ramsey."

Jonah didn't care. The Grim Reaper killed his parents. The mole had sent this dangerous man into Mount Vernon to threaten his friends. Lynn had been hurt, Mike tortured, and Trevor killed by the Grand Oracle.

"Agent Ramsey must go back and answer for his crimes," Marcus persisted.

"No." Jonah's voice was choked with rage and pain. "No."

Kevin knelt down to look Jonah in the eye. "What would Lynn say?"

The absurdity of the question momentarily broke through Jonah's fury. He glanced at the young Fallen Reaper.

Kevin returned the gaze. "Little man." He opened his emotions to Jonah and allowed his true feelings to show. His desire to protect Jonah, even from himself, surged forward.

Jonah's rage receded in the face of their mutual bond. When he met his godfather's worried gaze, all the things that Marcus had said to him at the hideaway registered. How would he use the incredible power he possessed?

The blinding hatred lifted and Jonah could think straight again. He resisted the urging of his Reaper nature and pulled his hands away from Ramsey's body.

Aside from sucking in a gagging breath, Ramsey didn't move. For a moment, Jonah feared he may have killed the man anyway. Then the agent's chest rose and fell, and Jonah relaxed. Ramsey wasn't dead, but he was totally mortal now.

CHAPTER FORTY
RALLY POINT

"Guardian vessel, identify yourself!" The challenging young female voice broke through the ship's speakers.

The rebels had noted their entry and the explosion of Ramsey's ship. No less than three armored rebel crafts had taken up positions around their own.

Mike watched the rebels dart around, seamlessly swapping positions and keeping the larger craft pinned in place. "Wow, they know how to fly."

That was as much as Jonah saw before he winced and huddled back on a bench in the rear section of the stolen craft, nursing his bruises and cuts. Trueblood offered to perform the Nistashi spell on him as soon as he boarded the craft, but he refused.

His healing process had been jump-started by taking Ramsey's power, but the man had inflicted serious damage. Kevin speculated it would take Jonah a couple of days of sleep to fully heal.

Ramsey lay on the floor against the back wall, cuffed and still unconscious. Kevin doubled-checked the restraints and then paused to set Lynn's retrieved blades beside Jonah. He hurried to the cockpit to drop into Jonah's vacant seat.

Jonah started to follow when Marcus got up, but his godfather gave him a look that was first furious and then sympathetic. "You should relax and let your body heal. I'll handle this."

"I'm okay." Jonah thought his voice sounded tired. He ached all over and smelled of dirt and otherworldly vegetation from his fight with Ramsey. Marcus crossed his arms and didn't move.

The Seeker's Compass

The warning blared from the speaker again. "Guardian vessel, identify yourself or we will open fire."

Realizing it was a losing battle, Jonah obliged his godfather and settled down.

Marcus nodded and hurried to the cockpit. He partially blocked Jonah's view as he leaned between the forward chairs. "Can I speak to them?"

The top of Mike's head, visible above the back of the co-pilot's chair, bobbed in affirmation. "Yes."

Jonah imagined his friend adjusting a set of controls.

Eventually, Marcus nodded and cleared his throat. "This is Marcus Armstrong, member of the Alliance Council. We've just escaped from the Central Archives."

The sound of a hushed conversation issued from the hidden speakers before the original voice returned. "Is the courier with you?"

Marcus exchanged a troubled glance with Kevin before saying, "I'm afraid I have sad news to deliver. The courier is dead."

A semi-transparent window opened, taking up the entire forward-view glass and showing the angry visage of an attractive young female rebel pilot. Her almond-shaped eyes narrowed, taking in Marcus and the group. "What happened?"

"The Grand Oracle killed him." Kevin's answer produced more shocked outburst from someone off-screen. "We have his soul."

The pilot's eyes widened, but she recovered quickly. "Give it to us."

Marcus shook his head. "I'm here as a representation of the Alliance Council and at invitation from your Elder. Do we have permission to proceed to your base? We will only hand over the courier's soul to the Elder. That was his final request."

The pilot turned in her seat, whispering to someone else again.

Jonah feared they would demand the courier's soul bottle anyway and then shoot them out of the sky.

Perhaps Mike sensed the same thing because he raised the spirit bottle into view. The pilot sat straighter in her seat. At the same time the person off-screen, a red-haired man, squeezed into view. The look of sadness in the man's eyes got to Jonah. It was clear he must have known Trevor.

Marcus gripped the back of Mike's seat. "This young man is a true Seeker." Marcus motioned toward the back of the craft. "And we have the Deliverer with us. Both young men befriended the courier and fought beside him. They share your loss."

The pilot's eyes snapped to Marcus. Now that she wasn't glaring at them, Jonah could see her eyes were a deep aquamarine and complimented her golden skin tone.

She shifted her gaze to the red-haired man, waiting for his decision. When he nodded, she turned back to Marcus. "Follow us. May the Deliverer quicken your journey."

The connection was cut. Mike tucked the bottle away and touched the ship's controls. It shuddered and begin to move, following the lead rebel ship.

Jonah relaxed as much as he could, but he also worried about the rebels' reaction when they reached the base. Would their awe wear off and the anger return? Trevor had touched a lot of lives, judging from the reactions. In a way, Jonah regretted ever doubting the boy.

Maybe he could ask Mike about Trevor when they returned home. That seemed so far away, even now. Jonah shifted his gaze out to the cockpit and the viewport. A squat mountain on the far side of a high plateau grew larger. Jonah called on the fading vestiges of Trevor's memories. *That's it.*

A wide rectangular opening near the top of the mountain turned out to be a hangar bay.

Kevin glanced at Mike. "Can you land us?"

"No problem." Despite the sluggish controls and the constant rattles from the craft, Mike guided the damaged ship through the bay opening and landed with a soft thunk.

Kevin patted the back of Mike's seat. "Not bad for a geek."

Mike shrugged and everyone left the craft to meet the rebels. Jonah consented to a helping hand from Kevin while Marcus helped Trueblood, but in short order, Jonah and Mike were standing side by side in front of the assembled crowd.

The Seeker's Compass **619**

Guardians, Archivists, and other Afterworld citizens had gathered in the rebel hangar to greet them.

The red-haired man from the rebel ship stepped forward with the young female pilot in tow. Jonah was surprised to see the man wore the uniform of Spire Guardian. "Where's the courier's soul bottle?" he demanded. A few of the gawking people seconded the man's question.

Jonah nudged Mike to pull out the soul bottle. When he refused, Jonah whispered, "It was Trevor's last wish."

Mike's face paled. He took the bottle from his pocket but passed it to Jonah and crossed his arms, hugging himself.

The rebel Guardian reached out and touched the bottle but didn't take it. "I was there when the Grim Guards attacked the meeting. I… I trained young Trevor." The man sucked in a breath to steady himself. Then he gazed at Jonah. "Truly, you are the Deliverer." He gave Jonah a respectful bow.

"Trevor," Jonah gulped, "I mean, the courier told me to bring his soul to the Elder."

The rebel Guardian straightened. "It is right that his soul ascend to the final plane." He motioned to a double door behind him. "The Elder awaits you."

"Marcus." Trueblood pointed to her injured ankle. "I'll never make the walk."

The female pilot raised her hand and motioned to someone near the back of the crowd. A woman in a plain white tunic moved through the people and over to Trueblood. From her way of inspecting the mage's ankle, Jonah guessed the woman must be a doctor or Healer.

She beckoned over a couple of men to help Trueblood to a side room.

When she saw Jonah's bloodied tunic, she paused. "You should come for treatment."

"No." Jonah didn't mean to yell but his voice rattled the hangar. People backed away, frightened. *Most won't understand and some will even fear you.* Jonah sucked in a deep breath to calm himself, but his voice still echoed with the words of past Deliverers when he spoke. "I have to see the Elder."

No one objected this time and the rebel Guardian and pilot led Jonah's group from the hangar. The Guardian remained stoic, but the young pilot's movements took on a reverent aura the further into the heart of the mountain the journeyed. She would glance back at Jonah and then hurriedly turn forward again. He didn't like it. The rebels already used his name as a parting blessing. What else could there be?

Soon, Jonah and his group stood before a large door made of smooth, dark stone. The pilot pushed the door open. She and the Guardian bowed, and motioned for everyone else to proceed.

Kevin peeked. "Wow." He entered with Mike right behind him.

Jonah paused at the opening to face the young pilot. "You aren't coming?"

The pilot met his gaze for a split second before averting her eyes. "We may not view his true face." She cast a quick glance at the Guardian for confirmation and then bowed again.

Marcus guided Jonah through the door. His breath caught because the cavern was beautiful. The floor was a deep emerald green, and glossy. But his feet didn't slip as he moved forward.

Toward the center of the space, seven pillars rose from the floor to the ceiling. Each had semi-transparent sides with multiple glowing white objects swirling around the interiors. The light from the objects hit the royal blue and violet patterns on the pillars and created ever-moving shapes on the walls.

"Awesome." Jonah's voice was hushed, as seemed proper in this place. The pillars reminded him of large soul bottles. Going on that idea, he let his Reaper side surge forward. "These are souls."

Marcus stopped in his tracks. "Are you sure?"

Jonah held his hand toward the nearest of the strange containers. Not only were these souls, they were powerful. "Yeah. I can feel them."

Kevin's hand hovered near his blades. "Remember the bottles in the Grand Oracle's place? I bet these are trapped souls."

As if in response to Kevin's words, the souls swirled around faster, emitting brighter light.

A deep baritone voice rolled from the shadows. "They are not trapped souls." The source, a tall, barrel-chested man, stepped into view. He wore bellowing robes of pale gold and matching sandals on his feet. The sash

The Seeker's Compass **621**

around his middle was emerald green like the floor. His snow white beard stood out in stark contrast to his ebony skin. And to Jonah's amazement, the man wore glasses.

The image of a wizened grandfather popped into Jonah's mind. As this being strode toward them in a dignified manner, the increased illumination from the swirling lights reflected off his bald head.

"These are ancient souls who've volunteered to stay behind and offer guidance to our resistance. I meditate and commune in harmony with them." He frowned at Kevin. "The soul bottles you witnessed are the Rulers of the Afterworld's perversion of the communing ritual."

Marcus had placed himself between the newcomer, Jonah, and Mike. He inclined his head to the man. "Prime Archivist. Or should I say Elder?"

The man took his time before nodding. "My real name is Prime Archivist Aristobulus, High Master of the remote Rocky Plateau Archives."

"That's a big title," Kevin whispered to Jonah as he crossed his arms, watching the man.

Jonah heard the awe in Kevin's quip and shared it.

"I never had the pleasure of meeting you, Elder, before my fall." Marcus moved aside to reveal Jonah and Mike. "This is Jonah Blackstone."

The Elder nodded, eager. "Yes, the Deliverer." His eyes shifted to Mike. "And you?"

"He's a Seeker."

Aristobulus pushed his glasses up on his nose and inspected Mike. "That is a remarkable honor, young man. There hasn't been a true Seeker in over two thousand years." He stood tall and patted his chest. "In fact, the last one was me."

Mike gawked at the man. "You're a Seeker?"

"Oh, not anymore. I worked with the last Deliverer toward the end. When he finished his work, my ability to open the inner compass faded." He held out a hand to Mike, but Jonah pulled the compass from his own pocket.

The Elder took it and caressed the device like a beloved possession. "The ability is temporary and bestowed on the one who's to help the Deliverer. I retained enough power to help your parents."

Marcus grunted.

Jonah gaped at the Elder. "You put the codes in the compass, didn't you?"

"Yes. I was able to enter the primary or surface level codes but not touch the inner compass."

Mike stirred. "And you helped Jonah's parents find the Protector's Ring and the Enhancer?"

The Elder bowed like he was happy that someone acknowledged that feat.

Jonah glanced at his godfather, who wore a pained expression. "Did you know my dad worked with the Elder?"

"No I didn't." Marcus worked his jaw. "It explains a lot and leads to many more questions."

Jonah blinked at his godfather's sudden anger. Strangely enough, he thought about Marcus and his dad and the final days of his parents. Marcus had accused his dad of not sharing information because his dad had worked with the Elder in secret.

All at once, Jonah had that perfect moment when an unpleasant but forgotten memory snaps into place. *The Elder.* He'd also been the one his father called for back in the chamber before Deyanira attacked. Jonah was sure of it, and had been ever since Trevor called the man Elder. Only now did he make the connection.

He activated one of Lynn's blades and waved it at the Prime Archivist while shouting, "You let my parents die!"

CHAPTER FORTY-ONE
THE ELDER

Kevin, the first to overcome his initial shock, grabbed Jonah around the waist.

Jonah continued to yell. "It's his fault."

Marcus stared at his godson, confused. "Jonah?"

"No! You don't get it." Jonah struggled in Kevin's grip. "My parents called for him the night they died." He pointed a blade at the Prime Archivist. "Didn't they? You're the Elder my dad called. But you didn't show up and the Grim Reaper killed them!"

Marcus turned on the man. "Is that true?"

"Yeah, it is!" Jonah shouted.

The Prime Archivist held up his hands and shocked Jonah when he nodded in agreement. "The young man is not totally wrong. I did not come when his father called."

"Why not?" Kevin asked, releasing Jonah.

"I couldn't return to that place. It had been compromised and I had already crossed to the Afterworld. Isaiah knew that, as well as the risks in rebelling against the Grim Reaper."

"You let them die," Jonah shouted.

"I could not have helped, young man. The Grim Reaper is more powerful than I am. Only the Grand Oracle could stand against him and they have common cause, for now."

Jonah's hands shook with anger and the fresh reminder of his loss. Marcus squeezed his shoulder.

Mike turned on the Prime Archivist. "Why couldn't you come back and help Jonah's parents?"

"I had to protect my identity and the rebellion on this side." The Prime Seeker exchanged a worried glance with Marcus. "I am sorry."

Marcus grimaced like he had a bad taste in his mouth. "I can't say I agreed with the secrecy, but I understand." He turned Jonah so they faced each other. "It's the reason we have the Alliance, Jonah. Our fight is in the mortal world. Your father understood that."

Jonah wanted to hate the Elder, and he did feel anger toward him. But even Marcus accused his father of doing things on his own. Jonah opened himself to a Reaper stare and then subjected the Elder to it. The man vibrated sincerity and conviction. But underneath, Jonah sensed falsehood.

Mike must have seen it too because he stirred and pointed at the man. "You're not the leader."

"He's right," Jonah joined in. "You're not the Elder, are you?" The anger threatened to return. Was this man covering for the one who could have helped his parents?

A tense silence filled the chamber until the Elder let out a long breath. In response, the seven containers glowed brighter and in the midst of the brilliance, short silhouettes appeared. After the light show faded, seven diminutive figures remained. The souls had taken on human forms.

As one, they stepped through the container walls and floated toward the group. Jonah tensed as the apparitions zeroed in on him and Mike. Each soul had aged skin and wizened features. The tallest was still shorter than Jonah.

At first glance, he mistook the dark skin tone and hanging garments for those of African Pygmies. But another name popped into Jonah's mind. His parents once told him about a short people called the Twa. *Yes*, Jonah thought. *An ancient, wise, and diminutive people.*

There were seven Elder Souls in all; four female and three male. Four, two female and two males, surrounded Jonah while the remaining three converged on Mike.

The Seeker's Compass **625**

When the Elder soul in front of Jonah spoke, it was with a blending of multiple voices. "We are the Elders." Their combined voices were similar to a well-tuned choir speaking in unison, but each voice carried a different note of a chord. "As you can see, we could not cross to your realm to help your parents. We are sorry for their loss."

Jonah gulped, not needing his Reaper stare to sense the truthfulness emanating from these souls.

"You are a Deliverer," the Elder intoned. It touched Jonah's chest with an ethereal hand. He stilled himself for the coldness associated with a Wraith's touch. In this instant, the contact was warm and calming.

Jonah's lingering pain from his injuries disappeared as well as his anger, sense of betrayal, and loss. He drew in a startled breath, feeling whole and energized. "Thank you." The Elder nodded.

A female Elder pointed to Mike. "He is indeed a true Seeker. He'll be able to consecrate new designation stones, if he believes in his power."

Mike stiffened when the woman pressed her palm to his chest. But after a moment, he relaxed, allowing the three beings to crowd around and touch him. The tableau reminded Jonah of a blessing ceremony, or the laying-on-of-hands from his aunt's church.

"He is in great pain over the loss of our courier." The female Elder withdrew her hands. "We also share your pain, young one, but the courier's soul will move on to its final plane of existence." She spread her short arms, indicating the cavern. "This is all an illusion. The true existence is out there, when you ascend. Therefore, we celebrate the courier's ascension."

Marcus motioned to Jonah. "Give them Trevor's soul."

Jonah withdrew the spirit bottle while thinking about the Elder's words. They touched something deep inside him. He gazed at the pillars. "You aren't trapped. You can come and go, to the other plane?"

The Elder's eyes brightened like two pinpoint stars. The effect was a thousand times more powerful than a Reaper Stare. Jonah knew his very soul was exposed to the being. "You are perceptive. The energy pattern, or spirit of the Deliverer, truly rests on you."

Aristobulus lifted the offered container from Jonah's hands. "Come."

Jonah assumed the invitation for him and the others because the Elders had already floated away between the seven pillars. They converged on the round fountain at the center of the cavern.

The Prime Archivist spoke in a voice like a teacher. "Spirits are energy patterns, young one. Have you ever wondered about geniuses in art, music, science, or political movements who seem to appear in every age? They are honored with the spirit energies of those disciplines, eternal patterns that appear when needed."

The pool of dark liquid in the fountain began to glow at the wave of the Prime Archivist's hand. "Deliverer and Seeker are names given to the energy patterns that come whenever the need arises and anoint the chosen vessels for a given time. You and your friend have those powers."

The Prime Archivist turned to Mike and frowned. "Your pain is the deepest. Would you prefer the honors?"

Mike took the place of honor beside the Prime Archivist. "What do I do?"

"Hold it above the pool." Aristobulus waved a hand over the water. "This is the well of souls, a natural pathway to the next plane."

Following the directions, Mike held Trevor's spirit bottle over the glowing liquid. The Elders joined hands and sang a peaceful hymn. The words were ancient and unknown, but the voices mixed in beautiful harmonies and touched Jonah's soul with peace and hope.

Mike's breath hitched in his chest and tears rolled down his cheek. When the Elders reached the climax of the hymn the bottle bucked in Mike's hand and Trevor's soul emerged. It hovered in front of Mike, who reached out and brushed his fingers against it. For a moment, the soul brightened.

A glistening shaft of light appeared, extending from the waters to the ceiling. Trevor's soul zipped around Jonah and the others one time and then zoomed up and into the light. After a short interval, the light winked out, plunging the pool into dimness again.

Jonah hooked an arm around Mike's trembling shoulders.

Mike shook his head. "I'm okay." He met Jonah's worried gaze. "Trevor said goodbye."

"It is done," the Elder souls intoned. They separated, each re-entering their crystalline container and giving up the human forms.

The Seeker's Compass

The Prime Archivist turned to Marcus. "I believe we have details to cover before you return to the mortal realm?"

Marcus inclined his head. "Yes, we do."

As he and the Prime Archivist walked away, deep in discussion, Jonah and Mike moved to one of the low benches lining the wall. The seats were wide and had thin cushions on them.

Mike perched on the edge of one, and Jonah joined him. Kevin hovered nearby, but far enough away to give them privacy. Jonah thought of asking Mike if he was really okay but was afraid of the answer.

After a long silence, Mike spoke. "I always knew what you were, but… to see you take someone's soul was…" He hugged himself while staring at his feet.

"Trevor asked me to do it. And I didn't take his soul."

"I know." Mike glanced at Jonah. "You almost lost control with Ramsey. I don't blame you."

"You think I'm an abomination?" Jonah didn't bother to hide his growing anger at the situation.

"I didn't say that." Mike pitched his voice lower. "I saw how afraid Marcus and Kevin were of you."

"Yeah, so did I." The thought pained Jonah. Not only had he frightened the rebels, he had also frightened Kevin and his own godfather. In a way, the Grand Oracle and the Grim Reaper were also afraid of him. Why else would they want him dead? "I scare everyone." Jonah's voice quivered.

He raised his hands, staring at them while recalling the sensation of pulling power from Ramsey. *Is this what it means to have the spirit energy of the Deliverer inside of you?*

Mike nudged Jonah's arm. "I'm not afraid of you."

The sincerity of Mike's words touched Jonah and helped to dispel his dark mood. "We're gonna be cool?"

Mike took a long time to answer. "Yeah. I need time to get over losing Trevor."

When Mike offered him a weak smile, Jonah's belief they would be cool with each other increased. He needed that. He didn't want to be alone with this heaviness of history and purpose. He suspected Mike didn't either.

Kevin stirred and moved closer to the boys, drawing Jonah's attention. He also noticed Marcus approached along with the Prime Archivist, who also held a thick book.

Mike blinked in surprise when the man offered him the book. He took it and ran his hands over the leather cover. "The Deliverer's Tales?"

The Prime Archivist smiled and patted the cover of the book. "I was there when the last Deliverer finished this." He turned to Jonah. "You're the new Deliverer and will need this book. Your friend is your Seeker and will translate it for you."

Kevin peered at the cover. "What will it tell them?"

The Prime Archivist met their combined gazes. "How to defeat the Rulers of the Afterworld."

CHAPTER FORTY-TWO
PARTING TOKEN

"What we need is our own portal." Kevin's statement ground the meeting with the rebels to a halt. He and Marcus stood in the rebel's staging area, in the midst of an argument with them about the risk of a journey to the Afterworld's pedestal room.

The problem was that the location of the chamber was close to the Grim Reaper's realm, and that worried many of the rebels. With no other option for returning Jonah's group home, Marcus wanted his godson to step in as the Deliverer and command the rebels to do it.

Jonah had resisted, not wanting to risk any more lives, nor encounter Deyanira again. That's when Kevin intervened.

The young Fallen Reaper shrugged. "Even if we secured the pedestal location on this side, Mike and Jonah are the only ones who can activate the ancient portals. We can't snatch them away to the desert cave whenever we need them." He glanced at Marcus. "Can we?"

Mike raised his hand. "I don't mind."

Marcus smiled at him. "Kevin's right. Having our own portal would allow us to connect directly to the portal you have here."

Mike wilted at that announcement. Since receiving the book, his attitude about the whole Seeker thing had changed.

"This presents us with an additional problem," Marcus concluded, stroking his chin.

Jonah leaned close. "So you don't want me to order them to do it?"

Marcus frowned at him, but Jonah didn't mind because he had a solution and the idea was simple as well as deserving. Plus, it would avoid going near the Grim Reaper's domain, at least for now.

He stood and everyone went quiet. The rebel Guardians sat straighter, waiting for his words. He gulped, reminded that they saw the Deliver almost as a religious figure. "Do you have something to stick the compass to a surface?"

After staring blankly at Jonah for half a second, the rebel pilot who had challenged their group earlier snapped her fingers and exited the staging chamber. She returned a minute later and handed Jonah a putty-like material.

"We use this to attach things to rocky surfaces. Will that work?"

"Perfect." Jonah hefted the malleable material in his hand.

Marcus raised an eyebrow. "What are you planning?"

Jonah grinned at his godfather. "I know where we can get a portal."

As soon as Jonah's group stepped through Deyanira's portal, Trueblood erected a protective shield.

Deyanira and several of her Grimnions hurried into the amphitheater moments after the group arrived. Her eyes widened in disbelief. The shock only lasted a second before the sorceress recovered and attacked with lightning and fire.

Trueblood didn't break a sweat as she fed power to her shield.

Jonah slapped the putty to the side of the portal and turned to Mike. "Do your thing."

Mike pressed the compass into the material. The code for the Deliverer's cavern was already entered. As Mike pressed the green activate button, Jonah turned and waved to an outraged Deyanira. The amphitheater disappeared before the evil Reaper's last barrage of spells could engulf them.

Jonah's group created a commotion when they appeared inside the Deliverer's cavern. Rubio, who had been in the process of entering the opening to the lower chamber, stopped in mid-motion, slack-jawed.

The Seeker's Compass

Jonah couldn't resist patting the side of the portal and saying, "Special delivery, from Deyanira."

Along with the portal, a bound and gagged Ramsey returned with the group.

Rubio grunted in surprise as he moved closer to inspect the agent. "I think the GBI will have a time identifying Ramsey. He's aged so much."

Trueblood crossed her arms, scrutinizing Marcus. "Interesting. I didn't realize the binding patterns slowed down the aging process."

Marcus frowned at her. "I told you. The trauma of *losing* his power had more to do with the aging."

Trueblood wore a rare smile on her face. "Rex confessed to me a year ago."

Marcus refused to meet her gaze, but he smirked. "The first person to mention this to Omar will get the worst assignments for a year."

Everyone laughed as the other Alliance people converged on the away team, the name Jonah and Mike had started calling the group.

*

The Alliance Council decided not to parade Jonah and the others around HQ. Marcus said Jonah's Afterworld dream-walk had convinced the group of the mole's existence. Until the Alliance could discover the mole's identity, they opted to send select personnel to the Guest House and question the group.

Kevin, Jonah, and Mike were shuffled from endless meetings and debriefings about the adventure. First, Rubio reviewed and recorded their individual narratives for the Alliance Council. Then various department representatives concerned with different aspects of the supernatural world asked their own questions.

After all that, Jonah had to tell his cousins and Wick all about the trip. Lynn grumbled because she missed out. Wick displayed equal parts wow and envy at not being present to witness mage Trueblood in action. Robert professed his simple relief at his little cousin returning unharmed.

Despite their denials, Jonah suspected his cousins and Wick had spent the bulk of their time playing video games while he risked his life in the

Afterworld. He didn't mind because he wanted to get his own time on the deluxe gaming systems before heading home.

That's exactly what Jonah did. He was into his fourth round, blasting through enemy fighters on the screen and beating his cousin Robert when Kevin and Mike entered the basement. Mike slumped into a big armchair, looking tired. Jonah understood because Mike had to endure a series of separate tests to determined any lingering symptoms from the Enhancer's mind boost.

Jonah set his game controller down. "How're you doing, Mike?"

"Fine." Mike screwed up his face despite his answer. "My mind is still going ninety miles an hour." He tapped his forehead. "Maybe the Elders or the compass did something to me."

Jonah nodded. "Don't forget the mind boost."

"How can I? It's weird. I… I started watching the Spanish channel."

"So…"

"I don't understand Spanish, but I followed the show." Mike looked perplexed. "When a commercial came on and I saw the text in Spanish, I realized what was happening."

"Wow, Mike. That's great." Jonah winced at the forced cheerfulness in his own voice.

"It's not." Mike frowned.

"We're all different. That's what you said," Jonah smiled.

Kevin snorted at the comment and sat on the couch beside Jonah.

Lynn, who reclined on a facing sofa with her brother, nudged Kevin's foot with her own. "Well, are they done with Jonah and Mike?"

Jonah sat up straighter, wanting to hear the answer.

Kevin shrugged. "Yeah, they are. Marcus is on his way here."

They didn't have to wait long before Marcus descended the steps. The tall Fallen Reaper paused, looking around the basement.

Mike gasped and pointed at a thick brown paper package in Marcus's hand. "The Deliverer's Tales?"

Marcus nodded and held out the bundle. "Yes."

Mike ripped off the packaging and let out a sigh as his fingers moved across the ancient cover. "We thought you were going to keep it?"

"It's coded and only you can translate it."

"Thank you, Mr. Armstrong." Mike opened the book and started reading. Robert and Wick huddled close to peek at the ancient book over Mike's shoulder.

Marcus wore a bemused expression on his face before announcing, "We promised your parents a fun yet educational tour of Monarch Associate's internship program. We should do that to keep up appearances."

Jonah couldn't believe he'd forgotten about the cover reason for coming to Atlanta. "When?"

"We'll get started tomorrow. Tonight, just relax and have fun. Pizzas are on me, although Mabel complained about wanting to cook everyone a decent meal."

Jonah's godfather remained true to his word. And the group relaxed, enjoyed pizza, movies, games, and just general silliness. Lynn spent increasing amounts of time on the phone to Rico. Wick did the same with Tamara.

Jonah wasn't the only one to notice. Mike did also, and that would inevitably lead to one of his bouts of quiet time. Each time, Robert would warn Jonah to give Mike space.

The next morning, the group visited the Monarch Associates building in northern Atlanta. They attended a genuine presentation on the internship program, given by people Jonah suspected didn't know about the Alliance.

After a flurry of phone calls home for permission to stay a few extra days, Marcus let the kids decide the attractions in and around Atlanta they wanted to see. Jonah enjoyed the outings so much, the trip to the Afterworld began to recede in his thoughts. Even Mike overcame his reoccurring periods of sullenness and started joking around.

All too soon, the time came for Jonah and his crew to head home to Mount Vernon. A quiet excitement filled the air as everyone gathered their bags on the morning of the departure.

Lynn stopped in his doorway, her bag slung over a shoulder. "You may be the Deliverer, but we're not waiting for you to drag around."

Jonah stuck out his tongue at his cousin.

She held up a fist. "I'm ready to get back to the blog."

"You mean Rico?" Despite taunting his cousin, mention of the clubhouse brought up an unpleasant worry for Jonah. "Do you think they're gonna take the attic from us?"

Lynn shook her head. "Marcus didn't tell you?"

"Tell me what?"

"When he replaced our computers last summer, Monarch Associates made an additional donation of computers to the center. In exchange, the director signed a agreement to lease us the attic. Unless they give us a location of equal size, we get to keep the space."

Jonah let out a relieved laugh. "That's cool. I bet her supervisor wasn't happy."

"He wasn't. Someone from Monarch went down there with the signed agreement. It's why Marcus was angry with Rex. We were always in the clear." Lynn pointed at Jonah's bag. "Get moving or I'll have Rico give you laps around the practice field when we get home."

"Ha, ha." Jonah zipped his own bag closed and left his room.

Mike, Wick, and his cousins were already there, along with Kevin. Jonah noticed at once that the Fallen Reaper wasn't smiling. Kevin also didn't have a travel bag. A horn honked from outside. Lynn peered out the open door and motioned the others to follow.

When Jonah reached the door, he didn't head outside. Instead, he sat his own bag down.

Kevin gave him a sideway glance. "Your ride is here."

"You aren't coming back with us." He didn't phrase it as a question because he knew what Kevin would say.

"Nah. I'm off on another assignment."

The Seeker's Compass **635**

"After all we did? Can't you get the Council to let you stay?"

"When you and Mike proved how special you were, Mandara became more of a pain about his people watching you."

Jonah kicked his bag in frustration. "I want you to stay."

"You can't get everything you want, Jonah."

"Why not?" Jonah looked into Kevin's serious face. "I'm the Deliverer. Mike's the Seeker. They need us. I can tell the Council you have to stay or–"

Kevin whirled on Jonah, shocking him. "Or what? You'll start making demands? That's not the way to act." The older boy's control slipped as his raw emotion spilled out. "You think I want to leave?" He snatched up Jonah's bag and crushed it in his grip while taking a deep breath.

"You were right, okay? I don't have any friends and…" Kevin faltered, staring out at the other kids around the van. "I can be myself with you."

Jonah was stunned by the boy's honesty and the knowledge that Kevin was just as angry about the separation. The difference was that Kevin as an Alliance member, had a job to do. "I'm sorry."

Kevin leaned against him. "I'll be back in a few months. I promise."

The goose bumps raced up and down Jonah's arms. The same effect appeared on Kevin's darker skin.

The boy slapped a hand over his forehead. "I need to stop making promises around you."

Jonah latched onto the comment in hopes of stalling the inevitable. "Why?"

"You'll learn one day."

Jonah crossed his arms. "Tell me now."

"Nope, little man."

Kevin hefted Jonah's carry bag in one hand and used his other to push Jonah outside and down the front steps to the van. He stowed Jonah's bag in the back and closed the rear door.

Jonah waited by the passenger sliding door. When Kevin came around, they touched fists.

Kevin smirked. "I'd tell you to behave yourself, but I know that won't happen."

"Funny." After a second goodbye wave, Jonah climbed inside the van.

Robert, Lynn, and Wick took the first two rows of seats. Mike had climbed in the very back, reading the Deliverer's Tales. Jonah joined his friend and stared out the side window at Kevin as the shuttle pulled away from the Guest House.

While his cousins and Wick begin to talk about what they planned for the rest of the summer, Jonah remained quiet. Once again, the deep certainty Kevin would keep his promise returned. Concentrating on the sensation helped to beat back the sadness Jonah experienced over their parting.

Fifteen minutes into the trip home, Mike snapped the old book closed and rested it on his lap. He pulled out his phone, fiddled with it for a few minutes, and then showed Jonah the screen. His buddy had pulled up the list of summer movies.

"We missed a lot." Mike scrolled through the information on his phone's screen. "Let's catch up when we get back."

Jonah grinned and in no time, they dived into all the reviews and info about the latest sci-fi, fantasy, and action releases. Maybe they did have the eternal spirits of the Deliverer and Seeker resting on their shoulders. But right then, they were like any other teenage sci-fi geeks planning the rest of their summer.

The shuttle reached Mount Vernon before either Mike or Jonah realized it. The first stop was Wick's house. Tamara waited for the young mage at the driveway.

Next was the Littleton's. Mike's spirits seemed better to Jonah as he got out at his home.

"Call me." Mike waved his cell phone before heading inside.

The Hightowers' home was the last stop. Rico leaned against his tricked-out car as the shuttle pulled to a stop. Jonah laughed because Aunt Imma hated that car.

Robert retrieved his bag and headed inside after a wave to Rico. Lynn wasted no time pulling their bags out of the back, hurrying to Rico and hugging him.

Ignoring them, Jonah reached for his own bag, only to discover something clipped to it. He turned the bag around and found his dad's Alliance badge fastened to the bag's strap. A note was also attached. Jonah ripped that loose and read it.

I got this from Marcus. Be good.

K.

Jonah smiled at Kevin's thoughtful gesture as he unhooked the gleaming badge and slipped it in a pocket. It was odd, but in a way, his dad's old Alliance badge represented as much to Jonah as the either Protector's Ring or Seeker's Compass.

BOOK THREE

AMULET
OF THE
GODDESS

CHAPTER ONE
GRIM PLAN

The Grim Reaper's summons tugged on Deyanira's soul, signaling the end of her exile. As if to underscore that fact, her Master's ship-of-bones arrived soon afterward to carry her to his Grim Keep.

Growing anxious, Deyanira quickly boarded and glanced up the ship's spiral stairwell. It led to where the steersman, and her fellow KIN, stood. The steersman's blood-red robe blew in the wind and his hands gripped the large ship's wheel made of bones.

"Hurry," she urged.

The steersman nodded and whirled his wheel. The large ship, the skeletal remains of a long dead leviathan, lurched into motion. Vibrations along the hull of the vessel increased until they hurtled over the ice floes of this area of the Afterworld.

Strong gusts of wind buffeted the craft and frigid air whistled through the portals: the eye sockets of the skull. Bits of ice crystals stung Deyanira's skin, forcing her brilliant, emerald eyes to mere slits.

Why would her Master call her back into his presence now? *Something must have happened.* She tilted her slender chin up, letting the bracing wind caress her pale skin and whip her lone, red braid around. The cold made her ritualistic scars ache, a pain she welcomed. *Better to be alert.*

The first signs of the Keep–double rows of towering, hooded figures–came into view. Ancient statues, a hundred feet tall, stood facing each other, scythes crossed. The rows of silent sentinels dwarfed the ship-of-bones as it zoomed between them.

The bulky shadow of the Grim Keep appeared against the bleak grey of the overcast skies. Its central complex was a mountain of rock, towering a thousand feet above the dreary surrounding. The various outer segments grew from solid rock in twisting patterns like roots jutting out of the frozen tundra.

As the Keep loomed ever closer, the awe-inspiring outline of a huge skull appeared out of the gloom. Carved into the rock face, the skull blazed with red fire. *Only the most powerful could summon that color of supernatural flames.* Deyanira shuddered at the display of raw might.

Soon, the bulk of the Grim Keep blotted out the dreary sky. The ship-of-bones slowed as it entered a natural overhang that created a cavernous opening at the base of the central formation. Turning from the eye-socket window, Deyanira descended the steps to the exit.

A dull, grating vibration reached her feet as the skull's maw opened. The flowing, red carpet, like a living tongue, had already extended to the guardhouse platform and solidified into a shallow ramp. Breathing in the frigid air, Deyanira pulled her hood over her head and marched off the ship.

A Grim Guard waited at the main gate, blocking her path.

"Well?" Deyanira said, gazing into the guard's bone-white mask. "Our Master has summoned me. Either lead me to him or move out of my way."

The guard turned and marched through the gate, Deyanira right behind. Once they entered the sheltering walls of the Keep, the sound of wind died away and the cold disappeared, replaced by the warm, moist air of the interior.

She followed the guard through the heart of the mountain until the corridor narrowed and closed in on each side. Adding to the oppressiveness of the place, veins of red rock meandered in the natural stone like blood dripping down the surface.

They reached a wide set of shallow steps cut into the rough stone, worn to glassy smoothness from centuries of use. As Deyanira prepared to climb the five stories to the arena, her mind raced.

Convocations of the KIN took place in the arena. A chill traveled down her spine because the arena was also used for special executions. She swallowed, calling on her long-repressed anger to push away the fear. If she had to die today, she would stand tall and not cower.

The sky had darkened to a sooty grey by the time Deyanira entered the arena. Black poles lined the outside of the circular area. Angel script, etched into the surface and glowing, covered each pole. On top of the poles rested onyx bowls filled with blazing, red fire.

Grim Guards stood in the darkness between each pole like living shadows. Their skull masks gave off a faint, white glow and the eerie, green illumination of their scythes produced a strange counterpoint to the red glare from the fires.

Deyanira's escort marched toward the center of the arena before coming to a halt and moving aside. That's when she noticed a person huddled on the ground, sobbing. He wore the grey robes of a Hunter, an agent of the Grand Oracle. *What's he doing here?* Her Master would reveal the answer, she decided, lifting her gaze to a high dais about twenty feet beyond the man.

The Grim Reaper stood robe-less with his head tilted back and his arms thrown wide. His bare arms were like corded, barren tree limbs, stripped of the bark. The red tint of his flesh had the smeared look of melted wax. It was not a product of reflected firelight, she knew. Something he'd done to himself long ago permanently marred his skin and turned his complexion a reddish bronze color. Even though his face was turned from her, the ritualistic scars were still very visible like jagged cracks along his bald head.

After a long moment, the Grim Reaper's back heaved and he lowered his arms, sated. A servant scurried forward with a robe. As soon as the Grim Reaper donned the garment, the hem writhed and moved as if alive.

He turned. All that was visible of his face was the glow of his angry-red pupils beneath the hood.

"Tell me why I shouldn't kill you, Deyanira?"

His voice curled around her, holding her in place until the guard gripped her shoulder and forced her down onto her hands and knees. The mortal in the Hunter robes jerked his head to look at her and Deyanira grimaced because she finally recognized the man. *Agent Hunter!* The once-arrogant man was little more than an emaciated figure now. According to the reports, Jonah Blackstone had sucked all the power from him, rendering him into this pathetic and frail husk.

Tremors rippled through the Afterworld at that news. Only a Deliverer could wield that kind of power. Hunter's eyes, once so full of pride, showed

Amulet of the Goddess **645**

abject fear now. He flinched and squealed at the eerie sound of a scythe cutting the air.

But the weapon came to rest against Deyanira's throat, not his. The ceremonial weapon's super fine blade cut into her flesh, drawing blood. She grunted, willing herself to remain still despite the hard, uneven stone gouging into her palms.

Her Master drew closer. When he spoke, his voice sounded like stone grinding against stone. Anger and fury radiated from him. "Tell me why I shouldn't banish your soul to everlasting oblivion!"

Deyanira gulped, feeling the scythe bite into her neck, followed by a stinging wetness. "I helped you kill the traitor, Isaiah Blackstone." She paused. "I found the ring…"

"And you lost it."

Deyanira wanted to protest. It wasn't her fault the Grim Reaper had allowed Jonah to defeat him.

The Grim Reaper glided closer while tracing a circle in the air with the index finger of his right hand. The hem of his robe reacted, reaching out to touch her face. "There are some who would have me kill you."

"That's easy for them to say," Deyanira replied while resisting the urge to recoil from the robe's touch. She spoke through a clenched jaw. "They hide in the shadows, throwing stones. Could the others do any better?"

The Grim Reaper stepped past her, balling his hand into a fist. The hem of the robe curled back on itself. A moment later, the guard withdrew the scythe, leaving a line of blood across Deyanira's throat. She risked a glance and found the Grim Reaper watching her.

He gestured. "Stand up. I called you here because I also wondered if someone else could perform better than you have done."

Deyanira stood at once and scanned the arena. They were still alone with the mortal, the servant, and the Grim Guards–until a single KIN entered the space. Per custom, KIN had to expose their faces to their master. When the newcomer didn't follow the ancient protocol, Deyanira's lip curled in disgust.

The Alliance mole bowed to the Grim Reaper. When he straightened, he threw back his hood to reveal a masked face. Deyanira noted that his form wavered from an enchantment that concealed his general features and made identifying him more difficult.

When he turned toward her, his filtered voice carried clear disappointment. "It's good to see you in one piece."

Deyanira didn't bother to acknowledge the taunt. She held her own chin high as she addressed the Grim Reaper. "Master, you were saying?"

"We are ready to proceed with my plans for the Wraiths, even a little ahead of schedule." The anger evident in his voice permeated the chilled air. "Our person within the Alliance expressed concern that you'll interfere again."

"What's this?" Deyanira overcame her caution and whirled on the mole.

The man crossed his arms and despite his masking magic, Deyanira could feel his smugness. "You prevented me from capturing the courier and ending the Afterworld rebellion."

Fury caused Deyanira's ears to ring, but self-preservation stayed her desire to protest. If the Grim Reaper had allowed this fool to say these things, she'd risk instant death to belittle it now. "Master, it's not true. I stopped Hunter from taking Blackstone to the Grand Oracle." She pointed a slender finger in the mole's direction. "This fool had lost control of Hunter by that point."

"And because of your feelings for the dead father, you helped the brat escape," the mole interjected. "Tell me, witch, is young Blackstone the son you always wished you had?"

Before she could stop herself, Deyanira had conjured green flames. "I warned you about calling me witch!"

"Enough!" The sky crackled overhead and the Grim Reaper's voice rolled over Deyanira and the mole like a tidal wave.

He made a hissing sound as he paced around them. "That isn't our most pressing problem. The half-breed has the Deliverer's Tales. That ancient book should have been locked away in the Central Archives."

A shudder went through Deyanira. If Jonah Blackstone had possession of that book, he could find the rest of the rings and... the Medallions. She wondered if the universe were playing a cruel trick on them. After more than two thousand years, this young boy burst on the scene and no one could stop him.

The Grim Reaper spoke just over Deyanira's shoulder, startling her out of her dire thoughts. "Now you understand the urgency! The mole has

Amulet of the Goddess

informed us the boy's friend is a Seeker! We must move ahead with our plans before they can grow stronger."

Even though Deyanira had a feeling deep inside that the plan would fail, what choice did they have? Well, she reasoned, clutching at a ray of hope, she could eliminate the troublesome mole when he returned in shame.

As if sensing her thoughts, the mole pointed at her. "Master, I humbly request you forbid Deyanira from interfering this time."

The Grim Reaper's glowing eyes bored into her soul and his will smashed against her mind. "You will remain in my Keep until the mission is over."

Deyanira sucked in a ragged breath. "Yes, Master." The oath wrapped around her body, binding her to the Grim Keep. To try and leave would mean instant, painful death.

The Grim Reaper gave a satisfied nod and turned to the mole. "If you fail, the leeway I showed Deyanira will not befall you."

The mole bowed.

"Either we control the boy," the Grim Reaper began while making a slight gesture with his left hand before the scythe whistled through the air again. It was followed by a heavy thud and then several wet splats. Deyanira turned, staring at Agent Hunter's headless body and the trail of blood leading to his head as it rolled a few feet away.

"Or you will bring him to me so I can personally witness his head roll." The Grim Reaper chuckled as he strode toward the exit, taking his Grim Guards with him. The mole paused long enough to glare at Deyanira in triumph before he followed.

Cold air wafted through the empty space and Deyanira breathed it in, calming her apprehension. After a backward glance to be certain she was alone, she held out her right hand toward the closest pole.

With a muttered counterspell, the pulsing, amber etchings faded to black. From the moment she saw the glowing symbols, she knew the Grim Reaper had found a way to prevent young Jonah from eavesdropping on their meeting. Now that she'd broken the protection, Jonah could see, or at least, hear her. Deyanira focused her thoughts on the source of all their fears.

Far away, in the mortal world, Jonah Blackstone jerked awake in his bed. Despite the throbbing in his temple, he was sure he'd dream-walked again. Well, almost. This time, he'd been blocked until the very end, when he saw an open-air arena under a dark, clouded sky, lots of red flames and… *Deyanira.*

Jonah's Death Sense spiked as one sentence hammered into his mind. *Beware, young Blackstone.*

CHAPTER TWO

MORNING VISITOR

Why did Deyanira warn him? Jonah wondered, rubbing his aching, sweaty forehead and scrunching up his face. He slumped back onto his pillow and stared at his dark bedroom ceiling. The evil Reaper had tortured him earlier this summer. However, Deyanira's Grim Hound managed to save his life, protecting him from Agent Hunter.

It made no sense. He closed his eyes, but true sleep eluded him. After tossing and turning for another hour, he glanced at his bedside clock and groaned. It was still a bit early to rise and dress for school. The chilled October morning hadn't even dawned yet.

Screw it, he thought, throwing off the warm covers. He rolled out of his twin-sized bed, which had become a little short after growing a few inches taller during the summer. Jonah was lankier and within half an inch of his cousin, Robert, in height now, which he thoroughly enjoyed.

As he left his bedroom and crossed the quiet family room, he stretched in that unrestrained way you can't help doing in the morning. Rubbing the sleep from his eyes, he entered the kitchen and stopped.

Aunt Imma and Uncle James were already seated at the round kitchen table. They each held a steaming cup of coffee and were talking to a stranger.

"Uh, good morning," Jonah managed as he wrapped his arms around his middle, trying to cover his rumpled t-shirt. The two inches of exposed skin below the hem of his sweatpants also embarrassed him. Only now did his mind register that he could hear the low rumble of a quiet conversation while approaching the kitchen.

The stranger had a well lined, deep chocolate face. His hair, a short afro, was salt and pepper. Dark blue mechanic's coveralls were visible beneath his opened, pale tan coat. And the man's serious expression morphed into a smile as he continued to scrutinize Jonah.

When he spoke, his baritone voice filled the quiet kitchen. "My God, he looks just like Janice. No denying him, huh?"

Uncle James stood and grinned, but the hand holding the coffee cup shook a little.

"Good morning, Jonah," his uncle began, already dressed for work in his trademark sports coat and slacks. Like Jonah's mom, Uncle James had a thin face, pecan tan skin, and brown eyes. This morning, his round eyeglasses were temporarily placed on the table. "This is your Uncle Amos Peacock." Uncle James gestured at the visitor.

Jonah waved but his Uncle Amos rose, leaned over the table, and thrust out a calloused hand. "Nice to meet you finally!"

"You too," Jonah said. He couldn't hide the confusion on his face.

Aunt Imma sighed and added, "This is your Aunt Ruby's husband."

An involuntary pit formed in Jonah's stomach. His Aunt Ruby was the woman in the pictures over the mantel. Ever since Jonah had arrived in Mount Vernon, almost two years ago, he experienced dread any time he looked at the woman's image.

He came out of his reverie in time to notice the furtive glance exchanged between the adults. There was something going on, and he didn't need his Reaper Stare to sense that.

Uncle James motioned toward the door. "I'll see you out, Amos."

Blinking in surprise, Uncle Amos waved to Aunt Imma. "Thanks for the coffee." He flicked his gaze to Jonah. "Good to meet you."

With that, the men exited the kitchen. Jonah tried to listen to their low conversation but Aunt Imma intervened.

"How about a big breakfast?"

Jonah gave up trying to eavesdrop. "It's not even Sunday morning."

Amulet of the Goddess

"Oh, that doesn't matter," Aunt Imma said in false cheeriness as she stood. She was a short, solidly built woman and at least a head shorter than Uncle James.

"It's nice to change up the routine from time to time." She loudly pulled out pans, cooking trays, and pots. In short order, she had grits bubbling on the stovetop, buttered slices of bread toasting in the oven, and strips of bacon crackling in the pan.

She asked Jonah to retrieve plates from the cabinet and also to prepare the orange juice. All the while, he couldn't help thinking she was keeping him busy so he wouldn't ask any questions. As if to prove it, each time he caught her gaze, Aunt Imma would turn to do something else.

Jonah's uncle returned with the morning paper, which he plopped on the table. After a quick word with his wife and a kiss on her cheek, he waved goodbye to Jonah and left for work. Jonah's aunt placed a big plate of scrambled eggs on the table, and another stacked high with buttered toast, along with a third plate full of crispy bacon.

She stood back, tightened the belt on her duster, and let out a long, satisfied sigh. "That should do it. Wake up your cousins, Jonah."

With that, she topped off her cup of coffee and hustled away to her room.

Jonah didn't need to fetch his cousins because the aroma of the hot breakfast had already worked its magic. Lynn strolled into the kitchen first, dressed in a new sweater. And to Jonah's surprise, she wasn't wearing her mid-top sneakers. This morning, she wore a nice pair of boots and her shoulder-length braids hung free, swaying as she deftly pulled out the newspaper's sports section.

It always amazed Jonah to watch her checking the scores as she ate breakfast. But this morning, she paused, paper in hand, and her eyes narrowed as she took in the big breakfast.

Her twin brother, Robert, appeared behind her a moment later, yawning. He was thin and lanky like his sister, and sported a perpetual bushy afro with neatly trimmed edges.

Robert stared in disbelief at the food arrayed on the kitchen table. "What's all this?"

Jonah shrugged. "Aunt Imma wanted to make a big breakfast." He grabbed a plate and piled food on it.

"It's not even Sunday," Robert said, his voice still full of questions. "What gives?"

Lynn prepared a buttered muffin and tea, then scooped some fluffy eggs onto a plate before she sat down. She eyed Jonah. "What happened?"

Jonah gulped down his first mouthful and said, "I caught them talking to Uncle Amos."

Lynn's eyes widened in response. Robert jumped up from his chair and rushed into the dining room to peek out the front window. He came back and slumped in his chair, frowning. "I can't believe he was here and didn't even bother to say hello to us."

Jonah didn't have an answer. He never even knew he *had* an Uncle Amos.

Lynn stared straight ahead, her butter knife tapping the edge of her saucer. "It has to be Aunt Ruby."

"Duh," Robert said around a piece of bacon that hung from his mouth. "We know he's married to her."

"Think, Robert." Lynn glared at her brother as if she were willing him to catch up. "It's been seven years..." she prompted.

Robert stopped chewing and his jaw dropped. "No way. But..."

"But what?" Jonah asked when Robert didn't elaborate.

Lynn put her butter knife down. "Aunt Ruby's been in a State Mental Institution for seven years."

Twirling a finger around his right ear, Robert also made coo-coo sounds.

"Robert!" Lynn admonished him. "But essentially, he's right. She ranted about the end times and the dead rising up to destroy the Earth."

"That went over well at family reunions!" Robert snorted, adding, "No one wanted her around. Uncle Amos argued with Dad and your mom. He accused everyone of choosing sides."

"Whoa," Jonah said, his breakfast now forgotten.

"Of course," Robert continued, "that could have been just old sibling rivalry. Aunt Ruby always hated your mom, as well as my dad, but more so, your mom."

"Why?"

Amulet of the Goddess

"Because Aunt Ruby didn't have the Sight," Robert made air quotes, "like your mom. That drove our aunt crazy." He gulped. "Well, you know what I mean."

The story stunned but also fascinated Jonah. "So, what happened next?"

"She got worse," Lynn continued. "Uncle Amos tried to hide Ruby's condition until she hurt several innocent people. By then, he couldn't do anything to keep her from being arrested." Lynn rose, discarded her tea, and crossed to the refrigerator. Inside, she had a large container of her custom sports drink mix. She loaded some into a squeeze bottle and returned to the table.

Jonah waited, eager to know more about his aunt. "And?"

Lynn sipped from the squeeze bottle before she continued. "Like I said, she got sentenced to a mental institution."

"Can we talk about something else?" Robert finished his second plate of breakfast before he leaned back in his chair.

"Fine." Lynn focused her attention on Jonah. "So, what do you think of our idea?" She raised a questioning eyebrow, waiting.

"About Aunt Ruby?"

"No. Advertising our services," Lynn corrected him.

Jonah glanced out the kitchen window, stalling for time. He had successfully managed to avoid giving Robert and Lynn his opinion on turning the Mount Vernon Social Club into a detective agency. Wick had taken a few cases because of the increase in ghosts and Wraiths being spotted around town. Wick said it was because Halloween was only four weeks away.

The young mage was the only one brave enough to advertise his interest in the supernatural. However, things hadn't gone so well with the first ghosts he encountered, so Wick reasoned that Jonah's unique ability to talk to spirits could be the clincher.

Basically, he wanted help in sending any lingering spirits on their way. But Jonah wasn't remotely interested in welcoming any further strangeness into his life.

Lynn nudged his chair with her foot. "Well?"

"Aren't you afraid of Aunt Imma and Uncle James finding out?"

"No." When Jonah raised a skeptical eyebrow, Lynn pursed her lips. "The way I see it, if anyone at church asks for our help, well, they aren't likely to mention it to Mom."

"Yeah," Robert agreed. "That goes for church and non-church folks. A lot of people claim they don't believe in the supernatural, but they really do." He nodded sagely.

Jonah frowned at his cousins, searching for another way out. "Lynn, you know the Tolerance Club's taking a lot of my time."

Lynn nodded. "Yes, I do, but we can walk and chew gum at the same time."

Robert, who had added a bowl of cereal to his morning helpings, snorted and shot milk and bits of cereal out of his mouth and across the table. "You sound just like Dad."

Lynn held her chin higher. "Well, it's a good saying." She tossed her brother a few napkins before turning to Jonah. "We're not talking about a case every day."

"Okay. Whatever. It's fine with me." As soon as the words left his mouth, Jonah suspected he would regret his answer.

"Good," Lynn said. "We'll put the ad in the next blog and post it on all the social sites."

"And we'll pass around flyers," Robert added, wiping up the spilled milk and tossing the sodden napkins into the trash can. "That reminds me." He ran to his room and returned with a printed sample of the latest blog in his hands.

He waved it in Jonah's face. "I did a nice job on these."

Jonah took the sample. He noticed the ad but the main article drew most of his attention. It was about sightings of a large, black cat around Mount Vernon. His friend, Danita Jackson, had written the article. A ninth grader like Jonah and Mike, she was also the leader of their reading group.

He lowered the flyer to stare at Lynn. "Danita wrote an article for you?"

"Yes, she did, and it's excellent. She explained the background behind all the misunderstandings of black cats throughout history. The Ancient

Egyptians revered cats because they represented Pakhet, the Goddess of the Hunt, or something like that."

Robert grinned at his sister. "Lynn's just impressed because Danita looks up to her. That's why she wants Danita to join the Summit team."

"She's also intelligent and a good writer," Lynn protested.

"Well," Robert continued. "I say no. She's too nosy, Lynn. How would we keep our other business away from her?" He elbowed Jonah. "Right? You know her."

Jonah's face warmed. Danita was brilliant, every bit as smart as Mike, even. But she was also scornful of anyone's belief in the supernatural. "Let's just deal with the ad first."

Lynn surprised Jonah by nodding. He was grateful when she let the matter drop. That allowed his thoughts to return to the significance of his Aunt Ruby release and Deyanira's warning. Was it just a coincidence that on the same morning he received the cryptic message, he also found out his Aunt Ruby had been released from a mental ward?

No, Jonah decided. Things were always connected when it came to him.

Robert caught his worried expression and patted him on the shoulder. "Little cousin, you need to get out more often."

"Ha ha."

"Seriously. I know a couple of girls who might be interested."

It was Jonah's turn to snort. "So do I."

When Robert laughed and went back to eating his cereal, Jonah slumped in the chair, brooding. Without warning, the title from an old, dark, fantasy novel his reading group covered last month popped into his head: *Something Wicked This Way Comes*.

CHAPTER THREE
HUMAN LIE DETECTOR

"Can you read his mind or not?" Brandon sneered as he crossed his arms and stared at Jonah. Besides being the local rich snob, the varsity boy's coach wanted to recruit him for the basketball team, something rarely done for any freshman.

Great, Jonah thought, *just what Brandon needed.* He squirmed in his seat as more of the kids milling around the Commons during this lunch period moved closer after hearing Brandon's challenging tone.

"Of course he can't read your mind!" Danita retorted, pushing her thick black-rimmed glasses up on her nose. She, along with Mike Littleton, Lorraine Hughes, Rodney Elkins, and Anthony Freeman, had commandeered one of the numerous lunch tables.

"Don't be ridiculous. That kind of thing doesn't exist," Danita insisted, sounding sure and superior. Anthony, who made valiant attempts at impressing Danita, nodded his agreement.

Before Jonah could respond, Mike rose from his chair. Like Jonah, he had grown a few inches by the time school started. "I told you, Brandon," he said while giving Danita an exasperated look, "Jonah doesn't read minds."

"Really? Then how can he tell if I'm lying?" Brandon's focus never wavered from Jonah. "I knew you were a freak, DC. You gonna open a palm-reading shop? I hear it runs in the family." The boy's buddies laughed at the stupid remark. "Go on, tell me if I'm lying." Brandon held out his palm.

"He doesn't read palms, either." Mike waved his thin arms into the air with visible irritation. "You have to ask him a question."

Amulet of the Goddess

"Mike!" Danita shouted, her short afro puff shaking as she stood. "You shouldn't encourage such nonsense." But many of the kids sneered at Danita and motioned for her to sit down. She did, but seemed put out. "It's ridiculous."

Brandon didn't appear to mind as he scrunched up his face, presumably thinking.

Nearby girls watched him with dreamy attention. Jonah shook his head. Even with his face screwed up, the girls thought Brandon was so handsome. Jonah wanted to gag.

"I got one," Brandon said.

Mike held out his slender right hand and patted the palm. "Pay first." Jonah stared at Mike as if he'd grown a second head. His buddy winked. "Don't worry."

Jonah wasn't worried; he was irritated. Mike had goaded him into using his ability on a tenth-grade girl. Despite all assurances, the little demonstration soon spread around the school like an internet virus. He expected the same to happen with this demonstration.

Brandon made a big show of opening his wallet and pulling out a crisp, five-dollar bill from a large wad of cash.

Mike scanned the immediate area for an adult, then he slid the money into his neat, tan pants. "Okay. Jonah's ready. Ask your question."

Brandon hooked a thumb at his friend Drew, who hovered in the background. "Does he like April?"

Danita frowned at Mike but she also couldn't hide her interest in anything that concerned Jonah. Lorraine let out a squeal of excitement and sat forward, more than eager to hear the answer. The large group of kids crowded closer to witness the show.

Jonah decided not to punch Mike and instead, put all thoughts out of his mind and focused on Drew. As a half-Reaper, Jonah could read the aura that people's emotions projected. It was how he determined the first student had lied. That use of his ability had also spawned rumors, causing some kids to consider him freakish, but most appeared pretty cool with the whole idea.

At least Lorraine, Rodney, and Anthony didn't seem to mind. Like Jonah, they were also members of the disbanded Teen Center Practice

Club. They were coincidentally around a few times when strange things happened to Jonah. That collective experience created a bond among the four club members, one that the other kids didn't share.

However, Danita wasn't a club member and she often voiced her doubts about his ability clearly. Jonah avoided her glare and focused on Drew, doing it purely for show. In truth, he didn't need to hear the answer nor scan the boy's emotions again.

Each time Drew glanced at Lorraine, Jonah sensed the boy's intensifying interest. But Drew would never let Lorraine know that, not with Rodney around.

"Yeah," Drew answered. "I do like her." He tried to smile. "She's not bad." A few girls whispered to each other, ensuring the comment would reach April's ears at warp speed. The rest of the kids waited to hear Jonah's verdict.

He gave Mike a scathing look because Drew wouldn't like the answer. The other kid who played this little game didn't like what he had to say. Convinced he was lying about his ability, she turned angry when he caught her in a lie.

"Well? Is he lying?" Brandon asked.

Without taking his eyes off his lunch, Jonah muttered, "He's lying."

The crowd erupted in catcalls and jeers. Brandon pounded his friend's shoulder but Drew appeared mortified. Jonah met the boy's anguished expression. *Wait for it*, he told himself.

Like clockwork, Drew's reaction turned to anger. "You're the only one lying!"

"He busted you." Brandon laughed even harder. "Who do you like?"

Drew's pudgy, caramel colored face darkened with embarrassment. "I told you." He thrust his hand toward Mike. "Brandon wants his money back."

"No refunds." Mike crossed his arms and stood his ground.

Brandon wouldn't let it go and slid an arm around Drew's shoulders. "Who do you like, Danita?"

Amulet of the Goddess

Danita gasped and Drew grew more embarrassed and angrier. When their gazes met again, Jonah thought he saw pleading in Drew's frantic expression.

"Can you tell?" Brandon asked, catching the brief glance between the boys.

An African-accented voice called out, "He doesn't read minds." The speaker's voice sounded muffled, like the person spoke through a filter. When the crowd parted, Jonah understood why. A tall, thin girl in a niqab approached the table. The veil that made her headscarf into a niqab was a black, mesh fabric that draped over her face, letting only her eyes show.

Murmurs broke out as she came to a stop only a foot from the table, clasping her coffee-colored hands together. "He senses the emotions of other people." She turned her covered head, speaking to Drew. "So it's not a good idea to get too emotional around him."

Jonah's insides went cold. It was one thing for people to think he was a little strange or for Brandon to pick on him. But to hear someone explain how his ability worked was something else altogether. Jonah caught the narrowed look Brandon gave him. The boy was a snob and a bully, but Jonah had to remind himself that Brandon wasn't stupid.

Last summer, Brandon and his friend, Antwan, had spied on Jonah at the request of a rogue GBI agent. Antwan caught Jonah phasing–moving from one location to the next in the blink of an eye. The Alliance, a secret coalition of human and supernatural beings that governed what people like Jonah could or should do, had to intervene.

There were Alliance members called Memory Charmers, who modified the boys' memories as a safety precaution. As a result, Brandon and Antwan were left with a one-hour gap in their respective memories. And of course, they became even more suspicious of Jonah. This girl had just given Brandon another piece of that puzzle.

Drew's face darkened to a shade of purple as he muttered, "Mind your own business!" Brandon, looking uncharacteristically cautious, gripped his friend's shoulder. But Drew shrugged him off. "It's not Halloween yet."

A few people laughed but most hissed.

"Hey!" Mike shouted as he thumped the yellow Tolerance Club ribbon pinned on his chest. "We don't allow intolerance or bullying around here."

Jonah wanted to slump in his chair because if this went any further, someone would want the real answer, and he didn't want to go there. Lorraine and Rodney had enough issues already. One moment, they couldn't get enough of each other. Then, the very next day, they would argue or pretend the other didn't exist. Rodney had already cast suspicious glares at Drew.

That's when something unexpected happened. Drew let out a yelp when an invisible force yanked his feet from under him. He landed on his back with a painful thump. People gaped at the boy and cast glances at the students closest to him. But Jonah knew better, having detected the crackle of magic in the air.

The mysterious girl's left hand fluttered slightly at her side just before Drew fell. *She had to be magical,* Jonah decided.

Although Brandon, too, glared at the girl, he seemed reluctant to say anything.

Her eyes remained fixed on Jonah as she crossed her arms. "I expected more from the son of Isaiah. You're supposed to be The One."

Jonah rose to his feet. "Who are you?"

The girl's intense eyes bore into his. "You never answered the question. Who does Drew like? Surely you can sense the *emotion* coming from him."

Drew's eyes widened as he scrambled to his feet and shoved his way through the crowd. Brandon chased after him.

The mysterious girl watched them leave, her own shoulders shaking with quiet laughter. "Pathetic." She whirled back to Jonah. "And you, playing parlor tricks."

Jonah stared at the girl in confusion. *Palm readers and parlor tricks?* Why were people mentioning those things? His parents, both dead now, worked as archeologists. His uncle was a newspaper publisher and his Aunt Imma, a very religious woman, was a hairdresser and wouldn't go near anything supernatural–or *Satanic*, as she often referred to it.

He pointed at the girl's left hand and whispered, "You're one to talk after what you did."

"Touché." The girl inclined her head before she turned and slipped through the gawking crowd of students.

Amulet of the Goddess **661**

Mike, who had watched the entire disaster in visible astonishment, stirred and leaned close. "Jonah, was she…"

Jonah nodded. "Do you know her?" Seeing Danita trying to fend off Anthony and listen to their conversation, he moved to the trash bin to throw out his tray.

Mike followed. "I haven't seen her around. She would stick out. The other Muslim girls don't cover their faces."

Mike scanned the students in the Commons. "Maybe she's really conservative."

"No." Jonah surprised himself with how sure he sounded. "She didn't want me to see her face."

"Oh." Mike's eyes narrowed as he watched Jonah. "Yeah. It's always about you!"

Jonah would have argued but just then, a small, anxious-looking, ninth-grade girl stepped beside the table.

Mike waved her away. "We're closed for business."

"Mike!" Danita objected as she smacked his arm. "Be nice."

Mike's shoulders slumped. "Sorry. Jonah has to get to class."

The girl eyed Jonah for a moment, clutching a folded bill in her right hand. Jonah opened his mouth to ask if he could help her when the amulet she wore sparkled in the sunlight. It was an ankh with a brilliant, green stone embedded in the circle.

The girl jumped at the same time a cold sensation ran down his back. It felt like someone had just opened a door to the chilly outside air. Spinning around, for a fraction of a second, he thought he saw the form of a boy. When he blinked, however, the effect vanished.

Jonah would have thought the boy was just a reflection in the window if not for the cold chill. When he turned back to ask the girl, he caught a glimpse of her running out of the Commons. *That was odd.*

Danita huffed and picked up her books. "Didn't you recognize her, Jonah?"

"No. Should I have?"

John Darr

"She's Latrell's little sister. You know, the boy who killed himself? You volunteered the Tolerance Club to help at his vigil."

"Yeah," Jonah said. He recalled hearing that Latrell had a little sister. "I didn't realize she was in our grade." His face warmed.

Anthony, still trying to impress Danita, blurted out, "Everyone knew that."

Jonah wanted to punch the boy.

"I'll talk to her," Danita offered, "and tell her not to waste her time on supernatural nonsense." She aimed a sad glare at Mike, who was too busy rooting around in his book bag to notice. Peeved, Danita hurried out of the Commons, taking Anthony in her wake. Lorraine and Rodney trailed behind them.

Once Jonah was sure no adults were watching, he punched his buddy in the upper arm. "I don't like playing the human lie detector."

Mike winced as he rubbed his bicep. "That hurt."

"Good."

Mike balled his hand into a fist, then decided against punching back.

Jonah pulled his book bag over a shoulder and headed for the stairs. "Did you see what just happened with that ninth-grader? Something scared her away."

"Yeah, I did," Mike said, falling into step with him.

"No, I meant something supernatural."

"Jonah, have you had any dream-walks lately?"

The question caught Jonah off guard and he paused at the bottom of the stairs.

Except for Deyanira's warning, his sleep had been undisturbed since before school had started. He decided not to mention the evil Reaper to Mike.

"No. Everything's cool. Why?"

"That girl in the niqab," Mike began as he climbed up the steps. "She worried you."

Amulet of the Goddess   663

"Well, yeah. She called me *Son of Isaiah*." Jonah couldn't miss the anxious face Mike pulled. "I didn't tell anyone about that, not even my godfather. So how could she know that name?"

"You're right. But now you're saying there was someone else in the Commons?"

"There was."

"I don't doubt you," Mike added. "I just hoped for more time before strange things started happening."

Jonah could sympathize. His own life had been turned upside-down with the death of his parents two summers ago; not to mention everything else that happened. His first school year in Mount Vernon was quiet and ordinary. Naturally, Jonah hoped this school year would also pass by with just the regular, mortal teenager stuff.

"Maybe the year will be quiet." Mike tried to make his voice sound hopeful. He spotted a tall boy beckoning him from the doorway of a classroom. "Oops. I'm late. See you later."

As Jonah watched his super busy friend hustling off, he too wished this school year would remain quiet, but sincerely doubted that would happen.

CHAPTER FOUR
THE TOKEN

Lorraine cornered Jonah at the end of the school day. She wanted the club members to wear bright orange ribbons complete with pumpkin heads at Latrell's vigil.

"Not only will it make a more visible statement than our regular yellow ribbons," she concluded, "but Halloween is in just four weeks. So it's seasonal too."

Lorraine beamed at Jonah and held up a sample ribbon. "Rodney designed the pumpkin heads. Each one is unique." She remained quiet and waited for his decision.

Jonah appreciated the amount of work–as well as Lorraine's barely contained enthusiasm. "Sure, why not?" he said.

Lorraine gave him a quick hug. "We'll bring them to the vigil tonight."

With the last bit of business done, Jonah headed out to his bike, his mind filled with homework, club schedules, and other things. He didn't pay attention when he dropped his book bag beside his bike as he'd done many times. Reaching out to unlock the chain, a shadow fell over him. The next moment, a large boy in a hoodie grabbed his book bag and ran.

"Hey!" Jonah shouted.

The boy sprinted across the sloping, grass hill and toward the outside patios where students ate lunch during school hours. Jonah shot off after him, trying hard to swallow the fact that someone stole his book bag! Though frayed and smudged, the bag was also one of the few things that remained from his old house in Virginia. Everything else had burned to the ground.

Jonah's rage at the boy propelled him forward and he gained on the thief despite being shorter. But as the boy reached the tall spruces screening the south side of the patio area, he dived into the thicket of bushes and phased.

"No! Wait!" Jonah shouted. He reached the spot where the boy disappeared and without stopping to think about his actions, he too, phased.

When he inhaled the mist of the aether, he recalled his training and focused. Soon, he felt a pinpoint of heat, the faint trail left behind by every person who phased through the supernatural realm. He concentrated on that, willing his mind to go in that direction.

The regular world snapped into existence around Jonah as he reappeared in an empty parking lot. He did it! He actually followed someone through a phase on his own. The reality of the situation caught up with him and Jonah paid closer attention to his surroundings.

The mysterious guy was several yards away. He still had Jonah's book bag slung over one shoulder as he headed for a pimped-out, former cop car.

"Hey," Jonah called out.

The guy froze for a second, then he sprinted for the car. Instead of getting inside and speeding away, the guy phased just short of the vehicle.

Jonah charged after him, pursuing the guy into a phase once again. In the aether, he felt the pinpoint of heat and willed himself to follow it. When the mortal world appeared around him again, Jonah was in for a shock: he was standing in his parents' hideaway.

The entire place, a lower, brick courtyard, and upper, smaller courtyard garden, once belonged to his parents. Back when they were still alive, they came here to get away and meditate. Now gone, they left the place to Jonah.

Jonah stood in the main courtyard. Before he overcame his shock, the hairs on the back of his neck bristled. A second later, the guy grabbed him from behind and pulled him into a bear hug.

"Let me go, perv!" Jonah shouted.

The guy laughed, his voice muffled by the face mask. "Perv? That's nice," he said in an amused tone. "You get too distracted, little man."

Jonah's eyes widened and he twisted around. "Kevin! What are you doing here?"

Kevin threw back his hood and yanked off his knitted face mask. The boy's deep brown eyes squinted in genuine amusement. "Why'd you call me a perv?"

"I..." Jonah slugged the Fallen Reaper in the chest. "You stole my book bag."

Kevin didn't budge from the punch. He was almost six feet tall and very muscular. But he frowned and rub the spot where Jonah hit him. When Jonah reared back for a second punch, he held up the book bag as a shield. "Just wanted to see if you could follow me through a phase, so cool it."

"You know I can." Jonah snatched the bag from Kevin and dropped it at his feet. "Rex told you." His irritation and surprise changed to a grudging happiness at having Kevin there. "Are you back?"

Kevin hunched his big shoulders and shoved his hands into his pockets. "No. Mandara is still pissed with me."

Jonah's annoyance flared at the mention of the Alliance's lead Fallen Reaper's name. "If Mandara is still mad, then how did you get here?"

"I asked Marcus if I could check up on you."

"My godfather said yes?"

Kevin nodded. "He's covering for me, but I have to get back to my assignment. That reminds me." Kevin pointed to the short row of brick steps that led to the upper courtyard. "There's something I want to show you."

Jonah only hesitated a moment before mounting the steps to the smaller, upper courtyard. An uneven, brick-covered path led from the stairway straight to the far side, disappearing into the surrounding forest. A second path bisected the first before vanishing into the trees. A sculptured rhododendron bush in a large, brick planter was placed at the center of this area.

Off to the right was an alcove, and that's where he spotted the shiny, brown box resting on the alcove's bench. He hurried over and discovered the box had a genetic lock. It was just like the one on the birthday cylinder his father had left him.

Amulet of the Goddess

"It's not my birthday," Jonah said.

"I know that," Kevin groaned. "Your mom's old office at HQ is being cleared out. Marcus had her stuff boxed up for you. But he thought you might want this now."

Jonah's hands trembled as he lifted the box. Sitting down, he rested it on his lap. This close, he noted the script that covered the surface, the same script as on Robert's archive box. He touched the small button, which he assumed was keyed for him. Sure enough, the symbol glowed and the genetic lock clicked.

When Jonah stared at the box without moving, Kevin asked, "Are you going to open it?"

"Yeah. It's just that, well, it's been locked since…"

"You don't have to look."

"But I want to." And Jonah opened the lid. The first thing he saw was a 4x6 color photograph. He reached inside to pick it up and realized it was the front of a small photo album. Jonah suspected, without opening it, that it contained his mother's photos of her family. These were the pictures she never displayed at home.

Jonah opened the album. The first picture was of his mother, father, and a small baby boy. They were all standing in front of a wooden bench with a brick wall behind them. He recognized the place. They had taken the picture right here in the hideaway. He wondered if that was the same time when they put his baby handprint on the alcove wall. At once, the tender memories caused tears to sting his eyes.

Kevin sat down beside him and rested his chin on Jonah's shoulder, pressing their cheeks together. "You'll be all right."

Jonah nodded, letting Kevin's physical touch strengthen him. He wiped his eyes and turned to the next photo. This one featured two young girls and a young boy. They looked just like Robert and Lynn. But Kevin pointed to the small date written in the bottom corner.

"That's your mom and uncle and–"

"My Aunt Ruby."

Jonah's stomach lurched and he made a small sound in the back of his throat. Every time he thought about her or saw a picture of his Aunt Ruby, fear prickled his insides.

668   *John Darr*

Jonah flipped to the next photo, glad to get to other relatives, including his grandparents on his mom's side. The last picture was a very recent one of his mom and Uncle James. They must have taken it just before his mom disappeared with his dad. Did she come here to see her family before that trip?

Kevin reached into the box and pulled out a small, sealed, manila envelope. Jonah hadn't noticed it beneath the photo album. He took it, being careful not to rip the paper, and opened it. Several pictures spilled out. He caught them, wondering why his mom would seal them up instead of putting them inside the photo album with the others.

Jonah gasped when he turned over the first photo. It was of Aunt Ruby. Her hair, a tangle of long curls sticking out in all directions, reminded Jonah of Medusa. She also wore a brown shawl over her shoulders and large, beaded earrings. Jonah could imagine the things clinking and clanking every time she moved her head.

His aunt and uncle had five kids in all, which were neatly arrayed around them. They looked like Jonah and his twin cousins. While gazing at the pictures, Jonah realized that his aunt never smiled. Instead, she smirked at the camera.

The final picture was of a small storefront with a strange, T-shaped doorway and a large, wooden ankh positioned above the door. The words, *Ankh of Life,* glowed in bright, neon letters across the left front window. Although the photo was black and white, Jonah could easily imagine garish colors on the letters.

He gazed at the picture, trying to decide if it were a bookstore or… she was a palm reader. That's when he spotted a neon palm in the lower right corner of the right front window.

The last things in the box were a folded note and three pieces of lacquered wood. He held those up. Viewed together, they displayed a beautifully drawn map. Seven locations of different terrains including a plateau, a forest, a valley, hilly land, and a meadow, were marked with a detailed drawing of stars.

Jonah grinned. "It's a triptych."

"A what?" Kevin frowned.

Amulet of the Goddess

"A triptych. You know, a piece of art divided into three separate parts. Together, they make one picture or scene."

Kevin reached out to run a finger along the surface of one piece.

"This is cool," Jonah said, placing them inside the box, "but why did my mom lock them up?"

Kevin shrugged and didn't offer an opinion.

Jonah decided to show the triptych to Mike later. That brought him to the final object in the box, the note. He opened it and read.

I'm sorry I couldn't stop Ruby before she hurt others. Don't blame yourself for what happened to her and Jonah. There's no way any of us could have known. Isaiah's furious and won't let you take Jonah back to Mount Vernon, but at least he's safe now and will grow up in peace. - S

A shudder went through Jonah, but he didn't know why. Who was S? Why had his dad been angry? Whatever the cause, Jonah wasn't surprised it had to do with Aunt Ruby.

Kevin nudged him. "You all right?"

"Yeah." Jonah slid the pictures into the envelope. He didn't blame his mom for not placing them in the album. He didn't want to see them again and he put the envelope and the note back inside the box. As soon as he closed the lid, the locks clicked into place.

Kevin settled his chin on Jonah's shoulder again and ran his fingers over the designs on the box's lid, remaining quiet.

Jonah welcomed the closeness with the young Fallen Reaper. But he could tell that Kevin was thinking about something. He nudged the older boy.

In response, Kevin pulled a small, wooden token from his pocket. "Here."

Jonah took the token. "Is this…"

"Yep. It's a way to call for help. Trueblood made that. We all have one. That's yours. We're working on something else, but it's top secret for now. Hold the token tightly in your hand," Kevin said. Jonah did, closing his fist around the object. "Then say or whisper 'Help' and it sends an alert to all the others with enchanted tokens."

The implications of the token registered on Jonah and he met Kevin's gaze. "You think something's gonna happen?" He feared Kevin would confirm his own feelings. First, Deyanira's warning, then learning about his aunt being released, and now this box with a note about his dad being angry over something that happened. "You do, don't you?"

Kevin shrugged. "Just being careful. Marcus, Rex, and Trueblood are traveling to the Afterworld to talk to the rebels. Mandara actually suggested they represent the Council."

"He wants Marcus out of the way," Jonah said, hating the man he had never met.

"We know." Kevin tapped Jonah's token-holding fist. "That's why you have that."

Jonah swallowed, trying to hold onto the brief spike of happiness. But it wasn't working because he knew Kevin would leave within minutes. He rose from the bench, gripping the box in both hands.

Kevin seemed to sense his disappointment. The Fallen Reaper remained seated but reached out to toy with the zipper on Jonah's jacket while staring at him in the eyes. "You okay? Everything all right?"

"Yeah. Why wouldn't it be?" Jonah caught himself because he didn't have to lie to Kevin about anything. He told the older boy all about Deyanira's warning and the weirdness at lunch with the mysterious girl.

Kevin gnashed his teeth together as he listened. His voice was tight when he said, "Deyanira could be playing with you. And that girl could have guessed about your abilities."

"No." He knew Kevin was just trying to cheer him up, and he didn't want that. "Tell me the truth."

"Well, why would Deyanira warn you? She hates you, remember? And the girl didn't set off your Death Sense. Just be careful." He tapped Jonah's hand again. "You have the token if you need more help."

Jonah nodded. "I'll take it with me tonight, to the vigil."

Kevin scowled and shot to his feet when he heard that. "I don't think you should go to the vigil."

"No choice. I'm representing my club tonight."

Amulet of the Goddess **671**

"Let the other kids do it."

"Why?"

"Because I can't be there to protect you, that's why."

Jonah gulped, moved by the pain in the boy's voice. "Kevin… I… you know, trouble finds me no matter what I do."

Kevin snorted. "That's the truth." But his hunched shoulders didn't relax.

Jonah hefted the box in one hand and opened his other palm to show Kevin the token. "Like you said, I'll have this in case anything happens. That's why you gave it to me." His words didn't reassure Kevin. Jonah could still sense the boy's tension. Something had him spooked. Why else would he risk getting in more trouble with his boss? "Why didn't you call me or text?"

"They stuck me in places where I couldn't use my phone." Kevin's hands balled into fists. "Mandara does it on purpose, to keep me away from you." He let out a sigh. "Watch out for his spy."

Jonah had all but forgotten the Alliance sent someone else to keep an eye on him. "Do you know who it is?"

Kevin scowled. "Marcus won't tell me."

Jonah didn't trust himself to respond because of the looming goodbye.

Kevin pulled him into a weak headlock and ruffled his picky afro. "Well, be careful, little man."

"I will," Jonah said, pulling free. He and Kevin walked down to the main courtyard in a comfortable silence.

Once there, Kevin lifted the book bag and held it so Jonah could slip the straps over his shoulder. When he did, Kevin turned him around and smirked. "Now you look like a regular nerd." He narrowed his eyes. "Wow. You've grown too."

Jonah grinned. "Oh, you noticed?"

"It's about time. I'll have to stop calling you *little man*."

Jonah toyed with the box, slightly nervous but willing to go further. "I thought I would always be your little man?" He glanced up into Kevin's face.

The young Fallen Reaper grinned. "Yeah, I guess so." He toyed with the strap on Jonah's book bag, lingering.

Jonah's heart beat faster as he gripped Kevin's hand and slid his fingers between the boy's larger ones.

Kevin wiggled his hand. "Jonah, I gotta go." He pulled his hand free of Jonah's, stepped back, and, as if mustering all of his courage, darted forward and kissed Jonah.

The first time was quick, the second longer. Jonah had never felt anything so wonderful. It was better than anything he could have imagined.

He hated it when Kevin pulled away. "I'll be back soon."

"Okay," Jonah whispered as Kevin phased. He closed his eyes, savoring the moment and the sensation of his first real kiss.

CHAPTER FIVE
THE VIGIL

The Tolerance Club had a table from which members could hand vigil attendees candles that were already lit. Jonah arrived later than he intended, but was proud to see his crew already taking care of business.

Sidling up to the table where Lorraine, Danita, and Anthony worked, he clipped on the new, pumpkin-head ribbon. "Everything going okay?"

"Yes," Lorraine answered. "Oh, Mike and his friend are passing out candles at the other entrance."

Jonah glanced at Danita, thinking she would know Mike's friend. She and Mike had grown up together on Morningside Drive. But Danita gazed back at him with a curious expression, like she was gauging his reaction to the news. Jonah didn't get that.

To avoid Danita's piercing gaze, he turned and peered through the gathering crowd, hoping to spot Mike.

Anthony cleared his throat. "I think we should walk through the crowd and hand out club pamphlets." Despite being his usual, take-charge self, he courteously waited for Jonah's decision.

"Sounds like a good idea," Jonah said.

Growing more curious by the second, Jonah scooped up a handful of pamphlets and skirted the edges of the gathering crowd. Anthony moved in the opposite direction. Suspicions blossomed in Jonah's mind about Mike as he walked. Aside from eating lunch together at school and their mutual club duties, he and Mike weren't hanging out as often anymore. In fact, they hadn't been to a movie together since school started.

With Kevin popping in and kissing him, the usual vivid awareness of being alone was absent. So why did he feel so moody now when he was practically walking on air after Kevin's visit?

His negative emotions spiked, forcing him to stop in his tracks. In addition, his Death Sense, the ability to detect mortal danger to himself or his loved ones, also prodded him with a painful twinge.

A raised conversation alerted Jonah that the crowd had grown thick around him. After handing out a few pamphlets, he tried to move to a more open area but bumped into another kid.

"Watch it," the boy warned. He turned and, seeing Jonah, added, "Oh. I didn't realize it was you."

Jonah blinked at the kid's surly tone. He also recognized the boy as the one who waved to Mike in the hallway at school. "You know me?"

Before the boy could answer, Mike slipped through the crowd to stand right beside him. "Jonah, this is my friend, Patrick."

Jonah remembered him from somewhere else now. "Aren't you in my Physical Science class?"

"Yeah." Patrick reached out to shake hands without any enthusiasm. When he did, his light coat slid up, exposing blue and yellow wristbands.

Jonah glanced at Mike's wrist, only to find the same colored bands there. A cool realization settled in Jonah's gut. The reason for Mike's absences and frequent tardiness to club events instantly crystallized. Mike had found a boyfriend. Jonah's new, turbulent emotions settled on a burgeoning dislike toward Patrick. He reached up to rub his aching forehead.

Mike stepped closer. "Jonah? We need to talk."

"I have to get back to the table," Jonah lied, angrily pushing his way through the crowd before Mike could say anything else. The more he thought about it, the more enraged he became.

In between the flares of his emotions, he wondered at the sudden mood change. This feeling of irritability and fury with his friend and the world was... odd. Still, seeing Mike with someone else didn't help matters one bit.

Rodney dated Lorraine. Anthony was vying for Danita. And now Mike and Patrick? It reminded Jonah how alone he was, even in the middle

Amulet of the Goddess

of a stupid crowd! No, he corrected himself, he and Kevin were moving forward. *So why am I pissed?*

In his rush to get away, he stumbled in the wrong direction, and was now headed toward the back of the field. When his Death Sense suddenly spiked, it only added a severe headache to his roiling emotions and Jonah clutched his head as he stifled a loud groan. Turning on the spot, he lifted up on his toes to see over and around the nearby people. It felt like a fiend was deliberately drilling spikes of tortuous pain into his skull. He thought of Kevin's warning and wondered if Mandara's spy could have been the reason for it.

That's when he saw her. A lone woman in a long, traveler's cloak stood near the stone dugout. The hood was drawn forward over her head, hiding her face in the shadow.

The crowd erupted with applause at something the vigil sponsors said. Jonah ignored the ensuing speeches and pushed through the press of people. By the time he stepped clear, the woman had vanished, along with some of the pressure on his mind. He searched around but didn't see her anywhere.

But how? he wondered, kneeling on the spot where the woman was standing. *Was she the reason for his emotional spikes?* Without warning, a sudden vision of a quiet train yard exploded in his mind. Jonah stifled another moan and grasped his head, knowing that's where the woman had gone.

Again, the question of *how* returned when it occurred to him that phasing was a Fallen Reaper power. But it wasn't the only way for supernatural beings to travel. Mages used vortices. Wraiths, in their gaseous form, could fly away on the air. There were also the portals and the Seeker's compass.

Jonah didn't know how the woman did it, but one thing was clear. She wanted him to follow her.

The raising of the candles surprised Jonah. With everyone's attention focused on the event, he had the perfect opportunity to get away. Throwing caution to the wind, he ducked behind the dugout and phased.

*

Even though Jonah wasn't following someone who had recently phased, he barely sensed the faint trail of magic in the aether. Rex, a friendly Fallen Reaper working with Jonah's godfather, never told him about that. Jonah filed it away, intending to mention it to the Fallen Reaper later. Right now, he concentrated on the magic, just as he did with Kevin's heat trail, and the real world exploded into view around him.

He was in a train yard, exactly as it appeared in the vision. Jonah whirled around, expecting an attack. When nothing happened, he took a moment to catch his breath.

The only sounds were the rattle of a train moving along tracks somewhere out of sight and the background drone of trucks rumbling on the distant overpass. Many of the rusted rail cars in this section sported broken wheels. It was more like a train junkyard.

His irritation peaked and he said, "I know you're here."

Something crashed against the side of a nearby train car. Jonah jumped at the sound and reached inside his pocket to grip the token Kevin had given him.

"Jonah Blackstone?" a woman's voice echoed, making it hard to pinpoint. But Jonah guessed it came from his left.

"Jonah?" This time, it was much closer and came from his right.

As he turned, trying to spot the slippery woman, he felt a familiar pressure. She was using a vortex to jump from one place to another around him while keeping out of sight. Her toying actions only compounded his frustration. "What do you want?"

"What do *I* want?" The voice was taunting. "You followed me. Brave, aren't you?"

Jonah felt her presence behind him as he pulled the token free of his pocket, preparing to activate it before she rushed past in a blur, brushing against his shoulder without attacking him.

The woman stopped at the far end of a boxcar and faced him. She was little more than a tall shadow but she made Jonah's Death Sense spike. The woman meant him harm, but not right now. He sensed mostly intense hate.

"I knew your father, young man," the woman continued, sounding like someone Jonah should have known but failed to place. "Despite all his

Amulet of the Goddess

faults, Isaiah was a powerful Fallen Reaper. He would have been proud to see his son using his abilities so adeptly."

Jonah took two steps closer toward her despite the danger. "Who are you?"

The woman laughed, sending a chill down Jonah's spine. Her heavy voice turned thoughtful in a mocking way. "Or perhaps you're more like your mom. Poor, poor Janice! Now she–" The stranger stopped and let out a low laugh. "I see your friends have arrived."

Jonah detected the telltale pressure at the same time a light flared behind him and a vortex opened. To his surprise, four huge men in black uniforms charged out, rushing into the train yard. Two flew by a stunned Jonah as they hurtled toward the woman.

Instead of opening a vortex, the woman wove her hands through the air before she vanished in an outpouring of dark, thick vapor. Jonah strained to catch a glimpse of her face in the reflected light from the spell, but it was useless.

The large men charged to the spot where the woman disappeared and studied handheld devices that glowed with a pulsing, eerie, orange color. Jonah wondered if the devices could detect magic.

A third guard remained by the open vortex with a young mage; while the fourth guy was standing right beside Jonah, regarding him with undisguised curiosity.

This close, Jonah needed to crane his neck back to see the man's brown face. All the men were well over seven feet tall and their muscled upper bodies were almost out of proportion with their lower halves. Each held an advanced club weapon in two-handed grips. Power sizzled along the length of the weapons, which made the hair on the back of Jonah's neck stand on end.

The man beside Jonah wore a black, military-style vest with the Alliance symbol on the left breast pocket. Below that were two short, horizontal, gold bars. Jonah recognized the commanding aura about the man as he touched a button on the side of his helmet.

"We have him, sir. The enemy fled upon our approach." He listened to a response Jonah couldn't hear. Then he clamped a large, gloved hand on Jonah's shoulder. "Come along."

Jonah didn't resist, but he gulped as he asked, "Who are you?"

The man blinked in surprise. "I'm the captain of the Alliance Guards."

Oh no, Jonah thought. Although he never knew anything about the Alliance Guards, he imagined their being here now couldn't be a good thing.

The Guard Captain nodded. "There's a Council member waiting to have a word with you."

This is it, Jonah thought. Visions of the intimidating mage, Rubio, waiting on the other side of the vortex, formed in Jonah's mind. Or worse, what if the perpetually mean-spirited Mandara finally showed up?

With those thoughts in mind, he let the Guard Captain lead him to the vortex. Jonah spared a glance at the young mage who produced the magical opening. The boy couldn't have been any older than Robert and Lynn. It amazed Jonah someone so young could already be an Alliance mage. And then he noticed the lack of an Alliance symbol on the boy's royal blue tunic. But he had to have been powerful and talented just to open and maintain a vortex like this one.

Maybe he's a trainee?

The boy didn't acknowledge Jonah but kept his chin up and his eyes forward with an important air about him.

The Guard Captain gestured at the magical opening. "After you, sir."

Jonah glanced back at the guard, screwed up his nerves, and cautiously entered the vortex.

CHAPTER SIX
THE HONORABLE COUNCIL MEMBER

Traveling through a vortex differed from phasing. For one thing, it took several more seconds because you had to walk or run to the next location. For another, the vapor that obscured your destination clung tenaciously to the body almost like cobwebs. And the vapory mist inside a vortex always managed to come into contact with every part of your body, despite the clothes you wore.

Jonah shivered, although he wasn't cold. Maybe he was biased, but he preferred phasing. Within seconds, the mist parted and he stepped into the Teen Center's attic clubhouse. Jonah paused, causing the huge Guard Captain to bump into him.

"Sorry," Jonah said, moving further into the familiar space.

In quick order, the other three guards stepped through, followed by the young mage, who closed the vortex.

The Teen Center, a renovated, old, Southern mansion with a commanding view of the hilly surrounding neighborhoods, was a popular destination for young people from all over the county.

Per an agreement with the administration, Jonah and his cousins were allowed to use the attic as their base of operation. It comprised two areas. The area to the right, the Summit, contained all the computers and monitors his cousins used to write their blog and maintain the center's website. Stray papers and computer parts littered the top of a smaller worktable, situated just beyond the computers. It was where the twins composed their blog.

On the left side of the attic was an old, slightly sunken sofa, two mismatched armchairs that faced the sofa, and a battered, brown steamer trunk in between. This is where the club regularly met.

Jonah's hopes rose when he saw a tall man in the blue tunic of an adult Alliance Mage. Slowly releasing the breath he held, Jonah felt relieved. He didn't have to face Rubio nor the mysterious Mandara, a Fallen Reaper who would have worn a Reaper's long coat. But that didn't mean he wasn't in big trouble.

The mage talked with an aide, keeping his back toward Jonah. His shoulder-length dreads bobbed as he emphasized something. When the conversation ended, the Alliance member turned and Jonah received a pleasant surprise.

The mage was Native American and his chiseled facial features looked very familiar. The man wore a genuine expression of relief as he bounded over to Jonah's group.

"Thank the ancestors you're safe!" He extended his right hand. "I'm so glad."

Jonah shook the mage's hand, feeling a little confused.

The mage stood back, taking in Jonah's appearance.

When he didn't introduce himself, the Guard Captain cleared his throat. "This is the Honorable Council Member and Mage, Symon Trueblood."

Trueblood frowned and shook his head, causing his dreads to sway around. "I wouldn't call myself *honorable*."

Jonah's jaw dropped. "Trueblood? You're related to Mage Trueblood? I mean…"

"That's right," the mage said. "Eleanor's my little sister." He spread his arms wide. "Yeah. It's hard to believe a guy as young as me has an adult kid sister." He laughed at his own joke.

The Guard Captain shook his head and the young mage trainee frowned.

Jonah suspected they all had heard that joke before. He grinned, never expecting an Alliance Mage to act like that.

Trueblood folded his arms across his chest and stared at Jonah. "That was a foolish thing to do."

Jonah's shoulders slumped, and he nodded. "Yes, sir, but..."

"But...?" Trueblood raised an eyebrow.

"She didn't attack me."

"True. What if the situation had turned south and she decided to hurt, or, even worse, *abduct* you?"

Jonah gulped because the mage's earlier playfulness was gone. In its place was a deep concern for him. Something worried the mage. Jonah reached inside his pocket and withdrew the token. "Kevin gave me this, in case anything happened. Plus, I can phase and fight."

The Guard Captain grunted in a satisfied way, eyeing Jonah with what looked like an approving gaze.

Plucking the token from Jonah's hand, Trueblood inspected it. "This is my sister's work." He winked at Jonah. "I showed her how to do it."

"Oh, really?"

"Yes." Trueblood dropped the token in Jonah's hand. "It's good to see you learning your powers," the Council member continued, "but following a stranger wasn't a good idea."

"She didn't mean me any harm." Jonah's face warmed at the obvious craziness of the statement. The woman definitely meant him harm. *Just not tonight.*

Trueblood raised a finger. "First, how did you follow her?"

Jonah averted his eyes, unsure of how the mage would take this part. "Well, I... I think she sent me a vision of where I had to go."

The Alliance people stirred. Trueblood rubbed his jaw, frowning as he peered at Jonah.

Jonah refrained from mentioning the woman had also spiked his emotions tonight. Instead, he asked, "Do you know how we follow someone through a phase?" The mage nodded. "When I phased, it was weird, but I could sense her magic trail and I followed it. I didn't need the images she sent."

"I've never heard of a Fallen Reaper who could do that," the mage said, sounding amazed. "That's remarkable, Jonah."

"You think so?" A cautious optimism crept into Jonah's voice. Unlike so many others, who got spooked when they learned of his unique abilities, Trueblood's amazement was genuine.

"Of course. You will do a lot of things no one else can. The Council knows that." Trueblood waved Jonah to the clubhouse section and then into an armchair. The mage sat on the arm of the sofa, trying to affect a relaxed air but failing.

"Tell me. What did she want from you?"

"Nothing. She was showing off and talking about my parents," Jonah confessed. "I never saw her face and…" The sudden sense of dread and worry that rolled off the Alliance mage stopped Jonah mid-sentence. "Do you know who she was?"

Trueblood made a dismissive gesture with his right hand. "She could have been anyone. The important thing is that you're safe."

Once again, Jonah wondered why an Alliance Council member would show up with his guards. "I'm in big trouble, huh?"

Trueblood smiled. "No, not as long as you show better judgment."

Feeling bolder, Jonah asked, "Why did you come, if I'm not in any trouble?"

"Well," Trueblood said, "I had one of those rare free moments in my schedule. So I decided to visit the young man who's been causing our enemies so much anxiety."

Jonah welcomed the cheeriness he heard, but also suspected the mage wasn't telling the truth. Sure, he could imagine Trueblood wanted to see him. In fact, Jonah fully expected the Alliance Council to summon him long before now. He realized they were watching at the field.

"Why are you spying on me? I mean, my godfather does that, and I know the Council sent someone to replace Kevin and keep an eye on me."

Trueblood studied his face but didn't contradict anything he said. "I thought it best if I saw the situation firsthand. And," he added, "you are the Deliverer."

An idea occurred to Jonah. He was the Deliverer, so why couldn't he ask for things? Kevin insisted he shouldn't do that, but for the first time, a Council member, someone besides his godfather, was right in front of him.

Amulet of the Goddess **683**

"Can Kevin come back?" Jonah asked. "You're on the Council. Couldn't you order Mandara to do it?"

Trueblood let out a roar of laughter but stifled it when Jonah frowned. "You need to learn more about Council politics. You don't order Mandara to do anything! Not unless you're the chairperson. Which I'm not." He chuckled to himself. "That being said, I'll see what I can do."

"Thanks," Jonah replied, somewhat reassured.

The mage sobered and leaned forward, scanning Jonah's face. "You look just like Janice." His smile was rueful.

Jonah blinked. "You knew my mom?"

Genuine amusement lit up Trueblood's face. "We were best friends. Me, her, and Omar."

"Omar?"

"Yeah. We all joined the Alliance at the same time. Janice escaped small town Mount Vernon to attend school in Atlanta. I was just off the reservation, all full of myself, young and stupid. And Omar was thousands of miles away from his home and everyone he knew and loved. We formed our own little mutual support pack." Trueblood's eyes had a gleam in them as if he vividly remembered old adventures. "We also had our share of trouble."

Jonah couldn't believe it. His mom had always been so… what? Could she have been like him and his cousins?

Trueblood seemed to read his thoughts. "Your parents would be proud of you, Jonah."

Jonah met the mage's gaze. "You were friends with my dad too?"

"Yes. He was one of the bravest men I ever met. And he sponsored my membership on the Council."

The sad truth of that statement hit Jonah with a sudden heaviness. "They never had a chance to tell me anything about the Council or…"

"I miss them too," Trueblood said. He pointed at Jonah's chest. "But you carry both your parents inside you. Whatever your father and mother were, so are you, now and forever. Never forget that."

The Guard Captain intoned, "Ashe."

The other guards and the young mage repeated the word in hushed voices.

A surge of pride, history, and belonging swelled Jonah's chest. He sucked in a breath and his lip trembled as he nodded. No one had ever said or done that to him. He wondered if the mage could have cast a spell on him, but suspected otherwise. There was no magic, just an energy more basic and powerful than anything else.

Suddenly, Jonah wanted to ask the mage about so many other things.

Trueblood intervened with, "I bet you're interested in how we followed you, right?"

Jonah hesitated, forcing himself to shift his thoughts to the new topic. "Well, yeah. I guess."

Trueblood snapped his fingers. "It was a location spell."

Jonah had been around Wick long enough to understand how those spells worked. "You needed something of mine. Like…"

"A piece of hair?" Trueblood laughed. "Let's just say not all the hair clippings at the barber shop end up in the trash."

Jonah didn't know how he felt about people keeping pieces of his hair. If the good guys could use it, couldn't the bad guys, too?

"I can guess what you're thinking," Trueblood added. "We made sure you left none of your hair behind. We are always aware of when you get your hair cut." He squinted at Jonah's afro. "Speaking of which…"

"That's okay," Jonah blurted out, causing the mage to smile.

The captain tapped his earpiece and drew Trueblood's attention with a nod.

The mage refocused on Jonah. "We should get you home."

Jonah only had a second to wonder if they would open a vortex to his backyard. Eleanor Trueblood had done that once and it was freakin' cool.

The mage stood and called out to the young trainee, "How late am I for my meeting?"

Amulet of the Goddess   **685**

The boy glanced at his watch. "Ten minutes."

"Excellent." Trueblood grinned at Jonah. "If you're gonna be late, then do it in style." He shook Jonah's hand. The Council member had extraordinary strength in his grip and he didn't release his hold as he said, "I don't want you wandering around all alone in the evenings. That's an order."

Jonah gulped. "Yes, sir."

"Sir?" Trueblood pulled a scandalized expression as he released Jonah's hand. "Don't call me *sir*. Makes me feel old." After an exaggerated shudder, he waved to the young trainee-mage. "Mr. Pledge, have you met Mr. Blackstone?"

The serious boy turned his attention to Jonah and shook his head.

Trueblood smiled. "Well, then, Thomas Pledge meet Jonah Blackstone."

Thomas's nod was formal and quick. Caught off guard, Jonah returned the gesture.

Trueblood frowned at the young man until Thomas strode over and offered to shake Jonah's hand. "Nice to meet you."

"Same," Jonah said. Like Trueblood, Thomas had a strong handshake.

"Mr. Pledge is finishing his trials and will become a full-fledged Alliance mage soon, and," Trueblood stage-whispered to Jonah, "his mom is on the Alliance Council."

Jonah's awe of Thomas instantly went up a notch. He was already on course to be an Alliance member and had a mom on the Council. No wonder the young mage carried himself so seriously.

But Thomas looked rather embarrassed at the sudden attention. He shuffled in place while staring at anything but Trueblood and Jonah.

"You two represent the next generation and should know each other," Trueblood continued. He patted the young mage on the shoulder and motioned toward the space in front of the attic window.

Thomas seemed relieved to do his job. He moved to the window and reopened the vortex with a practiced wave of his hand.

Jonah took a step toward the opening but the Guard Captain stopped him.

Mage Trueblood waved goodbye and then turned to the vortex and said to Thomas, "You think I have enough time to put a war stripe on my face? You know how Mandara hates that."

Thomas let out a moan and shook his head. "No, sir." Trueblood laughed as he stepped through. The Guard Captain removed his helmet and outer vest and handed those to the other guards. They exited through the opening next.

Thomas nodded to the captain and then, for a moment, he locked gazes with Jonah before stepping through and closing the magical opening.

Once they exited, the captain detached his weapon from its holder. He touched a button on the side, and it collapsed into a foot-long, black, octagonal cylinder. He reattached that to his belt and nodded toward the attic steps. "After you, sir."

At first, Jonah didn't like the large guard escorting him through the Teen Center. But he understood why the man got rid of his helmet and vest. Without them, he looked less like he was wearing a uniform.

Still, his size drew everyone's attention and Jonah hated that because it also made him the center of attention. However, the upside of the situation presented itself when Brandon and Antwan moved to block his path.

Brandon folded his arms. "What's up, freak?"

Jonah didn't hesitate to step toward the boy who didn't have the height advantage anymore. Before he could say a word, the Guard Captain pulled him back and planted himself in front of Brandon.

"Is there a problem here?" The captain's deep voice rolled across Brandon.

The bully stumbled backward while staring up at the imposing man. "Um, no." He hurried off with Antwan.

The Guard Captain snorted and motioned Jonah down the east wing and toward the side exit.

"You didn't seem afraid of that boy." The Guard Captain kept his eyes on the other kids as they neared the exit. "Admirable."

"I wasn't afraid of him." Jonah let his anger seep into his voice.

The captain nodded. "Good. It's important to stand up for yourself."

Jonah noted the tone of pride in the man's voice. He glanced sideways at the guard. "Do you think I made a mistake tonight?"

Amulet of the Goddess

"You were brave, that's for sure," the captain didn't hesitate to reply. "But always remember to have a second person with you, to watch your back."

Jonah nodded, taking the man's advice to heart. They reached the side exit to the Teen Center, and a large, black SUV was parked at the curb outside. The captain sprang forward to open the back passenger door.

Jonah paused before getting in. "My bike's still at the ball field."

The captain smiled. "It's in the back of the truck."

"Oh," Jonah said, looking stunned as he got in.

The captain slid into the front passenger seat and they started off. Jonah sat in silence, brooding about the sudden upsurge in his protection. He'd never seen these types of guards before. Even when Agent Hunter was in Mount Vernon, Jonah never had an escort.

What was Mage Trueblood afraid of? It had to be connected to the mysterious woman he followed. When the vehicle slowed to leave the center's parking lot, Jonah glanced out the window and jumped.

Across the parking lot, in the shadows of the tree line, two bright, red eyes stared back at him. But as soon as the truck started into motion again, the eyes blinked and disappeared. Jonah searched the gloominess as they zoomed by, sucking in a quick breath when he glimpsed the eyes bobbing through the trees, tracking his course.

Anyone else would have been terrified, but not Jonah. If he weren't mistaken, those eyes belonged to a Grim Hound. With his Death Sense quiet, he knew the beast wasn't there to harm him.

Soon, the SUV turned down a street with little tree cover and houses on both sides and the Grim Hound's eyes were lost from sight.

What the heck was going on?

CHAPTER SEVEN
MYSTIC WORLDS

Jonah's biggest fear was that Lynn or Robert would spot him getting out of the SUV. Once he put his bike in the backyard shed and entered through the kitchen entrance, the only person he saw was Robert, who was watching TV.

After nodding to his cousin, Jonah scooted through the family room and toward his own bedroom, feeling relieved. He should have known better. Lynn's hand gripped his shoulder before he could even enter his room. She spun him around.

Jonah guessed his cousin had been looking out the front window.

"Who was that?" she demanded. "Why'd they give you a ride home?"

Robert leapt off the sofa and was at their side in a second. "What did he do now?"

"He hasn't confessed yet." Lynn narrowed her eyes.

Giving in to the inevitable, Jonah waved his cousins into his room. He plopped on the bed while Robert leaned against the desk.

Lynn closed the door and rested an elbow on Jonah's chest of drawers. "Okay, spill it."

Jonah gulped and launched into his story about the vigil, the mysterious woman, and following her to the train yard.

"That was stupid, Jonah," Lynn hissed in frustration. "What if she had attacked you?"

Amulet of the Goddess **689**

"I had this." Jonah showed the token to his cousins. "I got it from Kevin, in case I need to call for help."

Robert took the token from him. "Kevin? When did he come through?"

Jonah told them about Kevin's visit, but he hesitated to mention the box. It rested on his memento shelf beside his dad's golden Alliance badge, although neither of his cousins seemed to have noticed it.

Robert let out a low whistle and passed the token to Lynn. "You've been busy today."

"You don't know the half of it," Jonah admitted.

Lynn tossed the token back to him. "So, what happened next? Why the ride home?"

Jonah avoided their inquisitive gazes by looking at the token. He turned it over in his hands. "Alliance Guards showed up and took me to the clubhouse. I met another Council member, Mage Trueblood's brother." He told them that Trueblood often hung out with his mom back in the day.

Robert gaped at him.

Lynn remained on point and asked, "How did they follow you?"

Robert laughed. "It had to be a location spell, right, Jonah?"

"Yeah. They had some of my hair."

"Dang!" Robert looked stricken. "Wick warned me not to leave my clippings behind! I thought he was just being paranoid."

Jonah shrugged. "I guess not."

"The more important question," Lynn continued, "is why a Council member would show up with his guards?"

"I didn't know they had guards," Robert added, scratching his head in confusion. "You don't think it has anything to do with our dear aunt, do you?"

Lynn pursed her lips. "Yes, of course I do! The mage is right: You shouldn't go out alone at night. Not until we know more. Got it?"

Jonah wanted to say, "Yes, ma'am," but feared he'd end up in a headlock. So he nodded and didn't mention the Grim Hound. When his cousins left him alone, Jonah pulled out his books and finished his homework.

Sometime later, he turned in. As he slipped under the covers, he realized that Mike's wish for an uneventful school year probably wasn't gonna happen.

*

During the night, Jonah had regular dreams about the brief image of Deyanira and the strange arena. By the next morning, he had an idea of how to interpret the sorceress's warning. Maybe she would be at her old store. He hadn't thought about the place or gone there in two years. But there was a chance he could find out the true reason for her warning.

When he told Robert and Lynn about his idea during breakfast, they all agreed to visit Mystic Worlds after school.

Jonah went through his day while avoiding awkward questions about his early disappearance from the vigil. Danita was the only club member to press for more information. Mike, catching Jonah's silent plea for help, came to his rescue and distracted her.

Free of Danita's questions for the time being, Jonah was fixated on getting to Mystic Worlds. As the time rapidly approached, Jonah prepared himself to face the dangerous sorceress and get the answers he sought.

Robert and Wick, who first jumped at the chance to come along, surprised Jonah by opting to remain at the mall. Lynn mumbled about them having something up their sleeves but she didn't elaborate. In fact, while they walked the few blocks from the mall to Mystic Worlds, Jonah suspected his cousin was in a sour mood. Something must have happened at school because Lynn wasn't that way during breakfast.

But he refocused his attention when they reached the location that used to be Mystic Worlds. Jonah let out a surprised groan at the sight of the brand-new sign above the store's front door. Mystics Worlds was now a New Age bookstore.

Jonah pressed his face against the front window to peek inside, fearing their trip had been for nothing. He relaxed when he spotted Deyanira's former clerk.

Glancing at Lynn, he nodded. "Let's do this."

The pleasant ding of the door chime made a strange counterpoint to the low buzzing of his Death Sense when he entered the store.

Amulet of the Goddess

Unlike Mystic Worlds, which had dark walls and shelves filled with strange knick-knacks, this new store featured pale blue walls. The bookshelves contained as many odd things and statuettes, but very few demons, dragons, or Reapers. Overall, the ambience was less oppressive and much more calming.

The configuration of the floor space hadn't changed, nor the chest-high shelves of books of all sorts. And the back counter was now soothing earth tones of green with a brown top instead of its former midnight black. The clerk finished with a customer and froze when he saw Jonah and Lynn.

The trio stared at each other for several tense moments until the clerk cleared his throat and smiled. "Ah, Jonah, isn't it? You're here to buy more books?"

Jonah didn't need his Death Sense to realize he was encountering the same noble Egyptian Wraith which had possessed the clerk before. But he wore different clothes now: loose pants, a flowing, colorful dashiki, a skull cap, and sandals on his feet.

Lynn nudged his arm and Jonah asked, "Why are you back here?"

The Wraith stood tall with a regal posture. "The host invited me in."

Jonah shuddered, failing to understand how anyone would willingly accept Wraith possession. He put that aside, however, and peered around at the half dozen customers in the store.

"Where's Deyanira?" When the clerk didn't answer, Jonah subjected the man to a Reaper's stare even though he had never tried using it on a Wraith-possessed person.

The clerk spread his hands as if he had nothing to hide. "I assure you," he answered, "since I've owned this store, Deyanira has never been in here."

Jonah didn't sense a direct lie to his question. But that didn't mean the clerk was telling the whole truth.

Lynn must have concluded the same thing because she took out her Reaper blades. In their current deactivated stage, the blades were eight-inch cylinders. But when transformed, they were fifteen-inch, razor-sharp, silver blades covered in Angel script. In addition, the weapons could hurt anything supernatural.

She pointed one inactive blade at the clerk. "Why would she warn Jonah?"

The clerk slowly retreated and moved to a corner display of calendars, further away from the other customers. His eyes remained fixated on the cylinder as he said, "Deyanira doesn't tell me her plans, young warrior."

"Why not? I thought you were her pet Wraith."

The clerk merely nodded as he shifted his gaze to Jonah. "She eventually deduced I helped you, young Blackstone, and has never fully trusted me again."

"Too bad," Lynn said before whirling on Jonah. "Well? Is he lying?"

Jonah nodded. "He's cherry-picking his words."

Lynn glanced around and activated one blade. Holding it close to her body, she shielded it from the view of anyone else. "I say we send this Wraith packing."

The clerk lifted an eyebrow. "In the middle of my store? I think not." He reached behind and underneath his dashiki. When he withdrew his hand, he was holding an ancient short sword very low at his side. "I've too much to accomplish to let you send me back to my realm."

Any other day, Lynn would have shown more common sense. But she stepped toward the clerk.

Jonah feared his cousin wouldn't back down, so he tapped her forearm. "Lynn, don't. He helped me with Deyanira."

Lynn shook with frustration as she deactivated the blade. "If anything happens to my cousin…" she warned before turning toward the door.

Jonah followed but stopped when his eye caught a display of potions books. He reached out to take one and held it toward the clerk. "You sell potion books?"

"Ignorant people erroneously assume that potions and natural remedies are no more than witchcraft." The clerk's voice adopted an eager tone.

Slipping the book from Jonah's hand, Lynn read the back cover and scowled.

"You should buy it," the clerk urged.

Lynn scoffed and dropped it back on the shelf. "You have got to be kidding."

Amulet of the Goddess 693

The clerked slipped his sword into the scabbard he had hidden beneath the dashiki and moved closer, ignoring Lynn's harsh glare. "Your parents were researchers, were they not, young Blackstone? Surely they trained you to value knowledge in all of its forms."

Lynn gripped Jonah's shoulder and turned him toward the door before he could respond. "Let's get out of here."

Jonah gave the eager clerk one curious glance before he exited the store.

*

Lynn fumed all the way to the mall, causing Jonah to worry about her surly attitude and distracted behavior.

"What's wrong with you today?" he asked as they entered the mall.

Lynn's stride never faltered but her brow wrinkled. She glanced sideways at him and let out a breath. "It's Rico. We had a big fight today."

With anyone else, Jonah would have assumed a fight meant an argument. But since this was Lynn, and Rico was also her regular dueling partner, he wanted to be accurate. "You do mean an argument, right?"

"Yes, an argument," Lynn said, a little too loud. A few people glanced in their direction and she lowered her voice. "I didn't see it coming."

"Well, that happens," Jonah said, but added to himself, *I guess*. He had no real clue about relationships.

"But not with me!" Lynn paused at the top of the first escalator and pulled Jonah to the side when he bumped into her. She waited until the people behind them passed before saying, "I've always been able to tell when we were heading for a fight and managed to avoid it. Most of the time."

Jonah nodded, pretending to follow her, and then suddenly, he got it. "You're using your intuition?"

Lynn's jaws worked as she mounted the next escalator. Jonah hurried to follow, eager to hear the answer to his question.

After leaning against the escalator's rail, Lynn finally said, "Yes, I was. But it didn't work this time. In fact," she glanced around, "Mom beat me in cards last night. Can you believe that? Normally, I could tell which cards not to play."

Jonah couldn't believe it. Not only was his cousin using her power–in her case, a super-strong intuition–but she had been using it regularly in her everyday life! What astounded Jonah even more was that Lynn watched him, waiting for his reaction, like he should have known the answer.

"Uh…" Jonah scratched his head as they reached the end of the escalator and moved down the concourse. He let it go when they approached Robert and Wick, who were waiting for them.

Robert sat on the bench with a couple of pretty girls leaning over him. Wick, who had a girlfriend, never shied away from performing. He stood beside Robert, creating balls of beautiful blue flame in his palms for the small crowd. Jonah didn't fail to notice that Wick scanned the area for mall security each time he did it.

The onlookers clapped and Wick snuffed out the flames before passing out cards. "Don't miss my show at the Teen Center this Saturday night!"

One of the girls made an awestruck sound as she took a sketch from Robert and showed it to her friend. Wick patted Robert's shoulder. "My friend's a part of the show." He flashed his lopsided grin at the small group.

Lynn slipped behind the bench and peeked over her brother's shoulder.

The girl who had received the last sketch watched Robert with an intense gaze. "Do you do private sessions?"

The sly grin on his cousin's face let Jonah know that Robert had indeed been doing private drawing sessions.

"No, he doesn't." Lynn clapped him on the shoulder. "Or at least, he better not be."

The girl's comical frown quickly changed as she took Robert's sketch pencil and wrote her number on a blank sheet of paper. That done, she flashed Robert a brilliant smile before strolling off smugly with her friends.

Lynn poked her brother in the head. "Seriously?"

Robert took his time tearing out the page with the number and folding it. "You're really gonna go there? I'm sure you and Rico are just studying when you two disappear." He glanced up at his sister, smirking. "And I know you must use your intuition to find the best spots for your *studying*."

Jonah's jaw dropped while Wick laughed like a maniac, enjoying the sparring.

Amulet of the Goddess

Robert seemed to score the point because Lynn didn't have a comeback.

Wick's laughing stopped as he studied her face. "I guess the bookstore visit was a bust."

"Yes, it was," Lynn answered.

"He knows something," Jonah offered.

Lynn huffed. "Jonah wouldn't let me send the Wraith back."

"Why not?" Robert asked as he began to sketch again.

Lynn glanced down at what he'd drawn and hissed, "Robert! You're sketching random people's thoughts?"

"Yeah." Robert avoided looking at his sister.

Jonah saw the jumbled, yet distinct, images.

"How long have you been able to sketch peoples' thoughts without them concentrating?" Lynn pressed him.

"Not long," Robert hedged.

Lynn threw her hands up in frustration. "It's unethical."

"Come on. I'm not digging for anything personal, just…" Robert's voice trailed off.

"I don't think you should do anymore sketches for a while."

Robert and Wick objected, Wick being the louder. "Lynn, he's part of my show! People are coming just for that. And we're starting to make good money."

Lynn crossed her arms. "Speaking of that, I think you're getting a little too flashy with your power. What if someone notices it's real?"

"Hey," Robert said, standing up, "just because your intuition is acting up, don't spoil our fun."

"Yeah," Wick chimed in. "I know what I'm doing, Lynn."

Robert peered at his sister and said, "Or are you getting a bad feeling about this?"

Jonah realized the taunt had rattled Lynn when, instead of punching her brother, she let her shoulders slump in a way he'd never seen.

Robert's expression changed in an instant. "I didn't mean that."

"We'll be fine," Wick added. "You'll see. And whatever's happening to you will soon pass."

Lynn stood tall and crossed her arms. "Maybe. But I still say we should be careful."

Wick nodded, but Robert watched his sister with a concerned expression.

Jonah thought she had a point. Wick and Robert were using their abilities more often than ever, and he had the Human Lie Detector gag at school. To top it all off, he chased after that woman at the vigil, even though it was, no doubt, a stupid thing to do.

Once again, Deyanira's warning came back to him. *Beware, young Blackstone.*

CHAPTER EIGHT
THE UNKEMPT CLERK

Jonah rapped on Mike's bedroom window and waited. Nothing. Everything was quiet inside the Littletons' split-level home. After several more taps on the ground-level window, Jonah gave up with an irritated huff.

While his cousins and Wick headed off to the Teen Center, Jonah searched for Mike to thank him for helping with Danita. And to apologize. Besides, he wanted Mike's opinion on everything that happened. But Mike wasn't home.

Images of Mike and Patrick, secluded somewhere while making out, popped into Jonah's mind, stoking a sudden jealousy. He was sure Patrick was keeping his buddy away from him. For a moment, Jonah fantasized about phasing the boy to the top of a tree or the middle of a busy highway!

Jonah gritted his teeth, waiting for the fit of jealousy to pass. What was wrong with him? The mysterious woman wasn't even nearby. Besides, why shouldn't Mike find someone? Especially after everything that happened with Trevor?

But Patrick? Jonah didn't get that one. He shook his head in bewilderment as he hopped on his bike and rode off.

At the entrance to Mike's cul-de-sac, Jonah stomped on the brakes. An idea suddenly occurred to him. Mike could have gone to work at his uncle's bookstore. It was still open.

Ten minutes after leaving the Littletons' home, Jonah rolled up to the front of Hackett's Book Emporium. The store was located inside a one-story house that had been rezoned for commercial use. An old-fashioned wooden sign hung above the front door.

Although Mr. Hackett could be a little intimidating, Jonah liked visiting the store. It smelled like a real bookstore and reminded him of the wonderful times his mom took him to little, out-of-the-way, secondhand shops. That was where he'd find the best books–the old ones with crinkled covers, smudges on the inside pages, and even underlined passages.

This evening, he was on a mission when he entered. Jonah glanced at the cash register, expecting to see Mike. But the counter was empty. A few customers milled around, cautiously avoiding the teetering stacks of books at the end of every aisle. Jonah moved further into the cramped store but stopped when someone directly behind him spoke.

"Can I help you?"

Jonah turned to find a short man with strange, sunken eyes, the kind that rarely blinked, staring at him. Sporting a mustache and goatee, the man wore a pale shirt and shabby, green slacks that covered his rail thin body and yellowish skin. He wasn't someone Jonah would have chosen to invite for dinner.

The man reached up to push a strand of his disheveled brown hair out of his face. "Yes?"

"Oh. I'm looking for Mike."

"He's not working today."

"Thanks."

Jonah edged around the stranger and headed toward the door when the man asked, "Are you a friend?"

"Yeah." The man's silence stretched on, growing uncomfortable, so Jonah added, "I'm Jonah."

The answer produced a sudden smile and the short man stood straighter. "You're Jonah Blackstone? Mr. Hackett told me about you."

Jonah nodded.

"My name is Alastor. Mr. Hackett hired me to look after the store while he's away." Alastor held out a thin hand.

Jonah hesitated because the man's overly long nails were uncut with mucky traces of dirt underneath. But he didn't see a way out when Alastor glanced down at his proffered hand.

Amulet of the Goddess

As soon as Jonah touched the man, he wished he hadn't. The palm felt clammy. He yanked his hand away and stoically resisted the urge to wipe it on his pants. "So, Mr. Hackett told you about me?"

Alastor tilted his head to the side, studying Jonah. "You like the Occult section, no?"

Jonah nodded, wondering if Mr. Hackett had also told Alastor to keep him out of that area. "I guess we can't go back there."

Alastor smiled. "Hmm, I approve of anyone's healthy interest in things beyond what you can see with your eyes." He gestured toward the Occult section of the store.

"Oh, no. I need to talk with Mike."

"He seems more focused on his social life these days."

Jonah blinked at the man's sharp tone. "Mike's cool."

Alastor retreated two steps while staring at Jonah's balled fists.

"I meant no offense," Alastor hastily added.

Jonah's ringtone, a sci-fi movie theme, blared out through the quiet store. He fumbled to answer the call while several customers glared at him. "What's up, Lynn?"

"Get to the Summit."

"Why?" Jonah whispered as he retreated toward the front door.

"We have a client. I'll try to wait, but hurry."

Jonah pocketed his phone and glanced back.

Alastor was watching. "Come back anytime, Mr. Blackstone."

Jonah nodded and slipped outside. There was something very off about Alastor. He wondered if the man were a Fallen Reaper. Or maybe even an Archivist. Jonah couldn't tell either way because fallen supernaturals didn't set off his Death Sense, not unless they meant to do him harm.

That thought didn't offer Jonah much comfort as he headed toward the Teen Center.

*

"Jonah!" Danita called out when he reached the door to the clubhouse.

Having taken over a bench outside one of the administrative offices on the second floor, she had her school textbooks perched on her lap, a spiral notebook in one hand and a highlighter in the other. Danita snapped the book closed and cradled it and the notebook in her right arm while tugging her heavy book bag over to him.

"What are you doing out here?" Jonah inquired. He offered to hold her bag open so she could cram her things inside. The backpack was already bursting at the seams.

"I was waiting for you to show up," Danita said, a little flushed. "I tried to persuade Latrell's sister not to come and see Wick, but—" She waved at the attic door.

It bore two signs: one for the Summit and a second one for the Mount Vernon Social Club. "So *that's* why they called me."

"Yeah." Danita dropped her book bag on the ground. "Are you gonna use your," she lowered her voice, "your hypothetical talent to help Wick?"

Jonah wasn't surprised Danita remembered every little thing she learned. "You really don't believe in anything that can't be tested and measured?"

Danita looked scandalized. "No, I don't, and neither should you."

"I don't get it," Jonah stammered, unable to resist entering the argument. "You're the leader of our book club! We read science fiction and fantasy books."

Danita sighed in a patronizing way that never ceased to rankle Jonah. "Those are books, stories, and fairy tales. And that's where those things belong! Not where people start believing them in the," she made air quotes, "real world!"

Jonah smirked at her. "You know, most myths are based on actual facts."

"Yes, regular, boring, explainable, and provable facts," she insisted. "It's just sad when people rely on mysticism to explain things they're too lazy to attempt to process with their brains and logic."

"Right," Jonah said, rubbing his forehead. "Anyway, I need to go—"

"Wait!" Danita gripped his forearm. "I asked Lynn about joining the editorial team for the Summit. She's all for it, but," she frowned, "I'm not sure about your cousin, Robert. Did she ask you yet?"

Amulet of the Goddess

"Well, yeah, but—"

"Did you support me?"

Jonah tried to avoid her expectant expression. "We haven't decided on it yet."

"Jonah, you know me." Danita opened her bag and pulled out a small notebook with frayed edges from extensive use. "I'm working on a second part to the black cat story." She flipped to a page and showed him. Jonah looked down at a badly drawn map of Mount Vernon and a big star near a north corner. Above the drawing, in bold ink letters, were *Black Cat Sightings*. "I've discovered several sightings of the cat in a park on the north side of town."

She closed the notebook and pushed up her glasses while giving Jonah a defiant look. "I'm gonna prove without question it's just some kids poking fun at people's superstitious beliefs."

That not only surprised Jonah, but also worried him. "Ah, that's not a good idea."

"Why?"

"It could be dangerous."

"I plan to go there during the day." Her uncertain glance belied her confident tone. "Just in case it's more, I would like you to go with me."

"Me?"

"Yes."

"But... But what about Anthony? He likes you."

Danita threw her hands up as if she were dealing with a little child. "Of course he does, Jonah. Anyone can see that."

"Well, then...?"

"He's okay, but I don't want him doing something stupid just to impress me."

Jonah snorted with laughter until Danita narrowed her eyes. He racked his mind to find a way out of the request, but failed. "I'll think about it, okay?"

"Thanks." She gave him a quick hug.

Jonah's face warmed. "I, uh, really have to go. They're waiting for me."

Satisfied with his answer, Danita nodded, grabbing up her book bag before she headed for the steps.

Jonah used his key to open the attic door while wondering why everyone seemed to be seeking his help or advice.

*

Robert and Lynn sat on the club's sofa, their backs to Jonah as he entered the attic. Wick stood beside them. Jonah's attention, however, was fastened on Latrell's sister, Alicia, who sat in one of the ratty armchairs.

Wick ruffled his twists as he sat down on the steamer trunk. "We believe you." He sounded reassuring.

"Oh." The girl's voice was small and fragile, Jonah thought. "No one else will. My mom gets angry with me."

"We understand," Lynn chimed in. "I'm glad Danita didn't talk you out of visiting us."

"Actually, I heard about Jonah at school." She paused as he slipped into the armchair opposite her and watched him for a quiet moment.

"Yeah," Wick said, giving Jonah an approving nod. "The Human Lie Detector. We should add you to the magic show." He grinned as he leaned forward over the trunk. "So, Alicia, tell us about it. You're seeing a ghost?"

"Yes," she said in an uncertain voice. "My brother."

Robert exchanged an eager glance with his sister. "He talks to you?"

"Yes."

"How?"

"He appears in his room sometimes and other places where I go." Alicia shivered and hugged herself. "My brother used to be nice, and we'd often talk, just like we did when he was still alive. But now he's scary. He yelled at me because I wore his ankh. He got so mad until I put it back."

"That's when he stopped appearing to you, right?" Wick asked. When the girl nodded, he snapped his fingers in triumph. "It must be the ankh! I bet he's attached to it."

Amulet of the Goddess 703

Jonah was glad when Lynn ignored Wick and asked, "What happened next?"

"He's haunting the basement, and tearing it apart. My dad keeps insisting that someone's breaking in, but I know better. And I think my mom does too." Tears glistened in her eyes. "I miss my brother."

Lynn moved to sit on the arm of the chair the girl was in, placing her own arm in a comforting way around the visitor's shoulders. "I wonder why he's staying around? Did he tell you?"

"He said he has something to do." She wiped her tears. "But I don't know what. He won't tell me."

"And you're the only one who can see him?"

Alicia shrugged. "I think my mom might sense him, but Latrell won't appear to her."

"Well, then, it's our job to find out why he's hanging around." Wick's confident voice seemed to relax Alicia for a moment.

"Oh," she squeaked, digging inside her pocket and withdrawing neatly folded bills.

Wick and Robert sat straighter, staring at the money.

Lynn spared them both a glance before saying, "You don't have to pay us."

"I want to."

"Yeah, Lynn," Wick seconded.

Lynn raised a fist and Wick slumped in defeat.

"I'll tell you what: Just pay us for the cost of the gas and we'll call it even."

Alicia nodded as she held out the cash. Lynn plucked out two bills and handed them to Wick. "Now, give us your address."

The girl did as Lynn asked while Wick scribbled it all down and Jonah listened. Alicia's parents were taking her to a family doctor the next day after school. Jonah had little doubt the doctor would be a grief counselor or psychologist. He recalled dodging his own bullet by not having to see a *doctor* after his parents died.

Alicia pulled out a house key and passed it to Lynn. "We always go out for dinner afterwards. We won't be home for a while."

Lynn nodded, all business. "Don't worry. We'll figure this out." She stood and motioned for Alicia to come with her.

Wick whirled on Robert as soon as Lynn and Alicia exited the attic. He frowned while holding up the limp bills. "A few bucks for gas?" He glared at Robert. "Your sister's gonna cheat us out of making any serious money."

Jonah agreed with him. "Why advertise if we're not gonna get paid for our services?"

"Thank you, Jonah." He turned to Robert. "Well, Bobby?"

Robert gave him a helpless shrug and kept sketching. Curious, Jonah leaned over to see what his cousin had drawn. The page showed a cluttered basement with things thrown around and turned over.

"That's her basement?" Jonah asked.

Wick came over to see it and whistled. "That looks serious."

Robert nodded. "Tell me about it." He glanced over his shoulder and said, "Lynn doesn't want to charge money because of how it'll look."

"How what will look?" Wick asked, confused.

"If our parents ever find out, she wants to say we were just using our abilities to help people. Charging for services will seem like, well…" He met his best friend's gaze. "…Like we're taking advantage of them."

Wick was dumbfounded. "We're helping people too."

"I know, but she doesn't want to be considered a cheap, charlatan palm reader." Robert stared at his drawing, unable to meet his friend's mutinous expression. "It's a thing with her." When he heard the attic door close, he hastily whispered, "I'll talk to her."

"You do that," Wick said before plastering a practiced grin on his face.

Lynn leapt up the steps a second later, snagging her squeeze bottle from the computer desk and sipping from it as she came over. "Can you do that spirit trap you're always talking about, Wick?"

"I need to get my stuff together, but yeah. Easy."

"Perfect. If her brother really is dangerous, I figure we can trap him long enough for," she patted Jonah's shoulder, "Reaper boy to do his thing."

"Don't call me that," Jonah fumed.

Amulet of the Goddess **705**

Besides his desire to use Jonah's ability to talk to dead people, Wick had also speculated that Jonah could open a rip or tear in the barrier dividing the realms. In doing so, he could send dangerous Wraiths back to where they came from. So far, all the ghosts Wick had encountered were less dangerous souls with unfinished business.

As a result, Jonah never bothered to try the technique. That didn't daunt him. It would be just his luck that on their first case, they'd get a real Wraith or an angry spirit.

Jonah glanced at the picture of the ruined basement again. That was exactly what he didn't want in his life: more weirdness. He would have asked Lynn if she had a bad feeling about this first job for the Mount Vernon Social Club, but he caught himself while the instinctive question was still perched on the tip of his tongue. Lynn's intuition was acting up now and she couldn't reliably sense anything.

A new, chilling thought occurred to him. What if her loss of intuition was deliberate? That woman at the vigil managed to spike his dark emotions. Could she have done something to Lynn? That threat frightened Jonah so much that he kept it to himself.

Besides, Robert and Wick were okay. And as far as he knew, all his powers were also fine. He realized he was just trying to cheer himself up.

When he noticed Lynn watching his reaction, he offered her a confident nod and said, "Let's do it!"

CHAPTER NINE
PECK OF POLTERGEISTS

Jonah sensed something was off. Latrell's spirit loomed in front of him, floating in the dark, damp basement. Yet the ghostly boy wasn't raving mad, nor did he appear even slightly dangerous.

Jonah whispered over his shoulder to the others, "What do you think?"

Robert and Lynn stood back. Wick, who wore his trademark fatigue pants, muscle shirt, and unlaced combat boots, was much closer. He reached up to ruffle his short twists as he peered over Jonah's shoulder. "I don't know, Padawan. Maybe he's stuck here because of unfinished business and isn't a Wraith at all. Talk to him."

Wick had already set up his spirit trap as planned. Robert drew a perfect circular sigil on the ground with red paint, and Wick set up a series of iron poles. As a precaution, Wick also linked all the poles with a single iron chain, since iron could hurt supernatural creatures.

But Latrell caught them all by surprise, appearing before the trap was even completed.

Tapping a pole with his boot, Wick said, "I guess I won't be needing this."

Robert called out, "Hey, I spent a lot of time drawing that sigil!" He pointed a spare pole at Latrell. "He has to be the one haunting this basement. Look around."

Lynn raised her chin while watching the apparition. "He can hear you talking about him," she said. "Do your thing, Reaper boy."

Jonah glared at his cousin. "You know I don't like that name."

Amulet of the Goddess **707**

"Tough. Find out what's going on and then send him packing."

"He's not–" Jonah stopped because Latrell flickered out of sight before he reappeared right in front of him. His first impulse was to back away, but Jonah held his ground.

Wraiths, ghosts, and spirits came in all guises, depending on the period in which they perished. In Latrell's case, death had occurred two weeks ago. Except for the black tunic and pants, he looked like any other kid at school.

However, the boy's haunted, unblinking eyes thoroughly unnerved Jonah.

He gulped and asked, "Are you the one haunting this place?"

Latrell shook his head and opened his mouth to say *no*. As a ghost, the boy didn't produce actual sound waves. Instead, Jonah heard the reply in his own head.

The plan to use his ability to talk to the ghost and help him with any unfinished business seemed straightforward. Now that he faced Latrell's ghost, however, Jonah had no clue where to begin. Could it be as easy as passing along a last word to a living family member?

What worried Jonah most was the information Wick had learned from his grandmother, a professional ghost hunter. According to her, all human spirits remained until after their funerals and their spirits were laid to rest. Others might linger a little longer to settle unfinished business but they too, eventually moved on.

Wraiths were different. They didn't have unfinished business. They were stuck. Period. That's why they grew so mean and violent. If left unchecked, a Wraith could turn into a dangerous poltergeist–or worse, a Phantom.

Jonah didn't know if Latrell was a Wraith or a regular spirit because the boy's funeral was still a day away. He glanced around the cold basement, rubbing his arms as the nagging doubt crystalized.

Narrowing his eyes, Jonah asked, "Do you have unfinished business here?"

Latrell nodded.

"I can help." Jonah waited but Latrell didn't explain. So Jonah waved his hands around, gesturing toward the ruined basement and the old, moldy boxes. The contents, mostly important papers and family photos, littered the damp basement floor. "Who did this, Latrell?" After seeing the boy, he didn't think the ghost could have been responsible for all the damage.

The young ghost shuddered and opened his mouth in a quiet scream while pointing behind Jonah. The next moment, Latrell flickered out of sight before he reappeared across the basement.

Robert yelled and Wick jumped away from his spirit trap.

An older spirit, a Wraith, clad in a black judge's robe and a powdered wig, stood in Wick's trap, glaring at the kids. The Wraith looked very solid as it sucked in a deep breath and bellowed at Latrell. *Don't tell the Reaper anything!*

Jonah winced, envying the others because they couldn't hear the Wraith. "I'm not a Reaper."

Liar! The Judge-Wraith tried to move and growled in pain when its body touched the iron chain. Dark welts appeared on his legs and wisps of ethereal smoke rose into the air. He whirled on Wick. *Release me!*

Wick blinked at the ghost. "Ah…"

"He says to release him," Jonah translated.

"Yeah, I kind of guessed that." Wick stood taller and peered into the Wraith's angry eyes. "No."

The Judge-Wraith went crazy, moving into a frenzied blur as he threw himself against the invisible container wall created by the trap. His thrashing was so violent that the floor shook beneath their feet.

Jonah's Death Sense spiked as six more Wraiths barreled up through the basement floor.

The trapped ghost pointed at Jonah and the others and shouted, *Attack!*

Wick whirled his hands and conjured green flames to fling at the Wraiths. The tactic caught one ghost by surprise. Jonah winced at the spirit's agonized howl when it disappeared.

Robert swung an iron pole at anything that approached him. A few times, he connected with a Wraith, causing sparks to erupt across the spirit's body.

Lynn grappled with a large Wraith, dressed like an inmate. The ghost grabbed her by the shoulders and pressed her against a wall. She struggled in its grip as it hoisted her into the air.

Amulet of the Goddess

"Take out the idiot in the wig," she yelled to Jonah. "The one who looks like an old judge!"

Wick blasted a second Wraith with diminished fire that injured the spirit but didn't vanquish it. "Do it now," he said, risking a glance at Jonah. "I can't keep this up."

"Yeah," Robert shouted between swings of his pole. "Do something."

"Do what?" Jonah asked.

"You're a Reaper," Robert answered. "Command them to leave. I don't know." A Wraith dodged Robert's makeshift weapon and knocked him into the mildewed boxes.

"Robert!" Lynn reached into her pouch and drew out her Reaper blades. "That's it. I've had enough."

In a fluid motion, Lynn brought her blades up, slicing through the body of the Wraith that was attacking her. The ghost screamed and its body flared before it exploded into ethereal fragments.

Lynn dropped to her feet and rushed to defend Robert. She cut the Wraith that was menacing him in half. As it burst into flames, Lynn whirled around. "Get your butt in gear, Jonah."

In the confusion, the Judge-Wraith dislodged an iron pole. It gouged out a section of Robert's constraining sigil.

"Oh, no!" Wick exclaimed just as the powerful Wraith broke the barrier, sending poles in every direction. The freed spirit slammed a solid fist into Wick's chest, hurling the young mage into a basement support column. Wick sagged to the ground, dazed.

The sight of his friends and family in trouble galvanized Jonah. He leapt on the old Wraith's back without thinking. He expected the Wraith to disappear, but it remained solid, allowing Jonah to wrap his hands around its gaunt face.

The Wraith tried to buck him off, but Jonah held on while mentally exploring Wick's idea about creating an opening to the Wraith realm. Since the basement lay in a direct line with the nexus point at the Crossroads, Wick theorized Jonah could do it.

The problem was that Jonah didn't know how to open a doorway between the realms. He agreed to try, however, because he preferred not to kill the Wraiths. His options were somewhat diminished anyway after Lynn and Wick managed to dispatch half the Wraiths.

Jonah closed his eyes. *Leave. Leave. Please, leave!* He repeated that over and over in his mind, but nothing happened.

His desperation increased as the Wraith turned on Lynn after it failed at trying to dislodge him from its back. Unlike the other Wraiths, this one was smarter and more powerful. He raised a hand and yanked boxes and other objects off the ground to hurl at Lynn and Robert.

Reaper blades weren't designed to deflect old pieces of kitchen appliances, but Lynn succeeded at it quite well. The Wraith upped the ante and went for an old sofa. The entire thing bucked and vibrated before rising into the air.

"Jonah!" Lynn shouted.

He concentrated, struggling to bypass his mounting fear as he imagined the magical energy source running beneath the floor of the basement. He reached out with his Reaper side and touched the power.

Jonah thought, *Leave.* Still, nothing happened.

Meanwhile, Lynn pushed Robert back but the sofa levitated in the air and followed them until they collided with a stack of boxes against the back wall and had nowhere else to go.

In anger over his failed attempts, Jonah shouted, "I command you to leave!" The Wraith wavered in its attack, the sofa poised to crash down onto Lynn and Robert.

Jonah felt a tug on his body and twisted around to see a rip forming in the air. The pull grew stronger by the second.

That's when he realized Robert was right. He was half-Reaper, and Reapers commanded spirits. Confidence and power surged into Jonah's body as he summoned his Reaper half. When he spoke again, his voice was deeper than normal and he knew how to phrase the command. "Go back to your realm."

The Wraith bucked and shouted beneath Jonah, but the pull of its own realm was too overpowering. Just as its body stretched thinner, Jonah slid from the apparition's back.

Amulet of the Goddess

No longer fearing the Wraith, Jonah pressed a hand to the body and shouted once more, "Go back!"

The rip widened like a weird, blossoming flower. The pull increased, sucking the angry Judge-Wraith and the three remaining spirits through it and swallowing them into the other realm. As soon as they disappeared, the crack between realms closed with a snap! The sofa, no longer held aloft by the Wraith's power, crashed to the ground, merely inches in front of Robert and Lynn.

Jonah collapsed to his knees, his chest heaving as a wave of dizziness overcame him. He felt hollowed out from the exertion required to keep the rip open.

"Way to go, Jonah," Wick whooped despite being a little unsteady on his feet. "I knew you could do it."

Lynn snorted before she deactivated her blades and pulled her brother from among the smashed, wet boxes.

Robert lifted his damp shirt away from his side. "This sucks."

Wick laughed at his buddy and didn't notice that Lynn's posture stiffened. She reached for her blades while glaring into the basement's far corner.

Jonah turned in that direction and realized Latrell had remained behind. That sealed it for him. The boy wasn't a Wraith like the others. "So, do you have unfinished business?"

Latrell didn't answer but stared at Lynn, his eyes widening. *Reaper blades.*

"She won't hurt you," Jonah said to the boy in a soft voice.

Latrell shook his head with a violent motion and jabbed a finger at Jonah. *You're a Reaper.*

"I'm not a Reaper." Jonah was quickly growing tired of saying that. Then something became obvious to him. "Wait. Is that why you set us up?"

I didn't set you up. My sister wasn't supposed to go to you, not like that.

Jonah stepped toward Latrell but the boy disappeared and didn't return, leaving them alone in the cold basement.

CHAPTER TEN
THE FUNERAL

Jonah, his cousins, and Wick all huddled in the Hightowers' den, talking about the Wraith attack. Latrell's odd behavior continued to baffle all of them.

Wick resorted to pulling his trusty lighter out of his fatigue pants, a sure sign of his churning thoughts.

Lynn crossed her arms, watching him. "Seems you were right."

"At least we got rid of the Wraiths haunting the basement," Wick agreed. "But now we're stuck with a new mystery."

Robert, who had changed into a dry shirt, added, "Maybe not now, but I know a way to find out."

"You mean Latrell's funeral?" Lynn tapped her bottom lip, considering the idea. "If it's a trap, I can't tell."

She strode around the living room in an agitated circle. "I hate this."

Robert's eyes widened. "Hey, what if dear old Aunt Ruby's involved?"

Lynn hugged herself while turning on the spot. "That's impossible."

"Why?" Jonah asked.

"First," Lynn said, holding up a finger to tick off her points, "Aunt Ruby's up in Titusville, staying with a friend."

"How could you possibly know that?" Robert asked, incredulous.

"I, unlike you, dear brother, did the proper thing and called our cousins to see how they were doing. They talked to their mom right after she

Amulet of the Goddess **713**

got out." When her brother made a disgusted face, Lynn glared at him. "Robert, no matter how we feel, she's still their mom."

Robert shook his head. "I wouldn't have done it."

"Right, whatever." Lynn frowned at her brother in dismay. Then she turned back to Jonah and held up two fingers. "Second, our aunt had no real magical abilities. That's why she hated your mom. She couldn't have been the woman you followed to the train yard."

"Oh," Jonah said.

Robert snorted but gave his sister a begrudging nod.

"With that question settled," Wick said as he snapped his lighter closed, "I think Jonah should go to the funeral."

"Why?" Lynn looked ready to argue.

"Think about it," Wick continued. "We weren't supposed to go to Latrell's house. It threw off their plan, whatever it was."

"Didn't I say so earlier?" Robert asked.

"True, Bobby," Wick admitted.

Lynn wasn't convinced. "The Wraith told Latrell to keep his mouth shut. So, he won't show up at the funeral."

"Yes, he will," Jonah answered for Wick. He understood where his friend was going. "He can't help it. Remember what Wick's grandmother said about spirits? Latrell's stuck here until after the funeral."

"And Jonah can talk with Latrell while knowing there's something up," Wick finished.

Despite Lynn's frown, Jonah nodded his agreement, liking the plan.

*

Oak Hill Cemetery was within a short bike ride of the Hightowers' home. Only after he arrived at the cemetery did Jonah realize he had no clue where to go. He found the groundskeeper and asked about the funeral.

When the grey-haired man gave him a once-over, Jonah was glad he put on the black pants and white dress shirt that he normally wore to church.

His plan was to find a hiding spot to watch the funeral, unobserved. But if he couldn't do that, he'd have to blend in.

The groundskeeper pointed out a prepared site. It was on a level spot, halfway up the adjacent, gently sloping hill.

The grave reminded Jonah that this was his first time in a cemetery since his parents' memorial service. As he coasted by the gravestones, he wondered if any ghosts would show themselves, aside from Latrell, of course.

He paused long enough to read the words on the substantial marble headstone already in place above the open grave. Latrell's birth and death dates sobered Jonah. The boy was only sixteen, the same age as Robert and Lynn.

The very thought of losing Robert or Lynn was unimaginable to Jonah, even though they had all been in extreme danger at times. As always happened, Marcus's warning to him about being careful took on new meaning.

He turned from the headstone, glancing around for a good spot to hide. Beyond the grave, at the crest of the hill, was a thick tree line. *Perfect.* Rolling his bike up to the thicket of trees, he chose a large pine and huddled behind it in his windbreaker. The day was crisp, but also bright and comfortable.

Nearly half an hour passed before a black hearse made its slow way up the curving cemetery road, followed by a long line of cars. It was like a living, mechanical snake. As soon as the hearse stopped at the base of the hill, a group of men exited the other cars and hurried to the hearse's rear door. Jonah felt a chill as the men pulled out a black casket, hefting it onto their shoulders, and carrying it to the gravesite.

A woman, whom Jonah suspected was Latrell's mom, exited the limousine with her husband. She was in tears while the father remained stoic, walking with stiff jerks of his legs. Latrell's sister, Alicia, trailed behind, solemn and quiet.

Within a short time, a sizable crowd of people had gathered, shifting on their feet. The minister, in a long, black robe and multi-colored stole, opened his Bible and the ceremony began. But Jonah wasn't interested in that. Instead, his eyes searched the surrounding land.

Amulet of the Goddess

A weather-beaten angel stood fifteen feet away, near the crest of the hill. Jonah paused when he felt a slight twitch in his Death Sense, but nothing happened. He continued his search until the twitch in his gut happened again. This time, when he turned to the angel statue, Latrell stood there, watching his own funeral with an unblinking gaze.

Out in the bright sunlight, Jonah noted Latrell's features. He was a little taller than Jonah, with his hair cut in a box fade that seemed to accent his thin, handsome face.

Once he was sure no one was looking in his direction, Jonah left the hiding place and made his way toward the teen. He was only a few feet away when Latrell's head snapped around to look at him. The move was so sudden and eerily inhuman that Jonah stopped short.

What are you doing here? Latrell asked, his voice echoing in Jonah's mind.

"Tell me what's going on."

Latrell fixed his eyes on the funeral. His ghostly jaws worked. *What are you?*

"I'm a half-Reaper. Why?"

I didn't know there were half-Reapers. Latrell gave a strange, hollow laugh. *I didn't know a lot of things until after… I died.*

"It's a long story," Jonah said. "So, are you gonna tell me what's happening?"

Latrell seemed on the verge of speaking when a sudden, low groan escaped his mouth. His little sister had placed a flower on the casket. A tear ran down Latrell's cheek, surprising Jonah. He never imagined a disembodied spirit could cry. He averted his eyes while searching for a way to get the boy to talk to him.

"I'm sorry about what happened." He peeked at Latrell. "I know how it feels, not having anyone to talk to."

You're gay? Latrell asked, focusing more closely on him.

Jonah hesitated. No one had ever asked him that question directly, not even Mike. They both kind of revealed themselves to each other during the Agent Hunter mess, the way two friends do when they suspect the truth in each other and just accept it.

For Jonah, something strange happened now. He didn't fear answering that question. True, Latrell was a ghost and not likely to tell anyone, but still, Jonah thought it revealed something about himself. At once, he realized Latrell waited for an answer, and he nodded.

Well, at least you didn't kill yourself.

"Maybe if we'd met each other, you wouldn't have done that?"

Pain flitted across Latrell's semi-transparent features. *I... wasn't all alone.*

Without conscious effort, Jonah opened his senses to his Reaper Stare. Feelings of sadness and regret rolled off Latrell. Jonah could understand the emotions, but if Latrell did have someone to talk to, why couldn't he have survived the bullying?

He reflected on his own run-ins with the bully, Brandon. In those moments, he relied on his cousins and friends to help him. Then again, no one ever bullied *him* for being gay, Jonah readily admitted, although others had been cruelly taunted. It was one reason he decided to start the Tolerance Club. Not only did he want to help other kids going through similar torment, but the club also grounded him to his mortal side.

After his recent experience in the Afterworld, Jonah harbored a deep fear that he could turn into a true oddball, someone unable to understand what normal people experienced. And he couldn't ignore the knowledge that something like suicide wasn't an option, not for himself, anyway. His godfather, Marcus, once told him that the Alliance wasn't certain what would happen if he died. Jonah might even turn out to become a super Reaper.

A commotion arose at the funeral that broke Jonah's train of thought. Latrell's mom had flung herself across the casket, wailing. His dad tried to pull her off, but his first attempts nearly overturned the coffin. The little sister looked too stunned to help.

Finally, one of the teenagers sprang from his seat behind the family and helped to pry the grieving mother's fingers from the lid. The rest of the crowd shuffled in nervous agitation as Latrell's mom slumped back into her chair.

During the entire episode, lights kept flashing from a photographer and a reporter who were standing among the mourners. The suicide already had several stories written about it. Some insensitive people even claimed that Latrell deserved what he got because of his sexual preference.

Amulet of the Goddess

Jonah noted the boy's angry expression. "What's wrong, Latrell?"

The ghost pointed toward the crowd. *I can't believe they came.*

Jonah thought he meant the reporters. "I saw a decent article about you in the paper. Not everyone's a jerk."

No, Brandon's parents. How can they dare to show their faces?

Jonah scanned the crowd and spotted four people standing slightly away from the rest of the group.

Brandon Warner, Senior, was a tall, light-complexioned man with a head full of wavy, black hair, peppered with gray. He wore an expensive, long coat and his demeanor was arrogant and dismissive, even when he was just standing still.

His wife was half a head shorter than him and thin. She also wore an expensive, long coat and clasped her gloved hands together in front of herself. With her chin tilted up and standing rigid as a plank, she watched the ceremony with a bearing that reminded Jonah of a movie queen.

The other couple, the Edwards, wore clothes as expensive as the Warners', but they seemed more resigned than arrogant. The man had a round face, glasses, and a short, neat afro. He was stocky, and essentially an older version of Drew. The mom was slender, with a thin neck that attractively showed off her pearl necklace.

Just behind and to the left of the couples stood Alastor, the clerk from Hackett's Book Emporium. He wore all black, but his hair was still unkempt. The truly eerie thing about the short man emerged when he looked straight at Jonah. As soon as he grinned, Jonah's Death Sense throbbed in unwilling response.

He thought of ducking behind one of the larger gravestones, then realized it was useless. Alastor nodded as if to emphasize that very fact before refocusing his attention on the memorial service.

A lot of kids bullied me. Latrell's voice shook with anger as he continued. *But Brandon and Drew were the worst.*

A pit of bitterness exploded in Jonah's stomach. Were Brandon and Drew's parents aware of what their sons had done? The graveside service ended while Jonah mulled that over.

Most mourners uttered soft, banal words to the stricken couple. Brandon's parents didn't even bother with offering their condolences. They, along with Drew's parents, retreated to an expensive sedan and hastily drove off.

Latrell's dad helped his mom out of her chair and led her toward the waiting cars. With the crowd steadily dispersing, Jonah grew anxious Latrell wouldn't linger. He fought to get his own anger under control so he could focus on what he needed to know. "Where does Brandon live?"

Why? Latrell's eyes narrowed. *What are you going to do?*

"Nothing. I was just wondering."

Latrell cocked his head to the side, studying Jonah. *He lives on my street. I'm not sure about Drew.*

The boy lived in Brandon's neighborhood. That explained the expensive headstone. It also explained why the Warners came. They had to know Latrell's parents.

Those connections only caused Jonah to feel the need to examine Latrell's situation even more closely. Not only did the boy fail to reveal anything about what was happening, Jonah still didn't know if Latrell was a ghost or a Wraith. "Are you going to move on?"

Latrell's eyes widened and he shook his head no. *I have unfinished business.*

"What?"

The ghost shrugged, looking like any other kid at that moment. *Maybe to do something about the bullies.*

Jonah heard the uncertainty in Latrell's voice. "I started a club at school to help kids that are being bullied."

That's cool. Latrell smiled. *You should help people like me... I mean, us.* He stepped closer to Jonah.

"Can't you tell me anything?" Jonah asked, searching the boy's ghostly eyes. They were a light brown. "Please."

I have an ankh in my room. It's on my dresser in a jeweler's box. Get it.

"Why? What's so important about that?"

The guy who gave it to me was the same one who talked to me before I died.

Amulet of the Goddess **719**

Jonah's jaw dropped. "Someone talked you into killing yourself?"

No.

"But–"

Never mind that. He had several custom-made ankhs. There's a sticker on the bottom of the box.

Jonah wanted to hear more about this person, but it finally occurred to him what the boy was asking him to do. "I can't break into your house. I mean, we still have a key–"

Everyone's heading to our house for the post-funeral gathering, Latrell said. He gestured at Jonah's clothes. *You'll fit right in.*

"I don't know…"

Just tell them you're from the club.

Jonah let out a breath and nodded. He'd come there to get more information. At least this was a lead. "Okay. What's the address?"

Latrell told him and then paused with a curious expression on his face. *Who are you?*

"Oh," Jonah said, thinking the boy must have heard his name in the basement. "My name's Jonah. Jonah Blackstone."

CHAPTER ELEVEN
MOTHER'S SORROW

Jonah's jaw dropped when he got off the bus and caught the first glimpse of Latrell's neighborhood. The homes along the beautiful, tree-lined street were grand—some with columns on the front porches—and all featured large front yards.

Kids didn't run up and down Latrell's street, shouting and playing with each other like they did in his own neighborhood. The sensation that enveloped Jonah as he walked along was a subdued peace. The impressive homes brought back Robert's comments about this neighborhood. Most of Mount Vernon's black lawyers, doctors, and other professionals lived here.

For the first time, Jonah wondered about Latrell's mom and dad's occupations. Drew's father, a successful dentist, had remained on the Hightowers' side of town. That impressed Jonah despite their son being such a bully. Maybe that's why Brandon treated Drew like a second-class friend.

Latrell's house was easy to spot because of all the cars lining the street and the curving driveway. Jonah's insides also knotted as he recalled the reception at the Garretts' after his own parents' memorial service. He hated the gathering and stormed off through the neighborhood. He wondered if Latrell's sister would do something like that, but didn't see the lonely girl as he proceeded up the driveway to the house.

Like all the others, this one was two stories, but all brick. As he drew closer, his Death Sense buzzed just before Latrell appeared in a second-floor window. He beckoned to Jonah, who almost pointed at his own chest in that hesitant way when a person's unsure they are the one being

Amulet of the Goddess 721

addressed. At the last moment, Jonah stopped in mid-motion. Latrell was invisible, but people might still have noticed him.

Latrell pointed down toward the front door and Jonah's heart climbed into his throat. *Remember the mission*, he chided himself. The front door was open behind the thick-paned, glass storm door. People moved in and out of sight beyond. Jonah screwed up his courage, opened the storm door, and entered the house.

The atrium was spacious with a long staircase to the right. Directly in front of Jonah was a huge funeral arrangement of flowers. The clashing, sharp scents tickled his nose, so he moved further into the house. To his left was a large living room filled with somber, black-clad adults. Straight ahead was a family room, much larger than the Hightowers'. Sunlight streamed through a row of windows that opened out to the backyard where more people had gathered.

His nerves tingled as he moved into the crowd, expecting someone to pounce on him, asking why he was there. Couldn't any of these people hear his heart pounding in his chest? *This is crazy*, Jonah thought, sliding through the adults. Without any conscious effort, he reached a table laden with food. Not the least bit hungry, Jonah turned away and that's when he saw kids outside on a large patio.

They were all his age and talked in little, nervous groups. In fact, Jonah realized there were more kids here than at the funeral itself. A boy, the one who had helped Mrs. Dickerson at the funeral, glanced inside, saw Jonah, and moved toward the patio door.

Jonah backed away and slipped into the midst of the talking adults when he discovered Alastor among the guests–watching him. Jonah considered just leaving until he spotted a second stairway that led to the second floor. Latrell stood on the midway landing, again beckoning to him. Once he had Jonah's attention, he disappeared.

As soon as Jonah mounted the first steps, someone tugged on his arm.

"Where're you going?" It was the boy from outside. He peered at Jonah.

"Uh, to the bathroom."

The boy pointed down a short side hall. "It's right there." When Jonah hesitated to respond, the boy added, "You started that Tolerance Club. Well, too bad it didn't help Latrell." His voice rose with his words.

Jonah didn't see a way out of this until Alastor arrived and placed a hand on the boy's elbow. "Excuse me, but I wondered if you could help me in the kitchen. The family wants to put out more ice."

"But…" the boy stammered, trying to extricate himself from Alastor's firm grip.

The little man must have been stronger than Jonah suspected because he hustled the boy away and into the kitchen. At the last moment before entering, Alastor glanced back at Jonah and nodded.

Despite the help, Alastor ignited a firestorm of questions for Jonah. He suspected the man had seen Latrell at the cemetery. Supernaturals could see ghosts and Wraiths, which meant Alastor was one. Jonah just didn't know what kind. He also realized he had stalled for too long, and hurried up to the second floor.

The first thing Jonah noticed was that Latrell's bedroom was neater than his own. He wondered if the boy's mom or a housekeeper had tidied up the room after the boy's death.

Latrell's full-size bed had a sea blue cover and multiple pillows on it. Jonah was envious of that, considering he still slept on a twin-sized bed. He shifted his gaze to the walls, where the boy tastefully hung black-and-white photos, all framed and neatly arranged. Judging from the expensive digital camera on the dresser top, Jonah guessed Latrell was really into photography.

A pang of regret hit Jonah and he wished he had only met the boy before his death. He crossed to a low worktable with a sleek reading lamp positioned in front of the room's main window. A closed laptop sat next to the lamp, with a couple of notebooks stacked off to the side.

This is where he'd seen Latrell. He reached out to touch the laptop when the boy spoke from behind him.

I thought you might not show.

Jonah spun around and hesitated before speaking fearing that someone might hear his voice.

Latrell nodded as he moved to stand right beside Jonah and point out the window. *That's where Brandon lives.*

Jonah leaned over the narrow desk to peek outside. The Warners' mansion sat further off the road and behind a slate wall and wrought-iron gate. *It must be nice*, Jonah thought.

Amulet of the Goddess 723

"Thanks." He glanced at Latrell.

The boy peered back, frowning. *It doesn't seem fair.* His supernatural body shuddered. *I should have been stronger. My sister will miss me.*

Jonah didn't know what to say until he realized he could be honest. "I still miss my parents, but I have to keep going." He lapsed into silence.

Latrell reached out his hand. The movement surprised Jonah and he stepped back before he could stop himself. Latrell jerked his hand away and instead crossed to stand beside the bed, his arms wrapped around his waist as if he were cold. *I didn't mean to try that.*

"It's okay," Jonah said, worried that he might've offended the ghost. When Latrell continued to stare at the floor, Jonah asked, "Where's the ankh?"

Latrell pointed at his dresser.

A small, wooden box with a handle carved into the shape of a mallard duck sat on the dresser. Jonah opened that to find five different neck chains and a small, black jewelry box. As Latrell said, the jewelry box contained the ankh amulet with the bright green, embedded jewel in the loop.

"I've seen this on your sister."

A rueful smile touched the Latrell's ghostly face. *I had to scare her to get it back.*

Jonah sucked in a breath. "That was you at the school when your sister came up to me." Latrell stared without answering. Jonah turned the box over. The small, white sticker attached to the bottom displayed the name of the jeweler in tiny letters.

"Cool. Got it." He turned to put the box back.

What're you doing?

"All I need is the clue," Jonah said, stopping before replacing the jewelry box in the larger box. "I can't take the ankh."

I want you to have it. Latrell came closer. *Please. Wear it, but not here. Wait until you get home.* Latrell's head tilted to the side as he listened to a silent call. He focused on Jonah. *Slip the box in your pocket. Hurry!*

Latrell's mom appeared in the doorway. Her eyes were puffy as she clutched a handkerchief in her boney hands. Her gaze skewered Jonah.

"Why're you in my son's bedroom?" She looked around the room like she suspected he'd stolen something.

"I..." Jonah made the mistake of holding up his hand, the one with the box.

Latrell's mom shot into the room and snatched the box from Jonah's grasp. "What are you doing with this?" she demanded. "It belonged to my son."

Her voice cracked as she sat on the edge of Latrell's bed. Her shoulders shook with quiet sobs, leaving Jonah feeling like an idiot. She wiped her eyes with the handkerchief and sucked in a shaky breath.

Her sad eyes met Jonah's again and she held up the box in a trembling hand. "Did you… did you give this to him? Were you… his friend?"

Jonah didn't want to lie to Latrell's mom, but he needed to explain why he was in the room. Before he could answer, Latrell appeared, near the doorway. He met Jonah's gaze, pleading with him to say yes.

Mrs. Dickerson stiffened. "He's here. I know it! I can feel him."

The words shocked Jonah. And her raw, emotional pain got to him, fueling his anger toward Brandon and Drew. Looking for something to say, he focused on his prepared excuse. "I run a Tolerance Club at school. We're setting up peer groups in honor of Latrell."

He didn't know how the woman would respond. She searched his face, her eyes tearing up before she dabbed them again. Without warning, Mrs. Dickerson rose to her feet. "Thank you. It's important to stand up to the bullies." She held out the box.

Jonah took it, unable to avoid feeling guilty for the slight deception.

"Do you hear me? Stand up for the others before it's too late." The woman's voice wavered at the last. She turned and fled.

Latrell disappeared as soon as Jonah opened his mouth to speak to him.

Left alone in the room, Jonah wanted to be anywhere but there. He hurried down the stairs, thankful he didn't run into Alastor or the troublesome boy before exiting the house. Only after he ran down the long driveway and rounded the curve in the street so he couldn't see Latrell's house did he finally slow his pace and relax.

Amulet of the Goddess

When he reached the bus stop, he leaned against the kiosk and let his mind replay that brief encounter with Latrell's mom. Her words still burned inside him, causing another mission to take form in his mind. Brandon and Drew needed to pay. And Latrell thought his unfinished business had something to do with the bullies.

The boy at the house was so right. What good had the Tolerance Club done Latrell? The way Jonah saw it, going after the bullies was just fulfilling the Mount Vernon Social Club's mission. Of course, that was assuming Latrell was a ghost and not a Wraith. Jonah ignored the nagging doubt for now. Even Latrell's mom thought he should stand up to the bullies. The problem was he didn't know what to do.

CHAPTER TWELVE
PERPLEXED PROPRIETOR

Jonah returned to school for the last half of the day with a determined frame of mind. When the time came to patrol with his anti-bullying crew, he hurried to his assigned trouble spot, eager to catch Brandon and Drew stepping out of line. But the bullies weren't around.

"I haven't seen them all day," Lorraine said as she finished her last shift.

"Oh, thanks." He waved goodbye to her and Rodney before catching sight of Mike heading down the bisecting hallway. Jonah reached the corner and spotted Patrick waiting by the exit. Wanting a word with Mike first, he leapt forward and grabbed his buddy's arm. "Hey, I'm telling Lynn and the others about the funeral. You should be there too."

Mike seemed hesitant as he glanced between Jonah and Patrick. It gratified Jonah to see real doubt in Mike's expression. But he also knew what his friend would say.

"Sorry, Jonah. I've already made plans, and I have a lot of work to do. Just tell me later."

Jonah checked his immediate irritation with his buddy. Mike looked tired, like he hadn't slept. He opened his mouth to ask about it, but Mike cut him off.

"Just call me later. Okay?" He joined Patrick before Jonah could even answer. The boys exchanged a few words before heading outside.

Jonah didn't get it. Mike acted like he didn't want to be around them anymore. *Or around me.* His frustration over the situation bubbled to the

Amulet of the Goddess 727

surface. He didn't need Mike's help to deal with the bullies, anyway. This was his decision.

Adding more fuel to his stewing anger, he believed the bullies only used Latrell's funeral as an excuse to skip school.

That thought was galling to Jonah, especially considering they were responsible for Latrell killing himself. A small voice of doubt popped into Jonah's head. *What if Latrell was lying?* But Jonah rejected that idea. Latrell's own anger was convincing enough at the funeral.

He would deal with that, but first, he already had a job to do for the club. The first place to start was finding out more about Latrell's ankh.

*

Jonah, Lynn, and Robert stood just inside the entrance to the jewelry store at Green Oaks Mall. The compact establishment, wedged between a vitamin store on one side and an electronic shack on the other, looked unremarkable to Jonah.

The jewelry store owner stood on the opposite side of the display counter, dressed in an immaculate, dark grey suit. "You interested in buying something for a pretty girl?" he asked Jonah.

"My cousin? Date someone?" Lynn asked. "I seriously doubt it."

Jonah glared at her. "You don't know that."

Lynn pulled a shocked expression. Robert, who was further back with his sketchpad open, cracked a smile.

"Well?" the jeweler asked.

Jonah shook his head. "No."

The jeweler sighed dramatically as he rested his hands on the edge of the display counter, careful not to smudge the glass itself. "In that case, what can I do for you?"

Lynn produced Latrell's small jewelry box. She opened it to reveal the ankh inside. "Did you make this?"

The man's eyes gleamed with pride. "Yes, I did. Exquisite, isn't it? That's real gold, by the way. And the stone is jade. They weren't cheap either."

Lynn snapped the box closed, smiling. "How many did you make?"

The man's demeanor changed as he peered at Lynn. "How did you get it?"

"We wanted to know who ordered it," Lynn pressed.

The jeweler's eyes narrowed. "Customer records are strictly confidential."

"But it was a birthday gift," Jonah said. "I simply wanted to send the person a thank you note." When the guy flashed a skeptical expression, Jonah added, "My aunt's insisting on it. She says it's the proper thing to do for such a nice gift."

"Well, uh," the owner stammered. "I can't. I value my clients' confidentiality."

Jonah gestured to a display of Halloween-themed rings. Some had little dragons engraved on them; others were embedded with blood-red, sparkling jewels, among other items. "What if I buy one of those?"

That offer seemed to irritate the man and he puffed out his barrel chest. "You can't bribe me and I won't give you any information." He leaned on the counter. "I suggest you leave immediately before I call mall security."

Jonah gulped. Mall security had recently chased him and Mike only a few months ago when Agent Hunter came after them. He doubted it would be wise to cause another incident so soon.

But Lynn crossed her arms, poised to test the man. "It's not illegal to ask questions."

Robert let out a startled yelp from behind. Jonah turned to find his cousin rubbing his forehead, like he had a headache.

"It may not be illegal," the owner said while taking out his cell phone, "but the mall security doesn't like its business owners being... ack!" The man stopped in mid-sentence, his expression instantly going vacant.

At the same time, Robert let out an anguished grunt. "His mind is... blocked all of a sudden," Robert hissed.

And Jonah's Death Sense also spiked. He pushed between Lynn and Robert as he spotted the niqab wearing girl from school on the opposite side of the concourse. Instinctively, he opened his Reaper Stare. The colors of her emotions were darker and riddled with something inky black, like a virus. *It's the evil intention behind her magic!*

Amulet of the Goddess 729

He blinked, shutting down the enhanced sight, and pointed. "She put a hex on the owner." With that, he took off around the curved end of the concourse without further explanation.

The girl turned and dashed in the opposite direction. Halfway down the concourse, she darted into a service hallway between two stores and burst through the metal door at the end.

Jonah ran after her, angered by the girl for more than one reason. Not only had she interfered with their case, but she was hiding under a niqab even though she wasn't Muslim. She was a sorceress, Jonah concluded, and he wanted to expose her.

He pushed through the doors, dimly aware of Lynn telling him to be careful. But his determination lent him speed and the corridor blurred. He was at the stairwell and leaping down at full velocity.

The girl had already reached the bottom, but Jonah landed right behind her a second later.

Shocked, she conjured a spell and hurled it at him.

Jonah dodged the attack, letting the walls absorb the impact of the spell with a surprisingly solid bang! that echoed in the enclosed space. He was fast, always had been, but he failed to consider the confined space. As a result, he hit the wall rather hard, temporarily dazing himself.

The girl laughed as she wove her hand and conjured a second hex. Jonah froze, knowing he couldn't dodge it this time.

That's when Lynn landed in front of him. She swiped her activated blades and shouted, "*Kulinda!*" The deflected hex responded with a low, snapping boom!

The slight hesitation in Niqab Girl's movement revealed her utter surprise at Lynn's unexpected arrival. She recovered quickly, however, and flung another spell. It was merely a distraction so she could open a vortex, the weakest one Jonah had ever seen. The edges were ragged and they undulated like it could collapse at any moment. Plus, it was very small. Yet the girl dived through anyway, head first.

Lynn's voice rang off the drab walls when she shouted, "Coward!"

Jonah rose to his feet. "How did you learn to do that?"

"Oh," Lynn blinked, looking a little embarrassed as she deactivated the blades. "When Rex came down to work with you, I asked him about the deflection move. He taught me how to do it."

Her answer impressed Jonah and made perfect sense. Rex was the only adult member of the Alliance who didn't hide everything from them. "Well, at least whatever's bothering your intuition isn't keeping you from successfully doing that spell!"

Lynn's eyes widened. "Robert!"

Jonah understood and he raced up the stairwell behind his cousin. They found Robert waiting at the entrance to the back hallway, looking spooked.

Lynn hurried to him. "Are you okay?"

"Yeah," Robert said, although he still rubbed his forehead. "What about the girl?"

"She got away."

Robert's expression fell. "We won't get anything from the store owner. She muddled his mind. I doubt he even knows his own name."

The news sickened Jonah. It was their fault the girl even attacked the store owner. "Maybe we should tell someone?"

Lynn stared down the concourse at the jewelry store and the owner. The man paced back and forth, talking to himself. Her shoulders sagged. "Hold on." She speed-walked over to the owner of the adjacent business, a woman dressed in a sheer, flowing, Indian fabric of vibrant reds and yellows.

After a brief conversation, the woman checked on the jewelry store owner. Lynn slipped away and came back to Jonah and Robert. "There. She's gonna call his brother."

"That's good," Jonah said, but he couldn't shake his sense of guilt and feeling responsible.

"We didn't know this would happen," Lynn offered, not looking any happier than he felt. After a moment, she nodded. "Come on."

Jonah thought they would leave the mall. However, once they descended the escalator, Lynn walked to the other end of the mall. She pulled her brother to an empty bench and plopped down beside him. Robert seemed to understand because he flipped open the sketchpad without being asked.

Amulet of the Goddess

Jonah crowded in close to see what he had drawn. The partial picture showed two customers standing at the jewelry store counter from the owner's point of view. The problem was, the faces weren't completed. Just the general shape and a few lines.

The dimensions of the two people were easy to see. One person was a man, as massive as a walking tank. He had thick arms and almost no neck.

The other person was thin and wearing a cloak just like the shadowy woman's cloak at the vigil. His inability to see her face only made Jonah more certain. Something caught his attention: her slender fingers and long nails. And Robert also included a fair bit of a strange amulet she wore around her neck. It depicted a woman dressed in Egyptian clothes, but her head was that of a lion with a solar disc for a crown.

The hairs on Jonah's neck bristled. He was sure he'd seen that amulet before, in an old book his parents had.

Lynn studied the drawing, then sat back, frustrated. "You drew the ugly amulet in detail! Why not the faces?"

Robert frowned at his sister as he rubbed his forehead. "I think they purposely obscured their faces while they talked to him. It was easier to focus on the amulet first. How could I know the girl would attack?"

"Well," Lynn said, "I can't tell anything about the woman, but," she tapped the drawing, "I saw that huge guy. He bumped into me at the store about a week ago. Knocked all my groceries out of my hands and didn't stop, nor did he apologize. The jerk!"

"You never mentioned that," Robert said.

"Until now, I didn't see the need to." Lynn wore a puzzled expression. "I wonder if he hit me on purpose."

"Could be," Robert said.

"Well, I've seen that woman," Jonah cut in. "She was at the vigil."

"Are you sure?" Lynn said. "You never saw her face."

"It's definitely her. Who else could it be?"

Lynn didn't have an answer for that.

Robert closed the sketchpad with an annoyed flick. "I'm sorry I couldn't get it all."

"That's okay." Lynn leaned into him. "It seems I'm not the only one they're attacking."

"Attacking?" Robert's eyes widened in horror at the idea.

"Yes, Robert. The more I think about it, the surer I am that something's deliberately being done to impede my abilities. Someone is doing it on purpose."

CHAPTER THIRTEEN
NIGHT PROWLER

Jonah's spirit was low when he returned to the Teen Center with his cousins. The woman who bought the ankhs was the same person from the train yard, but how did that help them? Who was she? And where could they find her now?

Lynn and Robert stopped just inside the atrium when they spotted Wick outside the West Hall, talking with the center's director. He held a poster advertising his magic show in one hand.

Not looking forward to rehashing the events for Wick, Jonah headed upstairs. "I'll catch you guys later."

He entered the attic and discovered Mike sitting at the editor's desk in the back corner. Jonah's buddy glanced up from his work, squinting through the eyeglasses he always wore when reading or studying. "Hey."

Jonah crossed to the desk, pulled a computer chair around, and sat. He hesitated a moment before saying, "Sorry about the vigil. I was–"

"A jerk?" Mike gave him a tired smile. "It's okay. I'm used to it."

"Funny," Jonah grumbled.

He avoided Mike's gaze and looked down at all the spiral notebooks, pencils, pens, and crumpled pieces of paper scattered over the desk. Mike even had the thick *Deliverer Tales* book, given to them while in the Afterworld, on top of the desk.

Jonah's godfather suggested Mike keep the book at the clubhouse. That arrangement also provided a space for Mike to work on the translations. The desk was the obvious choice.

The book's author recorded the tales in coded Angel script, and Mike was the only one who could decipher it. He intercepted the mind boost meant for Jonah. As a result, the incident transformed Mike into a Seeker, a Pathfinder, and a dutiful companion to a Deliverer.

After his awesome transformation, the Alliance Council had no choice but to allow Mike to translate the book. Of course, Mike had to travel to Alliance HQ and report his progress. Jonah used to keep up, but Mike hadn't mentioned any recent trips.

As Jonah watched his friend, he thought of all the times Mike claimed to be too busy to hang out. Work on the translation was always the favored excuse, but now that Jonah knew about Patrick, he felt certain that Patrick had become the real reason.

He grabbed a notebook and peeked inside. Mike's small, precise words covered every page, front and back. He felt a bit guilty about his lingering doubts. Mike had spent a lot of time in the attic working on the translations.

The situation raised a different question. When did he find the time to meet a new boyfriend? A spike of jealousy flared, giving him pause. He couldn't blame it on the supernatural attack by the mysterious woman. She wasn't here now, yet he was still jealous.

Why? He and Kevin had successfully attained a new point in their relationship before the Fallen Reaper returned to his Alliance assignment. And that's when Jonah hit on the problem. While Mike managed to find someone right there in Mount Vernon, Jonah couldn't even talk to Kevin.

And the older boy's whereabouts were also a secret. Kevin had accused Mandara of doing it on purpose. His incessant frustration with the Alliance also fueled Jonah's irritation. He dropped the notebook on the desk.

Mike glanced up from the laptop screen at him. "Jonah, we need to talk about Patrick and other things."

"Fine, but later."

"Jonah…"

"I have something to tell you." And Jonah recapped everything for his friend. When Mike continued to type and write, Jonah thought his friend did it out of spite because he refused to talk about Patrick. "Are you even listening to me?"

Amulet of the Goddess **735**

"Yes, I am." Mike recited everything Jonah said, but in a more concise form. "Happy?"

Jonah blinked in awe. He should have known Mike's enhanced mind would allow him to do more than one thing at once. In a way, Jonah was a little jealous of that too. "Okay. You heard me." He slumped in his chair.

Mike spared him a severe look. "I understand you being down because of the mall. But you have another lead."

"Yeah, yeah. The Niqab Girl."

"So, why are you acting pissed?"

Jonah chose his words carefully. "Brandon was one of the people bullying Latrell."

Mike pulled off his glasses. "That's news to me, but I'm not surprised." With a sad huff, he replaced his glasses and continued writing.

Jonah understood his friend's reaction. Mike had been on the receiving end of Brandon's bullying once. That made Jonah even angrier. "The Warners had the nerve to show up at the funeral. I'm surprised Brandon didn't come there just to gloat."

"He was in Atlanta on a tour of the State House." Mike paused in his writing and tapped the pen against his bottom lip. "His dad made him go in order to meet lawmakers and other important people. Brandon hated it."

"Why? I thought his snobby butt would love stuff like that."

"Brandon wants to play basketball, Jonah. And he's good at it; he even got accepted on the varsity team. That–"

"That rarely happens," Jonah finished. "Everyone's talking about it. So what?"

Mike exhaled, like he was trying to stay calm. "His dad thinks basketball is beneath his son's future career as a lawyer."

"Really? Oh, wow," Jonah said. For the first time, he didn't envy Brandon, not with a dad like that. He opened his mouth to ask a different question when he registered Mike's in-depth answer. "Wait a minute. How do you know all that?"

"They talked about the trip at school. Besides," Mike's oatmeal complexion darkened with embarrassment. "Don't get mad. Drew told me."

"You're still talking to Drew?"

"Sometimes. I'm trying to bring him back from the edge."

"He's one of the bullies!"

"Jonah, he only did that because Brandon made him do it." When Jonah gave him an incredulous look, Mike's shoulders slumped. "I know. He should have stood up to Brandon and told him bullying Latrell was wrong. I'm trying to get him to admit that, but it takes time."

Jonah wanted to tell Mike he was being stupid about Drew, but kept it to himself. This development changed his plans for scouting out Brandon's house. Knowing where the bully lived wasn't enough. If he ever intended to phase there, Jonah needed to see the inside of the house first.

For now, he would switch to Drew. That also fortified Jonah's resolve not to reveal his plan to Mike. Not only would he object, but Mike still considered Drew worth saving! As far as Jonah was concerned, Drew was even worse than Brandon.

"I'll see you later." Jonah stood. Then he remembered his mom's box. "By the way, my mom left me a triptych."

"Oh?" Mike gushed. "Was it in three pieces or all connected together?"

Jonah's earlier irritation evaporated at once. He loved how Mike knew what he meant without ever having to explain. Each could reference an obscure science fiction or fantasy movie and the other would instantly get it or even finish the quote. They were cool that way. Nerds. Best friends. "It was in three pieces."

"I want to see it." A real fire glimmered in Mike's eyes.

Jonah's face warmed with shame over his earlier shortness. "We can talk now, if you want to."

Mike seemed as if he wanted to do that. Jonah waited him out, hoping, but in the end, Mike said, "That's okay. I know you have other things on your mind. And I need to catch up on this work."

Jonah nodded. "Well, the triptych is in my room. I'll show you later?"

Amulet of the Goddess

"Yeah, that's cool." Mike continued watching him. "Where's your book bag?"

"At home. I'll finish my homework there." That was true. He needed to finish his own work and then prepare for his first scouting mission. "Check you later."

*

One benefit of focusing on Drew was that his family lived on the same side of town as the Hightowers. This neighborhood was older than Jonah's and had two positive attributes: Large tracks of undeveloped forest that ran along the back border of the neighborhood; and many of the mature trees near the homes had thick trunks. Perfect for hiding behind.

In the gathering dimness of evening, Jonah found several places around or near the Edwards' huge home to which he could phase. Jonah's sense of purpose increased as he headed home.

That night, around midnight, he snuck into his backyard. Having learned the year before that he couldn't phase into nor out of the Hightowers' property, due to the magical protections, it made things trickier for Jonah, but not impossible.

Situated beside the shed and out of sight of prying neighbors, Jonah phased to Drew's fenced-in backyard. He appeared beside the Edwards' shed, which he spotted earlier. After a few minutes, he determined which window belonged to Drew's bedroom: second floor, east side of the house. Jonah exited the backyard through a squeaky gate and snuck up behind a tree outside Drew's window.

He was too low to see inside the house, but that wasn't a problem. Jonah gazed into the tree's branches, allowing his eyes to adjust to the dimness. Once he was sure he had the spot in mind, he phased and reappeared on a thick branch. With a little shifting, he had a direct view into Drew's window. Thankfully, Drew had his blinds open and fully retracted.

Jonah concentrated, noting the placement of the bed, the chest, and desk. He shifted to see into a corner of the room. He had just decided on a space to phase–at the foot of Drew's bed–when the boy walked by the window and stopped.

Panicked, Jonah shifted behind the tree trunk, hoping the darkness concealed his movement.

The window clicked and slid open. "Hello? Who's there?" Drew stared right into the tree where Jonah hid. "Mike, is that you?"

Jonah's eyes widened and he phased to the ground but continued to stay flat against the tree. Then he felt a chill along his back at the same time Latrell's ankh amulet grew warm against the bare skin of his chest. "Dang it!" he whispered.

Jonah only wore the ankh to honor Latrell on this scouting mission. Now he realized that was a mistake because of the ghost's attachment to the piece of jewelry. The ghost could appear wherever the person with the ankh went.

He spun around to face Latrell's glowing form. "What are you doing here? Go home!"

Drew's window snapped closed like a gunshot in the quiet evening, startling Jonah. He suspected the boy would come outside to investigate and waved at Latrell. "Go!"

He can't see me.

"That doesn't matter. Now–" Jonah's Death Sense spiked as a low growl came from the adjacent yard.

Two bright orange cat eyes stared back at him from the darkness between the trash cans. That seemed to frighten Latrell, and the ghost disappeared. Jonah prepared to phase when he heard Drew's approaching footsteps, crunching the autumn leaves.

Oh no! If he phased away, whatever was stalking him would attack Drew if the stupid boy came into the side yard. Drew reached the backyard gate and stopped to turn on a flashlight. Jonah ducked behind the tree, barely avoiding the beam of light as Drew searched the side yard.

"Mike?" The boy's voice shook with uncertainty.

Please go back inside. But the gate creaked as Drew opened it. Jonah turned to see the orange feline eyes narrowing to slits. His Death Sense spiked harder. The creature would attack any second.

What could he do? Rush Drew and phase the boy to safety? That was the only option. Omar or someone else from the Alliance would have to modify the boy's memory afterward.

"Who's there?" Drew asked again.

Amulet of the Goddess

Just as he stepped through the gate, a chilling howl from a Grim Hound pierced the night air. Drew swore, followed by a heavy grunt of pain, and then Jonah heard the unmistakable metallic clack! of the flashlight hitting the brick steps.

A steady vibration reached Jonah's feet. Those were the heavy footfalls of a charging Grim Hound. The cat screeched out an angry feline growl before it leapt away, knocking over the neighbor's trash can. Seconds later, a huge, darkened shape rumbled across Drew's side yard, galloping right past Jonah and into the next yard, trailing the cat.

The beasts growled at each other as they raced off into the night.

"What the…" Drew said in a shaky voice. His rapid breathing was audible.

Jonah realized his own heart pounded away in his chest. Drew retrieved the flashlight, lingered a moment at the gate, and then hurried away. Once Jonah was sure the boy was back in the house, he phased to his own backyard.

Hidden in the shadows beside the shed, he slumped against the tree and tried to let his heart calm down as he regulated his breathing. Jonah had to credit Drew's willingness to come outside and investigate, even though that was dumb.

That was also too close.

Was the cat following him or Drew? Why would a Grim Hound suddenly appear to protect him? Unless it was Deyanira's Hound? Jonah didn't want to think about that. The Reaper's warning was strange enough. Would she send her Grim Hound to Mount Vernon?

And then there was Latrell. Jonah would have to talk to the boy and tell him not to follow him around. Of course, he could stop wearing the ankh. But that seemed a little rude if he were intent on helping the boy's ghost complete his unfinished business.

With everything that had just happened, Jonah harbored doubts about his plan for the bullies. He was prepared to save Drew's life instead of letting the cat have him. Marcus's comment from their Afterworld mission came back to Jonah. *You're not a killer.*

No, he wasn't a killer. But as the nervous excitement waned, his resolve to do something about the bullies stubbornly remained.

CHAPTER FOURTEEN
DIPLOMATIC RELATIONS

Brandon returned to school on Friday. But he and Drew acted subdued, preventing Jonah and his people from having any chance to report them. Jonah wondered if Brandon was down about having to come back to school on a Friday instead of staying in Atlanta. At least, Jonah hoped that was the case. *Or maybe his dad wanted him out of sight on the day of the funeral.*

Somehow, Jonah suspected Drew wouldn't mention his little scare from the night before. That didn't matter. He saw what he needed. Besides, the person Jonah really wanted to find was Niqab Girl. He didn't know what he'd do or say when he found her. He couldn't accuse her of attacking the store owner. If he did, she might try to hex him again.

As the school day wore on and none of the club members spotted her, Jonah wondered if she walked around *without* the niqab to hide in plain sight. Sensing his interest in the girl, Danita checked with her big sister, who often volunteered in the main office.

She stopped Jonah in the hallway before his last class. "No go. My sister refused to do it," Danita huffed, looking put out.

"That's okay." Jonah tried to cover his own disappointment. The girl was the only lead they had.

Danita perked up and said, "Guess what? People saw the cat on our side of town last night."

"Really?" Jonah winced at his failed attempt to sound surprised.

Amulet of the Goddess

She eyed him. "Yeah. I want to go to that park and soon." When Jonah frowned, she added, "You promised me."

"Okay. I'll hit you up later."

Danita grabbed his wrist. "You're still coming to the movies tonight, right?"

Jonah wanted to say no. He already had visions of Anthony constantly puffing out his chest for Danita while Rodney and Lorraine kissed in the darkened theater.

"Mike's coming with his friend," Danita said. Once again, she subjected Jonah to her calculating gaze.

"He is?"

"Yes."

For the first time, Jonah wondered if Danita knew about Mike and Patrick. That thought reminded him why he hesitated to go. Not only would he be the odd man out, but the person he liked couldn't be there either.

*

Jonah rode with Danita, Anthony, Lorraine, and Rodney to the movies. His desire to put the events of the previous night out of his mind was the primary motivation for going.

When Mike arrived with Patrick, Jonah noticed the two boys were careful not to reveal they were dating. Whenever Jonah joked with Mike, Patrick scowled at Jonah. It was as if the boy feared he liked Mike. That thought jolted his awareness about Danita's strange stares.

Not only did she know about Mike and Patrick, she was watching to see Jonah's reaction. A distinct surge of irritation with the whole situation overcame Jonah. He took a calming breath and made sure that he didn't sit near Mike during the movie.

Two-and-a-half hours later, Jonah was grateful for the mindless fun of the movie because it took his mind off Drew, Brandon, and everything else. As the group paused in the busy lobby of the theater complex, Jonah heard Brandon's snobbish laugh. He spotted the boy and Antwan near the games, talking to some girls.

"Let's hit the ice cream shop," Mike said, glancing out the atrium's glass windows. Patrick crossed his arms, glowering.

But when Danita and the others agreed, the boy didn't have a choice. They started for the exit but Jonah tapped Mike's arm.

"I need to use the bathroom. These are nicer than the ice cream shop's."

"Fine," Mike said, giving Jonah a curious look. "We'll get a table."

Jonah made his way through the crowd and headed in the general direction of the bathroom. Once his group had moved off down the sidewalk, he changed course and aimed for the sitting area adjacent to the games. He peeked around the wall separating the spaces. He didn't have a good reason to eavesdrop, plus, he really had to go to the bathroom after drinking his large soda. But he waited anyway.

Antwan craned his thin neck to look outside. "Our ride's here." His clipped African accent sounded irritated.

Brandon waved off his buddy, taking his time with the girl.

"My cousin's waiting in the car," Antwan insisted. "You know how she gets."

Brandon scowled at Antwan, but finally said goodbye to his little fan club. Despite needing to take a pee, Jonah's curiosity got the better of him and he exited the theaters behind the boys. A driver, of all things, waited by a large, black SUV with the door open for Antwan and Brandon to settle in.

Jonah's Death Sense spiked. The front passenger window rolled down and a pair of brilliant, brown eyes peered out of the darkened interior. It was Niqab Girl! Seeing her, Jonah did something he never expected to do: He stepped toward the vehicle.

The girl's eyes narrowed and Jonah could sense that she grinned at him. His Death Sense continued to throb. Despite that, he took another step, drawn by the mystery of this girl. That's when the SUV drove off. Jonah reached the curb and, remembering Lynn's advice, noted the license plate. That presented another problem because the SUV had a Diplomat's plate.

*

Amulet of the Goddess

A regular nightmare about the Niqab Girl interrupted Jonah's sleep. She chased him through the streets of Morningside Drive, firing hexes at him. Nothing Jonah did could deflect the attacks. Each strike was more painful than the last. Then, as he watched in horror, the girl transformed into a huge, black cat.

Sprinting at full speed to his house, he made it inside the front door right before the cat pounced on him. He slammed the door and leaned against it, breathing hard. Instead of pounding or colliding with the door, there was a quiet *knock, knock, knock...*

That terrified Jonah even more.

Again, *knock, knock, knock.* Jonah jerked awake in his bed, his covers tangled around his legs and ankles. He sat up, blinking and listening. This time, the knock was louder and harder at his bedroom door.

"Yeah?" Jonah mumbled.

Robert's muffled voice came from outside. "Get up, sleepy head. It's a beautiful Saturday morning, perfect for selling pumpkins."

Jonah groaned. "I'm coming." A faint glow came from his curtain, indicating it was near dawn. He shook off the weird dream as he tumbled out of bed and headed toward the shower.

After dressing, he slipped Latrell's ankh amulet around his neck. He wanted the ghost to show up so they could discuss his sudden appearances. At the last minute, he remembered his promise to Mike. Unlocking his mom's box, he took out the triptych and the mysterious note before placing both in his string bag.

*

Mike was just as sleepy as Jonah when they stopped by his house to pick him up before dawn. Wick, who sat in the front passenger seat, was wide awake like Robert. Once Mike settled in, they set off for the church.

Jonah was about to open his bag and show Mike the triptych when Robert took a corner too fast and a long, curved case in the rear of the van tumbled off the rear seat. "Robert?" Jonah asked, peeking over his seat at the case. "What's that?"

Robert glanced at Jonah in the rearview mirror. "Nothing."

Wick punched his buddy in the upper arm. "Tell him."

"Yeah, tell me," Jonah prompted, leaning forward to peer between the front seats. Mike even opened his eyes, looking just as interested.

Robert gave them an embarrassed glance. "I'm taking archery lessons, okay?"

"You are?"

"Yes." Robert narrowed his eyes as if daring Jonah to say something smart.

But Jonah thought that was the coolest idea. "Can you show me the bow?"

"Not now."

"When do you practice?" Mike asked.

"I go to the old Practice Club field on the weekends mainly," Robert confessed. He slowed as he reached the church and turned into the parking lot and glanced at Jonah. "I'll show you later, after we finish."

"Cool." Jonah looked forward to that. He never expected Robert to learn something like how to shoot an arrow from a bow. He wondered if Wick or Lynn would have suggested it or if the idea solely belonged to his cousin.

Jonah didn't have time to consider Robert's new skill because a huge truck was in the church's parking lot, its back wide open. The deacons and other young men from the congregation were lining up to unload the vehicle.

The boys went straight to work and soon dozens of pumpkins were littering the empty parking lot. A consignment of miniature pumpkins, good for making pies, was even included. Wick took charge of those. He caught Jonah's puzzled expression. "They're for the bonfire."

"Oh, cool."

By the time the sun was high in the sky, the south-facing lawn of the church that bordered the main road was adorned with neatly placed pumpkins. Jonah had to admit it was an impressive sight. Already, cars were slowing as people admired the grand display.

Amulet of the Goddess

A second crew of guys hung around during the sale to help customers by carrying the pumpkins to their vehicles. Done with their shift, Jonah and Mike headed to the Hightowers' van and climbed inside to wait for Robert and Wick.

Jonah took advantage of the opportunity to open his small bag and pull out the triptych.

"Wow," Mike gushed again as he took all three pieces and examined them. "It's beautiful! Did your mom make it?"

"I don't know."

Then Mike did something Jonah never thought to do; he connected the pieces. They made audible clicks as if the ends were magnetized. When he finished, the entire surface of the triptych glowed.

Mike's jaw dropped. "Very nice."

Jonah leaned closer to look. The seven stars pulsated as if they were animated. And fainter stars appeared below those, almost like reflections. The 3D effect was amazing. Then Jonah's own mouth dropped open when a label appeared beside each star. There were seven names in all: Phantom's Passage, Spector Ridge, Apparition Valley, Haunted Forest, Mirage Lake, Soothsayer Meadow, and Harbinger Plateau.

The names represented the terrain depicted at each location on the map. To Jonah, it was like looking at a video game fantasy world.

"It's been enchanted," Mike said.

Jonah waved his hand over the artwork. "Yeah, I can feel it too."

Mike glanced out the front window when they heard Wick's laugh. "You want to show them?" He raised a questioning eyebrow.

"Let's figure it out on our own." Jonah said it before he remembered that he and Mike didn't hang out as often anymore.

Mike nodded absently while running his thin fingers over the surface of the triptych. His eagerness to discover the map's secrets replaced his generally tired appearance. The work had driven away Jonah's morning yawns, but Mike still had puffy bags under his eyes.

Jonah wanted to ask if his buddy were sleeping at night, but Mike pulled the first piece of the triptych apart. The enchantment vanished, leaving the sections inert. However, Jonah could still sense the magic at a low, power saving mode.

Mike stacked the pieces and cradled them in his hand. "How's the case going?"

"Fine. Why?"

"Sorry for not helping more. I've been busy."

Jonah swallowed his taunt about Patrick and instead told Mike about the encounter at the mall with Niqab Girl. "And I found out last night she's Antwan's cousin! Can you believe that?" Jonah finished.

Mike's brow furrowed. "We were at the movies last night. How'd you find that out?"

"Oh, I saw Brandon and Antwan on the way to the bathroom." Jonah's face warmed a little. "I followed them outside and saw the girl in the car."

"Jonah!" Mike elbowed him. "That's why you had us wait for you at the ice cream shop?"

"Yeah. This is an important clue."

"Maybe." Mike scrunched down in the seat.

Jonah ruffled his afro, thinking. "We can watch Antwan's house and catch her."

"No, you can't." Mike turned in the seat to face him. "Don't forget, Antwan's dad is the brother of an Ambassador and a member of the royal family from his home country. Their house sits on a big piece of land on the north side. You can't even see it from the road."

Jonah's burgeoning enthusiasm waned. "I didn't know that."

"Yeah. And before you ask," Mike added, "Antwan had an older brother in school here and a couple of other cousins. Everyone knew about them."

When Jonah slumped back in his seat, Mike nudged him. "I'm sorry. His cousin is probably an exchange student. She could hide out in their house forever."

"So much for that idea." Jonah frowned, thinking about the girl. Without warning, his dream popped into his head. "Hey, is there a park near Antwan's house?"

Amulet of the Goddess

"Yeah. A really nice one. Our seventh-grade class had a cookout there. I think Brandon's mom arranged it. Why?"

"No reason."

Mike punched him. "Don't lie. Tell me."

"Okay." Jonah told him all about the dream and Danita's research into the sightings. "It's crazy, I know."

But Mike didn't laugh. He looked thoughtful. "Considering everything we've seen, that wouldn't be too much of a stretch."

"I wasn't serious, Mike. I was just wondering if Niqab Girl's a trainee with that woman in the train yard. Deyanira had a pet Grim Hound. What if that woman has a pet cat?"

"Or the girl?" Mike traded a look with Jonah. "Yeah, that's a definite possibility. But you're still stuck. Why not search for the big guy Robert drew? It couldn't be easy for him to hide."

Jonah agreed, but he didn't want to confront a guy that huge. Not unless he had a couple of those Alliance Guards with him. Besides, his suggestion couldn't work either. The Alliance, or more accurately, his godfather, would shut down anything he and his cousins were doing.

The club would have to find another way to discover what was going on, and fast.

Robert and Wick returned to the van and clambered inside. Jonah noticed that Wick had a small box with several of the miniature pumpkins inside.

"Who wants to see Robin Hood practice?" Wick asked as he grinned at Robert.

"I do!" Mike and Jonah chorused at the same time.

CHAPTER FIFTEEN
FAILED MAGIC ACT

Robert was fantastic at archery. "I started just after Lynn got her blades from Jonah's mom," he said.

Wick thumped Robert on the shoulder. "Tell the truth. You were chasing a girl who was into archery. Who knew you'd be so good at it?"

Robert grinned. "Thanks. I think."

Jonah didn't care why Robert chose the bow. He was simply impressed with his cousin's skills.

"This is a recurve bow," Robert explained as he held out the bow for Jonah and Mike to inspect. "My teacher has an authentic hunting bow from Tanzania. That one's a long bow. He's gonna let me borrow it for the bonfire."

"Why do you need a bow for that?" Jonah stopped fingering the bow to gaze at his cousin. "What are you wearing to the bonfire?"

"You'll see in three weeks."

"We have a lot of things to finish before the show tonight," Wick reminded him.

Robert put the bow away and stowed the case in the back of the van. "Let's go."

As they rode home, Mike asked to see the triptych again. He held the pieces in his hands, turning them over and examining the artwork. "Can I borrow this?"

"Yeah." Jonah didn't hesitate. Mike was a Seeker, after all, and Jonah trusted him more than anyone else.

Amulet of the Goddess

"Cool." Mike slipped the precious pieces into his jacket pocket.

When Robert pulled to a stop in front of the Littletons' house, Mike hopped out of the van and turned back to Jonah. "I'll meet you at the Teen Center tonight."

There was enough of a question in the statement to let Jonah know Mike sensed his persistent irritation.

"I'll walk home," Jonah told Robert. He got out of the van and stood beside Mike at the top of the Littletons' curved driveway.

Robert honked the horn as he and Wick drove off.

"Oh, boy," Mike said. "I know that look. You have to come tonight."

"Don't get me wrong," Jonah began, "I want to see Wick's show."

"But…" Mike prompted.

"I'm tired of being the odd person out, watching everyone else with their dates."

Mike blinked at him and didn't respond for several seconds. "Jonah, when are we gonna talk about things?"

"I don't want to talk about Patrick, okay?"

"I meant Kevin. I know there's something there."

Jonah realized he had a chance to do what he really wanted: talk to his best friend. "He kissed me," he blurted out.

Mike was stunned for several moments and then he laughed. "He did!?" When Jonah nodded, Mike shoved him. "Jonah, that's great!"

Jonah shrugged.

"How was it?" Mike asked, grinning at him.

"Good." Jonah couldn't resist smiling. "Really good."

Mike playfully shoved him again. "I knew it."

When Mike continued to stare, Jonah's irritation returned. "You want me to go and just watch you all having a good time? What about me? I don't even know where Kevin is. Sometimes I wished he hadn't kissed me. At least that way, I wouldn't still be thinking about it."

"Jonah, you don't mean that. And I'm sure that Kevin will show up. Marcus won't let Mandara keep him away. You just watch and wait."

"Maybe."

"But Jonah, we're all your friends. If you back out, people might get the wrong idea about you. Think that you're anti-social."

"I don't care."

"Yes, you do," Mike pressed. "Everyone likes being around you, Jonah, even if you don't notice or appreciate it."

Jonah pretended to be fascinated by the tuft of yellowing grass he worried with his foot.

"Jonah…"

"What?"

"You were different after our trip to the Afterworld. You were driven, always in charge. You started the club and a lot of kids joined just because of you. Don't start back-pedaling now."

The more Mike said, the more Jonah knew his friend spoke the truth. And that exasperated him even more. "I hate you."

Mike laughed again. "I'll see you tonight." He started down his driveway without waiting for a response.

"I'm not going!" Jonah called after him.

Mike reached his front door and went inside.

Jonah kicked at the tuft of grass one last time before he set off for home.

*

Jonah's group arrived early for the show because Rodney and Anthony were part of the band scheduled to perform as an opening act. Rodney played the keyboards and Anthony was a dancer as well as an announcer for the group.

Helping Rodney take his keyboard and equipment up to the stage was fascinating for Jonah. He volunteered to help wherever needed as the band members began setting up.

Amulet of the Goddess

Lorraine and Danita hung around the front of the stage, assisting the guys in any way they could.

After a while, the band's leader thanked Jonah for his kind assistance. Not feeling needed any longer, he decided to get a hot chocolate in the Cyber Café. The show wouldn't start for another thirty minutes or so and kids were already entering the hall.

His thoughts were on Mike's comments about Kevin as he bought a steaming drink. When he turned to find a place to sit, someone called his name.

"Jonah!" Alastor waved to him from a nearby table. "Over here."

Jonah hesitated.

Alastor continued to stare at him, seemingly forgetting the paper in his hands. Jonah didn't think he could just leave the guy hanging, so he crossed over to the table and sat down.

If Alastor sensed his hesitation, he didn't comment. Instead, the strange man leaned on the table and subjected Jonah to an oddly intense stare, one every bit as penetrating as a Reaper's Stare. Finally, he blinked and said, "You look like a man with a lot on his mind."

"Actually, I do…"

Jonah trailed off as Alastor lay down whatever he'd been reading. It was a story about Latrell's funeral in the Summit newsletter. Jonah had completely forgotten that Robert and Lynn had already covered the suicide.

"It's a sad story," Alastor continued. "I can't imagine being bullied so much that I'd take my own life."

Jonah tore his gaze away from the newsletter. "Yeah. I know." He focused on Alastor, a question coming to mind. "Why'd you help me at Latrell's house?"

"You seemed like you wanted to get upstairs."

"Yeah, but you didn't know why."

"I assumed you knew Latrell?"

"No. But my Tolerance Club started peer groups because of what happened."

"I heard. That was a very noble show of solidarity. Too bad something can't be done about the bullies." Alastor sipped from his iced mocha.

Jonah shrugged, his new doubts bubbling to the surface. "Bullies always get away with it."

"But just once, I wish someone had the power to do something. You know what I mean?"

Jonah shifted in his chair and faked a laugh. "Where's a superhero when you really need one?"

"I don't know," Alastor replied, his voice thoughtful. "I mean, if I had the power, I'd make the bullies pay. Shake them up a bit." A hardness came into the man's face and tone. "I'd show them they can't pick on people like that. Screw the consequences." He subjected Jonah to a brief, intense stare before sitting back and spreading his hands. "Listen to me. It's not like I was anything special in high school."

Alastor grinned, but the gesture seemed odd, like the man wasn't used to doing it. And this conversation was too close to the things Jonah already had occupying his mind.

Even so, he leaned back in his own chair and said, "You can't bust into the bully's house and jack him up."

"Of course not." Alastor frowned at him. "That would be foolish. The bully would claim to be the victim in that case." He paused, tapping his finger on the edge of his cup. "However, if the bully didn't know the identity of the person…"

As soon as Alastor said it, Jonah realized he'd need a disguise or a mask. He ignored his recent doubts while working through the various ways he could accomplish that. He had a full-faced mask that he planned to wear to this year's Halloween Bonfire. If he added a hoodie, Drew wouldn't know who he was. *Yeah, that could work!*

The distant sound of Rodney's band starting up reached the café. The thumping bass of whatever song they played vibrated the floor beneath Jonah's feet.

Alastor grimaced and stood. "I should go. You have a show to attend?" When Jonah nodded, the man waved. "Nice talking to you, Mr. Blackstone."

As Jonah watched the peculiar guy exiting the café, his thoughts returned to the plan forming in his mind. He could do this. In fact, he

Amulet of the Goddess 753

called it justice. A small voice in the back of his head warned him that he should be wary of Alastor. There was something suspicious about the man that Jonah couldn't nail down.

But this has been my idea all along, Jonah reminded himself. And he'd already scouted out Drew's house at substantial risk. All he needed now were the final details.

Jonah checked his watch, finished his hot chocolate, and headed for the hall.

*

He was shocked when he entered the West Hall. Not only did the wall of sound hit him but all the kids were packed in, creating a darkened mass of bobbing heads and swaying arms. The crowd moved in time to the opening band's music, which blared from a set of on-stage concert speakers.

Anthony danced around the stage with glowing strips attached to his gloved hands and the sleeves of his special shirt. His movements created lingering light shapes and swirls in the air.

The entire setup impressed Jonah, and he regretted not attending one of Wick's shows until now. Clearly, he had missed out on a lot. He went up on his tiptoes, searching the crowd before he spotted Danita and Lorraine in the glare of lights from the stage. They were right up front, dancing. And not far away, he recognized Rico and Lynn.

One of the disbanded Practice Club boys, wearing a black t-shirt that said CREW in white letters, paused on his way past him. "What's up?" the older boy asked. He noted the direction of Jonah's gaze and added, "You want an escort up front to where Lynn's standing?" He grinned. "We'll push the people out of the way."

Jonah laughed, thinking his fellow club member wasn't serious until the boy motioned to another of the older boys.

"Oh, no. That's okay."

"You sure?"

"Yeah. I'm… waiting for my friend, Mike," Jonah lied.

The boys nodded and exchanged quick handshakes with him before moving on, patrolling the crowd. There were others from the club, all wearing the same black t-shirts. It was a subtle dig at Brandon's crew,

754   *John Darr*

who served as security for the event. They were the official Teen Center's sponsored group ever since Brandon's dad had Jonah's club disbanded. Tonight, the guys wore their dark blue polo shirts with *Security* written on the left pockets.

Jonah ignored them and pressed further into the mass of chattering and dancing kids. He began to search for Brandon and Drew. But he didn't see either bully, which he found peculiar. Brandon never missed a chance to ruin their gatherings at the Teen Center. Yet tonight, he seemed noticeably absent.

Anthony went into a complicated series of turns, creating a vortex of multi-colored lights. When he stopped, he stood right behind the center microphone. People cheered as the band reached a crescendo and suddenly cut out, except for the continued thumping of the background drumbeat.

"Are you ready for the greatest magician in Central Georgia?" Anthony shouted into the mic. The crowd roared its eagerness and approval.

Jonah had to admit the boy's normal, show-off personality fit the occasion. He joined in the hooting and yelled "Yeah!" with the rest of the kids.

"Are you sure?" Anthony made a show of cocking his ear toward the crowd.

Jonah thought he'd go hoarse as he yelled with everyone else again.

"Then give it up for Magician Extraordinaire, Wick Jean-Baptiste!"

The place exploded in applause at the display of colored smoke that erupted from small tubes situated all along the front of the stage.

Wick emerged from the midst of the smoke just as the music kicked into high gear again. Anthony launched into his complicated moves with the light sticks and Wick joined in, like synchronized choreography, while producing amazing, syncopated puffs of blue fire in time with the music. It was spellbinding to watch. Wick was really quite good.

The talented, young mage ended with a burst of purple-colored fire over the heads of the crowd. Several ducked but others yelled with unbridled delight when it became clear the brief flare of fire was harmless.

Jonah was about to whistle when someone pressed in beside him. He turned to find Antwan's cousin standing there. She wore a hoodie to cover her head, but the mesh mask was still in place over her lower face.

"Pathetic," she said and her muffled voice was dripping with hate.

Jonah bristled at her comment. "Don't be jealous."

She turned her intense eyes on him. "Jealous? That fool is using real magic in front of mortals. He must know how dangerous that is." She pointed at the stage. Wick was into his regular opening magic trick, but mixing in real spells. "Look at him!"

"What about you?" Jonah asked. He kept his voice low, which made it hard to talk when people started clapping and cheering. "Dumping Drew on his butt and hitting that jewelry store owner with a hex."

He felt the girl's anger radiating out toward him, causing his Death Sense to throb. "Those were insignificant, subtle uses of magic."

"Yeah. Right! I bet that shop owner's still out of his mind. And you attacked Drew in front of a whole group of kids." Again, he sensed the girl's annoyance so he leaned closer to prod her more. "We almost caught you at the mall."

The girl laughed. It was strangely beautiful and very much at odds with what he was beginning to understand about her. He wondered if her laugh would remain that way or eventually become more sinister, like Deyanira's.

"Your cousin, Lynn, is far more adept with the blades than I thought," she said.

A grudging compliment was the last thing Jonah expected. He grasped for something else to say. "I know you're working with that sorceress."

"Your friend should be more careful," the girl said. She nodded toward the stage where Robert had begun his segment of the show. "Accidents often happen."

Jonah's insides froze at the threat. And his Death Sense spiked as Antwan's cousin spoke. He almost expected her to hex Wick and Robert at any moment.

But she remained still as she watched Robert drawing all kinds of things he'd taken from the first volunteer's mind.

Although his Death Sense finally quieted, Jonah's mind raced with the girl's cryptic threat. Now, more convinced than ever that she was a young sorceress-in-training, he had to stop her from completing whatever mission she came to do. The problem was that when he turned toward her again, she was gone, almost like she used a spell to vanish. Jonah knew better than that because he didn't sense any residual magic.

He searched the surrounding crowd, which proved hopeless in the darkened room. Closing his eyes, he summoned his Reaper Stare. But that too turned out to be a mistake. There were too many people pressed too closely beside him. Plus, the souls of young people were like brilliant stars and the vibrant colors of their emotions were more than enough to make him dizzy.

He couldn't search for the girl that way, but he could focus on her magic. However, each time he tried, Wick used a spell on stage, most often in between Robert's drawing stunts. Jonah's senses spiked so hard that he had to relent.

The situation provided further proof that Wick was summoning a lot of real magic in his show. A nagging doubt that the girl was right began to bother Jonah.

Focus, he warned himself as he opened his senses to detect the magic again. He was trying to filter out Wick's use of spells, but after a while, he just gave up. Not only did the process exacerbate a growing headache, but as far as he could tell, the girl wasn't using any magic.

Did she have a way to conceal herself? Jonah suspected the mysterious woman, whoever she was, must have trained the girl to be sneaky and hard to catch. He snapped his fingers as something the girl told Drew came to mind. *"You should be careful being emotional around him."*

Of course! All she had to do was calm her own emotions. That was the big downside of his Death Sense. Unless he were being directly threatened, or someone desired to hurt him or someone close to him, Jonah couldn't sense the person's true intentions.

At the same time, he realized the girl may have thrown off her hoodie and face mask to blend in with the crowd. In fact, she could have been standing right beside him and he wouldn't have recognized her.

Jonah let out a low growl of frustration and his heart raced with growing worry. A young sorceress in the crowd was a disaster just waiting to happen.

Robert's part ended and Wick let loose with an impressive, crowd-pleasing display of flickering, blue flames, set in time to the music. That's when it happened. The spike of magic produced a bright, hot flash of

Amulet of the Goddess

warning from Jonah's Death Sense. Wick's display of blue flames suddenly changed into green fire and surged outward in all directions. Unlike the purple and blue variety, these flames produced real heat and they bellowed out like lethal ripples, moving recklessly into the unsuspecting crowd.

Oh, no! Jonah thought as he watched the scene unfold in abject horror.

CHAPTER SIXTEEN
TOKEN CALL

If Wick's sudden fumbling around on stage weren't the first sign of trouble, the intense heat of the bright green flames must have been the next clue. People not only ducked, but they screamed and tried to run away. Those caught at the front of the crowd pressed into the ones behind them. In no time at all, the green flames ignited parts of the stage, and everyone panicked before the real stampede for the doors began.

Jonah shoved his way to the wall to let the jostling kids press past him. For the first time, their club members and Brandon's crew were actually working together. They shoved the doors wide open just in time for the kids to dive through. Jonah had to give the boys credit for wading into the crowd to help the unlucky ones who fell.

Shouts came from the front, where a few kids got knocked down. Jonah tried to edge toward the commotion, but it was difficult at best.

Meanwhile, Wick stood with hands outstretched toward the flames now threatening the stage and shouted, "*Washa!*"

Jonah had never heard Wick use the fire-casting word before. To his relief, the roaring green flames instantly became the harmless blue variety before they could burn anyone. As the hall emptied, Jonah observed several injured kids.

Helping one girl to her feet, she gingerly tried to place her weight on her left foot. She winced as Jonah lowered her to the ground. Another kid, a boy, cradled his arm while one of Brandon's team held paper towels against it. The other kids seemed mostly dazed rather than seriously hurt.

Amulet of the Goddess **759**

Once again, Jonah's Death Sense spiked. Off to the side of the stage, hidden in the shadows, he saw Antwan's cousin hurling a hex at Robert, who yelled before he dropped to the floor near one of the large speakers.

Jonah phased without a second thought, not caring if anyone saw him. Just as he reappeared at the side of the stage, from the corner of his eye, he saw the large speaker falling. Robert's shriek of pain followed.

Before Jonah could alter his focus and help his cousin, his Death Sense spiked again. The girl flung a hex at him, but he dodged it, plowing into a stack of chairs. Seizing the opportunity, Antwan's cousin raced out the back door and fled into the night.

Jonah rolled to his feet as a bright flash of reddish light came from outside. He felt the slight pressure of a vortex being opened.

Too late to stop the girl, Jonah stumbled onto the stage as Rico heaved the huge speaker off Robert. Lynn knelt down and muttered continuously to her brother who had tears streaming down his face. A pit formed in Jonah's stomach when he saw Robert's bloodied right hand. At least two of his fingers were bent at unnatural angles.

"Oh, my God!" Jonah whispered to himself.

Lynn met his gaze. "We need some ice."

"I'll get it," Rodney said, leaping off the stage and hurrying out of the hall.

Wick leaned over Robert, saying, "I'm sorry, Bobby. I'm sorry." He confronted the shocked faces of the other kids who remained inside the hall. "It was all my fault."

Robert's face had turned a ghostly pale by the time Rodney returned with the ice and the Center's Resource Officer.

Lynn took the ice and used her own scarf to wrap her brother's hand, securing the ice in place. She glanced up at the officer. "He needs to go to the hospital."

"I've already called the EMTs and the fire department. They should be here soon."

True to his words, the sirens sounded outside. EMTs entered the hall along with another officer, the firefighters, and, to Jonah's dismay, the Teen Center's director. After the last fiasco at his birthday party, Jonah was sure the woman would ban them permanently from the premises.

The professionals checked all the kids. The girl Jonah helped earlier did have a sprained ankle. Aside from the boy with the cut arm, the rest had only minor bumps and bruises from being trodden on. Brandon's security goons talked with the director and the Practice Club guys offered to help wherever needed.

In any other situation, Jonah would have expected Brandon's people to bad-mouth Wick. But judging from their nervous looks and shaky voices, he knew they weren't doing that.

Activity around Robert brought Jonah's attention back to his cousin. The EMTs were trying to move Robert toward the exit, but Lynn was stubbornly objecting.

"I need to stay with him!" she shouted.

When a second officer attempted to stop her, the Teen Center's officer waved to his buddy. "Let her go. I'll talk to them later."

Jonah tried to follow, but the Resource Officer stopped him. "You have to give a statement."

"But that's my cousin."

"I know." The officer withdrew a pad.

Jonah wanted to object until Rico came up beside him, looking just as pissed about not being allowed to go with Lynn. They exchanged a mutually sad glance before each told the officer what they witnessed. Jonah had to weave around what really happened. Even so, it didn't look too good for Wick.

The shattered, young mage was talking to the second officer and once or twice, he raised his voice. "I wasn't using explosives in my show." Wick darted to a box at the rear of the stage, throwing back the lid, and pulling out several small cylinders that looked like large firecrackers. He showed them to the officer. "These make a lot of harmless, colored smoke, that's all."

Wick and Robert had already planned for a way to explain the supernatural fire if the need arose. That impressed Jonah. He wanted to tell Wick it wasn't his fault. An evil sorceress-in-training had been here, acting on someone's orders. But Jonah never got the chance. Before he knew it, parents had already arrived.

Amulet of the Goddess 761

Wick's mom and dad had the same dark chocolate complexion as their son and they spoke with pronounced Jamaican accents. Wick's mom exuded a regal bearing, and she patted her son's slumped shoulders while her husband did most of the speaking. Her eyes surveyed the damaged stage, the toppled speaker, and finally, Jonah.

Jonah didn't know what to do, but he couldn't break her gaze until she nodded and turned back to the conversation. Since Wick's grandmother was a ghost hunter, Jonah wondered if the mom was also aware of magic and other things.

When she spoke, however, Jonah was sure of it. "My son knows his craft. He wasn't responsible for this."

"Then how do you explain the fire?" the Teen Center officer asked.

"Sabotage. I believe there were hard feelings between some of the kids here."

The officer looked stunned and Brandon's crew stirred. Wick's father stepped in, raising his hands in a placating gesture. "It was a simple accident, nothing more." He met his wife's gaze. She nodded.

Jonah recognized that look. There would be plenty of arguing later. Personally, he wanted to thank Wick's mom because she knew at once that something unusual had happened.

Perhaps the only thing that helped Wick was the fire chief's comment after examining the smoke makers. He agreed that the devices couldn't have started the fire, but he also couldn't determine what did.

Eventually, Aunt Imma arrived to take Jonah home. Rico tagged along, looking lost and uncertain.

"What about Robert?" Jonah asked as they climbed into their minivan.

"Your uncle is at the hospital." She sighed, like all the air was leaving her body. "Honestly, I always worried something would happen to Lynn, not to Robert."

Jonah hated that he was unable explain the real cause of the mess to his aunt. He rode home in silence while blaming himself for not stopping Antwan's cousin when he had the chance.

*

The long wait in the Hightowers' kitchen reminded Jonah of the time he, Robert, and his aunt were waiting for Lynn to come home after her mishap. She suffered a severe cut while saving Mike during the summer. This time, it was Robert who got injured.

Marcus's warning to Jonah, that his friends and family would get hurt, came back to him with a vengeance. Sure, he could also get banged up, and he did so way too often. But owing to his dual nature, Jonah had the ability to heal at a rapid pace. Unfortunately, Lynn, Robert, and Mike were mortals who didn't share that advantage.

It was at times like these when Jonah wanted to call his godfather. He needed to hear Marcus's calm voice assuring him that everything would be fine and the Alliance would handle it. Where were the Alliance adults right now?

Didn't they have someone here watching him? Where was that person? Jonah had never felt more alone and exposed than he did now and he wished Kevin were there. He bet the young Fallen Reaper would have caught Antwan's cousin with no problem.

The token. Jonah shoved his hand into his pocket and withdrew the small piece of wood. He rose and started for his bedroom before he changed his mind. His aunt would think he was upset and call after him.

Instead, he hurried to the bathroom at the end of the hall, closed the door, and sat on the closed toilet while gripping the token in his right hand. He concentrated and said "Help" three times, like Kevin had instructed him.

In response, the token grew hot in his palm for a few seconds and then it cooled. Was that it? What should he do now? Well, he couldn't stay in the bathroom all night! Without warning, the token went from cool to red-hot in a second. "Ouch!" he said, dropping it onto the floor.

After a shocked moment, he reached over and touched it with a hesitant finger to make sure it had cooled. He clutched it in his hand again. That must have been a response, but from who?

He flushed the toilet and ran the water to make it seem normal. As he exited the bathroom, his cell phone rang. He didn't recognize the number but suspected it had to be someone from his godfather's group.

Aunt Imma and Rico watched him with curious expressions as he crossed over to the patio door and stepped outside. "Hello?"

Amulet of the Goddess 763

"We received your warning," Mage Symon Trueblood said. His voice carried a trace of urgency. "Are you in immediate danger?"

"No. I'm okay, but..."

"Are you somewhere alone?"

Jonah didn't expect that question. "Yeah. I'm outside my house, on the patio."

"Hold on."

Jonah only had to wait a few moments before a vortex opened near the back shed. Symon Trueblood exited through the opening and quickly closed it. He walked over to Jonah but stopped in the shadows, avoiding the light that streamed out through the sliding doors.

"You were saying?" Trueblood prompted him.

Jonah told Trueblood everything that happened. By the time he finished, the mage had moved to the edge of the patio. There was a short silence.

"I suspect there's much more magic being used than you can appreciate, Jonah." Trueblood sounded as if he were selectively choosing his words. "I'll send someone else down to investigate as soon as I can."

"Who? Kevin?"

"He's on assignment again."

"You'll come, won't you?"

"I may not be able to. We rotate all the members of our group to camouflage our collective support for Marcus."

Jonah wanted to scream. Kevin had warned him and Mike about Alliance Council politics, but he hated hearing the harsh reality of it. "How soon?"

"Soon."

"What about the person the Council sent to watch me?"

Trueblood frowned. "You'll find no help there."

"You know who it is?"

"Yes, but we've taken an oath not to reveal anyone's identity."

"You mean you can't tell me? That's not fair."

"I am sorry." Trueblood sounded more somber than usual.

Just then, Aunt Imma let out a small sound of dismay from inside the house. Robert, Lynn, and Uncle James had just returned home. Robert's right index and middle fingers were bandaged and wrapped in a brace to keep them immobilized. His face was still pale and he looked tired and miserable.

Jonah scrambled for the sliding door and opened it just as his Uncle James loomed in the doorway. The man's eyes were furious as he gazed over Jonah's shoulder and saw Trueblood.

Jonah backed away and let his uncle exit the house. "Ah, Uncle James, this is—"

"I know exactly who he is, Jonah!" Uncle James narrowed his eyes in pure anger. "That man is Symon Trueblood, a mage who works directly for the Alliance."

CHAPTER SEVENTEEN
ROGUE'S GALLERY

Jonah couldn't believe his uncle recognized Trueblood. "You know about the Alliance?"

"Go inside and pull the blinds," Uncle James ordered.

"But–"

"Do it now, Jonah!" His uncle took a breath and added in a softer but final tone that didn't invite argument, "Please do as I say."

"Yes, sir." Jonah obeyed without another word.

"Who's that?" Aunt Imma asked Jonah as he reentered the kitchen.

Jonah blinked, reaching for a good cover story, and decided to be as honest as possible. "One of my godfather's coworkers. I told him what happened."

"Oh, that was thoughtful."

As soon as Aunt Imma turned to Robert, Jonah closed the blinds.

"You should lie down," Aunt Imma urged her son.

"I don't want to lie down," Robert objected. "I need to talk to Wick so he doesn't go crazy or keep blaming himself."

"You can do that later." She forced him to sit down on the sofa. "You lie back down for now." She read the pain medication directions.

Lynn watched from the entrance to the foyer, her arms crossed as her entire body kept trembling.

Rico had an arm around her shoulders. He whispered, "He'll be okay. I broke my fingers once when I flipped over the handlebars of my bike after running into a pothole."

"Not helping," Robert muttered. "I broke my fingers, not my ears."

Robert's sour mood seemed to affect Lynn the most. She shook her head from side-to-side. "I should have known. I should have felt this before it happened."

"Not that again," Rico sighed.

Lynn whirled on her boyfriend. "I sense when bad things are gonna happen. It's not my imagination!" She pulled away from Rico, marched down the hall to the front door, and dashed outside.

"Lynn!" Aunt Imma called.

"I'll go after her," Rico said and he followed Lynn.

Robert met Jonah's worried gaze as he rose to his feet again. "I'm tired and I don't need help."

Aunt Imma ignored his protest as she trailed him to his room. With the den cleared, Jonah returned to the patio doors and opened them a crack to listen. Uncle James and Trueblood had moved off into the darkness of the backyard, but their voices reached Jonah's ears.

"...told me you would protect my sister," Uncle James said.

"I *did* protect her."

"Really? Then what happened? Now my son and daughter are getting hurt. I won't have it!"

"We told you that Robert and Lynn would have to develop their skills."

"When they're eighteen. Until then, I'm responsible for them and Jonah."

A silence followed that comment. Then Trueblood said, "Jonah's not your son. You know what Janice and Isaiah wanted for him."

"He is my son, just as much as Robert!"

That statement touched Jonah. He still thought of his cousins as his cousins though, and not his brother and sister.

Amulet of the Goddess **767**

"I won't have you endangering my kids," Uncle James said.

"They are who they are, James."

"Not again."

When Trueblood spoke, there was real pain in his voice. "I miss Janice too. Every day."

"Don't mention my sister. It was your foolishness that provoked Ruby. And what happened to poor Jonah..."

"He's fine."

"No thanks to you! At least Jonah's godfather is level-headed and responsible. He wanted Jonah to stay out of all the trouble and that's why he sent him here."

"That was his parents' decision, and Marcus was only honoring their wishes. Jonah's becoming exactly whom he's destined to be. You can't stop that. No more than you could stop your sister."

"Get out of my yard."

"Fine, James. Tell Jonah I'll contact him later."

Jonah saw a brief flash of light when the vortex opened and quickly closed. Uncle James seemed to appear out of the darkness, walking purposefully toward the house.

When he caught Jonah listening, he let out a sigh and entered the house. "You heard?" Uncle James asked.

"Not everything," Jonah said. "I'm sorry."

"It's not your fault. None of this is." He looked very tired.

"So, you know about Lynn and Robert and me?"

Uncle James nodded and leaned against the breakfast bar to calm himself.

Jonah pulled out a kitchen table chair and sat.

Before Uncle James continued, Aunt Imma emerged from Robert's room, muttering about the state of his bed linen. She hustled to the hall closet and came back with clean sheets. Uncle James gave his wife a weary smile and pulled out a bar stool. Without warning, he said, "I always thought fate cheated the males in my family. Then Imma pointed out how I could make the right decisions on little information."

"You mean, you have the gift?" Jonah winced at using the word.

Uncle James looked thoughtful. "The gift. That's what your aunt–" He stopped, his eyes widening.

"Don't worry," Jonah said. "I found out about Aunt Ruby."

Uncle James blinked several times and then released a low breath. "Lynn and Robert have been talking too much."

"It's okay."

"No, it isn't. Listen to me, Jonah: Don't you worry about Ruby. Whatever happened is over."

If that were true, Jonah wondered, why was his uncle yelling at Trueblood and blaming the mage for his mom's death? Jonah hated the doubt that crept into his mind at his uncle's words. Did he not know what happened? Or was his uncle only trying to protect him?

A simple Reaper Stare would have done the trick, but Jonah resisted that idea. It didn't seem proper to use it on his friends and family.

"I can't deny that Robert has a variation of Lynn's ability," Uncle James said. "And his magic trick…" He looked Jonah squarely in the eye. "Given my sister's abilities, and your father's nature," he raised an eyebrow, "I realized you would be special, Jonah."

It was clear to Jonah that his uncle knew a lot but was also fishing for information. When he didn't answer, Uncle James rose. "Lynn's angry about losing her intuition, but it's really for the best. Those types of things always lead to unnecessary pain and suffering."

"Yes, sir."

Uncle James cocked his head to the side. "Have you called your godfather?"

"He's on a business trip. That's why I called Mage Trueblood."

"Business trip? I can imagine." He started for Robert's room but paused on the other side of the breakfast bar and said, "Steer clear of Trueblood and all this other business, Jonah. If the Alliance insists on sending someone while your godfather is away, tell them to send someone else. I'll tell Robert and Lynn the same thing. Better safe than sorry."

Amulet of the Goddess

His uncle was wrong. When it came to the supernatural, things had a way of forcing him into the very middle. If Trueblood were right, events were already in motion. No, he couldn't steer clear from it even if he wanted to. And he didn't want to, either, because there was something he had to do.

*

The rest of the evening passed quietly. Lynn didn't return home before Jonah headed to bed. Uncle James spent a long time talking with Robert. Far longer than he did with Lynn after she got injured. When Jonah peeked in on his cousin, Robert was fast asleep.

So Jonah slumped off to bed, his mind in turmoil. He liked the Truebloods. The sister had kicked butt in the Afterworld and saved his and Mike's life more than once. He couldn't imagine not being around either mage.

Feeling strangely keyed-up and anxious, Jonah slipped under his covers, put in his earbuds, and listened to music well into the night. Finally, his exhaustion overtook him and he slept.

Dream-walks, when they happened, seemed to occur just after Jonah closed his eyes. In this one, he stood in front of an impressive stone site with seven tall stone pillars evenly spaced around a large round platform of granite. Words, in an unreadable language, were etched in the flat faces of the pillars.

Too bad Mike isn't here, he thought. The place reminded him of the Georgia Guide Stones site, a granite monument in North Georgia. This monument was even bigger and it covered more area. At the center was a large, horizontal slab of stone.

For some reason, Jonah thought it was a sacrificial table. The idea popped into his mind on its own, along with sharp flashes of images of previous sacrifices. At first, he thought they were from some movie he shouldn't have watched. Yet the images seemed too real. But that couldn't be. He'd never seen a sacrifice in real life.

The flashes and thoughts left a sour taste in his mouth and an ache in the pit of his stomach. He shook his head and would have stepped onto the marble platform but he caught a slight distortion in the air in front of him. He stopped, knowing that it must have been a ward or some other kind of barrier. Jonah had learned that even during a dream-walk, any ward reacted to his astral body.

He took a step back and for the first time noticed someone moving in the shadow of a pillar. As he narrowed his eyes, peering into the darkness, he managed to make out enough details to identify Antwan's cousin, the girl in the niqab! She was still wearing the face mask and hoodie she wore at Wick's magic show.

Jonah's hands curled into fists. *Why was she here?* In answer to his unspoken question, someone in all black phased onto the marble platform.

It was the Alliance mole. Jonah remembered the traitor from a previous dream-walk in which the man had argued with Deyanira. Like then, he wore his Reaper long coat but also a hat and a mask to hide his true identity. And his outline seemed to waver as if it were distorted.

A flash of purplish light appeared, and the sorceress stepped through. It was her own version of a vortex, and very cool and frightening to witness.

The hulking man from Robert's picture came through the misty opening behind her. His eyes were a glowing, milky white, a sign of Wraith possession. As he lumbered around the center stone slab, he cast angry glances at everyone else.

But Jonah shifted his attention to the woman. Like the girl, she concealed herself in the shadows between the pillars. Jonah hoped she would lower her hood, but she didn't. Even with his ability to discern small details in the shadows, her hood was drawn too far forward to allow him to make out her face.

When she spoke, her voice sent chills down Jonah's spine. "You called us here, mole. Why?"

"I'm concerned with the mission's success," the mole replied with his slightly distorted voice. "Thank goodness tonight went exactly as planned." He waved a finger at the huge Wraith. "Your failure to control your brethren threatened the entire operation. They should have never attacked the Blackstone brat and his cousins."

"He banished my brethren back to the Underworld! A Wraith requires a long time to recover from that." He smacked his huge fists together. "I should have snapped the brat's neck."

"You'll be lucky if he doesn't send you back too," the mole scoffed. "Because of you, this girl had to take care of the store owner in broad daylight. And she also had to deal with the cousin tonight."

Amulet of the Goddess

Niqab Girl stirred. "I did what I needed to do."

"Yes, but I've been working overtime to make sure everything else remained on track."

"You just want to keep your head neatly attached to your body," the Wraith taunted.

"We should all be concerned with surviving, idiot!"

The Wraith growled and pounded the stone slab with his fist. The thing didn't budge, but it did creak.

"As for you," the mole continued to Niqab Girl, "are you even sure this barrier will keep the brat from eavesdropping?"

Jonah winced at being called *brat* yet again, but he didn't move a muscle.

Niqab Girl raised her hands. Magical energy crackled around her fingertips. "Deyanira trained me to do my job well."

The tension between the group was palpable, even to Jonah in his spirit form.

Then the woman laughed. It was low and mocking.

Niqab Girl turned her head toward the woman and lowered her hands.

The mole nodded and addressed the sorceress. "You, at least, must understand that careful, slow revenge is the best revenge of all."

The woman nodded and threw back her hood. But Jonah couldn't discover her identity because her face glowed, obscuring the features. When she spoke, her rich voice filled the air. "When it's over, Jonah Blackstone will belong to me, or–" she suddenly turned and looked right at Jonah. Her brilliant, orange eyes met his when she added, "You will die, young one!"

She waved her hand and pain engulfed Jonah's mind. He woke up in his bedroom, both hands clamped over his head. "Ow, ow, ow!" The severe headache lasted for several minutes, leaving Jonah on the verge of vomiting until the pain subsided.

As he tried to recall the meeting, a residual ache made his head throb. Had she put a spell on him to make it too painful to remember? He kept trying and when the pain finally subsided, he concluded that wasn't the case.

Eventually, he replayed the dream-walk and one thing became clear: The woman's eyes had vertical pupils, just like the cat that stalked him outside Drew's house.

CHAPTER EIGHTEEN
DARK AVENGER

Robert and Lynn were already in the kitchen when Jonah entered. Aunt Imma had prepared her normally huge Sunday morning breakfast. She was in her room getting ready for church while Uncle James sat on the patio, sipping coffee and reading the Sunday paper.

Robert looked so disgruntled and helpless in his hand brace that Lynn took pity on him and fixed him a plate of food.

When Robert held his spoon awkwardly in his left hand, Lynn's patience wore thin. "You can feed yourself."

"I know that, Lynn," he barked.

Lynn glared back until Robert slumped a little and added, "Thanks."

She nodded before starting on her toast.

Jonah sat down and piled his plate with hot food. Before he ate his first forkful, he glanced at his cousins. "Did Uncle James talk to you?"

Robert grunted but kept eating.

Lynn gave an angry huff and put down her toast. "Yes, he did. We're not stopping what we're doing."

"Cool." Jonah had assumed as much, but it was good to hear it all the same.

"Why didn't you tell us Trueblood came by last night?" Lynn asked.

Jonah nearly choked on his food. "Uncle James told you that?" Lynn nodded and waited for him to continue. Jonah told them everything he heard.

Even Robert stopped eating to stare at him in shock. "Wow. They really went at it. Our dad?"

"Yeah." Jonah waited. When his cousins didn't say anything else, he asked, "You're not surprised he knows about your powers?"

"No," Lynn answered. "Your mom was his sister. With all those gifted women on his side of the family, our dad had to know what was up."

"Then why keep the club a secret?"

"Because as you heard, our dad doesn't like the supernatural stuff. He knows about our powers but not how often we're using them."

Jonah nodded, wondering if the death of his mom and dad had anything to do with his uncle's opinion. But that brought up another subject. He put down his fork. "Did you find out why my mom stopped bringing me here?"

Lynn and Robert exchanged a worried look. "It had something to do with Aunt Ruby," Lynn finally admitted.

"What happened?"

"I'm not sure. But I remember the arguments. Instead of watching you, my dad asked Aunt Ruby to do it. When your mom arrived and found out, she went ballistic." Lynn's voice sounded hollow. She gazed across the kitchen, like she was recalling the critical moment. "When your mom came back with you, she looked tired. And you were asleep, I think. She and my dad argued again."

"Yeah, I remember that part," Robert chimed in. "Your mom cut her trip short and insisted on leaving that night." He pushed his plate away and leaned on the table. "That was the last time we saw you."

"Well, that is, until you came to live with us," Lynn said. "All this happened a few months before Ruby went totally crazy. But now that I think about it, her change started right after that night. Sorry."

He didn't want them to apologize. This was more information than he ever had before. To keep the conversation going, he described the note from his mom's box, one that he suspected came from Mage Trueblood.

Lynn nodded. "No wonder my dad was angry with the mage. But…" She faltered. "I think Dad also blames himself. Maybe that's why they can't stand to be around each other."

Amulet of the Goddess **775**

"Maybe." Jonah was bummed because he had no way to find out. His mom was dead. His aunt was in another part of the state, although Jonah had no intentions of talking to the woman anyway. If Trueblood knew something, Jonah doubted the mage would tell him. And then there was Omar, who insisted he ask Marcus. But Jonah's godfather was in the Afterworld.

Jonah wished he could have hit something. Adding to his frustration and anger were Robert's broken fingers and Lynn's diminishing intuition. Their last clue, Niqab Girl's location, was a bust because the girl stayed out of reach.

Jonah needed to act, but he wasn't sure how to do that. *Well*, he corrected himself, *that wasn't exactly true*. He already had a plan forming in his mind.

*

After church, Jonah spent the late afternoon in his room assembling his disguise. He intended to wear a black hoodie, black pants, gloves, and a full-face mask made of resin. It looked like a Komainu, a lion-like creature with boney ridges on the forehead and spiked cheekbones.

He pulled the mask on, adjusting the elastic straps. The material began to mold itself to his face. When Jonah glanced into the mirror, he was startled by his reflection. The only features about him that were still identifiable were his eyes. And the effect of narrowing them in mock anger was downright menacing.

A slow smile creased his lips. This was perfect! Drew wouldn't know him at all. Just to be sure, he positioned the hoodie over his forehead and moved his head from side-to-side. The mask remained firmly in place and the hoodie covered his afro.

Satisfied with his perfected disguise, Jonah stripped down and stowed the clothes in the closet. His judicious eavesdropping at school on Friday, plus, seeing Drew for himself in his room, revealed the boy stayed up late playing video games. Jonah bet Drew would do the same tonight. That suited him because he wanted the bully to be fully alert and scared when he suddenly appeared.

Jonah acted normal during dinner and even played video games with Robert afterward. He allowed his cousin to win, which was hard, given the adverse effect of Robert's brace on his usually adept gaming skills.

Late in the evening, Jonah sat at the kitchen table to go over his homework for the next day. He faked a wide yawn after a couple of hours and announced, "I'm going to bed."

Choosing a nice playlist of quiet songs on his phone, not the usual movie scores, to settle his pounding heart, he slipped under the covers. Falling asleep was the last thing on his mind because of his nervous anticipation.

Lost in his thoughts of what he had to do, it took him a moment to realize how much time elapsed. It was now ten until midnight, the time he selected to be sure his aunt and uncle were settled for the night.

Throwing off the covers, he put on the clever disguise, being careful not to make too much noise. He grabbed the mask, saving it until he got outside the house. At the last minute, he grabbed a handful of butterscotch candies and stuffed them into his pants pocket. Since his time in the Afterworld, he didn't get dizzy while phasing. But he planned to do a lot of it tonight, and that might take its toll. Better to be prepared.

The time on the clock radio changed to midnight. Jonah snuck out of his room, through the den, and, after turning off the alarm, he stealthily slipped out into the backyard. The autumn night sky was cloudless and there was a slight nip in the air. As he entered the shadow of the big tree near the shed, he shivered slightly, thinking the temperature felt even chillier there.

Jonah put on the mask and pulled the hoodie's drawstring tighter. Then he lowered his head, dropped his hands at his sides, and took deep breaths, settling his mind. *It's now or never. There's no turning back once I show up in Drew's room.* Jonah called up the images of Latrell, a troubled Lynn, disillusioned Wick, and finally, an injured Robert. The images pushed away any lingering doubts. That done, he mentally nudged himself into a phase.

*

Drew was exactly where Jonah expected to find him. In fact, the boy was reaching over to type something on his computer keyboard when Jonah suddenly appeared. Drew's eyes bugged out of his head and he stared at Jonah for a horrified moment, too shocked to say anything or even move.

Jonah took advantage of the surprise, lunging forward, and grabbing the front of the boy's t-shirt before phasing them both away.

They reappeared a second later inside the lower hallway of the high school. As soon as Jonah released Drew, the boy screamed and scrambled away to press his back against a wall.

"How did I get here?" Drew shouted.

Jonah watched, allowing the silence to build.

"Who are you?" The boy grew more frantic.

Jonah raised his arms and gestured at the surrounding hallway and the nearby bathrooms. It was a hotspot that the anti-bullying club often patrolled, and something else. He once noticed during one of his shifts that it was invisible to the motion detectors. He and Drew could move around without setting off any of the alarms.

"This is where you bullied him," Jonah said, careful to change up his voice. In fact, he spoke in a low and measured tone, trying to sound like Marcus.

Drew's eyes dilated even wider. "Latrell! Is that you?"

"No!" Jonah stepped toward him. "What did Latrell ever do to you?"

The bully cringed against the wall. "We were just having fun."

"Fun?" Jonah loomed closer.

Drew jerked away. "We never thought he'd kill himself."

Anger surged through Jonah. He grabbed Drew and hurled the boy against the opposite wall of lockers.

Drew cried out when he hit the wall and slid to the floor. "Please don't hurt me!" he begged as he curled into a defensive ball.

Jonah only dimly registered that he'd just thrown the hefty kid like he weighed nothing. It seemed like a spike of power must've entered his body. The lingering effects of the surprising extra strength suffused Jonah as he stood over Drew.

In desperation, the boy jumped to his feet and threw a punch, but Jonah easily blocked the attack. Moving with practiced grace, he gripped Drew and flipped the boy over a shoulder and onto the hard floor.

"Ow!" Drew squirmed in pain and tried to crawl away. "Please. I'm sorry!"

"No, you aren't!" Jonah gripped him by the ankle and phased again.

They reappeared outside Latrell's house this time, in the middle of the quiet street. Before Drew could react, Jonah hauled him to his feet and clamped a gloved hand over his mouth. Again, power augmented his movements, allowing him to hold the stocky boy with no problem.

"Did you tell his parents you were sorry?" Jonah hissed in Drew's ear. "I think you laughed it off with Brandon." Drew mumbled against the glove, but Jonah wasn't prepared to let him talk. "Did you tell Latrell you were sorry?"

Jonah phased them again to the roof of the high school, perching on top of the solar energy array. He hustled Drew toward the edge and a four-story drop. "Maybe people will think you took *your* own life."

Drew howled against the gloved hand before wetting himself.

The pungent smell hit Jonah a moment later. "Nice," he said, shifting to avoid being splashed by the growing puddle at their feet. Then he phased them again, sooner than planned, to get away from the mess.

They reappeared in Oak Hill cemetery. Drew let out a muffled scream when he saw the headstones. Jonah pushed him to the ground, right in front of Latrell's grave. He felt a savage satisfaction at the bully's raw fear. *Let him think he's gonna die.*

"I'm sorry!" The words tumbled out of Drew's mouth between wet sobs.

"Tell that to Latrell," Jonah growled.

Drew reached out his shaking hands toward the headstone. "I'm sorry, Latrell. I'm so sorry."

Jonah stood behind him. "Tell that to the principal too. Confess your crime."

"I will. I swear. Please don't kill me. I don't want to die."

"Latrell didn't want to die either, not until you and Brandon made his life utterly miserable."

Drew broke down into more sobs.

Jonah was sick of him. Besides, the dizziness had increased and he still needed to get himself home. He gripped Drew by the back of the neck and phased to the boy's bedroom, where Jonah shoved the bully onto the bed.

Amulet of the Goddess

"Remember," Jonah said. "Confess." With that, he turned and phased.

*

The mask and hoodie were suffocating Jonah. He stripped them off as soon as he entered his room and collapsed on his bed. His heart was beating so fast that he became light-headed and dizzy. Unwrapping a piece of candy proved difficult, as his hands shook. Once he managed that, however, and popped it into his mouth, he lay back on the bed and closed his eyes.

Several minutes later, the excitement wore off but his hands trembled again. He pushed himself pretty far tonight. Too far, if he were being honest.

No, the angry voice in his head answered. Drew deserved it. Brandon did too. He just hoped that Drew would come forward and snitch on Brandon. Then he intended to deal with Antwan's cousin separately.

After his head cleared, Jonah rolled off the bed, undid the black pants, and put them and the rest of the disguise inside a large shopping bag with handles. He pushed it into the back corner of his closet. As he lay in bed again, the events of the previous night caught up to him.

Did he do anything to give himself away? Jonah doubted that. But what if Drew told someone instead of confessing? *What would happen then?* Jonah wondered. Well, apart from Brandon, perhaps no one would believe the kid.

Jonah enjoyed the pleasant image of the snobby boy wetting his own expensive pants. He smiled to himself for a brief moment before a sobering fear intruded.

What if he had really hurt Drew? He threw the boy across the hall. Where did the sudden burst of strength come from? For once, Jonah wished he could go to Alliance HQ, sit down in one of their libraries, and read all about the powers of a Fallen Reaper. Well, there was Hackett's, but he didn't want to face Alastor right now.

Besides, he wasn't totally clueless about Fallen Reapers. It made sense that his Reaper half could provide him with extra power. But since he never was able to call on it before, he could only wonder why now? Jonah fumed because his godfather never explained any of those things to him.

As much as he wanted to dwell on that aspect of the evening, his mind wouldn't cooperate. His thoughts returned to his original question. Did he really do that for Latrell?

Maybe I did it for myself? He was quite satisfied with his actions. Someone needed to confront Drew.

Although his anger had waned, the deeper frustration and sense of isolation remained. No one could know about what he'd done. Lynn would kill him if she ever found out and Mike wouldn't talk to him for months, if ever again. This was his own private, little war on the bullies and now he knew he'd have to fight it alone.

CHAPTER NINETEEN
BAD-TEMPERED BULLY

School was uneventful for Jonah on Monday, which was fine because he felt lethargic from lack of sleep. What worried him was Drew's absence. He hadn't hurt the boy, not seriously. So why wasn't he around? Brandon and Antwan didn't act as if Drew had confessed. Not in the hallways, nor at lunch.

Doubts began to assail Jonah. Did he do the right thing? The voice inside his head was sure he did.

Toward the end of his lunch period, Jonah strode to his locker alone, still trying to calm his mind and banish his uncertainties. He had just removed his book for the next period when Mike came up. Jonah was shocked. Mike's eyes were heavy with bags beneath them. And his posture was somewhat stooped.

He leaned against the adjacent locker, watching Jonah. Although he seemed tired, Mike's eyes darted around, taking in everyone who passed by. He fidgeted with his own book. In fact, his hands never stopped moving.

"Mike? Are you okay?"

He seemed to have forgotten Jonah was there, even though he just walked up to him. "Yeah. Why?"

"You look like you haven't been sleeping."

Mike snorted. "You're one to talk! You look like the walking dead." He turned, leaning his back against the locker. "I'm fine."

Jonah began to suspect his friend needed the locker for support. "Where's your ribbon?"

Mike glanced down at his shirt and his eyes widened. Fumbling briefly in his pocket, he withdrew a bent, orange ribbon, and attached it to his shirt. "Happy?"

Jonah couldn't believe it. Mike was neat to a fault. His clothes were always clean and pressed and he seemed so put together. Today, his shirt was wrinkled, causing Jonah to doubt that he ironed it–and he even suspected he might have slept in it.

"I'm fine, Jonah. I just want to complete the translation. It's a lot of work and…" His voice trailed off. He shook his head and seemed to snap back to attention, narrowing his eyes at someone over Jonah's shoulder.

Brandon and Antwan sauntered by and snickered at them.

"Aw, you're so cute with the pumpkin ribbons!" He and Antwan laughed as they walked away.

"Idiots." Mike smacked the flat of his hand against the locker while glaring at the retreating boys.

Jonah was reassured by his buddy's reaction, and that reminded him that Mike would probably know about Drew. "Hey, have you seen Drew?"

"Nope. Why?"

Jonah hid his surprise by hooking a thumb at Brandon and Antwan. "It's only been those two clowns today."

"Oh, well, maybe Drew came to his senses."

"I doubt it," Jonah said. Now that he was on the subject, he was sure he could persuade Mike to give Drew a call. He just needed to prod his friend without seeming too interested.

Before he could come up with a way to do that, Patrick arrived and Mike's attention refocused like a laser.

"See you later," Mike said as he waved. Patrick gave Jonah little more than a suspicious glare before they walked off.

Thoughts of visiting Patrick one night in the disguise became more appealing by the second. Jonah slammed his locker closed and turned for class. That's when he spotted Latrell standing, or rather, floating in the middle of the hall. Streams of students walked through his ghostly body.

Amulet of the Goddess

It was interesting to watch the kids' reactions to his presence. Some shivered while others didn't seem to notice anything. And if the boy's presence wasn't weird enough, he turned and floated through the closed auditorium door. Jonah hurried after him.

The stage lights were on, shining down on semi-circular rows of folding chairs set up in concert formation. The band and orchestra agreed to combine for a one-time Halloween concert.

Despite the bright lights, Jonah had no problems spotting Latrell, who stood off to the side of the auditorium, near the back.

Jonah slipped down the row and stopped beside the ghost. "I know you're connected to the ankh you gave me." Latrell didn't respond so Jonah added, "What are you doing here?"

"I wanted to see you."

"You can't just show up unannounced." Jonah dropped into a seat while keeping an eye out for anyone who might overhear. "Why were you at Drew's?"

"Because you were." Latrell's ghostly eyes stared at Jonah's chest.

He wondered if the ghost could see the amulet beneath his sweater. "Well, stop doing that, okay?"

"I saw Brandon in the hallway. When you asked where he lived, I thought you'd do something to him."

"He was out of town. I…" Jonah hesitated, but was not sure why. "I visited Drew. I wanted to scare him into confessing his part in bullying you."

"You did that for me?"

Jonah nodded, expecting Latrell to smile. Instead, the boy looked worried. "What's wrong?"

Latrell didn't reply. After an awkward moment, he reached out to touch the pumpkin ribbon pinned to Jonah's chest. The semi-transparent finger passed through the fabric and chilled Jonah where it touched his skin. Meanwhile, the ankh around Jonah's neck flared with heat. The combination of cold and hot caused Jonah to suck in a startled breath.

Latrell pulled his hand away. "Sorry."

"It's fine." He held out his hand. Latrell hesitated before touching his palm to Jonah's. It felt weird, besides being cold. But Jonah imagined he could feel the texture of skin on Latrell's palm. "Can you make yourself more solid? One of the Wraiths in your basement did."

"That takes time and uses a lot of power." Latrell attempted a caressing motion with his hand but his fingers slipped through Jonah's. That seemed to sadden the boy and he withdrew his hand. "It's easier for a Wraith to share a mortal's body."

"You mean by possession?" Jonah shuddered. "No, thank you."

"But it doesn't have to be possession. That's forceful. A person can choose to share their body."

The eagerness in Latrell's voice worried Jonah. "I'm sorry, Latrell. I could never do that."

"Never?"

Jonah shook his head. In the back of his mind was a fleeting memory of something terrible that happened. It was connected to this subject. Despite the sense of dread that accompanied the notion, Jonah tried to call it up, but hit a wall. The more he tried, the more his head throbbed. He abandoned the effort.

Latrell moved closer, peering at him the whole time. "What was that? You looked like it hurt."

Jonah leaned away from the ghost. "I'm okay."

A band member walked onto the stage and moved around the back of the chairs. "My lunch period's ending," Jonah whispered.

Latrell nodded, then glanced down at his folded hands. "Thank you."

"You're welcome," Jonah replied but Latrell had already disappeared.

He stood and hitched his book bag in place while thinking about Latrell's cryptic request. He'd never let a Wraith share his body. Not even a sad boy like Latrell. Again, the wretched feeling that something terrible had happened to him pressed on the edges of his awareness.

Jonah's mind replayed the strange encounter all through his next class and afterward, until Mike came running up. He pulled Jonah to their first patrol spot, across from a boy's bathroom on the lower level. Jonah's face

Amulet of the Goddess **785**

warmed because it was the same location where he had phased with Drew the night before.

He wiggled out of Mike's death grip. "What's up?"

"Drew!" Mike gulped and glanced around, lowering his voice. "He and his parents came to the main office this afternoon. I was talking to the secretary when they marched in." Mike's news was interrupted by two fellow ninth-graders being rough with each other.

Once they turned the corner, Jonah nudged his friend. "Well?"

"He confessed to the principal that he bullied Latrell." Mike folded his arms, looking disgusted. "I tried to talk to him, and then he goes and does that!"

Jonah acted as if he were shocked by the news. "Did he report Brandon?"

"No, but Brandon would just deny it, Jonah. He's not dumb. And his father's important enough to make a big stink about it." Mike paused as a couple of girls walked by. "Drew should've been the last person to bully Latrell. I can't believe hanging out with Brandon means that much to him."

Jonah shrugged. "Maybe it does."

"Well, at least there's some good in him."

"What do you mean?"

"He came forward and admitted it," Mike pointed out. "So it must have been eating him up inside."

Jonah wanted to tell his friend that Drew had no intention of confessing until after his private visit, which scared him into it. The way Jonah saw it, if Drew were truly sorry, he'd have no problem telling on Brandon.

The last period bell rang. Mike pushed off the wall, and Jonah followed.

Before the end of the day, the entire school knew about Drew's confession, primarily through texting and instant chat apps. Jonah wondered if the boy would ever show his face again. The whole situation scared him a bit. He'd been the cause of this development, but it also set his resolve. *One bully down, one to go.*

*

Brandon proved to be a difficult target to watch. Between Jonah's school work, Practice Club meetings about the coming Halloween Bonfire, Tolerance Club, and other obligations, he couldn't scout Brandon's house until late in the day.

The other problem was the Warners' house itself. As Jonah had discovered while visiting Latrell's room, Brandon's house had a wall around it. Jonah borrowed Lynn's binoculars so he could spy on the bully from a distance. To his mounting dismay, he found that wouldn't work because the houses on either side of Brandon's also had stone or brick walls, as well as screening shrubbery.

Jonah's frustration grew as his search for a suitable hiding place proved fruitless. Plus, he was afraid someone would notice him loitering around the upscale neighborhood. As if proving Jonah's fear, Brandon exited his front gate.

For a critical few seconds, Jonah froze, unsure of what to do. Then he dived behind a nearby SUV. If Brandon caught him, the entire plan would be ruined. Only now did it occur to Jonah to phase away.

Feeling a bit embarrassed, he prepared to phase when he heard Brandon speak. "I told you, I don't care about law school."

"Brandon," his mother's urgent voice cut in. "Quiet. You're making a scene."

"What do you expect?" Brandon's dad said.

Jonah peeked around the edge of the SUV. Brandon's mother glanced up and down the street, as if she were worried about the neighbors overhearing. She and her husband were dressed in elegant evening attire. The dad's expensive coat was folded over his left arm.

"Your great-grandfather, grandfather, and I have worked hard to build our firm to the respected establishment it is today. You have no idea what they had to go through to stay alive, literally, in the South." He stepped closer to his son, towering over him. "We didn't work this hard to see you go out and prove a stereotype about young black men only being fit to play ball or wave a microphone around on a stage."

"But I'm good and I worked hard at it. The coach wants me on–"

"I'll have a word with the coach and extend my regrets. You will not be on the team this year, nor any future year."

Amulet of the Goddess

"Listen to your father," Mrs. Warner urged. "Our plans for you are much higher. A judgeship or even the State House."

Mr. Warner arched an eyebrow and his voice sounded dangerous. "You will comply with our wishes or you'll find out how hard things can be. Drew won't be the only one confessing. My protection for your chronic pattern of missteps will cease. Is that understood?"

"Yes, sir." Brandon sulked.

Seeing the arrogant boy so cowed was a new experience for Jonah. Again, he couldn't deny a smattering of pity for him. Just then, at the far end of the street, a black car came toward them. Jonah ducked under cover again as the car slowed, but not before noting it was a black limousine. The car pulled up until it was even with the Warners.

A huge man in a black suit that was stretched tight cross his large frame exited the front passenger side. Jonah sucked in a breath because he recognized him as the hulking man from Robert's sketch and Jonah's dream-walk. What shocked Jonah the most was the little, white skull the man wore on his left lapel.

Jonah had seen the small skull before. Mr. Warner had once escorted Agent Hunter and a serious-looking man in a dark suit and sunglasses around the Teen Center. Mike claimed the mysterious man was a security expert but Jonah remembered seeing the same small skull on the guy's suit coat.

So far, the only people Jonah had encountered wearing the small skulls were either Wraith-possessed or working with the Wraiths. That ignited a whole fury of questions about Mr. Warner.

What was he doing with this huge guy? Was Mr. Warner involved with the Alliance mole too? At least Brandon's dad didn't wear a skull on his expensive suit lapel.

The hulking guy gave the Warners a perplexed look. "You didn't have to wait here, sir. We coulda driven up to the house."

Mr. Warner glared at his son. "We were dealing with a minor problem."

The hulking guy shrugged and opened the back door.

Mrs. Warner got in, but Mr. Warner paused to speak to his son. "Your mother and I will be back this evening around ten."

Brandon's dad got into the car. The huge guy hurried around, moving quickly for his size. As soon as he closed his own door, the car drove off down the street.

That's when Brandon called out, "I know you're hiding behind the truck, freak."

Jonah's heart nearly leapt into his throat as he stood.

Brandon's face was a mask of fury. "I don't care what you heard—"

"I wasn't listening," Jonah lied.

"Then why are you here?"

Jonah moved around the vehicle to face the bully and gestured to the house across the street. "I was talking to Latrell's mom."

Brandon's face paled and he took a step away from Jonah. He seemed to realize he was showing fear and his face twisted in anger. "What did you do to me and Antwan?"

"I don't know what you mean."

Brandon jabbed a finger at him. "You did something to our memories." He moved closer. "I have a block. That's what Antwan's cousin said."

Uh-oh. Jonah was at a loss. He racked his brain, trying to stall and think of something to put the bully off.

Brandon noticed. "I knew it! What's going on?"

"Why don't you ask Antwan's cousin?"

To his surprise, Brandon scowled. "She won't tell me anything else about you, but she knows."

Jonah relaxed upon hearing that. He could be totally honest with Brandon. "I didn't do anything to you. I swear."

"Liar!" Brandon yelled after checking to make sure no one overheard him. "When I find out, you'll get it, freak." He spun on his heels and headed down the street.

With his original mission busted, Jonah decided to trail the bully. As he went along, he reflected on the unnerving conversation. Niqab Girl's willingness to keep Brandon in the dark was fortunate. *Maybe she didn't trust him either.*

Amulet of the Goddess

Brandon reached a nearby park, and Jonah discovered it was the same one Danita and Mike had mentioned. *Too bad the black cat wouldn't show up and eat Brandon*, he thought with savage pleasure.

But he didn't have time to dwell on that pleasant prospect because he had to pick a spot to hide in. He chose a large tree close to the picnic table where Brandon stood, and phased. Jonah's placement was perfect because he could overhear the boy's phone call.

"Drew told me someone was outside his house. That was right before he went crazy and confessed. So what?" Brandon paused to puff on a lit cigarette. "Why does your cousin want me to be careful?" He paused again, then threw his cigarette butt away.

"I don't like her bossing me around, Antwan. She's hiding what she knows about Jonah. I just saw the freak in my neighborhood. If she wants me to leave him alone, she better talk–or else." Brandon frowned and swore under his breath as he listened. "Fine. Whatever."

Jonah ducked behind the tree when Brandon turned on the spot, checking the area. "We still heading to the party tomorrow night, right?" He paused again. "Yeah, yeah. I'll meet you at your place. I'll be there at seven. I want to leave before my folks come home."

Jonah smiled. He knew exactly where Brandon would be the next evening. If he could see the boy's room–even if it were only in pictures, it would work. The main problem was that he didn't have any pictures.

As Jonah headed home for the evening, it occurred to him that Drew might have the type of videos or pictures he needed. And since Mike still talked to the boy, Jonah thought he could persuade his buddy to help. It was a slim chance, but his only option at this point.

CHAPTER TWENTY
ONE DOWN AND ONE TO GO

Jonah's first sight of Mike's bedroom convinced him that something was wrong. Mike's eclectic group of posters, everything from music groups to famous black scientists, still covered the walls. And the model planes of the famous Red Tails still hung on near-invisible threads from the ceiling.

But his two calendars that were filled with marks and circled dates that normally hung on the wall near the window were missing. Jonah thought he spotted the corner of one under a pile of books.

Mike had half his collection of supernatural, mythology, and alternative history books scattered around the room. And the starscape bedspread, which Jonah loved, lay hidden beneath the clutter of loose pages and magazines.

Jonah dropped his book bag on the only clear space of floor he could find, beside a beanbag chair.

Mike moved from an open book on his desk, to a notebook on his bed, and finally to another book on his dresser. He only paused for a few moments in between each move. All the while, he tapped a pen against his bottom lip while muttering to himself. Jonah feared this could have been a side effect of the mind boost.

When Mike tried to cross to his desk to repeat the circuit, Jonah jumped in front of him, blocking his way. Mike blinked as if he just remembered that he had let Jonah into the house.

He tried to step around, but Jonah gripped his thin arms and shook him. "What's wrong with you?"

"Nothing." Mike squirmed out of Jonah's grip and backed away, crossing his arms. "I need to finish these projects and my homework before I go to the clubhouse to work on the translations."

"Are you sleeping?" Jonah doubted that, especially after seeing the bed. And that brought up another point. "How come your mom hasn't noticed?"

Mike's face reddened a bit. "I sneak out early for school and…" He gestured to the corner of the desk and a couple of plates with half-eaten food on them.

That explained the foul smell. Jonah wrinkled his nose. "Is it the Enhancer or the compass?"

Mike blinked. "No. I'm fine with the compass. I only use it when they call, like when Marcus and Rex crossed over."

"What?! You saw Marcus?"

"Yeah. I didn't tell you?" Mike scratched his head. "I forgot. He said to say hello to you." Mike tried to get to the dresser again.

Jonah blocked him. "Mike, are you on something?" he asked, considering for the first time it could have been drugs but hating the very notion.

Mike glared back at him. "No, Jonah! I'm not on drugs." He threw up his arms in irritation. "Why did you come over?"

Even though Jonah had rehearsed his response, he hesitated to answer. The problem was that he didn't know if Mike would insist on all the details of the plan or not. "I need to ask you about Drew."

Mike stared at him as if he were trying to understand what he said. "Drew? Not that again."

"No, not that," Jonah said. "I wanted to know if Drew ever showed you pictures of Brandon?"

The abrupt changes that washed over Mike's tired, light complexion would have been funny at any other time. At first, he was shocked, then curious. "Don't tell me you like Brandon."

"No." Jonah grimaced and lowered his voice. "I don't like Brandon."

"Then why do you want pictures of him?"

"I don't want pictures of *him*. I wanted to know if Drew ever showed you Brandon's–"

"Brandon's what?"

"His house, what else?" Jonah could feel his face warming.

Mike shook his head and sat on the edge of the bed. He ignored the dislodged papers that slid to the floor. "I don't get it."

"I want to see if he lied about how rich he is."

"He didn't."

Jonah searched the messy room and spotted what he looked for. Mike's laptop was on the desk underneath a stack of papers. Jonah pushed the pages off and opened the computer. "Did Drew ever show you pictures?"

"He's posted stuff before, yeah."

"Show me." Jonah pressed his hands together in a pleading gesture and added, "Please."

Mike let out a tired breath, came over, and called up a social website. He opened a private photo album that Drew shared with his friends. Inside were tons of pictures and numerous videos. Jonah grew impatient with flipping through the photos. They didn't show enough of the background.

"Try the videos."

Selecting one that featured Drew, Brandon, Antwan, and two other guys, Mike leaned back to let Jonah look.

"Happy?" Mike asked.

"Not really." The video, taken at Brandon's home, showed more detail, but only in the kitchen area. The boys' mindless antics bored Jonah. "Do any of the photos show his bedroom?"

Mike's eyes narrowed. "Why do you want to see that?" Losing his focus, his eyes settled on the open books.

Jonah felt a bit ashamed using Mike's distraction to his advantage, but he tapped the laptop to get his buddy's attention. "Just show me, okay?"

After refocusing on the computer, and a moment of shuffling through the posted videos, Mike found a clip of Brandon and his buddies in the boy's bedroom. It was larger than any bedroom Jonah had ever seen and featured a huge bed, a very expensive-looking desk, and a computer. The

Amulet of the Goddess 793

dark wood dresser had a large mirror. Brandon also had a sitting area and what looked like a huge plasma TV and game consoles.

Jonah had only seen a room like Brandon's in magazines about expensive houses. *Gee whiz.* A big part of him was envious and he wondered if that was why Drew hung around the boy. On the plus side, the huge space made phasing there safer.

He rewound the video back so he could take in details of the room again but Mike snapped the laptop closed.

Jonah snatched his fingers out of harm's way. "Why'd you do that?"

"You're not planning on phasing to Brandon's house, are you?"

Jonah wondered how long it would take Mike to connect the dots. "No," he lied. "Why would I want to go to Brandon's house?"

Mike lowered his gaze as he rubbed his hand over the laptop cover. "Jonah, you have powers…"

"And?"

"Well, I'm not saying you would ever do this, but some kids might try to use their powers for stupid purposes."

Jonah couldn't face Mike's piercing gaze, so he crossed to the window. Mike came over and slung one arm over Jonah's right shoulder and the other underneath his left arm, hugging him.

Jonah relaxed a bit into the embrace. The hugs had become a comforting gesture whenever something was bothering one of them. There hadn't been any recently.

Mike rested his chin on Jonah's shoulder and whispered, "Tell me you aren't doing anything dumb."

"Tell me what's wrong with you," Jonah countered. He waited, wondering if Mike would answer.

"I don't know. I just have to work all the time. It's like… I can't stop myself." Mike shook him. "When are we gonna talk? I figured we'd tell each other about anyone we met."

"Then why didn't you tell me about Patrick?"

Mike let out a long breath. It was warm against Jonah's shoulder. "I didn't think you'd understand. Patrick's not supernatural. And after Trevor, I couldn't face being with someone in that world."

Jonah tightened his jaw. "I guess I can understand."

"And he's not my soulmate either. That person is still out there."

"Soulmate?" Jonah gaped at his friend.

"Yeah. You know, the right one for me."

"I got that. But how can you be sure?"

"Because, whenever I use the compass, it's like I can see possible futures, and sense the possibilities. In all of them, someone's out there for me, just over the horizon."

Jonah's jaw dropped. "You've been using the compass a lot, huh?"

"The Alliance asks me to do things for them."

"Oh, the top-secret stuff you can't tell me about."

Mike ignored Jonah's jab. "Patrick's just…"

"An idiot?" Jonah offered.

"No. A break from the weird. True, he can be a pain. He wants to move so fast and do… everything."

"You mean, like go all the way?" Jonah twisted around to see his friend's face.

"Yeah."

"Did you…"

"No! Jonah, I told you, he's not the one!"

"So you're saving yourself?"

Mike eyed him. "Yes, I am. You think it doesn't work that way for us, too?"

Saving ourselves for the right person. The idea hadn't occurred to Jonah. He wasn't at that point yet. "Did you see anyone for me in your crystal ball?" Jonah snorted.

Amulet of the Goddess   795

Mike shook him. "It's not hard to figure out your soulmate."

"Really?"

"No. It's Kevin."

Jonah couldn't deny Mike's words. The very thought of Kevin being his soulmate filled him with an old warmth deep inside. It was something from their first promise, and Jonah was reassured that it still remained. If only he and Kevin could be in the same state at the same time, things might be different.

Mike patted Jonah's chest. "Now, promise me you're not gonna do something dumb."

Jonah thought about it. What he had planned was the right thing. It worked with Drew, so it should work again. "I'm not doing anything wrong." His voice was steady because he was certain he was right.

Mike released him and crossed over to the desk.

For a moment, Jonah considered confessing everything to his friend. But his smoldering anger at Brandon and Latrell's subsequent suicide prevented him from doing so. Plus, Mike had gone back to shifting from one open book to another.

"See you later," Jonah called out as he grabbed his book bag and left.

Two hours later, Mike's questions still nagged him while he rode to the Teen Center. Jonah ignored the lingering doubt and locked his bike in the rack. He walked around the building and scrambled down the hill to the creek. As expected, no one was around.

With Brandon leaving his house so early, Jonah didn't have the luxury of waiting until midnight and sneaking out of his house again. So he chose the deserted area near the creek.

He pulled his disguise out of a newer book bag rather than his cherished older bag. He planned to hide the bag while he was away, but there was still a chance someone might find it. Better to lose the new one than his old one. After pulling the mask down over his face, he drew the hoodie forward to cover his head.

One thing was different: He wasn't nearly as nervous this time. Maybe that was because he'd already done this once, and gotten away with it. In fact, Jonah felt so cavalier, he predicted he'd be home in time for dinner.

He drew in a breath but froze when he heard the quiet crinkle of crushing leaves on the hill. He didn't move as he listened for additional sounds. It was a bird, he decided, hopping along the ground or a squirrel foraging for nuts. When he didn't hear another sound, he phased.

Brandon sat on his overly large bed, earbuds on. He was bopping his head to music when Jonah appeared. The boy let out a scream and jumped backward, slamming into his substantially hard headboard. Jonah smirked as he took a step toward the bed, delighting in Brandon's terror.

He reached out to grab the frightened bully when he suddenly felt a slight change in the air pressure. A dark shape appeared beside him. Jonah almost screamed, himself, when the newcomer grabbed his arm and phased him away.

Amulet of the Goddess

CHAPTER TWENTY-ONE
INTERVENTION

As Jonah plunged through the aether, he struggled to come to grips with the sudden change of events. He was also aware of who grabbed him. *Kevin.* When the outside world reappeared, Jonah immediately recognized his parents' hideaway.

He jerked his arm free just as Kevin released him. Thrown off-balance, Jonah stumbled forward and sprawled on the patchwork bricks of the hideaway's lower courtyard.

"No more vigilante work tonight," Kevin's muffled voice said. The young Fallen Reaper removed his mask.

Jonah scrambled to his feet and shoved Kevin in response. "Why'd you do that?" His own voice was muffled and he paused to throw back his hood and yank off his mask. "You messed up everything!" He tried to shove Kevin again.

The older boy blocked Jonah's attempt and pushed him away with an irritated huff. "I'm making sure you don't bother another innocent person tonight."

"Innocent?" Anger surged through Jonah. "Brandon's not innocent!"

"It's not up to you to decide that!" Kevin shouted back. He darted forward and grabbed hold of Jonah.

"Let me go!" Despite his struggling, Kevin managed to turn him around and hold him in a one-armed bear hug.

Jonah growled in frustration when Kevin checked his watch.

"Let me go!"

"Will you shut up?" Kevin hissed. "I'm waiting for an Alliance Council member, okay?"

Jonah's insides went cold. It was one thing for Kevin to catch him, but if a Council Member were coming, Jonah knew he was in big trouble.

After another glance at his watch, Kevin's impatient breath came almost at the same time a pinpoint of light appeared before them. The glittering shape expanded and formed into an undulating Alliance symbol of three interlocking circles with a pair of wings above.

Jonah's squirming ceased as the beacon flared and faded away before a vortex formed in the air. *Oh boy*, he said to himself, fearing the extremely serious Mage Rubio would appear through the magical opening this time. He had used the Alliance beacon before to announce his arrival.

However, the person who appeared on the other side wasn't Rubio, nor, to Jonah's surprise, was it Symon Trueblood, either. This Council person was short, bald, with large, black-rimmed glasses and an oversized, curly mustache.

As he exited the vortex, the mage continued a conversation with a young woman who also came through. The short mage signed a form she held out for him.

"Yes, yes. I'll take care of that when I get back." He motioned the woman back through and closed the vortex with an impatient gesture. After adjusting his royal blue tunic, he took quick, little steps toward Jonah.

"You've pulled me from important Council business, Mr. Brown." He had a stern-sounding voice that wouldn't have been out of place in a strictly run classroom.

"Sorry, sir. I know you're busy," Kevin replied in an unusually subdued and businesslike voice.

"Well, some things can be overlooked when it concerns the Deliverer." The mage adjusted his glasses and peered closer at Jonah. When he continued to fiddle with the spectacles, Jonah wondered if they were enchanted.

"You favor your mother," the mage said, "that's for sure. But I also see Isaiah in you." He beckoned Kevin closer. "Come, come. I have a lot of work to complete before the evening is over."

Amulet of the Goddess   **799**

Kevin shuffled Jonah closer. The man raised his right hand, the palm glowing. Jonah's first thought was that the mage would hex him.

As the short man waved his hand back and forth, Jonah realized what he was doing and squirmed even more fiercely in Kevin's grip. "Don't take away my memories!"

The mage's curly mustache twitched. "Really, young man, I'm not taking away anything. I'm not a Mind Bender."

Jonah stared at the mage in confusion. "A Mind Bender? What–"

"I'm merely determining if you've been hexed."

"What?"

"Be quiet," Kevin ordered, sounding more serious than Jonah had ever heard the boy before.

Jonah clamped his mouth shut and watched as the mage continued the examination, which consisted of a light pressure on his skull. The whole experience reminded him of the sensation he received when Robert read his concentrated thoughts. The instinctive thing for Jonah was to resist, and he did. *Get out of my mind*, he thought.

"He's clean," the mage announced, pulling his hand away with a jerk. "Thank goodness for that. You have a strong will, young man, as well as the maddening shortsightedness of all adolescents."

Jonah bristled at the dig. "Who are you?"

"I'm Council Member Mage Albrecht." He didn't offer to shake hands like Trueblood did and instead, Albrecht clasped his hands behind his back. "I work with your godfather from time-to-time."

"Where's Mage Trueblood?" Jonah asked.

Albrecht raised an eyebrow at Jonah's tone. "He didn't think it wise to return, given your uncle's feelings. And unlike me, he's not a certified Memory Charmer."

"Whoa." Jonah didn't know that members of the Alliance could do more than one thing. When his awe of the newcomer began to wane, he focused on the mage's original statement. "Why'd you think I was hexed?"

"Because," Kevin answered, "you went all Batman on Brandon and Drew."

Jonah was stunned and angered because that meant… "You were watching me the whole time?"

Kevin released him. "You bet I was! When I followed you to the creek, I thought you were sneaking out for a date. Then you phased away." Kevin wiggled an admonishing finger at him.

Jonah was about to argue his case when Albrecht cleared his throat to get their attention.

"As Mr. Brown mentioned," Albrecht began, "you can't use your powers for vigilantism. Marcus agrees."

"He's back?" Jonah's stomach churned at hearing that. "You told him?"

"Yes, we did," Albrecht answered. "Marcus is meeting with members of the Council." He glanced at his watch. "I really should have been there, but…" He gestured to Jonah.

"Sorry. I didn't mean for that to happen."

"Really?" Kevin chided. "You weren't sorry fifteen minutes ago."

Jonah wanted to jab the boy with an elbow but refrained with Albrecht watching him. "So, you thought I was hexed?"

"Given your ill-advised actions, yes." The mage's gaze penetrated Jonah, every bit as invasive as a Reaper Stare.

Jonah grimaced under the scrutiny. He boiled with anger at the thought of Kevin watching him without revealing he was even around. The situation reminded Jonah that there was another person secretly hanging around. "What about the Alliance person in town? I thought he was spying on me." Jonah sucked in a breath. "Did he tell you about Drew?"

"No, he didn't." Albrecht's voice carried definite tones of disapproval. "His name's Alastor."

"Alastor? The guy at Hackett's?"

"Yes. He's a Fallen Reaper," Albrecht added.

Then it all made sense to Jonah. The strangely intense stare that he thought was as strong as a Reaper's really was. Alastor had been scanning his emotions and goading him. The ensuing shame prevented Jonah from confessing to being fooled.

Amulet of the Goddess

Albrecht cocked his head to the side but didn't offer any consoling words like Eleanor or Symon Trueblood would have done.

Maybe Kevin sensed his mood. He patted Jonah's shoulder and said, "We should have warned you about Alastor."

Jonah shrugged. "I thought you couldn't tell me about him?"

"As a Council Member," Albrecht cut in, "I have the authority to share that information with anyone I deem fit. I think you and Kevin should know."

This was so different from his godfather that Jonah perked up at the unexpected opportunity. "So, is he working with the mole?"

"We think so," Albrecht answered. "That person almost ruined our talks with the Afterworld rebels."

And killed Trevor, Jonah thought but didn't add. As his mind raced through everything he knew about the Alliance insider, his jaw dropped. "I saw the mole arguing with Deyanira in a dream-walk one time." When Albrecht glanced at Kevin, Jonah wondered why the mage didn't know that bit. "I told Marcus about the dream-walk. The mole wore a Reaper's coat and covered his face with a mask and filter."

Albrecht shook his head. "With all that happened during the summer, that information was pushed to the side."

"Deliberately?" Kevin asked.

"That would be my guess. The mole wouldn't want the Council focusing on it."

"I can see that," Kevin added, "but why would he cover his face in front of Deyanira? She has to know who he is, doesn't she?"

"Not necessarily," Albrecht hedged. "But I think he covers his face in meetings with Deyanira because of Mr. Blackstone." He eyed Jonah, adjusting his glasses as he did so.

"Alastor knows about your dream-walking power and would have told the mole. Your recent experience seems to confirm it."

Kevin snorted. "And Alastor works for the Hardliners."

When Jonah nodded, Albrecht asked, "You know about them?"

"Yes, sir," Jonah answered. "They want to use me like a weapon."

"It's more complicated than that, but you are essentially correct. They know all about your various abilities."

"And the mole didn't want me to see his face," Jonah concluded.

"You would have told Marcus," Kevin explained, "and blown the mole's cover."

Jonah glanced between the two Alliance members. "Can't you do anything about Alastor or the mole?"

"We can't openly accuse Alastor of anything," Albrecht explained. "We're trying to gather evidence against him first, but he's very careful. If we move too soon, it could cause fractures on the Council. I fear that's the mole's ultimate purpose."

As the mage talked, something else occurred to Jonah. Agent Hunter had been ordered to leave him alone. Could this plan between the mole and his group have already been set in motion? *He knows all about your powers.* That thought scared Jonah. He didn't like strangers looking over reports on everything he could do.

Of course, he couldn't avoid telling Marcus everything, but he never appreciated the fact that his godfather reported to the Council, until now. Another, more ominous conclusion also became clear.

"Oh, my God," Jonah said. "If Alastor knew about my powers, he had to know about Robert, Lynn, Mike, and Wick."

"Yep," Kevin agreed.

Jonah began to pace back and forth, sensing he was on to something. "Alastor could have told the mole about Lynn's intuition. And they must've broken Robert's fingers so he couldn't draw what he sees in a person's mind." He paused to stare at Kevin and Albrecht. "Wick's magic act was ruined by Antwan's cousin. Everyone's been attacked except me!"

Kevin rubbed his chin while watching Jonah. "Well, they sent you out to get revenge."

"Taking advantage of my emotions? You mean they wanted to upset me about things? And attacking my family and friends..." Jonah's voice trailed off. He thought of every encounter he'd had over the past week, trying to fit it into the new information and awareness. When he came to the

Amulet of the Goddess **803**

bookstore Wraith, he wanted to kick himself. The clerk urged him to buy the potions book. Had he been trying to help?

"Could they be using potions?" Jonah asked Albrecht.

"Potions?" Kevin snorted.

Albrecht twirled the end of his mustache. "Potions… Yes, that's a fair point, young man. But I don't think you've been affected by a potion."

Jonah's nervous excitement increased. "Not me. I think they got my cousin Lynn and…" Just now the final piece clicked. "Mike! We have to go and check."

Kevin and Albrecht didn't make any moves to phase, nor open a vortex. Didn't they understand his exigency? He was about to ask that very thing when he felt the change in air pressure.

He turned in time to see his godfather appear, accompanied by Eleanor Trueblood. Jonah was relieved to have his godfather there. But he paused when Marcus drew closer with a grim expression on his face.

CHAPTER TWENTY-TWO
POTIONS MASTER

Jonah braced himself for the lecture when Marcus gripped him by both shoulders. But instead of yelling, his godfather subjected him to a concerned gaze. "Are you okay?"

Jonah nodded. "I'm all right."

A relieved smile tweaked the corners of Marcus's mouth. He looked around the darkened courtyard. "Can we have some lights?"

In response, Eleanor Trueblood raised her hands and muttered, "Illumens." Flares shot into the air and expanded into a small grid of pinpoints. They flooded the courtyard with soft, pale light.

"Thank you."

Eleanor nodded before turning to Kevin and talking in low tones. Meanwhile, Marcus walked around to the opposite side of the courtyard, taking his time. Jonah followed while wondering about his godfather's reserved mood.

When Marcus faced him, it was with a frown. "I'm sure you know why I came down from Atlanta," he began. "Your vigilantism concerns me, despite Alastor's obvious involvement."

His godfather's words were as alarming as a bucket of ice cold water being dumped on his head. "Sorry."

"I understand the temptation to act. And God knows we all make mistakes, Jonah. But we should always learn from them."

Jonah nodded.

Amulet of the Goddess

"That brings me to our second issue," Marcus continued, narrowing his eyes. "We need to discuss your knowledge about the bullies." An edge tainted his voice. "Latrell?"

"I talked to him at his funeral," Jonah confessed.

Marcus closed his eyes and massaged his forehead. "You shouldn't have done that."

"All I did was talk." When Marcus glared at him, Jonah suspected his godfather was scanning his emotions. "I've seen him a few times since then."

"This is certain to be dangerous, far beyond sending you after Brandon and Antwan." Marcus pointed an admonishing finger at Jonah. "Stay away from him."

"But—"

"I mean it. He's a Wraith and clearly working with the mole."

"What if he appears to me again?"

"Command him to leave at once!" Marcus said. "You're a half-Reaper."

"Okay," Jonah muttered, hoping that was the extent of his troubles but sadly suspecting it wasn't.

Marcus withdrew a thin, square box out of his inner coat pocket and held it in both hands. "You must learn to establish control, Jonah. There's a reason we have Memory Charmers like Omar and Albrecht readily available. We can't allow the larger world even a small glimpse of our existence. And we certainly can't tolerate our young trainees abusing their powers."

Marcus held up the box and cracked it open. Two wristbands gleamed inside despite the relative darkness. Both were a flat silver color with Angel script covering their surfaces.

"What are those?"

"I want to make sure you understand the seriousness of what you did." Marcus held the box closer. "Put them on."

Jonah's Death Sense prickled with a slight warning. When his hand neared the bands, he could sense the magic on them. For a moment, he thought they were shield bracelets, but his godfather wouldn't give him something with more power in it. Not as a punishment anyway.

"Jonah..." Marcus's voice took on an edge again.

Accepting that he had no choice, Jonah took the bands and slipped one over each wrist. As soon as he did so, the bands tightened and an unpleasant jolt shot up both arms and collided in his chest.

Jonah sucked in a breath, sensing that something vital had been stripped away.

"The bands nullify your ability to phase," Marcus explained.

A sense of betrayal overwhelmed Jonah next, followed quickly by shameful resignation. His shoulders slumped and his hands dropped to his sides. "How long do I have to wear them?"

Marcus's expression was unreadable. "I'd say a week should do it."

"A week?"

"It could be longer," Marcus warned. "Kevin will have to take you home." He turned and motioned to Trueblood.

"What about the Afterworld, and the rebels?" Jonah asked, ignoring the bands for the moment.

Marcus looked thoughtful. "They are well. It's dangerous work but it'll make a difference when things happen."

"What things?"

"Now's not the time to talk about it. We're due at Headquarters."

Trueblood reached them and graced Jonah with a smile. "It's good to see you again. I hope my brother didn't tarnish the title of mage."

"Ah, no, he didn't." Jonah stammered. "He's..."

"Different," Trueblood finished.

Marcus arched an eyebrow at Jonah. "Learn the lesson." His expression softened a bit. "I'll tell you about the trip some other time. Right now, go help your friend." With that, he placed a hand on Trueblood's elbow and they disappeared.

*

Mike radiated a tired excitement when he answered his front door. He peeked behind Jonah. "Where's Kevin?"

Amulet of the Goddess

"Let's talk." Jonah raised an eyebrow and pushed his buddy inside.

After greeting Mrs. Littleton, who was up in the kitchen, Jonah followed his manic friend down the short flight of stairs to the split-level home's lower floor. Mike turned for his bedroom but Jonah grabbed his arm and pulled him toward the family room.

"Well?" Mike asked as soon as they entered the room.

"Kevin wants to come in through the patio door."

"The patio? Why?"

"He's not alone. A Council mage is here."

Mike's eyes widened in fear. "Not Rubio?"

Jonah shook his head and moved to the sliding doors. "No. Someone else." He slid open the door and stood back.

Mike's eyes were riveted on the short mage as he and Kevin entered the house.

Albrecht glanced around the family room, taking in all the details. "Will we do it here?"

"No," Jonah answered. He nudged Mike. "In your room."

As soon as everyone crowded into the bedroom and closed the door, Mike asked Albrecht, "Who're you?"

The mage cast a spell on the bedroom door before giving his name, as if that were enough of an answer.

"He's a Memory Charmer, like Omar," Jonah explained.

"Wow." Mike offered to shake Albrecht's hand, but once again, the mage refused to do so.

Albrecht's earlier claims of being busy seemed to suddenly vanish, and he took his time surveying the room. He even crossed over to the desk to peruse the books he saw laid out there.

"Excellent! You're a voracious reader." The little mage bounced on his feet as he placed a square, black case on the desk. He turned to Mike, raising his right hand.

"What're you doing?" Mike exclaimed as he reared back and bumped into Jonah.

"He's just scanning you." Jonah leaned against Mike to keep him from moving further away from Albrecht. "He did the same thing to me. It won't hurt."

Albrecht let out a startled sigh almost as soon as he began the probe. "He's been affected. But it's curious." The mage's brow furrowed and he flexed his fingers while skimming all the titles on Mike's bookshelf. "You wouldn't have a potions book, would you?"

Mike blinked several times before answering, "No."

"What's the problem?" Kevin asked.

"It's not what I expected." Albrecht stepped right up to Mike and adjusted his glasses.

Since he wasn't the object of Albrecht's attention, Jonah could study the man's glasses up close and he discovered he was right. The lens wavered and adjusted at the mage's manipulations. They were enchanted.

Albrecht motioned to Mike's mouth. "Open please."

Mike's face reddened. "I haven't brushed my teeth–"

"Do it," Albrecht ordered. Mike obeyed. The mage leaned closer and sniffed before nodding. "Yes, just as I thought." He moved to his small case and opened it to reveal rows of glass vials, all individually labeled. Each had a black, screw cap on top.

Mike hovered over the mage's left shoulder, fascinated by all the vials of mysterious liquids.

"I'll need two small glasses of water," Albrecht announced after removing three of the vials.

"I'll get them," Jonah offered before racing to the kitchen. He asked Mike's mom for a couple of glasses and then returned.

Albrecht placed a spell over the door again and began measuring small amounts of the contents inside the vials into one of the glasses. He swizzled the mixture around before handing the glass to Mike and saying, "Drink up."

Mike obeyed without any fuss.

That impressed Jonah. He expected a little resistance. "So that'll fix my buddy?"

Amulet of the Goddess **809**

"Yes, it'll counteract the potion." The mage began mixing another potion in the second glass.

Meanwhile, Mike blinked and glanced around his room. Jonah watched the dawning horror on his friend's face. It seemed the potion was working faster than anticipated.

Mike gripped the sides of his head as he stared at the mess. "What did I do to my room? I remember, but…"

"Given the effects of the potion, you couldn't stop yourself, young man," Albrecht said.

Mike turned to him. "Yeah, it was crazy."

"How do you feel now?"

"Better. I mean, I don't want to keep studying." He glanced at this room. "Maybe cleaning up would help."

"Sit down first," Albrecht suggested.

When Mike hesitated, Jonah ushered him to the bed and sat down beside him. Albrecht followed and handed Mike the second glass of liquid.

"What'll that one do?" Jonah thought to ask.

Mike didn't wait for the answer but gulped down the second glass of antidote. As soon as he did, his arm went limp and he dropped the glass. Kevin caught it before it hit the carpeted floor.

When Mike slumped sideways onto Jonah's lap, Kevin grinned. "That's what it does!"

"Something to help him sleep," Albrecht added, a slight tinge of humor in his voice.

"Oh," Jonah said. He rested a hand on Mike's shoulder as a low snore escaped his buddy's mouth. "Uh, maybe we should put him in bed?"

"Here," Kevin said. He lifted Mike off Jonah's lap and cradled the boy in his arms. Jonah hurried to clear all the things off the bed by shoving them onto the floor. Then he pulled the covers back so Kevin could lay Mike gently on the bed.

Jonah finished tucking in his buddy before turning to Albrecht. The mage had already returned to his inspection of Mike's books. "Excuse, me," Jonah called out. "What was the potion?"

"Oh, that? It was an infatuation draft," the mage said.

Kevin snorted. "You mean, a love potion?"

Jonah gaped at them. "A love potion?"

"There's no such thing as a true love potion, Mr. Blackstone." Albrecht frowned. "An infatuation draft is designed to merely increase an existing attraction or interest."

"Why'd the cure work so fast on him?" Kevin asked.

The mage had returned to his case and he briefly paused in closing it. "It must be the change he went through to become a Seeker."

"Change?" Jonah tore his gaze from his sleeping friend to stare at the mage. "The mind boost just enhanced his mind, right?"

"Mr. Littleton experienced more than simple mind enhancement. The combination of the mind boost and the activation of the Seeker's compass changed his very nature." Albrecht's voice assumed an excited quality, like he was explaining a successful science experiment in class. "He's no longer totally mortal. He's part supernatural now, like all of us." Albrecht snapped his case closed with a flourish. "I surmise that's why the initial potion didn't work as planned."

"I don't know about that." Kevin gestured at all the books and notebooks around the bedroom. "He really loves reading and doing research. It just pushed it to a crazy level." He shook his head, but a smirk tweaked the corners of his mouth. "Leave it to you nerds to be more interested in reading a book than... well, you know."

When Kevin couldn't hide his sudden embarrassment, Jonah knew at once the older boy was thinking about their last goodbye. Shelving that pleasant memory away for a later, more convenient time, Jonah concentrated on the true culprit. *Patrick*. Somehow, that fool successfully managed to infect Mike with a love potion.

Kevin waved a hand in front of Jonah's face. "What's up?"

Jonah confirmed that Albrecht was examining Mike's books again and then whispered, "I'll tell you who did it later." He glanced at Mike surreptitiously.

Kevin's eyes widened. Then his expression turned sly, and he whispered back, "It wasn't you, was it?"

Amulet of the Goddess

Jonah slugged him in the arm. "No, it wasn't."

Once again, thoughts of phasing Patrick to the middle of a busy highway returned with exponential force. Jonah wanted to do that so bad now that he was already working out the details when two horrible realizations set in.

First, he couldn't phase Patrick (or anyone else) to any location as long as he wore the nullifying bands. Second, Mike described Patrick as non-supernatural. Presumably, that meant the boy didn't know anything about their world. So where would he get an infatuation potion?

The mole? No, Jonah decided. *It had to be the sorceress.* She was running around Mount Vernon and must have been behind all the attacks on his friends and family. Just when he needed his powers most, he was stripped of them.

CHAPTER TWENTY-THREE
PLAUSIBLE DENIABILITY

Jonah held the magic wristbands under the shower's spray, hoping they would short out. To his amazement, they repelled the water droplets. After drying off and dressing for school, he decided to test the bands while heading out back to the shed. He thought about the Practice Club clearing and tried to phase there. A sharp jolt ran up his arm and settled behind his eyes, resulting in an instant headache.

"Nice." Jonah squeezed one eye closed, making it difficult to roll his bike to the front yard. *That was stupid.*

"What's wrong with you?" Mike asked. He had just joined Jonah for the ride to school.

"Nothing." Jonah blinked his eyes, willing the headache to subside. "How're you feeling?"

Mike's smile was shy and slightly embarrassed. "Fine. I really needed the sleep."

Jonah could see that. Mike was once again as neat as ever and fully alert when they set off on the overcast, chilly morning.

Although Jonah was glad to have his buddy riding to school with him, he prepared himself. Mike must have had a lot of questions.

Sure enough, Mike glanced sideways at him and asked, "What happened to me?"

"Someone spiked you with a potion."

"What was it, Jonah? I don't remember anything after I drank from the

Amulet of the Goddess   813

second glass." He narrowed his eyes. "Tell me."

Jonah concentrated on the road ahead. "You sure?"

"Jonah!"

"Okay." Jonah took a deep breath and told him everything Mage Albrecht had said about the potion.

Mike paused at a crosswalk, his jaw working. "A love potion? That weasel!"

"Who?" Jonah acted innocent, but he knew exactly who.

"Patrick." Mike smacked a hand against his handlebar. "I'll kill him."

Jonah snorted. "You don't believe in fighting."

Mike glared at Jonah. His expression changed. "You could always phase him somewhere isolated and leave him there."

Jonah's insides froze. Mike didn't know about the vigilante stuff yet. "My godfather wouldn't like that," he said as they rode on.

They reached the high school a short time later. After securing their bikes, Mike leaned against the rack while gazing at the grey sky. "I'm not surprised."

"How so?" Jonah glanced around all the kids moving by.

"Well, he's pushy about making out," Mike answered in a low voice. "He's jealous of you and doesn't like us hanging out together."

"Tough." Jonah meant it. But talk of Patrick brought up another idea. "Maybe Patrick was supposed to distract you."

"Maybe." Mike kicked at the loose pebbles below the bike racks.

"Sorry," Jonah added.

Without warning, Mike slugged him in the arm. "You don't mean that. You hate Patrick."

"Well, yeah." Jonah rubbed his arm.

Mike hitched up his bag. "Anything else?"

Jonah feared how Mike would take the news that he was changed, so he just came out with it. "Albrecht said you're different now, like me and

Kevin."

Mike grinned. "I already know I'm part supernatural. The Alliance Healers told me the last time I visited HQ for a checkup."

"That doesn't bother you?"

Mike stared off, thinking. "No. The mind boost is permanent." He gazed sheepishly at Jonah. "Well, now I got my wish to be like everyone else. Right?"

Jonah recalled Wick assuring Mike that everyone had a hero inside them. Seeing that his friend really was okay with the change, Jonah smiled. "The club's meeting after school with Kevin and Albrecht."

"What about?"

"We need to figure out what the mole is doing. I'm sure it's about me."

"It's *always* about you, Jonah." Mike shoved him. "I'll be there." He glanced at his watch. "We're gonna be late."

Jonah bowed and motioned for Mike to go first. "Lead the way, Pathmaker."

Mike laughed. As they headed inside the high school, they talked about Mike being a Seeker before speculating on everything that had happened so far. With all the other things going on, Jonah was glad to have his best friend back.

*

Alliance adults crowded the attic clubhouse. Not only had Kevin and Albrecht arrived, but Mage Symon Trueblood and Rex were also there.

The big, blond Fallen Reaper bounded over to Jonah and Mike, pumping their hands like he hadn't seen them in a long time. "How're you doing, young fellas?"

"We're fine," Jonah answered, suppressing a grin. "What are you doing here?"

Rex grinned as he scratched his reddish nose. "You kidding? This is serious business. Marcus wants as many of our group as possible to know what's going on."

Amulet of the Goddess **815**

"He's keeping the Council occupied with his information from the Afterworld rebels," Trueblood said. He treated Jonah and Mike to friendly pats on the backs.

Trueblood and Albrecht wore their royal blue tunics today, and Rex was in his long, black Reaper's coat.

However, Kevin, who leaned against the back of the sofa, was still dressed like any other sixteen-year-old wearing a hoodie, jeans, and sneakers. No long coat in sight.

Jonah crossed to the sofa to sit beside the young Fallen Reaper while Mike retreated to the old editor's desk in the back corner. Jonah couldn't resist grinning when Mike let out a disgusted yelp at the messy desk and began to hastily straighten up the notebooks and loose paper. He stopped when Albrecht approached.

"Ahh, the translation of the coded text," the mage gushed. He and Mike began a spirited, quiet discussion of his progress.

Kevin whispered, "I thought we cured Mike."

Jonah elbowed him. "Be quiet!"

The attic door slammed. Lynn, Robert, and Wick bounded up the steps.

Rex let out a loud grunt when he saw Robert's hand and went over to inspect the finger brace. "Too bad your folks already know about this," he said, turning over Robert's hand. "I expect a healer may have been able to do something with it."

Robert gaped at the man. "Seriously? I could get it healed?"

Lynn stepped in. "Dad would go crazy if he saw you healed so soon."

Robert's sudden enthusiasm wilted. "Oh, yeah."

"Well, now wasn't a good time anyway," Rex concluded. He glanced at Trueblood, who nodded in confirmation.

The mage clapped his hands. "Everyone, this is Mage Albrecht." He gestured to the shorter mage, who seemed reluctant to break off his conversation with Mike. "He's also a member of the Alliance Council."

After Albrecht nodded to everyone, Robert raised his good hand. "Huh, we never really met you," he said, pointing at Trueblood.

The mage looked stunned. "Oh, I'm Eleanor's brother, Mage Trueblood."

"He's also on the Council," Rex supplied.

Robert whistled. "Really? How many people are on the Council?"

"Nine," Jonah and Mike said at the same time.

Jonah laughed and gestured for his friend to continue.

Mike stood up straighter like he was about to answer a teacher in class. "There are three mages, three Fallen Reapers, and three mortals."

"Correct." Albrecht gave Mike an encouraging nod. "We can talk about that later. Right now, we have more pressing matters." He motioned to Lynn. "I understand your intuition is being blocked?"

"Yes," Lynn answered, although she seemed guarded. Jonah could sense her deeper hope that the mage would have an answer.

Albrecht adjusted his glasses while scanning her but didn't move closer.

It was Trueblood who raised his hand with the palm toward Lynn. "May I scan you?"

"You're not a Memory Charmer," Jonah blurted out.

"No, I'm not." Trueblood smiled at Jonah over his shoulder. "I'm not scanning her mind for a compulsion. I'm looking for signs of a hex or maybe a potion."

"A hex?" Lynn looked appalled at the idea. She dropped her arms to her side and didn't move. "Do it."

Trueblood faced her again and muttered a complex spell under his breath. A soft, golden light engulfed Lynn's entire body. Sections of the glowing aura, particularly around her head, turned a dark green color, like a virus.

Wick ruffled his twists while gawking at the display. "Is that what I think it is?"

"If you mean a magical block, you're right." Trueblood lowered his hand but stopped because a dense, dark green haze surrounded the water bottle Lynn held.

When Lynn noticed, she dropped the bottle and backed away from it.

Amulet of the Goddess

"No way!"

Trueblood lifted the bottle and held it at arm's length. "It would seem your water's infected." He peered at Lynn. "Where did you get this?"

Lynn placed a hand over her mouth while staring at the bottle. She shook as she answered, "I have a large container of it at home, in the refrigerator. It's a mixture…"

Robert looked as sick as his sister. "That's wicked! Who would do that?" He glanced at the others. "I know. The mole. But how?"

"Robert has a point," Kevin said. "They couldn't get into their house. It's protected from that."

"It is?" Jonah asked, pulling his gaze away from Lynn's contaminated bottle.

Kevin nudged him. "Keeping you from phasing wasn't the only reason to protect your house."

Mike let out a shocked sound from the back desk. "That's why you had to phase to my backyard?" he asked Kevin. "The Alliance protected my house."

"Given what's happened," Trueblood said, "I think we should also protect the young mage's house."

Wick raised a hand in a hesitant manner. "I've already done that." When the adult mages all looked at him, he wilted a little. "Sorry."

"In this case, your actions proved correct," Albrecht said. He turned to Lynn. "It's obvious they infected one of the ingredients to your mixture before you got home."

Lynn covered her mouth again and her eyes went wide. "Oh, no! That huge guy rammed into me at the store and I dropped everything. I remember feeling that something was wrong, but I thought…"

"What?" Robert pressed her.

"I thought the feeling was about my fight with Rico. I should have known better."

"Don't you start blaming yourself," Robert warned his sister. "This isn't our fault."

818 *John Darr*

"Yeah," Jonah seconded his cousin. "That guy was a Wraith."

"It seems they've been watching you and planning this for a long time," Rex agreed.

"The mole and his people are behind all of this!?" Lynn shouted.

Jonah knew the look in his cousin's eyes. She wanted to hit something. And he agreed with her. But he had another target. "I bet it was the Alliance guy. He told the mole everything about us. Can we do something about him now?"

Jonah was gratified when Lynn seconded the idea.

But Trueblood frowned and Albrecht remained quiet.

Jonah turned to Rex in desperation. "You could do a Reaper's stare on him, couldn't you?" Like Trueblood, Rex didn't seem open to that idea, causing Jonah's irritation to flare. He didn't get why the Alliance adults thought they had to leave this guy alone.

Kevin tapped his shoulder. "Jonah, Alastor isn't a fool."

"So what?"

"He probably didn't know anything about this side of the plan."

Jonah spread his hands. "What difference does that make?"

"Plausible deniability," Albrecht explained. "He could honestly say he didn't know and pass a Reaper's Stare, even if we could manage to get the Council to agree to one."

Unable to respond, Jonah settled on exchanging an infuriated glance with Lynn, who looked just as angry.

Trueblood broke the silent tension first. "Jonah, I know you're frustrated with us, and believe me, no one hates hiding and subterfuge more than I do. I'm a what-you-see-is-what-you-get type of person." He placed a hand on Jonah's shoulder. "It's why your dad sponsored me for the Council, but even I had to learn to be more... subtle. The mole may just be the tip of an iceberg. Like any undercover operation when the goal is to ferret out everyone involved, the best way to accomplish it is to pretend you haven't uncovered their activities."

"Symon," Albrecht warned.

Amulet of the Goddess

"I'm not telling them any Council secrets." Trueblood gestured at Jonah and the others. "They're all intelligent young people, and we should treat them like that and not like little kids."

In that moment, Jonah didn't care what his uncle thought of Trueblood. He liked the mage.

Trueblood met each young person's gaze in turn, as if making a silent pledge to them. "You all understand? We're not doing nothing. We're building a case and trying to catch everyone that's involved. But that's dangerous and takes time. I'm trusting you all to keep that among yourselves."

Everyone nodded.

"Good!" He turned to Wick, who was unusually quiet. "Now, I understand you've come a long way?"

Wick's response surprised Jonah and interrupted his brooding thoughts about Alastor. Normally, the young mage was ecstatic at any chance to talk with an adult mage. But today, Wick fidgeted in a subdued, quiet manner. "I'm sorry about what happened."

"It wasn't your fault," Trueblood assured him. "Albrecht and I agree it was sorcery that caused your harmless flames to go astray."

Wick's posture straightened as he listened.

"You're a talented, young mage," Trueblood continued. "I assured the Council that you didn't lose control of your magic."

"You did?" Wick's eyes widened. "I mean, thanks."

Albrecht squared his shoulders. "That being the case, you've shown a lack of wisdom in so openly using your powers. On behalf of the Alliance Council, we're here to warn you."

"I understand."

"Don't look so glum," Trueblood said. "I'm staying behind in Mount Vernon for a few days to observe and coach you."

Robert leaned on his buddy's shoulder. "See? They aren't locking you up."

Albrecht approached Wick, peering at him through his big glasses. "A proper mage-trainee would have been able to stop the attack at once. If you had been in one of my classes, you would have done so."

"He should get formal training," Trueblood agreed, rubbing his chin and nodding, "like any other young mage."

Wick perked up.

Albrecht motioned to him. "Show me a flame."

Wick glanced at his buddy and hesitated, another response he had never done before.

Trueblood clapped his hands. "Don't be shy now. Show us your stuff."

Wick's frown twisted into his lopsided grin. He held out his hand and a ball of purple flame flared to life.

Albrecht made a disapproving sound but Trueblood was nicer. He raised his own hand and, with a quiet puff sound, a ball of purple flame appeared. Jonah could see the difference at once. Wick's flame, through impressive and pretty in a way, appeared weak and less distinct around the edges.

Trueblood's ball of flame was solid and almost perfectly round. Then the mage did something Jonah had never seen Wick do: He made his ball of flame smaller and smaller until it was almost a pinpoint of light.

"You're a natural, and I sense very powerful," the mage said. "No doubt it runs in your family, just like mine. But you need to learn finer control." He snuffed out his flame with a flick of his hand. "Don't sweat it. We'll turn you into a proper mage."

Wick's normal enthusiasm for magic returned and he grinned from ear-to-ear. Once again, Jonah felt a rush a gratitude toward Trueblood, this time, for alleviating Wick's dour mood.

Meanwhile, Trueblood turned to Robert. "Are your parents at home?"

"No."

"We should throw out that contaminated mix." He motioned to Rex. "Give us a lift?"

Rex held out a pair of keys. "You should learn to drive."

Trueblood grinned as he took the car keys and ushered Lynn to the attic stairs. "We'll be back," he said to Jonah in a perfect *Terminator* imitation. Rex laughed and followed.

Amulet of the Goddess **821**

"I think now is a good time to discuss some rules of conduct for mages-in-training." Albrecht pointed Wick toward the clubhouse section.

Wick gulped and said, "Yes, sir." He slouched to the sofa and sat down. Robert trailed behind and, when Albrecht didn't object, sat beside his buddy.

Jonah was happy for Lynn, Mike, and Wick. Despite solving the individual attacks, they still were in the dark about the mole and the sorceress. In effect, the club had reached a dead end.

Mike came over. "We should go."

"Where?" Jonah asked, distracted.

"Your house." Mike held up the pieces of the triptych. "I can tell you about my conversation with Patrick on the way."

"Who's Patrick?" Kevin asked.

Jonah motioned for him to keep his voice low. "We'll tell you on the ride to my house."

Kevin snorted. "Pass. I'll just meet you there."

Jonah grabbed the older boy before he could phase. "No. Ride with us."

"I don't have a bike. Smart guy."

"You can use Lynn's," Jonah explained. "It's outside and I know the lock code." He hefted his book bag on a shoulder. "Let's go."

CHAPTER TWENTY-FOUR
ANKH OF LIFE

A gust of strong, autumn wind blew fallen leaves across the street. Jonah's tires crunched them constantly as he, Mike, and Kevin rode to the Hightowers' house.

Releasing a loud yelp as a large acorn bounced off his head, Mike exclaimed, "Hey!" He paused in his story about Patrick to glare at the offending oak tree.

Kevin snorted, but Jonah prodded his buddy, "So, Patrick overheard Niqab Girl talking about love potions?"

"Not love potions, just potions in general," Mike answered, rubbing the sore spot on his head. "He checked out Mystic Worlds."

"Tell me that clerk didn't help him," Jonah interrupted.

"No, he didn't. When Patrick left the store, he ran into a woman in a cloak. She offered to sell him a potion."

Patrick's stupidity stunned Jonah. "That idiot didn't think that was dangerous? And he poured it in your soda? What if it had been poison?" His voice climbed to a near shout by the end.

Mike shrugged. "I know. But it shows how much he really liked me." Jonah glared at him and Mike didn't say anything else until they pulled into Jonah's neighborhood. "He meant well," Mike finally added.

Jonah opened his mouth to argue about that when Kevin veered close enough to shove him. "Stick to the point. Did Patrick see the woman's face?"

Amulet of the Goddess   823

Mike shook his head. "She remained hidden under the cloak's hood."

"We should get Robert to scan Patrick's pea-brain, anyway," Jonah suggested. And then he remembered Robert's injured hand. "Dang! Another useless clue."

"Maybe not," Mike countered. "She was wearing a strange amulet featuring a woman with a lion's head. Those can't be too common."

Jonah let out a sigh of disappointment. "Robert picked that out of the jewelry store owner's memory."

They reached the Hightowers' house and Jonah noted the rental car parked at the curb. Good, he thought. *At least Trueblood and Rex were still there.* The boys rolled their bikes into the backyard to lean them against the shed before hurrying inside.

Rex sat at the kitchen table, reading one of Uncle James's magazines. Lynn's empty sports mix container lay on the counter, drained of all its contents. Trueblood stood near the sofa, holding one of Mage Albrecht's small vials in his hand and watching Lynn.

Lynn sat on the sofa, leaning her head back with her eyes closed.

Trueblood searched Jonah's face as he held a finger to his mouth. "Not too loud. We're trying to encourage her to rest to let the potion work."

"What potion?" Jonah asked. "You made one?"

Trueblood chuckled. "Albrecht said there are only so many ways to block her power, and he came prepared with an antidote to neutralize the effects of them all."

Rex rose from his chair, which creaked in response. "We should go, Symon. Me and Albrecht need to get back to HQ."

Trueblood slipped the vial into his pocket and whispered to Lynn, "Remember, get some rest."

She nodded.

"Take care of them, Kevin. We'll talk later." Trueblood waved to Jonah and Mike, then he and Rex left the house like normal people.

As soon as the Alliance men were gone, Lynn's eyes popped open. "Okay. What's going on?"

Jonah motioned to Mike. "You explain while I get the box." He also listened to Mike who told a modified version of the Patrick story, making the boy out to be a girl.

Ducking into his room, Jonah snagged his mom's locked box from his memento shelf and returned to the family room. Mike went quiet while avoiding Lynn's thoughtful gaze.

"That *girl* gave you this love potion?" she asked. When Mike didn't answer, she let out a huff. "What's his name?"

Mike's face reddened.

"I already know about you, Mike."

"You do?" Mike's eyes widened. "I mean, how?"

"Doesn't matter." She raised an eyebrow.

"Patrick."

Lynn tapped her bottom lip, thinking. "Don't recognize the name." She looked up at Jonah. "Why didn't you tell us about this?"

Jonah shrugged.

Kevin intervened and offered to hold the box. He turned it around with the lock facing Jonah so he could activate it.

Lynn's eyebrow arched when she saw that. "Now you have a secret box? Where's mine?" Jonah heard the mock-outrage, a healthy sign that his cousin was feeling better.

Mike, who was clutching the triptych, disconnected the pieces and held them out. But as Jonah reached for them, the thought that kept bugging him finally crystalized. The first time he saw the amulet that Robert drew, Jonah thought it looked familiar.

Now, with his mom's box open and the photo album in sight, he knew where he first saw the amulet. Jonah dug under the photo album and pulled out the envelope with the pictures of Aunt Ruby and her family.

He could feel everyone's eyes on him as he slid the pictures free and searched through them. When he found it, Jonah's hand began to shake so badly that the other pictures slipped from his grasp.

"Jonah? What's wrong?" Lynn asked as she scooped up the dropped

Amulet of the Goddess   825

photos.

He ignored the question, his full attention remaining on the picture of Aunt Ruby and Uncle Amos. Around her neck was the woman-with-the-lion's-head amulet! It was exactly the same as the one in Robert's picture. That meant the woman was his Aunt Ruby all along!

Lynn peeked over his shoulder. He held up the picture. "It can't be!" Lynn hissed in disbelief. "She's in Titusville. Maybe the sorceress just has the same bad taste in jewelry."

"It's her, Lynn."

Kevin frowned at them. "You mean, your aunt?" Jonah and Lynn nodded in unison. "Here." Kevin thrust the box into Jonah's hands. He pulled out his phone and walked into the kitchen while talking in rapid tones with someone on the other end.

Mike peeked at the picture and his face paled. Then he let out a gasp and plucked a different picture from Lynn's hand. "Look!"

Holding the picture of the Ankh of Life bookstore, he pointed at the store's front window. "See the statuettes on the windowsill?"

Jonah's insides froze. Among the row of little figurines and statuettes was a free-standing replica of the amulet.

Mike and Jonah glanced at each other.

Lynn's face showed abject denial. "We should wait until we know if she's in Titusville or not."

"Well, you can stop wondering," Kevin said, coming over. "Trueblood and Rex went there and found the woman your aunt was supposed to be staying with. They're still talking to her, but the woman appears to have been hexed. Your aunt's been using her as a cover longer than a week."

"That settles it," Jonah announced.

Lynn shook her head. "But how? Our aunt never had any powers?"

"What if the mole's helping her?" Mike asked.

"He's a Fallen Reaper," Jonah said, "not a mage." He showed Kevin the picture. "We should check it out."

"That could be dangerous. I'm supposed to keep watch over you."

"You can watch over me there." Jonah jabbed a finger at the photo. "Besides, I'll be with Lynn and Mike."

"Yeah, the Mount Vernon Social Club," Mike added with a smirk.

Jonah grimaced. "Maybe we should change the name."

Kevin gave them both a deadpan look, not amused.

Jonah imagined that the older boy recalled what happened the last time he went along with one of their harebrained plans. It was the reason he was currently in hot water with Mandara. Even so, Jonah met Kevin's gaze and silently pleaded with him.

The older boy's resistance wilted and he eventually nodded. "Fine, but we only stay until dark. Then we leave. If anyone's there, we leave. If you irritate me," Kevin added, leaning closer to Jonah's face, "we leave."

*

The Ankh of Life bookstore must have seen better days, although Jonah doubted the store had looked any different when it was open. He estimated that couldn't have been for several years.

Copious cobwebs hung from the corners of dirty windows. The peeled paint and multiple years' worth of dead leaves had accumulated all along the front edge of the store to contribute to its obvious abandonment and neglect. The few other businesses on the shabby, narrow side street also looked long deserted and vacant, imbuing an uncomfortable eeriness into the location.

This tiny town was long past its heyday, Jonah decided. Gazing at the store, he could not stop thinking how much smaller it seemed in person.

Mike leaned against him. "Is it just me or is this place always spooky this time of year?"

"I bet it's creepy all the time," Jonah replied as he stepped to the front window. Most of the figurines, including the amulet, were gone. The few remaining items were toppled onto their sides. There was a clear circle on the otherwise dust-coated inner window ledge where the replica should have been. "I think someone's already been here."

"Yeah." Lynn pointed at the door. Loose cobwebs hung in the corners,

Amulet of the Goddess

as if someone had hastily yanked them away to reach the door handle.

Kevin pulled out his blades, glancing up and down the street to make sure no one was around. Only then did he activate them. "You remember what I said?"

Jonah nodded.

Lynn tried the handle but the door was locked. "Break in?"

"Better idea." Kevin held out his arms for everyone to grab hold, but waited for Lynn to activate one of her own blades. When she did and everyone was securely touching him, Kevin phased them inside.

Immediately, Jonah sneezed at the dust they dislodged by their arrival. Clear footprints on the filthy floor were further evidence that someone had been here. Not to mention, how everything was thrown around.

Mike pointed past the front sitting room toward a half-torn set of velvet curtains. "That way?"

Kevin took the lead, Mike and Jonah followed next, and Lynn covered the back. The arrangement was at once familiar and comforting to Jonah, especially since he had no powers as long as he wore the bands.

On the other side of the curtain, off to one side, was an office. The door was wide open and the contents of the shelves and the old desk were thrown across the floor. On the opposite side of the hallway was a room with a table and a large crystal ball. Covered in cobwebs, Jonah found it strange that it appeared untouched by the intruders.

Lynn's voice was hushed when she spoke. "My great-auntie owned the store until she died. I wondered if she left a will."

"I bet she did. Probably as a trust fund or something like that," Mike said. "You know, from what you told me, I bet your mom was supposed to take over, Jonah."

Mike nodded as if agreeing with his own assessment. "She would have passed it on to Lynn. I surmise the gift only appears in one heir each generation. I mean, that's how these things normally work."

Kevin poked Mike in the arm. "You sure Albrecht cured you?"

Mike flashed a silvery, embarrassed grin.

Lynn pointed into a side alcove and a heavily dented, metal door. "I guess our aunt couldn't get inside."

"More likely, her huge friend," Jonah said. He peered closer and added, "And that's why they couldn't get inside!" Dead center on the door was a genetic lock. Unlike the simple button on his birthday present cylinder or Robert's archive box, this lock was larger and round with strange symbols etched into the metal surface: three rows of symbols, one within the other, and all slightly raised.

Jonah suspected it was Angel script. He stepped forward and touched the lock, but nothing happened except for a mild tingle that he felt along the tip of his finger. Jonah tried again. Still nothing.

Mike peered at the lock and then Lynn inspected it. "I wonder…"

Lynn returned his gaze. "You wonder what?"

"Try it," Mike suggested.

"Why would it work for me?"

Jonah got it. "My mom managed to get my DNA. No reason she couldn't do the same to you when she visited."

"We're wasting time," Kevin prompted.

"Oh, all right," Lynn huffed. She pressed her finger to the lock and said, "Oh!" as the Angel script lit up. The symbols spun around, each circle turning at different speeds. When they stopped, there was a symbol in each row, all in a line, and the lock glowed a vibrant yellow.

With a hollow click! the rows of symbols retreated into the surface and the door swung open to reveal a workroom beyond. "No way," Lynn whispered in awe.

Jonah nudged his stunned cousin through first. He wasn't being chivalrous as much as betting her presence would diffuse any magical traps. The door had been keyed for her, after all. He relaxed when he didn't feel the buzz of magic, but then again, he might not have with the bands on.

Ancient texts, drawings, and more modern maps covered the surface of a large desk that was positioned against the wall adjacent to the door. The room's shelves were lined with ancient-looking books.

Kevin walked around the perimeter, inspecting everything. Mike perused the desktop with Jonah.

Amulet of the Goddess

Lynn gazed at a large mural on the wall above the desk. "This reminds me of something Robert would draw." She brushed her fingers over the artwork.

Everyone jumped when Lynn's phone rang. She yanked it out. "Yeah, hold on." She changed it to speaker and said, "We are all here."

"Where?" Robert's tinny voice asked.

"Yeah," Wick chimed in. "You're on a fun trip and didn't invite us? Hold on. We'll call right back." Lynn held up the phone in exasperation at the same time it rang again. She propped her phone against a couple of thick books when Robert and Wick made a video call this time. Their faces crowded into view on the small screen.

Mike flicked a switch near the desk. Not only did light flood the work area, but recessed lighting in the ceiling also came on and illuminated the wall.

"Whoa!" Robert said.

"That is wicked," agreed Wick.

"Jonah, it's just like the triptych." Mike pointed out the seven stars and typography of the wall map.

Robert glared at them on the phone's screen. "What triptych?"

"Long story," Jonah told his cousin. Mike was right. It was the same, only this had…

"Those are compass codes," Mike said before Jonah could. "And there're two sets." His eyes went out of focus for a moment. "They are mortal and Underworld coordinates."

Jonah nodded, growing excited at the news. "Hey, that means you can use the dialer in the Deliverer's cave to go to the other side!"

"Oh!" Mike exclaimed. "Like we did when we traveled to the Afterworld." He grinned. "We should try it. But not now, of course." He gestured around them.

Jonah was about to agree when he noticed the thin, hardcover, black books on the desk were actually journals. He opened one and recognized his mom's handwriting. Kevin came over and opened another.

Soon everyone was doing the same until Mike said, "I have the last one." He proceeded to flip through the pages at a brisk pace. When he finished, he took the other journals from Kevin, Lynn, and Jonah. In quick succession, he read through all of them. Jonah marveled at his ability to soak up the information so rapidly.

When Mike finished, he stared at the large map on the wall. "Your mom figured out what was happening."

"Mike, my mom's..." Jonah stopped

"I know, but she figured out what the map means." Mike pressed his hand to the open page of the journal as if he were trying to absorb the words through his skin. "Every seven years, on Halloween, those seven mortal nexus points align with the ones in the Underworld. When that happens, the nexus points become huge doorways, letting a lot of powerful Wraiths through all at once if..."

"A ritual isn't performed," Lynn said. She, too, gazed at the mural in rapt fascination.

Mike stood beside her as if they were the only two people in the room. "The person requires the amulet of Pakhet."

Lynn bobbed her head in agreement. "Pakhet. She's the goddess of the night and the hunt. If they have her amulet, they can call forth her full essence to lead an army of Phantoms and other Underworld creatures on a rampage across the mortal world."

Lynn sucked in a startled breath. "I remember now." She turned to Jonah. "Your mom used to tell me that story all the time when I was little. And... she had the amulet back then! Or a copy of it." Her eyes widened. "This must have been what my aunt ranted and raved about when they locked her up."

"Yeah, seven years ago," Robert said. His voice sounded even more hollow over the phone's speaker.

"But Aunt Ruby has the amulet now," Jonah pointed out. "So why break into the store?"

"Because she doesn't have the *real* amulet." Mike snapped the journal closed that he had been holding. "Your mom returned it to your great-auntie. She hid it to keep anyone from opening the nexus points." He glanced around the room. "I'm starting to think your aunts were the guardians of the amulet."

Amulet of the Goddess

Lynn laughed while also staring around the chamber. "Maybe so. It's clear our dear, old Aunt Ruby thought the real amulet was locked in here."

"Then we better close it up and go." Kevin glanced at his watch. "Time's up anyway."

Mike shook his head. "You don't get it, Kevin. The amulet's not here."

Jonah had a more pressing concern. "Ah, Mike? When do the points line up?"

Wick was the one to answer. "Isn't it obvious? It happens at midnight on Halloween. That's when the barrier between the mortal and Underworld is at its weakest point. *The Witching Hour!*"

CHAPTER TWENTY-FIVE
ALASTOR TRAPPED

Alliance personnel, including a couple of the huge Council Guards, flooded the old Ankh of Life bookstore. Lynn and Mike, who had never seen the guards before, reacted with shock to their impressive size as well as when the captain greeted Jonah by name.

But Jonah's attention was on Trueblood's demeanor. The mage looked as if someone had sucked all the joy out of his life. When he touched one of the black journals, Trueblood closed his eyes, and the pain was instantly evident on his face.

Jonah understood the reaction because he felt the same way when he opened his mom's lockbox. He expected to experience the same dull ache when he finally examined the rest of her things from her office.

Once the Alliance adults arrived, they ushered the young people out of the map room and into the crystal ball parlor. Mike poked the ball with a slender finger, carefully avoiding the cobwebs lest they cling to his hand. Lynn positioned herself at the doorway, straining to hear the conversations happening down the hall.

She moved away from the door just before Kevin stepped into view "We can go."

"What about the store?" Lynn asked. "I should lock the back room."

"No. They want to leave it open just in case Ruby comes back."

"Why?" Mike asked.

Amulet of the Goddess   833

"Because they want to catch her!" Kevin said. He held out his arms for everyone to grab hold of him and then phased them all back to the clubhouse.

Robert and Wick were eagerly waiting for their return. The boys hustled Lynn, Jonah, and Mike to the club area while Kevin returned to the bookstore.

Mike held back. "I have to go."

Jonah wondered if he were meeting with Patrick but he kept that to himself. As Robert and Wick proceeded to pepper them with questions about the old bookstore, Jonah let Lynn talk.

The gang knew all about the big plan and had already confirmed his aunt was working with the mole. But something else nagged Jonah. Why come after his friends and family but not him? There had to be more to the whole thing.

He said as much to the group.

"We need to dig deeper and unearth more of the puzzle," Lynn agreed.

"But how?" Robert asked, looking around. "We don't know where to find the mole's group."

Except for Alastor, Jonah thought.

"Can I borrow your blades?" Jonah inquired, breaking the tense quiet.

Lynn raised a questioning eyebrow, waiting for the explanation.

"I asked Rex to show me the deflection spell," Jonah lied. "I want to try it on my own."

Lynn shrugged and handed over the blades. She went back to describing the interior of the Ankh of Life shop to Robert, who already had his sketchpad out and seemed determined to manage despite his injured fingers.

Jonah used their distraction to head for the door. While the Alliance sent their trap for his elusive aunt, Jonah decided to pay the overly friendly Alastor a visit. With any luck, he'd get some answers.

*

Jonah almost faltered in his plan when he entered Hackett's and saw Mike working the register. But it was too late to change course.

"Hey, Jonah." Mike waved. "You came to talk about Pakhet's amulet?"

Jonah glanced around the store. "Actually, I came to see Alastor."

Mike frowned. "Does Kevin know you're here to see—"

"Mr. Blackstone." Alastor appeared at the end of the History aisle, his brown eyes darting between the boys. "Did someone mention my name?"

Jonah gave his buddy a slight shake of the head. Mike's frown deepened as he grabbed a pile of discount paperbacks off the counter and disappeared down the Romance aisle.

"Well," Alastor said, watching Mike a moment before turning to Jonah. "How can I help you, Mr. Blackstone?"

"I need to talk with you."

Alastor raised an eyebrow. "We can talk in the office." He led the way.

The last time Jonah had seen Hackett's crowded office was two summers ago, when Mr. Hackett asked him and Mike inside. Not only did he discover the bookstore owner was a talented fantasy artist, but the man's immense wealth of information about Fallen Reapers and the Protector's Ring had more than shocked them.

Only now did Jonah attach more significance to Alastor running the store while Hackett was away. He began to wonder if Alastor were the Fallen Reaper that Mr. Hackett claimed to know. That would make Mike's uncle part of the plot too.

That thought troubled Jonah as he sat on the grey folding chair and faced the cluttered desk. Alastor closed the door and leaned against the side of the desk. Jonah scooted his chair back, giving himself more room.

Alastor didn't appear to notice the move but clapped his hands together like they were old friends. "Well, what can I do for you?"

The sound of the man's false cheeriness goaded Jonah. He stood, pushing aside the chair, and activated one of Lynn's Reaper blades. He was dimly aware of the chair knocking over one of Hackett's numerous paintings but he didn't have time to worry about that. Alastor was his exclusive focus.

Amulet of the Goddess   **835**

The little man pressed against the closed door, keeping his eyes on the shiny weapon. "Careful with that, Mr. Blackstone. It's not a toy."

"I know how to use it." Jonah whirled the blade in his hand.

"So I hear."

"Yeah, I bet you did. I know who you are too."

"Really?"

"I heard about the Alliance Council and how you came to Mount Vernon to talk me into doing something stupid."

Alastor smiled. It didn't convey any happiness, just a sickening deceitfulness. "I didn't have to talk you into anything. I watched you scouting those houses on your own."

Jonah lost the effort to hide his surprise, causing Alastor to grin as he continued.

"The plan was already seeded in your devious, little mind. I merely helped it along."

Jonah's hand shook with anger and he had to concentrate to steady it. "You work for the Hardliners." With conscious effort, he refrained from shouting that Alastor also worked for the mole. That wasn't an option anymore, not after promising Trueblood he'd keep quiet.

"I see you've been talking with someone. Marcus?" Alastor gave him a questioning look. "No. He's too fond of keeping you in the dark. Perhaps Trueblood?"

Jonah wouldn't let the man distract him. The problem was that he couldn't accuse Alastor of working with his aunt or Niqab Girl, either. That would also indicate how much information the Alliance had on the man. But that didn't mean Jonah couldn't ask him about certain other things though.

"Why were you at the funeral? Why'd you really help me at Latrell's house?"

"I merely wanted to facilitate the development of your skills."

"Liar!"

Alastor raised his hands and grinned at Jonah again. "Why would I lie to you?" He tapped a dirtied fingernail against his forehead. "You can sense if my answer is the truth."

The more Alastor said, the more thankful Jonah was that his godfather was a Fallen Reaper as well as a lawyer. Marcus could make a statement that was true while excluding a whole bunch of damaging information. Jonah found it interesting that Alastor did the same thing now.

He was also reminded of what Albrecht said: Plausible deniability. Alastor was deliberately excluded from some parts of the plan so he could pass a Reaper's Stare.

"I'm not a weapon."

"I never said you were," Alastor agreed. "Now, put that Reaper's blade away."

Jonah wavered for a moment before he complied.

Alastor watched Jonah slipping the blade into his pocket. He leaned under the harsh light from the lacquered lampshade right above the desk. "That isn't yours."

"Yes, it is," Jonah lied.

"No, it isn't. First of all, you haven't chosen your own blades yet. Second, that one clearly doesn't fit you, although it did hum in your hand." Alastor slipped behind the desk and sat down. "Ah, yes. It must belong to your cousin, Lynn. Sometimes families tend to share an affinity toward particular blades."

The man's knowledgeable comments about blades ignited a flurry of questions in Jonah. And just as quickly, he realized this devious man was only doing it to distract him. Jonah couldn't let that happen because he feared Kevin would return to the clubhouse at any moment and discover he had slipped away. The young Fallen Reaper knew Jonah well enough to search here first.

Jonah reined in his natural curiosity and remembered his reason for confronting Alastor. "Why are you here?"

Alastor stared back in what Jonah thought was real surprise. "You honestly don't know? You were the first person in two thousand years to use a Protector's Ring. You defeated a Hunter by draining him of power."

Alastor leaned forward with his hands pressed flat on the desk. "We're still curious how you managed to do that."

"We?" Jonah asked. "You mean, the Hardliners?"

Alastor seemed disappointed when he nodded. "Apparently, you're destined to be The One. The Seers have prophesied your emergence." Alastor tilted his head to the side as he watched Jonah's expression. "And then there's your friend, Mr. Littleton. The first true Seeker in two thousand years."

"Leave him alone." Jonah's hands tightened around the blade cylinders.

"Of course, we also read about your Afterworld adventure with your best friend. It's nothing less than remarkable."

Jonah suspected the man of lying, hoping he'd reveal more details. But he had no intention of discussing his time in the Afterworld with Alastor. "I don't trust you."

Alastor spread his little hands. "It can't be helped."

That small gesture caused Jonah's temper to flare. Getting answers from Alastor was frustrating. One minute, he gave a real answer, then he'd hold back the details or explanation. Jonah had no doubt Alastor was still trying to goad him into doing something he preferred not to do. He returned the man's gaze, searching for a new approach.

Wait! If Alastor claimed he wanted to help, why not give him the chance?

Jonah sat up in his chair, acting like an eager student. "Why are they messing with me? You've seen everything. What do you think?"

Alastor's eyes widened. "That's an interesting angle, Mr. Blackstone."

"I really want to hear what you think." Jonah funneled all of his sincerity into the statement. It wasn't hard because he was genuinely interested in hearing what the guy would tell him.

After a moment, Alastor let out a nervous laugh. "I believe you, but there are some things you and your cousins need to discover for yourselves."

"That's what you want us to do. You're still using me, and seeing what I can do." Jonah nodded with the certainty of it.

"Of course."

"You're evil," Jonah said, unable to hide his pent-up frustration any longer.

A hardened look replaced Alastor's mocking amusement. The little man sat forward, hands folded but shaking with repressed emotion. "I am not evil. The people who used you are the evil ones, young Blackstone. They killed your parents."

"Don't talk about my mom and dad!" Jonah activated the blades.

This time, Alastor didn't appear afraid at all. In fact, he seemed satisfied at Jonah's reaction. "You have a right to be angry with the Alliance. You didn't ask for this burden, but it's been placed on your shoulders all the same."

Jonah struggled to put the man's words into perspective. He had to remember that Alastor worked with the mole and wasn't any ally.

"You can decide to do whatever you want," Alastor continued.

"That's what you want: A weapon."

Alastor shot to his feet, nearly banging his head on the low-hanging lampshade. "Be yourself. Embrace your power, no matter what the Alliance, the Grim Reaper, or the Grand Oracle say."

"You're just trying to push me into–"

"I know what happened to Agent Hunter," Alastor hissed, his voice more urgent and pressing. "Tell me, young Blackstone, how did Marcus and Kevin react to you?"

Jonah stared into the man's eyes. "What do you mean?"

"They were afraid of you, weren't they? Everyone is afraid of you. None of them will ever truly trust you. Not even the so-called Hardliners."

Jonah felt the pressure of the man's will on his own. Though frightened at first, something inside him automatically pushed back. The pressure relented and disappeared.

As a movie quote entered his mind, Jonah surprised himself and laughed. "Turn to the dark side? My hate will make me powerful?"

Alastor frowned at him, though Jonah didn't know if it were because of his statement or because he diminished the pressure. But the man quickly overcame his initial shock. "You are too powerful and too dangerous."

Amulet of the Goddess

Just as Alastor reached inside his coat pocket to withdraw his own blades, the office door banged open and Kevin charged in. His blades were already out and he brandished them at Alastor.

The little man leapt sideways and smacked into the wall, sending a pile of stacked books tumbling to the floor and knocking over several finished paintings. At the last minute, however, he seemed to come to his senses and left his own blades concealed.

"How dare you threaten me! I work for the Alliance Council!"

"So do I," Kevin snapped without lowering his blades.

"Mandara will find out about this!"

Kevin snorted. "Tell him. I don't care." He deactivated one blade and slipped it into his pocket so he could grab Jonah's arm.

Just before they phased, Jonah caught a glimpse of motion at the opened office door. He turned and saw a confused and wide-eyed Mike staring at him.

CHAPTER TWENTY-SIX
DANITA'S EXCLUSIVE

"Have you lost your mind?" Kevin yelled, not bothering to keep his cool.

Jonah hunched his shoulders and kicked at the loose brick in the hideaway's courtyard. "I wanted to get some answers."

Kevin gaped at him. "Do you know why you didn't get anything from him? Because Alastor isn't stupid, Jonah." The older boy stalked around the hideaway, visibly agitated.

"I'm sorry."

"You keep saying that, but then you go and do something stupid."

"You sound like Marcus."

Kevin's nostrils flared and he stormed right up to Jonah, standing over him. "If you think this is funny, let's go see what Marcus has to say about it."

"No. I don't. And I already said I'm sorry."

"Then mean it, and use your brain the next time."

Jonah shrank away from Kevin's anger. He had never seen the boy so worked up. As they locked gazes, Jonah could sense his deep concern. "Okay." His voice wavered.

The effect on Kevin was immediate. His expression softened as he gripped Jonah's hands, pulled him close, and kissed him.

Jonah didn't know how long they kissed. He lost track of time until a chill ran down his back. He thought it was just the wind or maybe the same jolt he and Kevin had experienced the last time they kissed.

Amulet of the Goddess

Kevin was the first one to pull away and in an instant, his Reaper blades were out and ready.

Jonah turned to find Latrell standing behind him. "What are you doing here?"

When Kevin moved toward the ghostly boy, blades raised, Jonah shouted, "Don't!" He grabbed the Fallen Reaper's arm to stop him, but Latrell had already disappeared.

"How is he still following you around?" Kevin asked. When Jonah shrugged, he let out a low grunt of anger and began to pat Jonah's coat and then his pants. That's when he touched the ankh. "What's this?"

"Well, we were kissing…"

"Don't even go there," Kevin growled.

Jonah dug the ankh out of his jeans pocket.

Kevin snatched it and held it up to Jonah's face. "Latrell can follow you around when you wear this. That's bad, Jonah, because he's a Wraith."

"We can't be sure about that."

"He's working with the mole. He gave you the clue about the ankh." Kevin shoved the ankh in his own pocket. "I know you feel sorry for him, but you have to face the truth." He checked his watch. "We need to go."

"Not yet." Jonah grabbed the boy's hand and held on.

"We have to. Mandara ordered me to check in every evening."

"Do you think Alastor told him already?"

Kevin frowned. "Yeah. Like I said, I don't care. I'll fight to stay here. Someone needs to make sure you don't do anything else stupid."

Jonah ignored the dig because he sensed Kevin's real concern and the deep desire not to leave him again. "Will you come back tonight?"

"No. I'll have to stay at the Guest House in Atlanta."

"Oh." Jonah gulped. "Say hello to Mabel for me."

Kevin sucked in a deep breath, forcing himself to calm down. "Jonah, you have to start listening to us."

842   *John Darr*

"I know." He leaned against Kevin and wrapped his arms around the older boy's waist. The Fallen Reaper's higher body temperature felt wonderful to him on a chilly evening.

Kevin stared across the courtyard, his face a mask of worry. "This is serious. You can't let your emotions take over, not now. It's exactly what they want."

*

Jonah had never experienced such a mix of opposing emotions and sensations in his life. On the bad side, he had to wear the power-nullifying bands, and he'd made Kevin furious with him. On the plus side, Kevin kissed him again.

As he and Kevin entered the attic, he was brought back down to Earth with a rude bump.

Mike, Robert, Lynn, and Wick turned to face them, all with matching serious expressions.

"What's up, guys?" Jonah asked even though he suspected Mike must have rushed there to tell everyone else what he witnessed. "Hey, Mike. Why aren't you working?"

"Why did Kevin burst into my uncle's store?"

"We'd like to hear the answer, too." Lynn's voice was tight. "But first…" She strode up to Jonah and held out a sheet of paper she'd been holding when he arrived.

Jonah took it. "What's this?"

"That is Danita's latest piece. She just emailed it to me." Lynn leaned against the back of the sofa. "You should read it." She folded her arms.

Jonah held the paper up to avoid her gaze. Mike crowded in to read over his shoulder.

THE GHOST OF VICTIMS PAST

None of us will forget the tragic news about the death of Latrell Mitchell. Despite your personal leanings, the premature death of a young person is always a shock and sad. The case of Latrell Mitchell took an unusual turn this week when Drew Edwards confessed to having bullied the boy before his suicide.

Drew made this confession to the school principal, his parents, and most surprisingly, to Latrell's parents. The Edwardses have promised that their son will receive some much-needed anger management therapy.

Jonah paused and lowered the page. He also tried to keep his face blank because everyone was watching him very carefully.

"This is great," he said. "Latrell's bully finally confessed. I thought Danita was writing about the black cat."

Lynn's eyes narrowed. "She was. You'll see; just keep reading."

Jonah didn't want to because he feared where the piece would go. But he did.

Many of you may know about my piece on black cats and superstitious beliefs. After reports of the black cat being spotted in Drew's neighborhood and discovering he saw it, I decided to question him for the next installment of my series. I've known Drew since the first grade, and while telling me about the night of the black cat sighting, he revealed something really unbelievable to me.

I found myself conducting an exclusive, impromptu interview with the troubled teen, being privy to the shocking nature of his confession. With some encouragement, Drew told me that he confessed to bullying Latrell because the boy's ghost visited him. That's right, reader!

In an encounter comparable to Charles Dickens's Scrooge, Latrell's ghost supposedly took the boy to various locales, including the high school hallway, Latrell's home, and finally, to the cemetery. According to Drew, as he lay sobbing in front of Latrell's grave, the ghost demanded that he confess his involvement in the matter.

Whether you believe in ghosts—I don't—or just think Drew ate some bad pizza before bed, one thing is for sure: The experience totally freaked out the kid. I don't endorse bullying of any kind, but should we thank Latrell's ghost for showing Drew the error of his ways?

Of course, I surmise this ghost was simply someone pretending to be the spirit of Latrell to scare Drew into doing what was right. But if any of you insist on believing in the supernatural, then I'll warn all the other bullies out there. Be careful or one night the victim's ghost might show up in your bedroom next!

Jonah flashed his cousins a nervous smile as he lowered the article. "That's really good. I like the bit about the ghost." His shaking hand betrayed his futile attempt to appear calm.

Behind Jonah, Kevin snorted.

Mike clamped a hand over his own mouth and backed away, his eyes showing dawning awareness.

Before Jonah could say anything to his friend, Robert hooked an arm around his shoulders. "Is there anything you want to tell us, little cousin?"

"Me? No."

"You sure, Jonah?"

"Yeah. I'm glad Drew confessed. He sounds like he needs mental help."

"Don't play dumb," Lynn warned, glaring at him. "Danita was more accurate than even she could appreciate."

"I don't…"

"Don't lie to us," Lynn warned.

"Jonah, Jonah, Jonah," Robert said. "Who do we know that can grab hold of someone and phase them from one location to another?"

"That's not what the article claims. Drew said it was a ghost."

"Drew explained everything to Danita," Lynn said, "including how it felt to phase. I asked her. You're just lucky she discounted it as utter nonsense, otherwise it would have been printed in bold there. That being said, what Drew described matched how we felt when Kevin phased all of us." She stood right in front of Jonah. "We all know it had to be you."

Jonah's shoulders slumped. He couldn't get out of this. It never occurred to him that Danita would interview Drew. "Fine. I did it." Jonah waved his arms in surrender.

Wick darted forward and gripped Jonah by the forearm, staring at his wrist. "What the…"

"Let him talk first," Robert said.

"But you don't understand, Bobby. This is a stun band." He gripped Jonah's other forearm and forced it up so the others could see the second band. "They're like stun cuffs."

Amulet of the Goddess **845**

Momentary surprise flitted across Robert's face when he heard that.

Jonah couldn't avoid it any longer and everything had to come out now. If he cooperated, maybe it wouldn't be too painful.

Robert peered at the bands. "Why does he have these on? Where'd you get them?"

Lynn tapped his arm. "Robert, don't you get it?" She turned to Jonah. "That's why Marcus came to see you, isn't it?"

Again, Jonah nodded, taking a deep breath before he confessed everything. And despite the imminent collective beat-down, confessing was a great relief until Lynn pulled him into a real headlock.

She ruffled Jonah's bushy hair. "Let's see if I have this straight. You didn't tell us that you went after Drew the first time." Lynn jerked her arms, tightening the hold.

"Ow! Yeah."

"Then," Lynn continued, tightening her hold again.

"Lynn!" Jonah squirmed in her grip.

"Quiet. Let's see, you go after the second bully. Only that time, Kevin must have interfered and you got into trouble for trying to be a vigilante superhero." Lynn twisted her arms a third time.

"Yeah. Okay, ow!"

"Anything else you're," she tightened the hold again, "forgetting to tell us?"

"No. I promise."

Lynn released Jonah, who took three staggering steps over to the sofa. The others huddled around him as he recited the highlights of his talk with Alastor.

Kevin stirred when Lynn glanced his way. "Hey," he said, "I've already yelled at him about it."

"Good," Lynn said.

Jonah braced himself for more, but Lynn and the others started discussing their next step.

Kevin tapped Jonah's shoulder and whispered, "I'm out of here."

Jonah hopped to his feet and trailed Kevin to the spot in front of the large attic window. The boys stared at each other, both knowing they couldn't hug or do anything else affectionate in front of the others.

"Bye," Jonah said.

After Kevin left, he started to rejoin the discussion but heard footsteps descending the attic stairs. Lynn, Wick, and Robert were still gathered around the steamer trunk, but…

Mike! Jonah hurried after his buddy and caught up to him just outside the Summit door. He grabbed Mike's arm.

His friend shrugged free. "Leave me alone!" His face darkened with real anger and he punched Jonah in the chest.

"Ow! Stop! Mike, I'm–"

"What if someone had seen you? What if you actually hurt Drew?"

"I didn't hurt him, and he deserved it. He bullied Latrell."

"You can't turn into a bully just to get even. That's wrong and it goes against everything we do in the club, the club which you started."

"I'm sorry I scared Drew. Okay?"

Mike pressed his hands flat against the second-floor railing, his breathing now heavy and fast. "You were totally wrong, Jonah." He turned his face away when Jonah stood beside him.

"I'm sorry. Really, I am."

Mike whirled on him and Jonah stepped back. "The worst part is: You lied to me. You already had plans to go after Brandon even though you promised me otherwise."

"Technically, I didn't promise and I didn't think it was wrong." Jonah realized too late that he said the wrong thing.

Mike's eyes flared with anger. "If it were right, then why did you find it necessary to lie to everyone?" He worked his jaw to keep from yelling further. "You knew we'd try to stop you! Just like Marcus had to do."

Mike moved away as Jonah reached out. "I can't get over you lying to me." He turned for the spiral stairway.

Amulet of the Goddess **847**

"Wait. Where are you going?"

Mike's angry expression shifted for a second and became guarded. "I'm going to the movies with Patrick."

"After what he did to you?"

"I talked to him. Well, I shouted," Mike said, adding, "he just wanted me to like him."

"Yeah, but there was the slight problem that he was being used by my aunt." Jonah slid closer to Mike. "Besides, Patrick just wanted to go all the way with you. He thought that potion would do the trick."

Mike grimaced. "I know that. And I can deal with him." When Jonah opened his mouth to argue the point, Mike grew testy. "We promised we'd help each other as Deliverer and Seeker. I guess you forgot about that." He hurried down the steps.

As Jonah watched his buddy stride across the atrium below before exiting through the front doors, he didn't know how things could get any worse than they were now.

CHAPTER TWENTY-SEVEN
BRANDON'S REVENGE

Every student read Danita's story about Drew on their mobile devices the next day. Jonah guessed that was a positive for the Summit's popularity, but he wasn't proud of what he'd done.

The muted, stinging sensation of the wristbands was an ever-present reminder of the price. He supposed that was the reason his godfather made him wear the wretched things. As bad as he felt about the *null-cuffs*, his private name for them, Mike's continued cold shoulder stung him even deeper.

He stubbornly refused to say a word to Jonah during their first joint anti-bullying patrol. By the end of the patrol, Jonah couldn't take it anymore.

Mike had already closed his locker and started to leave when Jonah tapped his shoulder. "Hey?"

Mike tensed at the touch and turned, clutching his notebook in one hand. His other hand was in his pocket. "What?" He refused to look at Jonah.

"I wanted to tell you something."

"You mean apologize?"

Jonah blinked in surprise, his own irritation rushing forward. "I already did that."

Mike's jaw tightened as he ground his teeth. "I'm helping the new club member on the last patrol today, so you'll be with someone else." With that, Mike turned and slipped through the students that were clogging the hallway.

*

Because Mike was a wizard at organizing things, Jonah let him handle all the patrol assignments for the Tolerance Club. When Mike handed Jonah his new assignment, and Jonah saw the location, he knew his buddy was simply getting even. Mike not only broke up their team by pairing Jonah with Anthony, but he also sent them to the opposite end of the school from himself.

Mike crossed his arms as if waiting for Jonah to complain further or assert his role as the club leader. Instead, Jonah snatched the slip of paper with the assignment on it and beckoned Anthony to come over before heading off to the secluded stairway.

The custodians used the area at the top of the steps to store extra supplies, broken touch boards, and the like. The doors to the roof stood at the far side of the space and behind a pile of old supplies.

Some student had evidently discovered the access door and created a narrow path between the boxes. The club had heard scattered rumors of students using it to catch a smoke on the roof. Occasionally, bullies took smaller kids in there for beat-downs.

He and Anthony posted themselves at the top of the stairs and spent the time talking about the upcoming Halloween Bonfire. Things were fine until Brandon showed up. The bully grinned up at them as he mounted the stairs before rudely shoving his way between Jonah and Anthony.

He pulled out a cigarette and a crooked smile appeared on his face. "What are you doing here, DC?"

Jonah stood his ground. "You're not supposed to be smoking in the school or on the roof." Anthony nodded in agreement.

Brandon made a show of lighting and taking a puff of the cigarette. "I thought you were just anti-bullying?" He held out the cigarette to Jonah. "Wanna try one?"

Jonah waved a hand in front of his face, trying to dispel the smoke. "Put it out!"

"Or what?" When Jonah didn't respond, Brandon laughed and glanced at his expensive watch. With a final snort, he threaded his way between the boxes and out the roof access door.

"Think we should report him?" Anthony asked.

850   *John Darr*

Jonah shook his head. "His dad will make too much of a fuss. Leave it."

Anthony's phone pinged and he checked it. "Hey. I need to meet someone. Mind if I head off a little early?"

"Nah. Go ahead."

Anthony took the first few steps and paused, turning back. "You sure about Brandon?"

"He's fine as long as he's alone."

With that, Anthony nodded and hurried away.

Jonah turned to peer at the sunlight streaming through the crack between the roof doors. He also caught the acrid whiff of cigarette smoke on the cool air current. Maybe he should have reported Brandon…

The door opened, cutting off that silent debate. Brandon stepped inside and threaded his way back through the box path. He stepped free and squared off with Jonah.

"You still here, DC? I'm starting to think you like me or something."

At that moment, Jonah realized all at once that Brandon was acting braver and calmer than usual, considering he was alone and without his usual admiring crowd. As soon as that thought crossed Jonah's mind, he sensed the person behind him. His assessment was rudely corrected when two people firmly grabbed his arms and legs.

Brandon wasn't alone after all. At the same time, a horrible realization occurred to Jonah. Not only did the wristbands nullify his phasing ability, they also muffled his Death Sense.

Jonah struggled, but he couldn't use any of the defensive moves that he'd mastered in Practice Club. Brandon dropped his cigarette on the ground and snubbed it out with a foot.

"Right on time, guys." He laughed as he loomed closer. "Hold the freak tight."

Jonah saw Brandon tensing up just before the boy threw the first punch to the face. A stinging pain exploded across Jonah's upper lip and nose before the sensation of wetness splatted on the top of his mouth and dribbled down onto his chin. He sucked in a startled breath, accompanied by fresh pain in other places.

Amulet of the Goddess

One of Brandon's buddies called out to him, "Watch it, Brandon. You don't want to leave obvious marks on him or we'll get into trouble."

A look of frustration transformed Brandon's face, like he didn't want to be told what to do. His expression subsequently turned thoughtful as he scrutinized Jonah's struggling form.

"You're right."

This time, Brandon delivered three solid punches to Jonah's midsection, causing him to gasp in pain as he struggled to breathe.

Brandon pulled back and smirked at Jonah. "Those were for Drew." He punched Jonah again in the stomach. "That one was for Antwan." Another punch. "And that one was because I don't like you."

Despite the excruciating pain, Jonah prepared to twist his body when Brandon reared back to deliver another punch.

"This is because I hate your stupid club." Brandon swung, and Jonah twisted. The result was having the bully's fist impact the side of Jonah's chest, hitting him squarely in the ribs.

That pain was even worse. Jonah's only satisfaction was Brandon's grunt of anguish. The boy cursed and shoved Jonah's head back, producing a sharp jab in his neck. "Let him go."

The guys did and Jonah sagged to the ground, still clutching his midsection. The blood from his nose ran down his cheek and pooled onto the cold floor. He listened to the boys laughing as they descended the stairs.

Jonah lay there, struggling to catch his breath while trying to ignore his injuries. In an odd way, he was reminded of his fight with Agent Hunter in the Afterworld. Before now, that was the last time he hurt so much. He touched his nose and winced. It wasn't broken, just bloodied.

He broke it two summers ago when he and Brandon had their first-ever duel. But this time was different. The continued dull, throbbing pain indicated that his healing factor wasn't working either.

Jonah struggled to his feet and made his way to the nearest bathroom. The tissues he used to staunch the bleeding came away scarlet red. He started to lift his sweater and winced. When he finally exposed his abdomen, he couldn't believe all the bruises.

Brandon's friend was right. The nose and busted lip were the only clear signs of the attack. Still, he worried that his relatives would notice even those. With his healing factor blocked, he would have to fully endure the pain of the attack just like any other regular kid. For all Jonah's desires to be normal, today, he wanted his powers back more than ever before.

*

His nose eventually stopped bleeding, but Aunt Imma noticed his constant wincing and the busted lip as soon as she came home from work.

"What on Earth?" She lifted Jonah's chin and inspected the bruise.

"It's nothing. Just a rough game of basketball."

Aunt Imma made a disapproving sound. "First Robert and now you."

She went off to her room to change out of her work clothes. Although his answer quieted anymore questions, he hated lying to his aunt. But he also couldn't tell anybody the truth. How would it look for the leader of the anti-bullying club to be victimized?

All the other kids would quit, Jonah decided. Then again, the work of the club was to get kids to report any bullying. Yet here he was now, refusing to do that too. Either way Jonah considered the situation, he felt like a fraud.

To ease his burning shame over the whole sorry ordeal, Jonah tried to concentrate on his homework. With his books spread all over the kitchen table, he worked there because it was less painful than moving the short distance it took to get to his room. His phone buzzed and vibrated, disrupting his attempt to study.

When Mike's ID flashed, Jonah dropped the phone on the table and returned to his homework. He didn't want to talk to Mike, not when he still blamed his friend for what happened.

The phone buzzed again with Mike's second attempt to reach him. Jonah glared at it, hoping his buddy would hang up. This time, Mike included a text message before he called the third time.

By then, Aunt Imma had returned to the kitchen and started pulling out items for dinner. "Why don't you answer your phone?"

"Yes, ma'am." *Dang it*. "What?" He hissed into the phone as his aunt clanked around in the pot cupboard.

Amulet of the Goddess   853

The silence on Mike's end told Jonah he wasn't scoring any points. But right now, he didn't care.

Mike let out a huff like he was counting to ten to calm himself. Then he said, "It's all your fault."

Jonah's stomach tightened. He had no clue what he did wrong this time and frankly, he was sick of people jumping on him. Before he answered, he rose slowly to his feet and lumbered outside to the patio. "What are you talking about? What did I do wrong this time?"

"Alastor! After you talked to him, he closed up the store and left town. I found a note saying I'd have to keep it open until he comes back."

"That wasn't my fault."

"Yes, it was. You and Kevin scared him off."

Jonah snorted and grimaced, clutching his stomach. "Alastor wasn't afraid of us."

"Well, you busted his cover. Either way, he packed up and left."

"He's probably just reporting to his boss. I'm sure he'll be back."

"No, he won't."

Jonah wanted to say *too bad*, but even in his sour mood, he knew that would set Mike off. "When's your uncle coming back?"

"My dad called him today, and he won't be back for two months. We have to work the store until then."

"So what's the problem?"

"I have to keep the store open, every day, after school. My dad thinks it'll build character!"

Despite his friend's anxiety, Jonah found the circumstances a little humorous. He fought to keep the amusement out of his voice. "I'm sorry, Mike, but I know you can handle it."

"I won't be able to do the things I want to do or see the people I want to see."

Jonah couldn't believe his friend. "Mike, how can you still see Patrick?"

"You should have to help me," Mike said, ignoring the question.

"What? Why?"

"Because I need your help."

The unexpected plea for help stopped Jonah's mounting anger in its tracks. "Well… ah, what about Patrick?"

"He's not a big reader. You know the store better and…"

"And?"

"And I may forgive you for lying to me."

Jonah rubbed his forehead, wincing at the start of a headache. If he did that, it could help patch things up with Mike. "When?"

"Get over here now."

"Now? But–"

Mike ended the call.

After clearing it with his aunt, Jonah slowly put his books away. He didn't look forward to the painful bike ride, but knew it would also be worth it.

Amulet of the Goddess

CHAPTER TWENTY-EIGHT
FIRST DATE

One unfortunate effect of Alastor's departure was the reduced operating hours. This forced the usual daily customers to mingle with the evening crowd. Jonah had never seen so many people in the store at one time.

He crossed slowly to the sales counter and waved. "I'm here."

Mike was all business. "Cover the register," he barked before moving off briskly to help a little woman find a rare book.

Reminding himself that it was worth it, Jonah eased behind the counter and spent the next two hours ringing up purchases. In no time, he had his own routine down. In between waiting on customers, he helped shelve the traded-in, used books, which they kept on the lower shelves only.

He experienced a pang of regret when he realized how much fun he and Mike could have had at the store, if he hadn't been such a jerk by lying. Things remained civil between the boys until an hour before closing.

Patrick came into the store. "What'sup?"

Jonah waved to the sullen boy just as Mike appeared from a side aisle with an arm full of paperbacks for the customer who was following him.

He hesitated when he saw Patrick and dropped the books on the counter. "Jonah, you handle this."

"Sure thing."

Jonah gave the customer a cheery smile, but did not fail to notice Mike motioning to Patrick to go to the back of the store and the office. Jonah rang up the customer as quickly as he could. After that, he moved from behind the counter, ignoring the prickles of pain, and approached the back of the store.

Patrick's angry voice carried out to him. "This sucks, Mike! I want us to go."

"It's my job to watch the store and close out everything afterward."

"Why can't Jonah do it?"

"Jonah has his own plans for tonight," Mike answered.

"Really? Admit it. You like hanging out in the books with your old boyfriend."

Jonah recoiled at that statement, grimaced, and shuffled backward. It was fortunate that he did because Patrick stomped away from the back office and barely glanced at Jonah while storming by. Mike came out and started straightening the books with agitated movements.

Part of Jonah was thrilled to see Patrick and Mike having problems. However, he didn't want to see his friend in pain, either. "Mike?"

"What?" Mike scanned the store. "Is something wrong?"

"No."

"Well, did you finish the used books?"

"Yeah, I did." *While you and your boyfriend were fighting.* Jonah took a deep breath as Mike began stacking magazines. "If you need me to cover for you tonight, I can. I'm not doing anything else later on."

Mike's mouth worked as if he repeated Jonah's words. "Seriously? I mean, thanks."

They faced each other in awkward silence. Jonah started to apologize when Mike sprinted for the front door.

Once again, Jonah reined in his mixed feelings. He'd only made the offer because he hoped Mike would accept his apology, not so he could chase after Patrick. He groaned as he reached the front door and peeked through the multi-colored glass. Mike and Patrick stood outside in the gravel parking lot, talking.

Remembering to be happy for his best friend, Jonah turned back to his work. His aching mid-section aside, he discovered he liked working the

Amulet of the Goddess

store alone. For one thing, he didn't have to hide his pain from anyone. In addition to that, the lower number of customers near closing time made it easy to help each patron individually.

Mike showed him how to close out the register and put things away in the safe that was located in the back office. *It was strange*, Jonah reflected. He loved bookstores, but never imagined working in one before, much less, owning one someday. He rang up a customer, who saw his happy expression and smiled back.

"Thanks for coming," Jonah said. He was about to turn and put away a stack of trade-ins when the door opened and Kevin strode inside. The tall boy stopped to take in the cramped store before crossing to the counter, all the while watching Jonah's expression with a neutral look.

"What are you doing here?"

Kevin hooked a thumb over his shoulder. "You're not supposed to be out on your own after dark, remember?"

"But I thought you had to check in regularly and were staying in Atlanta."

"I did check in and I'll head back to Atlanta. First, I have some news for you."

"Oh. How did you find me?"

Kevin grinned. "It wasn't hard. You're a boring kid, you know that?"

Jonah didn't bristle at the taunt. Instead, he smiled because he liked Kevin playfully sparring with him.

The final customer came to the register. Kevin moved aside and pulled a magazine from a nearby rack. Jonah finished with the customer and caught Kevin watching him out of the corner of his eye. Once the patron exited the store, Jonah took the trade-ins and eased around the counter.

He began shelving books in the Military Science Fiction section while Kevin watched his every move. "Didn't you have something to tell me?" Jonah asked.

"Oh, yeah." Kevin leaned against the bookshelves.

"We had Alliance Guards watching your aunt's old shop. Well, someone busted in."

"Was it my aunt?" Jonah asked, his hopes rising. "Did they catch her?"

"No, it wasn't her. And the person got away by busting out the wall in the back of the store to escape." Kevin rubbed his chin, looking thoughtful. "Almost like they expected the guards to bust in."

Jonah was disappointed, but at least Lynn had been right. "Aunt Ruby doesn't have the real amulet. That's good. It means she doesn't know where it is either."

"True," Kevin agreed, "but it also indicates she'll have to start looking in other places."

An unpleasant alternative occurred to Jonah. "Maybe she'll think I have it."

Kevin's gaze turned intense. "Well, she'd have to get through me first."

The comment thrilled Jonah so much, he made the mistake of reaching too high and had to suck in a painful breath.

Kevin was at his side in a second. "What's wrong with you?"

"Nothing." Jonah couldn't hide the fact he didn't want to reach up again.

Kevin took the book and slid it onto the shelf.

"Thanks," Jonah said. He tried to select the next book but Kevin took the stack and set them on the floor. He gripped the bottom of Jonah's sweater, but Jonah stopped him. "Kevin, don't."

"Be quiet." Kevin pushed Jonah's hands aside and lifted the sweater. The cool air on his bare skin slightly eased the pain.

Kevin hissed in anger as he examined Jonah's bruises. The boy's super warm hand felt wonderful.

"Who did this?" Kevin's voice was tight with suppressed anger.

"Brandon and his guys ambushed me."

"I'm gonna put my fist through his arrogant face!"

Jonah gulped at the raw fury in Kevin's tone. "You can't do that. I'm wearing these bands because I went Batman on him."

"I don't care. You could have a broken rib or two! Those stun cuffs must be interfering with your healing factor too."

Amulet of the Goddess

Jonah winced at Kevin's continuing examination. "Is it broken?"

"No. Just bruised," Kevin answered. He let Jonah's sweater drop but his hand lingered underneath it and against Jonah's abdomen for a moment. "Why didn't you let the school nurse check you out?"

"Are you crazy? She'd have reported it and then, everyone would know what happened."

"Brandon would have gotten in trouble that way," Kevin shot back.

"Yeah, and totally embarrass me in the process. The head of the Tolerance Club getting bullied!"

"Shouldn't you set the example by reporting it?"

Jonah gaped at him. "You really want me to do that?"

The young Fallen Reaper shrugged, his jaw clenching.

"Kevin?" Jonah waited for the boy to meet his gaze. "Don't do anything to him. Please. I don't want you sent away forever."

Kevin nodded, but Jonah knew he needed to distract the boy so he nudged the books with his foot. "Help me put those away."

Kevin obliged, slipping the books into the slots where directed. "Where's Mike?"

"Out with Patrick." Jonah didn't bother to hide his disappointment.

Kevin turned on him. "After what he did?"

"Tell me about it." Jonah was relieved to have Kevin agree with him. "I tried to talk to Mike, but he wouldn't listen. I don't get it."

"Well, I don't get either of you geeks," Kevin said with a laugh.

Jonah shoved him and regretted it when his bruises throbbed. Maybe he should have let Kevin pound Brandon into a pulp anyway.

Kevin slipped an arm around Jonah's waist and helped him walk to the front. Jonah didn't need the help but he loved the contact. "Hey, lock the door and turn the sign around."

"Lock the door?" Kevin smirked at him.

"You know what I mean," Jonah could feel his own face warming.

When Kevin returned, he glanced around the store. "What else do you have to do?"

"Why?" Jonah asked, curious.

"I can get us dinner and bring it back here."

Jonah began to mention that Aunt Imma had probably cooked something before he nearly kicked himself. Dinner in the bookstore with Kevin sounded wonderful! Plus, it presented an opportunity to be alone with him longer. The more Jonah considered it, the more he liked it. Besides, his aunt knew he was working at the store anyway. "Yeah, that's cool. I can close up things while you go and get it."

Kevin brightened at the idea and left.

Jonah went about his duties closing out the store and putting everything away. He had just finished dumping the trash out the back and was washing his hands when Kevin knocked on the door.

Jonah grinned. "You knocked?"

"This place is protected against phasing." Kevin held up the take-out boxes from a nearby restaurant. The enticing aroma of the hot food made Jonah's stomach grumble with anticipation. But Kevin also had a regular convenience store bag in the other hand.

He withdrew a cold compress from the bag and shook the packet as he pulled up Jonah's sweater. When the ice-cold compress touched his skin, Jonah sighed in relief.

Kevin stared into his eyes while he held the bag in place. Jonah could almost read the boy's thoughts.

"You promised."

"I'm not gonna touch the punk," Kevin said. "Come on."

Jonah held the compress in place as he followed Kevin to the Occult section, where Hackett kept a small table and some fold-out chairs. Kevin placed the dinners on the table and pulled out Jonah's chair for him.

They began to eat and soon Jonah asked Kevin about his time away from Mount Vernon. He was relieved when Kevin relaxed and told him about the missions. Jonah listened as the older boy's confident voice filled the quiet store. It was the longest Kevin had ever talked to him without pausing and Jonah loved it.

Amulet of the Goddess

Eventually, the Fallen Reaper finished discussing his assignment and gazed at him. "I need to get back soon."

Jonah swallowed. "Okay." All at once, he realized that sitting there in the darkened store, under the soft lamp light, he was having his first real date with Kevin. Well, with anyone! "Do you have to leave right now?"

"No," Kevin said, his voice tight. "I have a few minutes."

"What do you want to do?" Jonah's voice shook. But his anticipation spiked and his heart thudded in his chest when the older boy rose, leaned across the table, and kissed him.

CHAPTER TWENTY-NINE
GARAGE ATTACK

Jonah stretched and yawned, feeling refreshed. It was Saturday morning, and the night before, he'd had his first real date with Kevin. He rolled over, reliving the wonderful experience, and his mind suddenly registered there wasn't much pain. Sitting up, he threw back the cover and raised his t-shirt. The bruises on his abdomen were fainter, almost gone. He tentatively pressed his rib and received a very minor ache.

Yes! His healing ability had kicked in during the night. Relieved that at least one of his powers still worked, Jonah rose from the bed and got up. He took an extra-long shower and dressed for the day in a much better spirit. He even pulled on a light-colored sweater that Mike once told him looked nice against his skin color.

Even thoughts of his Aunt Ruby couldn't dampen his mood because he had an idea blossoming about how to find her. There was one person around who might have known his aunt's whereabouts: The store clerk Wraith. As weird as it was, the man had been honest after all. With a start, Jonah realized Deyanira had also tried to help him.

Beware, young Blackstone.

Jonah knew better than to think the evil Reaper did it out of any real affection for him. She simply hated the mole. Is the enemy of my enemy my friend?

Yeah, he would go and talk with the store clerk, but he couldn't go alone. The problem was Lynn already made plans to help Uncle James and Kevin

Amulet of the Goddess **863**

was off doing Alliance work. Jonah's next best choice was Wick. After a quick bowl of cereal, he fetched his bike and rode to the Teen Center.

Jonah entered the center and spotted Mike at once in the café. He crossed the atrium and sat at the table.

Mike was wearing one of the pullovers his big brother had sent him from college. He also seemed in a good mood this morning. "Thanks for closing the store."

"No problem." Jonah meant it. His night had turned out great. He smiled a little to himself.

Mike noticed. "Wow, you must be in a good mood."

"Why do you say that?"

"You're wearing that sweater I like on you and smiling. What happened?"

Jonah whispered, "Kevin stopped by last night."

Mike's eyes grew comically wide, then his grin turned wicked. "I see." He scanned Jonah's face. "What did you two do?"

Jonah smiled. "Nothing." Then, mimicking Mike when he had asked about Trevor, he mumbled, "We just talked." Mike reached across the table and punched Jonah's arm. Feeling better about his life, despite the predicted doom at midnight on Halloween, Jonah decided to clear the air. "I'm sorry I lied to you, Mike. You're my best friend and I promise—"

"Jonah, don't…" Mike's protest trailed off as his eyes flashed.

Jonah experienced an intense wave of goosebumps along his skin and pushed up his sleeve to examine his arm. "What the…"

"Be careful with your promises," Mike said, his voice serious. "We're part supernatural, so all promises carry extra weight. They told me that at Alliance HQ."

"You mean…"

Mike nodded. "You'll have to keep that promise."

"Oh, well. That's no problem. I was promising not to keep you out of the loop again." Jonah lowered his sleeve back into place. "By the way, your eyes flashed just then."

"So did yours. I think it's because you're the Deliverer and I'm your Seeker."

As a shocked silence slowly ensued, Jonah tapped the table. "Hey, I was thinking of going to Mystic Worlds and asking the Wraith what he knows."

Mike's jaw dropped. "Are you sure that's a good idea?"

"He's not dangerous. He helped me before. And he tried to tell me about the potions, remember?"

"Still." Mike pointed at Jonah's wrists. "You have those bands."

"Yeah. I was gonna ask Wick to go with me."

"He's upstairs practicing his spell casting."

"Cool. He's always complaining about not going on any of the good trips." Jonah rose but paused because he had forgotten something obvious. "You want to come along?"

"Thanks, but I don't think so." Mike leaned back in his chair, crossing his thin arms. "I want to make more headway on the translations. Tell me what happens when you get back."

*

"Let's be clear about this." Wick stopped Jonah just outside the former Mystic Worlds bookstore. "If Lynn finds out, this was your idea, okay?"

"Chicken," Jonah teased. He opened the door and entered.

Wick sucked in a breath when he crossed the threshold. "Whoa!"

"What?"

"I forgot they rearranged this place to dispel the magical energy." Wick scanned the store while ruffling his hair twists. "Yep. Look at the bookshelves. They're scattered like that on purpose. I bet there are sigils on all of them. Slick."

The store clerk approached and eyed Wick for a moment. "Mage?" His voice was low because there were other customers browsing among the aisles.

"Yeah, I am." Wick puffed out his chest, acting his usual confident self. That reassured Jonah. "I know why you have the bookshelves arranged like this."

Amulet of the Goddess **865**

The clerk nodded, visibly impressed. "You can't be too careful." He spread his hands in an inviting way and focused on Jonah. "How may I help you today?"

Jonah heard the genuine willingness in the man's voice. "Thanks for the potion warnings."

The clerk's eyebrow rose. "You neutralized that threat?"

"Yeah. And we know about the Pakhet legend and the amulet."

"Then you should recognize the great danger threatening this whole town," the Wraith added. "Be forewarned, young Blackstone. You must find the amulet."

"Sure thing," Wick said, "as soon as you tell us where it is."

"I have no information regarding the amulet's whereabouts."

Jonah thought the surprise on the clerk's face was sincere. He wasn't worried because he had another idea. "Does Latrell know?"

The clerk shook his head. "I doubt it. If he did, the Wraiths working with your aunt would also know." His eyes narrowed. "You do realize that the shadow of Pakhet still rests upon your aunt? She may no longer be herself."

"She's still a bad person—" Jonah stopped. The clerk held up a hand as a customer approached the back counter before moving away to help her.

Wick whispered in Jonah's ear, "Is he lying?"

"I can't tell," Jonah admitted. "The bands are messing with my Reaper's Stare."

The front door opened, cutting off their hushed conversation. Bright morning sunlight streamed through the entrance, casting an eerie glow around Niqab Girl.

She stepped aside while the clerk ushered the remaining customer out the front door. Her eyes, the only thing visible through her face mask, never left Jonah's face. "I'm looking for some books on powerful amulets."

The clerk closed the door and scowled at her while fingering an amulet hanging around his neck. It was in the shape of a flattened pyramid. He directed his attention to Jonah and Wick. "Is there anything else I can do for you gentlemen?" He flicked his eyes to Antwan's cousin briefly before opening the door.

"Nope," Jonah answered as he tried to pull Wick toward the exit. "Come on."

But Wick wore an uncharacteristic, enraged expression. "You're the one who messed with my magic at the show!" He raised his hand, calling on his magic.

Niqab Girl reacted in kind, stretching her right hand out. But she frowned and glared at the clerk.

Wick blinked and stared at his own hand as he tried several times to perfect a throwing motion but nothing except a brief spark appeared before it faded.

The clerk positioned himself between them. "There're no magic duels allowed in this store. It's neutral ground." He motioned to Wick and Jonah. "Please go."

Jonah had to shove Wick out the door. All the while, Antwan's cousin grinned at him.

Once they were outside, Wick tried to pull free of Jonah's grip, but Jonah succeeded in getting the young mage across the street and onto the opposite sidewalk.

Wick glared at the store. "Get out of the way, Jonah."

"That's not too smart." Jonah held up his wrist and showed off the band. "You want Trueblood and Albrecht to do the same thing to you?"

"She's gloating about the whole thing," Wick protested. Then he went still.

That scared Jonah. He followed Wick's gaze and spotted Antwan's cousin exiting the bookstore. She made a point of glancing at them before walking down the opposite sidewalk at a brisk pace. Wick set off down their sidewalk, keeping up with her.

Jonah followed. "Where are you going?"

"I need to find out what she knows."

"Following Antwan's cousin is pretty risky. The store clerk told us to beware."

Amulet of the Goddess

"He said *be forewarned.*" Wick continued down the sidewalk.

"Whatever. We should still be careful," Jonah said. He didn't know what to do. Wick was bigger than him and strong enough to push him out of the way and keep pursuing Niqab Girl. For a moment, Jonah considered calling Lynn or Robert even though that would only have made things worse.

"What are you gonna do when you catch up to her?" Jonah asked.

"Just have a nice talk with her." Wick flexed his hands.

Even with the effects of the bands, Jonah could sense the magic gathering around the boy.

Wick pointed at the retreating girl, who was now a block away. "We need to see where she goes. Come on."

"We already know she's hiding out at Antwan's."

"Maybe she's on the way to report to your aunt?" Wick countered. "You ever think of that?"

Jonah let out an exasperated sigh. "Lynn and Kevin would skin us alive if anything happens."

"Then we won't tell them. I have to do something," Wick pleaded. "We can't wait around until they find the amulet." He turned to Jonah. "I thought you would understand?"

"Excuse me." Jonah raised his wrists again. "No powers."

Wick ruffled his twists in irritation. "I have enough for both of us."

They crossed to the other side of the street and hurried to close the gap with Antwan's cousin. Wick fingered a shield bracelet on his right wrist, catching Jonah's attention. He noticed now that his friend had also given up his trademark unlaced, black boots for black high-tops that didn't make any noise on the sidewalk. Jonah wondered if Wick expected something like this to happen.

Up ahead, Antwan's cousin turned onto a side street between the shopping strip and a parking garage. Wick and Jonah broke into a run. They reached the corner just in time to see the young girl ducking into the parking structure.

A sudden thought struck Jonah and he glanced sideways at Wick. "She knows we're following her."

"Yep…" Wick pointed. Antwan's cousin sprinted to the far corner of the first level and into a stairwell. He led the way, weaving around rows of cars, and slipped inside the same stairwell. The girl's running feet made a huge racket, convincing Jonah she wanted them to follow.

The boys sprinted up the stairs. As they passed the fourth level, the exit door on the fifth level opened and closed with a loud bang!

Wick motioned Jonah to stop. "She may have just opened the door to fool us and then gone up to the sixth level."

When they didn't hear more footsteps, they continued their ascent and rounded the last few stairs to the fifth floor. Wick opened the access door as quietly as he could, poked his head out, and looked around.

"Okay, let's go," he said.

Jonah's Death Sense gave the mildest of twinges, almost imperceptible, as Antwan's cousin stepped into view, her arms crossed.

Wick frowned. "She's up to something." He fingered the bracelet again. A loud bang! came from behind them. Jonah and Wick whirled around to see a cargo van with the back raised off the ground. The huge man stood there using one hand to lift the whole rear of the vehicle. He wasn't wearing a nice suit today. Instead, he wore mechanic's coveralls. And his silhouette, outlined by the sun at his back, resembled a gorilla's. Once he had their attention, he let the van drop and it rocked back and forth.

Jonah recalled this was clearly the hulking man from Robert's drawing. As if to leave no doubt, the man's eyes flashed a solid milky white.

The girl spoke, and her voice filtered through her black mesh face wrap. "Why are you following me, Son of Isaiah?"

"I'm the one following you, evil witch," Wick said before Jonah could stop him.

"Wick," Jonah whispered. "Don't make her mad. The *Hulk* is a good friend of hers."

The Wraith sneered at them and spittle flew from his mouth as he shouted, "I should grind you two pathetic mortals into dust for what you did."

"I think we should leave now," Jonah suggested. He felt naked without his normal powers.

Amulet of the Goddess

Wick shrugged off Jonah's grip, refusing to move. For some reason, he wasn't afraid; in fact, he appeared strangely confident about challenging the Wraith.

Oh, well, Jonah decided. He stood his ground. "Where's my Aunt Ruby?" When they didn't answer, Jonah added, "You'll never get the amulet if you don't tell me."

The Wraith's eyes widened. "I told them you were too dangerous! It's better that I kill you now before you ruin everything."

In one quick motion, he grabbed hold of a nearby ticket box and ripped it from the concrete. Wick muttered a spell under his breath. The hairs on the back of Jonah's neck prickled just as light flashed in front of them and the two spells collided. Almost at the same time, the Wraith flung the ticket box toward them.

Wick jumped directly in front of Jonah. As he did so, the young mage turned his right side to the oncoming ticket box and held up the arm with the bracelet. A popping sensation washed over Jonah and a faint blue circle of distortion appeared around him and Wick. An instant later, the ticket box slammed into Wick's shield.

Even with the added protection, Wick fell backward into Jonah, sending them both to the ground. The box itself arched back through the air and hit the shocked Wraith squarely in the face. The huge guy stumbled backward and right over the edge of the parking garage, the ruined ticket box close behind.

An echoing thud reached them, followed by the lesser bang of the ticket box hitting the ground.

Wick got to his feet and helped Jonah up. "Sorry about that, Padawan. The shield stopped the ticket box, but it couldn't stop the kinetic energy." He glanced in the girl's direction, but Antwan's cousin was gone. "She attacked at the same time, but I don't think she expected me to deflect the hex."

Jonah's jaw dropped. "You've been practicing?"

"Yeah," Wick said, peeking over the concrete barrier that formed the edge of the parking garage.

Jonah joined him. Five stories below, the broken body of the man lay on large spools of industrial grade cabling that filled the narrow space between the parking garage and the next building. The tangled debris of the busted ticket box covered portions of the man's twisted arms and legs.

Jonah sucked in a breath. "He's dead."

"You didn't do it." Wick's voice shook, but that didn't make Jonah feel any better.

"If we hadn't followed her," Jonah began, "he wouldn't have tried to kill us, and..."

Movement below caught Jonah's attention. He pointed. "Look!"

The man's head twitched suddenly and he sat up. His left arm was bent at an unnatural angle under his body, so he took a moment to pop the arm back into the socket. Jonah and Wick winced when the crack of the realignment reached up to all five levels. If the mortal were still alive inside with the Wraith, that had to have hurt.

The Wraith glared up at them, got to his feet, and scrambled over the high fence. When he dropped onto the ground on the other side, he paused to gaze up at them before hobbling down the street and disappearing around the corner.

Wick let out a low breath. "I don't know if that's very cool, or very sick."

*

Jonah and Wick took turns retelling the parking garage adventure for Lynn, Robert, and Mike. Lynn congratulated Wick on saving Jonah's life. Mike remained quiet. Jonah suspected his buddy would say "I told you so" later.

But Robert got incensed with Wick for leaving him wondering where they were.

"Sorry, Bobby. You couldn't have gone with your busted hand."

Robert's face reddened in anger.

"He's right about that, Robert, but," Lynn speared Jonah and Wick with a steely glare, "they were both stupid to follow the girl."

Wick puffed up with anger. "She wrecked my show and hurt a lot of kids, Lynn. We can't let them get away with that."

Amulet of the Goddess

"You're the older one," Lynn countered, waving Wick silent. "If you had waited, I would have told you that I discovered where to look for the amulet." She punctuated her words by plopping into a chair in the clubhouse section of the attic. The others hurried over to join her.

She had her hands steepled like she was deep in thought. "I've given Mike's comments about my great-auntie a lot of thought." She smiled at him. "The Sight ability appears in only one woman in each generation of my family. I did some checking into the family records. All the women with the gift were buried in a family crypt."

"Whoa!" Wick said. "That is so…"

"Wicked," Robert finished. The two boys glanced at each other, and Jonah could see the eagerness on their faces.

He sat forward. "You know where, don't you?"

Lynn nodded. "Yes, I do."

CHAPTER THIRTY
FAMILY CRYPT

Jonah had ominous thoughts about visiting his second graveyard in as many weeks. This one was ancient, far older than the Oak Hill cemetery. The gravestones here were a dingy, dark grey from all the dirt and pollution that had accumulated over the decades. In some cases, it had been over a century since the person's death.

He, Lynn, Mike, and Kevin appeared in what they hoped was a remote corner of the cemetery. Lynn had anticipated the trip and done plenty of research to find pictures of the place, but unfortunately, they couldn't match the pictures with a map.

Kevin adjusted the hang of his Reaper long coat as soon as they arrived. The older boy acted perturbed, but Jonah thought he looked cool in it. Mike agreed, and of course, having two geeks admire the coat only made Kevin want to change it even more.

Jonah finally told him, "Take it off."

"Can't." Kevin ruffled the coat. "Mandara thinks it best to have the extra protection until things settle down. Trueblood agreed." He scanned the surrounding tombstones.

Mike held out the map he downloaded off the cemetery's website. Lynn shook her head and closed her eyes. After a moment, she pointed up the sloping hillside. Near the top were mature trees and rows of above-ground family crypts.

"It's up there," she announced.

Amulet of the Goddess

Lynn never faltered, leading them straight to an ancient crypt at the very apex of the hill. The angled roof was higher than the rest, and given its aged appearance, Jonah concluded it pre-dated all the others.

The oldest of the surrounding trees had huge branches that extended out and over the crypt, shrouding it perpetually in shadows. This morning, an eerie wind blew across the hilltop and Jonah huddled in his light jacket as Lynn walked right up to the building.

Impressive marble columns that framed the door and a wrought-iron security gate created a porch-like structure. Lynn pulled open the security gate and leaned in to examine the ornate metal door. Like the room in their great-auntie's old shop, this door also had a circular, genetic lock. Its status light blinked at them, waiting for the right person to touch it.

"I'm starting to think your mom must've owned stock in the company who makes these things," Mike quipped.

"You've got to admit, at least they work." Lynn positioned her finger over the lock. "Ruby and her Hulk friend weren't able to get through the door at the palm shop." She glanced at Kevin. "Think we should open this?"

"We're here. Plus, I have this." Kevin pulled a compass-like, golden disc from his pocket. About five inches in diameter, it had symbols evenly spaced around the outer edge of the surface and a large center button.

"What's that?" Jonah pointed at the device. "It looks like a flatter Seeker's compass."

Kevin exchanged a glance with Mike. "It's called a codex. Mike helped the Alliance create them."

Jonah gaped at his friend and knew this must be one of the top-secret things his friend couldn't mention.

Mike shrugged. "Sorry. I took an oath."

Lynn eyed the device. "So it's not a bomb?"

Kevin laughed. "No! It's an emergency transporter. It's like the compass except it only goes to one location, and anyone can use it. All you have to do is press the button and it takes you to a safe room."

"Really?" Jonah avoided pressing the center button and instead brushed his fingers around the outer edge. The device felt like it was made of the same metal as the Seeker's compass. He was instantly intrigued. "How did you make it?"

Mike opened his mouth, but Lynn interrupted. "Let's talk about that later. Okay?" She pressed her finger against the genetic lock and it lit up, followed by loud clicks from the vault door.

Kevin took that as his cue, put away the codex, and gripped the door's vertical handle. When he pulled the heavy door outward, a low moan escaped, sending a chill down Jonah's back. *It's just the wind*, he thought. Then the stale air, carrying the stench of death, emanated from the vault.

Lynn shivered and, with a quick backward glance at the others, she entered. Jonah screwed up his nerves and followed. The place felt larger inside than it looked from the outside. There were six crypts stacked lengthwise, three on either side of the structure. And in the very center stood a large, marble coffin. The name chiseled into the side facing the door was FOLAMI.

Jonah didn't recognize the name. He was expecting something like their great-aunt's given name, which he learned was Victoria.

Mike ran his fingers over the letters. "It's a West African name that means *Respect me.*"

"I knew that because I looked her up," Lynn said to him, slightly shocked. "But how did you know?"

"The mind boost," Mike answered.

"He can translate any language, spoken or written," Jonah added. "It's pretty awesome."

Mike shrugged at the comment and strictly focused on the name. "She must have been the first in the line. My guess is she was a freed slave."

"Yeah." Lynn nodded. "I read she was freed from slavery after the Civil War. Even before then, she was known to possess a lot of power. The story goes her owner wanted a prediction to help him escape the Union soldiers. Flame told him a lie and he was subsequently caught and shot."

"Wow," Jonah said. He touched the tomb—which was cold against his fingertips—thinking everything must've started with her. Moving around his ancestors' tomb, he gazed thoughtfully at the line of ornamental plaques along the right wall. Each identified its descendants and their specialty.

Amulet of the Goddess

All of these women were powerful mediums, psychics, and, in the one case, a Seer. Jonah found that interesting. The place exuded an intriguing sense of history. What boggled his mind even more was that he never even knew about this, and he adored history.

Since the bodies were arranged in chronological order according to their death dates, it was easy to find their great-aunt Victoria, the last one to run the Ankh of Life shop. But Jonah froze when he noted the next space below her crypt had a blank bronze plaque.

That slot was empty because his mom had been buried beside his dad back in D.C. In addition to his mom's empty slot, there was one more open niche. Jonah glanced at his cousin, Lynn, to see her expression. She met his gaze for a moment before focusing on Great-Aunt Victoria's crypt.

Mike pointed out the obvious. "It's sealed."

Kevin pulled a short crowbar out from the inner pocket of his long coat. He raised it and ordered the others to stand back before jamming it into the mortared edge of the covering stone. With a grunt, he shoved the tool clear through.

In quick order, he proceeded to knock away enough of the mortar to slip his hands into the opening. With a little effort, he ripped the cover stone away and revealed the black coffin within.

Lynn darted forward to help him pull it out far enough to rest one end on top of Folami's tomb. Kevin met her determined gaze and, on the count of three, they pried open the lid. Everyone gagged and covered their noses.

Their great-auntie was nothing more than a skeleton covered in a faded, long dress and purple cape that had a royal look to it. Her white hair was amazingly well preserved around her desiccated skull. That only added to the horror and oddity of the macabre sight.

Lynn, one hand covering her nose, pointed at a box in the woman's death grip. Kevin pried the skeletal fingers from around the box and handed it to Lynn. She, Mike, and Jonah retreated to the other side of the space while Kevin closed the lid and shoved the coffin back into the receptacle.

Jonah tapped the box, getting surprised by how thick it sounded. "Is it heavy?"

"Yes." Lynn hefted it.

Mike rubbed a finger over the engraved sigils covering the lid. "It's warded to keep supernaturals from detecting it." He pointed out the separate designs. "These are really powerful and complex."

"In that case, we'll keep it closed," Lynn said.

"And hand it over to the Alliance," Kevin added, joining them.

Lynn's objection was stopped before she could utter it because her face paled.

A minor tremor in his Death Sense alerted Jonah, but it was still too muted. Yet, if he felt that…

Something huge suddenly charged through the door and power-dived into Kevin, knocking him clear across the crypt and against the back wall with a solid bump. Jonah heard the codex and Kevin's blades clatter to the ground, but in the dimness, he couldn't spot them.

Kevin rebounded and grappled with the huge Wraith. He managed to gasp out to Jonah, "Get it out of here!"

Jonah realized that Kevin meant the codex. Mike was ahead of him and had already knelt to search the ground for it.

While Jonah hesitated, Lynn shoved the box into his hands and pulled out her own blades. Just as she moved to help, Niqab Girl stepped into the crypt and shot a hex at her. Lynn spun around just in time to deflect the first one. But her timing was slightly off and a second hex caught her in the side and sent her tumbling to the ground.

As the young sorceress turned on Jonah, he grabbed Mike and dived behind the center tomb. The hex hit with a loud bang! and shattered a corner. Heavy pieces of the tomb's lid crashed to the floor within inches of Mike's leg.

He managed to roll aside, letting out a painful grunt, and reached underneath himself, holding up Kevin's deactivated blades. Without warning, he shoved them into Jonah's back pocket.

"Mike, don't. Toss them to Kev–"

The side of the tomb took another direct hit, right above Jonah's head. Niqab Girl had shifted to the side to get a clean shot. Jonah and Mike hustled around in the opposite direction to keep the tomb between her and

Amulet of the Goddess   877

them. He realized their mistake too late. In focusing all of his attention on her, he failed to see the second Wraith-possessed goon who had entered the mausoleum before he rushed their position.

Jonah's first concern was to protect Mike by placing himself in front of his buddy. That proved a second mistake since the Wraith only wanted him. The large man pinned Jonah in a painful bear hug and started pulling him toward the door. Jonah tried to toss the box to Mike or just release it. The problem was the Wraith's hold was crushing the box against Jonah's chest.

Niqab Girl weaved her hands toward the ceiling of the crypt and shouted, "Kufanya!" Sigils that prevented any phasing instantly appeared all over the ceiling and walls.

At that moment, Ruby entered the crypt. She laughed at Lynn, who had struggled to her feet, looking murderous. "Thank you for opening the crypt, my niece! I could never have gotten in otherwise." She shifted her gaze to Kevin and the huge Wraith, still grappling with each other. "Leave him be, my pet."

The Wraith growled and hurled Kevin into the back wall. The Fallen Reaper used his hands to lessen the impact. He spun around, ready to keep fighting, but Lynn stopped him. In the quick lull, Mike darted from behind the damaged tomb and joined them.

Kevin took one of Lynn's activated blades and pointed it at the Wraith holding Jonah. "Let him go."

Aunt Ruby sneered, "He's coming with me. I have special plans for my nephew."

Kevin's arm moved in a blur and the blade zipped through the air at the Wraith. Less than a foot away, the weapon smacked into a barrier and ricocheted into one of the crypts. Niqab Girl, however, had erected a ward to guard their retreat.

Kevin let out a growl of frustration.

Jonah's insides burned with shame as the Wraith yanked him through the door and outside. He struggled, but it was useless without any powers. Aunt Ruby came next and Antwan's cousin last, her hands poised to cast a hex at the others. Once they were clear of the crypt, the hulking Wraith slammed the door and blocked it with two heavy, metal beams.

Jonah was getting a bad feeling about what was happening as he listened to Kevin's repeated pounding on the door. It actually bucked with each of his anger-fueled blows.

Ignoring the pounding, Ruby held up the amulet box and smiled. "I should have known. The old bat hid the amulet in a warded box to keep me from detecting it." She nodded to the huge Wraith.

The man made a show of holding up a remote. Two more Wraith goons scrambled away from the crypt. One dropped down from the roof and hustled over to the others. Jonah noted small square blocks of what looked like clay attached to the roof. They were just below the overhang.

Oh, no. "Don't do it."

"Watch your friends and family die, young Blackstone."

The Wraith holding him gripped Jonah's chin to force him to look.

"It'll be a tragedy to kill my niece," Ruby continued, "but you need to experience this emotional pain. You need to see their broken bodies."

"Don't, please, Aunt Ruby!"

Ruby leered at him and signaled the big Wraith to press the remote's button. When the charges went off, the crypt's roof seemed to jump half a foot into the air before slamming down onto the rest of the crypt. The entire structure collapsed in on itself in a tremendous crash of stone and debris.

Amulet of the Goddess

CHAPTER THIRTY-ONE
ALLIANCE GUARDIANS

Pieces of stone and marble slid loose and fell to the ground before the dust finally settled around the shattered mausoleum.

Jonah's voice was raw from shouting and tears streamed down his face. His friends and cousin had been cruelly crushed to death. How could his aunt be so evil that she would kill her own niece? He hated the woman now more than anything, even more than the Grim Reaper.

Ruby was ecstatic. "They all treated me like an outcast, even your mom did. Well, to hell with all those witches! I got the last laugh." And she did laugh. It sounded demented and totally devoid of any compassion.

"Shut up, witch!" Jonah screamed, even though it tortured his throat.

Ruby glared at him for a moment before taking a deep breath and her gloating expression returned. "You need to feel this pain, nephew." She motioned to the hulking Wraith. "Dig their bodies out. I want him to see."

The eagerness in the Wraith-possessed man sickened Jonah. His horror mounted as Ruby's obedient servant lumbered toward the heap of stone, plunging his huge fists into the rubble, and heaving off the first slab of marble. The brute flung it aside, careless of where it landed. In this case, it knocked off the top of a nearby obelisk headstone.

His obvious disregard for the dead and his willing depravity produced a deep desire inside Jonah to act. A silent growl worked its way up from his stomach and climbed into his chest. It was like a tidal wave of heat and energy. The Wraith holding him suddenly let out a scream of pain. And to Jonah's surprise, the goon's grip also slackened.

Somehow, despite the bands, a surge of power rippled through him.

Calling on his training, Jonah bucked his entire body and broke loose from the Wraith. *Yes!* He sprinted for the closest tombstones, determined to put as much distance as possible between himself and these lunatics. Most of all, he intended to survive.

Jonah thought he'd make it but the Wraith recovered faster than he anticipated. The man lunged and, wham! He hit Jonah between the shoulder blades. The blow lifted him off his feet and sent him tumbling over a row of tombstones. Jonah tried to tuck and roll but he landed too hard and slammed into the base of a large statue.

No, I won't let them win!

Fear and the primal need to survive drove all thoughts of pain out of his mind. Even as the heavy footfalls of the Wraith approached, Jonah again scrambled to his feet and pelted down the row of graves.

There, to his right! A dark shape leapt at him, and Jonah dodged to the left and into the next row over. Just as fast, he changed his direction, perhaps gaining a precious few more seconds because the larger man wasn't quite as agile.

The entire time, Ruby screamed in the background at the top of her lungs for her henchmen to catch him.

"Ah!" Jonah grunted in pain when something hot exploded against a nearby headstone; some of the flying pieces nicked his face. A hex. Jonah dodged into the next row to avoid another missile from Niqab Girl.

"Ruby!" Antwan's cousin shouted, sounding frustrated. "You've used up all your power. We should leave."

"I want the boy!" Ruby roared.

"We need to get the amulet to safety."

Jonah zigzagged through the gravesides, using the downhill slope to gain more momentum. One of the Wraiths leapt in front of him, forcing Jonah to double back up the hill.

Antwan's cousin created a vortex so she and Ruby could leave. Jonah made the mistake of staring at it for too long. The hulking Wraith charged in from the left and landed a solid punch into his shoulder. Pain paralyzed Jonah's left side, like he'd dislocated it.

Amulet of the Goddess **881**

His body spun into a large, stone angel, the breath as well as the fight knocked out of him. The hulking Wraith grabbed his arm and twisted it, causing excruciating pain. But the man seemed overly interested in Jonah's sleeve. Too late, Jonah realized that the Wraith had already figured out why he couldn't phase away.

Sure enough, the Wraith yanked up Jonah's sleeve to expose the band around his wrist, letting out an evil laugh as his eyes narrowed in malicious glee.

"We were ordered to bring you back alive, but no one said in one piece."

He lifted Jonah off his feet and threw him hard. Jonah landed at the base of a broken obelisk. The scattered pieces of it pressed into his back harshly. Though dazed by the anguish and pain, at the same time, he heard clicking sounds in his back pocket and felt something hard there. *Kevin's blades!*

Jonah pulled out the deactivated weapons. Just holding the blades brought up horrid images of Kevin lying dead in the rubble. Another surge of fury rushed through Jonah and the cylinders began to hum in his hands.

The large Wraith took his time stalking Jonah. "You're gonna pay for sending my fellow Wraiths back to the Underworld, you filthy abomination!"

Confident that he finally had a plan and a way out, Jonah activated the blades but kept them hidden behind his back as he leaned against the broken headstone. When the Wraith loomed over him, sneering, Jonah readied himself. He would have one chance only to surprise it.

"Let's see how you like enduring multiple broken bones," the Wraith taunted.

He reached down to snatch Jonah, and that's when Jonah acted by swiping the blades across the Wraith's chest. He was shocked at how easily the blades cut through the coat and shirt, like a hot knife through butter. Without any resistance, the blades sliced into the mortal's flesh beneath, scoring a deep wound in the man's chest.

As always happened, the cut sparked and bled. The Wraith inside the mortal screamed out in agony and pain. Jonah experienced a savage rush of satisfaction as the huge mortal stumbled away from him, seeking a safer distance.

The second Wraith paused in fear while staring between his wounded buddy and the sizzling, bloody Reaper's blades still in Jonah's hands.

Grateful for the man's fearful hesitation, Jonah regained his balance and jumped onto his feet. He was pissed and ready to make both Wraiths pay for what they had done. At that moment, he didn't care if the mortals lived or not. They were equally to blame for allowing the evil spirits to possess them.

Before Jonah could exact his vengeance, a Reaper blade whistled through the air and embedded itself into the second Wraith's shoulder.

Jonah blinked in surprise and whirled around to see Kevin! The boy's hair and his Reaper coat were covered with dust, but he was still alive!

Kevin's eyes radiated pure fury that matched Jonah's as he grabbed the injured, hulking Wraith and landed several consecutive punches. Kevin ended his barrage and hurled the man into the waiting SUV. The impact was so hard, all the windows shattered and the vehicle almost tipped over on its side. When Kevin moved in to finish off the man, the mortal opened his mouth in a silent scream.

The Wraith inside exited the mortal's body as a dark, gaseous stream of evil. Seeing this, the second mortal threw back his head and opened his mouth. The second Wraith exited its host body too. Suddenly drained of the Wraiths' power, the mortals sank to their knees.

With a high leap into the air, Kevin sliced at the escaping Wraiths but missed. The evil spirits fled off over the gravestones, heading down the hill and clean over the cemetery wall. Jonah had no clue where the Wraiths would find other host bodies. But he had the horrible certainty there were fools ready and willing to harbor them for the sick honor of it.

Kevin stalked over and gathered Jonah into a tight hug. All the tragic despair, hatred, and willingness to get revenge suddenly left Jonah's body. The embrace felt almost like the nullifying bands, except in this case, it nullified all his pain.

"Lynn and Mike are okay too," Kevin whispered, holding him tight.

A vortex opened and Kevin released him. Jonah tensed, expecting his aunt to return. He was ready, but he should have paid more attention to Kevin's relaxed pose. Instead of trouble, two Alliance Guards rushed out to subdue the mortal hosts.

Amulet of the Goddess

Only then did Jonah let out a breath as he also registered what a mass of pain his body was in again. He shook as the adrenaline of the fight began to evaporate.

Kevin slipped off his Reaper's coat and wrapped it around Jonah. "You okay?"

"I'm fine." He huddled in the surprisingly warm coat. "I'm sorry I didn't stop Ruby. She has the amulet and now she can work the spell."

Kevin tweaked Jonah's nose. "It's not your fault, crumb snatcher."

Jonah couldn't believe it. Kevin hadn't called him that in almost two years. The last time was the night his family's house in Virginia burned down, the night before he was sent here to Mount Vernon. The old nickname filled Jonah's body with warmth the same way it had the night Kevin made the first promise to him.

Now that Jonah understood what promises meant between two supernaturals, he grinned.

"Feel any better?" Kevin asked.

"Yeah." He did too, with Kevin standing beside him. The boys watched as more Alliance people arrived and inspected the now destroyed mausoleum. After a while, Jonah asked. "Where are Mike and Lynn?"

"They're both alive and well," Trueblood answered, walking over to them. He took in the situation a moment, frowning. "I think you should escort Jonah to the safe room." He handed Kevin a new codex.

*

The safe room wasn't exactly what Jonah imagined. It was a room, sure, but it was huge and circular, at least a hundred feet in diameter.

The first thing Jonah noticed when he arrived was the rather large sigil covering the center portion of the floor. Then he studied the glowing designation stone he saw on one side. That was as far as his amazement took him because Lynn and Mike tackled him a moment later.

"We thought they took you away with them!" Mike shouted as he pounded Jonah on the back.

Lynn gave him a genuine hug. "I'm glad you're okay, geek boy."

Jonah's throat tightened when she released him.

"Now that you're here," Kevin said, "I need to get back. Don't break anything while I'm gone." With that, he phased.

Jonah didn't want Kevin to leave him. Aware that the others were watching him, and waiting, he glumly hid is disappointment. "How did you guys get away?"

Lynn's face broke into an impressed grin as she gripped Mike's shoulder. "Show him."

Mike pulled out his Seeker's compass. "I used this to get us here."

"How? And why didn't you use Kevin's codex?" Jonah asked.

"A huge slab of that big tomb landed on it," Mike answered. "Smashed the center button." He glanced at Lynn. "And then she went crazy, saying we had to get out of there while Kevin was banging on the door."

"I didn't go crazy, Mike." Lynn nudged the side of his head. Then she shrugged and added, "I guess it took a while for my ability to truly come back, or maybe it was due to the situation. Like a flood, I suddenly got all kinds of impressions of danger." She shook Mike by the shoulder. "But your buddy used his quick thinking and managed to activate his compass."

She frowned and glanced around them. "You'd think this place would prevent anyone from getting inside without a codex device."

Mike held up the Seeker's compass, smiling. "I made the codex, and my compass has the coordinates inside."

It seemed odd to Jonah that his parents had given him the compass as a belated birthday gift, yet the device belonged to his friend now.

"How did you get away?" Mike asked, getting Jonah's attention. "Did Kevin save you?"

"I had his blades. Remember? You put them in my pocket? I attacked the Wraiths just before Kevin showed up. He was so awesome."

"Wow," Mike said.

Jonah turned on the spot, taking in the rest of the place. High overhead was a vent and a whirling fan. The faint air current it provided felt refreshing and cool. Around the edges of the space were a desk and chair, two comfortable-looking cots, a set of lockers, and stacked boxes marked as food.

Amulet of the Goddess **885**

Mike stood beside Jonah and explained all the features of the safe room. "And it even has a satellite hookup for internet and computer access to the outside world." He nodded to a large, wall-mounted screen. "You could stay here for a long time and be comfortable."

"Really?"

"Yes. There's a bathroom through that door and on the other side is a small place to heat up your food."

"It's cool," Jonah said, audibly impressed. "But it also reminds me of a jail, you know? Someplace to keep a person fully confined." Jonah caught the uneasy look on Mike's face and wondered at it. "Is this for Council Members?"

Mike crossed his arms, hugging himself. "Yeah, it can be. Or for anyone else who needs a safe place to crash."

"You mean, me?" Jonah waited. Mike finally nodded. "So, they built this just for me?" That worried him even more than the recent fight. "The Alliance expects something will happen to me?"

"I don't know, Jonah," Mike confessed. "They didn't tell me everything."

Jonah believed Mike, but he suddenly knew why the room felt so much like a cell. "There's no door to the outside," he observed. "How do I get out if I want to?"

"You wait until someone comes and gets you." Mike glanced at Lynn like he needed help. "Kevin has a talisman. I've seen one before. It's made of bronze-colored beads."

Jonah nodded, taking in that small detail. "And that's the only way out?"

"Yes. You hold onto someone else with the talisman."

"Can you use the compass to get us out of here?" Jonah touched the Seeker's compass with a finger. He hadn't held the thing in a while.

Mike hesitated, as if trying to figure out the meaning behind his questions. "Only if I have a talisman or I'm holding onto someone who does, yes, I can."

Jonah gave his friend a knowing smile. "Do you have a talisman?"

"No, I don't." Mike held up his hands when Jonah's eyes narrowed. "Honest. I wouldn't lie to you, Jonah."

"I suppose the Alliance made you take an oath not to tell me."

Mike's voice grew a bit testy. "Well, they didn't. And if they had, I'd just tell you that I can't talk about it, okay?"

Lynn finally spoke up. "What's your problem, hero?"

Jonah gestured around the place. "They built this specifically to lock me in."

"They designed it for your protection," Lynn said, narrowing her eyes at him.

Mike nodded in agreement.

Jonah disagreed. All this time, he assumed everyone was worried for him, but Alastor had a point. Marcus and Kevin were afraid of him. When he took Agent Hunter's power in anger, they stood frozen in place, unable to hide their own fear.

And the Grand Oracle called him an *abomination*. Had he also misread Trueblood's fear? Being here in this safe room made that seem more of a possibility.

To Lynn and Mike, he said, "Sometimes I wonder if everyone's afraid of me and what I'll do."

Lynn huffed and crossed her arms. "Stop feeling so sorry for yourself."

"I'm not," Jonah protested, but he secretly suspected he was doing that.

Mike at least seemed to understand his reference to their adventure in the Afterworld. He slid an arm around Jonah's shoulders. "I told you before. I'm not afraid of you."

"Neither am I, so get over it," Lynn said. She glanced up at a blinking light, high on the curved wall.

Mike jumped and pulled Jonah away from the center of the room. "Someone's coming," he explained.

A moment later, Kevin appeared. Jonah, Lynn, and Mike crowded around the young Fallen Reaper for an update.

"The two mortal hosts are being questioned at HQ," Kevin began.

"Aren't we at HQ?" Jonah asked.

Amulet of the Goddess

"Ha ha. Nice try." Kevin smirked at him. "The Alliance is covering up the true cause of the explosion and dealing with any eyewitnesses."

Jonah acknowledged that last piece of news with a nod, but he wanted to remain on track. "You're not gonna tell me where we are?"

"Nope. Security precaution." Kevin held up a hand to stop Jonah's next question. "And before you argue with me, I don't even know where we are."

Lynn pulled on Jonah's sleeve. "Give it a rest. Can we at least go home now?"

Kevin let out a long breath. "Nope, you can't."

Mike, Jonah, and Lynn chorused, "Why not?" at the same time.

Kevin backed away from their combined outrage. "Whoa, don't bite my head off! Marcus wants to see all of you in his office."

Jonah exchanged a glance with Lynn and Mike, knowing they were all thinking the same thing. *They were in trouble–again.*

CHAPTER THIRTY-TWO
PHANTOM'S PATH

Even before Kevin finished the phase, Jonah knew they weren't headed to Marcus's office. He could almost sense the extra protections they passed through, which Marcus's office didn't have. Sure enough, when the mortal world appeared around them, they stood on the rooftop of the Alliance HQ.

Mike let out a startled "Wow!" as he gazed out at the northern Atlanta suburbs, which were all visible from their vantage point.

Lynn remained quiet as she too scanned their surroundings. "Where are we?"

"Alliance HQ," Jonah answered. He motioned for his cousin to follow.

Lynn's eyes widened with heightened awareness before she gripped Mike's elbow and pulled him along.

Kevin had already moved toward the portico where Marcus stood, at the top of a short flight of marble steps. Jonah's godfather wore his Reaper's long coat and looked rather intimidating this evening.

Marcus wasn't alone. Omar and Symon Trueblood stepped into view. All three men wore similarly serious expressions.

Omar at least managed a warm smile once Jonah and the others reached the top of the stairs and entered the portico. "Good to see you again, Jonah. My God, you've sprouted over the past few months."

Jonah shrugged, feeling a little embarrassed at the unexpected attention. "I guess so."

Amulet of the Goddess

Omar grinned. "You'll be as tall as Isaiah soon."

A pit formed in Jonah's stomach at the mention of his dad. Omar didn't seem to notice because he moved on to greet Lynn and Mike.

But Marcus watched Jonah's expression. He wondered if his godfather regretted putting him in the bands, given what had just happened.

Marcus adopted a shrewd look. "You can relax, Jonah. I'm not angry about the cemetery. You had no way of predicting Ruby would show up. And Kevin informed Symon of your plan beforehand."

Jonah caught the way Trueblood avoided looking directly at Marcus. He could see the slight tension between the men. "Then what were you arguing about?"

Trueblood cracked a smile.

Marcus frowned. "We were talking about Alastor."

"What about him?" Jonah felt his anger toward the devious man surfacing, but he didn't care. "He left Mount Vernon. I had to help Mike keep his uncle's store open."

"Yeah," Mike agreed. "Is he here?"

"I'm sure he is," Marcus said. "But being here is a preferred change from Mount Vernon."

"That may be," Omar said. "But hasn't Alastor tipped his hand? Goading Jonah gives us more evidence against him. Perhaps Cedric will listen to reason now."

Kevin let out a loud, derisive snort.

"Who's Cedric?" Jonah asked, watching his godfather for the answer.

Marcus sighed. "Cedric Mandara. He's the leader of the Hardline Council members. That's a moot point for now."

He's not telling the whole truth, Jonah thought. There was something about Cedric, something that caused Marcus to dread any discussions about the man. It had to be more than the Council member just being a Hardliner, or sending Alastor to Mount Vernon.

"I called you here because it's time that you knew about your mom," Marcus announced.

"My mom?" Jonah's jaw dropped in astonishment. Lynn and Mike moved to stand on either side of him. He welcomed their support. "What about my mom?"

Marcus motioned for them to sit down on the large center cushion. Kevin hovered nearby.

Jonah waited for his godfather to continue, but it was Trueblood who began to pace with his hands clasped behind his back.

"It's nothing ominous, Jonah," the mage began. "It simply pertains to what's happening now." When Omar nodded encouragingly, Trueblood took a deep breath and continued.

"I've already told you how Omar, your mom, and I met. We joined the Alliance at the same time. What I failed to mention were the little adventures we enjoyed during the summers and our off-time. The room you found in the old palm reading shop is where we used to hang out."

"Really?" Jonah sat up straighter. Trueblood had confirmed his suspicions about the mage's earlier reaction at the Ankh of Life shop. "You recognized her journals?"

"I did. Me and Omar were there when your mom wrote most of them. You see, we had a project that we called The Phantom's Path. Those seven locations on the mural were part of it." Trueblood stopped his pacing and leaned against a column. "Your mom wanted to learn all she could about her power as well as the supernatural world. And me? Well, I became arrogant in my abilities. It didn't matter the subject nor how dangerous, I was supremely confident I could master it."

"And I was ready and willing to go along," Omar said. "They took me into their group like I was an old friend."

"What did you do?" Lynn asked the adults in general.

Jonah wondered if she used her intuition or her normal skill to sniff out a confession. She had done it to him enough times.

Trueblood clasped his hands together, twisting them in a nervous way that Jonah had never seen before. "It was really your great-aunt's prodding that piqued our interest in the Underworld. But once me and Janice were hooked, we went full tilt. As the youngest from a long line of shamans, spirit quests were second nature to me. You see, you have to get the right drugs and mix them in the right proportions—"

Amulet of the Goddess **891**

"Symon, that's too much information," Marcus said.

Trueblood ruffled his dreads, looking as if he were trying to regain his train of thought. "Oh, yeah. I guess that's not important. Anyway, all we wanted was to journey into the Underworld on a modified spirit quest."

The knot in Jonah's stomach began to grow. He gritted his teeth, preparing himself for what the mage might reveal.

"I met a Seer. Although the human host was,... older, the Seer herself had died at a young age. I... *flattered* her until she helped us."

Kevin covered the smirk that twisted his mouth.

Lynn frowned at the mage. "Seriously? You sound worse than my brother."

"Like I said, I was young and full of myself, okay?" A little of Trueblood's humorous nature returned as he smiled. But the mage quickly sobered and continued. "So, after, ah, convincing the Seer to help us, we began to go on a spirit quest into the Underworld. We only had two rules: Don't take anything and don't hurt anything. That was fine. Janice recorded our journeys, and Omar used his artistic skills to make the triptych and the mural."

Everyone turned to stare at Omar, who ran a hand over his bald head and down the back of his neck. It struck Jonah that he was stalling before he chose his next words.

"The trips were unlike anything I'd ever experienced," Omar began. "The Seer told us a lot of things and eventually showed us the areas of the Underworld called the Phantom's Path. Each location had a connected nexus point on the mortal side."

"And they also have designation codes," Jonah added. "Mike and I noticed that." He hesitated, reconsidering mentioning his desire to travel to the Underworld. With everything the adults were saying, Jonah was sure his godfather would nix the idea anyway.

"Yes, they do," Omar said, watching Jonah's expression. "Seven nexus points connected by an eighth location."

"But there were only seven locations on the map," Mike pointed out. "Where's the eighth?"

"We never found out," Trueblood answered. "When your Great-Aunt Victoria discovered what we were doing, she pressured Janice into taking something from the Underworld. Like I said, she was the one who turned us on to the plan anyway."

"What did you steal?"

"Pakhet's amulet," Trueblood admitted, looking a bit embarrassed. "And we may have hurt some of the guardian creatures around it called *Felines*."

"The Seer banned us from the Underworld," Omar added. "We gave Janice our pieces of the triptych and never returned. We thought she gave up researching the Phantom's Path. But it seems she continued gathering information on her own for a while. I guess she thought the goddess was the key to the eighth location."

"So," Jonah began, "what about our Aunt Ruby?"

Trueblood raised an eyebrow. "You've seen what a Seer can do, right?"

"Yeah, they read the future and make prophecies," Jonah said.

"Or warnings," Mike added.

"That's correct." Trueblood looked like he wanted to be somewhere else now, but he continued. "The Seer was more than a little angry with us and pronounced a curse on us. She said we had to forfeit our firstborn."

Lynn seemed the most spooked by that statement. She stared at Trueblood in concern. "Did that really happen to you?"

Trueblood blinked in surprise. "Who me? No, I'm a confirmed bachelor. And Omar," he glanced at Marcus, "well, he wasn't exactly worried about any actual firstborn." Trueblood's expression turned thoughtful. "Unless you were to use a surrogate–"

"Symon," Marcus cautioned him, looking uncomfortable with the subject.

"Fine. Anyway, Janice married your dad and everyone said it would be impossible for them to have kids. So we counted ourselves lucky and never discussed the curse."

"Then your mom got pregnant with you a few years later," Omar said. "We talked to her, but in the end, we convinced ourselves nothing would happen. For seven years, nothing did happen until the Wraiths contacted your Aunt Ruby."

Amulet of the Goddess

"Your mom explained the Sight to us," Trueblood took up the story, "when she revealed she had it." Trueblood pointed to Lynn. "And now, you have it."

Lynn nodded. "And my Aunt Ruby never had any real ability. That made her furious."

"Yes, it did." Trueblood stroked his jaw, watching Lynn. "I met old Victoria. She wasn't a tolerant woman when it came to people without abilities. She fawned over Janice while all but ignoring Ruby."

"When old Victoria died," Omar added, "Janice locked everything away. She wasn't interested in running the old shop and didn't want anyone else getting into it."

"Except me," Lynn raised her hand. "Jonah's mom coded the room specifically for me."

All the news left Jonah dumbfounded. He knew bits and pieces, but he never imagined that his demented aunt may have been a victim herself and that his mom and her friends had done something so reckless and cruel. He wanted to run away to have time to deal with it all.

Perhaps Omar sensed his thoughts or maybe he noticed the look in his face. He came over and stood close. "Don't feel sorry for Ruby. She made her own decisions. No one forced her down a dark path."

Jonah met Omar's serious gaze. He gulped, unsure if he wanted to know the thing he'd asked about before. "What happened to me, seven years ago?"

Omar's brow furrowed and he paused for a long time, his breathing audibly slow and even.

"Can you tell me?" Jonah pressed. "If my aunt is gonna hurt people, I want to know why."

Omar shook his bald head. "I agree with Marcus. Now is not the time to unblock those memories. But I can tell you what happened that night."

"I don't understand."

Mike nodded in agreement.

Lynn said, "I don't either. If you can tell him, why not unblock the memories so he can remember them, himself?"

Omar pressed his fingertips together, tapping them against his bottom lip while thinking. "Having the actual memories versus being told what happened can be a world of difference." He raised an eyebrow, prompting Jonah.

But Jonah still didn't get it.

"Consider this," Omar tried again. "When the Wraiths contacted your Aunt Ruby seven years ago, she was more than willing to put you through a traumatic experience in exchange for power. She subjected you to a forced Wraith possession, Jonah. Your mother found out and arrived just in time to stop it." Omar sucked in a shaky breath. "She called me to block your memories. Do you understand now?"

"No. I mean..." Jonah frowned. "Not really."

Marcus stirred. "In the Afterworld, when you took Trevor's power, you told us you gained some of his memories. That's because you touched his soul and transferred the memories into your own mind."

"When a Wraith possesses a mortal, it also touches the mortal's soul," Omar said, drawing Jonah's attention. "That person's memories and knowledge are open to the Wraith. But the reverse also occurs. The mortal has access to everything the Wraith has done."

Jonah's jaw dropped as he began to see the true significance of what Omar was trying to tell him. "You mean I saw the Wraith's memories?"

Omar gave Jonah's shoulder a reassuring squeeze. "I'm afraid you did. Can you imagine a seven-year-old boy seeing all that horror? Your mother wanted me to protect you from the ordeal of that vile Wraith's memories as much as from the pain of the possession."

"Your Aunt Ruby's up to her old game again, Jonah." Marcus stepped closer, towering over him. "We suspect she intends to subject you to a powerful Wraith again. It would explain why she tried to take you."

Kevin cursed under his breath. "That's why she needs him to be emotional."

"The attacks on your family and friends were meant to worry you as well as pull away their support," Trueblood explained. "Alastor goaded you into a fury over the bullies, and there's also his conversation with you before leaving."

Amulet of the Goddess

Jonah glanced at Kevin, recalling how enraged the boy had been about his confrontation with Alastor.

"Trueblood's correct," Omar agreed. "And the most obvious way to turn you into an emotional and mental wreck would be to open your block and allow all those horrible memories and images to flood your mind." He gestured at Jonah's head. "Someday, when you're older and stronger, maybe you *should* unlock those experiences. But right now, I'm afraid we'd just be playing into their hands."

Jonah sensed the utter sincerity in Omar's words. But the man's comments reignited his concern about the safe room. A ringing began in his ears. He paid distant attention to the conversation, tuning into his own, troubling thoughts.

"Isn't this convenient?" Lynn asked. "Ruby gets out just in time for the Witching Hour?"

"It's no coincidence, Lynn," Marcus answered. "It's part of a plan. We think Ruby went crazy because of a Wraith possessing her. As the time drew closer, her condition began to improve at an accelerated rate."

"It kept her crazy for seven years?"

"Time isn't the same for humans as it is for supernaturals," Trueblood added.

Marcus nodded in agreement. "The Grim Reaper and Grand Oracle have been working on their plan for over two thousand years. Only now are we glimpsing their end game."

Mention of the Rulers of the Afterworld only added to Jonah's feeling of betrayal. Unexpressed anger welled up inside him.

"Jonah?" Mike's voice seemed to reach him from inside his head as well as through his voice. "What's wrong?"

He's my Seeker. He can always find me. Jonah responded to the call and came back to the present awareness. Everyone stared at him, causing the ringing in his ears to return. "You don't trust me. You're all afraid of me."

"Jonah..." Marcus began.

"That's why you have the safe room." Jonah let all the bitterness and self-doubt he harbored inside spill out. "If my memory block fails, you can lock me away."

Lynn slid an arm around his shoulders to comfort him, but he was on a roll. "And now you say my mom did something she wasn't supposed to do and ultimately got a curse placed on me? And my aunt was bullied, which eventually sent her over the edge? What am I supposed to do when I face her? Tell me that!"

"Jonah..." Lynn tightened her grip, rocking him.

Trueblood came over. "That's Alastor talking. Forget whatever he's told you." He pressed his palm to Jonah's chest. "Remember what I said? Whatever your mom and dad were, so are you."

"Did she know? Did she laugh at my aunt?"

"No, Jonah." Trueblood's shoulders slumped. "Your mom loved her sister. That night, she..." He hesitated. "She tried to protect your aunt. Do you believe me?"

"Yeah, I guess so."

"Your parents were honorable, strong people, and you're even stronger. As far as Omar and I being afraid of you, we're not! You know why? Because inside, we know you're a good person."

Miko leaned against Jonah and whispered, "Told you."

Marcus met Jonah's gaze. "You shocked us, Jonah. That's all."

Kevin nodded. "And I'm not afraid of you either, little man."

Jonah's face warmed with embarrassment. Alastor, the mole, and his aunt were the ones manipulating his feelings and emotions, just as Omar said.

"If you ever face Ruby, I know you'll do the right thing," Trueblood continued. "Everyone has a past. Some people with ideal experiences and backgrounds turn out to be monsters. Others with wretched pasts become kind angels. It's not the experiences we endure, but how we allow them to shape us that determine who we are."

Jonah met his godfather's gaze. *I decided to be a vigilante.* In that moment, he understood why his godfather worried about him so much.

"It's okay, Jonah." Trueblood's voice was reassuring and understanding. "Everything that's happened was all about you. That's a lot to deal with."

Marcus came over. "It's been a long day for all of you. Time to go home."

Amulet of the Goddess

CHAPTER THIRTY-THREE
BANDS OFF

Jonah awoke refreshed. The bruises from Brandon's ambush were gone and the nicks from the battle in the cemetery were even fainter. Once again, his beleaguered healing factor had snapped into action. Better yet, his sleep hadn't been disturbed by nightmares or dream-walks. The net effect was that he felt prepared to go to school and fully ready to face whatever Monday would throw at him.

Due to the reworked club assignments, Mike and Jonah were patrol partners again. Jonah's pride in his group increased because they handled every situation that day without incident. The only thing to impact his good mood was Brandon's superior swagger around the hallways.

The boy was smart and didn't openly gloat about their run-in. But that didn't stop the bully and his friends from snickering at Jonah every chance they got.

Brandon, being Brandon, couldn't resist taking things further. During lunch, he passed by Jonah in the cafeteria and deliberately bumped into him. He grinned and in a voice full of false concern said, "I'm sorry. Didn't mean to hurt you!" Then he laughed and walked off with his friends.

Jonah glared at him with the tray shaking in his furious hands.

"Don't fall for it," Mike warned.

Jonah sucked in a deep breath to calm himself. Keeping his head down and letting his body heal was proving more difficult than he expected. He could sympathize with Lynn and the frustration she experienced over losing her Sight.

He had taken his power for granted. It was a vital part of himself, like his hands, arms, and legs. To go without it was not only humbling, but also infuriating.

He doubted he'd ever complain about not being normal again.

*

In addition to staying away from trouble while he healed, Jonah's desire to know what happened to him seven years ago was no longer so urgent. In a rare moment, Jonah actually agreed with his godfather. He didn't want to remove the block if it meant he had to relive the Wraith's memories.

The new information about his mom, Trueblood, and Omar just added to all the other concerns swirling in his head. By Tuesday afternoon, Jonah opted to finish his homework at home, alone. He still valued those moments away from others and guessed he always would.

But he wasn't trying to be anti-social. He intended to finish his homework early so he could go by Hackett's and hang out with Mike. Notebook and textbooks scattered across the kitchen table, Jonah bowed to his mountain of homework. He made good progress until Kevin arrived.

"Am I interrupting?" Kevin asked as he entered through the kitchen door and pulled out a chair.

"No." Jonah rubbed his tired eyes and pushed aside the book he was reading. He experienced a pang of doubt, wondering if Kevin had bad news or not.

"Don't worry about Ruby," Kevin assured him. "The Alliance is searching for her."

"I'm not worried about her." Jonah opened and closed the cover of his textbook. "I just hate waiting for something else to happen. If we can't find my aunt, we need to find the eighth nexus point."

Kevin slid his hand inside the book to stop Jonah's repetitive movement. "I asked Trueblood about it. He doesn't think the site is a nexus point."

Jonah nodded. "Mike said the same thing." Reminded of his plans to meet his buddy, Jonah glanced at his watch. "I need to finish my work."

Kevin laid his hand on top of the textbook, palm upward.

Amulet of the Goddess

Jonah brushed his own fingers across Kevin's and intertwined their fingers. "I really have to study."

"I know." Kevin's eyes remained fixed on their clasped hands. "I guess you want to be ready for tonight?"

Jonah gazed at him, confused and a little excited. Did Kevin have something planned for them? This was the first time, since their impromptu date a couple nights ago, that they had been alone together.

"I was gonna go and see Mike at his uncle's bookstore," Jonah said. "Why?"

Kevin paused and his brow furrowed as if he didn't believe Jonah. He pushed up the sleeve of Jonah's shirt to expose the band. "This comes off tonight. Did you forget?"

"What? No," Jonah lied, because he *had* forgotten about the deactivation of the bands. It wasn't his fault. So much had happened to him, it was hard to keep all the events straight.

"Wow!" Kevin fingered the band. "I thought you'd have that marked on your calendar. You geeks like your schedules and appointments so much."

"Funny." A smile spread across Jonah's face. "Are you gonna be here?"

"Yep. I have to return the bands to HQ."

"I mean…" Jonah trailed off as he hesitated to ask what he really meant. "We can… do something."

Kevin smirked. "Like what?"

"Maybe phase around."

"To where?"

"*Around*," Jonah repeated. "Maybe we'll end up at the hideaway." His face warmed.

Kevin frowned. "There's nothing there. Plus, it'll be pitch black. What are we–" His eyes widened for a comical moment.

It heartened Jonah to see him really considering the idea.

But Kevin shook his head. "It's too dangerous with Ruby on the loose."

"The mole doesn't know about the hideaway," Jonah pleaded.

"Can't you cover for Mike tonight?" Kevin suggested.

"Oh, yeah." The idea hadn't occurred to Jonah. On the plus side, he wouldn't have to hide anything from Mike. "Yeah. I'll ask him."

"Cool." Kevin reached over to ruffle Jonah's hair. "We can do dinner again."

Jonah heard the eagerness in Kevin's voice. They were thinking the same thing. *Make out.*

As if he couldn't wait, Kevin leaned clean across the table, his face nose-to-nose with Jonah, and kissed him. When he pulled back, Jonah let out a frustrated huff.

Kevin stood up and slid the chair back in place. "Call me and tell me what you decide later. All right?"

Jonah nodded, afraid he couldn't speak. After Kevin left, he slumped back in the kitchen chair and stared at the door. It took an act of supreme will to refocus his mind on the homework. Even then, Jonah couldn't remember anything he read or wrote.

*

Jonah flopped on his bed after dinner. He called Mike, enduring his jokes and innuendoes, but set up everything for the evening. As the time drew close for the bands to deactivate, Jonah began to worry about Kevin. The Fallen Reaper was a no-show so far.

"Kevin will be here," Lynn said as she, Wick, and Robert crowded into Jonah's room. "He has to take them back, right?"

"Yeah." Jonah squirmed under the combined attention. They watched him as though they expected him to drop dead, sprout wings, or grow a second head.

"Be still," Lynn ordered.

"You want to trade places?"

"I didn't act like a vigilante. You did." Lynn leaned against the closed door.

Wick sat at Jonah's small desk while Robert crossed over to the window, splitting his attention between what was outside and Jonah. As the bedside

Amulet of the Goddess

clock changed to read *five fifty-nine*, everyone stared at Jonah in hushed silence.

Lynn walked over and pushed his head. "Come on."

"Fine." He sat up and stretched his arms out on the bed in front of himself, palms up so they could see the magical bands. Six o'clock came and still, nothing happened.

Lynn sighed. "He said six?"

"Yeah. That's when they first got activated."

"Maybe," Wick started, "his clock was slightly off–"

Jonah sucked in a startled breath just as the bands flared before popping loose from his wrists and becoming three sizes too big in an instant. The feelings that suddenly surged back into him were staggering. He took long, deep breaths, welcoming the part of himself that was sorely missed. All at once, he was whole again.

Wick grabbed a band as soon as Jonah slid them off his wrists and held it up to inspect it.

Lynn took the other. "We should lock these up in Robert's box, just in case."

"Lynn, please." Wick reached for the second band. "I won't do anything bad with them."

Jonah tuned out the argument for the time being. With his powers regained, he could phase around whenever he chose to. And his Death Sense would also be working again.

"Take my side, Bobby." Wick waved his friend forward. Lynn crossed her arms, ready to argue both boys down, when a knock came at the front door.

Lynn slipped out of Jonah's room while calling out to Aunt Imma, "I'll get it!"

Jonah recognized Kevin's low voice as he greeted Aunt Imma. Moments later, he followed Lynn into the already crowded bedroom.

As soon as Jonah saw Kevin wearing the Reaper's coat, he knew their plans were a bust. "What happened?"

"Work. Sorry." Kevin withdrew the slender box from his coat pocket and opened it.

Wick's face fell. He held up the bands, a pleading look in his eyes as he turned to Kevin. "Can I hold onto one?"

"Sorry. Albrecht's orders."

Wick took his time placing the bands in the box. He ran a finger along the edge of one, like it was a long-lost possession.

Kevin snapped the box closed and met Jonah's disappointed gaze. "It's not my fault."

"Whatever," Jonah mumbled, not bothering to conceal the dissatisfaction in his voice.

Lynn watched them. "What's not your fault?"

Kevin slid the box in his coat pocket before answering. "Jonah wanted to celebrate by phasing around Mount Vernon tonight. But he can't do that now. It would be too dangerous."

Lynn narrowed her eyes, "Weren't you gonna help Mike at the store for a couple of hours?"

"Yeah. Me and Kevin were gonna phase around afterward, you know, before I came home." Jonah pouted for Kevin's benefit. He wanted the boy to feel as bad as possible for messing up their plans.

"Well," Kevin added, avoiding Jonah's direct gaze, "since I can't stay tonight, an Alliance Guard will watch you."

That news excited Wick and Robert, who exited the room. Jonah listened to their footsteps retreating toward the front door. Lynn gave Jonah and Kevin one last suspicious look and then left the room.

Kevin threw up his arms. "I'm sorry. Mandara says he needs me for something important." Kevin made air quotes on the last word.

"He's purposely keeping us apart!" Jonah plopped back on his stacked pillows when another thought occurred to him. He sat up again. "You think he knows?"

"What? That you're a horny, little teenager?" Kevin grinned.

Jonah hurled a pillow at him. "About us."

Amulet of the Goddess

"There is no *us*, yet. I guess." Kevin sat on the edge of the bed. Jonah leaned against his back, resting his chin on Kevin's shoulder. His skin tingled where it touched the enchanted coat.

"This sucks."

"Yeah," Kevin agreed. "But I have to get back. He's probably watching the clock." Kevin stood up.

"I hate him," Jonah said. Kevin frowned at the comment and Jonah noticed. "What is it about Mandara that gets everyone so worried whenever I mention him?"

"Nothing."

"But–"

Kevin kissed him, cutting off the mild protest.

"Wow," Kevin said when they stopped kissing. "I'll remember that whenever I need to shut you up." He slipped out the door, narrowly avoiding Jonah's second thrown pillow.

CHAPTER THIRTY-FOUR
MIDNIGHT READING

Mike stayed on and kept Jonah company at the store. He and Patrick weren't doing so well after all. Or so Jonah hoped. Mike said he was done messing around with someone who was not good for him. Jonah considered asking why but dropped the sensitive subject.

The boys sat on stools behind the counter and talked about any and everything, including Kevin and what Jonah did and didn't know about the boy. Once again, he was reminded of Kevin's promise to tell him about his First Death. All Fallen Reapers had original lives before joining the Undead.

"Trevor told you about himself," Jonah reminded Mike.

"Yeah, he did." Mike folded his arms, thinking. "I got the impression he needed to tell his story. Maybe he sensed something would happen to him."

Jonah thought about that. "You're just better at this than I am."

Mike leaned into him. "No, I'm not. Trevor didn't hesitate to do anything."

Jonah raised a questioning eyebrow and Mike scowled at him.

"I don't mean that, Jonah."

"I still don't believe you two just talked," Jonah laughed.

Jonah sobered as he thought about Kevin. How would he handle anything Kevin revealed to him? The Fallen Reaper hinted more than once

Amulet of the Goddess

that not everyone died a noble death. Those thoughts invaded Jonah's mind as he and Mike finished closing up the store.

The Alliance Guard escorted both boys home, stopping by Mike's house first. Once Jonah returned to his house, he peeked out the bay window in the den. The Alliance Guard's black SUV remained parked outside for nearly fifteen minutes before driving off. They were probably waiting to see if he went anywhere, Jonah decided.

He was about to move away from the window when he saw two red eyes across the street, staring back at him. His heart leapt into his throat. But unlike two years ago, now he had a lot of experience with Grim Hounds. And, with the bands gone, his Death Sense was working as normal. He didn't sense any danger from the beast.

It must have been the same one that chased off the cat outside Drew's house. Throwing caution to the wind, he opened the front door and stepped out onto the front walkway. The eyes continued to watch him but the Grim Hound remained in the shadows.

Jonah moved away from the house, his senses on alert as he stopped near the end of the driveway. Come on, he urged the beast.

It responded instantly, emerging from its cover beneath the neighbors' overgrown bushes. The Grim Hound was huge. Jonah concentrated on it and sensed its familiar tug. It was Deyanira's Grim Hound.

The beast padded across the street, eerily silent, considering its size. It was like a black, moving shadow and would have struck fear in anyone else. But Jonah wasn't afraid. As the beast drew closer and extended its snout, Jonah stretched out his hand. The Grim Hound sniffed his hand before moving closer to nuzzle him, like a fond pet.

Jonah patted its large head and received a low, satisfied rumble from the creature in response. "What are you doing here?"

The Grim Hound stared at him with its red-in-red pupils.

"Did Deyanira send you?"

The Hound bobbed its head in the affirmative.

That intrigued Jonah. He scratched it behind the ears. The creature let out more low rumbles and bumped against him. Jonah was imagining he could have the strangest pet of anyone in the neighborhood when his

Death Sense suddenly spiked. The Grim Hound's body went rigid too and it turned its ears toward the west, pointing up the quiet street.

Jonah peered into the darkness, but he couldn't see what had alerted him. He wondered if it were the black cat or someone who was working with his aunt. The Alliance's warning became very real.

The Grim Hound growled at what Jonah couldn't see. Within seconds, the presence receded and disappeared. The Grim Hound relaxed as it released a low, mournful sound.

"I should get inside." He petted the creature once more and turned toward the house. The Grim Hound followed. Jonah paused on the front porch, genuinely amused. "I can't take you inside. You're too large."

The Grim Hound nuzzled him again before it set off around the side of the house. For some crazy reason, Jonah knew where it was heading. He re-entered the house and hurried into his bedroom. Even before he reached his window, he saw the red eyes staring through the window at him.

He pressed his face to the window and watched the Grim Hound circle on-the-spot three times right outside his window before it finally settled down, like it intended to stand guard.

As weird as it seemed, the creature's presence reassured Jonah, even if the Grim Hound actually belonged to Deyanira.

He changed and climbed into bed, hoping for a nice dream about the date he should have had with Kevin. Instead, he endured a nightmare of sorts. It wasn't a dream-walk, although it contained extremely real visions, like Jonah was actually living through them.

In one horrible dream, he was an ancient Berserker, a crazed and powerful warrior, cutting down enemy after enemy. The sounds of the blade hitting another blade and slicing through flesh and bone were authentic. The screams as the smaller warriors died were too real. Even the horrid and unbelievable smells were so vivid and vile to Jonah that he didn't know what to make of them.

The Berserker reveled in the gory nightmare, enjoying every moment of it. Then the dream changed in the way dreams often do.

Next, Jonah was a medieval High Church official, an Inquisitor, pronouncing judgment over a group of male witches. At their feet lay their

Amulet of the Goddess

royal blue cloaks, and on each man's forehead was branded the Alliance symbol. The wounds had long since healed over, suggesting the men had done this to themselves as a sacrificial badge of honor.

But to the crowd of filthy peasants shouting, spitting, and even urinating on the condemned, the symbols only signified their evil allegiance to Satan.

Jonah knew better, both as himself and as the Grand Inquisitor. These men represented a threat to the Grand Oracle's plans. That was why he had to burn them alive. Jonah marveled at the man's knowledge and nefarious intent, now laid bare to his own perusal.

"Burn them!"

Men with torches set the piles of wood and brush ablaze. The condemned, all mages, muttered silent incantations before turning the flames into the harmless blue variety. Jonah—or rather, the Inquisitor—raised his hand and changed the flames back to angry red fire. The peasants didn't even consider a religious man using an incantation as anything suspicious.

They all focused on the real, bone-chilling screams of the mages. Jonah couldn't look away because the Inquisitor's eyes were also riveted on the spectacle.

The mages' skin blistered, blackened, and burned before splitting open to reveal the crimson, angry flesh beneath. Their final, agonized screams echoed in Jonah's mind as the scene changed again.

This time, something was very different. It wasn't the past, but the present, or maybe even the future. Downtown Mount Vernon was on fire and he could see it in the distance. Jonah, or whomever he currently inhabited, stood in his own neighborhood. Large, black cats and Grim Hounds roamed the streets, attacking innocent mortals and ripping them apart in an orgy of violence.

With the wave of a hand, a circular window opened in the air near him. Scenes from all over Mount Vernon appeared there. Angry Phantoms and super-powerful Wraiths, zooming through the streets, cutting down anyone they caught outside.

At Jonah's feet, he saw his relatives' destroyed house. It looked like a bomb had gone off dead center and ripped it wide open. Uncle James, Aunt Imma, Robert, and Lynn's broken bodies lay sprawled among the other debris that buried the front lawn.

Mike and Wick were among them. Jonah tilted back his head and laughed, but the sound was not his own voice at all. It was the mixed voices of his aunt and the goddess, Pakhet.

Kevin ran up to him, his Reaper's coat ripped and cut. He pleaded, "Jonah, stop this! You have to resist!"

Jonah laughed again, raising his hand, and blasted Kevin with a powerful hex. He watched in smug satisfaction as the Fallen Reaper sailed clear into the next yard, where he landed and didn't move again.

Trapped inside his aunt's head, Jonah's soul screamed out in horror and protest. Everyone he loved was dead at his feet and it was all his fault.

The scene changed yet again, surrounding Jonah in total darkness. For the first time, he wasn't witnessing events from being inside someone else's mind.

"Will you resist, young Blackstone?" a voice asked out of the darkness.

Jonah whirled around, but he couldn't see the speaker. "Who are you?"

"Will you do all in your power to fulfill your destiny and stop what you've just seen?"

"Yes." Jonah meant it with all his soul. He didn't want to kill his family and friends. He wasn't like Aunt Ruby, nor was he a killer.

"Do you swear?"

"Yes, I do."

A pale hand reached out of the darkness and gripped Jonah's forehead.

He awoke in his own bed, and his own room. Sitting up, he pressed a hesitant hand to his forehead and then hugged himself, rocking back and forth. That was the most terrifying dream yet. So much of it seemed real. He threw off his covers and looked out his window, but the Grim Hound was gone.

Not ready to close his eyes again yet, Jonah stumbled out of his room and into the kitchen. With shaky hands, he poured himself a glass of cool water and plopped down at the kitchen table to sip it.

Whenever one of the scenes from the dream popped back into his mind, he pressed his eyes closed tightly and willed it to go away. He flooded

Amulet of the Goddess **909**

his mind with only nice and beautiful memories. Eventually, he imagined being with Kevin, which seemed to work the best.

He glanced at the clock and groaned. He didn't want to go back to sleep now and raised the glass to sip more water just as the kitchen doorknob twisted.

Fear gripped Jonah and he sloshed water down his chin and chest. "Dang it!" He jumped up to grab a paper towel and dry the front of his pajamas.

Lynn entered the house and paused when she saw him. "What are you doing still up?"

"Not waiting for you to come home," Jonah snapped back. He took a deep breath and said, "Sorry," when Lynn raised an eyebrow at his curt tone.

She stepped into the kitchen and set her purse on the table. "What's up? Another dream-walk?"

Jonah shook his head and sat down. "No. A nightmare." He paused, not knowing if Lynn would understand, but felt he needed to tell someone or he'd go crazy. The first thing that came to mind was the last part of the dream. He swallowed and said, "I have the feeling that whatever happens next, it's gonna be up to me to end it. Me alone."

"How do you know that?"

"It's just a feeling. I can't explain it."

Lynn moved her purse aside and sat opposite him. She stared at Jonah with an indeterminate look before placing her hands on the table, palms up. "Give me your hands."

"Why?"

Lynn tilted her head to the side, willing him to get it.

Jonah did. "You want to read me?"

"I practiced a little, back before Aunt Ruby interfered with my powers." She wiggled her fingers. "Come on, before I change my mind."

Jonah slid his hands into hers. She tightened her grip, but not too tight, and closed her eyes. Jonah didn't know what to do. The last time a Seer read his future, she merely touched him.

He was wondering if Lynn would have a similar reaction when she bucked in the chair. Her eyes flew open to reveal slightly clouded pupils, but not as bad as an actual Seer.

Jonah recoiled and leaned as far away as their clasped hands would allow. "Lynn? Are you okay?"

"I'm fine, Jonah." Her voice was hollow and deeper than normal but her eyes remained wide open. The little jerks of her head to the left and right unnerved Jonah. It was if she were watching a movie on the insides of her eyelids.

Jonah's stomach churned because he suspected she was seeing what he dreamt. He didn't want her to see that last part, not where they were all dead.

A startled moan escaped Lynn's mouth. She released his hands and lowered her head to the table. The kitchen was eerily quiet as he waited for her to say something.

"Well?" he prodded.

Lynn raised her head and met his worried gaze. Her eyes had gone back to normal but her brow furrowed. "You're right. It will be up to you alone."

"What did you see?"

She shook her head and rose. "I can't be sure. Mostly just rapid jumbles of images from other times. It must have been…" She let her voice trail off as she grabbed her purse.

"Lynn?" Jonah wanted to ask her so much more about her power and what she thought it all meant, but he could tell she didn't want to talk about it. At least, not tonight.

She paused by the breakfast bar. "When the time comes, I'll fully endorse your decision to face your destiny alone." With that, she hurried off to her bedroom.

My destiny? Jonah knew she had seen everything then, including his promise to the voice in the darkness. And he recalled something else that happened. When he made that promise in the so-called dream, he experienced the familiar goosebumps along his arms.

Jonah didn't know how, but he clearly sensed he'd made a real promise to a supernatural being.

Amulet of the Goddess 911

CHAPTER THIRTY-FIVE
WRAITH IN THE ATTIC

Lynn was back to her normal self at breakfast. Jonah played along and never mentioned their late-night reading session. He had something else to worry about now, besides an evil aunt on the loose. Wick had come by before school and sat at the kitchen table beside Robert.

Jonah learned that he, Robert, and Lynn wanted to summon Latrell. "He has to know something," Wick insisted as he ended his little speech.

Frankly, Jonah never once considered the idea, partly because he pitied the boy. "I don't know."

"He admitted he was part of the plan. They even gave him an amulet," Robert pointed out. Wick nodded.

When Jonah frowned, Lynn nudged his chair with her foot. "Why are you stalling? I thought you wanted to find the eighth location?"

"I do." Jonah couldn't meet her eyes because he thought Latrell had suffered enough while a mortal. And besides, he wasn't sure what the boy might reveal. Latrell had seen him and Kevin together. "It's not fair to him."

"Jonah…" Lynn blew out an exasperated breath. "He's a Wraith! He will go crazy eventually and probably haunt his sister or something."

"You can't be sure of that."

"I agree with Jonah on that point," Wick interjected before raising his hands to hold off Lynn when she whirled on him. "We should summon Latrell, but the boy may not go crazy. Not all Wraiths are crazy."

"Yeah," Robert jumped in. "Some are mad, evil, and homicidal. Take your pick."

"The Seers aren't like that." As soon as Jonah said it, he blushed. Seers weren't exactly normal people either. "Well, that bookstore Wraith warned me about the danger. He's all right."

A haunted look came over Lynn's face when Jonah mentioned Seers. "We'll do it this evening, and no more stalling. Halloween's in two days and we haven't found the eighth location yet."

Wick glanced at her. "Four sound okay? That should give us enough time to ask our questions."

"That's the plan." Lynn poked Jonah in the shoulder. "You be ready to do your thing. No excuses."

"Yes, ma'am." Jonah saluted her. He half-feared she would pull him into a headlock, but she left the house without a second comment.

*

Mike and Jonah sat in the clubhouse side of the attic, at the old card table. Their books and notebooks were spread across the surface as they did their homework. The old sofa and armchairs had been pushed apart and the steamer trunk was moved aside to make room for Wick's spirit trap.

Despite all attempts to distract himself, Jonah grew more apprehensive as the time to summon Latrell drew closer.

"It'll be all right, Jonah." Mike reached over and tapped his hand. "You'll see. They won't hurt him."

"I'm not worried about that. It's something else." Jonah closed his book and slid it inside his book bag. "I'm scared of what Latrell might say when he shows up."

Mike's eyes narrowed. "What do you mean?"

"The last time he appeared, I was with Kevin." Jonah raised an eyebrow until Mike's own eyes widened.

"Oh." He leaned closer. "Latrell saw you two kissing?" Jonah nodded. "Wow. And you're worried he'll tell your cousins?"

"Yeah. Wouldn't you be worried?"

Amulet of the Goddess 913

"No." Mike bit his lower lip as he sat back in his chair, thinking. "I doubt Latrell would do that to you, Jonah. Maybe you should tell them though, just to be safe."

Jonah didn't get a chance to voice his thoughts about that idea because he suddenly felt the telltale shift in air pressure.

Mike sucked in a breath as he, too, noticed.

Kevin appeared near the large window. He spotted them at the card table and strolled over. "Thanks for calling me." He paused as he maneuvered around the spirit trap. "It sounds like a good plan."

"Yeah," Jonah said without any real enthusiasm.

"What's wrong with you?" Kevin asked.

"Nothing."

Mike gave him a disapproving glare and said, "Jonah's worried because Latrell caught you two kissing."

Kevin had just grabbed a chair and he paused in mid-motion, watching Jonah. After a moment, he shrugged and sat down at the table.

Jonah shoved him. "You don't care if he mentions it?"

"Honestly? I don't know. It's not like I have to worry about any relatives knowing about me, remember?"

Jonah couldn't tell for sure, but he detected a little bitterness in Kevin's tone and he suspected why. Not only had Kevin been the youngest Fallen Reaper, but unlike Jonah's dad and godfather, who'd been Reapers for decades, Kevin had only been one for a short time.

The older boy told him about a family–a mom, dad, and little brother–still living in Chicago. In that moment, he wondered if that was why Kevin was so willing to tag along with them, even if he got into trouble with Mandara and the Alliance.

"I'm sorry," Jonah said, not knowing what else to add.

"Don't sweat it. Go ahead and summon Latrell early."

"How did you–"

Kevin playfully tapped Jonah's forehead. "I know your wicked, little mind."

Mike stood. "You better hurry if we want to hide it from the others."

"We're not hiding it from them," Jonah said, realizing the hypocrisy of the statement. "We'll just talk to Latrell first…"

Mike glanced at the candle stands visible between the sofa and chairs. "What if we can't do it?"

"I can."

"You don't have the amulet."

"He doesn't need it." Kevin eyed Jonah. "He can summon Latrell to him whenever he chooses to."

Jonah nodded in agreement as he held up a hand with the pinky finger extended. "You in? I'm being up front with you."

Mike finally nodded and locked his own pinky finger around Jonah's. Kevin smirked at them. With fifteen minutes left before Wick and the others were due to arrive, Jonah hurried to turn off the overhead lights before closing the dark blue curtain over the attic window. The desk lamps and floor lamp near the sofa would remain on.

Jonah stepped between the candle stands and positioned himself at the edge of the sigil design. He wanted to leave plenty of space for Latrell.

Mike lifted the final link of chain off the trunk and stood close, his expression determined. "You ready?"

Jonah took a deep breath and closed his eyes. He pictured Latrell and reached out with his Reaper power, mentally calling to the Wraith. Then his lips parted and he said, "Latrell, come to me. We need to talk."

Mike gasped at the same time a fog of coldness hit Jonah. He opened his eyes and found Latrell standing right in front of him. The extreme nearness of the spectral boy caused Jonah to stumble backward, almost tripping over the chains. He had to make an awkward leap to avoid pulling everything down.

Mike overcame his own shock and clicked the final length of chain in place.

Latrell reached out for Jonah. *What's wrong?*

The spirit took a step and bumped into an invisible wall. His eyes widened in fear when he noticed the sigil below his ghostly feet.

What's this, Jonah? Let me out!

"It's okay," Jonah said. "I wanted to talk to you." He turned to translate for Mike and Kevin. "He said–"

"I heard him," Mike assured Jonah.

"Me too," Kevin added.

"Really?"

Kevin sounded impatient as he explained, "Fallen Reapers can hear ghosts, Jonah."

Mike shrugged. "I'm changed, remember?"

Latrell watched their conversation. Once it ended, he turned on Jonah. *Why trap me?*

"We need answers," Mike said as he moved to stand beside Jonah.

Latrell stared at Mike for a quiet moment before turning back to Jonah. *Let me out!*

"If you answer my questions, I will."

"Why are you here?" Mike fired at the boy. "Why did you give Jonah that amulet?"

I wanted him to have it, Latrell said.

"Why?" Jonah asked, his voice beginning to rise. "Are you part of my aunt's plan to open the nexus points?"

Latrell's face showed signs of shock. *You know about that?*

"Yeah, I do. And the Phantom's Path."

As soon as Jonah uttered those words, the attic door opened.

"We got company," Kevin announced.

The ghost boy went crazy, blurring into motion as he repetitively hit the invisible barrier over and over.

"Latrell, it's okay. They're just my cousins."

Latrell stopped whirling around, but he continued to tremble with fright as Lynn, Robert, and Wick stepped into the attic.

Lynn ran over. "Jonah! Why didn't you wait for us?"

"I wanted to talk to him on my own."

"How did you summon him?" Robert asked as he hastily crossed to the filing cabinet.

Wick called out to him, "No use looking in the Seeker's box, Bobby." He walked around the circle, peering at Latrell. "Jonah can summon Wraiths because of who he is–a Reaper."

Lynn tossed her braids with an angry flick of her head and glared at Kevin. "You let him do it?"

Kevin grinned. "Alliance override."

Lynn huffed and focused her attention on Latrell with a fascinated expression. "What did you learn?"

Jonah shrugged. "Nothing, yet."

I don't know anything. Latrell rotated his vaporous body, trying to keep everyone within sight while Mike translated for Lynn, Wick, and Robert.

Lynn shook her head. "I'm not buying that. We know you distracted Jonah."

Jonah gave his cousin a sharp look. Kevin had been the only one to suggest that so far. He had the growing suspicion that Robert, Wick, and Lynn were holding frequent, private discussions about him.

"Where's the eighth location?" Lynn asked.

Latrell gave a sudden, violent shake of his head. *I don't know! It's secret and they guard it. The goddess of the hunt would hurt me if I tried to find out.*

After waiting for Mike's translation, Lynn narrowed her eyes at the ghost. "Did you even try?"

Latrell lowered his head. *Yes. Her Felines are worse than Grim Hounds. They can tear a Wraith or mortal apart.*

"Felines?" Lynn asked. "You mean the creatures that guarded the amulet in the Underworld?"

Yes. Latrell looked between Jonah and Kevin. *Reapers like to call on Grim Hounds, but the Felines are just as bad. The goddess also uses them as her symbol and harbinger. At least, that's what I was told.*

Amulet of the Goddess

"Of course!" Wick pulled out his lighter, flicking it open and closed so fast, his hand shook. "The black cat everyone's been seeing around town is a Feline. I bet you!"

Jonah had seen one outside Drew's house and several in his nightmare about Mount Vernon on fire. And, if he weren't mistaken, there must have been one outside his house the night Deyanira's Grim Hound came to him.

Latrell confirmed Jonah's sinking feeling when he said, *That one wasn't a harbinger. It was her shadow transforming into the cat and roaming around.*

"That's impossible!" Lynn shouted. "My aunt—"

It's not your aunt doing it! Latrell became more agitated by the second. *Whenever her shadow falls on a mortal, she gains limited power. But they have to be careful not to drain themselves. If the person is magical or special, Pakhet can bestow more abilities on them. It's why she possesses special people.*

"But in our aunt's case...," Lynn began.

"She keeps draining herself," Jonah finished. "That's what Niqab Girl said to her in the cemetery."

"Okay," Robert said, "but transforming into a cat has to use up a lot of her limited power."

Lynn poked Latrell with her finger, then quickly pulled it back. "That's what she's doing, isn't it? Our aunt is so power hungry that she would stoop to doing stupid tricks, just to show off."

The finger poke startled Latrell but didn't seem to hurt him. *Yes. She is.*

"Danita!" Mike shouted.

"What about Danita?" Jonah didn't like Mike's horrified expression.

"She wants to prove someone's using that cat purely to exacerbate people's superstitious fears."

Lynn's eyes widened. "I may have encouraged her when she turned in the piece about Drew." She stepped closer to Mike. "What has she done?"

Mike gulped. "She knows where the cat has been appearing most often. She went there this evening, hoping to take pictures or a video..."

Lynn swore under her breath and rushed to her computer. "I'm guessing you and Kevin have never been there?" She flicked her eyes toward Jonah and then back to the monitor.

"No, I haven't." He turned to Kevin, who shrugged and crossed to Lynn's side.

"Latrell?" Jonah faced the boy. "She'll hurt Danita, won't she?"

The ghostly boy nodded. Jonah motioned to Wick. "Let him go."

"But what about the eighth site?"

"He's telling the truth. I can sense it on Wraiths too," Jonah said.

"Oh." Wick unhooked one chain, then used a knife to scrape away a portion of the sigil.

Latrell waved to Jonah. *I'm sorry.*

The apology sounded genuine. "It's okay. We're all being used."

Latrell nodded before he disappeared.

As Robert and Wick joined Lynn and Kevin at the computer, Jonah hurried to the curtain, pulled it aside, and opened the attic window. Cool air rushed across his face.

He closed his eyes and quested out using his Reaper powers. Just like with Latrell, Jonah concentrated on his connection to the Grim Hound. He pictured the beast in his mind and within a second, he connected. *Come to me. Now.*

"Jonah? What are you doing?" Mike whispered from right behind him.

"Wait."

A loud, deep bark sounded from below the window. Kevin exclaimed a curse in the background.

Jonah leaned out the window. The huge Grim Hound was below, peering up at the window with its red-in-red eyes. "Find Danita," Jonah said. He knew he didn't have to yell for the creature to hear him. "She's in the north park. Protect her. Understand?"

The Grim Hound bobbed its head in acknowledgment before it streaked off like a rocket. The speed of the hounds always amazed Jonah, but he had no clue if it would reach Danita in time.

Mike gripped Jonah's shoulder. "That was a Grim Hound."

"You—you could see it?"

Amulet of the Goddess

Mike nodded, his eyes wide. "When did you get a pet Grim Hound?"

"Shhhh," Jonah warned his friend, but it was too late.

Lynn and Kevin had already stepped away from the computer.

Kevin looked the angriest with him. "Jonah, what was a Grim Hound doing here?"

"A Grim Hound?" Wick called out. "Where?" He hurried over to peek out the window.

"I doubt it's there now," Kevin replied, crossing his arms.

Jonah knew he had to explain part of it. "I think Deyanira sent her Grim Hound to watch out for me."

No one said a word for several shocked moments.

"We can talk about it later," Jonah announced. "Right now, we need to save Danita, right?" He raised his eyebrows.

"Oh, we're gonna talk later," Lynn warned.

Kevin shook his head, grabbed Jonah's arm, and said, "We'll be back."

CHAPTER THIRTY-SIX
PAKHET'S SHADOW

Kevin and Jonah's first stop was the Hightowers' house.

"Get your Reaper's coat," Kevin told a confused Jonah.

"Why?"

"It'll protect you from a Feline's claws. Hurry."

Jonah did, ducking inside the house and returning in record time. The last stop was inside Kevin's hotel room. The young Fallen Reaper's coat lay across one of the double beds. He snatched it up while Jonah slipped into his own coat.

"Follow me," Kevin said before he phased.

Without hesitating, Jonah dived into the aether after the boy. Seconds later, he reappeared in a clearing in the middle of a deep forest of pines. He glanced around without seeing any sign of a park.

Kevin turned and pointed off to the north. "The park borders the national forest here. Lynn thought this was a good place to avoid any people."

"She's right," Jonah agreed, but he worried they wouldn't find his friend in time. "Danita could be anywhere."

"Think, Jonah. I know you're probably connected to the Grim Hound. Where is it?"

"Oh, yeah." Jonah closed his eyes and concentrated. He felt the beast's presence at once. "It's…"

"Phase. I'll follow."

Amulet of the Goddess

Jonah obeyed Kevin and phased. They reappeared not far from a jogging trail. Nearby, two huge, dark shapes slashed and fought with each other. The deep, angry growl of the Grim Hound countered the higher-pitched snarl of the Feline.

Danita wasn't far away, sprawled on the ground and holding her injured arm. Her slashed jacket sported a red stain. Danita stared in shock as the supernatural creatures tumbled and tussled with each other.

Her attention was so focused, she didn't hear Antwan's cousin stalking toward her from the opposite direction, her hand raised and ready to hex.

Jonah phased right in front of his friend and used his Reaper's coat to protect them both from the attack. Danita screamed and struggled, but Jonah held her tight as an unpleasant tingle shot up his back. Thankfully, nothing else happened and the enchantments on the Reaper's coat worked their magic.

Kevin appeared next to them, using his own body as a shield. He deflected a second hex into the trees with the swish of his blades. The thwarted attack splintered a trunk. "I have a bandage in my left coat pocket," he said.

Jonah fumbled, pulling the bandages free, and huddled next to Danita. He met her terrified gaze. "You're okay now."

He helped her stand and she clung to him, whimpering in pain as they moved away from the fighting beasts. Kevin covered their backs until they reached a safe distance. Jonah checked Danita's wound and discovered three deep, bleeding cuts on her forearm.

He did his best at cleaning the cuts and putting the bandages on. All the while, he winced at the sounds of the fighting creatures and Kevin's continued blocking of hexes.

Danita moaned at his clumsy results.

"Sorry," he whispered.

As Jonah completed his work, a vortex appeared in front of them. Antwan's cousin stepped out and hurled a hex, but Kevin moved in a blur and blocked the renewed attack.

Frustrated, the girl turned on the Grim Hound and caught it with a hex. The beast yelped and let go of the large cat. But the Grim Hound recovered quickly and growled in defiance at the young sorceress and the

Feline. Instead of charging, the hound drew even with Kevin as they faced off with the girl.

The Feline's outline shimmered before it transformed into Aunt Ruby. The evil woman didn't appear weakened from the injuries she suffered, made evident by her torn clothes. With her eerie, glowing, orange eyes, she looked even more powerful.

When she spoke, it was Pakhet's tones intertwined with her own, just like in his nightmare. "So, my sister's son is The One? The Deliverer? Release all the limitations the Alliance has imposed on you. Embrace your true power and destiny, something your dear, old mom never could."

"Leave my mom out of this!" Jonah screamed. He moved forward, but Danita clutched his arm for dear life, pulling him back. Unwilling to leave his friend, Jonah settled on making sure that Danita remained behind him. "You don't know anything about my mom."

Ruby laughed. "Poor child, you fail to understand that she's responsible for all this. Refuse me now, young one, but when I release the true goddess of the hunt, your friends and family will be the first to suffer from her wrath. At the Witching Hour, the beginning of their end will be at hand."

When she whirled her arms, Jonah and Kevin tensed, expecting a renewed attack. But Aunt Ruby produced an outpouring of supernatural power that obscured her and Niqab Girl's escape.

The Grim Hound let out a whine of frustration and bumped against Kevin, who hesitated before he patted the beast on the head.

Danita stared at the creature in mounting shock.

"You can see it?" Jonah asked.

She nodded, as if afraid to speak. And then she fainted. Jonah caught her and lowered her to the ground. He knelt, cradling her head in his arms. His own body trembled with the prolonged release of pent-up, nervous tension.

The Grim Hound moved closer to sniff her. Jonah reached up and scratched the hound behind the ears. "Thanks for saving Danita." The beast growled in a strangely modulated fashion.

Kevin stepped closer. "We need to get her to safety."

"Well, it's good she fainted," Jonah pointed out. "We can phase her to the clubhouse without her ever knowing."

Amulet of the Goddess

"That doesn't matter," Kevin said, frowning.

His meaning became clear to Jonah. "Don't let them take her memories away."

"Those are the rules. And Danita's not cool with supernatural things anyway."

"She could see the Grim Hound. That has to mean something."

Kevin deactivated his blades and shoved them into his pocket. "It means Danita's seen someone die, in person."

Jonah stared at the Grim Hound and then into Danita's face, wondering whom that person could have been. After a moment, he met Kevin's gaze. "I know what it's like to have your memory blocked. I don't want her to go through that."

"You're not the only one having to deal with a memory block," Kevin snapped before he stopped himself.

"What?" Jonah's eyes widened. "You've been–"

"You didn't feel this way about Brandon and Antwan," Kevin interrupted him.

"They deserved it," Jonah shouted. He couldn't believe Kevin would go there. "Plus, we had to hide what they saw. I phased Antwan and…" Jonah trailed off at Kevin's raised eyebrows.

The young Fallen Reaper reached down and lifted Danita into his own arms. "I'm just telling you what Marcus's argument will be."

"Do you think it's right?" Jonah wanted Kevin to agree with him.

After a moment, Kevin let out a low breath. "I trust you, Jonah. If you say she'll be okay, I'm with you."

Jonah relaxed when he heard that. "You'll tell that to Marcus and the others?"

"Yeah, I will. But it's not our decision."

*

Kevin's prediction was right on target. No sooner did the Alliance members arrive to inspect Danita, than they took over the situation. Jonah and the others stood aside and watched as a Healer repaired the gash on her arm.

Trueblood opened a vortex. "Back to the clearing."

An Alliance Guard held Danita in his massive arms and turned for the opening.

"Wait," Jonah protested. Kevin pulled him back, but Jonah struggled. "Why take her back there? That's dangerous."

Trueblood's posture relaxed for a moment as he met Jonah's concerned gaze. He stepped away from the vortex. "We have people in place. It'll look like an animal attacked Danita, and a passerby scared off whatever it was."

"But–"

"Let us do our work." The mage motioned the Alliance Guard through the magical doorway.

But Jonah couldn't let Trueblood go without at least trying to do something for Danita. "I don't think it's fair to extract her memory. Kevin agrees with me."

Kevin, who looked like he wanted to stay out of this argument, nodded when Trueblood glanced in his direction.

"It's the standard policy for a reason," Trueblood stated. "No special treatment."

"But it doesn't work all the time," Jonah countered. "It didn't work with Brandon and Antwan. They just became more suspicious of me." He stopped himself from mentioning the recent fight. "What good is that? There have to be other ways to do this. Or just talk to the person instead of yanking their memories clean away." Jonah's voice rang off the attic rafters when he finished.

For a moment, he thought Trueblood would be angry with him, but the mage watched with a bemused smile on his face.

That bothered Jonah. "It's not funny."

"I'm not laughing at you, Jonah. It's just that you are so much like your dad," Trueblood assured him. "Isaiah always saw through the pretensions of

Amulet of the Goddess **925**

the Alliance and their efforts to make people uncomfortable by clinging to outdated rules."

"He–he did?"

"Oh, yeah. It's why we became good friends." Trueblood gestured to his dreadlocks.

"I was a rebel from birth and drove the elders of my tribe crazy." A thoughtful gleam entered his eyes. "You make a good point. We do have other options available besides memory charms and blocks. There's no reason to continue using this all-encompassing approach."

Jonah never accepted the possibility he'd actually win the argument. "So, you'll give Danita a chance?"

Now Trueblood frowned. "I'll mention it to the Council, but I'm afraid for tonight, it's just the status quo for Danita. I'm sorry." He nodded to Kevin and stepped through the vortex.

Robert, Wick, and Mike all congratulated Jonah on his convincing argument.

Even Lynn couldn't avoid grinning as she congratulated him. "Not bad, hero."

"And don't worry about Danita," Kevin added. "Alliance people will stay around to protect her. She'll be fine."

*

Jonah grew concerned when Danita didn't show up by lunch period. "Did you see her this morning?" he asked Mike.

"No, I haven't. I'm sure–"

"She's okay," Jonah finished. A little irritation entered his voice. "Everyone keeps saying that." He rose and threw away his half-eaten lunch. "I'll check with you later."

Jonah knew Danita liked books as much as he did. So he went to the school's library and that's where he found her, squashed in a back corner, hunched over a stack of books.

She glanced up at his approach and smiled. "Hi, Jonah."

"How are you?" Jonah dropped into a seat across from her.

"What? Oh, I'm fine." She narrowed her eyes, growing curious. "How did you find out?"

Jonah never expected her to ask that question. "Ah, Mike told me."

Danita frowned for a second, then her face smoothed. "I probably mentioned it to him. Anyway, it was scary."

"What do you remember?"

"Well, I was searching the woods for the cat when it suddenly showed up and attacked me."

"And…" Jonah prodded, wondering what the Alliance could have taken from her.

She frowned. "It hurt my arm." She pulled up her sleeve to show him the large bandage.

Seeing the injury produced an involuntary, sympathetic ache in Jonah's own body.

"I fell, but, after that, I remember nothing," Danita continued. "I blanked out. Someone heard my scream and came to help." She nodded more to herself than Jonah. "They spotted something running off when they approached." Her hands shook a little. "I guess I was pretty lucky."

"At least you're all right." Jonah's relief was genuine, but it was chilling to see a Memory Charm at work on someone he cared about. Brandon and Antwan didn't matter to him. Danita, however, was his friend, and that made the whole thing more frightening.

"You were right," Danita said as she reached across the table to grip his hand. "It was dangerous to go there alone. I'm sorry I didn't listen to you."

"That's okay."

"No, it isn't. Now I don't have the last part of my story. I wanted to get it finished today because Halloween's tomorrow."

"You still want to prove people are just being superstitious?"

"Of course." The fire in her eyes reassured Jonah.

Still, he couldn't let it go. "But what about the cat?"

"It was just a black cat, Jonah."

"It hurt your–"

Amulet of the Goddess 927

"There you are!" Anthony Freeman interrupted, popping up on the other side of the bookshelf. He froze when he saw their clasped hands.

Jonah and Danita jerked their hands apart.

"I was just checking on her." Jonah stood.

Anthony worked his jaw, clearly wanting to say something or maybe even fight.

Thankfully, Danita reached out and pulled him into a chair beside her. "We're just friends, Anthony. You know that."

"Yeah, whatever," the boy groused.

Jonah hurried off when Danita puffed up, ready to argue. He hoped to be spared having to witness any of that conversation.

CHAPTER THIRTY-SEVEN
GRIM ATTIRE

Saturday morning dawned with a grey, overcast sky. *Just perfect*, Jonah thought, glancing out his window. Today was the day—or rather, tonight was *the night*. Aunt Ruby would open the nexus, although the Alliance still hadn't located the eighth site. And there was also the inevitable awareness that his moment of decision was soon coming.

Jonah expected Lynn to mirror his growing anxiety, but she seemed in high spirits when she met his curious gaze at the breakfast table.

"Glad you're happy about tonight," Jonah grumbled, pulling out the cereal box.

"We're making the right decision—or you will be."

He was pouring milk in his bowl but tilted the carton upright just enough to stop the flow. "But what if things go wrong?"

"Then they're meant to go wrong. But I doubt that."

Jonah set the milk carton down rather hard. "When I make my decision?"

Robert exited his room and Lynn shushed Jonah. She made a show of focusing on the folded newspaper in front of her.

After breakfast, Jonah and his cousins rode their bikes to the Practice Club clearing, where transformations were already underway. Bags of decorations and other items lined the edge of the clearing while long tables had been set up for the massive spread of food from local restaurants.

Amulet of the Goddess **929**

Local firefighters stacked wood for the bonfire near the center of the field. They lived in the neighborhood and volunteered to make sure everything went off without any problems.

Jonah, Robert, and Lynn joined the other kids decorating the surrounding trees with Halloween-inspired items. They hung orange and black streamers and set out the real, miniature jack-o'-lanterns from their church pumpkin sale. Tonight, they would all be lit up with small candles. Copious amounts of skeletons, pumpkin heads, and bats soon could be seen dangling from overhead branches.

On the paths from the nearby school and the makeshift parking area, fake pumpkins were neatly arranged that would light the way. The temperature was expected to be a cool fifty degrees. *Not too bad*, Jonah concluded.

And it would be cloudless too, something Rodney appreciated for his band. He worked with the group erecting the portable stage at the north end of the field.

The preparations brightened Jonah's mood. He could almost forget that somewhere out there, his deranged aunt wanted to unleash a goddess and her Phantoms on the town.

He had just helped another club member hang a streamer of miniature paper skeletons when Mike poked him in the back. Jonah turned. "Hey."

"I wanted to ask you something." When Jonah nodded, Mike asked, "Can I borrow your coat?"

Jonah glanced at Mike, who looked warm enough in his own light coat. "Uh, what's wrong with yours?"

"Not this one." Mike laughed and then leaned closer. "I meant, your Reaper's coat."

The request surprised Jonah, but he didn't mind. "Sure, no problem."

"Cool. It should hang just right."

Although Mike was correct and they were within an inch of each other's heights, Jonah had already noticed an added benefit of the enchanted coat. Before school started, he wore it once, on the same night his godfather gave it to him as a birthday present.

The incident with Danita was his second time wearing the coat, and in between those two occasions, he had grown taller. Only when he took it off to hang in his closet did he notice the enchanted garment had actually lengthened to compensate for his recent growth spurt.

"Yeah," Jonah agreed. "We can go by my house when we leave here."

Mike flashed a thumbs up and ran off to finish hanging the remaining decorations. As Jonah surveyed the clearing, he thought Kevin had a point when he opted out of helping. With all they knew about the supernatural world, it seemed odd to celebrate Halloween like this. Still, Jonah wished the Fallen Reaper had hung out all the same. Not only did he feel safer with Kevin near, he was also craving some alone time.

It occurred to Jonah that he and Kevin could have worn their matching Reaper coats. He imagined everyone would have assumed the coats were from some fantasy film, but that didn't bother him.

By late afternoon, and with everything done, Mike followed Jonah home. He gushed over the feel of the coat as soon as Jonah handed it to him. "It's lighter than I expected." He slipped it on his own thin frame. "Oh." His eyes widened.

"What? Did it hurt you?"

"No. I..." Mike shook his head. "Light jolt, but it's okay now."

Jonah grinned. "It was adjusting to your height."

"Really? Cool!" Mike admired himself in Jonah's mirror. "This is really nice. Why don't you wear it more often? It looks so good on you."

Jonah shrugged. He could get away with putting it on during the winter. But it looked so formal and dark. Maybe he could wear it to church sometime. A dress shirt and tie would fit well. "I'd look too goth in it."

"Hmmm." Mike turned his profile to the mirror. "That's precisely the look I want tonight."

"What about Patrick?"

"He's too image-conscious to wear more than a mask."

Jonah had a sudden thought. "Does he know what you have planned?"

"No, and he also doesn't dictate what I can wear." Mike sounded confident, but Jonah knew the signs in his friend. Mike bit his lower lip when he was unsure about something, and he worried that lip right now.

Amulet of the Goddess

The conversation reminded Jonah that, aside from his idea that he and Kevin could have dressed in their long coats, he didn't have a costume. Even though he never said it out loud, he just planned to go as himself and keep busy working. Now that seemed like a really lame option.

He sat on the edge of his bed, regretting his choice not to have put more thought into the matter. "My mask would have been perfect to wear."

"You can't." Mike whirled on him. "What if Drew or Brandon shows up? They'll recognize it in an instant."

"I said it *would have been* perfect." Jonah threw up his hands. "I'll think of something else."

Mike took off the coat, slipped the hanger in, and gently folded it over his arm. "You only have a few hours left." He checked his watch. "Well, I have to go. And thanks for letting me wear this."

"Big date." Jonah tried to keep the envy out of his voice. He didn't think he succeeded, judging by Mike's expression.

"Jonah, we can't do anything about your aunt. The Alliance is watching all seven locations. They'll be ready to handle anything that comes through."

"Yeah, I guess so," Jonah muttered.

"That's not the real issue, is it?" Mike said while running his fingers over the fabric of the coat.

"I just know it'll come down to me. It always does."

"We'll be right there with you." Mike's confident tone made Jonah feel even worse. "Don't forget, we have the safe room to protect you, although I know you don't like it."

Jonah forced a smile. "Actually, it's pretty cool."

Mike seemed to relax and he motioned to the door. "Walk me out."

Jonah rose and followed his friend. "See you tonight," he said when they reached the front door.

Mike waved and left. As his friend walked up the street, Jonah tried to see the bright side of things.

*

Jonah still hadn't thought of a costume to wear by the time Robert came home. His cousin paused to get a carton of juice from the kitchen before turning for his room. He had a long case slung over his left shoulder.

Jonah pointed. "What's that?"

"You'll see." Robert beamed at him as he marched into his room and shut the door.

Jonah would have guessed it was the bow, but the case was different, and more expensive looking. He tried to imagine what his cousin planned to wear and concluded he'd find out soon enough.

Lynn pranced out of her room and into the kitchen. She wore dark green tights under a full-sleeved, earth-green jacket, the perfect image of a fantasy elf.

She tugged on two fabric sheaths tied to her emerald green sash. "I can store my blades inside these and leave them activated. Just in case."

"That's cool," Jonah said, admiring his cousin's clever costume.

Instead of the usual white-blond hair the movies favored, Lynn kept her hair in braids, plaited tightly to her head. The hairstyle highlighted her grey eyes and thin face.

She spun on her heels and called out, "Robert!"

Robert exited his room, wearing similar green tights and a short green cloak studded with glittering, stuck-on gems. He also carried an authentic-looking, African long bow over his left shoulder.

As Jonah watched, Lynn used makeup to accent Robert's already angular eyebrows even more so. Together, they were stunning to see.

"Wow, guys."

Robert tilted his chin upward. "You dare speak to me, mortal?!"

Lynn shoved him while Jonah laughed. Despite the fun, he began to feel out of place with everyone else. Even Mike had a plan, and a date. Jonah frowned, hating that he wasted his great mask to play the vigilante. Now he couldn't wear it.

He slumped into the kitchen chair, his earlier excitement over the bonfire rapidly waning. Robert and Lynn exchanged a glance.

Amulet of the Goddess

Jonah caught it. "What?"

"Something told me," Lynn said as she winked at him, "that you didn't have a chance to come up with a costume for yourself. So, I already took care of that."

"You did?" Jonah sat forward. "What did you get for me to wear?"

Lynn held up a finger. "Just wait." She busied herself sprinkling glitter on Robert's tunic. Several minutes later, someone knocked on the back door. Robert opened it and a wizard entered.

Jonah couldn't believe it. Wick was dressed as a typical fantasy wizard, complete with a long, scraggly beard, a crooked, pointed hat, and a tall, knobby staff. What didn't go with the theme was the heavy, black robe he had draped over his arm.

Wick greeted him with a dramatic voice. "Greetings, Padawan."

"I'm surprised you didn't come as a Jedi," Jonah said.

"I thought about it, but this seemed more on the mark."

"Yeah, right." Jonah laughed. "Trueblood and Albrecht don't look like that."

Wick shrugged and pulled a large, plastic bag from under the heavy robe and held it out to Jonah. "This is for you."

Jonah took it and peeked inside. A full-face skull mask and a foldable, fake scythe were inside it. He pulled out the mask for a closer look and discovered it wasn't a cheap one from the superstore. It was well crafted and substantial, gleaming a metallic white even under the pale kitchen light.

Wick held out the black robe to him and Jonah's stomach knotted. "You're kidding, right? I can't go as a Grim Guard." He experienced a quiet moment of panic as he recalled the real Grim Guards from his dreamwalk.

"Why not?" Wick asked, failing to perceive his momentary shock. "It's perfect!"

"But…"

Robert draped the robe over Jonah's shoulder as he promptly propelled him toward his bedroom. "Go change. We have to get there in time to greet the first guests."

Jonah experienced an unpleasant pit in his stomach when he changed and looked at himself in the mirror. A Grim Guard stared back at him. The skull mask was even more form-fitting then the Komainu mask and downright spooky to see. Given the quality of the mask, Jonah wondered where Wick could have gotten it.

This is so weird, he thought. He started to smile behind the mask when a sudden image from his recent nightmare popped into his head. The power of it was so real that Jonah stumbled backward, his legs bumping against his bed. He yanked off the mask and struggled to calm his breathing.

He was shocked at his own expression in the mirror. Worse, his legs began to shake, forcing him to grip the edge of his chest just to remain on his feet. He hated this moment of weakness. Yet the urgency of the onrushing decision couldn't be denied. He had a path to take, and Lynn agreed.

For a moment, he wanted to rush out into the family room and demand that she tell him exactly what she had seen. *No, I can't do that.* He pushed away the panic by calling up the memory of his parents. Even at the end, he witnessed the resolve on his dad's face and his mom's acceptance.

We did everything out of love for you.

Jonah sucked in a ragged breath as something unusual happened. Strength of purpose filled his chest. His breathing slowed and he stood taller as Trueblood's fortifying words came back to him. *Everything your parents were, so are you.*

His parents were brave, and so was he. Jonah wiped a tear away with a rock-steady hand. He decided to walk forward, bravely meeting whatever challenge he had to face. After slipping on the mask, he gazed at himself again in the mirror and thought, *I'm ready.*

CHAPTER THIRTY-EIGHT
HALLOWEEN BONFIRE

Two huge, sci-fi troopers stood at the entrance of the practice field. Given their size, Jonah had no doubt they were Alliance Guards. The men augmented their regular uniforms with fake armor plates on their chests, legs, and arms. But their stun weapons were clearly evident.

As Jonah approached, he recognized the guard on the right. It was the captain who fetched him the night he chased after Aunt Ruby.

The captain smiled and gestured to himself, showing off the armor pieces. "What do you think?"

"That is so cool," Jonah said as he came to stand beside the man. He held out his right forearm, giving Jonah a closer look and tapped the surface of the fake armor piece. It looked real, but was actually no more than hardened plastic that was painted to simulate battle damage. "Did you make the armor?"

"Oh, no. My son did these for us. He's rather gifted at product fabrication."

"Your son? Is he here?" Jonah scanned the area, eager to meet any kid who could create something as realistic as the armor. He also wondered if the captain's son would be as huge as his gigantic dad.

"I'm afraid he doesn't want to hang around his old man." The captain's voice did not even try to mask his weariness. "I think the only reason he did these was because he loves being creative."

Jonah nodded while trying to hide the sudden sadness he felt at knowing he would never get a chance to be in the same place with his own dad.

Right then, he'd have given just about anything to see his father one last time.

The captain patted Jonah's shoulder and his expression revealed a knowing compassion. "Sorry."

"It's okay," Jonah said, anxious to switch to another subject. "How well can you move in the armor?"

The captain adjusted his stun weapon and suddenly shocked Jonah by whirling it around before snapping it back into place. "The design is practical enough, but we can detach the pieces in seconds if the need arises."

Jonah nodded and adjusted his robe. Despite the heaviness of the garment, he could also move around quite freely with it. Only now did he consider the necessity and advantage of being able to do that.

He was fidgeting with his mask when Anthony marched up, dressed as a X-Wing pilot. He seemed a little aloof, more so than normal, with Jonah.

"We're working the entrance with…" Anthony nodded to the Guard Captain.

"Cool."

Anthony crossed to the other side and took his post without another word. Jonah made a note to talk to Danita again. Or maybe he should have just had it out with Anthony? Thinking of her, he scanned the small number of club members and their friends already positioned on the field.

He spotted Danita, dressed as an Amazon warrior. Jonah blinked several times, and glanced over at Anthony. The boy was watching him. *Yeah, we'll have to talk.*

More kids began arriving and soon occupied Jonah's full attention. Many people had gone all-out with their costumes. Others were cheesy and cheap. Still others were obviously quite thoughtful, like a girl who was walking around in a cloth-covered, wire-framed coffin with her face painted a sickly green.

Several of the kids hovered around the huge Alliance Guards, arguing over which video game the costumes came from.

Jonah snickered when the captain waved the gawking kids through the entrance, urging them to hurry with the constant phrase, "Move along!"

Amulet of the Goddess

Mike, having chosen to dress as a traditional vampire, looked sleek and handsome in Jonah's long coat. Jonah didn't even recognize him at first. As expected, Patrick wore a simple half-faced mask, the least you could do and still be allowed inside.

Jonah decided to have some fun. He stepped in front of the boys and turned his scythe horizontal just to block their way.

Patrick looked defensive but Mike peered into Jonah's mask, and nodded.

Jonah pointed the scythe at Patrick without speaking.

The boy puffed out his chest. "A half-mask is okay."

People behind them got restless or shifted to the other line, bypassing Anthony.

Deciding he had played it out long enough, Jonah said, "It's too lame, Patrick. That's why you can't come in."

Mike laughed and said, "That's a good costume."

Patrick didn't find it funny at all.

After receiving an annoyed glance from Anthony, Jonah waved them forward. That's when he saw Brandon and Antwan approaching with their dates. The boys both wore expensive, store-bought pirate costumes. Their dates were clad in period dresses. *Gee whiz*, Jonah thought. He searched the crowd for Drew, but didn't see the boy anywhere.

His senses tingled when he spotted a girl in a bone-white mask that covered her face. It had the merest suggestion of a mouth and vertical, cat-like slits for the eyes. Jonah was certain it was Antwan's cousin. She wore a dark nun's habit, but the girl's tall frame and signature movement were unmistakable. Plus, it didn't hurt that he easily sensed the magic in her.

She shifted to his line, intending to enter right past him. When she drew even, she paused with her mask only inches from his. "Interesting choice in costume, Son of Isaiah." Jonah heard the amusement in her voice. "See you later."

The mysterious girl slipped by and instantly seemed to evaporate into the gathering press of kids. Jonah pulled out his phone and typed a quick text message with one hand while waving people through with the other. *She's here.*

He and the others had previously set up a texting group.

White Mask.

Jonah's phone buzzed with a response from Lynn.

I see her.

Jonah exchanged duties with another Practice Club member as soon as he could, and then entered the open-air party to find Lynn. She nodded toward the far side of the stage, where Rodney's band was already well into their first song. Antwan's cousin stood near Brandon and Antwan but she remained aloof, watching the surrounding crowd.

Jonah, Lynn, and Robert traded off watching her, but the girl remained tethered to her cousin for most of the evening. When Wick took over the task, Jonah could finally relax. He pushed up his face mask, leaned the scythe against a tree, and eagerly enjoyed the party. Lorraine grabbed him for a dance to make Rodney angry, or so he suspected. They danced for two songs.

He was grateful for Danita's interference when Lorraine tried to rope him into the third straight song. She pulled Jonah away while smiling, "He promised we'd dance."

"Fine." Lorraine whirled around before she stormed off.

"I think she and Rodney are at it again," Jonah said.

"Of course," Danita agreed while she hooked her shield to a catch on her back, freeing her hands. She and Jonah danced to a slow song. She gazed into his eyes and Jonah had to admit the contacts really set off her large, brown eyes.

"Thanks, anyway," he said.

Danita smiled. "You looked like you wanted to get away."

"I did," Jonah whispered while glancing around. "But I don't want Anthony mad at me again."

"Don't worry. He's helping his dad bring in more drinks from his truck."

"Oh. Nice costume, by the way. It's so eerie." Jonah meant it. He had always considered her a bookworm and geek, just like him and Mike. He never even noticed that she had a female body.

Danita beamed at him. "Jonah Blackstone, was that a real compliment?"

Amulet of the Goddess **939**

"Ha ha. Everyone jokes." He produced a mock frown.

Danita laughed and then jiggled his hand, her expression conspiratorial. "What's going on? I saw you doing a lot of texting."

Jonah gulped, trying to come up with a valid excuse. "Nothing. Just keeping in touch with the rest of the club members."

Danita's eyebrows drew together as she leaned against him. "This feels familiar somehow. We've never danced before, have we?"

Oh boy, Jonah thought, fearing her memory block wasn't working.

His phone buzzed with a message and he tried to shield it from her view as he read. Wick wanted to change up. "Look, I have to take care of something with the party. See you later?"

Danita nodded, giving him a curious look. Then she folded her arms, striking an unintentional pose that matched the warrior theme of her costume. Unable to resist the urge, Jonah snapped a quick picture with his phone before he slipped through the crowd.

He found Wick near the base of the short hill on the east side of the gathering. "What's up?"

Wick pointed to the side of the clearing where Brandon was holding court. "She's stuck with them all evening. Seems pretty strange to me."

"Tell me about it."

"Well, I need a break." Wick motioned to his girlfriend, Tamara, who was dressed as an Egyptian priestess. Jonah gaped at her when the duo disappeared into the throng of dancing and laughing kids.

A motion at the top of the hill caught Jonah's attention and he turned to find two red eyes peering at him from the shelter of the trees. Jonah hurried up the hill and the Grim Hound bounded forward to nuzzle against him. It let out a low, satisfied growl when Jonah petted its head.

"You can't keep that as a pet," Kevin said. He stepped into view, wearing his Reaper's coat.

The Grim Hound sniffed him and nudged Kevin's hand until he consented to pet it.

Jonah smiled. "I thought you weren't coming."

"I have to keep an eye on you, especially tonight." Kevin motioned with his chin to the surrounding trees.

Jonah peered into the darkness and made out several more Alliance Guards, complete with the added fake armor. They stood at intervals around the clearing. "I didn't know they were here."

"We're trying to maintain a low profile."

Jonah pointed in Brandon's direction. "Niqab Girl is here too. That can't be good."

Kevin raised a small device to his mouth and spoke in quiet tones. One of the Alliance Guards motioned to another, who descended the hill and moved into the activity on the field.

Without thinking about it, Jonah stood beside Kevin with the Grim Hound between them. They were like two silent sentinels outside the flow of normal activity while still being on the lookout for trouble.

At eleven, the bonfire was lit and everything become louder and much more raucous. Jonah glanced at Kevin. "You wanna dance?"

"Not with you," he deadpanned.

"Oh? Whom do you prefer to dance with?"

Kevin shoved him and whispered, "Maybe later."

The Grim Hound went rigid. Its ears twitched as if it could hear something they couldn't. Then it took off through the woods and trotted around the outskirts of the gathering. Its heavy footfalls dwindled as it went further away.

Jonah gazed at Kevin. "What was that–"

A loud squeaking came from Kevin's device. Movement around Jonah alerted him to the presumption that all the Alliance Guards must have gotten the same call.

Kevin listened, his face growing more somber by the second.

"What happened?" Jonah moved right up against him, trying to overhear, but he couldn't make out the words.

Kevin lowered the device. "Wraiths are streaming out of the nexus points."

"But it's not even midnight!" Jonah pointed out.

Amulet of the Goddess

"I know. But the nexus is opening." For more than a few minutes, Kevin listened to more messages, and his voice grew hard. "They're all opening! Wraiths, Phantoms, black cats, and even Grim Hounds are coming through and causing trouble for mortals."

Jonah experienced a flash of fear. It was the dream happening all over again, except this was real. "The Alliance is handling them, right?"

Kevin balled his hands into fists as he shook his head. "Grimnions have begun showing up in places, adding to the chaos. The Alliance is stretched thin, trying to keep all the mortals out of harm's way while taking on the Wraiths."

A voice streamed out of the device in Kevin's hand. Jonah recognized it as the Guard Captain. "Kevin! Several Phantoms have penetrated the Crossroads. They're headed this way."

Before Kevin could respond, a light flashed inside the gathering of kids. It was Antwan's cousin. When she had Jonah's attention, she nodded, whirled, and fled through the crowd.

Jonah's legs moved automatically as he sprinted down the hill and into the bonfire party, giving chase.

"Jonah, wait!" Kevin called.

But Jonah couldn't respond. The flickering heat from the bonfire and the incessant yells of the kids became an annoying distraction as he strictly concentrated on following the girl. She was quick and seemed to disappear and reappear among the other kids.

A rowdy football player stepped right in front of Antwan's cousin. Without missing a beat, she held up a glowing hand and knocked the player sideways, straight into his friends. The display of lights shocked some of the kids but most laughed and clapped like it was part of an act.

Jonah wasn't far behind, pushing his way through the clueless kids. Another flash of light only produced more yells. People noticed him running and sidestepped out of his way. That allowed him to glimpse the girl as she slipped past the rope barrier before dashing into the darkened trees.

He plunged ahead into the gloom and ran through the stand of trees that surrounded the clearing. Just as he got into the vast expanse, he managed to make out her dark silhouette waiting for him.

Something's wrong.

He skidded to a stop at the same moment his Death Sense spiked. Light flared and the girl cast a spell at him. But Jonah had no intention of standing still and making himself an easy target. He charged forward and phased before the spell could hit him. For a split-second inside the aether, he managed to keep his focus and come out of the phase, landing almost on top of her.

Antwan's cousin stumbled back before somersaulting away. Using that moment of awkwardness to her fullest advantage, she sprinted toward the ravine. In the dead of night, all that appeared was a large, black chasm. The girl turned at the last minute to cast another spell. And Jonah prepared to phase again when Kevin unexpectedly appeared in front of him and deflected the attack.

A group of Alliance Guards caught up with them. And that's when the eerie howls reached his ears. Phantoms–glowing, ghostly apparitions as terrifying as the Grim Guards–zeroed in from all directions. Unlike the Grim Reaper's personal minions, these beings wore ragged but flowing, white robes covering what looked like ancient, decayed knight's armor.

Each carried a shield and a long sword. Though their bodies glowed with ethereal light, their faces remained hidden in the pitch black of their battle helmets. All that was visible to their enemies were the tiny, bright specks of light that represented their eyes. Their howls were worse than a Grim Hound's bark in their shrillness, which nearly froze Jonah's blood.

The Alliance Guards were unaffected. They snapped into motion, using their stun weapons to defend themselves and Jonah from the Phantoms' swords. The clanking of weapons colliding with other weapons was so deafening that Jonah was thankful the bonfire music muffled the raging battle. None of the mortal kids had a clue that a primal struggle between two opposing forces raged around them in the darkness.

Kevin stuck close, blurring into motion to hold off Phantoms with his Reaper blades. He scored some hits, but the armor the Phantoms wore prevented him from easily dispatching the creatures back to the Underworld.

Jonah welcomed the protection, but he also wanted to fight. He had his chance when a Phantom came for him. With his power humming in his ears, Jonah extended his hand before Kevin could intervene. He swiftly

Amulet of the Goddess **943**

opened the rip to the Underworld. The Phantom didn't have time to stop and it tumbled straight into the opening.

When the other Phantoms swerved away, giving him and Kevin a break, Jonah thought it was because they feared begin consumed by the rip he had just opened. Then his Death Sense flared and he knew better.

The mole appeared, along with several milky-eyed Grimnions carrying their signature, handheld scythes. The Alliance traitor pointed right at Jonah. "Kill the boy now!"

That ignited a firestorm of activity as every Alliance Member moved to protect Jonah. He didn't want that, of course, but what could he do? For the first time, he wished he had his own blades, or even the Protector's Ring. He vowed to take that up with his godfather if they all survived.

A roar greeted his ear as Deyanira's Grim Hound took down a Grimnion that had broken away and was headed toward the gathering. *They're trying to split us up.*

He patted the Grim Hound. "Go. Protect Danita and Mike." The beast barked and streaked off, taking out another Grimnion on its way.

The Guard Captain finally made it to Kevin's side and yelled, "Get Jonah to the safe room so we can protect the other kids. Go!"

Kevin pulled out the codex, gripped Jonah's arm, and activated the device. The clearing instantly disappeared, and the next second, they found themselves in the safe room. A group of milky-eyed men stood in a loose circle around them.

The mole had compromised the so-called security. And now, he and Kevin had inadvertently transferred themselves right into the enemy's hands.

CHAPTER THIRTY-NINE
CENTRE POINT

"Watch out," Kevin shouted. Pushing Jonah to the side, he drove a blurred fist into the face of an attacker at their immediate right. By doing so, Kevin and Jonah successfully avoided the first volley of stun shots from the other Grimnions.

Kevin and the bad guy smashed into the lockers, but it was Kevin who whirled back and pushed Jonah to the floor. He used his own long coat to cover them both, just as the Grimnions fired again.

Jonah's nerves were frayed as tendrils of power played over Kevin's enchanted coat. The Fallen Reaper grunted in pain, taking the brunt of the assault that somehow managed to leak through the protections.

The mole's order for his men to attack finally made sense. The Alliance traitor knew the Guard Captain would have sent Jonah here, since it was the only way to get him alone. And the mole must have given those guys a working codex. The traitor's level of access to top Alliance secrets scared Jonah.

Just when he thought Kevin couldn't take anymore, there was a change in the air pressure and the assault came to an abrupt halt. Loud grunts and the dull thuds of delivered punches filled the room. Kevin stood up and Jonah could see what was happening.

Five Alliance Guards that appeared in the room were taking on the Grimnions. One of the guards was down, his blood pooling on the floor from a vicious slash across the upper arm.

The Guard Captain had another Grimnion in a two-handed, overhead grip. He brought the struggling guy down on one knee, cracking the henchman's back.

Amulet of the Goddess

Jonah stared in shock as the dead man sprawled out on the floor.

The captain noticed his reaction. "No time for the niceties."

In short, brutal exchanges, the bodies of all five Grimnions soon littered the safe room floor. All of them appeared dead. Without intending to, Jonah reached out with his Reaper side and gulped. Their mortal spirits or souls were already gone. He shivered as he stood up to survey the scene.

The Guard Captain checked on his injured teammate and pulled out his communications unit. "Team one to Marcus." He waited. Static and the clamor of fighting filtered out of the speaker.

"Marcus here."

Relief flooded Jonah when he heard his godfather's voice.

"We secured the safe room for now, but its location has been compromised."

"Acknowledged. Sending a second package."

Kevin pulled Jonah away from the center of the room. A second later, Mike, Robert, Lynn, and Wick appeared. Excluding Mike, who held his Seeker's compass in his hands, all the others looked stunned and ruffled.

"Jonah!" Mike, rushed forward along with Lynn and Robert to hug him.

"What about the bonfire and the other kids?" Jonah inquired. He wanted to ask a million other questions but midnight–*the Witching Hour*– drew ever closer.

"They're fine," Lynn said, waving Danita's fake warrior shield. "The Alliance people who stayed behind broke up the party and sent everyone home. The Phantoms were only interested in you, and they ran off once you left."

"Oh," Jonah said. He pointed at the shield in Lynn's hands. "What are you doing with that?"

"Trueblood enchanted it to deflect their spells."

The mage's fast thinking impressed Jonah. He also suspected that Lynn suggested the change. Instead of asking, he glanced at Mike. "Was Danita okay?"

"That Grim Hound protected her."

"All right, everyone!" The captain signaled his team. "We have to move. The mole will know something has gone wrong and eventually send more people."

He snapped his fingers and the guards moved as a unit, surrounding the kids, with Jonah and Mike at the center. A teammate helped the injured guard to his feet.

With everyone in place, the Guard Captain nodded to Mike.

Looking more composed than Jonah would have expected, Mike held up his Seeker's compass. It hummed with power and Mike's eyes glowed. Jonah and the others shot worried glances at the floor when it started vibrating beneath their feet. Loud clicks came next before a space appeared around the edge of the sigil design.

Jonah had to shift aside when a thin pole extended from the center of the floor and stopped at waist height. Mike clicked his compass into an opening at the top and the device instantly lit up.

The whole setup awed Jonah. It was a modified version of the travel platform they had used before. He only had a moment, however, to marvel at the newer design when Mike chose a location and activated his compass.

*

"The entire sigil is an emergency transport option," Mike explained as the group reappeared at the hideaway.

The concept intrigued Jonah too much to be angry with his buddy for not telling him about the modification. "How long did you work with the Alliance on the room?"

Mike shrugged. "Ever since we returned from the Afterworld."

Robert and Wick examined the platform, uttering quiet comments about adding the device to their video game as a way to move between levels.

Lynn stood beside Kevin. Both watched the Alliance Guards fan out around the small clearing, setting up a perimeter.

"Are we going up to the courtyard?" Kevin asked.

Lynn shook her head as she met Jonah's gaze. The time for his decision rushed forward.

Amulet of the Goddess **947**

He turned to get the captain's attention. "How do we know the mole hasn't already found out about this place? I mean, he ruined the safe room."

"This is safe, Jonah," Kevin said, sounding irritated. "Marcus never shared that information with the Alliance, not even the Council."

"But what about Trueblood and Albrecht? They're on the Council."

"Yes, but they're also part of Marcus's inner circle."

"As am I," the captain added, "and my team. We're all determined to find the mole."

Jonah relaxed at hearing that news but a knot developed in his stomach when he glanced at his watch. It was already eleven forty-five. The Witching Hour was only fifteen minutes away and they still hadn't found his aunt. How could he face her and do what he had to do? Maybe it would have been better to let the goons just take him.

But that couldn't be right. It didn't feel like the correct decision somehow. He glanced at Lynn who merely stared back. At a loss for what to do next, Jonah turned to the others and asked, "What are we gonna do about Aunt Ruby?"

No one had an answer, which further irritated Jonah, making him grow impatient. He prepared himself before he suggested they return to the safe room alone when Mike yelped and pointed at the device in Kevin's hand.

"What's that?"

"It's a codex," Kevin answered in confusion. "What else would it be?"

Releasing an exasperated huff, Mike took the device and examined the surface. "It's not the same as the ones we use."

"How can that be?" Jonah crowded closer. "You had to make them, right?"

"Yeah, but…" Mike trailed off. "None of the prototypes were designed for the safe room. We did tests first. Once they perfected the process, the Alliance Council picked a location for the safe room in secrecy. I guess that backfired though, huh?"

Jonah agreed, but something else worried him. "Are you saying you don't know where this one goes?"

"No, I'm just saying they made me use different locations during the tests. The Alliance chose the destinations. The mole could have easily used his contacts to pass along his own destination, claiming it was just another test."

Kevin swore under his breath. "I took that from a Wraith back in the safe room. I bet they planned to use it to take Jonah to Ruby."

"If that's true," Lynn began as she came over to examine the device, "can you tell where this one goes?"

In answer, Mike closed his eyes. The symbols on the enemy codex glowed and pulsated with light. When Mike reopened his eyes, they had turned a rich amber color. Given his unblinking stare, Jonah doubted his friend even saw the present. It was if he were peering through space and time.

"It's for a place called Centre Pointe," Mike announced. After blinking his eyes several more times, they returned to their normal color. "That's in central Georgia."

"Yeah," Jonah agreed. "It's an ancient monolith site, like the Georgia Guide Stones but much bigger."

He glanced around at the confused faces. Mike and Wick were the only ones who nodded.

"My grandmother told me about Centre Pointe," Wick began. "Old rumors circulated for decades that spirits haunted the place, particularly during this time of year."

"But what is its significance?" Robert asked.

Wick shrugged. "No one knows, nor who built it and why."

"Well, that's clear now," Lynn said. "It has to be the focal point for Ruby's ritual."

Jonah did not fail to note the resigned tone in his cousin's voice and the way she kept meeting his gaze. He swallowed hard because the time had come, and he was sure of it. Now, at the actual moment of decision, Jonah wasn't afraid.

"Centre Pointe is the eighth location!" he said. "The one that controls them all."

Kevin frowned at him. "How do you know that?"

Amulet of the Goddess

"It just makes sense," Wick answered, earning a warning glare from Kevin. "Think about it. Wraiths and spirits haunt the place."

"In that case, we need to tell Marcus," Kevin said to the Guard Captain.

The captain tossed his communication device aside. "No go. We have to assume they already compromised our communications channels."

"Then I'll phase to his location and–"

"That won't matter," Jonah interrupted. In his mind, he was already walking on the path he had to take. *Will you sacrifice yourself for the sake of others?* He said yes in the dream. Now he was primed to face the real decision.

"Jonah, we have to do something," Kevin insisted.

Every pair of eyes turned to Jonah who shook his head. "My aunt's already opening the nexus points. We won't have enough time to break through a ward." He hoped Kevin would accept his coming decision, but knew the Fallen Reaper wouldn't. "The Alliance is busy fighting Wraiths and keeping mortals safe. That was the plan all along. Keep them busy so the mole could get to me." Jonah's voice grew more confident as he spoke.

"We have to try." Kevin turned to the captain for support.

Jonah gripped the boy's forearm and turned him back. "No, Kevin. My Aunt Ruby will finish the ritual and unleash Pakhet before the Alliance can stop her. The only way to end this is if I go alone."

Everyone objected to that idea, everyone except Lynn that is, as Jonah expected. He pressed on. "It's about me. Wraiths always need a mortal host to do the most damage in this realm. My aunt's body is limiting Pakhet's power. But if she had me…"

"You're the Deliverer," Mike said, an expression of horror consuming his face at the idea.

Kevin remained defiant. "How can you get through? Huh?"

"She wants me. She'll undo whatever protection she has."

"No. You can't do that!" Kevin made an imploring gesture to Lynn. "Back me up on this."

But Lynn shook her head, causing Robert to gape at his sister.

"You can't agree with him!"

"I do, Robert." Lynn took a deep breath and drew herself up. Jonah always thought his cousin possessed a regal bearing in those unguarded moments. But tonight, she carried an air of supreme power about her. Lynn raised her chin as she surveyed the expectant faces around her. "I've seen it already with my Sight. Jonah has to embark on this part alone."

Robert looked like he might puke. He shook his head, but his shoulders slumped in glum acceptance. Wick couldn't hide his own grim expression.

The captain gazed at Jonah with a determined look in his eyes before gracing him with a curt nod. "Your orders, sir?"

"Watch over everybody. And listen to my cousin."

The captain grinned. "I already have. She was the one who told us to follow you to the safe room."

The guard's words only deepened Jonah's reverence for Lynn's gift.

Kevin's knuckles cracked in the sudden silence as he worked his fist. "I'm coming with you."

"You can't. Either my aunt will conduct the ritual while you fight or…" Jonah couldn't finish the sentence.

"They'll kill you and take Jonah anyway," the captain said.

"I don't care!" Kevin's voice echoed through the clearing.

"Kevin," the captain moved beside him, "You're a member of the Alliance. We must make hard decisions sometimes. The young man—" he gestured to Jonah, "the Deliverer is right."

"Plus," Wick said, holding up his watch, "we're nearly out of time. The Witching Hour will occur in less than ten minutes."

Kevin whirled around, glaring at everyone. "What are we supposed to do while Jonah sacrifices himself?" He turned on Jonah, his emotions washing over Jonah like a tidal wave. "What if you're wrong? What if you …"

"I won't be," Jonah replied, finding it odd to suddenly be the secure and calm one. "I resisted them when I was seven, and I'm much stronger now. Besides, I'm ready."

Kevin reached out and stopped himself for a fraction of a second before going ahead. He pulled Jonah into a tight hug and only released him when the captain gripped his shoulder and pulled him back.

Amulet of the Goddess **951**

Lynn stared up into Kevin's anguished face. "Don't worry. We have a part to fulfill too, just not with Jonah yet. Trust me."

Jonah used her distraction to wipe his own eyes. He reached out for the counterfeit codex and Mike gave it over before he slipped out of Jonah's coat.

"You should wear this too." Mike's voice quivered.

Jonah smiled. "Trust Lynn. It'll turn out okay." Mike nodded but he didn't look convinced. All at once, the certainty that Mike had a bigger role to play overcame Jonah. A voice rang in his ears and his mind. He didn't know if it were the revolutionary spirit of the Deliverer inside him or not. But his own voice was steady and sure as he added, "You're my Seeker, my Pathmaker. Open the way when the time comes."

Mike blinked and his posture straightened. This time, when he nodded, all doubt was gone from his face.

Jonah threw aside his heavy, black cloak and donned his Reaper's coat, savoring the unique but familiar feeling of having it adjust to his body. He stood tall, taking one last moment to meet everyone's gaze with his own and reached Kevin's intense eyes last.

"I'll be okay," he said. "I promise." With that, Jonah pressed the activation button on the codex and left his friends and family behind.

CHAPTER FORTY
RUBY'S STORY

Jonah instantly experienced a horrible moment of déjà vu. The codex had deposited him at the bottom of a shallow hill and just below the impressive stone site called Centre Pointe, the eighth location, which was just as it appeared in his dream-walk.

Seven tall, stone pillars rose high above him. All were spaced around a large, seven-sided raised platform or stage made of granite. Even from where he stood, he could see incomprehensible words etched on the pitted, marble sides of the pillars. At the center of that was a large table of stone.

His aunt was standing there, her body glowing with a shimmering, yellow outline. Her arms reached toward the sky and she tilted her head back, uttering words that Jonah couldn't hear because of the constantly billowing wind. The clouds overhead churned and roiled as if they would soon spawn a tornado.

A dome of magical energy protected the entire ancient site, just as Jonah had predicted. Debris, kicked up by the wind, slammed hard against the barrier and flared, illustrating the danger to anyone who dared try to get through.

As soon as Jonah appeared, he had to dodge and duck the Phantoms that patrolled the outside of the dome. Even now, Felines and Grim Hounds loped from the surrounding darkness toward him. But Jonah wasn't afraid. As one Phantom zoomed close enough to harass him, Jonah raised his hand and ripped an opening to the Underworld.

The Phantom let out an inhuman screech before it reversed course. After that display of power, the others were wary and kept their distance. But that didn't stop them from brandishing ghostly swords at him.

Amulet of the Goddess

Grim Hounds and Felines continued to stalk him, matching his progress up the hillside, snarling and hissing.

Jonah moved right up to the barrier until its magic pulled on his skin. His aunt sensed his presence. She lowered her arms and gazed at him with orange, cat-like eyes that were definitely non-human. Waving a hand, she produced an opening in the barrier, that was just big enough for him to enter.

No going back once I step through, Jonah warned himself. Summoning all of his courage, he cautiously entered.

Antwan's cousin hurried toward him from one side, but she stopped short. She also scanned the hillside, no doubt, looking for Alliance people.

"I'm alone," Jonah told his aunt but not the others.

Ruby motioned and a Grimnion patted down his long coat and pockets. He quickly found the fake codex and took that. Once he moved away, Ruby finally spoke.

"So, you are your father's son after all." Her voice was deeper and strongly accented now. "He, too, would have come on his own in order to save the others. It would have been a useless gesture, of course, just as your attempt will prove to be." She shouted to her minions, "Take him!"

Jonah didn't resist when two Grimnions darted forward to grab hold of him. The stronger than normal humans had no problem lifting him and carrying him to the stone slab. They laid him on top of it, spreading out his arms but keeping his legs together. *Almost crucifixion style*, Jonah thought.

For the first time, Jonah experienced real fear. His heart rate increased even faster when a different Wraith-possessed goon approached, carrying several long, cement nails and a huge mallet in his hands.

Jonah's dread spiked because he recognized the Wraith. He also sensed its unique hatred for him. This was the same hulking Wraith that he previously cut and whom Kevin kicked around. The mortal wore an expression of savage fury.

Struggling proved futile because the Grimnions held him fast. The man dropped the nails on the slab and they clattered against the hard surface. He grinned in triumph while taking his time to choose the first nail. Positioning the tip right over Jonah's palm, he forcibly pressed the sharp end into the flesh.

It took all of his effort but Jonah restrained his urge to respond violently and refused to utter a sound as the pain mounted. The Wraith frowned, visibly disappointed. He positioned the mallet over the nail's head next and with a malicious grin, raised the mallet, ready to strike the nail and plunge it through Jonah's hand, thereby nailing him to the slab.

Jonah couldn't move, nor could he call upon his power, owing to the effect of the barrier. He tried to mentally prepare himself for the agony he was about to endure. As the Wraith brought the mallet down, a hex fortunately hit the man's mallet arm, causing him to miss the nail altogether. The mallet splintered the stone slab where it impacted, sending stone shards and slivers flying. One nicked Jonah's cheek, drawing blood.

The Wraith whirled around, his eyes blazing with fury as he shouted at Ruby, "Why? You told me I could do it!"

Ruby smirked. "I lied."

The Wraith growled, raising the mallet again.

Ruby hit him with another hex, but this time, it froze him in place. Jonah marveled at his aunt's growing power.

"I said no! I don't want to inhabit a broken body, fool!" She twisted her hand and the Wraith let out a scream of pain. "Obey me or I'll send you straight to the Underworld myself."

The Wraith managed to nod before he dropped the mallet. When Ruby released her hold, he slumped to the ground.

A rustling of cloth came from Jonah's left, accompanied by the quiet crunch of shoes walking softly on grains of sand or dirt.

"Are you going to thank me, nephew?" His aunt waved her hand and magical bonds appeared to hold his feet and hands in place. The Grimmions that previously gripped him backed off.

In a fit of stubbornness, Jonah refused to shift his head or look at her. The soft hiss of fabric and quiet footsteps grew louder. Jonah could feel the heat of his aunt's body leaning over him. When he felt her exhaling a deep breath on his face, Jonah jerked his head to the side.

His aunt laughed. "So defiant! And so much like my sister. You have her features."

Amulet of the Goddess

"Don't talk about my mom." Despite his personal intent to not respond, he turned to look into his aunt's lean face.

She, too, resembled his mother, except for the crazed look in her wildly dilated pupils. Her cheeks lifted in amusement, reducing her eyes to mere slits.

"Why shouldn't I talk about her? She was my baby sister. I knew her long before you arrived, child." Aunt Ruby nodded. "Yes, I wiped her bottom when she was just a baby. I raised her as much as our parents did. So," she gripped Jonah's face by his cheeks and squeezed. "I have every right to discuss Dear Sister."

She gave his face a little shove and released him.

When she laughed, Jonah yelled, "I know what you're gonna try. It won't work." Before Jonah could restrain himself, he blurted out, "It didn't work the last time because you're only a palm reader!"

Antwan's cousin gasped, turning her masked face to watch Aunt Ruby.

Jonah charged on. "I heard they laughed at you and jeered, calling you a palm reader because you didn't have any real power."

Aunt Ruby's reaction baffled Jonah. He expected her to yell back or hit him. Worse still, she could have let the Wraith come back to nail him to the slab after all.

Instead, she remained unmoving for a second before crossing her arms. "Yes, you're so much like your mother. Arrogant in your abilities. Disdainful of others whom you don't think measure up."

"I'm not–"

"Silence!" Ruby's voice rolled across the hillside. She paused to collect herself again. "You're right. I wasn't able to do it last time. You were more powerful than anyone thought. This time, you're an emotional wreck. I can see all the anger and pain over everything that's happened."

Aunt Ruby drew closer, the gleam in her cat eyes unnerving Jonah. "And when the Witching Hour comes, and the barrier between the mortal and supernatural world is at its weakest, the goddess will take you. And this time, you won't be able to resist."

Ruby glanced off to Jonah's left. He turned his head and saw an hourglass floating in the air. He didn't know the exact amount of time remaining, but judging by the minuscule amount of sand in the top portion, he knew the Witching Hour couldn't be more than five minutes away. Ruby leaned over him, running her soft hands over his face. Jonah shuddered and jerked as much as the restraints would allow.

"Don't touch me!"

"I'm your aunt. Family."

"I don't care." He swallowed and tried to calm himself. Ruby was correct. His emotions were raw. One moment, he'd think about the doomed Latrell, or Lynn's pained demeanor when her power was blocked, and the ensuing sadness he felt threatened to overtake him. And the next moment, he would remember Robert and Danita's wounds, or all the kids that were injured at the magic show, and he got furious. The incessant jerks that pulled him in different emotional directions were mentally exhausting.

In an attempt to get his mind off that, he spoke to his aunt. "Why?"

Her eyes widened. "Why? Because I was always the one that had to make sacrifices. I raised your mother and uncle. I had to find a job at an early age to help the family out. When they were old enough, they all got to go off to college and earn their fancy degrees."

Ruby leaned against the slab, fingering the beaded necklace that hung low on her bosom. "You don't know about the women in our family, do you? Only one lucky female from each generation got the *Sight*. They became famous or wealthy in their time. After all I sacrificed for my family, did I get the gift? No! Your mother was the chosen one! As an added insult, my brother, James, even got a trace of the *Sight*. I was nothing more than a *palm reader*."

Ruby spat out the phrase while glaring at Antwan's cousin. "I became the pariah of the magical community, especially by those women who were gifted as sorceresses. I was nothing to them, and brusquely pushed to the side like a fallen leaf."

She whirled around to face Jonah again. "Then, the Wraiths approached me seven years ago with an offer. If I could give you to them, they promised to make all my life's dreams come true. They said they would grant me the spirit of a Seer!"

"A Seer?" Jonah asked before he could stop himself. "You want to become a human priestess?" All this trouble and death simply because she wanted to be a Seer?

Amulet of the Goddess   **957**

"Yes!" Ruby's eyes grew wide and wild. "They can call on the Wraith prophets to possess their bodies. When that happens, whole vistas of time and knowledge open up: the ultimate *Sight*. I would become a true prophetess and legitimately take my rightful place among my peers."

Jonah thought about the Seer he met before his world turned upside-down. She was a frail, old woman, almost entirely unnoticed. She wasn't flashy like his aunt, nor did she try to show everyone her ability. Jonah began to wonder if the Wraiths would honor their promise and actually give his aunt that privilege.

"My dreams were within reach," Ruby continued, "until you happened." She peered into his eyes. "Little Jonah Blackstone resisted the Wraith. Then your mother came and rescued you." Ruby gave a sad, little laugh. "Your father wanted to hunt me down, but Janice prevented that. Even so, my own family ostracized me. My husband and kids shunned me. And they locked me away in that awful place for seven long years. But the shadow of Pakhet came to visit me."

Jonah's aunt thrust her hands into the air, like she had just received the Holy Spirit in church. "I kept the faith!" she shouted. Then she lowered her hands and stared at him. "Eventually, they came back to me and renewed their promise. All they wanted," she poked Jonah's cheek with a finger, "was you!"

That statement unstopped his tongue. "You can't trust them."

Ruby laughed. "The Wraith King will keep his promise to me."

"Ruby?" Antwan's cousin said. "What are you talking about? You're supposed to deliver Jonah to the mole when this is over, not to the Wraith King."

"And what can the mole or Deyanira offer me?" Ruby asked, whirling to face the girl. "She's wholly concerned about you, her precious sorceress-in-training. Neither she nor the mole care about me! Only the Wraith King can offer me what I truly desire."

The girl moved quickly and raised her hands to cast a spell. Jonah sensed the magic gathering, but the girl didn't expect to find betrayal from another source. The Wraith Ruby had embarrassed instantly came to her aid. He knocked Antwan's cousin in the shoulder, causing her spell to miss Ruby before it flashed against a pillar with a loud crack!

The Wraith followed up with a solid blow to the girl's face. Jonah winced at the sound of her mask splintering. The lower half flew through the air and smashed against another pillar like a porcelain cup. Antwan's cousin dropped and didn't move. For a moment, Jonah worried she might be dead.

Ruby snapped her fingers. "Chain her! The cuffs will nullify her power."

The Wraith picked up the girl in one arm like she weighed nothing and dropped her at the base of the pillar where her broken mask lay. He chained her hands at the wrists and then wrapped the chain around the pillar. The girl's head lolled to the side. The upper portion of her face was hidden by the remaining half of her mask.

Ruby leaned over Jonah. "You see, I never had to worry about them betraying me. I was in control all along. Even that treacherous Alastor didn't suspect my true plan." Ruby cackled like a madwoman. "They have no idea. The Wraith King wants this to happen right this time. After Pakhet has her ride tonight, leaving a wake of chaos and destruction, she will reward me."

"What about the mole?" the Wraith who tied up Antwan's cousin asked. "He may also come."

"I'm not stupid." Ruby gestured around her at the pillars. "This place is protected against that kind of meddling by Reapers. And besides, he only had two codex devices."

She leaned close over Jonah and hissed in his ear, "That's right. You can't fight it this time. No mother or father to save you now. Give in to the despair and fear. It'll only hurt if you try to resist. I tell you that merely as a kindness, nephew."

Ruby stood and held the real amulet aloft. "Prepare yourself." With that, she slipped the amulet's chain around Jonah's neck and let it settle on his chest. "The Witching Hour is upon us."

Amulet of the Goddess

CHAPTER FORTY-ONE
WITCHING HOUR

The air above Jonah stirred and twisted in waves on itself. Aunt Ruby resumed her incantation, and her modulated voice rose to a fever pitch. Jonah struggled but accomplished little more than violently turning his head from side-to-side. Despite his attempts to shift his gaze from the gathering magical energy in the air high above the slab, he couldn't resist for long.

His aunt may have been a simple palm reader, but her strident voice filled the site, and even seemed to mix with the shifting air. She stumbled while uttering the strange sounds, as if she had memorized or was recently taught the spell a short time ago.

Jonah suspected that must have been the case. He heard the nervous stammering in his aunt's delivery. What she lacked in finesse, she made up for with her growing intensity. And the spell worked. The pull of the magic on his skin increased before a painful jolt to his mind occurred. For a horrible minute, something awful flashed through his head and he sucked in a startled breath.

As his aunt continued, another flash of unrecognizable memory appeared in his mind, accompanied by a relentless, stabbing pain. He grunted and his head jerked, but his eyes remained wide open, staring into the contorting air. Jonah heard himself panting and fear seized him. *Were those the blocked memories?* The brief images produced so much shock and pain that it horrified Jonah.

Despair threatened to overwhelm him. He felt helpless, unable to even look away from what was coming next. As if in answer to his pain, the air ripped apart and a brilliant light enveloped the entire stone slab. Jonah blinked into the blinding light until his eyes adjusted—or, rather, something moved around on the other side, thereby blocking the light. He caught glimpses of blurred shapes that reminded him of buildings.

The rip widened and Jonah saw a glowing, amber eye. Fear choked him and he wanted to yell, but his throat was dry and nearly collapsed. The shape moved and its other eye peered through the rip, narrowing in clear malice. Waves of hate boiled through the opening, buffeting Jonah with their intense force and power.

Somewhere off in the distance, as if magically magnified, the soft dong of a church bell penetrated the growing roar from the rip and extreme elements. Jonah noted the continued strikes of the bell. Four, five, six… His whole body trembled. Seven, eight, nine… This was it. Pakhet was due to come through and possess him and he couldn't save himself nor could he fight back.

Ten, eleven, twelve… The rip burst open, instantly forming into a ragged circle above his head. Jonah had a full view of Pakhet. Just like the amulet, her body was that of a woman but she had the head of a lioness. She was sitting on a glowing throne. The angry, orange eyes flared and she wailed a bone-chilling battle cry before she launched herself toward Jonah. Ruby's chanting stopped and she scrambled away from the slab and hunkered between two pillars, watching.

Pakhet roared loudly as she rushed out of the rip and engulfed Jonah. Every inch of his inflamed body ached. He screamed in helpless anguish and bucked when the goddess's essence flowed into his open mouth, nose, eyes, and ears. Once that ordeal ended, his head exploded with severe pain. Then something deep inside Jonah resisted.

No!

A new source of strength flowed into him and he reacted to the pain and the flagrant violation of this body. Pakhet's hold was unmitigated and felt like a million arms wrapped about him, smothering him. Jonah called on his Reaper power and yelled in his mind, *Get out!* When he let up, the pain only increased as Pakhet pulled him deeper and deeper toward darkness. Jonah knew he'd be lost forever if that happened.

He imagined grinding his teeth and pushing back with all of his strength

Amulet of the Goddess

while screaming in his mind, *I command you to get out!*

All at once, he experienced a wrenching sensation of motion. He seemed to tumble forward, which was odd, considering he still lay on the table. But in his mind's eye, he saw himself being propelled upward before flying through the rip in the air. As he crossed over, the goddess was torn away from him. But Jonah thought she must have hooked her tendrils into him because it felt like he was being cut. Searing pain flared all over his body, as if she were scraping his skin raw.

The forward motion changed and he fell faster and faster until he hit the dirt-covered ground. A wave of nausea came next and he rolled over, gasping for breath, and barely managing not to vomit. That's when he registered he wasn't at Centre Point anymore. He was somewhere else. He saw a crowd of people and a group of bound witches in the foreground.

Jonah shook his head. Unlike his recent nightmares and the Wraith's memory fragments, this time, he wasn't stuck inside the Inquisitor's mind. He was free to move around the medieval setting. Jonah rose slowly to his feet and shifted through the crowd of poor, dirty peasants as his nausea faded.

He stalked around the witches, all of whom were tightly bound to stakes. The uneven noise of the crowd grew in volume and cheers. A space opened and the Wraith, disguised as an olive-skinned priest this time, marched out.

Like the Inquisitor in the previous nightmare, this high priest clutched a Bible to his chest and his eyes glowed milky white. Jonah wondered how all the people failed to notice that. *Maybe only I can see it because it's his memory.* It didn't matter though and Jonah resisted the urge to back away and hide.

As the priest took his place at the head of the crowd, Jonah fastened his gaze on the man's face. Eventually, the Wraith turned to stare back at him. Pain sliced through Jonah's head again. He winced, but managed to maintain his eye contact and even moved closer. All that mattered anymore was the Wraith. He could sense the events playing out around him and any eye contact rushed along the flood of memories. When the pain became unbearable and his legs faltered, the scene shifted again.

It stabilized, and Jonah blinked in surprise because he found himself alone in the attic clubhouse. Everything inside the space was the same as the mortal realm, except for his colorless vision. It wasn't black and white, however, just a muted wash of blue, like he was strictly an observer of the place.

"Hello?" Jonah's voice sounded hollow and alone in the empty space.

That unnerved him even more. He scrambled to his feet and hurried up the attic steps, bursting onto the second floor of the Teen Center, where he stopped because no one was around. What about downstairs? After searching the entire Center, Jonah gave up and returned to the attic.

I must be all alone in this weird version of the mortal world, he thought before he dropped into a desk chair. Only now did he register that he could even sit in it. *Was this a dream-walk or a nightmare?* There were strange elements that defied both.

More importantly, where am I?

"Prepare yourself, young Blackstone." The accented voice came from behind him. He shot to his feet and whirled around to find the Egyptian Wraith standing near the steamer trunk.

The Wraith's Egyptian attire and ancient breastplate looked entirely out of place in the clubhouse. He watched Jonah, the amulet around his neck shining like a bright star.

Jonah couldn't believe his eyes. "What are you doing here?"

"I came to warn you."

"Too late. Pakhet already tried to possess me."

The Egyptian nodded, folding his hands behind his back as he strolled from his spot behind the sofa over to the attic window. He looked out. "She may yet succeed."

"How?"

"Look around. Where do you think you are?" When Jonah didn't answer, the Wraith continued, "What do you remember happening at the Witching Hour?"

"I..." Jonah paused, rubbing his still-throbbing head. "I saw Pakhet. She lunged out of a rip above me and... and she flowed into my mouth and

Amulet of the Goddess **963**

eyes and..." Jonah shuddered.

"Pain?"

"Yes."

"And then what? Think and remember."

"I felt like I was falling, going back through the rip."

The Egyptian held up a finger. "You didn't fall through the rip when you resisted the possession. In her fury, Pakhet yanked you through the doorway."

"Why?"

"It's simple. Even in your present emotional state, as long as your soul remained intact, you were too powerful and could still resist. But if your soul was forced out of your physical vessel, as it is when you take your dream-walks..."

"My body..." Jonah's jaw dropped.

"... is still lying on the stone slab at Centre Point, free of your soul and wide open." The Egyptian watched Jonah. "All is not lost, young one. Both you and Pakhet have entered this realm."

Again, the Wraith went silent while watching Jonah's reaction. "Here's one bit of fortunate news. As long as you wear the amulet..." He pointed to the amulet around Jonah's neck and finished, "no other Wraith can take over your body. It connects your soul to hers."

Jonah didn't think that was good news at all. "What about her?"

"She landed in the furthest reaches of the Underworld. She must find her way back. Make no mistake: She will. There's a doorway that leads back to your body, young man. You must cross through it before she does. Otherwise, the goddess will trap you here forever."

"But I don't understand this place."

The Egyptian nodded. "It's a modified form of dream-walking. Your unique nature will allow you to shape this portion of the Underworld according to your memories."

Jonah's eyes widened. "My memories?"

The Wraith inclined his head. "Now you begin to understand. The block is dissolving. Your aunt was right about trauma breaking through it. As it dissolves, you'll recover the memories from seven years ago, including–"

"The memories from the Wraith who attacked me," Jonah finished. "Omar told me about that."

The Egyptian leaned forward. "He's a wise Memory Charmer. That is why you must prepare, young Blackstone. You must experience these memories before you can find your way back. My advice: Don't fight them, despite all the pain or what you see. Accept it and move forward."

"I did that in the last memory, just before coming here."

"Good. Your instincts have served you well."

"Wait a minute," Jonah said. He rubbed his head, thinking. "Three nights ago, I had a terrible nightmare. It was about places and people I'd never seen–"

"Those were also the Wraith's memories. Your previous block was fractured, which was your aunt's plan."

Jonah's upper lip trembled, recalling the fragments of memories. "They were bad scenes. All the fighting, killing, and death…" Jonah shook his head. "I was seeing things through his eyes and feeling what he felt."

The man nodded. "I'm sorry. He was a Wraith. You may experience the memories in the same way here, or not. The Underworld works differently. You may even be an objective observer, as a way to protect your mind."

"It did!" Jonah said. "I was outside the Wraith's mind, almost like a dream-walk."

"Then remember," the Wraith admonished, "the quicker you accept, the faster you'll get through the pain." His mouth opened, but he said nothing else. Instead, his eyes narrowed. "I'm sorry."

Before Jonah could ask why, pain exploded in his head again as the next memory yanked him away from the attic clubhouse.

Amulet of the Goddess

CHAPTER FORTY-TWO
HELL ON EARTH

This new memory was of a colonial village near the sea. The tall masts of sailing ships could be glimpsed over the tops of the shabby buildings surrounding the clearing. Occupying the dead center was an enslaved male, stripped naked. Blood oozed from angry welts, which covered every inch of his glistening, ebony body. Still, the punisher was only resting.

He abandoned the wooden peg he'd been using as a seat and took a drink of water from a ladle. Satisfied, he unfurled his long whip and tested it, producing a sharp snap! that caused the watchers to stir uncomfortably. When he was ready, he started the brutality again.

Each lash of the whip produced a spray of blood that splattered across the ground and the crossbeam holding the poor man. Jonah averted his gaze, but something caught his eye. He looked, wincing with each blood-spilling blow of the whip, willing himself not to get sick.

Blood and open wounds on the poor man's lower torso obscured a symbol. At first glance, it resembled a tribal tattoo or marking. Jonah suspected the slavers probably thought the same thing, but he recognized it. It was the Alliance Symbol, branded on the man's body, just like the mages did in that awful dream-memory.

This man had been singled out because he was part of the Alliance! But if he were African and the symbol was used as a tribal marking, that meant a much larger Alliance, with members from many cultures and many peoples.

The whip sliced into the slave's already puckered and damaged flesh. Jonah finally averted his eyes. He didn't have to watch this horrible scene to follow the Egyptian Wraith's admonition.

Spotting the offending Wraith was easy. Tall and dressed as a ship's captain, he motioned for two servants to bring horses forward. A third servant attached the condemned man's wrists and legs to ropes and then to the horses. The animals were moved apart until the unfortunate man was suspended in the air, his leg and arms straightened painfully out.

Jonah knew what would happen. He read about this form of torture in one of his parents' books. His sense of revulsion and horror propelled him forward. He stood close, gazing into the Wraith's eyes until the captain turned and looked at him. The constant throbbing pain increased as the whole memory passed between them. Jonah saw the horrible thing to come, but he gritted his teeth without breaking contact.

Once again, the pain mounted and he stumbled until the scene changed. Jonah fell back and hit solid ground. The world around him came back into focus, indicating he had returned to the clubhouse.

He collapsed on the solid-feeling floor and sucked in breaths as his excruciating headache subsided.

"What did you see?" The Egyptian's voice was soft, but urgent.

Jonah rolled on his side, resting his head on the floor. He let his breathing slow considerably before he answered. "The Wraith was having a man flogged and…" His voice faltered.

The Egyptian nodded in understanding and moved closer. "Did you resist?"

"I don't know how to resist what I'm seeing." Jonah swallowed. Memories of the last headache caused him to feel a bit nauseous again. "How long will this last?"

"Until you've integrated all the memories."

"I don't want to integrate them!"

Jonah got the point even though the Wraith remained quiet. If he thought that way, the pain would only get worse. And he could never return to his body. "I saw the Alliance symbol on the slave's body, just like the forehead of the medieval mages. How long has the Alliance been around?"

Amulet of the Goddess **967**

"From the moment the Grand Oracle and Grim Reaper took over, others have fought and tried to resist them. The Alliance, as a group, is almost as old as the Rulers of the Afterworld. Their rise to power has never been stronger than it is today. You are their most prized possession."

Jonah lifted his head, staring at the Wraith in disbelief. "I'm not a weapon."

"Don't be so naïve, young one. Why do you think the Wraiths have tried twice now to possess you? You successfully escaped the clutches of the Grim Reaper and the Grand Oracle."

"That still doesn't make me a weapon," Jonah said while hauling himself into a seated position.

"You really don't know what the Alliance has planned for you? It's not surprising, I guess."

"What does that mean? What are you saying?"

"Time grows short. You must work your way through the memories and return to your body. I can only help you so much."

Jonah rose to his feet, glaring at the Wraith. "But you're not helping me!" He aimed a kick at the back of the sofa and flipped it over. The solidness of the furniture was reassuring, however, in its own way.

The Wraith was unmoved. "I'm trying to help you—"

"Then do it!" Jonah raised his fists. "Stop lying to me. How are you even here?"

The Egyptian stood tall. "You summoned me."

"No, I didn't."

"Yes, you did. When you first came to this way station, your soul called out for help. I came through at the Witching Hour when the drain on myself was at its minimum. Your summons led me here."

Jonah gaped at the Egyptian, not fully trusting him. "Why do you call it a way station?"

"Because, out there beyond these walls, our realm, the Underworld, exists. But you created this bubble to hide from the truth."

"I don't understand."

"Each time you resist a memory, your weakened block strengthens, and you come here." The Wraith paced around Jonah. "A memory block says as much about the recipient as it does about the Memory Charmer. Do you know why they tell the receiver to *let go*, young Blackstone? Without the subject's willing participation, the block could never completely work."

Jonah thought about the time he spent with the Alliance members. He'd seen Omar tell Antwan to let go of the memories.

The Egyptian nodded. "A sufficiently powerful intellect could never succumb to a Memory Charm."

"So, each time I return here…" Jonah began.

"You're allowing the block to solidify and wall off the memories." The Egyptian gestured around him. "This is a place of great importance to you. Your friends, family, and allies all travel through this location. It's only natural that you would choose it now as a place of refuge."

That was true, Jonah thought. The attic clubhouse was a central part of his life. But he could tell there was more than that. He scanned the Wraith while summoning his Reaper sense. "You're not telling me everything." An air of deception or half truth permeated the ghostly warrior. Jonah grabbed the Wraith by his breastplate and shoved him across the room.

The man was agile and turned the backward motion into a controlled tumble. Even so, he looked irritated by Jonah's unexpected response.

Jonah stepped toward him. "If I summoned you here, I can just as easily send you away."

Fear touched the Wraith's face. "If you do that, who'll help you?"

"You're not helping me now." Jonah raised his hand, fingers spread. "Talk, or you go back to wherever a Wraith belongs. Tell me now!"

The clubhouse shook with Jonah's power. The walls creaked and bits of ceiling fell around them.

Despite glaring at Jonah, the Wraith answered. "Hell on Earth. That's the Grim Reaper's ultimate plan. He's creating more Wraiths than normal because he's managed to block untold numbers of mortals from moving on. He would prefer to make himself a god in his own right, granting and denying rites of passage to all mortal souls."

Jonah's anger cooled as he considered the Wraith's words. "Okay, I get that, maybe, but what about you? Why don't you support him?"

"Because he would deny all of us passage, keeping us in this realm forever. He promised full access to the Afterworld for the Wraith King and all faithful Wraiths. But our King doesn't trust the Grim Reaper. He wants to use you as a weapon against the Rulers of the Afterworld."

"But…" Jonah raised his hands to his head as he turned on the spot. "I still don't know why you're fighting your own people."

"Some of us believe our king would be as bad or worse than the Grim Reaper," the ancient warrior explained, "if he had ultimate power to grant or deny passage to the final destination. We refuse to exchange one tyrant for another." The Egyptian moved close enough to touch Jonah's shoulder. "You are The One who's destined to restore the balance."

"You mean, bring balance to the Force?" Jonah asked. He couldn't resist the quip and needed the brief respite from all the building tension and worry.

The Wraith frowned at him as if seriously considering his comment. "Essentially, yes. The Seers and I have invested our faith in you."

That sobered Jonah again. "But why do you trust me so much?"

The Wraith hesitated and sighed. It was strange to see the ghost do that. "Because you are my descendent."

"What?! You're *my* ancestor?" Jonah's eyes widened.

"It's why I could hear you and respond to your summons." He raised a finger. "Stay focused on the task at hand."

Jonah gulped and nodded. "So you want me to take control of my body and…"

"Be yourself, young Blackstone. Merely fulfill your destiny and set things right."

Jonah gazed at the man, sensing total honesty from him this time. "What if I do the wrong thing?"

"There's good in your heart, young one. That is the quality inside you that prevented the Wraiths from possessing you." He cocked his head to the side. "I'm certain your memories confirm the evil of most Wraiths that are still stuck in between."

"Yeah," Jonah agreed. "What do you mean by *in between?*"

"Simple. Why do you think I'm not a raving ghost?" He gestured around them. "Those demented Wraiths are the ones who don't fully cross over to our realm. They're left *in between*; they can see and hear mortals but are unable to touch or interfere, except in rare occasions. The futility of their ambiguous position drives them crazy."

"Latrell said he was trapped in between."

"It's our king's own form of punishment." The Wraith frowned.

"Why doesn't he stop Wraiths like you?"

"He would, if I were not so careful. Once granted access, a Wraith can go and come, at times. Unless the king decides otherwise and withdraws the privilege from us."

Jonah narrowed his eyes. "You're hiding out in here, aren't you?"

The Wraith didn't move for a few seconds. Then he nodded. "You are perceptive, young one. You are also accepting the truth. I can feel the block fading again."

At his words, another memory yanked Jonah away.

CHAPTER FORTY-THREE
PAKHET'S SPAWN

Jonah groaned and dropped to his knees. The transitions were taking a heavy toll on him. When he was sure he wouldn't vomit, Jonah raised his head and froze. He was fully expecting yet another horrible memory from the Wraith but instead, he found himself facing a large, old-style, four-poster bed against the wall opposite him. At least two people moved back and forth in the darkened bedroom.

One was a skinny, black man with glowing, milky white eyes. The other looked like his mom. Jonah gaped at the woman. It was his aunt, albeit a younger, leaner version. She muttered under her breath, waving her hands back and forth over a young boy strapped down to the bed.

Jonah stood up for a better look and stiffened. A pallid, younger version of his own face lay among the damp pillows. Jonah pressed his back against the wall in horror as his mind caught up to the situation. This was the time his aunt sadistically subjected him to a forced Wraith possession.

When his younger self bucked and twisted, Jonah knew with horrific certainty that the Wraith was already lodged inside him. Writhing in anguish, younger Jonah cried out in severe pain. His aunt's eager expression sickened Jonah. The woman showed no compassion for the torture he suffered. Anger and rage made his blood boil.

Younger Jonah's hands slipped free of the restraints and he flailed around. Aunt Ruby leaned over the boy, pressing her weight on top of him to keep him down. Older Jonah tried to strike her, but his attack went through Ruby's shoulder without any adverse effects.

No longer able to contain himself, Jonah roared in frustration as his younger self released a piercing scream. At that moment, the bedroom door burst open to reveal his mom. She drew her Reaper blades but faltered at the threshold, visibly torn between her struggling son who was pinned under Ruby's weight, and the helper Wraith, which swiftly pulled out a scythe.

His mom snapped into conditioned motion, diving forward and coming in low under the Wraith's swing. She cut him across the chest with one blade and stabbed him with the other by thrusting up through the base of the man's jaw. The eyes flared as the Wraith and the human died.

Ruby leapt from the bed, her arms raised.

Jonah's mom pointed one blade at her. "What've you done to Jonah?"

"Only what I had to do…"

Jonah's mom let out a growl and used her blade to cut the amulet from around her son's neck. She dropped the object to the ground and drove the blade through it. When the amulet flashed and popped, the Wraith's form instantly detached from younger Jonah's body.

His mom whirled and cut the Wraith's head from its body before it could escape. The spirit dissolved into more fragments.

Ruby had bolted around the bed, heading for the dresser. She grabbed a shotgun, leveled it at his mom, and fired. The explosive sound of the gun startled Jonah. However, his mom's deflection spell created an invisible barrier in front of her, causing the bullet to ricochet before it punched a huge hole in the bedroom wall.

Janice Blackstone leapt over the bed, almost coming down on Ruby, who tried to raise the gun and fire again. His mom sliced upward with one blade, severing the barrel. The other blade cut into Ruby's hand, splattering a spray of blood across the wall.

Ruby gasped in pain, dropped the gun, and cradled her injured hand. She darted to the window and plowed through, shattering the glass and taking half the curtains along with her.

Jonah's mom halted at the window and turned to check on her son. He could see the warring emotions on her face. At last, her shoulders relaxed and she dropped her blades on the bedside table. Sinking onto the edge of the bed, she warmly gathered younger Jonah into her arms.

Amulet of the Goddess

She hummed an old hymn as she rocked her son. A creak came from the hallway and two people loomed in the darkened doorway. Jonah recognized Symon Trueblood's silhouette from the dreads. The other was Omar.

"Where is she, Janice?" Symon stepped inside, wearing his blue mage tunic.

Janice nodded toward the window. "Gone."

"I'll catch her."

"Ruby knows all the hideouts in the back woods."

Symon pointed at the dark stains on the floor and wall. "You hurt?"

"No. I cut her."

"That'll make it easier. And she used magic tonight. It should leave a trace." With that, Symon nodded and hopped through the broken window before fleeing into the night.

Jonah's mom beckoned Omar to the bed. "Help me. He's trembling." As Omar leaned on the opposite side of the bed, young Jonah grunted, then began a series of spastic jerks.

Omar's brow furrowed in worry. He leaned closer, rubbing his hands together. "Are you sure?"

"He's suffering, Omar."

"That Wraith must have left wicked memories behind. He'll have nightmares if…"

"Do it." When Omar hesitated, she gripped his hand. "I appreciate what it means to you, but he's my son. And this is our fault."

A look of guilt and sadness crossed Omar's features. He nodded, placing his hands on little Jonah's head. She had to restrain her son because he continued to jerk at odd moments.

"Jonah?" Omar's rich, deep, African voice was soothing. "Jonah, let them go. Let go of the memories. Those aren't yours. I know you're scared." Omar's arms and shoulders jerked and his head tilted back as he grimaced.

Young Jonah shouted out, his voice clear and frantic. "I have to warn him. He's in danger." Then he went limp, shuddering again.

"No, Jonah." Omar lowered his chin and said, "Let it go. Don't hold on."

Again, Jonah spoke in a clear voice. "Dad! You have to get out of here. He's coming!"

Omar, brows drawn together and hands shaking, kept his eyes closed as he spoke in an urgent tone. "Say something, Janice. Maybe your voice will get him to relax. I've never seen anyone hang on so relentlessly."

"Jonah, it's me. Let go, sweetheart. Please." Younger Jonah's body seemed to relax and the trembling subsided. "That's it. Let it all go."

"That's it," Omar echoed. "Let it all go, Jonah."

A soft glow appeared over Omar's hands and settled on little Jonah's forehead. After a long moment, Omar removed his hands and sat back. He hunched his muscular shoulders and hugged himself. "It's done," he said, closing his eyes. "That Wraith was horrible. Your sister should be…" His voice faded softly.

Jonah's mom peered into Omar's saddened face. "How long will the block last?"

"It should last until he's an adult." Omar opened his eyes and met her gaze. "Unless you choose to remove it."

She shook her head. "I'll never tell him what happened here."

"I understand, Janice, but it's part of who he is. If Jonah's anything like Isaiah, he'll find out one way or the other."

"Omar…" She faltered and focused on stroking her son's wet forehead. "What was that about Isaiah?"

"Janice…"

"I'm his mother."

Omar frowned. "I only got bits and pieces, but Isaiah and Marcus were in a restaurant and everyone died, except them."

The horror in his mother's eyes mirrored Jonah's own. He remembered that strange dream. Omar had been performing the Memory Charm on Brandon and Antwan when the procedure managed to trigger one of Jonah's blocked memories.

The Alliance adults convinced Jonah it was part of the general block. Now, however, he knew better. That memory predated this event in his life.

Amulet of the Goddess

"That's all I could see," Omar continued. "How could the Wraith have that memory? It's almost like it was Jonah's, except long forgotten." Omar raised an eyebrow. "He's never been to a Memory Charmer before, has he?"

"No." She met Omar's gaze. "He hasn't. And don't tell Isaiah about this."

"Janice, it's his right as a father."

"He'll kill her."

Omar shrugged while Janice rocked her son back and forth. Little Jonah's breathing was even and unlabored now. In fact, Jonah thought his younger self might have even dozed.

"She's my sister, my family. I fear what would happen to Isaiah if he killed her. He may be angry now, but someday, he'll regret it. I won't add that burden on him."

"Things will be worse if you don't tell him," Omar warned. "He's a fair man, Janice, but he and his brother are too much alike when they get angry."

My dad's brother? How would he know my dad's brother? Omar was magical, but still lived a normal lifespan. Jonah's dad had been a Reaper for decades, and his mortal family were all dead.

Jonah only just now realized his mom had remained quiet while gazing at his younger self and stroking his damp forehead. "Fine, but I'll tell Marcus and the others first. If we're all there, Isaiah will listen."

Omar peered into her eyes. "You sense that?"

"It's a narrow possibility. But if I tell him alone, he'll run off and kill Ruby."

"I trust you. But..." Omar squeezed one of her hands and his expression grew somber. "Why couldn't you sense this?"

"It's always hardest dealing with family. It's a blind spot that we all have."

"I see." He nodded in understanding, but his expression remained sad. "What's wrong?"

"Now that I've experienced this..." Her voice trailed off as she slid her fingers through young Jonah's short afro. "I'll never be able to bring him back here to Georgia."

Omar's jaw dropped. "You're that sure of it?"

She nodded. "Jonah won't be able to grow up with his cousins, not like we wanted." She wiped away a tear. "I may have a way to bring them together, eventually." The sadness in her voice was painful for Jonah. Did his mom predict that something would happen?

Jonah moved closer until he leaned over his mom and his younger self. He knelt down while gazing into her tear-streaked face. *Mom.* He hadn't seen her in two years. He reached out a ghostly hand to touch her own.

Janice shuddered and looked around. "Who's there?"

Her reaction and the question startled Jonah so much that he leapt back before he could stop himself and fell through the wall.

Intense pain split his skull, causing him to cry out as he stumbled and sprawled on his butt. But he forgot the pain when he gazed around at the new memory. He was in a throne room, straight out of a dark fantasy movie. Or maybe a horror movie, he corrected himself.

The ground on which he sat had a patchwork of deep brown, black, and burning red rocks. The red portion shot through the other stones, like veins or blood, Jonah decided. Overhead, the ceiling was a shiny, black material that reflected the color from the lit torches lining the walls. The place was in a word, oppressive.

A Wraith knelt on the ground several feet away. Jonah wasn't sure if it was the Wraith from his memories or not, but he suspected it could have been. Not far from the kneeling figure, curved, black steps led up to a glowing, red throne. On the throne sat a figure, his features hidden in the shadows.

Jonah could see the outline of a crown on the being's head, perched above two angry red eyes. *The Wraith King?*

A motion to the left of the king's shoulder drew Jonah's attention. An image wavered on the flat section of the wall. Jonah sucked in an angry breath as the Grim Reaper's visage came into view. He had the hood of his robe pulled forward, obscuring his face. Like the Wraith King, all that was visible was the glow from his angry eyes.

The Grim Reaper spoke, his gravelly voice making Jonah's nerves stand on end. "What news do you have for me?"

Amulet of the Goddess

The Wraith King motioned to the Wraith on the floor. "My servant failed in his attempt to take over Jonah Blackstone."

"I know of your failure," the Grim Reaper said. His voice carried danger in it. "Why haven't you sent this spirit to everlasting oblivion?"

The Wraith King nodded. "I understand your anger, Master, but this fool has important information." He gestured. "Speak."

The Wraith kept his head bowed, not daring to look at either being. "When I tried to take the boy's soul, I discovered something unexpected."

"And what was that?" The Grim Reaper asked.

"His impossible birth only became possible because of Pakhet's essence."

"What's this?"

The Wraith King stirred. "Master, Pakhet's amulet enhances the fertility of the one who wears it."

When the Grim Reaper nodded, the kneeling Wraith hurried on, "The mother possessed it before she conceived. The boy's body…"

"Would make a suitable host for the war goddess's essence," the Grim Reaper finished. "His body could contain the full power and achieve the first part of my plan."

"That is so, Master." The Wraith King inclined his head. "We should wait until the next alignment."

"That's seven years away! What about the aunt? We'll need her again."

"One of my minions still possesses her. We can control what she does until then."

"I want her separated from any influence by her family. Perhaps locked away for the duration would be best?"

"It will be done, Master." The Wraith King bowed.

As the Grim Reaper's image disappeared, the Wraith King rose from his throne.

He raised a glowing hand toward the Wraith on the floor. "As for you…"

Jonah ran forward and peered into the doomed Wraith's terrified eyes. A second before the Wraith King tortured or killed his servant, the memory shattered.

Instead of returning to the attic, he landed in a field of war in some far country of the distant past. Jonah suppressed a wave of panic and willed himself to accept the new memory without resistance.

Quicker than before, he found the Wraith, an arrogant captain this time, and made eye contact with the spirit-possessed person. The scene shifted. In the new scene, he discovered the Wraith taking possession of a foreign soldier who was in the process of beating and shooting a group of protestors.

Jonah was glad to turn his back on that. He preferred not to see the bullet-riddled bodies hugging the wall. After making eye contact, the scene changed again; and when it did, something amazing happened. A part of Jonah opened up, a part that didn't flinch away from what he saw, and the pain suddenly began to recede.

The process of moving from memory to memory sped up until the scenes were little more than a blur. An entire vista of memories stretched out before him. Even though he couldn't consciously see all the details, he had each one. That strange, strong part of him accepted it, propelling him forward. Each new scene flashed by with little more than an irritating bump against his soul's body.

Up ahead, Jonah sensed as much as he saw the approaching darkness. Fear returned because a frightening sense of finality loomed ahead. Jonah wrapped his mortal fears in the shielding calm of his Reaper side. Memory after memory flashed by until the darkness was upon him. All sense of forward movement ceased as he stumbled and fell in the total absolute nothingness of this scene.

With the darkness came the undeniable sense of Death, with a capital D.

Amulet of the Goddess

CHAPTER FORTY-FOUR
YOU CAN'T CHEAT DEATH

The ticking of a clock echoed through the darkness. *No, not a clock*, Jonah realized. *It's a tap. Yeah, it's actually a tapping.* He focused on the muffled sound of a cane hitting a concrete sidewalk. It was important.

A grouping of blinking lights appeared, drawing Jonah's attention. He thought they were far away, but it was difficult to tell without any reference points. Slowly, a nighttime sky dissolved into the blackness and around the lights. Then, more sounds came: Cars, the dull, sliding thumps of many people walking, and music.

In the background, the tapping continued, punctuating all of the other noises. *Strange*, Jonah thought, *it reminds me of a ticking clock*. Time was slipping away rapidly. What could he do, all alone in the darkness? There were no Wraith's eyes to stare into that might possibly end this memory.

Out of the darkness, a hazy scene coalesced into shapes that grew sharper and clearer, soon revealing the bustling activity of city life. Jonah stood on a street corner, his eyes darting here and there, taking it all in. In the distance, the flurry of twinkling lights morphed into the illuminated upper portion of the Eiffel Tower.

Of course! This was the full memory he remembered glimpsing earlier in the summer. It had to be the same one that Omar referred to in the previous scene while talking to his mom. He would finally know the truth of the experience. But why Paris? What happened here?

All around him, Parisians hurried along. Some even walked right through his immaterial body. Although it didn't hurt, Jonah was unnerved by the sheer number of collisions. He whirled around, trying to find a clear spot on which to stand, and that's when he saw a younger version of himself. He was only a few feet away in his pajamas, his eyes wide with wonder.

I don't understand about the dream-walks yet.

It was odd to see himself again in a memory. This version of himself was younger than the last by a year. Jonah ignored the people walking through him as he moved closer to the younger Jonah. Then he heard the tapping again, only stronger, more methodical, and more insistent.

He and his younger self looked around, mirroring each other as they peered into the nighttime crowds. But Jonah remembered the sound came from a pale man. That's when he spotted the source.

A thin, pale man wearing a long, black overcoat, stark white shirt, black tie, and black top hat strolled through the crowds. Parisians moved out of his way as if he were a skiff, cutting through living waves. The man carried a long, black cane with a large, silver handle and silver tip. The tip made the tapping noise. With his top hat tilted back, his eyes never wandered from his destination.

Jonah's dread and fear grew exponentially. One glance at his younger self and he realized the feelings weren't his own. Even though this was just a memory, he was experiencing a sympathetic reaction inside himself.

The pale man reached them and nodded his head in greeting to little Jonah. And then he looked squarely into older Jonah's face as he continued past, never breaking his stride. Jonah shuddered and rubbed his arms just as little Jonah did the same thing.

They turned, watching the pale man proceed toward a restaurant. The dread from his younger self threatened to overwhelm him. It was right at that point when Omar's voice had intruded the last time. He and Jonah's mom lured him away from the memory. But they weren't here now.

Jonah knew he had to get inside that restaurant. He nudged himself into a phase and a moment later, stood at the front doors of the upscale Parisian locale.

Little Jonah appeared right next to him. The younger boy didn't hesitate to dart through the doors, literally, and go into the restaurant. Jonah followed. It was dark inside, elegant and full of hushed conversations in

Amulet of the Goddess

a variety of languages, but French dominated most of them. Little Jonah seemed to know where he was going as he weaved around the crowded tables and toward a back section.

Jonah followed and soon heard a familiar voice that caused his heart to jump into his throat. His dad sat at a table with three other people, two of whom Jonah didn't know, but the third was Marcus! A stab of fear hit Jonah and he glanced at his younger self. They had to warn his father. The strange man was coming for him.

"Dad!" they yelled at the top of their lungs, their voices mixing, younger and older, in a weird chorus of sound. But no one in the restaurant paid any attention to them, just as Jonah expected. The younger Jonah didn't understand so he yelled again.

"Dad! You have to leave! Get out! He's coming!"

Jonah's dad paused and glanced around. After a brief, puzzled look, he went back to his conversation. Marcus gave him a curious rise of the eyebrow, but his dad shrugged it off.

"Dad!" Little Jonah shouted yet again. His voice sounded so fragile and fear-stricken. Jonah wanted to tell his younger self that their dad couldn't hear him. At least, not yet. Maybe if he joined in, using his own voice, they could get his dad's attention.

Jonah opened his mouth to call out when a piercing scream filled the restaurant. More yells followed before the sound of dishes crashing to the floor and heavy thuds filled the room. Every person in the restaurant turned toward the commotion.

The pale man had entered the restaurant. His cane never stopped its incessant tapping. Behind him, bodies littered the floor. Like a wave, people in front of him also collapsed. Some suffered horrible spasms while others sprouted lesions and scars on their faces. All succumbed to horrible, painful deaths.

The carnage spread across the restaurant as waiters, the maître d', and customers perished wherever they stood or sat. Distant crashes and thuds even came from the kitchen. *Death.* The man was Death, personified.

Jonah turned back to his dad, but Death suddenly stood in front of him, peering down at younger Jonah. The coldness that emanated off the being chilled the young boy and Jonah, despite his long, insulated coat.

The effects of Death continued to spread around the restaurant until it reached his dad's table. Two of the diners fell immediately. Only Jonah's dad and Marcus remained on their feet. When Marcus pulled out his Reaper blade, Jonah's dad grabbed his arm and forced it down.

"Dad, run!" young Jonah shouted. Death smiled at him and raised a boney finger to his lips.

"Shhh. Your daddy can't sense you here, but Death can. One day, you'll be able to call out to him, when you're stronger." He met older Jonah's gaze. "You understand what I mean."

Little Jonah didn't, but older Jonah did. He gulped, loath to relive that memory of his parents' last stand.

"Now be a good boy and stay here while I have a talk with your daddy." Death raised his eyes from little Jonah to look at Jonah once more. "Both of you." He flicked his boney hand and rooted Jonah's body to the spot. Only his eyes could move, following the being's progress to the table. He suspected the same thing probably happened to his younger self.

Isaiah Blackstone turned to face Death, but the being flicked his hand, causing the chair to bump into Jonah's dad's legs and forcing him to sit down. The same thing happened to Marcus. Both men sat rigidly in their seats.

Walking around to other side of the table, Death waved his hand and sent the dead dinner companions flying across the room. They knocked over tables on the way to the far wall, which they hit with sickening thuds.

Death dusted off a chair, sat down, and leaned his cane against the table. After spending a minute to examine the unfinished meals, he pulled two half-finished plates toward himself and began to eat. "Exquisite."

Jonah's dad talked through a clenched jaw. "You can't take me now. You promised."

"I don't want you yet." Death ate another bite of food and took his time chewing it.

"Why are you here?"

Death put the fork down. "I'm here because of you, Isaiah Blackstone. When I told you how to rebel and to demand the ancient trial, you made an oath to me. And your wife also accepted the terms when you married

Amulet of the Goddess

her. Now that you have a son, you seem somewhat inclined to forget your vow."

He poured wine into a glass, then lifted it to his nose to sniff before taking a sip. "I don't care who's on top in the Afterworld. Nor do I care what the Grand Oracle hides in his pathetic repositories. In the end, everyone comes to me." Death lowered the glass and took another bite of food.

He swallowed, pointing his knife at Jonah's dad. "Even the Grim Reaper will face the ultimate harvest. It is the way of the universe. I will devour the souls of you and your wife."

Marcus struggled to move. "Did you have to kill all those innocent people?"

Death seemed perturbed by the question. "I assure you that unlike the Grim Reaper, I never take mortal souls except at their appointed time." He put down his fork and seemed in no hurry while sipping more wine. "All these people were destined to perish tonight in a terrorist gas attack."

"That's the way you'll play it?" Isaiah asked.

"Like you really care." Death smiled. "The only reason you're still alive is because of the Reaper blood in your veins. Don't worry; you'll still have your allotted thirteen years with your son. But mark my words, if you don't stick to the agreement for him, I will have you and your wife sooner than you can appreciate. The cosmic balance rests on the boy's future."

Death stood up, took his cane, and walked around the table until he was directly beside Jonah's dad. "You, of all people, should know that you can't cheat Death."

With a wave of his hand, the dead people disappeared from the restaurant. Then the tables faded, followed by the walls. Nighttime Paris also dissolved into the blackness until only Jonah's dad, Marcus, Death, and of course, Jonah and his younger self were left.

Everyone remained immobile, including young Jonah, even though Death had removed the invisible force holding them. Jonah moved closer to his dad, taking in his features. It had been two years since Jonah last saw him and tears welled up, threatening to spill.

When Jonah reached out to touch his dad, his dad inexplicably began to fade. Jonah thrust his arms out, trying to wrap them around his dad and hold on, even for a moment longer.

"No!" It was too late. His dad and Marcus were gone, along with younger Jonah. He was alone again in the darkness.

Except this time, the pale man stood nearby, his cane in hand. He ticked it against the ground as he strolled closer. The light followed him until both he and Jonah were perfectly lit.

"You understand about your father's fall?" Death's slightly Southern accent carried a note of curiosity.

Jonah nodded. "He went through a test. That was different from other Fallen Reapers."

"Precisely. His mission was to produce you." Death pointed his cane at Jonah. "The vessel of the Deliverer's spirit and power. Only a special birth could produce someone like you, half supernatural and mortal, both sides gifted, in their own ways."

Despite the fear, Jonah's anger flared. "Then why did you kill my mom and dad?"

"We all must play our parts. Your father accepted his role, despite the consequences and all."

Jonah's eyes blurred with tears. He remembered the way his mom and dad stood so tall in that chamber when they sensed him watching, like they… like they fully accepted what would happen. Jonah wiped the tears. "What about the Grim Reaper? How's it fair that he can screw things up?"

Death laughed and moved around Jonah, studying him. "Why do you think you're here, young man? If more powerful supernaturals were to interfere, that would further upset the balance. The Grim Reaper was mortal once. It's only cosmic justice that a mortal must overcome him."

Jonah's heart ached with the knowledge that his parents had to sacrifice their lives in order for him to survive. He shook his head, trying to deny his parents' final words. *Everything we've done is because we love you.*

Death peered into his eyes. "Accept the truth along with the burden. You are what you are, young man." He pointed his boney finger at Jonah's forehead. "You took in the Wraith's memories. Your Reaper half did that, dulling the pain and shock from your mortal side. It was the instinctive thing to do and something you would have learned years ago if your mother hadn't interfered."

Amulet of the Goddess

"My mom saved me."

"Did she? Because of her love and fear, she held you back from fully developing. Then your parents tried to hide from the truth of your birthright, sheltering you in secrecy for years. They wanted to have a normal son, but you, young man, are so much more."

Everything we've done is because we love you. Jonah couldn't ignore the words.

Death nodded. "Yes, even then, as misguided as they were, they acted primarily out of love." He waved his cane and below them, a scene wavered into view. It was like standing on a glass walkway high above an empty street. Jonah didn't recognize the shabby rows of mom-and-pop businesses.

Then his eyes came to the blinking, lavender palm in the window of the old Ankh of Life store halfway down the dingy side street. "That's my great-aunt's store!"

"And also the doorway back to your body." Death inclined his head toward the scene.

Jonah noticed a gathering darkness at the far end of the main street, perhaps ten blocks away.

"What's that?"

"The goddess has made her way to the doorway. She's gathered the Wraith King's Phantoms to fight with her." Then Death pointed toward the storefront. Streams of vapor whirled around the shining door. "Your aunt has also summoned Wraiths to bar your way."

Jonah gaped at the vision because the faces of Wraiths appeared in the vapors. Ice water flowed through his veins. So much wasted time! He had to get back, yet he didn't know how. In desperation, he turned to Death.

"Can you help me?"

Death raised an eyebrow. Jonah realized he must have sounded foolish for asking. Yet, for a second, he thought the being might refuse.

"If I were to render aid," Death finally said, "you would have to make an oath to me, here and now."

Like my dad did. "I'll do it." Jonah glanced at the advancing darkness of Pakhet's spirit.

"Do you understand the nature of oaths to us?"

"Yes, I do." Jonah said, his fear growing as the darkness moved another block closer to his aunt's store.

"Very well." Death leaned closer. "Remember, you can't cheat Death." The being placed his cane on Jonah's right shoulder. "Do you swear to fully accept your destiny and do all in your power to correct the imbalance, even if it means sacrificing your own life in the future?"

Jonah gulped, finally understanding what Death meant about the oath. But he also experienced a moment of déjà vu. It was the line from his dream. This was the moment! He glanced below. The Darkness rolled down the next block, picking up speed. Jonah met Death's intense gaze and repeated the words from his dream. "Yes. I swear."

Thunder shook the floor as Death lifted the cane. "Then I will help you."

Before Jonah could ask what he planned to do, Death disappeared, leaving him behind. "Huh, hello? What about me?"

Jonah turned on the spot while below him, on the street, the cloud of darkness dissolved into multiple Wraiths, their bodies like thunderclouds and now only a few blocks from his aunt's store. Behind them loomed the larger evil of the goddess essence that wanted his body. Jonah was about to call out again when Death reappeared.

"It's done."

"What did you do?"

Death gave him a severe look. "I fulfilled my part of the bargain." He moved so fast, he seemed to phase before he stood right in front of Jonah. "Now, perform your duty, Deliverer." With that, he touched Jonah's forehead with two boney fingers and light flared around them.

The next second, Jonah stood in the Underworld version of the attic clubhouse. The Egyptian Wraith hurried over to him. "You've done it!"

Jonah nodded. "I have to get to my great-aunt's store. That's the way back to my body."

"Then do what you would in the mortal world. Phase." The Wraith reached out a hand to stop Jonah. "Remember that you can also shape this realm around you."

Amulet of the Goddess 987

Jonah didn't understand but he didn't have time to figure it out. He pictured the street in his mind and phased. He reappeared on this realm's version of his aunt's side street, just outside her business. The cloud of angry Wraiths, Phantoms, and Felines rounded the corner and bore down on him.

CHAPTER FORTY-FIVE
THROUGH THE DOORWAY

Several regular Wraiths streaked toward Jonah as soon as he appeared. He raised his hands to defend himself when green fire shot overhead, effectively slamming into two of the gaseous beings. They screamed in agony as the flames consumed them. The others scattered, diving to either side. Jonah ducked and heard a brief swish before the solid thunk! of an arrow finding its mark. More death screams followed.

"Jonah! Get your butt in gear!" Lynn's strained voice came from behind him. He turned and his jaw dropped. Not only was Lynn's spirit here, clad in elf garb and holding gleaming Reaper blades, but Wick was also present, his glowing hands conjuring fire with ease. And Robert had also come. He held a bow in his hands and was firing off dozens of glowing arrows like a cool version of Legolas. Happily, Robert's spirit version of himself didn't have any broken fingers.

Behind the group stood Mike, his eyes ablaze, holding his hands aloft. Jonah wanted to shout for joy as Kevin and four Alliance Guards charged from the Deliverer's cave and into the Underworld. Mike had to use the Deliverer's seal to open a pathway to this location.

Of course, Jonah realized. *The designation stones!* He and Mike both noticed each location on the triptych had assigned codes. In the mortal world, each designation stone had six symbols etched into the surface. *Why wouldn't the same apply to the Underworld version of the stones?* Jonah thought as he searched the ground at his feet.

What he saw shocked him. Instead of a single designation stone, the individual symbols formed a huge circle. His Death Sense spiked,

Amulet of the Goddess

interrupting his moment of discovery, and alerting him that he had temporarily lost focus. Dodging to the side on instinct, he avoided the swipe of a sword from a Phantom that streamed right over his head.

The Egyptian's advice crystalized in his mind and he knew what to imagine. In a split second, he held two gleaming Reaper blades of his own. The weight of the familiar weapons reassured Jonah and he snapped into action, whirling and slicing as he backed toward his cousins and Wick.

"How did you guys get here?" Even as he shouted the question, the answer came to him instantly. *Death*.

Robert was skewering another Wraith with an arrow through its open mouth when he replied, "A strange guy dressed in all black showed up and said he could take us to you."

"Lynn didn't trust the dude," Wick said, nailing a Wraith of his own with green fire. "At least, she didn't until Kevin vouched for him."

"That's when Mike knew what to do and opened the portal to this place," Lynn answered, her blades never pausing for a second.

Jonah nodded toward the glowing, T-shaped door that led into this version of his great-aunt's store. He noticed the large, digital clock situated above the entrance and considered asking about it when the advancing vanguard of Pakhet reached the side street.

"We can handle this," Kevin announced. He blurred into motion and cut down a Phantom with two upward slices of his blades.

The Alliance Guards had spread out and were battling the undulating feline shapes that leapt at them from all sides. The guards' sizzling weapons flashed and slashed through the air as the men bravely fought. As valiant as they were, Jonah couldn't help but worry; for every creature they smacked down, it seemed two more charged in to replace it.

Wick turned and fired off a shot at the advancing darkness itself, which now rolled across the sky above them like an all-consuming storm cloud. But all that did was anger the goddess. Tendrils shot out in all directions, morphing into the forms of individual Phantoms as they swiftly approached.

Wick held his left wrist aloft, and a shield sprang up around him. The closest Phantoms collided with the barrier, howling in fury when they tumbled past. Others swooped in to hack away at the shield with their swords but thankfully, all failed to break through.

Meanwhile, Robert and Lynn were holding their own against the swarm of regular Wraiths charging down on them from the store roof. Jonah worried for Robert when he noticed his quiver only had one arrow left. But as soon as his cousin took that one, the quiver instantly refilled.

From Jonah's perspective, Wick seemed to be in the most peril. Minions of the goddess continually dived and battered the young mage's shield, besetting him from all sides. Jonah sprang forward into the thick of the assault and sliced away. Like angry wasps, the Phantoms turned and swarmed over him.

But Jonah anticipated their reaction and he phased all around the street, keeping the Phantoms frustrated. Plus, each time he reappeared, he'd take down another before phasing away again.

Kevin appeared beside him and they moved in sync with each other. Jonah could feel the older boy's presence for the split second he entered the aether, and he respectively adjusted. With Kevin instinctively doing the same, they became a blur of lethal blades that the Phantoms couldn't penetrate.

The distraction worked. Wick lowered his shield and attacked the Phantoms from behind. He fried at least four of them with green fire before they realized their imminent danger. When they tried to refocus, Kevin and Jonah moved in and overwhelmed them.

Freed to adjust his attack on the regular Wraiths, Wick combined a shield explosion and green fire to decimate most of the group that was hampering Lynn and Robert.

"Hah!" he shouted.

With the Alliance Guard holding back the Grim Hounds and Felines, the makeshift strategy seemed to be working well. At least, it was until a bellowing tendril of energy streaked down at Wick from behind. Colliding with him, it knocked him several feet down the street. The cloud spiraled up before diving for Robert and Lynn next.

The twins stood their ground. Robert shot several arrows straight into the cloud. Pakhet let out angry, disembodied screams of fury as each one hit its target. If a tendril drew close enough, Lynn sliced it and cut it with her Reaper's blades.

The goddess circled overhead, *giving up that plan*, Jonah thought. Then the cloudy substance hit the ground and solidified into feet, legs, a torso, and finally, the head.

Amulet of the Goddess **991**

Jonah stared in amazement at the giant, beautiful Egyptian goddess that stood at least thirty feet tall.

She wore a short, red-and-white skirt, cinched in the front with a golden ring and white fabric tie. Golden sandals adorned her feet and segmented, sleek, gold armor encased her legs. Armored bracelets covered her forearms and her fingers ended in long, lethal-looking nails. In her left hand was a short, curved, Egyptian khopesh sword, and with her right hand, she held a long staff with a curved handle featuring a cobra's head at the end.

Her face was Aunt Ruby's instead of that of a lioness. She wore a battle helmet with fringes that dropped down and barely managed to cover the tips of her exposed breasts.

"Whoa!" Robert gushed, his mouth hanging open. Sinking his bow even lower, he and every other guy stared in openmouthed awe at the goddess.

Lynn smacked her brother across the back of his head. "Get a grip, Robert!"

Robert gestured at the giantess's voluptuous chest. "But they're huge!"

"Must I remind you? You're ogling *your aunt*!"

The reality of the situation apparently dawned on Robert all at once because he responded with gagging sounds. "Agh! I'm gonna be blind for the rest of my life!"

Jonah noticed Kevin staring and elbowed him. "What are you looking at?"

Kevin smirked. "I'm not blind."

Jonah didn't think it helped that this representation of the goddess seemed to be striking a pose.

When Pakhet pointed her cobra scepter at Lynn, Jonah's cousin raised her enchanted shield instinctively and braced herself.

But Pakhet spoke in their aunt's voice. The power of it rolled across the scene. "You should serve me."

"No way!" Lynn shouted back.

Pakhet turned her eyes on Jonah next. "You're a child of my power. Serve me! Ignore your bargain with Death. I'll show you the true nature of the Deliverer's spirit. Together, we'll rule this mortal world."

"Sorry. But I can't help you." Jonah was proud that his voice sounded so calm and sure. He was also aware of the others giving him curious glances.

"Very well. Then prepare to die." She waved her hand and hordes of Phantoms instantly appeared both in front and behind Jonah and the others. Phantoms outnumbered them by a thousand to one. This was the main army, which she planned to rampage across the mortal world, starting with Mount Vernon.

Jonah's group backed up, moving toward each other, and forming a loose circle. They would fight as best they could, but Jonah couldn't figure out how to manage so many spirits on their own. As if in answer to his unspoken plea, a shiver ran down his spine and the Egyptian Wraith appeared beside him. The man nodded to Jonah as he pulled out two long, black poles with curved khopesh blades on both of the ends.

Lifting his eyes to Ruby's towering figure, he shook his head. In a flash, his ebony features transformed. The nose elongated into a snout with extensive, sharp teeth and his head also became longer and more angular. Jonah gaped at the man because his head soon changed into the black dog's head of Anubis.

Anubis raised his sword.

Around Jonah's group, more apparitions began to appear. All were women, clad in glistening, shining armor that barely covered their attractive bodies. Golden shield pieces were artfully wrapped around their forearms and lower legs and they all wore golden sandals. Long, thin, intricate braids fell to their shoulders. The most prominent weapons were the slender, sharp knives located at the end of the gauntlets they all wore.

Each one had glowing, narrowed eyes and they crouched, facing the Phantom army, ready to strike.

"Who are they?" Jonah asked in a quiet voice.

"The daughters of Pakhet, warriors who normally serve the goddess," Anubis answered.

Jonah found it odd to see the dog's mouth move as regular words tumbled out. He also noticed the Egyptian Wraith's normal cadence had taken on a barking, guttural quality.

"So they're on our side, right?" Jonah asked.

Amulet of the Goddess

Anubis nodded. "They disapprove of the negative aspect of the goddess being used by the Wraith King and your aunt." He turned his snout toward Jonah. "Normally, the user of the amulet can choose or dictate which aspect of the goddess comes forth, be it positive or negative. But the Grim Reaper and Wraith King have used their powers to summon the huntress and they fuel her with a blinding rage."

Jonah's eyes widened because he recognized the larger meaning for himself. He could use the Deliverer spirit for good or evil too.

"Traitors!" Aunt Ruby yelled. She raised her armored right foot to stomp on Lynn and Robert.

Jonah's blades glowed brighter in his hands and he leapt to his cousins' defense. "Leave them alone!" He didn't bother to run but micro-phased right under the huge foot, scoring two deep gouges in the metal. He hoped he managed to penetrate into the flesh beneath.

The goddess wailed in agony and staggered back, giving Jonah a chance to plant himself between his cousins and the hostile being.

That's when he saw Wick, who was entirely cut off from help. Jonah ran for the goddess and phased on top of her left shoulder. Jabbing a blade at the ornamented collar she wore, he intended for it to be more of a distraction than any real attempt to cut her. The shock of the attack, however, caused the goddess to rear back and swing at him. Jonah had already phased to the street below. In a moment of unbridled fury, she pointed her huge scepter at him and fired. The blast took out half the structure beside this version of his great-aunt's store.

The explosion also acted as a signal, alerting the rest of Pakhet's Phantom army to commence their attack. But the warrior women moved like ghosts themselves. They shifted in and out of sight while also gathering in groups to help each member of Jonah's team. They sliced away at the enemy, racking up a heavy kill ratio in seconds.

Jonah dodged a second blast from the goddess and phased again. This time, he reappeared beside her left leg. He caught Kevin doing the same thing on the giantess's right. But Pakhet was quick. She swiped at them with her khopesh sword. Kevin used his blades to block, but the raw power of the goddess sent him tumbling along the street and right into a tree.

The blade caught Jonah's coat just before he phased away, causing his body to spin. That motion continued as he appeared on the other side of the street. He rolled into the wall, banging his head.

He couldn't focus long enough to move as Pakhet leveled the scepter at him and fired. But Wick dived in front of Jonah and activated a protective shield. The power of the shot pressed them both against the wall, but the shield held–for the moment.

"You have to do something," Wick said, his voice tightening with the effort to keep the shield in place.

"What? Change myself into a giant mummy or something?"

Wick gritted his teeth, strictly confining his attention to protecting them.

Around them, Pakhet's minions cornered the rest of their group. Eventually, she would stomp them to death, if nothing else. That's when he noticed the sparkling amulet she wore. Jonah stared down at the replica around his neck.

That was the connection! His mortal body still wore the actual amulet. He tapped Wick's shoulder. "As soon as I'm gone, help Lynn and Robert."

"Gone?"

"Just do it, Wick."

Jonah readied himself as the goddess prepared to fire on them again and shouted, "Now!" As soon as the shield disappeared with a popping sound, he charged forward, waving his arms as a distraction and trying to draw her aim. When the goddess shifted her weapon, Jonah phased.

He reappeared on her left arm and jammed his right blade into the hand holding the scepter. He didn't wait to see if she dropped the weapon, but ran up her arm and dove right for the amulet. Clutching his remaining blade with both hands, he plunged it into the outer metal of the amulet and mentally urged the weapon on, willing the metal to melt like butter so he could drive his blade further inside.

And he succeeded. A gaseous darkness swallowed him up instead of real flesh, blood, and innards, which would have ensued if the goddess had actually possessed a physical body. Around him, the substance that made up Pakhet convulsed into spasms. Jonah could also feel the vibrations from her continued stomping.

He hoped that Wick had time to raise a shield over his cousins; otherwise, this would have been for nothing. And it would also be futile if he didn't get moving with his hasty plan. Jonah curled himself into a ball and opened his Reaper self to the goddess.

Amulet of the Goddess

"You want me? You got me."

As expected, once he connected to her soul, memories from her experiences through the ages flooded Jonah's mind. He protected his mortal self from the sudden surge by allowing his Reaper side to fully engage in the experiences. Like before, he surfed the memories without being affected or traumatized.

The goddess's essence reacted to his invasion by causing tendrils to coalesce around him, entangling and holding him in what she thought was a death grip. Jonah welcomed it, even wanted it. Only when he called on his power to vanquish her did the goddess realize her mistake.

But Jonah held on doggedly, refusing to let go. *No! you won't get away!* He summoned all the command he had, relishing the sureness of his Reaper heritage inside.

He also manipulated his long coat. It writhed and the ends shot outward, intertwining with the spirit's essence and grasping it tightly.

Pakhet's struggle intensified, trying to expel him, but Jonah's coat clung to her. That's when the cracks appeared. Memory after memory, going back for thousands of years, shattered like glass and immediately disintegrated. Pakhet screamed again.

Jonah concentrated and imagined his power rushing through the being. She may have been powerful and old, but he was the Deliverer, a spirit that was just as old and powerful. As the tendrils were extricated from his coat, the true amulet came into view, shining like a familiar beacon in the larger darkness.

With a thought, his blades activated and he used the Reaper's coat to propel himself forward, like a squid thrusts itself through the ocean. As he neared the glistening amulet, Jonah reared back before driving his blade straight into the heart of the jewel.

Fractures raced across the amulet and it shattered at the same time the blackness around Jonah also exploded into a million flaming fragments. That proved unfortunate because he found himself over thirty feet up in the air. Too stunned and weary to phase, Jonah plummeted toward the ground. Before he hit, however, Kevin appeared and caught him, phasing both of them safely to the street below.

The Fallen Reaper lowered him to his feet. Before Jonah could thank him, the goddess exploded with an outpouring of supernatural energy that rushed away from them in a shock wave.

"That was *wikid* cool," Wick whispered, plainly awed.

Jonah nodded his agreement, only now taking note that Robert, Lynn, and the four Alliance Guards had also survived.

The Phantoms ended their attacks at Pakhet's demise and now, they were all wailing in their final death throes. The women warriors waded into their midst and cut them down like saplings. Only the regular Wraiths remained behind.

Wick called, "I've been waiting all night to do this."

The staff in his hands glowed as Wick twirled it overhead and shouted in a perfect Gandalf-like voice, "You shall not pass!"

When he brought the staff down, a wave of forcible energy shot out, knocking all the regular Wraiths back and away. Broken and defeated, most scattered or disappeared.

Above them, the clouds still churned impatiently.

"You dissipated Pakhet's energy," the Egyptian observed, still in Anubis form. "But you must take care of the remnant still residing inside your aunt. Free the goddess from her control."

"He's right," Lynn agreed. "You need to get back and stop Ruby."

Kevin gripped Jonah's shoulder and pushed him toward the door. "Go. We'll cross over after you leave." He nodded with his chin.

Mike had already reopened the doorway to the Deliverer's cave. When a few remaining Wraiths zeroed in on him, Mike raised his hands and opened other doorways in the air, right in front of the spirits. That caused them to slip into other locations before they could reach him.

"Wow," Jonah said, clearly impressed.

In the lull of action, Kevin lifted him up. "Get going now, little man." Heaving Jonah through the glowing doorway, he swiftly shoved him back into his real body.

Amulet of the Goddess

CHAPTER FORTY-SIX
WRAITH TO THE RESCUE

Jonah sucked in a ragged breath and opened his eyes. At once, he knew something was horribly wrong. Although he had returned to his physical body, he sensed he wasn't alone. Someone or something else pressed against his consciousness.

For a horrid moment, he feared the remnant of Pakhet had inhabited his body anyway. As he summoned his Reaper power to expel the invasive spirit, he heard the familiar voice of the Egyptian Wraith in his mind.

Calm yourself, young one. I will leave your body now.

And Anubis did, but it was unpleasant. Jonah's muscles locked, rendering him helpless as the Wraith streamed from his body. The most shocking part was when it exited through his mouth and eyes. The sensation was excruciating, causing Jonah to pity mortals who willingly opted for this.

As soon as the Wraith was free, all sensation and control returned. His body and rigidly contorted muscles relaxed even though he was still held fast to the slab by Ruby's spell.

His Aunt Ruby stumbled from her hiding place between the stone pillars. The Egyptian Wraith, now merely a tendril of billowing smoke with the Anubis head, snarled and attacked her, driving her back.

Then he changed directions and dived at Aunt Ruby's Wraith-possessed henchman. When the Wraith impacted the man, he disappeared inside the mortal's body, causing the man to collapse to the ground while bucking with spasms. Seconds later, both Wraiths emerged from the mortal's body and whirled around the site, locked in mortal battle.

They collided with the pillar that Antwan's cousin was chained to before barreling right over Jonah, causing him to shudder when they swept by.

Jonah glimpsed the enemy Wraith's true form. He was some kind of serpent, with a head that looked like a fabled dragon. Whenever the Wraith's reptilian body was visible in the vapor, Jonah could see it wrapping itself around the Anubis Wraith.

Several times, the battling Wraiths forced Ruby to duck as they smashed against the pillars. Jonah, who silently urged on his ancestor, thought the impacts were entirely random until the Wraiths whizzed by him again and hit a different pillar. The stone fractured and bits fell away, breaking the restrictive sigils Ruby had skillfully emblazoned on the surfaces.

Power surged into Jonah and he pulled himself free of Ruby's magical locks. With her own abilities diminished, Ruby let out a frustrated yell and charged him, clutching a knife in her hands. Jonah twisted just in time and the knife scraped against the stone. The tip broke and would have cut him in the back if not for his Reaper's coat.

He swung his left hand, catching Ruby in her chest. The woman only staggered a step before stopping. She was much stronger than he expected. Her enraged eyes changed to the bright orange of a lioness.

She held out her hand and produced one of the strange, purplish vortices. "Attack!" she shouted to the remaining Phantoms on this side. With that, she leapt through the vortex and disappeared.

Jonah rolled off the slab and prepared to fight, but the Phantoms disappeared instead of attacking him. To his surprise, the Felines and Grim Hounds also turned and bounded away at inhuman speed into the surrounding darkness.

Behind him, the reptilian Wraith expelled a death shriek as Anubis ripped out its ghostly throat. The enemy Wraith exploded into fragments, leaving a battered Anubis behind. The canine eyes met Jonah's before he nodded and disappeared.

Kevin, Lynn, Robert, and Wick arrived a moment later. Jonah turned to them, unable to hide his mounting fear. "They're going for the others."

Lynn's own face paled. "Dad!"

"What?" Robert asked.

"She hates him as much as Jonah and his mom."

Amulet of the Goddess

Robert's jaw dropped. "We have to get there."

"A little help this time," Kevin said to Jonah. "Phase to the street in front of your house. Don't try the backyard."

Jonah nodded as he grabbed Wick's forearm and phased home.

*

"Oh, my God," Lynn exhaled as soon as they reappeared.

The reason for Kevin's orders became clear in an instant. The Hightowers' home was now a raging battlefront. Marcus, Rex, Eleanor, and Symon Trueblood were all outside on the front lawn, fighting off Phantoms, Felines, and Grim Hounds. Behind them, a dome of protection covered the entire house and backyard.

Inside that bubble of protection stood Anthony, Rico, Tamara, Danita, and Uncle James. The kids huddled together, gazing in shock at the combat going on all around them, while Uncle James stood with them.

Deyanira's Grim Hound fought alongside Marcus and the others, taking on any other Grim Hound that attacked. Marcus finally noted their arrival and motioned them closer.

Kevin and Lynn held their blades out and fended off anything that came their way. Overhead, a stream of Phantoms dive-bombed the shield, hitting it in one spot and sacrificing themselves to weaken it.

"Our barrier won't last much longer," Symon called out to Marcus. He waved his hands and conjured a huge, black bear that lumbered around, making the ground tremble like an earthquake as it took down random Felines and Grim Hounds.

His sister, Eleanor, had her wand out to conjure her fiery phoenix. The huge, flaming red bird soared into the air, emitting an ear-splitting screech. It intercepted the Phantoms, but many managed to make it through before they swooped down to plow into the shield.

"It's our aunt," Jonah told Marcus. "She still has power."

Despite Trueblood's phoenix, the Phantoms blasted a hole through the barrier, which caused the entire protective dome to collapse. A flash of purple vapor bloomed in the backyard as Aunt Ruby stepped through, right in front of Uncle James.

"No!" Lynn shouted. She grabbed Jonah's hand. He didn't need any explanation before he phased them.

Aunt Ruby raised her hand and fired a hex at her own brother. But Lynn was there in an instant, raising an enchanted shield. She knocked the hex away and brandished her blades at her aunt. "Stay away from my dad!"

"Yeah," Robert shouted. He joined his sister a second later with his bow and arrow in hand.

Jonah, Kevin, and the Alliance adults crowded around the kids to protect them as they fought off the dwindling numbers of Phantoms. The ghostly knights seemed more interested in preventing Jonah and the others from interfering. His group couldn't interfere anyway because their aunt had erected a protective barrier around herself, Lynn, Robert, and Uncle James.

Ruby cackled like a mad woman. "Watch your son and daughter perish just to save you, James!" She attacked her own niece and nephew. When Robert and Lynn rebuffed her, the tricky woman tried to hide her surprise by summoning her remaining power from the goddess's essence to slip in and out of the aether. Jonah's jaw dropped as his aunt used a technique similar to the one Kevin taught him.

But Robert and Lynn acted as one. Witnessing their coordination convinced Jonah, more than ever, that the twins communicated with each other without talking. Or maybe Robert shared his sister's intuition. As Ruby ducked and dodged, appearing at random around them, attempting to reach their dad, Robert and Lynn never failed to meet her either with a blade or bow.

"Whoa!" Wick said. "Who knew Robert had it in him?"

Ruby scored a hit to Lynn's shoulder and followed that up with a swipe of her hand. The enchanted shield soared away and landed off to the side. Ruby shoved her niece away. Robert faltered for a second over his sister's condition.

Recovering quickly, Robert whirled around to face Ruby each time she appeared in a different location. Even with Lynn down, he seemed even more capable of tracking their aunt and protecting his dad. He pulled back on his bow, ready to let an arrow fly when the mole appeared inside the barrier.

Amulet of the Goddess

The Alliance traitor moved in a blur and knocked Robert's arrow aside before it could hit Ruby. The traitor continued his movement, grabbing Robert's right arm and deftly slicing off his hand with a Reaper's blade.

Everyone screamed at the same time and rushed forward. The mole threw down some shiny objects. They sparked and a barrier sprang up around him, Ruby, and Jonah's cousins. It meshed with and fortified the shield Jonah's aunt had already erected.

Inside, Robert's shock displaced his own ability to make any sound as he dropped to his knees beside his sister. The mole yanked the bow free and broke it in two. He gripped Robert by the afro, pulling his head back and exposing his neck. Jonah's cousin cried out in pain while cradling the bloody stump where his hand had formerly been.

Ruby raised her hands, ready to hex her own brother, when the mole shouted at her.

"We don't have time for revenge. Do it now and let's get out of here!"

Marcus and the other Alliance adults attacked the mole's barrier with everything they had, but it stubbornly held.

The shocking turn of events stunned Jonah, as did the fear at having to watch his cousins and uncle die in front of his eyes. But he was wrong. They all were wrong.

Ruby whirled in his direction and her magical power spiked, something he didn't think she could accomplish. Before Jonah could move away from the barrier, she hurled a hex that penetrated the shield and hit him squarely in the chest.

Marcus screamed his name, but the hex had already engulfed his body. The pain was unbelievable but thankfully, only lasted seconds.

One moment, he cried out; and the next, he was high above the scene, looking down on his physical body as it dropped to the ground, spread-eagled. A large, dark stain marred his chest.

Kevin reached his side first and dropped to his knees, cradling the limp body. Marcus whirled to attack the mole but the traitor and Aunt Ruby had already fled the scene.

Ruby killed him! Jonah screamed for someone to spot him floating above. *Mike! Marcus! Kevin!* But no one heard him.

That realization accompanied a sudden lurch before he spiraled downward into total darkness, screaming for help that would never come. He was dead, and his soul was hastily being sucked into the Underworld.

CHAPTER FORTY-SEVEN
SEER'S BLOOD

Jonah was alone, in total darkness, and terrified. He called for help until his voice was hoarse from the effort. "Mike, hear me!" he tried one, last time. "You're my Pathmaker!"

Nothing except absolute, nerve-wracking silence. He huddled on his knees, his entire body shaking with sobs and complete incredulity over what had happened. His aunt had been the one to kill him! It wasn't supposed to happen that way.

He would never see his friend, Mike, again. He could never argue and poke fun at his cousins. The memory of Robert losing his hand made him feel even worse. And he didn't even know if Lynn were still alive.

Marcus was gone, and Kevin could never hold him again. Jonah swiftly descended into total despair. Is this what Death meant by that promise? Had he been tricked? He didn't know how long he remained huddled and sobbing, consumed by the horror of being alone for all eternity.

A quiet voice punctuated the silence, calling his name. Jonah ignored it. When he heard the voice again, he thought it was a trick concocted by his addled mind until the Egyptian Wraith's voice spoke again, only much stronger.

"Young Blackstone? Are you all right?"

Jonah raised his head and wiped his eyes. Slowly at first, the attic clubhouse materialized around him. The Egyptian Wraith stood nearby with a worried look on his noble face. But that didn't abate Jonah's fears. "Is this Hell? Am I doomed to repeat the same thing over and over forever, and always return here?"

"First of all, it's the Underworld, not Hell." The Wraith arched an eyebrow. "That's a fiction produced by the Grand Oracle and Grim–"

"Why're you here and not Anubis?"

The Wraith was shocked. "How do you know about that?"

Jonah thought the Wraith was joking with him. "What do you mean? You changed into Anubis when we fought Pakhet. I went back and stopped her but... but... my cousin... my aunt killed me," Jonah finally said. "And I came here to the Underworld."

A mixture of emotions played across the Wraith's face before settling on unmasked awe. He darted forward. "You've seen the future. What happened?"

Jonah stared at the Egyptian in disbelief. How could he see the future? "I... I died. My aunt killed me."

The Wraith drew back. "That's a possibility that hasn't happened yet."

"I don't understand," Jonah shot back while rising to his feet. "I lived through it all. It was real!"

"I warned you, this realm can do strange things," the Wraith insisted. "And your power could have made it possible to view the future as if it had already happened."

For the first time, Jonah's abysmal shock and despair began to recede. "You mean it really was a vision?"

"Have you ever experienced a vision before?"

Jonah thought back and nodded. "Yeah. I had one of Pakhet using my body to destroy Mount Vernon and all my friends and family. That was a nightmare. This was... real."

"Of course it felt that way. You made it real."

"So, it won't happen?" When the Wraith didn't answer at once, Jonah's fear returned but he wouldn't give in. "I'm gonna stop it from happening."

"It's difficult to alter what you've already seen. Most often, the very actions you take become the ones that combine to ensure the future you saw."

Jonah shook his head. "You said it was just a possibility. Now you're saying it's gonna happen? Make up your mind!"

Amulet of the Goddess

"I'm sorry. The future is always fluid."

But Jonah was thinking from another angle about what he experienced. It wasn't just a vision about the final fight. He also saw everything that led up to it. He pointed at the Wraith. "Look at me now. In the vision, you knew that I'd recovered the memories. My Reaper side did it." Jonah spread his hands. "Well? Did I do it or not?"

The Wraith narrowed his eyes. A second later, he said, "You have."

Jonah nodded. "I need to stop what happened next, and I will."

"How?"

"I know where to start. The Underworld version of my aunt's store is the doorway to my body."

"If what you say is accurate, then you must do what you would do…"

"…in the mortal world. I know. I have to phase there," Jonah finished. He lifted his chin. "Let's go, and bring your swords."

*

Several regular Wraiths streaked toward Jonah and the Egyptian Wraith as soon as they appeared outside the Underworld version of his great-aunt's store. He raised his hands and imagined two flaming Reaper blades like he did the last time, instantly conjuring a pair.

"How did you…?" the Egyptian Wraith asked, even as he brandished his swords. "Oh, of course."

They proceeded to defend themselves. All the while, Pakhet and her army drew closer.

"I need to pass through the doorway and stop my aunt."

"What about Pakhet's essence?"

Jonah dodged a Wraith but another immediately appeared, blocking his way. "I fought her. You said I dissipated her essence."

"Then you must do the same thing again." He sliced a Wraith in two and the ghost screamed as it flared before it died. "To go over now would be useless. Your aunt would draw a steady power stream from Pakhet."

Jonah's frustration mounted. He wanted to get straight to his aunt so he could end this. If things went the normal way, Robert and Lynn would suffer. As he thought about that, green fire shot overhead, slamming hard into two of the gaseous Wraiths. They screamed in agony as the flames consumed them.

A welcome swish and the thunk! of Robert's arrow finding its mark came next.

"Jonah!" Lynn arrived still clad in the elf garb. She was holding her gleaming Reaper blades. Wick was there too, conjuring fire, and Robert held his bow in his hands, firing off glowing arrows.

Behind them stood Mike, his eyes ablaze and his hands held aloft as Kevin and four Alliance Guards charged from the Deliverer's cave. Just like before.

Jonah took command and called out to the Guard Captain, "Put one of your people with Robert, Lynn, and Wick. You're with me and Kevin."

"Jonah?" Kevin asked.

The Guard Captain snapped into motion, arranging his people. That done, Jonah said to Wick, "Watch your back."

Just then, the bellowing dark cloud that was actually Pakhet streaked overhead. When she dived at Jonah's friends, they held her off now that they were better coordinated and expecting her.

Pakhet circled overhead, giving up that plan. The cloudy substance hit the ground and solidified into feet, legs, a torso, and finally, the head. She was a gigantic, beautiful Egyptian goddess, at least thirty feet tall, fully clad in protective armor.

"Don't forget that's our aunt, Robert. No gawking," Jonah taunted his cousin.

"What…? I…" Robert sputtered and his face reddened.

"That goes for you too," Jonah said to Kevin as he elbowed him. He raised his face to look Pakhet in the eyes. Even as she lifted her huge sword, Jonah called out, "Lynn's not gonna join you and neither am I, so kill the speech, Auntie."

Pakhet glared down at him. "Insolent."

"Yeah, my godfather hates that about me."

"Very well. Prepare to die." She waved her hand and hordes of Phantoms

Amulet of the Goddess 1007

appeared both in front and behind Jonah and the others. They were outnumbered by a thousand to one, just like before.

But Jonah stood tall, although his friends and family shifted nervously. "Don't worry," he told them. "We have help."

"I like your spirit, son, but these are bad odds," the Alliance Guard Captain said.

Jonah ignored the comment and turned on the Egyptian Wraith. "I need Anubis and the daughters of Pakhet. Now!"

The Wraith arched an eyebrow but didn't bother to ask any questions.

He lifted his eyes to Ruby's towering figure and shook his head. In a flash, his ebony features transformed into a black dog's head.

Anubis raised his right hand and sword while, around Jonah's team, a new group of apparitions appeared. All were women in glistening, golden armor, and they crouched, fully poised to strike the Phantom army.

"Protect my friends and family," Jonah ordered the women. Then, not waiting for Pakhet to smash them all, he yelled, "Attack!"

The women warriors and the Alliance Guards snapped into action, so swiftly that Pakhet's army was caught entirely off guard. *Good*, Jonah thought. He needed that surprise to last a moment longer.

Phasing atop Pakhet's shoulder, now that he knew what to do, he dived right for the amulet. He willed the metal of the amulet to melt like butter under his blades so he could plunge his weapon inside.

As soon as he did, Jonah curled into a ball and opened his Reaper self to the goddess. "You want me? You got me."

The goddess's essence reacted to his invasion and her tendrils flowed around him, entangling him. Jonah responded by manipulating his coat to do the same. The garment intertwined with the spirit's essence and held fast.

With the knowledge of what happened before, Jonah called on his power to vanquish the goddess. He waited for the reaction, and sure enough, the tendrils released his coat and in the process, revealed the true amulet. Once that happened, he used his Reaper's coat to propel himself forward, reared back with his right arm, and jabbed his blade into the very heart of the jewel.

Cracks and fractures raced across the amulet before it shattered. The blackness around Jonah also exploded into a million flaming fragments. Prepared this time, he phased to the street below as the giant body began to dissolve with the outpouring of disseminated energy. The last bits of the powerful goddess essence rushed away from them in a shock wave.

Like before, the Phantoms broke off their attacks and wailed their final death throes as the women warriors cut them down.

"That was wikid cool, Padawan," Wick whispered, still visibly awed.

"I know," Jonah agreed. He pointed at the regular Wraiths that remained behind. "Now do your Gandalf move."

After giving Jonah a puzzled look, Wick twirled his glowing staff overhead and shouted in a perfect Gandalf impersonation, "You shall not pass!"

When he brought the staff down, a wave of energy and powerful force shot out, knocking all the Wraiths back and away.

Jonah turned to Kevin. "I need to get through the door to deal with Ruby. You leave after I'm gone."

"Wait!" Kevin called out.

"Come on, Anubis." Jonah motioned to the Egyptian Wraith. With that, he ran for the door and dived through.

*

Happily returned to his physical body, Jonah didn't resist this time when Anubis left him but attacked his aunt and the other Wraith. While they fought, Jonah tried to think of a way to change what would happen. He managed to take down Pakhet's essence in the Underworld, but he still had to stop the events from occurring at his house–or at least, alter them.

Anubis broke the final restrictive sigil and a flood of renewed power surged into Jonah. He pulled himself free of Ruby's magical locks and went through a kind of strange replay as he combated his aunt. He was acting strictly on auto-pilot now.

Eventually, she held out her hand and produced one of the strange, purplish vortices. "Attack!" she shouted to the remaining Phantoms on this side. With that, she leapt through the vortex and disappeared.

Amulet of the Goddess

Once again, the Phantoms vanished instead of attacking him, and the Felines and Grim Hounds bounded away at inhuman speed before fading into the surrounding forest.

Just then, the reptilian Wraith let out a death shriek and Anubis ripped out its ghostly throat. The enemy Wraith exploded into fragments, leaving a battered Anubis behind. The canine eyes met Jonah's, who nodded and promptly disappeared.

Jonah was ready when Kevin, Lynn, Robert, and Wick showed up. He told them, "Aunt Ruby's going for Uncle James and the others."

"A little help this time?" Kevin said to him.

"Yeah, I know: Phase to the street in front of my house. Don't even try the backyard."

Kevin shook his head.

Jonah was about to grab Wick's forearm when he noticed Antwan's cousin was still chained to a pillar. With the sigils gone, she should have gotten her powers back, unless the chains themselves were enchanted. He hadn't paid attention to the girl the last time. Now, he saw a way to do something different.

"Give me your blade," he told Kevin, the plan only now forming in his head. They deliberately left her chained, but if he could free her and convince her to stop the mole, maybe that would be enough to alter the final outcome.

Kevin scowled but handed over a blade. Jonah rushed to the girl and cut her chains with two swipes of the weapon. Like throwing a switch, she leapt to her feet, hands raised and ready to hex.

Jonah held up the blade to protect himself. Wick, Lynn, and Kevin were at his side in an instant, ready to back him up.

"Cool it," Jonah told the girl. "Can you get to the mole?"

She smirked. "I'm not telling you."

"I didn't ask you to. Tell him what Ruby did."

The girl lowered her hands a fraction. The frown on the visible portion of her face told it all. "Why do you want me to do that?"

"Because we both have a problem with my aunt. I'm guessing the mole does too." At the last moment, Jonah remembered someone else who wouldn't have approved of Aunt Ruby's betrayal. "And Deyanira won't like it either. She sent me her Grim Hound, after all."

The girl stared at him for a long time. Too long in Jonah's opinion because they needed to get home. Finally, she nodded. "One day, we'll have you on our side."

With that, she produced a vortex and stepped through.

"Why'd you let her go?" Wick asked, pointing toward the spot where the girl once stood.

"I had to. It's the only way to change things."

Kevin frowned at him. "Change what?"

Jonah met Lynn's gaze, but didn't answer. Instead, he gripped Wick's arm and phased home.

CHAPTER FORTY-EIGHT
HOME FRONT

Before they could even arrive, Ruby's Phantoms had already breached the Alliance's ward around the Hightower house.

"No!" Lynn shouted. She grabbed Jonah's hand and he phased them into the backyard.

To make up for lost time, Jonah reappeared right in front of Uncle James. Lynn raised the enchanted shield to block Ruby's hex. Then she brandished her blades at her aunt. "Stay away from my dad!"

"Yeah!" Robert shouted, joining his sister a second later with his bow and arrow in hand.

Jonah moved back with Kevin as the Alliance adults crowded around the kids to protect them as well as to fight off the dwindling numbers of Phantoms.

Like before, the ghostly knights seemed more interested in keeping Jonah and the others from interfering, and he knew why.

Jonah stayed clear as the familiar events played themselves out again. If the mole appeared, he had to be ready.

Ruby ducked and dodged, appearing at random around the twins, attempting to reach their dad. Robert and Lynn met her either with a blade or a bow.

"Whoa!" Wick said. "Who knew Robert had it in him?"

Ruby scored a hit to Lynn's left arm and followed up with a swipe of her hand. The enchanted shield soared off and landed on the side. Ruby shoved her niece out of the way, causing Robert to falter for a second.

But he recovered, whirling to face Ruby and forcing her to evade once more as he protected his dad. Jonah's insides squirmed. It was right about now that the mole should have appeared to change the course of things. As the seconds ticked by and the traitor still hadn't arrived, Jonah knew his plan had succeeded.

Because he was thinking about that, he failed to notice that Ruby also realized something was off. She pulled away from Robert and turned toward Jonah. That's when Jonah understood how stupid he'd been. Whether or not the mole showed up, Ruby still had every intention of killing him since she couldn't use him. He was not out of danger yet.

As his Death Sense spiked, Jonah dived for the shield and came up with it at the same time his aunt fired. The enchanted shield repelled her attack, but it still managed to stagger him. His swift tactic, however, shocked and distracted her. She was so focused on him that she ignored Robert who bared his teeth and narrowed his eyes. He released his arrow and it flew straight and true, hitting Ruby directly in the chest.

The shock on her face as she clutched the protruding arrow was priceless.

"How dare you shoot me?"

"You're lucky. I was aiming for your version of a heart," Robert spat out.

"Ungrateful..." She never finished her words because she crumbled to the ground.

The remaining Phantoms let out anguished cries. Jonah opened the rip between the realms and quickly dispatched all the Phantoms back to the Underworld.

The frightened looks his friends gave him would have stopped Jonah any other time. But he pushed that aside. He hurried over to Lynn, who, with the help of Robert and her dad, was sitting up and trying to shake off the negative effects of Ruby's hex.

Jonah shifted his attention to his aunt. Pressing his hand against her forehead, he summoned his Reaper power and felt it surging through him as the appropriate words popped into his head. "You are released from your bond. Come out!" he commanded.

His voice shook the ground, startling everyone. The goddess essence obeyed and withdrew from his aunt. Even in her pain, Ruby struggled and

Amulet of the Goddess

her grasping hands strained to hold onto the essence, as if she wanted to draw it back into her body.

The woman's feeble attempts disgusted Jonah. In the end, however, she was too weak and limply slumped to the ground, unconscious.

The goddess essence, now free of his aunt's evil influence, transformed back into its natural form: A regal female with large, expressive, dark eyes. Judging from the muttered comments he heard around him, Jonah suspected everyone else could also see her true form.

The goddess peered into his face, looking deeply into his soul. "Well played, Deliverer."

Her gaze shifted to something over his shoulder and she bowed.

Jonah turned to find the Egyptian Wraith floating there. His fight with the reptilian Wraith left his ghostly garments ripped. But he returned the nod with a regal bow of his own.

The women warriors soon joined the entire gathering and ministered to their goddess.

Jonah watched, relieved at the demonstrative change in Pakhet's demeanor. The Egyptian Wraith must have sensed his thoughts because the being stepped closer and spoke to him in a quiet voice.

You wonder at her change, young one?

"Yeah," Jonah admitted. "I mean, you told me every spirit of power has a negative and positive aspect."

The Wraith blinked in surprise. *Yes, that's correct.*

"And the Grim Reaper and the Wraith King brought out her negative aspect."

Again, correct. He gestured at Ruby. *Your aunt was a willing vessel to them. But once you freed Pakhet...*

"She reverted back." Jonah's eyes widened.

The goddess isn't just the huntress. She also bestows fertility, as well as other kind blessings. He peered at Jonah. *Power is always neutral. It's how you use it, whether for good or evil, that reveals what resides in your own heart. Understand?*

Jonah did now. He had inadvertently allowed his anger over Latrell's suicide to turn him into a bully. He winced at the memory and checked to make sure Marcus wasn't listening. "Have you been talking to my godfather?" Jonah grinned at the Wraith's perplexed look.

Pakhet's form began to glow, drawing their attention. "Come, sisters." She raised her arms and, along with her warrior women, disappeared in a flash of light.

After a stunned moment of silence, Marcus gestured to Rex. "Get Ruby to the healer. Fast."

Rex complied, picking up Aunt Ruby's limp body and phasing away.

"Don't help her!" Robert screamed. His voice sounded raw with anger.

Symon Trueblood gripped his arm. "You don't mean that, Robert. She's your aunt and you won't want her death on your conscience."

Robert stared at the mage in defiance.

"He's right," Jonah agreed, entering the argument. "The Wraith inside her drove her crazy. It was only following orders to do it. I saw it all in a dream-walk."

"Jonah, she was already evil," Lynn countered. She was on her feet but a little unsteady. Rico held on to her.

"I know that, but…" Jonah couldn't believe he was defending his aunt, the woman who had tortured him seven years ago and tried to kill him just now.

He was glad when Uncle James stepped forward. "Lynn," he said, placing his hands on her shoulders, "no one can be pure evil and good at the same time."

"It's the Grim Reaper's fault." Jonah's voice had risen. "He's behind all of this."

His uncle nodded and pulled Robert and Lynn into a tight hug. Jonah hesitated until Uncle James grabbed his arm and pulled him into the hug too.

"Thank God you're all right," he said in a voice choked with emotion.

When he released them, Lynn nodded to her father with a knowing look on her face. "This is why you talked Mom into visiting her friend in Savannah."

Amulet of the Goddess **1015**

Uncle James smiled. "You're not the only one with uncanny ability." His smile faltered when he met Symon's gaze. Lynn whispered something to her dad. He nodded before walking over and offering to shake the mage's hand. "Thank you for protecting my family."

Symon grinned. "That's just part of the job."

Jonah whispered to Lynn, "What did you say to him?"

"It's a secret." She glanced sideways at him. "I knew you'd fix things."

Jonah gaped at his cousin. "You knew?"

Lynn refused to answer. Instead, she held out a hand to Rico and he came over and wrapped his arms around her.

Jonah realized his cousin had seen everything that night she held his hands. That's why she got so spooked. Yet, she still trusted him to figure it out. That thought sobered him.

While Jonah slowly registered the idea, the other kids rushed forward to surround them. Tamara was already hugging Wick and talking in hushed, urgent tones with him.

Anthony patted Robert on the back, congratulating him, while Danita rushed to Lynn's side. "That was so amazing! I never saw anything like that." She took the shield and turned it over in her hands.

Mike tapped Jonah's shoulder and leaned close. "I told you."

Jonah whispered to his friend, "You told me what?"

In answer, Mike nodded at Danita, Anthony, Rico, and Tamara.

Jonah noted the other kids revealed their nervousness by a slight shakiness to their voices, or the not-so-hidden trembling of their hands. But they were excited rather than terrified.

He got it. Mike insisted the other kids joined his Tolerance Club because they liked or admired him. And Rico already knew Lynn had abilities. No doubt the others had followed Rico here, into the danger, instead of running home.

"Maybe," Mike whispered. "It's time for the Mount Vernon Social Club to expand its membership."

By now, Rico had already extricated Lynn from the Danita fan club and they walked a little way off, leaving Wick to answer questions.

Robert watched his sister walk away, smirked, and said, "I bet Rico's trying to talk Lynn into wearing one of those warriors' outfits next Halloween."

Jonah would have laughed if not for Uncle James looming behind them, frowning. "That's not gonna happen. Your mom would kill all of us." He clapped Robert on the shoulder. "Not bad with the bow and arrow."

"Thanks." Robert grinned as he clutched the bow.

Uncle James tapped his son's right fist. "Do I want to know how you healed so fast?"

"Not really," Robert said.

"Well, in that case, I think you should wear the brace a little longer." Uncle James raised his hand to stop Robert from objecting. "At least two more weeks. We don't want people asking questions."

"But that'll suck!"

Uncle James squared his shoulders, looking stern.

Robert's shoulders slumped. "Yes, sir."

Jonah was about to tell his cousin of all the times his own mom made him wear bandages long after his bumps and cuts had healed. The intense curiosity of the other kids forced Jonah to reconsider mentioning that aspect of his abilities.

Robert must have sensed his thoughts because he whispered, "The guy in black fixed my hand so I could help out."

Jonah's eyes widened when he heard that. Death said he had helped, but at the time, Jonah had no clue what the strange being might have done. That only reminded Jonah of his oath to Death, something he didn't want to think about at the moment.

"What are they doing?" Danita asked, pointing at the Trueblood siblings.

The mages walked in a circle around the scene, waving their hands all around. For a moment, their spells undulated in the air, moving away from them and toward the surrounding neighboring houses.

"We're strengthening the deflection charms to keep prying eyes away," Symon explained after joining the group. "They should last until we clean up this mess."

Amulet of the Goddess

"Still, I think we should move inside," Marcus suggested, motioning everyone toward the house.

Kevin and Jonah stood back, observing the activity.

Jonah wondered what would happen to his friends. "Memory charms?"

Kevin shrugged. "Most likely, unless they agree not to talk."

Even though Jonah had argued for Danita being given a chance, he never thought about this aspect of it. "Would the Alliance trust them?"

"They'd have to take an oath just in–" Kevin jerked and swore under his breath because the Grim Hound trotted over and licked his hand.

Jonah laughed and petted the beast. It nuzzled against him. "Thanks for protecting my friends and family." The Grim Hound bobbed its head. Then it looked away as if someone called it. Jonah understood. "You're gonna report to her, aren't you?" Again, it bobbed its head and made a strange, growling sound. This close, Jonah could feel and hear the subtle rhythm, and nature of the growl. It was a language.

He closed his eyes as the Grim Hound repeated the modulated growl. The vibrations stimulated his mind and slowly formed a mental image. In a moment of clarity, Jonah extended his hand and opened the rip to the Underworld.

The Grim Hound took a playful nip at his hand before it turned and leapt through the opening.

*

Marcus, Eleanor, and Symon had all the young people gathered together in the family room. The Guard Captain was the only one of his team to enter the house and he took up serious space. Uncle James provided people with something to drink, but everyone was restless and no one seemed thirsty.

Lynn and Robert excused themselves and headed to their rooms to change. Wick had yanked off his hat and wig before he sat with Tamara, who looked intensely interested in what Marcus would say.

Danita and Anthony clung to each other, looking scared and uncertain despite Mike whispering reassurances to them.

Rico leaned against the mantel, arms crossed and trying to look brave, but not succeeding.

Jonah stood in the kitchen because whenever someone looked at him, he saw the questions in their gaze. He thought Robert and Lynn had the right idea and headed for his own room.

Marcus stopped Jonah in the hallway and whispered, "Trueblood told me of your impassioned plea for a change of policy. So we'll talk to each person and offer them an option." He searched Jonah's expression. "That is what you wanted?"

"Yeah, it is. Thank you."

"You're welcome." Marcus straightened and scanned the quiet crowd of kids waiting for him. "Are you going to stay?"

Jonah glanced at his dirty, long coat. "No." While Marcus stepped back into the den to begin his comments, Jonah retreated to his room. He was about to close the door when Kevin slipped inside and closed it for him.

He had already taken off his long coat so he waited for Jonah to slip out of his own. Then Kevin wrapped his arms around Jonah's waist and hugged him for a long time, rocking him back and forth. They listened to the low voices coming from the den and didn't care at the moment.

Jonah welcomed the embrace, settling into it, along with his general sense of safety and closeness whenever he was with Kevin. Without warning, he began to shake as he came to terms with everything they managed to accomplish. It seemed impossible, but they were all still here and safe, for now.

Kevin rubbed Jonah's arms until he stopped shaking. The Fallen Reaper's higher body temperature enveloped Jonah, and he loved it. While they embraced, Kevin used his enhanced hearing to relay what Marcus said to the others. The kids weren't told everything, just enough for them to decide which way they should go.

Jonah knew there would be a lot of questions in the coming days if his friends chose the oath and not the Memory Charm. After a long moment, Jonah leaned back and glanced into Kevin's eyes. The older boy looked down before brushing his lips against Jonah's. Just as they kissed, a knock came at the bedroom door. They released each other, though neither wanted to do so.

"Yeah?" Jonah called out.

Amulet of the Goddess

Mike opened the door and peeked inside the room. Jonah saw someone moving past his buddy in the background and heard the sounds of people leaving the house.

"Sorry," Mike said as he closed the door behind him. "I didn't mean to interrupt."

Kevin waved off the apology. "I guess Marcus is finished?"

Mike nodded and his eyes sparkled with excitement. "Everyone's gonna take an oath instead of the Memory Charm."

Jonah pumped his hand in the air.

"Then I'll have to go." Kevin released a long breath. "We have a lot of cleanup work to finish before the morning." He gave Jonah a quick hug before leaving the room.

Mike looked stricken. "I'm really sorry." He sat on the edge of Jonah's bed.

"It's cool," Jonah assured him, pulling off his sweaty shirt. "What's up?"

"Two things. Are you gonna ask Danita and the others to join the club?"

The question caught Jonah off guard. "Well, not tonight."

"I know that. But they'll have a lot of questions for you."

"We'll deal with that later." Mike gave him a frosty look and Jonah added, "I promise," before he could stop himself. Right on cue, goosebumps raced up his arm. "Dang it."

Mike grinned while his eyes flashed, indicating a sealed promise. "That takes care of that."

Jonah eyed his friend, wondering if Mike had bluffed him into making the promise. "What's number two?" he asked.

"Oh, I wanted to know if I could sleep over here tonight."

Jonah paused after tossing his shirt in his dirty clothes bin. "Why? You afraid to stay at home alone?"

"No." Mike frowned. "All the action's here."

Jonah couldn't disagree with that. And it would be nice for a sleepover. "Yeah." He took a fresh shirt out of his drawer and pulled it on. "What about your parents?"

"I called them." Mike glanced at the door. "After okaying it with your uncle, they agreed. My mom's bringing over some clothes and other stuff for me."

The front doorbell rang right on cue. Jonah stepped out of his room just as Uncle James answered. After talking with Mike's mom, he closed the door and held up a small gym bag. "This is for Mike."

Mike ducked into the hallway and took the bag. "Thanks."

Uncle James proceeded into the family room and started picking up cups and stacking them in the dishwasher. He noticed Jonah standing at the entrance. "You and Mike okay?"

"Yes, sir."

"Well, if you use any dishes, put them in the dishwasher when you're done. I'll run the load in the morning." With that, he patted Jonah on the shoulder and headed off to his own room.

Jonah glanced at Robert and Lynn's closed doors and decided they must have turned in for the night. He fetched two juices for himself and Mike, who was stretched out on the bed and patting the empty space beside him.

Jonah obliged. They were both skinny but still pressed tightly together on the small bed.

Mike poked him in the side. "You need a bigger bed. Aren't you afraid Kevin will tumble off?"

Jonah flashed him a scandalized expression and shoved him back. But they settled down, side-by-side. Jonah turned on some music to help cover their voices and Mike rested his head on Jonah's shoulder as they talked about everything.

It was wonderful for Jonah, talking with his best friend again. Sometime later, Mike went silent before Jonah heard his buddy's soft snore. He slumped down into a more comfortable position, being careful not to awaken Mike.

After propping up a pillow, he leaned back and closed his eyes, falling quickly into a sound and dreamless sleep.

Amulet of the Goddess

CHAPTER FORTY-NINE
THE DARK AVENGER RIDES AGAIN

Jonah and his cousins didn't have the luxury of sleeping in late the next day because of school. He at least got to enjoy the change of pace with Mike sitting at the kitchen table, eating breakfast and talking with them.

Once at school, Jonah was surprisingly alert as he and Mike walked through the halls. The activity of ninth grade seemed way too normal compared to what they had gone through the night before. Jonah, however, welcomed the normal and wanted to put some distance between himself and all the things he had discovered. He would never forget a bit of it, but that didn't mean he had to dwell on them either.

Perhaps Mike thought the same thing because he distracted Jonah by doing the Human Lie Detector gag again. This time, Jonah actually had fun. It also helped that the person in front of him today was telling the truth, a rare but welcomed change. There had been enough lies, secrets, and half-truths to last him a lifetime.

"That went well," Mike said as he threw away their lunch trays and gathered his things.

"Yeah, it did."

Mike paused, regarding him. "You aren't mad at me about the Human Lie Detector?"

"Nope. It took my mind off what happened."

Mike stopped fidgeting with his book bag and sat down. "Jonah, do you remember all those memories from the… Wraith?" Mike glanced around, but no one paid any attention to them.

"Yeah, I do."

"That's horrible."

Jonah shrugged. "Yes and no. Since they weren't my memories, I can treat them like scary movies I've seen. I remember them, sure, but they don't bother me as much. You know what I mean?"

Mike frowned. "I guess so. But what about your aunt and what she did seven years ago?"

"At least, now I know what happened. That's a good thing. I don't have to wonder about it anymore." He smiled at his buddy and gathered his book bag. "Seriously. It's cool." Jonah leaned closer and whispered, "My Reaper side can handle a lot."

He laughed at Mike's expression as they walked to the next class.

*

Jonah and Mike had their regular monitor duty that afternoon. Even before they arrived on post, they heard the laughter and catcalls. Above it all, Jonah recognized Brandon's snide voice.

They rounded the corner and found the boy and a few of his buddies. In the center of the group was a girl. Jonah recognized her as Heather, someone who once considered joining his club.

Mike also recognized her and let out a grunt of disbelief. He marched up to the boys just as Brandon pushed Heather.

"She's kissed more girls than you, Wayne," the bully taunted while tweaking Heather's long, single black braid.

Heather's eyes narrowed in anger as she clutched her books to her chest, trying to break through the hostile ring. Mike came to her rescue and shoved his way between the bigger boys, acting braver than Jonah expected.

"Back off, jerks."

Jonah joined him. "That's right."

"We were just talking, weren't we, Heather?" Brandon winked at the girl.

Jonah shoved one of the guys out of the way so Heather could leave. She sniffled as she hurried down the hall and out of sight.

Amulet of the Goddess

Brandon and his buddies sneered at her.

Mike faced Brandon. "You know bullying isn't allowed."

"Whatever. Come on, guys," Brandon said. He looked straight at Jonah and mimed smoking a cigarette before walking off.

Mike huffed. "He's getting worse."

"I know," Jonah said, watching Brandon swagger down the hallway with his friends. "Hey, I'll catch up with you after class."

Mike gave him a searching look before shrugging as he left. Jonah waited a second and then turned in the opposite direction. If he hurried, he could still make it.

He burst into the nearest bathroom, aiming for the farthest stall, slamming the door, and locking it. Jonah took a deep breath and thought about the shaded spot next to his backyard shed. In a second, he'd left the bathroom stall behind and was standing beside the tree in his relatives' backyard.

Jonah hustled into the house and went into his bedroom, where he threw open the closet doors. His heart pounded in his chest from all the apprehension. He had already promised not to do the vigilante thing again. But as he pulled out the paper shopping bag with the mask, hoodie, and black pants inside, he suddenly didn't care if he had to spend another week in Marcus's magical wristbands.

After making sure everything was still inside, Jonah returned to the secluded spot beside the shed outside. He huddled in the shadow of the tree, thought about the bathroom stall, and phased.

When he burst out of the confined space seconds later, he startled a boy who hadn't been in the bathroom when he left.

"What the… " the boy's eyes widened. "I swear no one was in here."

Jonah wondered if he'd caught the boy smoking or doing something else that was forbidden. He glanced back at the stall he exited. "You were peeking in the stalls?"

The boy's face darkened with embarrassment. "No!" He hurried from the bathroom.

Jonah grinned until he realized he'd be late to class himself. He could endure the detention because there was something he needed to finish for Latrell as well as himself.

*

Coming up with an excuse to dodge a suspicious Mike after class wasn't easy. So Jonah told him what he had planned. Mike's light complexion darkened in anger.

"You wanted to know," Jonah reminded him. "Brandon deserves it anyway."

"What about your godfather?"

"I'll be more careful this time." Jonah raised his eyebrows, praying Mike would agree.

"Fine," Mike huffed. After a moment, he nodded and grinned. "Just don't get caught."

With that out of the way, Jonah ducked into a bathroom and changed his clothes. He kept the mask hidden until he reached the out-of-the-way staircase that led to the roof access door. He ascended halfway up before pulling the Komainu mask over his face and tugging the hoodie's top over his head.

That done, he climbed up the rest of the steps to the storage area. Jonah didn't have to wait long for Brandon and his buddies to enter. Whatever Brandon was saying to his friends died in his throat as soon as he noticed Jonah, whose face was hidden behind his mask.

The shock on the bully's face was worth all the risk. Brandon's buddies didn't notice his reaction at first because they were too busy moving around Jonah from either side to block his retreat.

Wayne was the first to realize that Brandon wasn't acting normal. "Hey, what's wrong? You look like you've seen a ghost."

Brandon regained some of his snide arrogance. "What do you want? Halloween's over."

Jonah pointed at the boy, whose face instantly drained of color.

"Brandon?" Wayne's voice betrayed his nervousness.

That seemed to snap Brandon out of his fear, and he motioned to Jonah. "Hold him."

Amulet of the Goddess

Jonah expected that. As Wayne and the other boy closed in, reaching for him, Jonah stepped backward and phased. Wayne and the other boy grabbed empty air while Jonah's micro-phase put him about two feet behind the boys' grasping hands.

They couldn't stop their forward momentum and tumbled into each other, letting out surprised grunts. Wayne recovered first and took a swing. Jonah blocked it at the same time he sensed the second boy coming from behind. He phased and reappeared behind that boy in a crouch.

With a sweep of his leg, Jonah caught the boy by his ankle, causing him to lose balance and fall into Wayne. Both went down in a wild flurry of arms and legs. Jonah sprang to his feet and charged at Brandon. The bully let out a high-pitched scream but, despite his fear, Brandon stood his ground.

When Jonah came close enough, Brandon swung at him. Jonah blocked the first punch and used another micro-phase to dodge the second attack. He appeared behind Brandon and slapped the boy across the back of the head.

Brandon howled in frustration and turned, already swinging. Jonah ducked, phased again, and smacked Brandon on the head with the flat of his hand again. When Brandon whirled to face him, Jonah backed away.

Come on, run at me!

Brandon snarled and rushed forward, just as Jonah predicted. At the last second, he phased, allowing Brandon to plow into the metal shelves behind him. He heard a satisfying crack! followed by Brandon's muffled howl of pain. The boy fell backward onto the ground, blood seeping between the fingers he used to cover his nose.

Jonah resisted the urge to gloat or say anything at all.

"Brandon!" Wayne shouted as he charged at Jonah, who grabbed the boy and twisted him around. A surge of power augmented Jonah's strength as he moved. Wayne let out a startled yelp before his feet left the ground.

Jonah hurled the boy into his friend and both subsequently smashed into a stack of old monitor boxes. The boys slumped to the ground, dazed.

Brandon shrank away from Jonah, mumbling beneath the hand that still clutched his bloody nose. Jonah slipped behind the bully, pulling him to his feet, and phased, taking Brandon along.

*

Jonah told Mike everything as they walked to their bikes after school. And to his relief, Mike laughed before catching himself.

"You shouldn't have done that."

Jonah pulled a skeptical expression. "Really? You gonna tell on me?"

"Of course not."

Jonah unlocked his bike and hitched up his book bag. "Good. I'd hate to have to visit you one night in the mask." He faked a scowl at Mike.

"Don't try it," Mike replied, unconcerned. "I'm fantastic at opening portals. I'd hate to send you somewhere too strange."

Jonah shoved him. "You were freakin' cool!"

They set off for the Teen Center and Mike explained how he came up with the defensive move. The boys were still talking when they reached the door to the attic clubhouse where they found a wrapped package right outside.

"It has your name on it," Mike pointed out.

Jonah plucked the package off the ground. It was heavy and clearly held a long box inside. He took it up into the attic space before opening it. Inside were a pair of Egyptian swords.

"Wow," Mike gushed, running his hands along the dark, aged metal. "These are real."

"They are, and I bet they belonged to the Egyptian Wraith."

Mike gaped at him. "Why would he give them to you?"

Because I'm connected to them, the Wraith replied. He silently appeared behind them in the clubhouse area of the attic. And Latrell was with him, looking calm.

The adult Wraith bowed. *You can call on me, but if you take my swords, I can appear without you having to do that.*

Jonah walked over, Mike trailing behind him. "But why give them to me?" Even as he asked it, Jonah had the feeling the Wraith was going away. "What do you want me to do?"

Open the doorway to the Underworld. We'll both go through.

Amulet of the Goddess **1027**

"No," Jonah protested. "You'll go to the farthest reaches of the place if I do that."

It's okay, Latrell answered. *He's gonna show me how to avoid going mad.*

"That's good, Latrell, but why can't he just take you over? He can go back and forth at will. Can't you?"

Only at certain times, the Egyptian Wraith explained. *I can't take another spirit with me and I want to help the boy.*

"Wait," Mike spoke up. "There's another option."

"You mean your defensive move? Won't that send them somewhere weird?" Jonah asked.

"I don't mean that way, Jonah." Mike pulled out his Seeker's compass. "I can open a portal to the Underworld and send you to one of the seven locations on the triptych."

The Egyptian Wraith gave him an impressed look. *You would do that for us?*

"I'm the Pathmaker, and Jonah's my Deliverer." Mike's voice was strong and sure. "And you helped us. I'm only returning the favor."

"We can't just pop into the Deliverer's cave, can we?" Jonah asked. He liked the idea but could they get away with it? "Aren't there any guards?"

"Jonah! I'm the Seeker. I have a special pass to use the portal whenever I want." His sureness wilted. "I'll just tell them I'm doing research for Alliance HQ."

Jonah's doubts faded as the idea took hold. "Okay. Let's do it." He turned to the Egyptian Wraith as Mike called up the Deliverer's cave code on the compass. "See you there?"

Yes. The Wraith nodded before he and Latrell disappeared.

Jonah remembered to grab the box and take it with him. Here he was, about to travel halfway around the world in the blink of an eye to help two spirits pass into the Underworld. *So much for a normal life*, he mused as Mike activated the compass.

CHAPTER FIFTY
DELIVERER NEXT TIME

Over the course of the week, Danita finished her series on the black cat, still advocating her insistence it was all superstition. Jonah found her position odd considering she'd made an oath with the Alliance and knew the supernatural existed. It was Mike who pointed out Danita was only denying it as a cover so people wouldn't notice her sudden change in attitude.

Jonah doubted it were that simple, but he didn't argue. Even weirder still, none of his friends asked him any questions. They reacted to him just the same, or tried to. Jonah also noticed a slight change in Anthony's demeanor: He was less cocky.

Local news reported a series of strange yet coordinated acts of violence on Halloween night. The common consensus was that a small group of individuals organized the violence using social media with the goal of disrupting and causing mayhem. Jonah knew the Alliance was pushing that narrative to obscure the real events.

When Marcus arrived at the Hightowers' house early Friday evening, Jonah feared his godfather had already found out about their unauthorized visit to the Deliverer's cave.

After talking with Uncle James and Aunt Imma, who had recently returned from Savannah, he stopped by Jonah's room and knocked on the door. "May I come in?"

Jonah was lounging on his bed, reading a book for his book club, and waiting for this moment. He set the book aside and leaned against his headboard. "Sure."

Amulet of the Goddess

His godfather wore suit pants, a medium blue dress shirt, and a dark tie, like he just phased down after a day at work in the Alliance law offices.

"How are you?" Marcus asked, entering the room and resting an elbow on the dresser top. He must have seen Jonah's grimace because he laughed. "I realize everyone keeps asking you that question."

"Yeah, they do. But I'm fine. I found out my parents tried to protect me, but I'm stronger than everyone thinks, right?"

Marcus nodded. "You are. Perhaps keeping you away from the supernatural world wasn't the best thing to do, but you can't fault your parents for that."

"I don't." Jonah unclenched his hands now that his godfather hadn't mentioned the trip to the Deliverer's cave. Still trying to avoid it, he said something else. "What about the amulet?"

"It's safely tucked away at HQ. We've made repairs to the Centre Pointe columns, now that we understand its true significance."

"Do you know who built it?"

Marcus shook his head. "I hear Mike is looking into it with a few of our best historians."

Jonah nodded. He expected Mike to work for the Alliance as a lead historian one day. He already had access to more than Jonah did. But thinking about his buddy just now reminded Jonah of his other friends. "Danita and the others took oaths, but how does that work with them? They aren't even part supernatural."

"No, they aren't, but the oath is still binding. Of course, we explained what would happen if they ever tried to violate it."

That interested Jonah, but he wondered if his godfather would answer when he asked, "What would happen?"

Marcus shrugged. "Nothing bad. They would probably just get tongue-tied."

Jonah gaped at his godfather, trying to imagine how that would play out. *Was he being literal?*

His godfather narrowed his eyes. "What's really bothering you?"

Jonah should have known he couldn't hide his real concern. Ever since he recovered his memories, one thing remained at the forefront of his thoughts, even though he incessantly tried to avoid it. *Paris.*

"I saw a memory," Jonah began. "One that Omar thought a different Memory Charmer hid."

Marcus glanced out the open bedroom door. Jonah heard the TV along with his aunt and uncle, who were talking in the kitchen.

But Marcus lowered his voice anyway. "What was it?"

"When I was five, I had a dream-walk and saw you and my dad in Paris."

Marcus's face went slack.

"I saw Death too," Jonah continued. "He came into the restaurant and told my dad he would die. He talked about the way my dad fell and said he had to stick to their agreement about me. What did he mean? You never told me the whole story." Jonah paused to take a breath and calm down.

Marcus frowned. "I'm sorry, Jonah. The time never seemed right to explain everything."

"My parents knew they would die. Death said he gave them thirteen years to spend with me."

True pain and regret seemed to radiate off Jonah's godfather. "Yes, they did, but he did not say how or when. Well, perhaps your mother knew. That's why they ran on their own the night they died. We would have stayed with them and, well, possibly also died in an attempt to save them. Isaiah and Janice would never have allowed that."

Jonah experienced a fresh wave of pain and revelation that the dreams provided. It was a lot to take in, and he imagined it would require some time to sort out. Mike often suggested he write everything down. That way, he wouldn't have to worry about remembering and could go back later.

It was a good idea, Jonah eventually decided. And that reminded him of the other thing Mike suggested. Jonah hopped off his bed and unzipped the small pocket on his backpack. He pulled out a thumb drive and held it out to Marcus.

His godfather took it with a puzzled expression. "What's this?"

"My mission report. Mike thinks I should start writing them down." He felt a little guilty because he didn't mention his glimpse into the future in

Amulet of the Goddess **1031**

the final report. Except for telling Mike, Jonah decided not to reveal that aspect of the Underworld experience. Besides, it involved Lynn, and she already made it crystal clear she wasn't ready to have people gawking at her.

"That's very astute. This will help," Marcus said as he slipped the drive in a pocket. "I'll read it when I get back to my office."

Jonah hesitated to mention the last thing that bothered him. Of course, his godfather seemed to sense that. Before he could ask, Jonah blurted out, "There's something else I heard when my mom and Omar were talking after they saved me."

A serious expression settled on his godfather's face but he waited, listening.

"Omar insisted my mom tell my dad what happened, and he mentioned my dad's brother and–" Jonah paused when he caught the slight flinch in his godfather's eye, and he hopped off the bed. "You said my dad's family died a long time ago and he was also a Reaper for a long time. I looked it up. Omar wasn't even born when my dad was a mortal. So how could he know about my dad's mortal brother?"

"Jonah..." Marcus moved to the window.

Jonah suspected his godfather wanted to put more space between them. That thought spurred him on. "Did he tell Omar and you about his brother?" Jonah pressed. "Why?"

"Many members of your father's family died on that tragic day." Marcus steepled his fingers, staring at them as if coming to a decision. Finally, he met Jonah's eager gaze. "Your father wasn't the only one to become one of the Undead and eventually, a Fallen One."

Jonah dropped onto the bed, staring at his godfather in skeptical astonishment. "What? Where? I have an uncle out there?"

Marcus raised his hands. "Yes, you do, but–"

"I want to meet him."

"All in good time."

Jonah was finding it hard to get his head around this. He felt betrayed by Marcus. "Why didn't you tell me?"

"Your father and his brother never agreed on anything, including your birth. He had nothing to do with your life, which was strictly his own choice."

"He never wanted to see me?" When Marcus reluctantly nodded, Jonah's growing interest in this man waned. "Is he also part of the Alliance?"

"Yes, and Jonah, I'll tell you about him, but not today." When Jonah crossed his arms and frowned, Marcus added, "I'll reach out to your uncle and see if he wants to meet you. Okay?"

Jonah nodded. This was so busted. The more he thought about a man who never came forward, especially after his brother and sister-in-law died, the more Jonah decided he didn't want to meet him. "Don't even bother."

"You're angry now, and you have the right to be. Once I contact him, we can decide then." Marcus began kneading the back of his neck, a sure sign of agitation with the subject. "This leads into my next topic. The time is coming when the things your parents and I did to protect you must end."

"You mean protecting me from the bad guys?" Jonah snapped, still visibly angry. "They've been coming around anyway."

"I don't mean that. But even there, you're protected in ways you don't appreciate." Marcus took a deep breath. "No, I'm talking about the work and politics of the Alliance itself."

"The Egyptian Wraith told me I was a big weapon."

Marcus winced. "That was a bit much, but you do have powers. Soon, you'll take your place in the Alliance's mission." Marcus peered into Jonah's eyes. "I'm uneasy over your familiarity with this Wraith. They can be very dangerous."

"Not him. He's helped me all along by telling me about the potions. He also fought with us in the Underworld. And…" Jonah swallowed. "He's my ancestor. That's why he helped me," Jonah added as he realized something else. "That's also why he worked with Deyanira at first, just to get close to me."

Marcus blinked in surprise. "Isaiah never mentioned…"

"Maybe my dad didn't know. Like you said, I'm different." The statement didn't bother Jonah anymore. And he wondered if that could have been the reason his uncle stayed away. *He didn't want me born.*

Amulet of the Goddess

"Your parents wanted you to be a normal kid before that burden fell on you. I can support their point of view. I've tried to keep it that way, but we all knew it would come to an end eventually."

"What are you saying?"

"I think you've reached the turning point. Albrecht told me your block is gone."

Jonah recalled the experience in the Underworld. "My Reaper side could handle it all."

"That's remarkable, and only proves my point. You're a powerful young man."

A smile tweaked the corners of Jonah's mouth. "So, are you shipping me off to the Alliance army?"

Marcus laughed but it was relaxed. "No, Jonah. Nothing like that. You've proven you can do amazing things. People will want you to do more in the near future. Be prepared."

"Oh," Jonah muttered, considering his godfather's comment. He bet it had something to do with Alastor and the Hardliners. Everyone wanted to use him, it seemed. Jonah ignored those thoughts. They would only open up the memories and conversations with the helpful Wraith and remind him of his promise to Death. That scared him more than anything else.

He caught his godfather scanning him with a partial Reaper stare. Jonah didn't want to go there, not right now. He fully intended to keep his promise with Death, but he had no plans to tell anyone about it, not even Mike or his cousins. Well, maybe he could tell Kevin.

Marcus shifted and Jonah switched to something else. "Will you tell me about my dad's fall?" he asked.

"Why don't you come up to the office one Saturday? I'll tell you everything I discovered. Bring your cousins and we can show them around Washington. Okay?"

Jonah nodded, liking the idea. They could go during the coming winter break.

Marcus came over, gripped Jonah's shoulder, and held on, applying a little pressure. "By the way," he began, "you don't know anything about young Brandon being found on the rooftop of the school, do you?"

Jonah was ready for this. He had plenty of practice calling up feelings of innocence and denial. He did that now, hoping he could fool his godfather. But Marcus surprised him and didn't resort to a Reaper stare.

Jonah let out a breath. "No."

"Really? A custodian discovered the boy, screaming his head off atop one of the solar collectors on the high school's roof. No one could figure out how he managed to get up there."

Jonah didn't squirm because it suddenly occurred to him that he could be genuinely happy. After all, Brandon had tried to bully someone else and finally paid for it. He smirked, thinking about that. "What did Brandon say?"

"He claims Latrell's ghost grabbed him and put him up there." Marcus shook his head. "His parents are furious because a picture of the helpless young man has already gone viral." Marcus paused, giving Jonah a questioning look.

"Yeah, that means it's all over the internet," Jonah explained.

"Well, they threatened to sue and the administration fought back, saying that given Brandon's antics, it was more likely a prank by him and his buddies that backfired." Marcus glanced around the room. "We never took that mask that Kevin said you wore. Do you still have it?"

Jonah gulped. Not seeing any way out of this, he fetched the mask from the closet. Marcus held out his hand.

"Brandon's evil," Jonah said, handing over the mask. "Me and Mike caught him bullying someone else. He—"

"I understand." Marcus turned the mask over in his hands. Jonah wondered if his godfather planned to put him in the null-bands again. Instead, Marcus gave him a tired smile. "We asked you to stand up to evil. Still, you're pretty young."

Jonah stared at his godfather in disbelief. "So, you're not mad?"

"After all that you've experienced, I believe that if you had done this to young Brandon, and I'm not saying you did, you would have only done it out of concern for others and not as a way to show off your powers. That makes a huge difference."

"So, the wristbands again?"

Amulet of the Goddess **1035**

"Why? You didn't confess to going after Brandon. That being said, something else could be appropriate at this point."

Jonah's stomach clinched. What would his godfather want this time? Something worse than the null-cuffs? He steeled himself for the bad news as his godfather peered at him.

"I decided," Marcus began, "a promise from you would help me rest at night."

Jonah gulped, relieved. "Seriously?" Then the complications occurred to him. What if Brandon got out of hand again, or one of his other buddies?

Perhaps Marcus could sense his conflicting emotions because he lifted an eyebrow. "I still have the wristbands."

"Okay," Jonah blurted out.

Marcus extended his hand.

After hesitating, Jonah grasped it. When Marcus arched a skeptical eyebrow, Jonah said, "I promise I won't do any more vigilante stuff."

Given his recent experience with promises, Jonah prepared himself for the physical reaction. A sharp prickle had already raced up his arm and settled in his chest. For a second, he thought he saw curly, thin lines appearing on his and his godfather's hands, almost like writing.

Did this happen every time he made a promise? Before he could read the letters, the writing disappeared in a muted flash.

Marcus nodded and released the grip with a satisfied look on his face. He returned the mask and patted Jonah on the shoulder for real this time. "Take care."

After his godfather left, Jonah leaned against his headboard, thinking for once in his life, he was okay with that promise. He did what he had to do. And as far as talking about his father, he was also okay with waiting. Jonah wasn't sure he wanted to go into his dad's history at the moment. He also found it interesting that he didn't want to meet his uncle, either.

What he needed now was a rest. The mundane, ordinary everyday teen stuff to worry about would give him a much-needed break. He could be the Deliverer some other day.

*

That evening, Lynn and Robert crowded into his room after dinner. Jonah prepared to tell them everything, including news of a long-lost uncle, when he caught the expressions on their faces. "What's up?"

Robert glanced at Lynn before answering. "Uncle Amos called our dad about Aunt Ruby."

Jonah gulped and decided it would only be polite to ask. "How is she?"

"She's back in Milledgeville," Lynn said. "Our uncle hopes one day she'll be well enough to come home." Lynn frowned, like that was the last thing she wanted.

"I guess Uncle Amos can't know about what happened, huh?"

"No," Lynn agreed, surprising Jonah when she smiled. "There's one good thing. Dad and Uncle Amos were considering celebrating Christmas together this year. That way, you can meet the rest of your cousins."

Robert brightened. "I haven't seen my cousin, Stan, in a long time."

Jonah settled back, listening to his cousins talking about his other cousins. Lynn apparently wanted to attend the same college as Stan. Jonah smiled, and the tension began to leave his body. It was like a dark cloud had lifted now that their Aunt Ruby was no longer on the loose.

He eventually told them about Marcus's comments and, honoring his promise to be open, he told them exactly what he did to Brandon and why. Robert and Lynn high-fived him.

"Good for you!" Lynn said.

The front door closed and a second later, Uncle James peeked inside Jonah's door. He held up a tub of gourmet ice cream. "Who wants some?"

Robert and Lynn raced for the door, leaving Jonah alone. He hopped off his bed and paused when he noted the Ankh of Life bookstore picture lying on his desktop. *Why did I leave it out?* The answer was obvious.

The picture represented his mom and all the adventures she, Omar, and Trueblood had undertaken. That place was a connection to her. Making a sudden decision, he plucked the picture off the desktop, opened his mom's lockbox, and slid it into his mom's picture album, instead of the brown envelope with the pictures of Aunt Ruby and her family.

It's my picture album now, Jonah reminded himself. Positioning the box back on the memento shelf, Jonah hurried to the kitchen. The prospect of enjoying gourmet ice cream with his family shoved all thoughts about his aunt and the Amulet of the Goddess clear out of his mind.

Amulet of the Goddess

ABOUT THE AUTHOR

John Darr is a native of the state of Georgia. As a graduate of Columbus State University with a B.A. in Communications, and with work on his M.F.A. degree at Howard University in Washington, D.C., John has over twenty years of experience as an author, screenwriter, independent filmmaker, an educational television producer, screenwriter teacher, and technology specialist. His current projects include two YA Urban Fantasy book series; The Jonah Blackstone and Forest Heights series. He's currently working on a third adult Fantasy/Science Fiction series, Omega Quest Chronicles, as well as completing the screenplay adaption of the first Jonah Blackstone book, The Protector's Ring. Visit him online at www.johndarrbooks.com.

OTHER BOOKS BY JOHN DARR

Jonah Blackstone Series

Book One: The Protector's Ring

Book Two: The Seeker's Compass

Book Three: Amulet of the Goddess

Book Four: The Destiny Medallion: Conspiracies

Forest Heights Series

Book One: My Prince, My Boy

Book Two: Satyr's Melody